CRUSADER

THE SANCTUARY SERIES

VOLUME FOUR

Robert J. Crane

CRUSADER
THE SANCTUARY SERIES
VOLUME FOUR

Acknowledgments

You'd think that with a book this size, the acknowledgments would correspondingly drone on and on, but I'm going to try and keep this brief. Unlike, you know, the book itself.

Heather Rodefer once again Editor-in-Chief'd her way through the entire, 400 typed page, 10 Point Times New Roman beast of a manuscript. She calls it my Encyclopedia. Let me tell you something, Ms. Editor-in-Chief - Encyclopedias don't have a plot. I'm pretty sure Crusader does. Somewhere in there. Muchas gracias, Heather.

Deb Wesley again kept me on track with the technical details, reminding me of things like the fact that horses would not be able to descend a spiral staircase. Whoops. Also, she helpfully substituted the words, "Whicker" and "neigh" for all the whinnying that happened. Just a little variety, you know. It helps. Thank you, Deb.

Robin McDermott took time out of her life to go over everything in fine detail and let me know I was calling Ryin Ayend by both his names on pretty much every occasion I referred to him. Sorry, Robin. It's fixed now. For that and a thousand other error corrections (and getting your Gmail address suspended while mailing the book to me in 30 pieces of scanned text) I thank you.

Paul Madsen helped give the book another good look over as final error correction when it was nearly ready to go. My thanks to the great Paul, who waited patiently for the book for...well, almost as long as the fans.

Thanks to two of Cyrus's biggest fans who read through to make sure I was on track with this story, David Leach and James Boggs. Their feedback was invaluable.

Once again the cover was designed by the incomparable Karri Klawiter, who should really be making a fortune as a mind reader. I'm glad she's not, though, because I need book covers.

Editing was once more handled by the great Sarah Barbour, who did this *while she was on vacation* and even did a second pass, heroically going back for more when I would have thrown in the towel, personally! Her dedication amazes me.

Much gracias also to my group of secret sprinters, who helped me drive through to the end of this work at high speed. Mad props, all.

Last in the roundup, but never least, is my parents, who came to stay with us during both the 2nd draft and 3rd draft of Crusader, which allowed me to work late in the night on the manuscript. Thank you both. Also, my wife and kids, who are the reason I do this and the reason I get to. Love to you all.

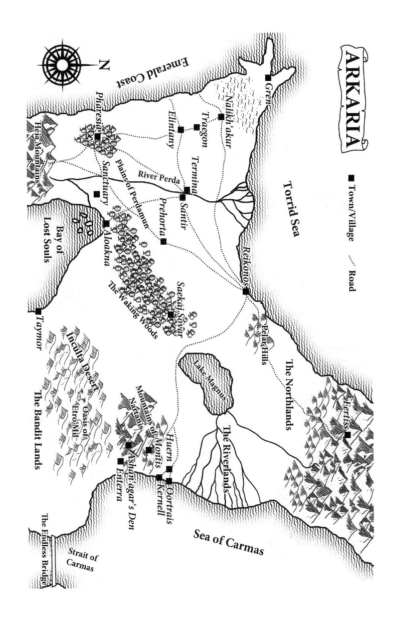

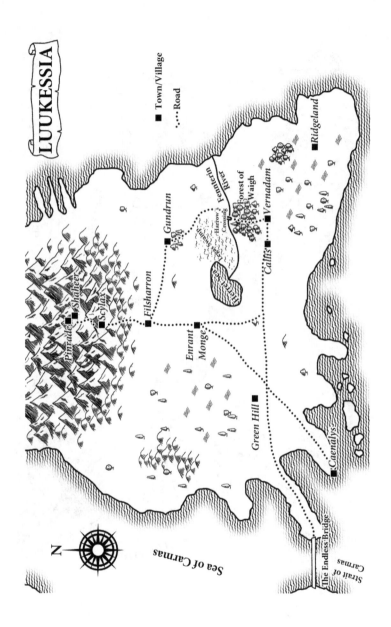

NOW

Prologue

Fear consumes us, the diary read. *It owns us, makes us its chattel and property, takes hold of our lives and enslaves us to it. There are only three ways to best fear. The first is to care nothing for anything, including your own life. The second is to confront it and thus build courage by facing your demons. The final is to believe so deeply in some cause that you are willing to walk through any fire, no matter how scorching, because of that belief. Unfortunately, all three of them are difficult for a coward such as myself, and of the three, one is of little appeal to anyone.*

The rains had left with almost as little warning and fanfare as they had arrived with, and Cyrus Davidon stared out the window, Alaric's journal clutched in his hand, mulling over his path. The room smelled faintly of wet wood and mildew; no great shock since the rains had blown into the Council Chambers of Sanctuary next door. All around him rested broken tables, smashed bookshelves, even a shattered painting—*though that was my work rather than that of ... well ...*

The only sound in earshot was the crackling of the fire and the popping of the torches. They gave the air a sort of sickly smell, sweet, of oil burning, perhaps. Cyrus realized for the first time that it could have been magic burning, for all he knew. They were magic torches, after all, lighting and unlighting as needed. He leaned his left hand against the chair, feeling the pain within, and as he shifted, the ring on his finger caught on the inside of his gauntlet. *I've been sitting here like this for too long,* he thought, putting the journal aside. The lettering was elegant on every page; not quite a surprise though close, as Cyrus could not recall having seen the Master of Sanctuary write much of anything for himself during the time Cyrus had been a member of the guild.

The rains had stopped at some point after nightfall, Cyrus dimly realized. It was after midnight now, and the strain on his eyes had been considerable. Putting aside the book, he stood and heard the cracking of his joints. He sighed. *I sound as though I'm about to fall apart.* He chuckled ruefully at the thought. *Soon, perhaps.*

He paused, pondering. *What Alaric said in the journal—I'm afraid. Fear. How long ago did I master fear? When I was at the Society?* He did the arithmetic in his head and found it unfavorable. *How long ago did I stop feeling the pinch of fear?* He thought about it for another moment but received no argument from himself. *Then. I stopped truly fearing after ...*

He let out a swift exhalation, as though he could purge the thought from himself, and tasted bitterness almost tangibly in his mouth. *Alaric was right. There are few enough ways to truly purge fear from your life, and I believe he might have figured them all out. Not caring about anything is certainly a swift way to do it, and I did that for long enough to know. Confronting it is easier* in conjunction with the third ... he blinked. *Believing in something enough to die for it, well ... that's the most difficult of them all.*

His eyes worked their way back to the book again. He'd read most of it during the night, much of it from times long, long before he had even met the man known as the Ghost of Sanctuary. There had been new insights, fascinating ones, things he hadn't fully understood—until now. *But what would it say about the time I spent in Luukessia? What was he doing in that time, what was he thinking?* He found himself walking back to the chair unconsciously. Sitting back down, he picked up the journal of Alaric's thoughts—and the other. *Vara's.* He stared at the dull cover, the dark leather binding of it, ran his hands along the front as though he could feel it through his gauntlet.

He sat them both on his lap and opened them, skimming through the pages of the first until he found what he was looking for: a date. He read for a few paragraphs and his jaw dropped. *Ah. So that was it.* He turned his attention to the other book, Vara's journal, the handwriting only slightly less flowing, and opened it, jumping through the pages until he found the one that fit. It was wrinkled, the parchment rumpled as though it had been exposed to water.

Damn you, Cyrus Davidon ...

He looked up, around the empty room and toward the darkness outside. "That's a hell of a way to start a journal entry." His eyes fell back to the page and he read on, trying to absorb it all, flicking back and forth from one journal to the other, reconciling what he knew of that year with what he didn't, fitting the pieces of it together in his head. It all crept in, slowly, much like the darkness outside, and he did not want to stop reading, even when he heard a noise of something from within the walls, something quiet but certain, something very much alive … in a place that was not.

FIVE YEARS
EARLIER

Chapter 1

Vara

Damn you, Cyrus Davidon, Vara thought as the sounds of battle rang through the halls of Sanctuary. *You were not meant to be gone this long.* Her sword felt heavy in her hand as she ran down the stairs from the tower, a horn blaring all around with shouts of "ALARUM! RAIDERS!" loud enough to roust even the near-dead. Her plate metal boots slapped against each step, ringing out in a clatter and clang that would have reverberated through the entirety of Sanctuary on a normal day; now they were well drowned out by all else that was going on.

Six months he's been gone. Six long months. With every step down the stairs she felt the hard metal through the leather footcovers she wore underneath her boots. *When the day comes that I see him again, I'm going to let our General know exactly how poor his sense of timing is.* There was a smell wafting up the stairs, a scent of blood and fire, and not of the smokeless flames produced by Sanctuary's torches, but of real fire, of battle and death.

She jumped the last flight of stairs, vaulting over the few others who were storming down, to find the foyer awash in chaos. There was battle, and fire, and blood all; armor and swords, axes and arrows, all winging their way over the sweeping stone architecture of the usually peaceful halls of Sanctuary. The room was packed with dark elves in the blackened steel armor of the Sovereign's forces, warring with the motley and unmatched army of Sanctuary. She saw Sanctuary rangers, human, elven and dark elven, wearing cloaks of green and brown, warriors in armor of flat steel and dull hues, some with surcoats of red, blue and white; all of them clashing with dark elves in their dim armor, like the forces of light arrayed against the legions of dark.

And dark appears to be winning.

She watched as a dwarf clad in silver mail was cut down by a cleaving attack from a dark elf, who let out a shriek of triumph as his foe dropped to the ground, dead. Vara took it all in, a tingle running through her. She felt it slipping through her, six months of rage, pent-up anger and frustration. There was a taste of morning breath in her mouth, the bitter, acrid flavor of waking still there, and it only felt more appropriate when coupled with the anger surging through her now.

Damn you, Cyrus Davidon.

She channeled her fury into a yell that rang out over the battle. She leapt, not a small leap but a great, ungainly leap of twenty feet, using the mystical strength granted her by armor and sword. She brought her blade down on the dark elf who had slain the dwarf. He stared at her flight, wide-eyed, as she landed upon him and pierced him through his armor. She left a great rent in it, cutting through it as though it were nothing more than old, tattered parchment.

The melee lay open before her, half the heads in the room on her, watching. The clash of swords, the clang of blades, the sight of hundreds of bodies pressed against each other, and yet something familiar prickled at her mind even as she rushed forward, sword in motion to deal with the next dark elf, and the next. There was an aura of low-hanging fog, of something passing beneath her feet as she brought down a sword and split the metal helm and skull of a dark elf while whirling to land a hard-edged slash against another enemy.

Something moved out of the corner of her eye—several somethings, actually, as this was a full-fledged battle—but this one more pronounced. It was big and green, with black robes and a sash around the shoulders that bore the markings of a healer. The troll, Vaste, brought his staff down on the neck of a dark elven warrior whose blade was only inches from Vara's side. The warrior's skull cracked, a sickening noise of bones and wetness echoing in her ears as the body hit the floor and was trampled under the troll's feet as he moved on to his next opponent.

"That's okay, don't thank me or anything," Vaste said under his breath. "After all, why bother to be grateful to me for saving your life?"

Had she not been an elf, and possessed of the exceptional hearing that was a hallmark of her race, she might not have heard him. "I'll thank you later, should we both survive this. As it is, you may have done nothing more," she laid her blade across the throat of another dark elf, "than buy me a temporary reprieve; we seem to be somewhat outnumbered."

"We're not, actually," Vaste said, his hand glowing and pointed into the distance. Vara turned and watched as a healing spell settled on a human ranger whose face was slick with blood pouring from a gouge in his throat. Skin closed up, leaving only the spilt blood as a mark of the death that had nearly visited the man. He shouted his thanks and plunged twin blades into a dark elf whose back was turned. "It's just that most of our force is arrayed on the wall against the army that has us surrounded."

"Did it not occur to anyone that the Sovereign of the Dark Elves would simply teleport a force into our midst?" She caught the blade of one of the dark elven attackers on hers and turned it aside, spinning him about while she plunged her sword into the back of his neck.

"I don't know. Did it occur to you?"

She narrowed her eyes, but she was turned from him, dealing with two dark elven warriors that came at her with axes. "Fair point."

"I'm sorry, I didn't hear that?" She couldn't see the troll's face, but she heard the smile in his reply.

"I said focus on the battle, you malodorous pile of rubbish." She struck down the first of her foes with an offhand attack, keeping his body between her and the second as the dark elf sunk to his knees. "Where is Fortin? He could turn the tide of this contest in mere seconds."

"Visiting his estate in the Elven Kingdom, I believe," Vaste's voice had a sudden strain to it and she turned to find him holding back three dark elven warriors who were pressing their advantage and driving him toward the doors to the Great Hall, where another battle appeared to be taking place. "He does so love to commune with the rocks and boulders; who would have known that a rock giant had a sensitive side? Certainly not me, but then again I rather enjoy his 'batter your enemies with superior strength until their skulls become a fine paste' approach."

"Aye," she said, moving to help Vaste but finding herself cut off by three strong dark elven warriors. "We could use a bit of that right now." She found herself boxed in, the one on the left driving her back while the one in the center pushed at her with an oblong blade that hosted a right angle at the tip. She watched Vaste block attacks with his staff, the focusing crystal on the tip of it glowing a ghostly white. "Do our forces outside even know that we've got enemies in the damned foyer?"

"I would have to guess that this is a coordinated attack." Vaste's words came out in great, shuddering gasps as he exerted himself, striking a killing blow against one of the dark elves menacing him. "They're probably making an assault on the wall even now."

"Bloody hell." Vara saw the white, toothy grin of her center assailant as he thrust his great sword at her and she dodged, countering with an abrupt lunge, her sword at full extension. Her movement caused her to avoid strikes from the dark elves on her left and right, and she let her attack carry her through, striking the dark elf in the mouth with her blade. She felt it slide in, watched his grin dissolve in blood and broken teeth, then pulled her sword left, jerking it free and striking against the neck of her foe to the side. She pirouetted and brought it across the throat of the one to her right. With athletic ease she jumped over the bodies of both of them as they fell and moved toward Vaste, who had acquired another attacker.

"Oh, good," the troll said as she struck down the first of his assailants from behind, without warning, causing two of the others to pivot to face her. "I was beginning to worry that perhaps I just wasn't that important to you."

"You truly aren't." She crossed swords with the next that came at her. The clash of her mystical blade against her opponent's cut steel, chipping his sword.

"At least until you need a healing spell," Vaste said. "You ungrateful tart. I bet if I was a warrior wearing black armor, you'd feel differently."

He said it lightly, with just the hint of a barb, but when it reached Vara's ears, it curdled and she felt heat rush through her veins, setting her blood afire. She struck down the next two enemies with reckless disregard for her own safety, catching a wound to the shoulder that slid through the joint of her armor. She ignored it, felt the searing pain of it and set it aside, letting the thought of the warrior in black burn her internally. *Six months, you arrogant bastard, and not so much as a scrap of news; I hope Terian caught you right in your pompous, overmuscled arse with a blade—*

She felt a pain that was nowhere near her shoulder, a pain so acute and stunning that she hated herself for feeling it. Guilt washed over her, halting her uncharitable thought midway through, leaving her with only the same familiar mantra that had been rolling through her mind for the last six months: *Damn you, Cyrus Davidon. Damn you for your arrogance, for your idiotic nobility, your lack of consideration—and for leaving, most of all. Damn you for all of it.* She buried her blade in another foe, then another.

Something caused her to shudder. The thin fog that had seemed to creep into the room was gaining in volume, rolling over the floor and swirling into the center of the foyer. Behind her, she could still hear the wail of the horns, the slamming of doors and the roaring of fires bursting out of the hearth across the room, warning the residents of Sanctuary of the attack in their midst. All of that seemed to calm, along with the swell of the battle as the mist rolled to the center of the room, rising from the floor into a man-sized pillar, gaining definition and swelling into a figure.

Worn, battered armor appeared out of the cloud along with a helm that covered all but the mouth of the man within it. A sword of darkened metal swept out of the fog, cutting neatly through seven different assailants who surrounded the mist. The cloud dissipated and flowed to the other side of the room, near the hearth, gathering behind a cluster of dark elven warriors. It sprang into a pillar once more and out came a sword, stroking neatly across the bodies of the foes arrayed about it, then dispersed once more and moved to a spot near the lounge, where it became a tornado of mist and exploded, puffs of the smoky air evaporating to leave behind Alaric Garaunt, the Guildmaster of Sanctuary. He sprang forth from the smoke, his mouth contorted in fury and the sound of his yell rained upon the foes that he struck down a moment later.

Pieces of Alaric's quarries flew across the floor, rolling in among the bodies and the blood that was already slickening the stone. Vara cut her way through a dark elf and found herself standing in the doorway to the Great Hall, looking within at the place where the guild dined. More than a dozen dark elves had funneled into the Great Hall and were battling with Sanctuary defenders scattered among the tables. There was a smell of hearty stew mingled with baked bread, at odds with the crimson-covered surfaces and the bodies that lay amidst the upturned tables. The clash of blades and the screams of fury and pain warred with the simple, homey scent of the meal being prepared within.

Vara's eyes flew over shattered tables and broken chairs to see Larana, the mistress of the kitchens, hovering in the air, feet at least a head above Vara's own height, her druidic magic issuing forth from her hands. Blasts of coarse flame shot forth to consume the dark elves who were moving forward to attack her, a wave of heat from the fire washing over Vara even at this distance. Her hand came up out of instinct, as if to protect her from it. When she lowered it again, a passel of flaming corpses lay about the Great Hall, thick, black smoke gathering above at the high ceiling.

She paused to watch the normally mild, quiet druid, eyes aflame, float toward her remaining enemies, driving them back toward Vara, who braced and attacked as the dark elves ran into her in ones and twos, turning from Larana with panic in their eyes, the flames driving them to focus more on what they were retreating from than what they were running to. Vara stepped into them, sword moving horizontally in a slash that killed three of the first four with one stroke and sent the other to the ground, crying in low guttural noises that choked the air.

Vara stopped, turning to look back to the melee still proceeding in the foyer. Larana's eyes met hers, the druid's gaze a bright, verdant green that reminded Vara somehow of life—and the end of it. "They'll be needing help mopping up in the foyer," Vara said, and Larana nodded, drifting gently a foot off the ground before she flew forward, past Vara and into the battle.

There was a shift, Vara could tell, as she charged back into the fight in the foyer, blade in hand. Where before there had been wall-to-wall melee, now only a few dark elves remained, backed into a corner to the left of the doors that led outside. The moans of the injured filled her ears. She ignored it all as she shouldered her way through the crowd toward the dark elves standing off in a line. They were backed into the corner, staring down the members of Sanctuary who stood opposite them. Larana hovered menacingly nearby, and Vara could see other spellcasters, waiting to break the uneasy peace. Warriors of Sanctuary had crowded to the front, and a small distance, the length of a sword or two, was all that separated the dark elves from being overrun by the larger numbers.

"I am an officer of Sanctuary," Vara said when she reached the front of their line. "You are surrounded, outnumbered, and soon to be headless, your skulls adorning pikes on the top of our walls as a warning to your countrymen of the folly of assailing us." She stared with cold eyes at the last of them, and the enemy stared back as one, not questioning, a cold, unfeeling mass, their irises the striking dark-elven reds, yellows and purples, otherwordly. *Demons.* "Surrender and you'll be shown the hospitality of our dungeons, but at least you'll be alive."

There was a quiet moment before something broke it. "In the name of the Sovereign." A dark elf close to the back of their formation near-whispered it, but she heard. Another took up the call, louder this time. "In the name of the Sovereign." Then another. The heavy smell of smoke and iron lay upon the air, burning her eyes with its pungence.

"Oh, bloody hell," Vara whispered.

"IN THE NAME OF THE SOVEREIGN!" It grew to a chorus, then a chant. Their shared voices all offered up to the heavens, they banged their mailed feet against the floor as though trying to make the Sanctuary army flinch with their effort. Vara grasped her sword tighter and she felt the tension in the ranks behind her as others did the same, knowing that the charge was coming, and that it would be short and bloody. There was a rattle of swords and behind her the noise of tense breaths being drawn. Another smell reached her nose, flooded it, the scent and feeling of humidity, of mist in the air, and she saw it swirl around her feet, so dense that the stones of the floor disappeared beneath a thick layer of the wafting, whitish clouds.

The mist gathered and swirled into the corner behind the dark elves, who continued their rage and bluster, making a fearsome racket that drowned out almost all else in her ears and made her head ache from the noise of it. A solid mass began to take shape behind the dark elves, who were oblivious to the sight of a perfect cloud forming in the corner. It grew in size and volume and turned darker, a storm gathering unto itself, until finally a hand swept out following the point of a sword, and Alaric Garaunt appeared behind them from within the depths of it. Vara saw three fall with the first attack as the Ghost's ancient blade, Aterum, swung high and sloped a bloody line on the brown stones of the wall to his side as it descended.

Vara could hear the collective intake of breath around her, the Sanctuary soldiers waiting, their line formed to contain the last dark elves. They watched as the screams and chaos consumed the dark elves and shattered their formation, as the elvews, so prepared for bloody sacrifice and shouting their willingness to die for the Sovereign only moments earlier, fell to pieces under the onslaught of one man behind them. It was short and bloody, covered in the swirl of fog and mist, and in the end it came down to a final dark elf, and Alaric held him out at the edge of his blade, the warrior trembling. There had been twenty or more of them in the corner before the Ghost had appeared, and the last seemed to realize this, his breath coming in shuddering gasps, his sword clenched in his fist, navy skin around his knuckles turned sky-blue from the strength of his grip.

Alaric stared down his sword at the dark elf, who dropped his weapon with a clatter, and began to raise his hands. The Ghost stared down, his lone eye unflinching. Vara caught an almost imperceptible shudder down Alaric's arm and the sword began to move, sliding through the belly of the dark elf, who gasped and looked up at Alaric with wide eyes.

"You have sieged and invaded my home, slain my brothers and sisters." Alaric's voice was low and as filled with malice as Vara had ever heard it. "Let this be a warning to you and yours; there is no mercy for those who would do such things." His palm reached out and the dark elf shuddered as a surge of power shot from Alaric's gauntlet, the energy of the spell sending the dark elf into the wall at such a speed that Vara could hear the splatter of his flesh and blood even as she turned her head not to look.

When she turned back, Alaric stood, red splotching the battered surface of his armor, looking coldly down at his hand as though it were something foreign to him. "Alaric?" Her voice was barely above a whisper but it stirred him as though drawing him from a trance. "We have been attacked from within; we must make preparations to protect ourselves. We must either shut down the portal or station a small army here to deal with additional assaults should they come. We need a messenger to go speak with Thad at the wall; we may have to reinforce the guard there if the dark elves are attacking."

The Ghost stared back at her, quiet, almost lifeless, before finally nodding his head underneath his massive helm. "Let it be done." He looked through the crowd until his eye came to rest on Larana. "Go to Thad. See if the dark elves have begun their attack in earnest." He looked again through the crowd until he found a grizzled man in armor, whose face was exposed through the front of his helm. "Belkan ... you will form a guard and keep watch on the foyer every hour of the day and night. We cannot shut down the portal, lest we strand Cyrus's army in a foreign land without retreat or any way to get a message home." The old knight looked suddenly weary though he still held Aterum in his hand.

Larana did not wait for any further instruction; she surged forward over the head of the crowd, running on air and seeming to slip through the crack of the main door without it opening but barely. Vara watched her go then walked slowly toward Alaric, who remained still, unmoving, a statue of steel and flesh. "Alaric," she said quietly, "are you quite well?"

He did not move at first, but when he did it was only to move his head ponderously to look upon her with his one good eye, an almost imperceptible smile upon his lips. "A goodly portion of our army is away in a foreign land under the command of our General. We have not heard from them in six months though they were to have been gone only three. We have been surrounded by the legions of the dark elves, most aggrieved at us for our part in defending the Elven Kingdom during their recent invasion, and now they have gone so far as to use a wizard to slip an elite force of their soldiers into our home using a spell I felt certain was unknown to any but our own spellcasters. If that were not enough, only half a year ago we slew the God of Death himself." The smile grew slightly larger, and all the more grotesque in its obvious falseness. "Tell me, child— why would I not be quite well?"

"As long as you're keeping a good perspective on things." Vaste's voice rang out from just behind Vara, but she heard the usual irony only on the surface; there was a deeper sense of darkness hidden from all but those who knew him best.

A shout of alarm came from behind them and Vara turned. A point of magical energy had appeared in the center of the foyer, over the great seal that was placed in the middle of the room. It crackled and glowed, shedding green upon the face of Belkan across from her, his sword braced in his hand and pointed toward the brightness. She saw others mirror the action as the spell grew in its intensity as the seconds ticked by. She gripped her sword more tightly as the front door burst open and Larana shouted (*of all people,* Vara thought; *it would be the worst if she were the one shouting*), "We are under attack! They have siege towers at the walls!"

The sparkle of magic at the center of the foyer grew brighter; something began to coalesce within. *Another round, then. Let's have at it, Sovereign of the Dark Elves. Send me all you have, every last one of your bastard children and all the sons of whores you slap into armor and call warriors. Send them all and I'll throw them back at you, bloody and shattered. Throw your whole army at us and I'll take them one by one, grind them up and heave them back to Saekaj Sovar, march through your city, and leave it in ruins the way you did mine, you right bastard—*

The spell magic faded, leaving not another small army but a lone figure. A druid, a human man, a little shorter than she but not by much, his eyes dark and already looking around at the carnage and bodies that lay strewn across the foyer. He let out a short, sharp breath as his eyes walked over the scene.

"My gods," Ryin Ayend said as the last of his spell faded, "what has happened here?"

"You have missed much in your absence," Alaric said, walking toward the druid with a slow, shuffling gait. "And it has been long since we have heard from any of your brethren."

Ayend paused, a subtle cringe on his face, a slight twist of pain and discomfort. "Things have … gone astray in Luukessia. We have had some … unforeseen difficulties."

There was a low whistling sound from outside that seemed to grow closer, swelling into a loud squeal as Vara threw herself to the ground in front of the hearth. The massive, circular stained glass window above the front doors exploded inward as a huge rock—launched, Vara was certain, by one of the catapults surrounding the walls of Sanctuary—burst through and landed with a crash, rolling through the foyer and sending bodies flying, until it came to rest in the Great Hall, butted against the ruin of one of the large oaken tables. Moans of pain and screams of loss issued forth from the path of the boulder, and Vara pulled herself back to her feet, shaking the little pieces of colored glass out of her hair.

"Unforeseen difficulties?" she said, in a most rueful tone drawing the attention of Ryin, who was pulled to his feet by Alaric from where he lay not far from her. His eyes were glazed, fixed on the door to the Great Hall and the boulder lying within. His jaw hung open. With the window shattered, sounds from the outside filtered into the foyer, and a low roar could be heard in the distance: the maniacal, chanting sound of an army, the low rumble of the siege machines, and the sound of other rocks hurled from catapults impacting elsewhere, the flat thump and shaking of the ground as they hit. "Yes, we've experienced a few of those ourselves since your departure." With that, she looked back to the broken window, the blue sky visible beyond and listened again, to the sounds of battle, the sounds of war, of all the different kinds of hell waiting just outside the Sanctuary gates to be unleashed on them.

Damn you, Cyrus Davidon. Damn you for leaving me like this ...

Chapter 2

Cyrus
Six Months Earlier

Cyrus Davidon had a dream he was running. A pair of red, glowing eyes were following him somewhere as the fear grew within him. When he awoke, he was on a beach. He sat up in his bedroll, a heavy sweat rolling off his skin even though the air was filled with a pleasing coolness all around him. The sands sloped down to the Sea of Carmas, where the waves lapped at the shore, the ebb of low tide bringing small breakers onto the beach at regular intervals, the low, dull roar of the water a kind of pleasant background noise.

His breath came erratically at first as he tried to catch it and control it, taking long, slow gulps of air as he swallowed the bitterness that had been on his tongue since waking. A hundred fires lit the night around him, providing heat and warmth for his army, protection against the light chill of the tropical winter. The smell of smoke hung around him, of lingering fish on the fire, hints of salt in the air.

A light breeze came off the sea as the wind changed directions, bringing the smell of sulfur and rot. He sniffed and the scent of the seaweed down the shore became lodged in his nostrils, reminding him of the Realm of Death, where only days earlier he had led an assault that killed the God of Death, Mortus. The memory came back to him, of the listless and unmoving air in that place, of the image of death itself, a clawed hand as it reached out, grasping for Vara ...

Just over the sound of the waves against the shore, Cyrus could hear chatter from around some of the fires where the members of his army sat huddled for warmth. He turned his head to look; there were warriors and rangers, men and women of no magical ability, still talking, laughing and boisterous.

"I would have thought two days march would have cured most of them of their enthusiasm," came a voice at his side. Cyrus looked back to see the face of Terian Lepos lit by the fire, the orange glow flickering against the deep blue of the dark elf's skin. "They were tired enough yesterday from the long march on these sands, I suppose. But now they're back at it again, all full of excitement, eager to get into their first battle." The dark elf's face was narrow and his nose stuck out, coming to a point, his hair black as obsidian, and he wore a half-smile that couldn't look anything but cruel in the low light.

"They'll get over it quick enough once they've been in it." Cyrus's armor creaked as he turned to face Terian. He pulled off a gauntlet and ran his fingers across his bedroll. Sand covered the surface of the cloth. He felt the tiny grains, like little pins as he brushed against them, a few of them glimmering like shards of glass in the light, and he remembered other sand, in another place, a whole pit of it, with red blood pooling and holding it together in great lumps—

"Trouble sleeping?" Terian's words drew Cyrus back to the present. The dark knight sat slumped a few feet away, legs arched in front of him, his new double-handed sword resting across them, a cloth in his hand, polishing the blade. Cyrus saw the little glint of red in the steel, a hint of the magic that the weapon carried.

Cyrus let a half-smile creep onto his face; the blade had come from a dark elf whom Cyrus had defeated in the city of Termina while defending it from the dark elven army. He felt a pang at the thought of Termina as it led to thoughts of Vara, a stirring pain in his heart and guts, and the half-smile disappeared as quickly as the waters receded down the shore. "Just a nightmare," he said to Terian. "It won't be trouble unless it happens over and over again."

The dark elf nodded, face inscrutable. "Those sort of dreams tend to find me when I'm troubled during the day, as if to follow you into your bed and attack you when they know you're at your weakest." He took his shining eyes off Cyrus and turned them back toward the fire. "But I suppose you'd have more experience with those than I would."

Cyrus caught the knowing tone in the dark knight's voice. "I suppose I would." With a low, deep breath, Cyrus pushed to his feet and felt his armored boots sink into the sands. He felt unsteady at first then caught his balance. His breath caught in his throat as another thought crossed his mind, of Vara, of what she had said to him the last time they had spoken.

"Something on your mind?" The low rasp of Terian's voice drew

Cyrus's attention back to him. "You're not usually the silent type." The dark elf took a breath and a slight smile caused his white teeth to peek out from behind his dark blue lips. "Someone, perhaps? Someone tall and blond, with a heart as icy as her eyes?"

Cyrus stared back at Terian, and caught the glimmer of understanding there. Cyrus deflated, his shoulders slumping as the weight seemed to drag him down even as he remained on his feet. "What ..." he began to speak, but his words came out in a low croak. "What do you do ... when someone that you ... when someone close to you ... betrays you so thoroughly?" He felt the bitter taste of what he said and remembered the last words she had spoken to him. *We will not, cannot be. Not ever ... I thank you for trying to comfort me in my hour of need, but I'll have you take your leave now.* He slid his fist back into his gauntlet and felt it clench.

"What do you do when someone betrays you?" Terian's voice was dull as he repeated the words. "That's an excellent question." It hung there between them as Cyrus watched his old friend. Terian ran his cloth down the flat facing of the sword, polishing the side, rubbing the metal.

After a moment of silence, Cyrus looked around, the waves still crashing, inevitably, on the shore around him. He waited, but Terian seemed frozen in thought, staring at the black, endless sea in the distance, listening to the lapping of the tides. The blue skin on his hand stood in contrast to the red metal of the blade and the white cloth. "Terian?" Cyrus asked. "Are you all right?"

The dark knight didn't answer, his hand still moving in regular rhythm, up and down the blade. His fingers slipped, over the edge, and jerked. The dark knight stared down dully as though he couldn't quite fathom what he was seeing. Liquid welled up, and the first drops fell to the sands. Cyrus stared at it, and remembered again of a time long, long ago, long before Sanctuary.

"Damn," Terian said mildly. The dark elf stared at his wounded hand.

"I'll get Curatio," Cyrus said, starting to move.

"No," Terian said, and Cyrus heard the dark knight's armor rattle as he got to his feet. "I'll go. I should have been paying attention." He clenched his fist and Cyrus watched a thin stream of red run out of his palm and form a droplet on the base of Terian's wrist. The dark knight's expression was still formless, almost indifferent to his wound. "But about your question ..."

Cyrus stared at him. Terian's eyes seeming to fixate on a point beyond Cyrus, as though he were looking through the warrior, not at him. "Yes?"

Terian's gaze came back to him, found his, and there was something in it that Cyrus couldn't define, some depth that made Cyrus think of an open window, curtains stirred by a breeze only slightly to reveal furnishings inside. He caught a hint before the curtains blew back into place and hid the room within from view once more. "I don't know. You got your vengeance, once upon a time, didn't you? For your friend, after he died?"

"After we were betrayed?" Cyrus remembered, with a knot in his stomach, Narstron, his oldest friend. *Of how he died.* "Not revenge. Not really. Besides, this is ... different."

"Is it?" Terian took his hand and brought it to his lips, pursing them to catch the next drop before it fell to the ground. "Hurt is hurt, right? Pain is pain."

Cyrus recalled the gut-punch pain, the agony of realizing later that people they had been allied with had betrayed him. Vara's words came back to him again: *We will not be, cannot be. Not ever ...*

"No," Cyrus said. "It's not the same." He weighed the sensations, the loss of his oldest friend, the anguish of it all, and found it ... lacking.

"I suppose," Terian said. "Death is a much more ... permanent wound, and the vengeance so much more ... deserving."

Cyrus stared out again, across the dunes, without answering. The hundred fires left spots in his vision as he cast his gaze over them then turned his eyes again toward the sea. Endless, infinite, and deep beyond any measure he could fathom. *The sea goes down, perhaps forever.* The blackness it contained was akin to the darkness within him, the empty cold that threatened to swallow him in despair. He felt a hand clap him on the back as Terian turned and walked away. He did not watch the dark knight go, absorbed as he was in his own thoughts.

It's warm enough; I shouldn't feel a chill. But it was there. The pain of losing Narstron had been bitter and hard, had laid him low for days, long days filled with a despair that choked out any happiness or possibility thereof in the future. It had been darker than the days when his wife had left him—*darker than any save for those at the Society of Arms ...*

Until now. The little points of light that the fires had left in his vision seemed to coalesce, to flash in front of him, to give him an image, one that he wanted and yet wished he could blot from his memory. A face, her skin as pale as the northern snowfields, her hair as yellow as the gold he carried in his purse, eyes as blue as glacial ice. He felt the same pang, again, inside, the dagger wound that she'd left him with.

Cyrus tasted the bitterness on his tongue again, the sadness that clung to him like a cloak. He looked back to his bedroll and knew that his slumber was over for the night. The moon hung in the sky overhead, far above him, and he drew an uneasy breath. The morning was far, far off, many hours away, and yet it would come, inevitably, and he would marshal his armies and drive them across the bridge that he had seen by last light, the one that stretched over the infinite sea, over the unfathomable depths, one that he'd been told led to a new land and an uncertain future.

And perhaps, somewhere over there, I will forget about her—the blond-haired elf with the pale skin, and her words, the ones that had cut him deeper than any pain that the warrior in black armor had ever felt in his life.

Chapter 3

Sunrise found Cyrus staring out across the water, watching as the red disc rose over the horizon. The chatter of the young warriors and rangers had died down only a few hours earlier, and he had been left alone with his thoughts, staring across the Sea of Carmas as the first members of his army began to rise. Cyrus heard the sound of footsteps in the sand behind him and turned to see Curatio, his pointed elven ears catching the light and casting shadows on the side of his head.

"You're up early," Curatio said, making his way over to the fire next to Cyrus, a small loaf of bread in his hands. "Or perhaps late." The elf broke the bread and offered Cyrus a half, which he took. "Terian said he was talking to you when he cut his hand last night." Curatio wore the scarf of a healer, a long, rectangular cloth sash that remained untied, wrapped around his shoulders and hanging loose, the ends reaching to his waist. Runes were stitched into it in dark lettering, but the white color told all who saw that he was a healer, a spellcaster with the ability to mend wounds and restore life. "You haven't been up since then, have you?"

Cyrus gnawed on the loaf, which was fresh, still warm. He looked up at the healer in surprise and drew a smile from Curatio. "Magically conjured bread. It'll be down to the spellcasters to keep us in bread and water as we march onward, especially for the next few days as we traverse the bridge."

Cyrus picked a large piece out of the doughy center and ate it, shifting it around in his mouth, enjoying the soft flour taste. He grasped a piece of the crusty exterior. It broke between his fingers and he popped it in his mouth, listening to the crunch between his teeth. He looked south and saw the Endless Bridge, something he had seen only once before. It was stone and sloped up to a hundred feet over the water, with enormous supports that reached above the span every few hundred feet, symmetrically placed pillars of stone lining its avenue. It extended into the distance, beyond the horizon, and the stone seemed to glitter in the light of the sunrise.

Cyrus smacked his lips, stopping before he took another bite. "Leaves me feeling a bit ... empty inside."

Curatio's smile cooled. "The bread? Or something else?"

"Leaves me feeling weak," Cyrus said, lowering the bread. "And the last thing I want to be when I'm marching into an unknown country is weak." He turned and looked into the distance where the horses were tied to trees at the edge of the beach. "How are the horses?"

"They've been curried, their feet have been picked out, and Martaina is saddling them now," Curatio said, his eyes following Cyrus's. "She's quite the wonder with animals, that one. She's got a few others helping her, but she seems to be taking excellent care of them."

"Good," Cyrus said without emotion. "The more we have delegated to good people, the more we can focus on what's coming."

The elf's face lost its smile gradually, fading as the lines slackened and Curatio turned serious. "And what might that be?"

Cyrus took another bite, a heavier one, and chewed, answering only after he'd swallowed about half of it. "Battle. Longwell says we'll be passing through an unfriendly Kingdom on the other side of the bridge. Says they'll have pickets out, riders, you know. They may throw trouble our way to keep us from passing."

Curatio's eyebrow rose, sending his ageless face into a very slight display of amusement. "Pickets? Outriders? A scouting party of what? A dozen men on horseback? Versus our fifty on horse and thousand afoot?" A light chuckle came from the healer. "I wish them the best of luck."

Cyrus didn't join the laughter. "They'll present themselves, they'll threaten, but Longwell says the outriders won't make much fuss. This Kingdom, it's the one by the sea—Actaluere, Longwell called it—it has holdfasts between the bridge and Longwell's father's lands. They may send armies out to halt us once they know we're here."

Curatio's eyebrow twitched slightly higher. "Do you think they'll succeed, General?"

The elf's odd formality stirred Cyrus's irritation. "Not if we're careful, they won't. But even a hundred men with no magic could wipe out an army ten times their size if they were to catch us sleeping." Cyrus clutched the bread tighter. "We have a journey of several weeks across their territory. That's a long while that they could cause us problems, and a very long time to maintain an all-hours watch, especially after a hard march every day."

"Good practice," Curatio said, taking a bite of the thick, hard crust of his bread. "After all, we are here to season our young and inexperienced recruits."

"A march of several weeks, with the threat of attack hanging over us every hour of the day?" Cyrus looked at the bread in his hands and was suddenly no longer hungry. "That will season them, all right." He stood, and looked over the stirring army. "I'd rather have peace from them, though, and stay at their inns, buy fresh food from their people, spread our gold around their realm on our march than seed their lands with sword and fire." The sergeants of the army were shouting now, yelling their displeasure at the recruits, stirring them out of their stupors as the sound echoed down the shore.

"Aye," Curatio said softly behind him as the the noise of the rousing army carried on, "always better to have peace than war. But in my experience, it's not always a luxury we are afforded."

It took another hour to get everyone fed and formed up to move. They reached the bridge after another hour's walk, and took a break in the shade by the span. The stone bridge was wide enough to accommodate ten columns of their troops walking side by side. After the army was formed up again, Cyrus began the procession to lead them over. He kept his horse, Windrider, in front of the army, a few yards ahead of the rest of the mounted members of Sanctuary. The steady clip-clop of hooves against the stone of the bridge lulled him.

It will not work, Cyrus. It can never be, you and I. For I am elf, and my life is long and my duties are as great as my sorrow. We will not, cannot be. Not ever. Vara's words echoed over and over in his mind as the gentle wash of the water lapping against the supports of the bridge beat a steady rhythm in his consciousness. The sun shone down from overhead, but the salt air and sea breeze kept him cool, even in his black armor. *Not ever.*

The sound of someone next to him jarred Cyrus, causing him to look up. As soon as he saw who it was, he relaxed. "You," he said with a sigh.

"Me," Aisling said. Her hair was white, flush against the navy skin it framed on her face and an exaggerated amount of cleavage was on display under her traveling cloak, which was open. Her usual leather armor was gone, replaced by a cloth garment of deepest red that hugged her belly and her upper body.

Cyrus stared at her, his expression in near-disbelief. "Are you wearing a bustier?"

Her eyebrows danced up and her lips pursed in a smile. "I'm surprised you know what that is."

He looked away, shaking his head in annoyance. He hadn't intended to give her any sort of encouragement. "My wife used to wear them." He looked back, slightly uncomfortable. "From time to time."

"Oh?" Her voice trilled in interest. "You were married?"

"A long time ago." He turned his head to look at her, a little too much frost in his voice, even to him. "Try not to pretend you didn't know."

She shrugged expressively, exaggeratedly, and as though every bit of chill in his words had melted somewhere between the two of them. "I was just being polite. Of course I've heard the rumors about you being married. I've heard a great many rumors about you. But then, I've heard a few about myself as well and not always true, so I prefer to glean the fact of them directly from the source before I go believing something I hear in passing, no matter how good it sounds."

Cyrus felt the breeze off the sea stir the hair under his helm and reached up to take the metal contraption off, securing it to a hook on his saddle. With that done, he ran his hand through his hair, felt the slight sweat that had developed on his forehead, and wiped it onto the sleeve that stuck out of his gauntlet. Once done, he looked back to Aisling, who still rode next to him, watching him, almost expectantly. "And what rumors would you have me dispel?"

"Just one," she said, but the slyness and her smile were gone, replaced by something else: an almost primal hunger, as though she were thirsty and waiting for a single drop of water to fall upon her tongue.

"Just one?" He looked back at her. "Then what? You'll ride back into the line and trouble me no more?"

"For today, yes." The hunger on her face grew, an insatiable curiosity. "I make no promises about tomorrow."

"Ask your question, then." He felt his hands on the reins, on the leather, felt them squeeze tightly against the dry material that lined the inside of his gauntlets, felt the hint of perspiration on his palms. "Ask and then be gone."

"Is it true ..." She started and then stopped, but the desire had grown in her eyes. "Is it true that you and Vara ...?" She didn't finish, as though she couldn't bring herself to ask the question. "I mean, in Termina you were together, but I heard ... it was rumored ..."

"It's true," he said, bowing his head, feeling the despair overwhelm his desire to snap back at her, to growl, to tell her to ride off the edge of the bridge. "It's all true." He twisted his neck to look at her. "Now say it and be done." He spoke with no acrimony, his voice was dry and hollow.

"Say what?" She looked at him, and all the emotion he had seen writ upon her face was gone, replaced by a slight furrowing of the lines of her brow, a puckering of her full, purple lips.

"Whatever racy suggestion you're going to throw my way," Cyrus said, still wary. "Just say it. Get it over with."

There was a subtle flicker in her eyes, and the curiosity washed from her face, replaced by something else—*genuine regret*, Cyrus thought. "I'm sorry," Aisling said. "I can't think of anything like that right now. All I have to say is ..." Her lips curved with just a hint of wistfulness, "... I'm sorry for you that it didn't work out." She nodded at him and slowed her horse, falling back into the line with the others that followed behind him.

Cyrus rode on. The bridge stretched before him as far as he could see—and so did his pain.

Chapter 4

The days ran together, one upon another, until all Cyrus could remember was the bridge, the endless grey stone that went on infinitely into the distance. On either side the waters were blue, and a cool breeze ran through the cracks in his armor, keeping the heat of the sun at bay. By the end of the third day, Cyrus imagined throwing himself over the side into the water below, letting his armor drag him down, down to the bottom of the sea, letting his boots sink into the sand, the water rush into his lungs, drowning all his despair along with him ...

The conjured bread grew old by the fourth day, and Cyrus was sick of chewing it, the light airy flavor turning to nothing but mush in his mouth. The conjured water was even worse, less satisfying somehow. Without wood to burn, they slept without fires at night. The only flame available to them was that conjured by wizard and druid, and there were only five of those. Three times a day, long lines were cast over the edge of the bridge and fish were caught, but it was a paltry amount, enough to feed but a few and as flavorless as the bread.

The others steered clear of Cyrus, as though they could sense his foul mood, save for Aisling and Curatio, each of whom made at least one attempt per day to speak with him. Curatio's efforts were squarely in the realm of morale, of worry about the army's waning enthusiasm as the journey across the bridge dragged on. Cyrus spoke in a perfunctory manner, and at the beginning and end of each day attempted to deliver a somewhat motivational speech urging them onward, mentioning that green lands and fresh meat were somewhere over the horizon.

His conversations with Aisling, on the other hand, were another matter entirely. The dark elf had taken to speaking with him in a cheery manner. Cyrus kept the acidity of his responses low, usually not deigning to answer rather than say something that might drive Aisling away. In something of an odd move for her, Aisling had steered well clear of any innuendo in speaking with him—a fact that by the fourth day was not lost on Cyrus.

"So you were born and raised in the Society of Arms in Reikonos?"

she asked him.

Cyrus gripped Windrider's reins tighter. He could feel the horse tense under him, and he ran his gauntlet along the side of the horse's neck gently. "No. I was dropped off there at age six, after my mother died."

"Oh," she said. "Did you know your father at all?"

He thought back, thought about memories from so long ago that they swirled together. "Not well. He died when I was very young, and he was away in the war off and on for a year or two before that." Cyrus tried to remember his mother's face and failed, only a blurry haze where it once had been, the only distinguishing feature being bright eyes, as green as the summer grasses in the plains outside Sanctuary. "I don't really remember my mother either, come to that."

"That's a shame," Aisling said. "What do you remember? About your childhood, I mean?"

Cyrus thought about it, trying to stir some memory in his brain. He felt his nostrils flare and the salt air of the sea loomed large in his mind again. "Meat pies," he said softly, almost too low to be heard. "My mother used to make them. Big, hearty ones, with beef and pork and chicken all crammed into a doughy crust." He could almost smell them, taste them, even though it had been more than two decades since last he had tasted the ones his mother made. "Every time Larana makes them, it brings me back to sitting at the wooden table in our house, eating dinner." He squinted his eyes and the horizon grew fuzzy, blurring. "I can almost picture her when I think of eating meat pies." He remembered brown hair framing the green eyes, and the soft touch of a hand along his face to wipe off dirt or grime. "What about you?" He looked to her and caught a faint blush of darker blue on her cheeks.

"Another time, perhaps," she said, a coy smile covering her embarrassment. Drops of rain splashed upon her head, the first signs that the dark skies above them were preparing to loose their fury. She steered her horse away from him as he watched her go, suddenly regretful at her departure.

He called a halt to their travel as the downpour became so heavy that they could scarcely see the bridge in front of them. Cyrus sat against a pillar as the rain washed down, gathering in puddles that became nothing but rippling rivers running over the sides of the stone bridge in great waterfalls. He looked back at the outline of shapes behind him. He felt a pang and knew that when the rain let up, he'd need to check with the other officers to make certain someone hadn't wandered to the edge of the bridge to relieve themselves during the storm and been swept off by the deluge.

As the rain poured down, rattling his helm, he sat in the shadow of the pillar, Windrider next to him. He looked up at the horse, which whinnied. "Soon," Cyrus said. "You'll have fresh dirt under your hooves soon. Another day at most."

The snort of reply caused Cyrus to crack a smile. "Well, if this rain lets up, anyway. What's wrong, you don't like conjured oats?"

Cyrus could swear he heard a slight growl in the horse's whinny as Windrider answered him, and he looked into the shapes to his side, shrouded in the rain. "I don't like it either. But we'll be there in a few weeks ... and after that, we'll be home ... sometime. A couple months, maybe."

Cyrus could almost hear the thoughts of the horse as he whinnied. He shook his head, wondering how pitiful he must be to think he was talking to a horse. He looked up at the beast, white coat and mane looking grey in the rain. "Then what? I don't know." Cyrus's eyes settled again on the horizon, the darkness ahead where the bridge disappeared into the pouring rain only a hundred feet in front of him. "I don't know what happens when we get home."

Chapter 5

The end of the bridge came into sight by midday next. The storm had passed, giving way to blue skies and intermittent clouds, white, puffy and without a trace of the dark greys that had blackened their crossing on the day before. The sight of green shores sent a murmur through the army at Cyrus's back, enlivening them with energy that had been absent in the last few days. When he reached the end of the grey stone bridge, Cyrus dismounted and walked onto soft ground once more, the cheers of his fellows bringing the ghost of a smile to his face. With a wave of his hand he beckoned them forward as he moved out of the way and the army surged onto the shore as the sun began to set behind them.

The shores were white and sandy, with a beach laid out in either direction to the north and south, curving inland before it reached the horizon. Cyrus could see the red disk of the sun, settling in a half-circle over the water, turning the sapphire surface red. Behind him, he heard his army moving in jubilation, the noise of boots on stone fading as they streamed off the bridge and began to make camp. He had sent Longwell and a few others ahead on horseback to scout above the berm that ended at the inland edge of the beach. He had no desire to be caught under the attack of a hostile force while the Sanctuary army recuperated from their march.

"It's been a long week," Curatio said, appearing at his shoulder.

"Aye." Cyrus stared at the sun, now only a slight edge showing above the waves.

"Perhaps a day of rest might be in order for tomorrow?" Curatio's tone held the air of suggestion only. Cyrus turned and raised an eyebrow; the healer outranked him on the Sanctuary Council, being the lone occupant of the station of Elder, an honorific one step below Guildmaster. Still, Curatio had presented his idea as mere recommendation. "To give our new recruits a chance to enjoy themselves, to give their feet a rest before we head into hostile territory for the next month or so?"

Cyrus watched the waves crash over the shore. He felt a tug

inwardly, the strange and insatiable desire to march onward, to keep going until they reached the castle of Longwell's father, to smite anything in his path. Yet somewhere beyond that was an overwhelming urge to linger, to remain away from Sanctuary and all the inherent problems that would greet him upon their return.

Cyrus rolled his helm between the metal joints of his fingers, listening to the steel scratch against its equal. "We've found fresh water nearby?"

"Aye," Curatio said. "And tracks just inside the woods ahead suggest that there are wild boars in the area. A day of rest could allow for a hunting party to track them—"

"Then we feast upon roast pig and fresh fish?" Cyrus drew a deep breath, and it was almost as though he could feel sundown approach the way an old friend would come to visit. "It'll be good for our morale, I suppose. And as you point out, we are likely to be under stress of worry from potential attack over the coming weeks. Very well. A day of rest is ordered."

Curatio's hair was speckled with silver, but never had his age been more evident than when he smiled, very slightly, back at Cyrus, and the warrior knew he had been maneuvered most expertly. "Duly noted. I'll take care of it." With a slight bow, Curatio turned and began to walk away.

"What would you have said if I'd ordered us to march on?" Cyrus didn't watch the healer, but he heard Curatio's leather shoes stop, the sound of the sand they kicked up on each step coming to a halt.

"I would have tried to convince you, of course." The healer's answer was crisp, serious, and muffled because Curatio had not turned to face him as he gave his answer. The footsteps in the sand resumed, and Cyrus heard the elf move away, back to the sound of camps being set up and fire being started. He pondered Curatio's answer again, and listened once more in his mind to the inflection. It had been very cleverly given, Cyrus thought.

It was also, Cyrus knew, a blatant lie.

Chapter 6

Thanks to the efforts of Martaina and a few of the more experienced rangers, there was indeed wild boar meat waiting for them the next day at breakfast. The smell of the roasting flesh awoke Cyrus, and he sat up to look at the fires along the beach. Many of them bore spits, and recruits talked while circled around them, their voices loud, with much merriment being made. Cyrus could see even at a distance that there were bottles being passed around, spirits of varying kinds that had made the trip from Sanctuary.

Cyrus pulled himself up next to his fire, a small one down the beach from the others. Someone had added logs to it during the night and done so quietly enough that Cyrus hadn't awakened. "Aisling," he said in a low whisper. The next nearest fire was a hundred feet away, and he could see Terian's shadow next to it in the pre-dawn light, his sword once more across his lap. Curatio and Longwell lay around their fire, still sleeping; he could tell them by their garb.

He looked down the beach in the opposite direction. The angle of the curves on either side told him that they were on a peninsula. He snuck a look back at the joviality around the fires, at the silent stone bridge that watched over them, and began to walk, his boots kicking up sand. He looked again behind him; no one seemed to take any notice as his footsteps carried him away from his army.

His hand fell to the scabbard and the hilt of his sword as though he were looking for reassurance. His blade, Praelior, was still there, ever-present and ready to be drawn. He felt the urge to pull it loose and practice with it. *Later. When we're out of sight of the camp, perhaps.*

Tall grasses reached out from the treeline on the berm above the beach, a deep patch of grass that looked as though it would stretch to Cyrus's waist. The chirp of crickets from within was loud, and the trees hanging over the patch of grass waved in the wind, their branches rustling. Somewhere behind them, Cyrus knew the sun was beginning to rise, even though he couldn't see it yet.

"You're not supposed to wander away from the army." He turned to find Aisling standing behind him, a few feet from the grass, a thistle in her hair.

Cyrus let his hand drift away from the hilt of Praelior, where it had come to rest when she had spoken to him. "You don't think we can make an exception for the general who leads said army?"

"Mmmm," she seemed to purr as she considered it, her face pensive. "I think we're in a foreign land with enemies an uncertain distance away." He caught a glint of light in her eyes. "It would probably be better to play safe than be sorry."

He felt his face set in hard lines, an unamused smile only barely there. "You don't think I could take on an entire non-magical army by myself?"

She raised an eyebrow at him. "I believe that if anyone could, it'd be you—but I also believe that you might need more than luck in order to do it."

Cyrus's hand tensed again around Praelior's grip. "I have more than luck."

"Oh, indeed," she said as she began to walk toward him, her small feet leaving little indentations in the dry sand, small craters where her worn leather boots trod. "But perhaps you'll accept that having more help would be ideal, especially if you mean to wander far afield."

"And that'd be you, would it?" He looked back at her, wary.

"Unless you fancy going back to camp and rounding up some others?" She looked at him coolly in reply, impassive.

"What I fancy is doing what I want, when I want, and not being questioned about it."

"Too late for that," she said, smug. "It was too late for that the day after you took your officership. Maybe even the day after you joined Sanctuary. It's hard to go unnoticed around here, even when you're one of the small folk. As an officer and the general of this expedition, it's well nigh impossible."

"I just need to walk—to get away for a bit." He said it with every element of patience he could summon from within.

"Until you what? Walk her right out of you?" She smiled, but it wasn't a happy smile. "You'll be walking a good long time to pull that off, til your feet bleed and your bones rub down to powder. Even then, you'll be lucky to get her out of you before there's nothing left to get her out of."

Why am I talking to her about this? "This isn't your concern," he said.

"It kind of is. You are my general, too. Our expedition counts on you."

He felt a great weariness. "I'm not some sort of communal property that belongs to the whole guild or the army. I'll lead, but this is a day of rest."

"And you're looking so very restful."

"Why are you here?" He spoke in near-silence, his words almost drowned out by the breaking of waves off the shore.

Aisling did not respond at first, and she turned to look back to the forest, staring into the dark spaces between the boughs of the trees, eyes piercing them as though she could see things hidden within. "Because you look like you could use a friend."

"I have friends," Cyrus said, too quickly.

"Do you?" She drew her gaze away from the woods and onto his eyes and he felt himself look away first. "I see a man who leads an army, and who hasn't had a soul talk to him directly in days but the Elder of Sanctuary and myself. The Elder to relay commands and establish order, and myself—for my own reasons, of course."

"I'd find great mystery in your words," Cyrus said, looking away from her and back to the waves and the shore, "if not for the fact that I have known 'your reasons' for as long as I've known you. Your intentions have been made plain; you needn't bother trying to be my friend when we both know that my friendship isn't the part of me you're interested in—"

She stepped in front of him, eyes blazing. "I've never been coy about my intentions toward you, but you fault me for it nonetheless. Would you prefer I dance around it, exchanging biting insults with you? That I berate you for little or no reason and never let a kind word break through my imposing facade?" She stepped closer to him and he caught the scent of her breath, cinnamon, as she brought her face only inches from his. "Are you so steeped in the way of pain and combat that you can't accept honest, sweet words? Does every advance that interests you have to come couched in the agony of bladed phrase and stinging words?"

Her hand was on his cheek, her fingernails tracing delicate lines down his face. She leaned in closer to him, and he felt the pressure of her nails increase even as she lowered her voice to a whisper. "Do you want me to hurt you? Is that what it takes?" She held her hand still, the pressure constant, her nails pressing into his cheek.

His hand came up and seized her wrist, yanking it away. "No," Cyrus said, throwing her hand away from him. "That's not what I want."

She edged closer and he felt the press of her against him through his armor. "Then what does it take?" Her soft breathing seemed to surround him, filling his senses, drowning out the crashing breakers and the chirps of the crickets. "I'm not her. I'll never be her. But I could be …" He could feel her push against him, saw her stand on tiptoes to bring her lips to his, "… what you need right now." He turned his head and her lips found his cheek, and the delicate kiss she left there sent a surge of feeling through his whole body. "I can do … what she hasn't, what I know you need … it's been a long time, hasn't it …?"

"Long time," he said, echoing her, the truth stumbling from his mouth. He wished he could force it back in there, along with everything else that had happened in the last month, but it was there, nonetheless.

Cyrus felt the moment fade, and as Aisling leaned up to kiss him he gently shook himself free of her. There was no anger in him; only wistfulness and a deep sorrow. "I'm sorry. I don't need what you think I do—and I'm not what you need, either."

She looked suddenly very small to his eyes, but she summoned her courage and spoke again. "Do you even know what you need right now?"

He thought about it and heard his own breath as he inhaled then exhaled, thinking. Inhale, exhale. "I don't. But I don't think that me— really me, inside, not my urges, but me—I don't think that's what I need."

She nodded, but it was subtle and slight, a barely-there movement of her head. "If you don't know what you need—really need—then how do you know what I need?"

Without waiting for him to answer she turned and soundlessly she stalked off into the grass, disappearing at the treeline with only a single glance back at him before she faded away behind a tree trunk.

The last look was nothing but regret, pure and longing—and with life of its own.

Chapter 7

The celebration went on throughout the day. Cyrus could hear it from where he stayed, out of sight down the shore, swinging Praelior at imaginary foes, feeling the sweat from his exertions rolling down his face.

It will not work, Cyrus ... He saw himself in the Realm of Death, his blade cutting into the chest of a demon knight, his sword biting into the bulging muscles of the creature, its breath foul and heavy with the stink of fetid rot, of death itself, on the day that he challenged the might of Mortus, the God of Death, and survived ...

It can never be, you and I ... He brought Praelior around in a slice that he imagined caught the ready neck of a dark elven footsoldier, landing at the seam of his armor. In his mind he was back on the bridge in Termina on a long, cold night that followed a day filled with infinite promise. He could almost feel the chill, even in the tropical air.

For I am elf, and my life is long and my duties are as great as my sorrow ... He brought the blade down on the skull of a foe who wasn't there, a goblin, heard the satisfying crack of sword on skull in his mind's eye. He remembered the night that he and Sanctuary had invaded Enterra, the night that he had claimed the scabbard that rode on his hip, that made Praelior whole, a weapon unmatched in the world of men, and he could sense the clinging desperation of the moment when Vara had died in the depths, when he'd watched Emperor Y'rakh drop her to the ground, her golden hair spilling onto the floor ...

We will not, cannot be ... He stopped and reversed his grip, holding Praelior above his head and thrust it toward the ground, burying it into the head of Ashan'agar, heard the howl of he who was once the Dragonlord, and remembered the feel of the wind on his face as he rode the back of the beast into the rocky ground of the Mountains of Nartanis.

Not ever ... Cyrus felt himself in another place, before swords, before blades and armor, where the sand was thick with the blood of the fallen. He felt himself breathe heavy, cold air, the aroma of sweat around him. His eyes found his foes, and there were more of them than he could count. He felt the rush of fear, and tried to quiet it, but—

Not ever.

His eyes snapped open and he turned, Praelior pointed at a figure standing at a distance from him, hands open and outstretched. Cyrus's eyes widened in the realization that he had moved on instinct, had known that someone was there unconsciously and acted before being truly aware of it himself. He saw who it was, and took a deep breath, then another, long, loud gasps, causing his chest to heave with the exertion he'd just undertaken. He looked at the arm that held Praelior and it trembled. He lowered the blade from where it pointed at a figure before him. "Odellan."

"General," Odellan said. He wasn't wearing his helmet, but it was under his arm. The elf's armor was polished to shine, the same set he wore when he was an Endrenshan—a Captain—in the Termina Guard. The surface of his breastplate was lines and art, carvings in the metal that gave it an artistic touch that Cyrus's straightforward black armor lacked. Odellan's helm was similarly adorned, with winged extensions that rose above his head and down on either side of his face as well. It rested now in the crook of his elbow, and the elf's face was relaxed, his blond hair stirring in the sea breeze. "I didn't mean to disturb your training."

Cyrus slid Praelior back into the scabbar, and managed to get his breathing under control. "Walking the beach is hardly disturbing me, Odellan. You just surprised me, that's all."

Odellan nodded, inclining his head to the side. "I'm impressed you heard my approach with your back turned and the waves crashing as they are. Your hearing must be near-elvish in its efficacy."

Cyrus pulled a gauntlet from his hand and used his sleeve to wipe the sweat from his forehead. "I take it you're out for a walk?"

"No, actually," Odellan said. "Sorry to interrupt you, but I had a purpose. Longwell was looking for you, wanted to discuss the course for tomorrow."

"I'll find him shortly," Cyrus said, sniffing. "Is there still an abundance of boar? I find myself more hungry than I thought."

Odellan allowed a smile, an oddity on the face of most elves Cyrus had met in his life. Only in the last few years, in Sanctuary, had he gotten to know them more closely and seen behind the somewhat straitlaced facade typical of their race's conduct with offlanders—non-elves. "I can't imagine why—days of insubstantial bread and water supplemented by bony fish not quite to the taste of your palate?"

Cyrus felt a quiet chuckle escape him. "I suppose not." He felt a rumble in his stomach. "I'm going to get something to eat. Are you going to keep walking down the beach?"

"No," Odellan said, falling into step beside Cyrus as the warrior began to make his way toward the encampment. "I'll accompany you, if that's all right."

Cyrus shot Odellan a sly look. "Why wouldn't it be?"

Odellan's returned expression was near-inscrutable. "I'd heard you were feeling decidedly unsociable of late."

"I see," Cyrus said. "Doubtless the rumor mill supplied you with reason enough for my desire to remain … isolated."

"Indeed," Odellan said with a nod. "Even a newcomer such as myself can't help but be exposed to discussions among the rank and file of why our revered General—a man they refer to in hushed tones as 'Cyrus the Unbroken'—has gone from a charismatic brawler with a decidedly outspoken persona to a black hole of despair, the very image our elven artists look to when trying to capture the mood of our society this last millenia."

Cyrus halted and Odellan walked another pace before stopping. Cyrus's eyes narrowed at the elf. "Some of that was funny, and I can't decide how I feel about that."

Odellan raised an eyebrow. "Only some of it? I was trying to keep a playful tone throughout."

"The 'Cyrus the Unbroken' bit was a tad grim; otherwise you succeeded."

"Ah, that," Odellan said, looking back at him. "It seems there's a story that goes along with it, though I've yet to hear it told the same way twice."

"And the rumors about the reason I'm as black in the mood as an elvish artisan? Are those told the same twice, or do the details vary with the telling?"

Odellan cast his eyes down. "Those seem to be almost the same every time. A dashing young warrior, a rising star in the Sanctuary firmament, casts his eyes upon an elven paladin of legend, spills the secrets of his soul to her, and receives naught but anguish for his reward." Odellan tilted his head, his expression pained. "It would be hard for even the most accomplished embellisher of stories to mistake a tale so plain as that one."

"That's never stopped rumormongers from trying."

"As you can tell, the broad strokes of that one convey all the important bits," Odellan said. "Whether anything else happened, we all get the gist." Cyrus caught a flicker of something behind the elf's eyes, some pain within. "Heartbreak is no great joy for any of us, but no one will disturb you if you don't wish to talk about it—"

"I don't," Cyrus said, resuming his walk. "It's nothing personal, but my ... adversities are my own."

"Well, that would make it personal, wouldn't it? Still, I understand completely." The elf gave Cyrus a curt nod. "And I shan't bring it up again." Odellan hesitated. "Save but to say that if ever a day comes when you wish to discuss it ... I am the soul of discretion."

Cyrus felt the muscles in his body tense and then relax, the full effect of Odellan's offer running through his mind. "It's kind of you, Odellan. I doubt that day will come, but I appreciate the offer."

"A kindness I fear is all too small a repayment for those you've done for me." Odellan's silver boots had begun to collect small clumps of wet sand, and the shine on the top of his metal-encased feet was not nearly so polished as his breastplate. "After all, you saved my life and the lives of countless of my people in Termina and then brought me from exile to a place where I can do some small good, I hope."

"More than small, I would think," Cyrus said as they passed the embers of the fire he had slept beside. The sun had risen in the western sky and was hanging high above the sea, day in full and glorious bloom.

The smell of roasted pig was in the air, and Cyrus could see Martaina Proelius next to a boar that looked to be fairly intact, and the ranger gave him a smile as he approached. "Hungry?" she asked.

"Indeed I am," he said, his voice suddenly scratchy. "How's the boar?"

"Oh, he's dead," she said, taking a knife from her belt and carving a slice from the haunch. "But tasty. It's nice to see you seeking the company of others again, sir, even if it is only for a meal."

"Well ... not only for a meal," he said, eliciting a wider grin from the ranger. He took a bite of the meat she had given him. "That is good." He shifted the meat around on his tongue, tasted the curious flavor of something beyond meat and fat. "There are spices in this."

Martaina grinned with obvious pleasure. "I found some familiar plants over the berm; it made seasoning these beasts all the sweeter."

"Well done," Cyrus told her, beginning to turn away. "Well done indeed."

"General," she said, causing him to turn back. "Remember that you're among friends here."

He gave her a wan smile and turned back toward the officer's fire, Odellan at his side. "Even if I forgot, there seems to be no shortage of reminders."

"These people love you, General." Odellan said it with quiet certitude. "The veterans, the ones who came to help you train the newest, they have been through fire and death with you and have followed you off the very map." He shook his head. "I wish I had commanded such loyalty when I was in charge of the Termina Guard."

"I daresay you commanded more in your last battle," Cyrus said. "My people have a very good chance of resurrection if they should fall. Your men knew that the fight for Termina would cost many of them their lives and they stood with you anyway."

"They fought for King and country and for their homes, for the lives of their brethren," Odellan said with a quiet shake of his head. "That is a powerful motivator, and one that is lacking in guilds such as Sanctuary. At first blush, I should think guild life would be the purest sort of mercenary company, a people banded together for mutual gain, undertaking adventure, exploration and battle in the farthest and most dangerous reaches of the world for the wealth and riches they can reap. Yet it is not so."

Odellan's mailed fingers rested on his helm, his eyes seeming to trace the lines of the carving upon it. "I watched Sanctuary stand against the God of Death—a god! Something not seen by living eyes in generations of your people! Yet it was not Sanctuary that broke but Mortus. Of those who stood with you, only one of them shouted in fear, and none of them lost command of themselves or ran. I should imagine that any mercenary company would have trembled when he descended from the air above us. I would think that even the Termina Guard, who held against the certain death that the dark elves levied against us, would have quailed at the sight of a god, of death, of the endless sleep.

"You say that these people stand with you because they know there is a chance of resurrection if they fall. I remind you that many of them stood with you then, in the Realm of Death, when there was no chance at all if they died. It is not because of King or country or riches or gain that the army of Sanctuary stood with you then or that they are with you now, here beyond the edge of the world." The fire in Odellan's eyes burned brighter. "They believe—in you, in the cause, in what we are doing here. The veterans believe enough that they would die for it." Odellan turned his head and looked back to the still-burning fires that littered the beach. "The newest have been sent here to find that conviction for themselves."

Cyrus stopped and looked with Odellan down the beach, at the thousand souls under his command, waiting for his word to march forward on the morrow, into battle, pain, and possible death. "I don't know what kind of belief I can give them." He shook his head, and the little mirth that he had felt when talking to Martaina dissipated like a wisp of smoke after a fire has been put out. "I'm carrying a weight of my own right now. I'll do my duty, help forge them in battle and keep them from danger as best I can, but ... belief?" Cyrus shook his head. "That's something they'll have to figure out for themselves."

"You're right, they do," Odellan said. "But you will show them the way."

"I don't know how I can do that," Cyrus said, "when I'm not sure what I believe in anymore."

"You still hold true to duty—honor—purpose. These are things you wear like your armor." Odellan stared at Cyrus, and Cyrus looked back at him. "You are here at a time when you'd almost assuredly like to be elsewhere. You're doing your duty to your guild and holding true to a friend who asked for help."

Cyrus cleared his throat. "It sounds pretty when you say it like that, and I told myself the same when we were leaving Sanctuary, that I was here to do my duty and fight for the guild and what we stand for." He looked back at the bridge, the long stone causeway that stretched over the horizon, and lowered his voice to a whisper. "But I had a long time to consider it on the bridge. I don't think that's why I'm here anymore." Cyrus heard a hollowness in his words, in his tone, something brittle and empty, and the slow dawning within him of something he had yet to fully admit to himself.

Odellan stared back, impassive. "Why do you think you're here?"

Cyrus looked back at the bridge again, the endless bridge. The seas were so blue beneath it, the skies only a slightly lighter shade above the horizon. And in the distance, far in the distance was ... nothing. Nothing visible. His horse was nearby. He could climb on Windrider and ride, just ride—

But not back to the bridge. Not over it.

"You certainly said it well when we left," Odellan said, jarring Cyrus away from his thoughts. "You spoke of duty and nobility of purpose, of helping others in need, and you said it with conviction enough that I believed you." The elf didn't look judgmental, and he said it matter-of-factly. "So if that's not why you're here, then what is it? What compelled you to lead us over the bridge, if not your honor and desire to help a friend?"

Cyrus saw in his mind's eye the image of himself on Windrider's back, of a long gallop down a winding road in a far off land. He saw villages, mountains, forests and cities. Castles passed him by and he rode through jungle and swamp. Nothing he saw was familiar yet all of it was. Behind him, all the while, was the specter of something else, something that drove him onward, that would not let him rest.

Her.

"I meant it when I said it to them," Cyrus whispered, meeting Odellan's gaze at last. "I just ... I don't know that I believe it anymore. I feel ... empty inside, like all the wine has been poured from my cup and there's not enough left but to ripple at the bottom when something happens—as though the littlest things can bring me only the slightest of joys now. A month ago, a year ago, I would have come here for duty, for honor, for all those things." He shook his head ever so slightly and a pained expression crossed his face, anchored in place by the realization that had now fully formed within him. "But that's not why I'm here now.

"I'm here because I'm running—from her."

Chapter 8

"General," Odellan said in a low whisper of his own, so low it was almost inaudible to Cyrus's ears. "You are wounded, sir. You are wounded in a way that no healing spell can cure. The cut runs deep, to the quick of you. That is to be expected. But you are still the same man who undertook this mission, and whatever your reasons, I know you and I have seen what you believe borne out by what you do, which is the truest guide." Odellan's finger came to land on Cyrus's black breastplate and tapped on it, twice, for emphasis. "This wound will fade in time, and you'll be left with what was inside all along—a purpose forged in fire. No matter what else happens, you'll do your duty. I'd stake my life on it—and I have."

"I hope you're right," Cyrus said, not feeling the same certainty as the elf. "I certainly hope you're right."

Cyrus shuffled to the officer's fire and noted a few others standing around it—Nyad, her red robes billowing around her like a cloak, Ryin Ayend standing next to her, too close to merely be considered friendly or familiar. Curatio and J'anda were there, J'anda watching Cyrus, a light smile upon his blue face. Samwen Longwell waited with them as well, the long handle of his lance resting against his dark blue armor. He was careful to avoid running it across the white surcoat he wore over his ensemble. "General," Longwell said with a nod.

"This is where I take my leave of you," Odellan said in a whisper.

"Stay," Cyrus said, turning back to him. "I'd like you to sit in on this."

Odellan hesitated, clearly torn. "I'd certainly like to. But I am a new recruit in this guild, and it would be improper for me to be sitting in on a war council not a week into my tenure here. Other recruits would be most aggrieved if this particular honor bestowed me came to their attention—enough so that it would cause complaints to come your way, surely—"

"Send the complainers my way," Cyrus said in a low, gravelly voice. "I may even invite them to sit in as well, if ever they've led an army against a horde of dark elves." He smiled at Odellan, causing the elf to return one weakly before Cyrus turned back to the waiting Council. "Hello, all," Cyrus said, then paused. "J'anda," he said to the enchanter, who inclined his head and smiled back at Cyrus, "I don't recall you being with us when we left Sanctuary."

"Indeed I was not," the enchanter said with his customary smile, "but after a day or so of contemplation, I realized that heading into an unfamiliar land, filled to the brimming with men and armies, you may have need of my particular skills." He bowed with a flourish.

"Well," Cyrus said with a slight shrug, "I can't say I'm sorry to see you." He looked around the impromptu circle. "Before we get started, I want to apologize for my ... reclusiveness on our journey thus far."

There was an air of discomfort around the fire, the officers shifting their gazes to each other, wearing pained expressions, until Terian spoke from behind Cyrus. "Somehow we've managed in your absence, oh great and mighty." The dark knight brushed past Cyrus, the point of his pauldron clanking against Cyrus's armor. "I think we all expected that what happened between you and Vara would put you out of commission for a while longer." His eyebrows arched upward, almost leering. "Did you manage to put her behind you or does she remain on top— metaphorically speaking, of course," Terian said with a wicked grin. "We all know that you didn't actually get that far—"

"He didn't?" Nyad turned to look at him, her mouth agape in a way that made her look slightly mawkish. "I'd heard you and she had finally consummated your torturously prolonged courtship after we got back from Pharesia!"

Cyrus felt a flush of red run through his cheeks and looked down.

Before he could answer, Terian spoke again. "Hah! The last time Cyrus had relations was probably back when there was only one position." There was a glimmer of spite in Terian's eye as he turned to look at Cyrus, something beyond the give and take that they exchanged along with their usual banter.

Cyrus shook it off, pasting a fake smile on his face as he feigned amazement. "There's more than one position now? What new devilry is this?"

"That's enough," Curatio said, stern in a way Cyrus hadn't heard from the elder elf before. "We have things to discuss, and I'm certain that if Cyrus wishes to talk about his personal matters in Council ... well, I would immediately suspect he was some sort of enchanter masquerading as Cyrus."

"It wouldn't be me," J'anda said. "I have many less depressing people to be if the mood strikes."

"Thank you, Curatio," Cyrus said. "I think there was a word of support buried in there, somewhere. But you are correct, we have matters to discuss. We enter hostile territory tomorrow." He looked to Longwell for confirmation.

The dragoon swung his lance around and buried the three-pronged head into the sand, where it stood upright. "We are already within the bounds of the Kingdom of Actaluere, but their nearest village is quite a few miles from here and we're unlikely to run across any patrols this far out. Tomorrow, and every day that follows as we go deeper into their Kingdom, the greater chance we stand of running into hostile forces."

"Can we go around their Kingdom?" Nyad asked. Her face was screwed in concentration, as though she had other questions waiting to bubble forth. "After all, as I understand it, we're not here to combat these people."

"You are correct," Longwell said, his lilting accent stirring the words pleasantly. "My father's Kingdom—called Galbadien, by the way—is not at war with Actaluere. But neither are we allies. The King of Actaluere is Milos Tiernen. He is a younger man than the other two Kings of Luukessia, and cunning. He spent a few years on a galley trader, doing business with the gnomes across the Sea of Carmas, and he learned to be even more shrewd than he already was. He controls the area north of here for quite a distance yet, and we'd have to skirt a very narrow border between his land and the northern King's—that's the one my father is at war with. The northern Kingdom is called Syloreas, and is ruled by a very grizzled man named Briyce Unger. He is completely without guile, a conqueror born, and he and my father have squabbled over their borders since each of them took the throne only a few years apart from each other. His men are the ones we are here to fight."

"What can we expect in terms of resistance as we cross Actaluere?" J'anda shifted his sandaled feet on the beach.

"Hard to say," Longwell said, looking at each of the Council in turn. "Each of the keeps throughout the Kingdom would fight for its own defense unless they summoned aid or the King were to call them together for some purpose—invasion, war, whatnot. Each of the three Kingdoms in Luukessia is much the same, more fragmented and feudal than Arkaria by far. The Kings rely on their barons and dukes to keep the order in their own lands."

"So even after we cross their borders, it would be a while before they could bring their full might to bear—if they were of a mind to," Odellan said, his fingers resting on his chin, deep in thought.

"I don't mean to be rude, but I thought this was to be an officer's meeting?" Ryin asked. "May I ask why a new recruit is here?"

"Sure, ask away," Cyrus said. "The fact that they're so divided works to our advantage. We'll be halfway across Actaluere before they can put up an army worthy of our concern."

"Do not rule out treachery," Longwell said. "I would not put it past King Tiernan to attack us in the night, when we least expect it."

"That would be to our advantage as well, I suspect," Odellan said.

"Excuse me," Ayend said in annoyance. "But I've yet to get an answer to my question."

"Yes, you did. You didn't ask why Odellan was here, you said, 'May I ask why a new recruit is here?'" Cyrus shrugged. "Subtle distinction but important to getting the answer you seek—in one case you're asking for permission to ask a question, in the other you're asking the question."

"I should have expected nothing less from a petulant child—" Ryin let out a snort of disgust.

"I'm having a strategy meeting to organize the next phase of our march," Cyrus cut him off, cool as steel. "If you want to have a temper tantrum about why a man who has led an army is sitting in on my planning session, I suggest you do so while teleporting yourself back to Sanctuary."

The silence hung in the air until Terian broke it. "I haven't had this much fun since that time I got kicked out of the guild for standing back and letting Orion squabble with that dipshit gnome. You two should fight; I put my money on Cyrus." Terian looked to Cyrus, who met his gaze. "Maybe after you're done kicking his ass, he'll let you relieve your tension with his wizard squeeze." The dark elf waved vaguely at Nyad. "Unless you're just saving it all up for battle. Which would explain a lot, come to think of it—"

"Enough." Curatio's voice crackled across them all. "Ryin, Cyrus is General and in command of this mission. Including a former guard captain of the elves who is quite experienced is a wise and prudent course of action; surely you must see that." Curatio's tone was soft, but Cyrus heard the iron beneath it. The healer's eyes cut over to Cyrus, ignoring Terian entirely. "General, if you'd care to continue."

"Not much more to say, I think." Cyrus looked around the circle. "We'll travel by day because it's an easier march. I'll want watches around the clock, sentries keeping an eye on everything—and no one on watch more than one night in a row. We need everyone well rested. I also want outriders scouting during the day, experienced rangers who will know how to escape getting caught by hunting parties. We'll stay in villages and inns as much as we can manage, buy local goods and food, spread some gold around, which will be good for us and for the locals. Hopefully that will give Milos Tiernan cause enough to let us pass uncontested." He turned to Longwell. "How long will we be traversing Actaluere?"

Longwell frowned, pensive. "I would say nearing two months. Perhaps a month and a half if we make haste, but two months is more probable. I suspect it will be a week, two if we are fortunate, before Actaluere becomes aware of our presence here. After that," he shrugged his shoulders lightly, "another week perhaps before they challenge our resolve, if it comes to that."

"We'll make ready on the morrow, then," Cyrus said. "We'll need to be vigilant as we cross their territory." He turned his head to Nyad. "We won't be going around. I'll have Martaina organize the rangers for what we talked about. She is the most senior ranger with us, yes?" Catching a nod from Curatio, he went on. "Odellan, Terian, Longwell and I will coordinate with the warriors and other front rank fighters, setting up watches and preparing for the imminent conflict with Actaluere's army."

"Let me caution you," Longwell said, "I was guessing when I said how long it would take for them to rally. It could be shorter. They could band together two or three holdfasts worth of knights and infantry and make a challenge to us tomorrow if they saw us walking about."

"Duly noted." Cyrus gave Longwell a curt nod. "We'll prepare as if they'll be waiting for us behind every corner, and we'll march as quickly as we can without causing our army to wear out. The next two months will be hard, harder on morale than on our bodies, methinks. They'll grow lean from the march, but it'll be the mind that feels the friction of this before their feet do, this constant motion forward. Our army will tire of looking around every turn in the road for the enemy, and complacency will set in. We need to remind them of the urgent need for constant vigilance, especially among the veterans, the watchers. They'll be the most prone to overconfidence."

Cyrus turned his eyes toward the berm and the trees beyond. "They're out there, somewhere, and we need to march out of here tomorrow as though they know we're already here and that they're waiting for us in ambush. We need to carry that feeling, without fatigue, for the next two months." He looked back at the Council, at all of them, saw the disinterest in Ayend's eyes contrasted with the rapt attention from Odellan. "Because the only threat to us now is that we don't—and then they'll overwhelm us when we least expect it."

Chapter 9

They marched out the next day, over the berm and along a path that carried them inland. By the end of the day they had passed through coastal swamps and long grasses at the side of the path and had grown tired of palm trees and algae-covered ponds. A week passed as they followed the same routine: breaking camp as the sun rose, marching for two hours then taking a short break, followed by another two-hour walk at which point lunch was served (meat from whatever could be hunted, foraged berries and plants supplemented with conjured bread and water). In the afternoon there came another two or three more marches before they ended their day finding a suitable campsite.

Some days they would make camp earlier or later depending on what the scouts told Cyrus. Good ground was critically important, and Cyrus planned their final stop of the night around finding defensible positions on level ground. Edible plants and game were plentiful, providing the army with sustenance and keeping the grumbling to a minimum. From time to time they stayed in inns, buying local animals from farms for slaughter, and ale from the tavern keepers, who seemed pleased at the amount of gold that came to them in exchange for what they gave. Complaints about the length of marches were more frequent, though after the second week only the most disgruntled even bothered any longer. Most took the long days in stride, accepting of the direction they were heading.

"What do we do about the ones who want to go home?" Ryin had voiced the thought after only a day's march past the bridge.

"Tell them that the bridge is back that way," Terian pointed behind them, "and invite them to be on with it."

As the second week died, Cyrus could feel the tension that had surrounded them upon leaving the beach dissolve, the quiet marches giving way to laughter and joviality, the evening campfires going from being solemn events where all were watchful to festive occasions.

"I'm trying to decide if I like them better like this or worse," Cyrus said to Curatio one night in the second week as they sat by the fire,

Cyrus chewing on a roasted haunch from a herd of goats that Martaina's rangers had bought from a local farm.

"So long as the outriders and the watch take their duties seriously, we'll be fine," the elder elf told him. "This journey will be hard enough on their spirits and their bodies without driving constant fear into them. They wake early and go to bed early, and live their lives on their feet in all moments between. Remind the watchmen of their duty with all the fury you'd waste on the ranks of the army, and spare the others the misery." Curatio took a sip from a skin of wine from the last village they had visited. "Their feet give them enough of that, I suspect—I've healed enough blisters in the last two weeks to know that much."

They passed a moment in silence, Cyrus chewing on a piece of meat. "Alaric sent more than half the Council on this expedition."

Curatio grunted in acknowledgment, and when Cyrus said nothing in response, the healer spoke. "Is there a question to go along with that observation?"

Cyrus continued to stare into the fire that crackled and popped in front of them as it caught hold of a branch that had slipped to the edge of the fire. "He knew what happened between Vara and I, didn't he? He thought I wouldn't be up to the task of commanding the expedition on my own."

"Alaric and I did not part on the best of terms, so I wouldn't feel qualified to tell you what he might have been thinking when we left," Curatio said. "But I will tell you that the officers that are here volunteered to be here—in fact, every officer volunteered to come." Curatio hesitated. "Save one, of course."

"Of course. She was hardly in a fit state to go on a long pilgrimage, after all." Cyrus felt his lips become a grim line. "Nor do I think she would have wanted to be burdened by the company she'd have had to keep while on this jaunt."

"Alaric knows people," Curatio said. "That's his gift, really, to know people, to see into their hearts. It's not some magical power, just a keen insight into the soul. If he sent more officers than was strictly necessary, it is not because he didn't trust you. It's because he sought to aid you in a time when he knew you would be going through great difficulty."

He looked at Curatio, who remained stoic, staring into the fire.

"You've lived for 23,000 years. Any advice on getting through this ..." He blanched as he felt the pain rising within, "'great difficulty'?"

Curatio did not move, did not stir, did not even seem to breathe. When he broke his silence, his voice sounded like a whisper caught on the wind. "Did you love her? Well and truly, more than anyone you'd loved before?"

Cyrus heard the quiet scrape of the fingers of his gauntlet as he ran them across his greaves, heard the sound of the breeze coursing over him and stirring the leaves of the forest that surrounded them, smelled the meat on the fire. "Yes. More than anyone. More than the woman I married."

"Then no." Curatio moved at last, reaching for a piece of dried wood behind him and tossing it upon the fire. "I don't have any advice that will help you."

Over the next seven days they marched into more populated areas. The coastal swamps gave way to green fields, orchards with citrus trees as far as the eye could see, fields of sugar cane and countless other farms. The army began to pass people on the road, horse-drawn carts, small children playing, all of whom moved aside to gawk at the army of Sanctuary as they went past in neat formation. Eyes widened at the sight of dark elves; Cyrus saw a small child run in terror upon seeing the handful of goblins who marched with them.

As Cyrus rode past· the onlookers, he felt someone slip into formation next to him, at the head of the army. He blinked when he realized it was Martaina, her usual carefree happiness gone, replaced by a taut expression, the lines of her face all angled, her eyes darting in all directions.

"What is it?" Cyrus asked.

"I've been seeing watchers," she said, turning to give him all her attention. "In the woods, in the trees. At distance, to be sure, but they're there. We've got shadows, and they're following us about the countryside."

Cyrus looked around, trying to spy to the horizon, across the fields, but all he saw were groves of trees on one side, long grass on the other, and a road that wended its way into the distance. "If you say you saw them, I believe you. Human eyesight is can't compare to yours."

"They're out there." She chewed her lip. "Not many, not yet.

Maybe a dozen or two, it's hard to tell. I think they have spyglasses, because I see the shine of light off them from time to time. They're definitely watching and waiting but hard to say what for."

"Scouting party, maybe. Longwell!" Cyrus called behind him, and the dragoon dutifully trotted up to join he and Martaina. "Our rangers have sighted watchers keeping an eye on us."

Longwell's serious face grew more drawn. "Should have figured. We're only a day's ride from Green Hill, which is Baron Hoygraf's keep. One of Luukessia's most singularly humorless chaps. If there was to be a fight for us on this side of Actaluere, it would be from him."

"This would have been good to know," Cyrus said. "You think this Baron Hoygraf will try something?"

Longwell gave a broad, expansive shrug. "Only a little more than any other titled defender of the realm of Actaluere whose game we're picking off. The animals we eat are his property by the laws of the land. None of them will take kindly to our treading across their roads either, especially with an army. I'm certain word has reached their capital, Caenalys, by now. Hoygraf would be his leading edge if their King means to move against us. He'll be operating independently of King Tiernan for now, which should be a cause for concern." Longwell dipped his shoulder, almost contritely, apologizing for the news he was delivering. "Like I said, he's a humorless bastard."

"How many men does he have at his command?" Cyrus asked.

"A half-thousand, perhaps, at his hold. Maybe a few score more but not many." Longwell's hand pointed to the horizon. "He'll be able to secure reinforcements if he calls for his bannermen from nearby holdfasts, but it'll take a few days."

"He won't be a serious threat in a direct battle until then," Cyrus said. "But we'll still need to keep careful watch. Unless the people of Luukessia have no use for treachery?"

"Oh, they have many uses for it," Longwell said with a half-smile. "Many."

They rode without incident for the rest of the day and camped that evening on a grassy plain, a thousand stars lighting the skies above them. Cyrus fell asleep with his mind on a blond elf, her words fading in his ears, and awoke when Odellan shook him shortly after midnight.

Cyrus sat up and looked into the face of the elf, whose helm was hiding his fair hair. "What happened?"

Odellan's mouth was a thin line. "We lost a scouting party."

"Lost?" Cyrus got to his feet. "I presume they were too experienced to get 'lost' if they were a scouting party."

"One veteran ranger named Mikal, a human," Odellan said. "Had a couple new warriors and rangers with him. They were sent to the north during the night to reconnoiter the farms above us, see if there was any sign of trouble. They didn't report in when they were supposed to."

Cyrus rubbed his eyes. "How overdue are they?"

Odellan's grimace became worse. "Six hours."

"All right," Cyrus said, his hands feeling at the hilt of Praelior at his side. The rush of strength from it gave him a jolt, helping him wake. "I don't want to become too alarmed yet. They may have had good cause to detour around something, or perhaps found something that they're taking a closer look at. We'll wait, for now. We'll give them until sunrise, then go looking for them."

"You don't want to send searchers after them now?" Odellan looked concerned.

"Purely at a gut level, yes," Cyrus said. "But six hours could be reasonable caution on their part, taking care to get back to us without getting themselves into trouble. There are a host of possibilities, and I don't want to get overexcited when we have no idea what's happened to them."

"So we send a search party at dawn?" Odellan's body was frozen in a hesitant state, stiff and formal.

"No," Cyrus said, causing the elf to blink. "Then we go looking for them. All of us—the whole army. If something caused one scouting party to disappear, I'm not taking a chance on sending another into the same trap. We go in force."

Odellan cracked a smile. "Aye, sir."

The night lasted long, and Cyrus never returned to the ever-elusive sleep he had found before. Instead he stared at the campfire, watched the flames dance, the hues of orange at the top, the whitish heat at the base of it, and he saw a shade that seemed familiar. The fire swayed in the wind, and he saw the yellow at the heart of it, the same color as her hair, and it moved, like the swishing of her ponytail …

The sun came up as it always did and brought with it a surprise. A

rider with a flag of truce was brought to Cyrus at dawn, Longwell and
Odellan escorting him. The man was stout, red of hair and beard, both
of which were long and reached to the middle of his chest and back. He
approached Cyrus's fire, with Longwell and Odellan flanking him.
Neither looked particularly happy to Cyrus's eyes, and the warrior felt a
chill inside as the man approached, his face freckled and aged, his chin
held high.

"My name is Cyrus Davidon," he said upon greeting the envoy, "of
the army of Sanctuary."

"My name is Olivere. I bring the compliments of Baron Hoygraf,"
the envoy began, "who speaks in the voice of Milos Tiernan, King of
Actaluere." Olivere wore darkened steel armor with a blue surcoat that
had a shark upon it, leaping out of a field of water.

"I accept his compliments," Cyrus said, "and wonder what would
possess the good Baron and the King to be sending an emissary to me."

The envoy smiled, a cunning smile that caused Cyrus's concerns to
congeal inside him like old blood. "You march an army through their
lands without their leave to do so and kill game from their fields, fish
from their streams. You're fortunate that you've received an emissary
and not darker tidings."

"Come now," Cyrus said, in as friendly of a tone as he could
manage, "we've made no hostile movements against your King or your
Baron. We're passing through on our way to Galbadien to aid in their
war against Syloreas. I have no quarrel with your King or Baron and
will even pay them a toll for using their roads or killing their game if
they would so like."

"I'm afraid that's unacceptable," the man said. "Having an army,
hostile or no, traveling through the heart of the peaceful Kingdom of
Actaluere, is not something that Baron Hoygraf will permit. It is
considered an act of war. However," the envoy said, his smile becoming
more genial, "should you turn your force around and take them back the
way you came, we will grant you safe passage back to the bridge, so
that you may return to your foreign homeland and inform them of the
graciousness of Baron Hoygraf of Actaluere and our primacy over the
spiteful Kingdoms of Galbadien and Syloreas."

"Hmmm," Cyrus said. "I had a feeling we might come to this
particular sticking point."

"Oh?" The man cocked his head, and his red beard shifted with him, lying flat against his dark armor. "You don't wish to turn around, I take it?"

"Wishing has little enough to do with it." Cyrus turned his back on the envoy. "I've committed our force to act on the behalf of the King of Galbadien, and I keep my word." He turned to the envoy. "That's something you should tell your Baron about me—about us, I should say, the army of Sanctuary and myself. We keep our word and our commitments."

"I see," Olivere said. "And I take it that my peaceful words shan't change your mind?"

"Doubtful," Cyrus said. "So try making your threat, instead."

"Very well." Olivere smiled, a smarmy, disingenuous smile this time that made Cyrus want to bury his sword in the man's face. "You realize that you're missing a war party, I take it?"

"I realize that you've taken our scouting party," Cyrus said, eyes narrowed. "Are they dead or alive?"

"They live, for now," Olivere said. "Had you been reasonable and agreed to go back to the bridge, they would have been released immediately. As it is, if you turn back, we'll return them to you there before you cross. If you don't turn back, we'll kill them, one per day, until you either return to the bridge or we're forced to bring our army against yours." He leaned forward to Cyrus, and the smile got wider. "And their deaths won't be quick nor will they be painless."

Cyrus stared into Olivere's eyes, saw the twisted pleasure, the taunt within, and Cyrus felt something grow very cold within him, a chill that seemed to ice his skin and bones like the frost on winter mornings in the Northlands. He looked behind Olivere to Longwell. "How far away is Green Hill?"

"A few hours ride," Longwell said, concentrating. "Why?"

"Get the army moving," Cyrus said. He looked back to Olivere. "Carry this message back to your liege. I will be at his gates with my army within hours. If my people are not safely delivered to me upon our arrival, I will burn his keep and kill all his men. And it will not be quick," Cyrus said with malice, "nor will it be painless, especially in his own case."

Olivere's eyes flickered, and the man withdrew his head from where it had been leaning forward, the wicked light in his eyes smothered. "Green Hill is a fortress. You'll spend months trying to lay siege to us—months you don't have. The Army of Actaluere is already in motion and will fall on you sooner than you expect. We have watchers in the hills by the bridge, and we were informed of your arrival the day you set foot on our shores. We've been watching you since you camped by the bridge, indulging in your pitiful excess by lounging for an entire day after your journey." Olivere's lips turned up in a cruel smile. "The King of Actaluere rides with an army of ten thousand men, ready to meet you on the field of battle. Your pitiful force stands no chance."

Cyrus leaned toward Olivere and beckoned that the envoy should lean closer to him. "Last month," Cyrus whispered, "I went up against an army of one hundred thousand with only a few hundred." He pulled back, a coarse, soulless grin on his face. "Do you think your ten thousand scares me?" Cyrus looked to Odellan and ignored the slightly stricken look on Olivere's face. "See him safely back to his horse." He focused on Olivere, stared the man straight in the eyes. "Warn your liege. I have more at my command than you can possibly weather."

Cyrus watched the envoy be led away as Ryin Ayend joined him, still yawning and rubbing the sleep from his eyes. "What was that all about?" the druid asked.

"The Baron who's in charge of the nearby holdfast captured one of our scouting parties during the night and is threatening to kill them unless we leave these shores," Cyrus said.

Ryin froze midway through stretching an arm over his head. His tanned face became hard lines in a moment, mouth slightly open. "I take it that you bypassed calm reflection of peaceful remedies to this situation? You mean to show him the error of his ways by burning his home to the ground, yes?"

"Is that going to be a problem for you?" Cyrus gave the druid have an icy glare.

"Not necessarily," Ayend said. "But I do think we should consider options that might result in less conflict before rushing headlong into battle."

"I asked him to release our people," Cyrus said.

"Did you 'ask' politely or was there some component of a threat attached to it?"

"Now, Ryin," Cyrus said, all too patronizingly, "you've known me long enough to recognize that when someone threatens me, or any of my people, they're not going to get much in the way of politeness in return."

"Aye," the druid said, voice cracking, "that's what I was afraid of."

The news spread through the camp as the army was awakened, and Cyrus found himself surrounded by the other officers. The last embers of the fire had begun to die down, and Cyrus ignored the last few logs that he could throw upon it. Curatio was pensive, as was J'anda. Longwell and Odellan spoke in hushed tones at the edge of the knot of officers. Ryin and Nyad huddled close together, as if for warmth, but no words were exchanged between the two of them. It was Terian who watched Cyrus with a certain intensity, who finally broke the morning quiet.

"So we break down the walls, take our people back and drag our enemies' entrails from their still-writhing bodies?" The dark knight's face was twisted, spiteful.

"I'm not opposed to that if it comes to it—save for perhaps the grisly entrail removal portion of it," Ryin said. "But are we certain there is no other way?"

"They could give our people up peacefully before we get there," Terian said, "and then we walk inside and drag their entrails out of—"

"They're in a keep," Ryin said, shaking his head. "Are we really prepared for a siege? This could take weeks or months."

"No, it won't," Cyrus said, cutting across the words of argument that came from J'anda and Terian before they could begin. "In Arkaria, it might take that long. But this is Luukessia, a land that has never known magic, yes?" He looked to Longwell, who nodded in confirmation. "This will take less than an hour."

"I'm sorry, I don't mean to discount the power of spellcasters since I am one," Ryin said, staring at Cyrus with a sort of scornful distaste, "but I don't think they add as much to sieging a castle as you might think."

"Ever laid siege to a castle?" Terian asked, looking at Ryin.

"Yes, once," Ryin said, his arm wrapping more tightly around Nyad, almost defensive. "In the Northlands, when I was with my old guild. A group of bandits had taken it by subterfuge and we were employed by the Confederation to help lay siege to it. It took close to a month. We magic users had little to nothing to do during the time, just sat back and waited."

"The other side had magic users as well?" Cyrus said. "To put up defensive spells on the ramparts to block invasion, and such? Because that would be the only reason they wouldn't have used you in the siege, assuming your leader was competent."

"You mean ... oh, I see," Ryin said, nodding his head. "Oh. Oh, my."

"Yes," Cyrus said with a thin smile. "The possibilities are near-endless. Rally the army. We march as soon as they're ready."

Campfires were doused, packs were gathered, blades were hoisted, and the army was moving minutes later. Cyrus was at the fore, with the officers and Odellan riding in a tight-knit group around him. "This will be a two-pronged attack," Cyrus said. "The first prong is the army at the gates. The other is a smaller group of veterans." He turned to Odellan. "You're on gate duty."

Odellan's eyebrows raised. "Where will you be?"

"With the other prong, cutting into their delicate entrails."

The day was sunny and bright, an absolute contrast to Cyrus's mood. It was as though all the darkness he had carried with him had been given shape, the mournfulness turned to rage and now pointed at a target which he could feel good about spearing with his blade. They crossed over hills and through valleys, until at the crest of a ridge a castle appeared in the middle of a green, grassy valley below.

It was surrounded by a moat, with a curtain wall almost thirty feet high the entire way around. There was a drawbridge that began to rise as they drew closer, with a little village less than a mile away from the walls. Cyrus saw a stream of people in the village square, a hubbub of activity, as though they were evacuating, heading south in a cluster.

"Do they think we're going to attack their town?" J'anda asked. "We've been so nice to their countrymen." The sun was high overhead, beating down upon them.

"The smallfolk who are left unprotected in villages tend to bear the brunt of any war in Luukessia," Longwell said. "They likely believe we will act as every other invading force would and start by sacking the village."

"Keep our people clear of the village," Cyrus said, measured neutrality in his tone. "It seems to me those folks had nothing to do with their Baron's decision to commit suicide, so we'll have no part in wrecking their lives." He looked back at them. "Pass the word. I don't expect we'd need to worry about it with a seasoned Sanctuary army, but these people are new, some of them may be from armies where that was permissible and I want them to understand—anyone sacking, looting, burning or raping will be killed and left to rot in this land—that sort of behavior is simply not tolerated in Sanctuary."

"But we can sack, loot, and burn the castle, right?" Terian looked around. "Right?"

"That depends on how the Baron responds to our arrival," Cyrus said.

They followed the road outside the village. The cool mid-morning air still bore the chill of the pre-dawn even though the sun shone down on them now, casting shadows through the pines that were scattered along the path. The smell of the trees filled his nose, the sharp scent as present as the crunch of the needles under the hooves of their horses. The army marched behind Cyrus, and he looked up at the white stone curtain wall, shining in the sunlight, and saw heads peeking from behind the ramparts. The castle had towers at each corner, and across the battlements Cyrus saw spears poking up. *To lay siege to this castle in a traditional way, I'd need siege towers, catapults ... and lots of time. But I have no time to spare for bastards such as these.*

Blocks were set a few feet apart, creating teeth on the battlements, parapets in a line for archers to fire down at approaching armies from behind cover. Cyrus watched them coldly, analytically, trying to decide how best to approach. The curtain wall was square and went all the way around, a thirty-foot ascent no matter which direction they approached from. Though he couldn't see it, he suspected that the Baron's chambers would be toward the back of the castle, past the courtyard—a bailey, he had heard them called—and it would be a guess whether the prisoners would be kept in quarters there or in the dungeons.

"One hour," he said under his breath as he brought Windrider to a halt. "One hour," he said more loudly, to the officers behind him, and he heard the words passed back to the army on foot behind them.

A slight breeze stirred his hair under his helm. He looked up at the battlements, heard hushed voices from behind them. The drawbridge was up, a mighty wooden brace separating him from the walls by a moat filled with brown, grimy water. It stank from stagnation and the castle's waste. He saw slick walls next to holes in the edge of the battlements, and knew he wanted to go nowhere near the water nor the front gate, either.

"Pass the word for Martaina and Aisling to come forward," Cyrus said, and he heard the murmur of voices behind him. Martaina appeared at his side almost instantly, her horse edging past Longwell's to stand next to him. Aisling was slower to appear, taking her time, showing up almost a minute later, her traveling cloak hiding her features in the light shadow created by the cowl. "Ah, good, there you are."

"You summoned us, oh great and mighty General," Aisling said, each word coming out as a curse. Her bustier was gone, and she was clad in the familiar leather armor that he had always known her to wear.

"Shelve your issues with me until later," Cyrus said. "We've got people being held hostage in that castle. Do you have your bow?" He turned to look at Aisling, and she stared back, defiant, before reaching under her cloak and pulling out a bow with a fox carved near the grip. "Good." He took a breath. "You'll need it, I suspect."

"Hail," came a voice from above them. Cyrus looked up to see Olivere staring down, his red hair and beard visible, leaking out of a cavalier's helm. "I have passed along your message to the baron and he has one for you in return."

Cyrus felt his jaw click into place, felt his teeth bear down. "Let's hear it, then."

"Oh, no," Olivere said, teeth bared in a broad grin. "You'll see it."

With a flourish, the envoy stepped aside and two guards joined him, lifting something under the edge of the battlement. "Make ready with your arrows, ladies," Cyrus said, tense, waiting for what he suspected was coming. "I'll need someone willing to take a swim if they do what I think they're about to."

"I'll go," Ryin said. "I can use Falcon's Essence to—"

"No," Cyrus cut him off. "I need someone to swim."

The three men behind the rampart came up again, this time with a struggling burden. It was a woman, a human in the garb of one of

Sanctuary's rangers. Her face was bruised and her clothing was in disarray, her leather armor missing, and her underclothes were ripped and tattered. She said nothing as the men lifted her and set her upon the ramparts, but she struggled, a spiteful look of hatred burning in her eyes as she glared at her captors.

"Calene Raverle," Martaina said in a gasp at Cyrus's side. "She looks like the hells have had at her."

"Something has had at her, that's for certain," Terian said, his voice low and menacing. "And by something, I mean animals that don't deserve the mercy we'd show a dying dog."

"You had your warning," Olivere said, "army of Sanctuary!" With a push from Olivere, Calene Raverle screamed and was loosed from the battlements. She fell almost ten feet before the noose around her neck caught her.

The crack of the rope reaching full extension caused Martaina to cry out, but Cyrus kept his eyes on Calene Raverle. He had seen her before, in the Realm of Death, he realized, had passed her by when they were teleporting out. He had seen her face among the other rangers throughout the journey, and he realized he didn't know a thing about her—not even her name, until Martaina had said it. He stared at her now, though, looked at her face, her dead eyes, staring at him accusingly. Cyrus stared back.

"Get her down," he said in a voice so low and guttural he didn't even recognize it as his own. An arrow flew from his left, from Aisling, and the rope broke, sending what had been Calene Raverle falling into the moat where her body landed with a splash, then floated to the surface. "Someone go get her." Martaina made to get off her horse and Cyrus held out a hand to stop her. "Not you. Keep your bow ready to fire." He didn't watch for her nod.

Odellan stepped in front of him, shedding his armor piece by piece as he made his way to the edge of the filthy moat. The elf jumped in, causing Cyrus to grimace. "That was my responsibility, I suppose," he said, so low it was almost inaudible to his ears. He caught a worried look from Martaina on one side and an almost imperceptible nod from Aisling on the other.

Odellan grasped the body and swam back to the edge of the moat, where he was helped out of the water by Longwell and Scuddar

In'shara, a Sanctuary warrior from the Inculta Desert. Cyrus watched as Odellan handed the body up first, with care and reverence, as others stepped forward to handle it.

"Curatio," Cyrus said, low enough that he knew that those watching on the battlements above them couldn't hear it, "take her to the back before you do it. Then join me up here again. We go in ten minutes."

"Aye," he heard Curatio say.

"Admirable, what you've done for your comrade. You have one hour," Olivere said from above them, "and then we will execute the rest of your people. One hour to begin your journey home, or all of your people will come to a sudden, tumbling end, just as that one did."

Cyrus looked up at Olivere, but could only see the shadow of the man's face. "I can tell you truly treated her well as a prisoner, and I assume you've extended the same courtesies to the rest of our people that you've taken."

He heard a laugh from behind the parapet, and Olivere's voice was tinged in humor. "You come at the head of an army into a foreign land, bringing the threat of sword and fire to our holdings, but you expect great civility in the treatment of those captured in the course of your transgressions?" Olivere let out a humorless bellow. "You presume too much, foreigner. Count yourself lucky we haven't executed all of your people yet—though that hour is drawing nearer."

"I expected civil treatment because while I have come at the head of an army," Cyrus said, "you have yet to seen our 'sword and fire.'" He gave Olivere a grim smile, one he was certain the envoy could not see at the distance they were apart. "But soon, I think, you will."

"Bold threats," Olivere said. "Perhaps I should tell the baron you've refused his offer and to just send me the other prisoners now?"

"The remaining prisoners are your only hope for mercy at this point." Cyrus's hand lingered on the hilt of Praelior. "Kill them if you must, but remember my words, Olivere. You are trifling with the wrong people."

"You have one hour. Start marching." Olivere disappeared behind the battlements, leaving Cyrus staring up at the castle walls, a cold, seeping fury blanketing him, making him immune to the warm rays of the sun.

"Plan?" Aisling said from his left.

"Kill every last one of them and let Mortus sort them out," Terian said. "Oh, wait, we killed Mortus a few weeks ago, didn't we? All right then, kill them all and let them remain unsorted."

"The following people will come with me," Cyrus said. "Mendicant, J'anda, Ryin, Terian, Longwell, Curatio, Nyad, Martaina, Aisling and …" he looked around and caught sight of a familiar robed figure toward the front of the army, "Scuddar In'shara. Odellan will remain here in charge of the army and continue to watch them."

"And you'll be …?" Odellan asked, pure curiosity on his face.

Cyrus let a bitter smile seep out. "Taking an afternoon run."

Chapter 10

Curatio rejoined them minutes later, and Cyrus gave a subtle nod to Ryin, who began an incantation under his breath. Cyrus had explained the details to those he had selected once Curatio returned from the back of the army. Cyrus felt a gentle wind rush over him and he looked to the healer. "Is she ...?"

"She'll be fine," Curatio said brusquely. "Physically, at least."

"I had hoped that the resurrection spell would allow her to forget what happened." Cyrus stared at the castle walls. "I take it that ...?"

"No such luck." Curatio reached into his robes, keeping his face impassive, and his hand emerged with a small but wicked looking mace. He pressed a button on the handle and half-inch spikes popped out along a horizontal line on the ball of the mace.

"Don't you worry about that button getting pressed accidentally in your robe?" Cyrus said, looking at the weapon, eyes wide.

Curatio stared at it and cocked his head, indifferent. "It has happened, once or twice."

"And?"

Curatio shrugged. "I'm a healer. It's a rather simple fix."

"Ah." Cyrus turned his attention back to the castle. "All ready?" He heard words of affirmation behind him, the subtle agreement of those going with him. "Mendicant, Nyad, J'anda and Ryin, follow directly behind me, Aisling, Martaina, Longwell, Terian, and Scuddar, you're up front. Curatio—"

"I'll be up front, too," the healer said, and rolled his wrist in a circle, spinning the mace around by a leather strap, making it blur as though he were about to throw it like a hammer.

"You're the only healer we're taking with us," Cyrus said.

"Then you should probably watch my back," the elf said without emotion, "and I promise they'll not strike me down from in front."

Cyrus shifted his gaze to Scuddar, Longwell, and Terian in turn, his eyes carrying a warning. *Protect him.* He received nods in return from all but Terian, who was paying him no mind.

"Let's get this carnival of slaughter underway," Terian said, placing his helm on his head. It bore spikes like devil horns, curving six inches into the air. When coupled with his spiked pauldrons and darkened steel armor, it gave him a demonic appearance. Cyrus saw the gleam of red in his sword and shook his head—*truly, the dark knight lives up to his title.* He darted forward, causing Cyrus to gesture to the others to move as he ran after Terian.

Cyrus felt his feet leave the ground, as the subtle pressure of the earth against his metal boots lifted away with his next step. He continued to run, the wind of his motion stirring his beard and hair, and he looked upward as he felt himself rise with each step. He kept the battlements in his sight, saw the faces peeking from behind the parapets, mouths open in shock at the sight of a war party—his war party—charging at them while running on air.

Martaina and Aisling had their bows unslung and were firing as they ran. Cyrus saw arrows striking some of those who were leaning out of cover, heard them scream as the arrows struck home and he watched as one of them staggered and fell into the murky, disgusting moat below. Another screamed and came out from behind cover in time to catch another arrow, this one through the chest, sending him to his knees. Most of the castle's defenders weren't even wearing armor. *Arrogance. That will cost them.*

They crested the wall and Cyrus lunged over a battlement, Praelior in hand, driving his sword into a soldier who was waiting for him on the other side. The man had shouted in alarm and begun to run away as Cyrus punched his blade into the man's lower back. Cyrus saw him jerk, tensing at the pain before going limp. There were roughly ten defenders left along the battlement, and most were so awestruck at the sight of invaders coming over their seemingly impregnable walls that all but three were running to staircases that led down into the bailey, the courtyard below the wall.

Cyrus looked down as he swept Praelior across the chest of one of the castle's guards who had chosen to fight. The man fell to the courtyard below. The bailey was an open area with a few carts filled with hay and other goods and stables off to the left, which gave the air an aroma of horses. Twenty or more knights were in the courtyard below, and a battle cry went up from their number. They had been standing in formation, their armor covered with the same blue surcoats that Olivere had worn to treat with Cyrus.

"Nyad, Mendicant," Cyrus said, and pointed Praelior at the knights below. He heard the murmur of the wizards casting spells behind him as he watched the knights spring into motion, their helms covering their heads save for slits for eyes and holes punched to breathe. They had split into two parties, one storming each staircase when the spells struck—flames encircled them in a solid wall and then they rose within the wall as well. A blaze taller than a man seemed to grow out of the ground itself, swirling around the knights, drawing shouts from them at first, of alarm, then of pain that degenerated into shrieks and cries. Cyrus watched as the figures within the fire seemed to melt away, falling to the ground in a slick motion, like water poured out of a cup. A horrendous smell of charred, burnt flesh wafted over the courtyard as Cyrus and his party stared down into the burnt remnants.

"We're clear to the living quarters," Martaina said, her bow still nocked and pulled up to fire.

A few pitiful moans made their way to Cyrus's ears; the last surviving defenders who had run from the battlements had arrows protruding from them and were scattered between the walls and the stairwell. Cyrus looked to his right, where Martaina stood, then to his left, where Aisling had already slung her bow on her back. He caught sight of two of her victims, moaning, saw the fletchings of the arrows protruding from the soldiers' groins, and winced. He looked at Aisling, who shrugged. "For Calene," she said simply.

"Keep a close formation." Cyrus stepped over the edge of the wall and drifted down into the courtyard. "I'm sure there are more of them inside the living quarters. Swords up front, spellcasters behind." He caught a look from Curatio that was pure heat. "Except you, warrior priest. Go ahead and dispel the Falcon's Essence, Ryin." Cyrus felt the wind beneath him dissipate and the clunk of his metal boots hitting the ground echoed through the bailey. "J'anda, you know what to do."

"I always know what to do," the dark elf said. "For funerals, you send flowers, for a dinner date, you bring wine, and for those times when your significant other has been putting on weight, you say nothing at all."

"Very suave," Terian said. "What do you do when you're in a

foreign land and an army of thugs has kidnapped members of your guild and is holding them hostage?"

"Ah," J'anda said with a light smile, "I have the perfect answer for that as well."

They made their way across the stone courtyard, the yellow blocks reminding Cyrus of grains of seasoned rice as the midday sun cast shadows under the ramparts. The living quarters were at the opposite end of the drawbridge. Scuddar was operating the mechanism to open the bridge while Cyrus and the others made their way toward the wooden doors. "Barred?" Cyrus asked as he approached.

"You taking bets?" Terian was beside him. "Because I'd guess yeah. You think they're oblivious to all this commotion?"

"Thus far," Cyrus said, "intelligence hasn't been their strong suit." When he reached the door he leaned back, Praelior in hand, and felt the strength of the sword surge through him. With a mighty kick he splintered the doors, breaking them from their hinges and sending them twisting inward, falling to the ground with a thunderous clatter. A throne room lay before Cyrus, small of scale, with eight ranks of soldiers, twenty across, shoulder-to-shoulder, standing in his way. These were wearing plate mail, he noticed, as he stared at them, unimpressed.

"I'm here for Baron Hoygraf," Cyrus said, and pointed his sword at the unmoving statues, their armor giving them the appearance of being posed. "Anyone who doesn't want to experience unspeakable pain, move out of my way."

The soldiers remained, their steel armor locked in place, their spears lowered, shields side by side in an impenetrable wall. Cyrus let out an annoyed sigh. "Perhaps you're laboring under the impression I'm going to charge you down. I'm not. Although if I did, I assure you that your spears and shields are of no concern to me. Are any of you going to surrender? We breached your castle in minutes and have killed every one of the guards you've sent at us thus far. Does that not frighten you? Do you not feel a twinge of uncertainty that such an impossible thing could happen?" He watched them, looking for some sign of emotion, but their helms concealed any thoughts they might have had. "Very well then. Just remember, you chose unspeakable pain, not me."

A strange twinkling of light filled the room. "J'anda?" Cyrus asked. "You gonna be okay?"

"There are rather a lot of them," the enchanter said, his voice strained. "You'll excuse me if I don't talk; I'd like to get this over with."

"That's what she said." Terian's voice was low but amused and Cyrus caught a glint of humor from the dark knight when he said it. "And by she, I mean Nyad."

"Oh, yes, I see, very funny," Nyad said from behind them. "Because I'm a woman who enjoys sexual relations, I must be a horrible, disgusting person. You're just jealous, you syphilitic, whore-mongering nightmare."

The lights cascaded in front of the soldiers, and Cyrus saw reflections of eyes inside their helmets, watched the first few of them slacken, the points of their spears drifting downward. "What is that?" he heard one of the soldiers in the back ask, but no one answered.

Then the front rank of the soldiers dropped their shields as one with a great clatter that rang through the hall. They turned in a single motion, raised their spears, and thrust them forward. Cyrus watched as they hit home, in the joints of armor, through gorgets and into necks, and there was shouting as the first three rows of the formation turned on the next, and a melee commenced as the soldiers of Green Hill tried their best to kill one another. Cyrus saw one of the armored soldiers slip a sword under the breastplate of another, watched two others decapitate a third, and he felt a slight smile creep across his face.

"They'll do this until they're dead," J'anda said, and Cyrus looked back to find the enchanter with his eyes closed. "I only needed less than half under my direct control—the others I simply made blind to our presence."

"Can you maintain this?" Cyrus asked.

"At least until they're all dead, yes," J'anda replied, a hint of a smile on his lips. "Go forth and give my regards to the Baron when you meet him."

"I'm gonna stick a sword up his ass," Terian said. "Is that what you mean by regards?"

"Good enough," J'anda said. "Now, if you'll excuse me ..."

Cyrus led the way, skirting the side of the battle, angling toward a hallway to the left of the red velvet padded wooden thrones that sat in the middle of the hall on a raised dais. He walked down the long, grey hallway, motioning to the rooms on either side and letting Terian and Longwell kick open the doors. He heard the screams of women, the cries of children, and then heard the doors shut and the footsteps of Terian and Longwell beside him again moments later. *Smells like fear.*

He reached another commanding set of double wooden doors, with candles lit on either side of the hallway to offset the darkness that had crept in after he left the main hall. There were no windows and the hall came to an end up ahead. Cyrus turned at the door, pushed on it, and found it barred. "This is it," he said. "Hoygraf lives until we have a conversation." Cyrus saw Scuddar push past Nyad and Ryin to join them. "Scuddar, I take it the army is in the castle?" The desert man nodded. "Are they seeing to the dungeons, then?" Another nod from Scuddar, who wore robes that stretched from his face to his feet, *an odd bit of attire for one who uses a sword, but then Scuddar is something of a rarity.* "All right."

With another thunderous kick, Cyrus broke down the doors in front of him and let Martaina and Aisling sweep past, their bows already firing. Arrows caught two sentries unprepared; Martaina's landed in the neck of her foe, Aisling's once more in the groin. Other guards were arrayed around the room and began to move to engage the Sanctuary force. Cyrus swept two of them aside with a strike that broke their swords neatly in half. Scuddar, Longwell and Curatio took down enemies of their own, and Cyrus saw a bolt of lightning streak through the air and wrap around three guards surrounding another man who huddled at the back of the room.

The one who wasn't hit by the lightning was clearly standing apart from the others. He wore a red cloak with a fur collar, and his clothing was more sophisticated than most of what Cyrus had seen in Termina or even Pharesia. His hair was black, his face was pale, pale white and his beard was scraggly and black. When he came up from his knees after watching his men downed by Ryin's lightning spell, there was visible anger etched on his face and a fury in his pale blue eyes.

"Halt!" The man called out, his voice carrying no sign of strain and in a tone that led Cyrus to believe he had never once been disobeyed— *at least not without the perpetrator going unscathed.*

Cyrus reached out and cut down one of the guards that had halted at the man's command, then another, and another. "Oh, I'm sorry," he said, when the man turned his furious eyes on Cyrus, "I didn't listen when you told me to turn back, Baron Hoygraf. I didn't listen when you said you'd kill my people. Do you really expect me to stop now?" Cyrus thrust Praelior through the last of the standing guards, sliding the blade through the guard's chest and the breastplate he wore as though it weren't even there.

"But in fairness," Cyrus said, advancing on Hoygraf, who backed into a wooden hutch, causing the contents inside to clatter like glass, "you didn't listen to me either. I told you that I would destroy your keep, kill all your men, and give you a painful end if you didn't return my people, and now here we are, and I've nearly kept my word." There was a bustle behind him and Cyrus turned to see two of his army shoving their way into the room, dragging a haggard figure along with them. "Oh, good, my old friend Olivere." Cyrus looked at the Sanctuary warriors. "I take it you cleared the dungeons and turned loose our compatriots?" One of the warriors nodded, his crooked front teeth bared in a smile. "Were they similarly harmed like Calene?" The smile of the Sanctuary warrior disappeared, replaced with a scowl that made the crooked front teeth look much more intimidating.

"See, you shouldn't have done that." Cyrus turned back to Hoygraf. "Terian? Would you kindly make Olivere aware of the gravity of his liege's mistakes?"

"With utmost pleasure," Terian said, and Cyrus could hear the grin in the dark knight's words without turning to look at him. A moment later, Olivere screamed, even though Terian hadn't taken so much as a step toward the man. A smell emanated around them, of pestilence and illness, the rancid stench of boils opening to the air. The scream continued, growing in pitch, and Cyrus watched the hard lines on Hoygraf's face dissolve, his eyes going from narrow to wide as he watched Terian's spell take effect on his envoy. Hoygraf's jaw dropped, and the Baron let out a little exhalation of horror.

"Oh, Baron," Cyrus said. "You tortured and beat our people, had your soldiers do unspeakable things, but a little spell makes you wilt like a flower on the hottest day of summer?" The stench worsened as Cyrus circled Hoygraf, and watched the Baron turn away. Cyrus looked to Olivere, who was now covered in burst, bleeding pustules and writhing on the ground. "That's right, I forgot. You don't have spellcasters in Luukessia. But we came from over the bridge, so you had to know it was a possibility that you were up against something of this sort."

"Illusions and trickery." Little flecks of spittle came from Hoygraf's lips when he made his reply. "Your sort is the worst of demons and devils, the curses of all manner of evil that comes from your side of the bridge. You don't belong over here, in this blessed land of our ancestors, you filth."

Cyrus felt his hand drift forward, the tip of his sword pressing into the throat of the Baron. "Filth? You call us filth yet you had no issue with brutalizing our women rangers when you captured them."

"Women need to know their place, and if they wish to stand in the line of battle next to the men, then they should know the injury of—"

"Dear gods, just shut up," Cyrus said, pressing Praelior's tip into the Baron's neck, causing blood to run down his throat in a thick line. "You disgusting, wicked pile of shite, you're lucky I don't give you similar injury to theirs with my sword."

"You unnatural beasts," Hoygraf said. "King Milos Tiernan marches this way as we speak—"

"And when he gets here, he'll find us gone," Cyrus said. "If he's lucky, he won't meet us in battle, because I think—and you might agree with me—my army is going to be too much for him to handle. We have wizards, druids, healers and enchanters, and every last one of them will be turned loose to wreak havoc. All we want is to pass through your lands, and every day you asses make me waste here is another day I'm going to make your lives miserable. Your best bet is to let us go on, so we can stop making your lives miserable and start doing the same to Briyce Unger, who I'm told is no friend of yours."

"He is not," Hoygraf spat. "But do not think you will be allowed to simply walk through our territory uncontested—"

Cyrus pulled his sword from Hoygraf's neck and stabbed it into the Baron's stomach, burying it in his guts. Hoygraf screamed, grunted, and moaned, falling to his knees. Cyrus took care to keep the sword steady as the Baron fell, not letting the blade move. "Let me make this clear to you. You are impotent against us. Your army, even if it numbers ten thousand, will fall before our magical wickedness like wheat falls to the reaper. Your threats against us possess all the efficacy of a castrated bull

trying to mate and none of the grace. And speaking of castrated ..."
Cyrus let his eyes fall down, drawing a look of panic from the Baron.
"Kidding. That's too easy for you."

Cyrus looked back to Terian, who had Olivere by the collar. The
envoy's eyes bulged from his head and he was still. "I think he's dead,
Terian. You can drop him now."

"Oh?" Terian looked down, let Olivere drop to the floor, then
turned back to Hoygraf. "Then this is the last of their kind left alive in
the castle. How shall we finish him?"

"We don't." Cyrus motioned toward the door, and he heard the
others begin to move toward it. Cyrus stood and let the blade of his
sword slip from the Baron's abdomen. "I've heard a stomach wound is
the most painful way a man can die. I took care to make sure I didn't go
too close to the bottom or the top, just right in the middle." He craned
his neck to look down at Hoygraf. "I think I got it about right. It'll
probably take you a few days to die from that, and it's not going to be
much fun while you're doing it.

"So we're just going to leave you here," Cyrus said, backing away
from Hoygraf. "I think you'll have enough time to communicate to your
King what I've said to you, but just in case, I'll have Longwell leave a
note." He nodded at Longwell, who blinked and began to look around
for parchment. "I'd give you a long sermon about how raping is wrong
and how attacking strangers who have done you no harm is unkind, but
frankly," Cyrus said with a sneer, "you'll be dead, so I think the lesson
will be irrelevant to you. Besides, your impregnable castle has been
breached and all your soldiers have been killed. We'll be escorting your
women and children to the town down the hill where they can wait for
your army before we burn this place to the ground. I think that everyone
who could benefit from the lesson will have learned it." He nodded.
"Best of luck, Hoygraf." He met the Baron's wide, pained eyes. "Enjoy
your slow, agonizing death."

Cyrus stood and turned to find that all but Terian and Longwell had
left the chamber. He looked to Longwell first. "Write something that
reflects my threat that if they interfere with our crossing, we'll burn
every holdfast between here and Galbadien. If they leave us be, we'll be
out of their lands in a month or so—and their villages will be all the
richer for our passing."

Longwell nodded. "I'll try and be diplomatic about it, but I'll come up with something in that vein."

"Diplomatic?" Cyrus raised an eyebrow at him. "I've left the Baron gutted in his own castle. The moment for diplomacy has passed. Make it a threat, make it obvious, and let the King know that the consequences for failing to follow my directive will be the absolute destruction of his entire Kingdom. I will leave a swath of scorched earth ten miles wide as I exit this land, and if Milos Tiernan wants that on his head, so be it." Cyrus turned and started for the door, but Terian caught his eye, causing him to stop.

The dark knight watched Cyrus with a very subtle smile. "Every time I think I've got the measure of you, Davidon, you surprise me. Alaric would have just executed this Baron and been done with it, if no other suitable justice was to be found. A slow, painful death?" Terian's smile faded. "I would have thought you ... beyond that."

"Let the gravity of the crime be reflected in the punishment," Cyrus said. "If there is no justice in this land for him to answer to, let him answer to the natural laws of his own mortality."

"I see," Terian said, and his smile vanished. "An excellent point about letting the crime be reflected in the punishment. An excellent point, indeed."

Chapter 11

"They have a full complement of spices," Martaina said, coming from the kitchen of castle Green Hill, a large sack slung across her back. "We can take enough food from here to feed us for a few days." Cyrus sat at the head of the table in the dining room, a plate of food in front of him, the aroma of succulent mutton chop and fresh vegetables wafting up at him as he took a bite of the lamb. He could hear his soldiers eating in the throne room, where trestle tables had been set out. Others were in the courtyard, while still others he had entrusted with the task of sorting out whether anything in the castle was worth taking.

"They have wine as well," J'anda said, entering the dining room behind her, a goblet in hand. "It's not quite like the vintages of the Riverlands, but it's far from atrocious." The dark elf made his way over to a padded chair and sat down, leaning his head back. "Is there any chance we could stay here for the night? I would love to take advantage of having a bed to sleep in for the first time in weeks."

"You and everyone else, I daresay." Curatio held a goblet in front of him as well, a sparkling silver one that he took a deep, delicate sip from before replacing it on the flawless white tablecloth.

"So are you going to turn loose the army on the castle?" Aisling stared at Cyrus from where she leaned against the doorjamb leading into the hallway to the kitchens. "Let them have a little plunder for their troubles here?"

Cyrus picked up the napkin that sat at his right side and dabbed his face with it in an exaggerated show of politeness that caused Terian to roll his eyes and J'anda to guffaw. "I don't think so," he said with a shake of the head. "Letting them run loose through this place, tearing it to pieces? Sounds like a recipe for losing discipline. Not to mention the fights it'd likely start over who gets what loot. No, we'll take what foods we can carry, the spices, and we'll go through the weapons to see if there's anything that would be worth parceling out to the army, since," he coughed, "there isn't anyone left alive to fight here. Any other objects ..." He shrugged. "I don't want to feel like we're looting, but I suppose this isn't that different from any other expeditions we've mounted, save for the fact that here our foes are human."

"Damned right," Terian said with a snarl. "If this was a castle of dark elves you wouldn't think twice about dividing up the spoils from them, so why wouldn't we add the assets from ransacking this place to the guild bank? There's likely some jewels or something, isn't there?" He looked to Longwell, who seemed to be lost in his own thoughts.

"Hm?" The dragoon looked up when the others in the room turned their attention to him. "Oh, yes. A Baron of his station would likely have a number of precious stones, gold and silver, and I daresay that within the armory you could find more than a few swords and axes that would be better than some of the things I've seen our warriors toting about. Luukessian steel isn't mystical since we don't possess magic, but it's of good enough quality. And there are certainly a few mystical weapons that have made their way to our shores," his hand grasped the hilt of his lance, "though not many."

"Is it considered acceptable to plunder your conquests in Luukessia?" This from J'anda, who held his goblet up to his nose and took a deep inhalation of his wine before sipping again.

"Oh, yes," Longwell said. "Conquest is much more brutal here than in Arkaria, you might have noticed. Looting and pillaging is perfectly normal when you conquer, much like we saw from the dark elves in Termina. Also, without weapons and armor that can add strength or the ability to use magic, many women are treated like chattel and considered part of the spoils of war." He looked around the table and saw the looks on the faces of Nyad and Martaina. "Not that I endorse such thinking myself, but you heard the Baron—and he is not alone in his way of thought."

"Pardon me?" Martaina looked at the dragoon in askance.

"Well, women are forbidden to own property," Longwell said. "They are considered to be subject to the rules of their husbands, subject to their whims."

"So, what?" Aisling's purple eyes flashed in anger. "I'm supposed to kowtow to some man because he thinks he's stronger than me? That I'm good for cooking meals, relieving his tensions in the night, making plump babies, and nothing else?"

Terian eyed her up and down. "You're pretty thin; I doubt you could make a very plump baby with those hips."

Her hand moved fast, fast enough that Cyrus barely saw it. The dagger was out and thrown before Cyrus could shout a warning. Terian dodged it, barely, and it embedded in the stuffed padding in the back of Terian's chair. He clucked softly at her and smiled. "I'm keeping the dagger."

"As what? A memento of the only occasion when a woman paid you attention without gold filling her purse in exchange?" She smiled sweetly at him but it was all fake, and Cyrus could see the venom beneath. "I've got better ones; ones I save for people I actually mean to kill."

Far in the distance, Cyrus could hear very low whimpers from Baron Hoygraf, alone in his quarters on the floor above. "I doubt we'll change the male-dominated hierarchy of Luukessia today, so let's shelve this discussion."

"I suppose you're okay with it if we get to this land his father rules," Aisling pointed at Longwell, "and he tells us women to sit in the back line of battle, or worse, in the prep tent."

"I presume your father won't tell me how to run my army?" Cyrus looked at Longwell, who nodded confirmation. "Besides, if I'm not much mistaken, the attitude in this land is not wildly different than what I've heard about life in Saekaj Sovar." He stared hard at Aisling, and she looked away. "Since it's considered the norm, I want officers and our veterans to go over the castle, top to bottom, and decide if there are things beyond food we should take with us as spoils. Half of the value will go to the guild bank for the effort expended to take the castle. We'll burn everything else."

"Half of the haul will be a small fortune with a holdfast as rich as this one," Longwell said, approving. "What's to be done with the other half?"

"I want it given to the two women whom the Baron captured and ... well," Cyrus said, lowering his voice. "We can't undo what was done, but perhaps if they've joined Sanctuary for adventure and thought the better of it, they can take the recompense and it will at least give them some options where they might not have had any before."

"That will likely be enough to allow them to live a fairly well-off life," Longwell said. "Unless I miss my guess on the size of the Baron's treasure hoard."

"Good." Cyrus took the last bite of mutton then slid his chair back from the table. "Work through the night if you have to, but I want it all set to travel tomorrow morning. Take the animals out of the stables and give every one of our people that was captured their own horses." He stopped in thought. "I hadn't wanted to bother with wagons while we were traveling down the beach to the bridge, but now that we're in Luukessia, I expect we could take some wagons with us, yes?" He looked at Longwell, who nodded. "Good, that'll spare us having to send one of our wizards or druids back to Sanctuary with the spoils, and we may yet have a need for some of those items to trade later in our journey." He looked at the faces around him. "Anything else?"

No one said anything, but there were a few shrugs. Cyrus smiled. "Then I'm going to go steal a few hours sleep in the Baron's bed."

J'anda threw a wadded-up napkin at Cyrus.

"What? You're not the only one that longs for a soft bed, my friend."

"Hmph," the enchanter said, teasing. "Perhaps I'll join you later."

"Hah," Cyrus said. "Just don't wake me, whatever you do." He left and turned to go down the hallway. "If someone wants to drag the Baron down to his own dungeons, I wouldn't complain."

"He probably would, though," Longwell said. "I think I can hear him complaining now."

"Complaining, whining, dying—when it's a raping, murdering, bastard doing it, who cares which it really is?" Martaina asked.

Cyrus felt his feet clank against the stone as he walked down a hallway that led to the Baron's quarters. The torches burned, giving it a smoky aroma that filled his nose. There was a soft whisper of leather on stone behind him, causing him to hesitate. "If you've come to proposition me, even if I were amenable, I'm far too tired for that tonight."

Aisling walked past him, her shoulder bumping gently against his armor. "You didn't speak up against their treatment of women in this land."

"I gutted the Baron who captured our people and raped our women," he said, staring at her as she turned to stand opposite him, only a few feet from his face. "I gave away half the guild's spoils so we could try and give the women a fresh start if they decided they wanted to leave behind this adventuring life. I don't know what else you want me to do."

"It's not only about what you do," she said in a low whisper, "sometimes it's about what you say—or don't say."

Cyrus let out a deep sigh. "I'm in love with a woman who wields a sword better than any man I've ever met save one, a woman who wears heavier armor than I do, who can beat the ass off almost any man she's ever crossed swords with. Do you really think I have a problem with women being the equal of men in any capacity?"

"Perhaps you're just a glutton for pain," she said acidly. "But if you feel that way, why didn't you condemn it when Longwell told us how it was over here?"

"Because I was too busy listening to Longwell condemn it while he tried to backpedal away from his society's embracing of male superiority," Cyrus said, leaning against the wall to his left, resting his glove against it. "I just assumed that we who are here from Sanctuary, where we have a few women officers who help run our guild, would all know that I feel that way." He paused and glared back at her. "Where is this coming from? Me? Or how things are back in Saekaj?"

"Maybe both," she said, arms crossed. "You can't tell me it's the same for humans, either. How many women are taken into the Society of Arms compared to men?"

"Fewer," Cyrus said, resting his weight on the wall.

"Half as many, I've heard, just in the first trial," Aisling snapped. "Because the orphan girls who are slight of body are taken to the Wanderers' Brotherhood and trained as rangers rather than thrown into the Society's Blood Families."

"Which is good for them," Cyrus said, "because it gets brutal there."

Aisling's eyes narrowed at him. "Are you saying girls can't handle a fight like that?"

Cyrus didn't back off. "I've seen many that could. But most were eliminated, yes."

Aisling's face broke into a frozen smile, distorted, without any sense of mirth to accompany it. "Pretty little things."

"Yes," Cyrus said. "And they were weeded out by the first trial and sent to be scullery maids or serving girls because it was deemed that if they should continue in the Society or the Brotherhood they'd be nothing more than pretty broken things."

"So what's the difference between that and here?" Her voice was cool, and her eyes held a hint of disgust. "You can't tell me some of those scullery maids, in the houses they worked in, got any better treatment than our female warriors and rangers at the hands of the Baron's men."

"No, but I also can't do anything about them, either," he said, annoyance rising. "I'm not in charge of Reikonos or the Society of Arms or anything, really, save for Sanctuary's army here in Luukessia and my own self. So if you really think I'm tacitly endorsing their treatment of women, or anything else—pigs and chickens or crops and fields, for example, I'm not. I'm trying to do the best I can to do right by my people. That's it. Radical societal transformations will have to wait for someone both more visionary and less likely to strike down someone who pisses him off with a sword."

"They might need the sword and the will to use it if they're going to radically transform a society in the way you've described."

"Why are you here?" He leaned in closer to her. "Is this because you think I'll change my mind and give in to your advances if you argue with me more? Because—"

"Don't insult me by suggesting I'm only here because of some unquenchable desire of my loins to have you," she said, her voice hot with her temper. "I've made clear my interest and you've made clear your lack of. That's fine. I'm giving you my opinion, that's all." She didn't smile.

"Duly noted. But you've never been much of one for formalities or arguing, so forgive me," he said, "for suspecting ill intentions. I didn't mean to insult you by suggesting—"

"Yes, you did." She slipped back a step, but it was so subtle he almost didn't notice, so perfect was her balance and movement. "But that's all right." Her smile was back, but it was hollow, unreal. "I've come to expect it."

"I'm sorry," Cyrus said, and meant it. "I'm sorry if I've been unkind to you."

She smiled, and her expression was more genuine but still tight. "I believe you. And I bid you good night." She turned and drifted into the shadows of the hall, and he could barely see her as she walked along, toward the throne room.

Cyrus entered the Baron's quarters to find him on the ground, lying on his side, moaning. Hoygraf's eyes found Cyrus as he entered the room, and looked around at the rich surroundings, the tapestries and furniture, made as exquisitely as any of the pieces he'd seen of note in Sanctuary. "You know, Baron, you had a pretty good life here before you went and stuck your head in the dragon's mouth."

The Baron had a layer of white, dried spittle around his mouth and he grunted, his reply low, straining to get out. "And will ... again ... after you leave."

Cyrus squatted a few feet from the man and looked at him. "I have my doubts you're going to pull through this, honestly. But I tell you what," he said, cheery as anything to the dying man, "if you do pull through by some miracle, I'll have one of my women—maybe the one you hanged on the wall of your castle—put another knife in you. And I bet she'll be less charitable and more efficient in her choice of targets than I was."

"You ... are scum ..." The Baron forced his words out in grunts.

"I find insults like that have more effect coming from someone who has the moral credibility to muster some righteous outrage with it," Cyrus said with a taunting air. "Maybe a priest or something. But from you?" Cyrus leaned closer to the Baron. "Tell me something—did you let your men have their way with the captives or did you get in there and lead from the front?"

The Baron's cold eyes found his and the man moaned in a guttural pain. Sweat beads were falling off his forehead and he was already pale, paler than he had been before. "Does it matter at this point? Will it save me if I didn't?"

"No," Cyrus said with a shake of his head. "They were your men, after all, and in spite of whatever lies you might make up, I have no doubt that the beatings and all else happened with your permission, if not your direction. This is just a chance for you to ease your conscience before you die."

Hoygraf set his jaw and when he spoke, it sounded like his teeth were grinding. "I have nothing on my conscience to be rid of."

Cyrus viewed the Baron with cool indifference, watched the blood trickle from between his fingers where his hand rested on his belly. The air in the room stank of excrement and other things. "Are you a married man, sir?"

The Baron looked up at him with hateful eyes. "Presuming you have not killed my wife in your haste to wreck my holdfast."

"I have killed no women in my siege," Cyrus said. "The women of the castle were escorted to the village, so I presume she is just fine, wherever she may be. I was only curious about her reaction to your efforts to violate members of my army."

"She understood well that you foreigners and your loose women badly needed a lesson in manners and their place," the Baron said between clenched teeth. "My wife knew her place."

"I'm sure you showed her that place often, and with considerable urging from the back of your hand," Cyrus said. "I'm going to have my guards move you to the dungeon so my people can have a nice evening of sleep without the benefit of your slow, miserable death to waken them. I trust we won't be able to hear your screams from up here?"

"You are such a bastard," Hoygraf said to him. "If ever I get a chance to repay you for this—"

"You won't," Cyrus said. "Here, let me help you up." He pulled the Baron to his feet and dragged him to the door, opening it to find four guards outside. He blinked at them in surprise, three humans whom he recognized but didn't know by name, all armored and clad as warriors, and Martaina. "Can you have this—" he gestured at Hoygraf, who he was dragging, "taken down to the dungeon?"

"Certainly," Martaina said, and nodded at two of the guards, who each took an arm and began to drag the Baron away.

"Sweet dreams, Baron," Cyrus said. "Have a lovely night thinking about your life and all the things you've done to bring yourself to this point."

"All I'll be thinking of," Hoygraf said as the guards turned him to speak, "is cutting your head off and showing your body to you before you die."

"Did I do that to you?" Cyrus asked, holding his hand to his chest, feigning a wounded expression. "No, I simply exposed your innards to the light of day so that you could have a chance to expunge some of the darkness within." Cyrus let his expression turn cold. "And there's so much darkness within, Baron." Cyrus waved in his direction and the guards carried him away, the Baron grunting as they turned the corner.

Cyrus turned to Martaina, grim thoughts now covering his countenance. "Make sure that our women who were captured are provided ventra'maq." He thought about it for a beat. "Do we have any with us?"

"I have some," she said smoothly, without emotion. "I'll make sure they get a dose each."

Cyrus frowned. "Your husband is back at Sanctuary." When Martaina did not react, Cyrus suddenly wished for the ability to pull his words back from the air and banish them somewhere dark and far away, where they would never have been spoken. "Oh. Carry on, then." He turned and started back into the Baron's quarters, too sheepish to look at Martaina when she stopped him.

"There's a woman who asked to stay behind when we took the others out. She says she's the Baroness," Martaina said, seemingly undisturbed by Cyrus's comment. "She's asking to speak to the conqueror of the castle."

Cyrus thought about it for a long moment. "Have her escorted up. I seem to have put her husband on a slow path to the grave; the least I can do is hear her out and explain why he's fated to die."

Martaina grimaced. "Are you sure you wouldn't rather I did that?"

Cyrus cocked an eyebrow at her. "Do you really want to?"

The elf's grimace smoothed out, returning her ageless features to an expressionless mien. There were no wrinkles at the corners of her eyes. Cyrus could not tell how old Martaina was and had never asked. "A woman married to a man like that likely knows the danger of the day that the wrath he has wielded is loosed upon him. I wouldn't be surprised if she expects to be told he's dead already. She's most likely here to collect his body for burial and to plead for some of her possessions that were left behind."

"I expect I owe her the courtesy of an audience and an explanation," Cyrus mused, still thinking it over. "I appreciate the offer, though. Have them bring her up."

"Very well," Martaina said. "I'll see to it." She turned and crisply walked down the hall. Cyrus watched her receding back, her green cloak gone, revealing instead her green cloth shirt and pants, something designed to blend into the forests and thickets she seemed born to hide within.

Cyrus walked back into the Baron's quarters and waited. His eyes were drawn to the place where the Baron had lain, where a red puddle had already begun to dry into the rug. He almost flinched at it, thought about covering it up with something, anything, but decided against it. *Perhaps she won't notice.*

There was a soft knock at the door. "Enter," Cyrus said, and it swung wide to admit a woman in a green dress with a flowing skirt and a hem that dragged on the ground. Both her hands clutched at the top of the skirt around her waist, lifting it off the floor only slightly, reducing the drag against the carpeting. "Come in," he said, taking note of her flowing brown hair and emerald eyes. She was young, younger than he, and her bosom was neatly displayed by her neckline. Had it not been for a few slight tears in the fabric, he would have assumed she put it on to impress him rather than believe she had been in it all day without anything to change into.

Cyrus rose from the chair and heard his armor squeak in protest. The chair protested more loudly at his weight, but he kept his gaze on the Baroness, met her green eyes without flinching away, tried to infuse his own expression with as much warmth as he could manage. He felt a pang of sorrow for what he was about to have to tell her, but there was nothing for it. "My name is Cyrus Davidon of the guild Sanctuary."

"I am Cattrine, the Baroness Hoygraf." She performed a curtsy, dipping her head and shoulders. Her hair was piled upon her head in an elaborate hairstyle. He watched as her gaze was drawn to the bloodstain on the rug behind him and coughed to turn her attention back to him. She gave no reaction beyond a subtle flicker of her eyes.

"I am pleased to make your acquaintance, Baroness," Cyrus said, inclining his head in greeting. "I assume that it is quite the opposite in your case, which is understandable." He swept his hand around, offering her the chair he had been sitting in.

"No, thank you," she said, her eyes filled with a quiet intensity. Try as he might, Cyrus could not see any deceit or anger burning within them. *She is either indifferent to her husband's plight and is carrying out mere formalities or she is superior at keeping her thoughts far below the surface.* The Baroness's lips upturned very slightly, in a formal smile that held no genuine warmth of its own. "I trust you know why I am here?"

"I had assumed you wanted your husband's body returned." Cyrus took two steps to his lef to a cabinet that held a silver tray on the top of it. Bottles of exotic glass, shaped in ways that Cyrus had not seen from glass blowers in Arkaria rested across the top of the bar. "Would you care for some refreshment?"

"Certainly, you may offer me some of my husband's own liquors," she said without a trace of acrimony. "I recommend the spiced rum from the Isle of Remlorant."

Cyrus looked across the bottles again at the unfamiliar writing upon them. "I apologize ... although we speak the same language, your land's methods of writing differ considerably from my own."

He heard her cross the room to him, felt her brush against him, and a pale forearm reached in front of him, plucking an ornate glass bottle from the bar. It was tall, and the glass was multifaceted, reminding him of an exceptionally large gemstone. "That was quite the novelty," the Baroness said, reaching for two glasses from the cabinet next to her, "I almost thought I was about to be served a drink by a man." She poured a small quantity of the liquor into one of the glasses, and Cyrus caught a strong hint of alcohol in the air as she did so. "By the man who killed my husband, no less." There was no bitterness in her tone, Cyrus realized, just an aura of tiredness, of weariness, and the smallest hint of emotion. "Do you trust me to pour your cup, sir?"

"I trust that if you poison me, my healer will revive me from death," he said as she poured a second cup full of clear liquid. "A feat I daresay he wouldn't repeat for my poisoner."

"I have no interest in poisoning you," she said, her hands clenching the glass. "It profits me naught to have you dead, as I have no interest in pointless vengeance."

"Your husband is not yet dead, Baroness," Cyrus said, and watched her entire body stiffen. He was at her shoulder, but she turned her face so that he could not see. "Do not take too much hope from that, though, as he is mortally wounded and will pass before much longer."

She was shorter than him by a head and a half at least, Cyrus realized, though she was still tall for a woman. She had angled herself so that he could not see her expression, but he saw the lines of her body, saw her left hand clutching the glass she had poured and saw it shake subtly, the liquid within rippling from the motion. "I see." Her tone was dull, duller even than when she had spoken a moment before. She turned to Cyrus and he saw no trace of tears on her pretty face, nor any other emotion either, but the dark circles under her eyes hinted at more than she freely gave away. "Where is he now?"

Cyrus hesitated. "He remains in the dungeon, where he will stay until he expires."

"I see," she said again. "This is his punishment for defying you?"

"This is his punishment for kidnapping my people and causing grievous bodily harm to them." Cyrus studied her cool eyes, and he saw no hint of reaction at his accusation. "But you knew what he did, didn't you?"

Her eyes didn't even widen. "I didn't know that he did that, but I know my husband." She took a long, slow sip of the spiced rum in her cup, her eyes downcast, but when the glass left her lips, her eyes rose and met Cyrus's. "If it is as you say, and he is not long for this world, then even with the crimes he has committed, I would plead to you for leniency and ask you to allow him to die in comfort, in a bed, down in the village."

Cyrus took a sip of the rum and felt it burn all the way down. "Not here, in his own bed?"

The Baroness stiffened. "I would not presume to tell you what to do with this castle now that you have taken it."

"Your husband did terrible things," Cyrus said. "I am not inclined to let him free in his last hours."

The Baroness set her glass down and took a step closer to Cyrus, still separated from her by the cloth of her skirts. "I ask you not for clemency, sir, but leniency. If he is to die, then I suspect he is in pain. Am I wrong to want to lessen it?"

"Not wrong," Cyrus said, taking another sip, a longer one this time. "But what he did—"

"Was cruel and capricious, I'll grant you," the Baroness said. "But I appeal to you for mercy—you, who are now master of his house by conquest."

"I'm not master of his anything," Cyrus said. "We'll be leaving in the morning on our way to Galbadien, where we were headed before your husband provoked me into this wasteful action. The things we take from your keep are only recompense for what we lost here." He hesitated. "The rest will be burned."

"Sir Cyrus, perhaps you do not understand the full weight of what becomes yours," the Baroness said, leaning closer to him.

"It's actually 'Lord Cyrus of Perdamun,' if you want to be formal," he said, feeling a slight blush in his cheeks from the rum. It was good, and he seldom drank spirits or wine. "'Cyrus' is also fine." He turned his head to the side and downed the rest of his glass as she leaned her body against him. "I'm afraid you do me no service, madam. I am leaving on the morrow. I have no desire to enter into a protracted battle with your King. I have business in Galbadien, business with Syloreas and its army, and all that I have here is concluded."

"When my husband dies," she whispered, "I am no longer a Baroness, no longer of the House Hoygraf. I will be a fallen woman, from a fallen dynasty, and subject to beg on the streets for whatever scraps of food I might get, or be taken up as wife by some charitable stranger, but as the wife of the dead Baron Hoygraf I am sullied, impure, undesirable."

Cyrus stared down at her, felt the blood run hot in his veins. *It has been far, far too long.* "Of the many things you may be, I assure you that undesirable is not one of them."

"Do you have a wife back in your homeland? Or someone you are promised to?" Her other hand came up and stroked the stubble at his cheek.

"No," Cyrus said, sensing danger before him, "but neither does that mean I feel that just because I defeat a man in battle, I can take his wife as though she were chattel."

Her hand slid around the back of his neck and drew him closer to her. "Even if she were to be content—nay, happy—with such a pairing?"

Cyrus slid his hands up and gently took hers from around his neck. "Not even then. Madam, I am sorry for your loss—though your husband is not yet dead—but I cannot accept. Where I come from, women are not property to be exchanged along with gemstones and animals when a man's keep is conquered."

She seemed to crumple in his sight. "Here they are nothing but—and without your aid, I am not only property but worthless property."

"I am truly sorry for that," Cyrus said, inching away from her. "If you wish, you may come with our army under my protection—but not as my woman or any such thing of that sort."

She bristled. "As a harlot? A traveling woman, there for the pleasure of your men?"

Cyrus raised an eyebrow. "No, we don't have any of those. You'd accompany us as a free woman, whose rights and person are inviolate. Any such offense against said person would result in grievous penalties. When we return to Arkaria, you are welcome to make your own way in our society, which I suspect you'll find to be slightly more ... favorable. If not, then I wish you the best of success here in Luukessia. Regardless," he said, feeling the regret seep through him, "I will allow you to take your husband back to the village if you'd like, to die in a bed."

"Thank you," she said, ashen. "But in all honesty, my husband is a monster, an inhuman beast with appetites as copious as they are revolting. His death in a dungeon is a fitting end for the atrocities he has perpetrated on others ..." her lip quivered, "... and myself. I came to you because I am a woman who had much to lose, on the cusp of nothingness, and I wished to see the man who might spare me from it, if he were amenable."

"I'm afraid I can't grant you that which you would have of me," Cyrus said. "I am simply not so cavalier in my choice of marriage partners, and to propose that we wed after ten minutes of conversation is not in my character. The consequences could well be dire for both of us should we be forced to live with each other for the rest of our lives."

"I assure you that I am a good wife, sir—dutiful, faithful, and true. And in the matter of conjugal relations, I am willing and frequent in—"

"That's about all I need to hear," Cyrus said. "I trust in all you say, but believe me—none of it will sway me." He shook his head. "I apologize, but I must cut our audience short as my day will begin rather early tomorrow. Will you be returning to the village?"

"I suppose," she said, a strand of hair falling out of place on her head and into her eyes. "I was offered a bed for the night by one of the families down there, and as I have no bed here—" She looked at Cyrus once more, and he saw hope and regret in her.

"If you want to come with us and travel to Arkaria, we'll be on the road for quite some time, but I can promise you it's a place where women are not property." He drew himself up. "You'll be safe with our army, but it is going to be a long journey."

"I will consider your offer," she said. "If you will consider mine."

"I can't take advantage of you in that way," Cyrus said, "and make no mistake, it would be taking advantage. You would be with me because I hold the power to restore you to a modicum of your former station. But I have only the basest desires for a willing slave, which it sounds like you are offering to be." She started to open her mouth to protest but stopped, falling silent and bowing her head. "My offer remains open, if you want to leave behind the idea that you'll ever be beholden to a man again. I can see in you a woman who chafes under the bonds of your society."

She stared off into the distance, and Cyrus realized she was looking around the room one last time. "I thank you for your offer, sir, but Luukessia is my home." Her green eyes met his, and he saw only coolness in them now. "I bid you well, and since you would not have me stay here, good night." She curtsied for him, and a few more strands of her hair broke loose from the elaborate bun that she wore atop her head. She picked up her skirts and turned, walking toward the door. He hurried over and opened it for her and she let a stretched, worn smile cross her lips, one that never quite reached her eyes. With a subtle incline of her head toward him in thanks, she left, and he closed the door after her.

Cyrus went through to the bedchamber, alone, and began to take off his armor. Some pieces, like the mailed gloves, had come off frequently. Others, like his breastplate and backplate, felt as though they were stuck on, they had come off so rarely of late. A tub of lukewarm water waited for him in the corner; it had been hot before he had spoken with the Baroness. His underclothes peeled off with some difficulty and he slipped beneath the water, felt the grime wash off his skin. Something else remained, though, some taint or dirt he couldn't remove no matter how hard he scrubbed.

Chapter 12

Cyrus awoke after a fitful night of sleep. The Baron's bed was massive, almost as big as Cyrus's bed back at Sanctuary. This one was carved entirely of wood, however, and had four posts that reached the ceiling, with hanging curtains for some illusory privacy should someone else be in the room. There was a chill from where he had left the window open, a thin port that allowed blue sky to filter in from outside along with crisp morning air. Cyrus felt the heavy covers over him, soft cotton cloth that smelled of other people.

He rolled out of bed, felt the cold on his skin, and went rummaging for underclothes in a wooden dresser. The first drawer he opened presented him with women's undergarments. "Oh," Cyrus said after staring at them for a moment then shut the drawer. He walked across the room to the armoire on the other side and opened it to find male attire. He selected a cloth shirt and pants that he proceeded to stretch until he fit into them comfortably. Once finished, he began to strap on his armor.

Before placing his helm upon his head, he walked to the mirror and took a long look. His hair had grown long, long enough to place into a ponytail. His beard had also come in thick, black, and heavy. He sighed, thinking about how much more he had liked it when his face was bare and dismissed the thought. "I'll shave again when I'm back home," he said. "And not before."

When he opened the door to the Baron's quarters, he found Martaina outside with the same three guards. She didn't look tired at all but stood stiff against the wall at attention. "Have you been out here all night?"

When he spoke, she seemed to stir, angling her head to look at him. "Of course. There was a concern that some of the Baron's men had hidden away in the castle, and we couldn't take a chance on them getting to you in the night."

Cyrus felt a smile struggle out from beneath his stony facade. "Then ... shouldn't someone have been in the room with me?"

Martaina's eyes flashed, and her jaw tightened. "I suggested as much, but Curatio believed that a thorough search of the room before you turned in was a good enough precaution."

Cyrus suppressed a snicker. "Ranger, horse whisperer, master archer, guard—tell me, Martaina Proelius, is there anything you're not proficient at?"

He watched the emotion fall off her face, little cracks of it, hiding behind a wall she built in the span of a second. "Very little," she said with an emotionless smile. "Very little, indeed."

"Did you manage to get all the valuables taken out of the Baron's quarters last night when you swept through?" Cyrus gestured for Martaina to follow him, which she did.

"We found quite a few riches, yes," she said, stepping shoulder to shoulder with him. Martaina was taller than most of the other women in Sanctuary, only slightly shorter than six feet tall. "I think we found most everything of value."

"Consider taking some of the liquor if you're into that sort of thing," Cyrus said, feeling a slight ache behind his eyes. "I get the feeling it wasn't cheap, any of it."

"I'll inform Terian. I think he would perhaps get more use out of it than any of the rest of us that are here."

Cyrus smiled. "Because Andren isn't here, you mean to say."

"I mean to say."

They emerged in the throne room to find it largely clear of people. Only a few souls lingered, engaged in quiet conversations. Cyrus passed through the entry doors to the courtyard, Martaina still at his side, and the sunlight caused him to blanch. "What time is it?" he asked.

"Nearing nine o'clock," came the soft voice of J'anda Aimant. The enchanter sat on a wooden chair just outside the door, lounging in the shadow of the rampart over his head, his feet on another chair in front of him. "We assumed that since our General was unready to move forward, it might be safe to wait a while longer before hustling to be ready ourselves." J'anda had a silver goblet in his hand and a bottle of wine was on the ground next to him, the cork removed. He took a drink from the goblet after holding it up in silent toast to Cyrus.

"I take it you've insured that the Baron's wine cellar didn't go unattended?" Cyrus asked.

"I only took a few choice vintages. With Longwell's help, actually.

I thought all humans spoke the same language, but these Luukessians have the most curious handwriting. It looks nothing like any of your words."

"That's because the writing of humans in Arkaria is based on the elvish alphabet," Martaina said.

"Ah," J'anda said after taking another light sip. "Now that you mention it, I never noticed before, but yes, I see it now. But your letters are so peculiar compared to theirs."

"They have more than we do," she replied. "So they had to have added some at some point."

"Is the army ready to move?" Cyrus asked, looking between J'anda and Martaina.

"Soon," J'anda said, unconcerned. "Curatio is in the dungeons, taking a final look around, and, if I'm not mistaken, examining our dear, soon-to-be-departed Baron."

As if on cue, Cyrus heard a great outcry from somewhere inside, and there was a slamming of doors within the keep. A few people joined them in the courtyard, leaving the confines of the throne room behind. Cyrus heard loud footsteps within, and Curatio and Terian emerged, the dark knight looking strangely satisfied and the healer a bit flushed. "What was that?" Cyrus asked.

"The Baron still has some fight left in him," Terian said. "He got very upset when Curatio tried to look at his wound, so I was forced to settle him down."

Cyrus felt cool trepidation run through him. "How is he?"

Curatio sighed. "Not well. I suspect he has an infection, something I'm not able to cure. He appears feverish from a distance, but that could just be from the pain of having a large hole in his middle."

"I know that's the sort of thing that would tend to put me in a sour mood," J'anda said, irony dripping from every syllable.

"Well, have him dragged out," Cyrus said without emotion. "As cruel as I am, I don't want to burn the man's house with him still in it. We have a message for him to deliver, after all." He turned away as Curatio gestured to two warriors standing near the entry to the throne room, motioning them back inside.

Cyrus walked out across the drawbridge and felt a slight current of air as he crossed the filthy water below. The army was present, for the most part, on the other side, but not assembled nor ordered at all. They stood about, in clumps of people, talking in subdued circles. Cyrus could see empty bottles strewn on the ground and suspected that the Baron's wine cellar had been well and truly pillaged in the night. "I hope no one's too hung over to march today," he said as he passed a clump of soldiers. Laughter greeted his words even as he caught sight of a couple green faces in their midst.

Windrider waited with the other horses, already saddled. Cyrus approached him and ran an ungloved hand across his back, causing the horse to whinny at him. He brushed the back of Windrider's neck and whispered to him before turning back to see Martaina staring at him from next to her own horse, an eyebrow raised. "He seems to understand me," he explained, feeling slightly embarrassed.

"He does," she said. "That one is the rarest breed I've ever seen. That's not just an ordinary horse—or even just an exceptional one, for that matter. Where did you find him?"

"He's Sanctuary's horse," Cyrus said. "I've been riding him since the first time I had need of a horse, as I recall."

"Since the day Alaric paired you with him, you mean." Cyrus turned his head to see Curatio already mounting his steed, a slight smile on his face."

Cyrus frowned. "I suppose he did, at that. Anyway, I've always gone back to him since then." He ran his hand through Windrider's mane and was rewarded with the horse turning his head to brush against Cyrus.

"That's quite a horse," Martaina said, "I'd keep him close."

Cyrus put a foot in the stirrup and climbed up. As he settled himself, he saw Odellan a few paces away. "Odellan," Cyrus said, drawing the elf's attention. "Did you stay out here all night?"

"No, sir," Odellan said as his horse trotted over to stand next to Cyrus's. "All of our soldiers slept behind the walls last night, myself included. We bunked in the barracks in shifts, so everyone got some time in a genuine bed."

Cyrus shot a look at Martaina, who looked away innocently. "Well, almost everyone." He looked beyond Odellan to where a few horse-drawn wagons were parked at the far edge of the army. "Is that our spoils?"

"Indeed," Odellan said. "We've made out rather well. The injured prisoners we freed—including Calene—will be riding in the wagons the next few days. The six of them that were men seem to be holding up rather well. They were only beaten, after all. Calene and the other woman—Sinora is her name—are slightly worse for the wear. Calene seems to be adapting, but Sinora may be riding the wagon the rest of the trip."

"Let's talk about this later," Cyrus said as a familiar figure rode up on a horse. Today her hair was down, wrapped into a ponytail behind her, the long brown strands standing out against the white shirt she wore. Gone was the dress, replaced by immaculate white breeches that went all the way to her ankles. Her boots were worn, brown cowhide, and she wore a navy overcoat that fell to mid-thigh. Her eyes were visible as she approached him, the green standing out against her garments and her face. A few stray hairs blew around the sides of her head as she brought her horse to a canter, then a stop next to him.

"Baroness," he said. "A pleasure to see you."

"I believe it's soon to be simply Cattrine, if it is not already." She remained proud, her head held up. "I have mulled over your offer and believe it is in my best interest to leave this place behind."

"I see," Cyrus said. "Very well then. Follow my commands and keep up." He looked at her horse. "That looks like a solid animal; I doubt you'll have any trouble in that regard."

"Thank you, Lord Davidon," she said, oddly formal. "I shan't present any problems for you."

"Good to know," he said. "How familiar are you with the lands between here and Galbadien?"

He saw the first hint of emotion as the corner of her lip curled slightly in response to his inquiry. "I am an expert rider, sir. I have been over the entirety of Actaluere, from the southern shores to the northern and eastern borders. I have even been," she said with a hint of pride, "all the way to the bridge to your land and on it, though only for a short distance."

"The well-traveled sort," Terian said as he mounted his destrier. "Which makes sense, considering who your husband was." The dark knight smiled wickedly. "I bet he broke you in quite well."

Cattrine's eyes narrowed. "I think I hear an inference from you that

I don't care for, sir. Don't think that simply because my fortunes have been lost in the last day that I'll take any sort of insults from some blue-skinned devil. I am a lady, sir, and if you won't accord me the respect due—"

"You'll what?" Terian moved his horse close enough to hers to look her in the face, and Cyrus saw nothing but pique in the dark elf's expression. Cyrus started to tell Terian to back off her, but there was a flash of metal and Cyrus saw a dagger at the dark elf's throat.

"I'll ask you to take a step back," Cattrine said in a low voice.

"Get away from her, Terian," Cyrus said.

The dark knight backed his horse away, a few steps at a time, and Cattrine sheathed her dagger under her cloak.

Cyrus cleared his throat. "I trust that the rumor of this will spread through the ranks—and let them know that the Baroness," he heard her cough, softly, "excuse me, the former Baroness, is under my personal protection and any harm that comes to her will be revisited upon the giver a hundred-fold." Cyrus turned his gaze on Terian, who was already glaring at him.

There was a ripple of quiet agreement, but no one said anything of distinction. Those close in attendance held the awkward silence until Cyrus broke it. "Is everyone with us?"

"The last of them are coming out of the castle now," Longwell said, pointing to the drawbridge, where a few stragglers carried large burlap bags, and a few carried other outsized objects. Two men struggled with the Baron, dragging him over the drawbridge. Once he was over, they dropped him limply to the ground and left him there, filing away back into the neatly ordered rows of the army's formation.

"Very well," Cyrus said, and turned to Odellan. "Let's start heading east. We've lost enough time in this place." He looked around and caught the Baroness's unflinching gaze and he blinked. "I mean ... uh ..." She did not say anything, merely stared at him with an eyebrow raised, without emotion until he looked away first. "I don't know what I meant." He looked back at Nyad and gave a subtle nod, which she returned. With a slight extension of her hand she pointed to the castle Green Hill—*a hellhole if ever there was one*—and Cyrus saw black smoke rise from within it, small puffs going up into the sky.

"All right," he said, "let's start this convoy moving." He urged

Windrider forward at a canter, following the muddy dirt path that cut through the green fields and hillocks.

He checked after a half a mile, just to be sure that the army had fallen in. It had, a long line of marchers, with a few wagons visible at the far back of the column, bringing up the rear. A few of the officers and veterans on horseback rode alongside the column rather than at the front with the other horses. Odellan and Longwell were the most obvious, their armor in shining silver and deep blue, respectively. Longwell's white surcoat had appeared as clean as ever, showing no signs of the battle yesterday. Behind them, some distance back, a pillar of black smoke rose into the heavens.

Cyrus's wandering eyes found Curatio in deep conversation with J'anda, the two of them especially cheerful this day. The sun shone down; Cyrus could feel the warm tropical air of spring and wondered if the mild winter around Sanctuary had broken yet, if the occasional patch of white, frosted grass that could be found in the mornings had disappeared. It was like seeing the first signs of age, the little bits of silver streaking hair, leeching the color from the strands.

He thought of Reikonos, of the bitter snowfalls that encased the city in winter, the white snows that would pile up while one slept, waking to find the world changed the next morning. He thought of the uneven roofs of the city, the high and low buildings situated next to each other, the towers beside one-story dwellings. He thought of the slums, of the deep valley that saw direct sunlight only at midday and of how bitter and dark it became in the winter. He wondered if the dark elves had surrounded the city or if the humans still held them at a distance.

Cyrus thought back to a winter in Reikonos, the worst of all of them, and it was like a thread of oddly colored string in a tapestry; unfamiliar, unmatching, that looked nothing like the rest of the weaving. *When was that? I was young ... first year at the Society? Yes ...*

"What were you thinking," Terian's voice whipsawed Cyrus out of his memories, "having her come along? Are you so hard up to get laid that you've taken to embracing the wives of your enemies before they're even dead?"

"Are you a little testy because she held a knife to your throat?" Cyrus tried to keep his tone indifferent.

"That's hardly the closest anyone's gotten to me with a blade," Terian said, and Cyrus heard the groan of metal in the dark knight's gauntlets as he gripped the reins of his horse tighter. "We're in the middle of this hostile Kingdom. Her husband ordered the capture of our people and personally tortured and beat them."

"You're not telling me anything I don't know," Cyrus said.

Terian's face turned a deeper blue, darkening, almost purple. "Then why did you have the wife of an enemy who you personally gutted and left to die a slow, torturous death come along with us? She could be a spy, she could be harboring a desire for revenge—she could just be here to try and get close to you so that she can slip a knife in your back."

"She had a chance to do that last night," Cyrus said. "She's coming with us because with her husband's death she loses everything. I offered her a chance to come to Arkaria, to make a new life in a place where she's not reliant on a man for everything."

Terian's flush subsided and his face loosened, settling into a kind of disbelieving wonderment. "And you believed her? Did she try to sleep with you?"

"Lately, who doesn't?" Cyrus asked warily.

"Umm, me," Martaina said from over Cyrus's shoulder. He looked back and saw the elf raise her hand in the air.

"I was joking," Cyrus said. "But duly noted, and thank you."

"I don't know how to take that," Martaina muttered under her breath. "But you're welcome."

"She tried to use her feminine wiles on you," Terian said, bringing Cyrus's attention back to their conversation. "She's getting close to you to exact revenge."

"Revenge would be easy." Cyrus shook off the dark knight's concern. "I'm not worried about that. And if she 'used her feminine wiles,' as you said, it's probably because the women of Luukessia have no other weapon to use. We're in a land where women don't carry swords and are subject to men's whims. What else are you going to use when force of arms is denied you? Sharp words?"

"I find they get me where I need to go."

"Because you can use a sword to back them up," Cyrus said. "The women of Luukessia have no such option; they're not trained with weapons, and if you're going to take a blade to a skilled swordsman, you damned sure better have the element of surprise on your side, otherwise you're going to get cut into tiny fillets. So what else is she supposed to do? She tried to persuade me, it didn't work. I didn't give her what she wanted, I offered her an alternative that she decided to avail herself of."

"Which involves following in your wake for the next few months," Terian said, shaking his head, "being in perfect striking distance—I mean, she already has a knife. You should at least take that from her."

"I think not," Cyrus said. "If I were a woman in the middle of a foreign army, with the upbringing she's had, married to the monster she was, I'd carry ten swords, three spears and a battleaxe just so I could feel safe. I remain unconcerned about her dagger."

Terian's hand went to his throat, fingers playing in a line across it. "Something you might learn—and I hope you don't—there's an old quote from my people. 'A woman can slit a throat as easily as a man.'"

Cyrus looked at Terian with undisguised amusement. "Are all your people's sayings that dark?"

Terian stared at him blankly. "Perhaps you're mistaking darkness for truth. It's a hard, bitter, and cruel world, and the people you think you can trust aren't always what they seem."

Cyrus raised an eyebrow at him. "Weren't you the guy who once told me that you can't stand people who aren't what they appear to be?"

Terian blinked, bewildered. "I ... what? I said that?"

"When we were about to kill Kalam, the black dragon. You were talking about the Alliance and why you hated them." Cyrus smiled. "It always stuck with me because it was the first time any of you officers had bothered to explain why you detested the Alliance. And of course," he said grimly, "about a week later, you left Sanctuary. You know, to 'roam the world' or whatever." Cyrus cocked his head in curiosity. "You know, you never did tell us what you did while you were 'roaming.'"

Terian's eyes, dark purple, had been focused on him until the last. The dark knight seemed to lean back in his saddle, and Cyrus watched him swallow hard. "You know what I was doing."

"No, I don't," Cyrus said. "We may have this easy familiarity, but you're not exactly the easiest guy to get to know on a deeper level, Terian. The Gatekeeper suggested you were doing things that wouldn't make any of us proud, but I don't know what you were up to. You could have been dancing in an all-male revue in Saekaj, for all I know." Terian's eyes narrowed and Cyrus shrugged, a smile on his face. "Well, that wouldn't exactly make me proud of you, but hey, we all hit rough times ..."

"I think I liked you better when you were moping and brooding over the loss of your blond elf-princess," Terian said with a note of bitterness.

Cyrus felt a stab of pain within. "Yeah, well ... I'm sure I'll be back to my old self any day now. I doubt that I can shed the pain of her easily, like a snake shedding its skin."

"How do you know if it's easy for a snake to shed its skin?" Terian stared ahead, looking at the road in front of them as he spoke. "Just because it happens often? It could be painful as all hell, trying to leave behind something you've lived your life in like that. It could be as tough as leaving behind family, upbringing ... anything you've carried with you."

Cyrus turned to look at the dark knight. "Is that like you, then? A dark knight in the service of Sanctuary, trying to shed the wicked parts of your training?"

"Probably." Terian turned his head and the mask was there, visible for Cyrus to see, nothing underneath it, no lines on the dark elf's face. "I was raised to serve Yartraak, the Lord of All Dark. At seventeen, in my eighth year of training with the Legion of Darkness, I, along with all the other budding dark knights, was expected to seal that oath of loyalty with a soul sacrifice." He let that hang in the air between them.

"What's a soul sacrifice?" Cyrus stared at Terian, who kept his eyes ahead.

"Don't ask questions you don't want to know the answers to." Terian turned his head, and Cyrus caught a glimpse behind the mask—a cool, calculating look lay on the face of Terian, something Cyrus hadn't seen from him before. "They might scare you, after all, shake your pretty little worldview and crush all your ideas about honor and virtue and nobility in the world."

"Maybe you've forgotten who you're talking to," Cyrus said, feeling the irritation rise within him. "I'm not Alaric."

Terian let out a low chuckle. "I suppose not—stabbing your

enemies in their guts and letting them squirm to death, taking their wives away before they're even dead? You know, I would have had a whole new level of respect for you if you'd told me you had slept with her." Cyrus turned to look at Terian in disgust. "I know," the dark knight said, "it'd be low, I'll admit, but let's face it, she's pretty and you're ... well ... I hesitate to say you're not a man in your urges, but ... I mean ... come on, Cyrus, it's been since before I met you, hasn't it? Do you just feel nothing down there?" He narrowed his eyes. "Are you a eunuch?"

Cyrus gave him the hard glare, and Terian shrugged. "Just asking. Most men who hack and slash with a sword for all the days of their life tend to be fairly free with the other sword as well, if you take my meaning. So is it something to do with the God of War?" Terian cracked a smile. "Did Bellarum order his initiates to keep armor between them and women folk at all times, or something? Was there a command to avoid sex at all costs, even when offered to you by beautiful women of varying races and species?"

"No!" Cyrus shouted his answer then looked around, drawing the curious stares of others. He ignored Martaina's giggles behind him, and when Curatio caught his eye, the healer looked away as did Odellan. "It's not that," Cyrus said.

"Please tell me you weren't holding out for Vara," Terian said. "Because that would be ... actually, that would be comically amusing." The dark elf snickered, then straightened out his expression. "Though not for you, I suppose."

"I was." Cyrus let the words out, scarcely believing them. "I actually was."

"Oh dear gods," Terian said. "You don't mean you're a ... I mean, you never? Not even with your wife?"

"What?" Cyrus stared at him, uncomprehending. "No, of course I did with Imina—my wife," he said, when he caught the confused gaze from Terian. "But she was the ..." he lowered his voice. "The first ... and the last."

Terian let out a sharp laugh, like a bark, then cut it off. "Sorry. The first and the last? What the hells, man? You've been divorced since before I've known you. And not before? What, did you marry when you were sixteen?"

"I ... no, I didn't even meet Imina until I was nineteen or so." Cyrus caught his breath. "I don't know. After her, I was focused on building my guild, and there wasn't really much chance to—" He flushed. "You've seen where we lived when we were in the Kings of Reikonos. I didn't want a public exhibition, and frankly, it's not as though I met many women. Every now and again, I'd see my ex-wife, and we'd ... well, you know. But that was it."

"Yeah, but again, you've been with Sanctuary for ... what? Over three years now?" Terian looked at him with guarded disbelief. "You've been an officer for most of that time, and I hate to break this to you, but the women say you're easy on the old eyeballs, so I think you'd have had an offer or two. I'm saying if you really wanted to—"

"I came close once," he said. "With Nyad." He looked around and didn't see the wizard in the formation with them. He caught sight of crimson robes further down the column. "When we were out on the recruiting mission. I mean, I had started to come out of the melancholy I was in after Narstron died, but, well, we were close to it, and she—" he flushed again, "—she found out about how I felt about Vara and stopped me."

"Ouch." Terian grimaced. "Nyad never stops anybody." He looked behind them. "Guess there had to be a first time, but I'm a little shocked it was you. But since then, there have been offers, right?" He looked around again. "That ranger, Aisling? Hasn't she been on your trail for a while?"

"Yes," Cyrus said. "But Vara ... I don't know. I always ... held out this hope in the back of my mind that Vara and I could ... you know. It seemed like we were right there—she told me she felt the same way about me, and ..." He sighed. "Everything ... just completely fell apart."

"What did she say to you that night?" Terian looked at him, and Cyrus could see the curiosity, curiosity and something else. "The last night in Sanctuary, before you came downstairs and offered to go with Longwell?"

Cyrus felt the tension run through him, felt his muscles ache, smelled the fresh air and the outdoors. "She said ..."

We will not, cannot be. Not ever ... I thank you for trying to comfort me in my hour of need, but I'll have you take your leave now.

"She said that it would never work between us." Cyrus heard the words echo in his mind, heard the quiet around them, felt the seeping darkness of her quarters as she had said them. "That she would outlive me by so long, that her pain would be so great that it wasn't worth it to her."

"Ouch." Terian let out a low whistle. "She knows how to drive the dagger deep, doesn't she? I mean, you'd think she'd had a hundred years of experience doing it to say something like that."

"She was just trying to …" Cyrus let the words hang there. "Cut me loose with as little pain as she could."

"Still. That's the easiest she could come up with?" Terian shook his head. "Brutal. It was just brutal. She could have at least given you a roll in the proverbial hay for your years of pining before she booted you from beneath her sheets."

"Oddly enough," Cyrus said, "I don't think that would have helped." There was quiet for a few minutes, unbroken by either of them until Cyrus said finally, "I haven't told anyone that yet. Thank you for listening."

"Why wouldn't I?" Terian asked.

"You've been a little strange lately," Cyrus said. "One minute you act like my friend Terian, then the next it's like you're channeling Vara."

"That's low," he said, wincing. "I've been your friend for a long time, Davidon." The wince disappeared, replaced by a knowing smirk. "Can you think of anything you might have done that would change that?"

Cyrus thought about it and shrugged. "I can't think of anything. But I wondered if maybe I'd done something to piss you off."

"Yeah. Well …" Terian said, pensive, "… you did give me this very impressive sword." He pulled the blade from his scabbard, holding it up. The steel held a bright red edge to it and it glimmered and shone, the mystical power beneath the forging obvious in the daylight. "This is a blade given by the Sovereign to his truly great dark knights, the ones of such skill and virtue that they remain unchallenged in the realm of personal combat. It's a rare honor to get one of these and they say the red in the steel is from the blade, drinking the blood of its enemies to grow stronger." He smiled, a very slight one. "So that's noteworthy, isn't it?"

"I suppose," Cyrus said, inflectionless. "Such a trivial thing, though. I wasn't ever going to use it."

"Ah, yes, trivial things," Terian said, a bitter smile on his lips. "It's funny how the things we think are so trivial really aren't. But that's all right," the dark knight said, his smile widening, the bitterness leaving it. "I'll make good use of it." He stared at the length of it and swung it to the side, causing his horse to shuffle footing with the change in weight. Terian laughed. "It'll drink the blood of my enemies." He looked back to Cyrus, and nodded his head in gratitude.

"Every last one of them."

Chapter 13

Weeks passed as they traveled across the land. Cyrus stayed at the fore of the expedition save for once per day, when he would ride along the sides of the column and speak to the soldiers. They nodded and smiled at him, giving him hope and encouragement and taking his mind off Vara.

Aisling seemed to avoid Cyrus in the days that followed the castle siege. She nodded and smiled politely at him but made no attempt to initiate conversation. Uncertain of what to think or feel, he nodded courteously when he saw her and even doffed his helm but said nothing more than pleasantries.

While Cyrus spoke with the Baroness only occasionally to check in on her—to little effect, she would answer politely but offer little else—she seemed to be getting along well with almost all his other officers. He regularly saw her riding with J'anda and Curatio as well as Nyad and Ryin. Occasionally he would also see her speaking with Longwell or Odellan, or Martaina. Once he even saw her talking with Aisling. Both of them had been looking at him when he turned around, and they averted their eyes quickly, leaving him with a distinctly embarrassed sensation, his ears burning.

The weather changed as the weeks wore on. The sun grew warmer, and they made the turn into croplands, where corn dominated the fields, along with grains of all sorts. The days grew longer, and the breeze carried less chill. The hills gave way to long stretches of flat plains, with just the slightest roll to them; they reminded him most of the Plains of Perdamun, of Sanctuary and home—and of an elven girl that he could not get off his mind, no matter how he tried.

"We're less than a week from my father's castle," Longwell said to Cyrus one day as they were passing a field with a fence of stone that encircled it. The skies were grey, a light drizzle of rain making its way down upon them.

"So we'll be heading to his castle, not the front line?" Cyrus looked at the dragoon. Odellan rode on the other side of Cyrus, listening to them both.

"Aye," Longwell said. "It has been something akin to six months since my father first sent his messenger to us; it would be difficult to tell where the army is after such an interval." Tightness creased the dragoon's face. "If it is as bad as he said in his message, we may not have far to go to find his army."

"That doesn't sound as if it bodes well," Odellan said, the light rain trickling down over his armor.

"It didn't bode well when my father contacted me." Longwell looked glum. "He knew it would be an exceptionally long journey to send someone after me. I didn't tell them exactly where I'd be, because I didn't know anything of Arkaria when I left." He paused, frowning. "Nor was I of a disposition to tell him at the time either, I suppose. I only told him I was going over the Endless Bridge to find a strong army to join. His messenger tracked me down based on whispers of my involvement in the defense of Termina."

"That's a hell of a walk if you don't have have a wizard to teleport you." Cyrus heard Windrider whinny. The rain was chill, the little splashes of water bouncing off his armor and into his face.

"I think he hoped I'd have found a strong army I could bring back with me," Longwell said. "Syloreas has long been our enemy, back thousands of years, since the three Kingdoms began."

"Perhaps you could give us some history of the conflicts of this land," Odellan said.

Longwell looked at the elf with dull eyes and an amused smile. "Certainly. They fought constantly; not ten years would go by without one of the three Kingdoms declaring war on another and pressing the attack. Sometimes there were defeats, occasionally a Kingdom would be conquered for ten or twenty years—I think Actaluere was actually put under Syloreas's boot for almost fifty years once, but that was several thousand years ago. Every time, eventually, the people would rise up, throw off the lazy army with the help of the other Kingdom, and the cycle would start again a few years later."

"Oh my," Odellan said. "That makes the sordid history of the elves and dark elves look quite peaceful by comparison."

Cyrus stared at Longwell with a raised eyebrow. "No offense, but your people sound as bloodthirsty as the trolls. That's an awful lot of wars."

Longwell shrugged. "I didn't start them. And I was only involved in one of them—the last war, between all three Kingdoms."

"Who started that one?" Cyrus asked.

"Syloreas," Longwell said. "Briyce Unger began with an invasion of Actaluere's northern borders, and my father," he said, rising tension apparent in his voice, "decided it would be an opportune moment to deprive Syloreas of some of their southern lands while they were distracted with an invasion thrust that nearly reached halfway to Caenalys, the capital of Actaluere. What my father hadn't anticipated was that Briyce Unger would turn his armies around when he heard that we had begun assaulting his border and march them directly there to hammer us."

"What did Actaluere do?" Odellan asked.

"Not a damned thing," Longwell said bitterly. "They tossed out the remaining garrison troops that Briyce Unger had left behind, then sat their army back and waited until Unger and my father's forces had done a good amount of damage to each other. Then King Tiernan of Actaluere launched an attack on our border, taking two cities away from us and leaving Unger unpunished."

"Can you really blame him?" The Baroness's voice came from behind them, startling Cyrus and causing him to turn. She sat on horseback, following only a few paces behind them. "He saw an opportunity to get Unger out of his territory and take two jewels out of Galbadien's crown with minimal effort while you and Syloreas were busy bleeding each other dry in the north. King Tiernan ended the war he hadn't even started with more territory, while Galbadien and Syloreas both lost half their armies." She shook her head and smiled. "Your father got perfidious and thought to turn our war to his advantage, but Unger's bullheaded pride worked against him. Your father was outsmarted by Milos Tiernan. There's no shame in it; Tiernan's shrewd above all else."

"That was treachery," Longwell said, reddening. "My father gave Milos Tiernan a perfect opportunity to get revenge on Syloreas for invading their territory; it could have been mutually beneficial for both our Kingdoms and instead Tiernan stabbed my father in the back."

The Baroness kept an infuriating smile perched upon her lips, giving her an impish look that caused Cyrus more intrigue than he cared to admit. "I thought it was an exceptionally clever way to pit two enemies against each other to maximum advantage. After all, it wasn't as though there's ever been any sort of peace or alliance between Actaluere and Galbadien—only a few years without war between us."

"No formal peace, but no formal war either," Longwell said. "It was basest treachery."

The Baroness shrugged. "See it however you like; Milos Tiernan walked away from the conflict with more territory and an army ready for the next war. Your father's Kingdom limped away just as Syloreas did, with countless young men dead, less territory than when you started, and forced to concede what you'd lost. If the point of war is simply honor and not winning, you're still doing it wrong. I hear tell your father's soldiers are just as savage when sacking a town as Briyce Unger's are."

Longwell did not answer, and seemed to slump slightly forward on his horse, his eyes focused ahead. Cyrus watched the dragoon for a long moment, and when it seemed unlikely he would ever speak, he did. "I cannot argue with that." Longwell rode off a moment later, after the silence had hung in the air. He rode toward the back of the column, ignoring several soldiers who hailed him along the way.

"If you'll excuse me," Odellan said, "perhaps I should speak with him—and inspect the column while I am at it."

"Certainly," Cyrus said with a nod. Odellan turned his horse and rode away. Cyrus turned to speak with the Baroness, but she was already gone, ensconced in a conversation with Nyad and Ryin, the three of them riding side by side.

The next week passed quickly, the flat lands over which they traveled speeding their journey. Longwell seemed to come alive again a few days after the conversation with the Baroness. He had been sulky and withdrawn, causing Cyrus to privately wonder if he had been that depressing to be around when they had first set out on their journey.

Only a few days later, they came around a bend in the road and something enormous became visible on the horizon. Cyrus was riding at the front of the column as he almost always did, and when the silhouette began to take shape as the sun was starting to set behind them, he wondered if perhaps it was a cloud bank.

"That is the Castle of Vernadam," Longwell said, riding to the fore to come alongside Cyrus. "That is my father's home."

"Not yours?" Cyrus asked.

He caught a glimmer of regret from the dragoon. "Once perhaps. Not anymore."

They bedded down for the night in a clearing, and as the campfires lit the sky, Cyrus stared into the distance, where he could still see the faintest shadow of the castle on the horizon. He heard someone move next to him where he stood at the far edge of the army's camp, and he turned to see the Baroness, clad in her riding outfit but with a blanket wrapped around her to guard against the chill of the early evening.

"There stands Vernadam," she said, almost whispering, "a place I never thought I would see, not in my lifetime."

"No?" Cyrus looked over to her, saw the wind stir her hair. "The borders of your lands don't seem too hostile to crossing, if it were for just a person by themselves."

She looked over at him, her glazed eyes returning to focus. "Women do not travel alone, and the Baron does not travel this far outside his holdfast."

"How long were you married?" Cyrus watched her. She didn't answer him quickly, as though she were taking her time coming up with the right reply.

"Only a year or so," she said. "It was a very quick arrangement, really."

"Hm." Cyrus nodded, looking at the fire. "Less than a year and already happy to leave him behind. He must have been a real monster."

"As though you don't already know." He could feel her bristle.

"I know what he did to others," Cyrus said, reaching for a branch and stirring the embers of the fire with it. "I know how he treated strangers in his land who meant him no harm. So, yes, that gives me some idea of how he might treat his wife."

"You have no idea," she pronounced, and her words were stiff. "Beatings were commonplace. Whippings he saved for occasions of special displeasure, which seemed to happen whenever he was drunkest."

"You're not making me sorry I left him to die," Cyrus said, holding the branch steady, letting it catch fire. He watched the flames lick at the healthy bough, saw the first black scoring appear upon it.

"As you said, I've been married for a year and I was glad to leave him to die," she said stiffly. "I never considered myself a cold or vicious person, but perhaps I am." She looked away and her eyes fixated again on Vernadam's shadow in the distance. "I certainly was not much of a wife, to hear my husband tell it."

"I doubt you gave him any cause for beatings or whippings," Cyrus said, letting the branch drift through a pile of ashes. "Because there is no cause for such things, not between husband and wife. He did not seem the sort of man whose justification I would accept as anything other than the petty anger of a man denied something."

"Denied?" She looked at Cyrus and wore the faintest half-smile. "I denied him nothing. Not my body, at all hours, not his favors, requested day and night. He came to me often in the hours of the morning too early to be measured by any light, and I would give him that which he craved so fervently, no matter how asleep I was. Once, he came to me when I was in a deep grog. I moved too slowly for his liking, so he dragged me by the hair out to the courtyard where he bound me to a post, naked, and had his way with me in front of all of his men and the servants and everyone." Her lip quivered, but her eyes smoldered like the fire. "So that he could show them—and me—that he ruled his household with a firm and unyielding hand. When he was done, he left me there for a day, without food or water, like a common thief or drunk, and forbade the doctor to see to my injuries."

The twigs at the end of Cyrus's branch caught on fire at last, and he pulled it out of the flame, holding the length above it, the smallest reaches of it burning with a light of their own. "How did you get saddled with him?"

She looked away again. "My brother gave me to him in marriage, in hopes of gaining his favor." She looked back at Cyrus. "Since my father is dead, my brother was well within his rights to give me to anyone he wanted to."

"And now?" Cyrus watched the slow burn of the twigs spread up the branch. "Now that he's dead, wouldn't your brother want to marry you off again, to someone else?"

"No," she said simply. "Because now I am damaged, imperfect."

Cyrus frowned. "Because you've been married before? By that

standard, I suppose I'm damaged and imperfect, too." He raised an eyebrow. "Which I actually am but not because of being married before."

"No," she said. "Because of the scars. Because of the whippings, the beatings ... and ... other things he's done to me." She swallowed hard. "He used to say that he had left his mark on me, that no other man would ever want me, or would ever have me, after what he'd done."

"I don't, uh ..." Cyrus looked at her. "I'm sorry, I mean, I've seen you in a ... somewhat revealing dress ... I guess ....I mean, I didn't see anything."

"You wouldn't." She shook her head, very slightly and perched on her lips was a rueful smile. "The men and women in the courtyard the night he dragged me out and tied me to the post, they saw. But he kept it ... all well below what the rest of the world would see. Women are expected to maintain a certain standard of propriety, after all." He saw a single tear flow from her left eye, down her cheek, to rest on her defined chin. It was a perfect droplet, just the one, and it lingered there. "The simple loss of my virginity to my husband would not be considered enough to defile me for life, to make me untouchable to other men for marriageable purposes."

"Ah," Cyrus looked at the Baroness again, saw the smoldering anger in her eyes, and felt it touch him. *My emotions are muted and best they remain that way. I already feel less remorse for leaving the Baron as I did. Men who dominate and abuse women in such a manner are scum, but I fear my anger with him would have me become a torturer were I to fully loose it upon that wretch.* He looked back at her; she was undeniably beautiful, stunning even, to his eyes, which had become somewhat jaded of late, filled to the top as they were with the intoxicating beauty of a she-elf who had hurt him so.

The Baroness is different. She seems ... not helpless. Far from it. But wounded. Like me. She possessed an air, a quality of genuine and natural beauty. She seemed to sense his gaze and turned to look at him. "And you?" she asked. "You are not married?"

"Not anymore." He sniffed and threw the branch into the fire, smelled the smokiness of the wood filling the crisp air.

"Is she ... gone on?" The Baroness looked at him carefully, probing.

"She was still quite lively when last I saw her, which was a year or two ago," he said. "She left me."

"Left you?" There was a rising curiosity in the Baroness's voice. "You allowed this?"

"Allowed it?" Cyrus suppressed a laugh. "I gave my full consent when she asked for the divorce decree. She didn't want to be married to a warrior who was always traveling, always gone, always in danger."

Cattrine frowned, as though contemplating something impossible. "Is that ... does that happen often in your land? A woman leaving a man when she is unsatisfied?" She blushed. "I don't mean to suggest she was unsatisfied by you. I'm certain you're very satisfying." She blushed deeper, a crimson shade in the firelight.

Cyrus watched her with some amusement before he shrugged. "It happens. More among the elves than the humans, I'm told, but it happens among my people as well."

"Fascinating," the Baroness said, her skin lit by the flickering of the fire. "Your world is ever so much different than my own."

"If you think that's different, you should see Sanctuary," Cyrus said.

"Your guild is called Sanctuary, yes?" The Baroness looked at him once more, her hand resting on her leg, her knees pulled up to her chest. "But there is a place called Sanctuary as well?"

"Our guildhall, yes."

"What is it like there?" Her voice carried a combination of awe and wistfulness.

"It's in the middle of the Plains of Perdamun, a long, wide stretch of grasslands. When you teleport into the plains, you have to run south through a field of wildflowers to Sanctuary. They'll be in bloom now, I suppose, all the colors on display ... red, blue, purple and orange. It's like a rainbow growing from the ground, and if you're with a druid, and they cast the Falcon's Essence spell, you can run right over them, watch them rock in the wind as you pass, stirring them. The main tower appears first, looming above you like a spire sticking out of the ground, then you see the other towers and the wall ... it's built with a curtain wall like a castle, but it's like no castle you've ever seen."

"The wall goes around for a mile or more ... encloses gardens, stables, an archery range ... and in the middle of it all is Sanctuary."

Cyrus smiled at the memory, the thought of the stone blocks that comprised the guildhall, of the stained glass window glowing in all its colors above the main doors. "It's gorgeous. One of the ... warmest places I've ever been. It was ..." His smile faded. "Home."

"You miss it." Her voice punctuated the quiet against the crackle of the fire against the logs.

"I suppose."

"Were you always in Sanctuary?"

"No. I was born and raised in Reikonos, the capital of the Human Confederation."

"Was that where you learned to fight?" She hugged her knees closer to her chest. "Was that where you got your sword?"

"I learned to fight there, but I got my sword—this sword," he tugged at the hilt of Praelior, "later, when I was with Sanctuary."

"Did your parents teach you how to fight?" She looked at him with genuine interest, and he felt himself warm, something unrelated to the fire.

"My father was a great warrior, but he died when I was far too young to learn how to fight. No, I learned in the Society of Arms—where they send all young men and women who wish to learn to master the fighting arts."

"Women, too?" Cattrine looked vaguely impressed. "You had women train alongside you?"

"Yes," Cyrus said. "Some of the older boys would take it easy on the younger kids, knowing they could crush us without difficulty. Some of my roughest fights were against the girls. They did not yield an inch, regardless of age."

"It did not ..." She searched for a word, "humiliate you, being defeated by a woman?"

"Heh," Cyrus said. "Every defeat was a humiliation, and there was no more shame in being beaten by a girl than by a boy. Sometimes there was less. Some of those girls had a pain threshold that made me look pitiful by comparison." Cyrus felt his expression change. "I haven't talked about this in years until a couple months ago. And again now. I don't talk about these things. How'd you do that?"

She smiled. "I asked. Doesn't anyone else ever ask you about yourself?"

A thought of Aisling flashed through his mind, settling within him, leaving an uneasy feeling. "Not particularly," Cyrus said.

They were quiet for a minute then the Baroness spoke. "What is her name?"

Cyrus blinked, then looked at her, at the orange light casting a warm glow on her face in the soft light. She coaxed him with a hint of a smile. "Who?" he asked.

"The woman." She smoothed a wrinkle on the knee of her pants. "The one you think of all the time. The one they say you ran across the bridge to get away from." She dropped her voice an octave, and he strained to hear her next words. "The one who broke your heart."

"Vara," Cyrus whispered. "Her name is Vara."

"She was not your wife, was she?"

"No," he said. "She was not."

There was a moment's pause, and he heard the Baroness slide across the ground toward him, heard her inch closer, felt her only a foot away. "What was it about her that drew you so?"

"I don't know," Cyrus said quietly. "She wasn't kind to me, not from the beginning. But there was something about her ... a draw, a pull between us that was unlike anything I'd ever felt."

"What was she like?"

"Sharp of tongue, quick to anger," Cyrus said, "a terror with a blade, and a wielder of magics that could knock a man flat." He paused. "A fighter. She's ... a fighter, at least that's how I remember her."

"It makes sense that a man as strong as yourself would be drawn to a woman possessed of great strength," the Baroness said. Her face spoke of other things though, and held a drawn, harried look. "I suppose that it must be a great attraction, to find a woman so much like yourself." She seemed to draw back from him, her confidence crumbling. "My life must seem very dull and pitiful to someone who adventures in far away lands and rides the back of a Dragonlord—"

"No." Cyrus turned all his attention to her, sweeping away thoughts of Vara. "Not at all. My life is ... well ... filled to the brimming with madness, but that doesn't mean I don't have great respect for the way others live. Besides, it sounds like you've been in more peril than I have, living with the Baron." He paused in thought. "Who told you about the Dragonlord?"

"Curatio," she said, looking back to him. "They all tell the most amazing tales of you, of your exploits."

"Oh?" Cyrus looked away. "They exaggerate. Most of them weren't that interesting."

"So you and Sir Longwell and your lady elf did not hold a bridge against an army of one hundred thousand for an entire night?" She looked at him with genuineness, and he felt a prick of conscience.

"No, we did," Cyrus said. "But that was not the whole story. There were others helping us on that bridge, and we had additional forces on bridges to help guard our flanks." He shrugged. "There's just more to it, that's all."

"In all of the stories they tell, you seem so brave," she said with a voice filled with wistfulness. "So fearless. Are you not concerned with death?"

He let a ghost of a smile creep across his face. "Death doesn't concern me."

She cocked her head at him. "No?"

"No," he said with a shake of the head. "I killed him two months ago."

"What?" She blinked. "Oh, you mean your God of Death. Mordo—"

"Mortus," Cyrus said, the vision of the four-legged, eight-armed god flashing through his memory. "His name was Mortus."

"They say you have died before," Cattrine said. "I have heard the tales that western priests hold the power to return life."

"Some do." Cyrus nodded toward Curatio, who sat at the next fire, his back to them, staring into the flames. "He does. But only for an hour after death, and only when the death was caused by battle, or injury—he can't heal natural illnesses, like fever or sickness."

"What does it feel like ... to die?"

"Depends on how you go about it. I've never enjoyed the sensation any of the times I've died, from what of it I remember. Coming back might be worse but better than the alternative, I suppose. Makes you sick," he said in answer to her unasked question. "Powerful nausea, an ill feeling that settles in your stomach, and you come back weak, like you're sitting on the edge of slipping back into death at any moment and a good sneeze will carry you back to the other side."

"Is it … does knowing you won't die … not forever, anyway," she halted, trying to find her words, "is that where you get your fearlessness?"

"I'm not fearless," he said. "Not exactly. I just don't scare easily. They taught me in the Society of Arms how to bury the fear, how to master it. The natural instinct is to run from that which you fear. That doesn't work for a warrior, we're supposed to take the hits without flinching, to commit to battle so hard that our opponents back away knowing they'll have to stand toe to toe with our fury in order to best us. That doesn't work when you're afraid all the time." He looked away. "So they taught us that any time you fear something, you come at it with all your strength—not stupidly, mind you, but to attack it—and almost always that thing you were afraid of turns out to not be so bad. Because fear's not tolerated in a warrior, not in the Society of Arms." He took a deep breath. "Neither is running."

"Could you teach me?" She sat next to him, and he could scarcely hear her breathe. "Could you teach me to be as fearless as you? Because I …" She looked away, and he could feel the vulnerability within her, at the surface, and he wanted to reach out, to touch her shoulder, but refrained. "I am afraid all the time. It kept me in a place I hated, kept me prisoner to a man who hurt me, and made me …" she swallowed heavily, "… made me come to you, offer myself to you without even knowing you, just to hold on to what little I had." She turned back to him and straightened. "I don't wish to be afraid anymore. I want to go to this new life—whatever it turns out to be—because I want it, not because I want to run away from what I had."

"I don't know," he said. "I learned most of it in an arena—the place where they put us from the time we were kids, where we'd fight day in and day out." As he spoke he could feel the sands around his bare feet, as though he were there. "They started us from a young age, and you learn to revel in it." He thought about it for a moment. "Or hate it. Some came to truly hate it. They didn't last. Either way, I don't think that you necessarily need to fight in order to banish your fear. You lived under the thumb of a man who was so far beyond cruel as to defy any explanation. I'm certain it was difficult for you, to feel … trapped, that way. I have felt … similarly before."

"Oh?" She was next to him, closer now, and he could feel the warmth of the fire, mixed with his life's blood coursing through his veins, reminding him that he was alive, and that she was a woman who had offered herself to him in ways that he wanted, needed. "I find it hard to believe that a man such as you could have felt that way."

"It's true," he said. "Long ago, I was on my own for many years, without anyone to turn to or to trust." He felt his face harden as the bitter pangs came back to him. "I ... I'm sorry." Emotions, strange, similar, crippling in their own way, washed over him and he stopped talking for a beat. "I ..."

"What?" He felt her at his arm, her hand resting upon the plate of his shoulder. "What is it?"

He swallowed heavily. "I think ... I have come to the point of sleep, for the night. I suspect tomorrow will be a long day."

He felt her freeze against his side, and slowly her hand withdrew. "I see."

"If you'll excuse me ..." He stood and looked down at her, saw the regret behind the eyes as her hand came to rest on her lap, slow, like a snake coiling back up, and she smiled but not sincerely.

"I should turn in as well." Her smile faded. "I've lost my appetite for conversation anyway."

"I apologize," Cyrus said with a deep bow. "Perhaps someday I'll continue my story, but it's something I haven't spoken of ..." he thought back, tried to remember his time with Imina, and realized he had never told her either. "Ever. Not ever." He forced a smile—a thin, tight one. "Forgive me, madam." He bowed again and went to his bedroll, still bound up by its cord. He untied it and spread it across the ground by the fire.

"I understand," the Baroness said, getting to her feet. "What I told you, about what the Baron did to me—I've never told a soul that. Some of his acts were seen, obviously, others not. But even those that know, I never ... confessed or made mention of because to do so would seem to make it ... more real, I suppose. There are other things, varied and horrific, that I would not wish to speak of, not ever." She held herself up, and Cyrus saw her wither in the light. "Little venoms that I will keep in my soul until the day I die." She straightened. "Should the day ever come that you wish to expunge yours, I would willingly listen. And perhaps," she licked her lips, "trade you for a few of my own, that it might lessen the sting of them."

"Perhaps." Cyrus stood next to his bedroll, staring at the woman before him—so close to broken, yet so unbowed. He marveled at her and felt the crass urge to take hold of her, to kiss her—"Good night," he forced himself to say. "I will see you upon the morrow."

"Good night," she said, and turned to leave him. She took a few paces and stopped, turning back. "Why?"

He had already begun to lie down, and paused, crouched on one knee. "Why what?"

"You were married," she said. "You had this Vara, whom by all accounts you loved, and yet you never told anyone of these dark days in which you felt alone and desperate and had no one to trust?" She seemed unsteady, as though afraid to overstep her bounds, afraid of his reaction. "You have friends, and people who respect and admire you. Yet in all these people, in all your closest confidants, you found no one you could speak of this to?"

Cyrus felt his mouth go dry, and his head took on a slow spin. He took a sharp intake of breath and felt the sting of what she said, yet curiously he felt no anger or resentment for broaching the question. "There are some who know, but not because I told them," he said at last. "And much like yourself," he lied, "perhaps I didn't want to speak of it as it would become ... real to me. I have long said that things past are best left there. They are done, why give them new life by speaking of them?" He tried to smile but failed and knew it, so instead he lay down on his bedroll and stared straight up, into the sky and the few stars he could see beyond the light given off by the hundred fires around him. After a few moments, he heard the Baroness's steps pick up and fade as she walked away.

Imina. Narstron. Andren. Vaste. Terian. Alaric. Niamh. Vara. Some closer than others, and yet I would not tell a single one of them. Not one. He felt a strange weight in his chest, as though a great stone were upon it. *Because after all this time, and all that I've been through, in truth ...* he felt an odd satisfaction as the truth came to him, *... I'm just as alone now as I was then.*

Chapter 14

They had nearly reached the castle by midday next, when the sun was hot overhead and the feeling of spring had subsided and been replaced by the sensation of early summer. Cyrus felt the rays of the sun heating his armor and him within it, causing him to sweat, and wondered if this were what pottery in a kiln felt like. The smell of horses was especially heavy, and the conversation from the ranks of the army behind him was louder, more boisterous, now that the months of travel had come to a close and their destination was in sight.

The last taste of the conjured bread was still with him as Cyrus felt a crumb fall out of his beard. *Perhaps I should get rid of the whiskers,* he thought. *Or at least shave and let them grow out again. They don't seem to be doing me any favors by getting this long.*

The castle Vernadam was close on the horizon, and Cyrus could tell it was bigger than any castle he could recall ever seeing. Though perhaps not as tall as the Citadel in Reikonos, it was quite large, easily larger than the sprawling monstrosity of a palace in the elven capital of Pharesia. The castle itself was built on a steep hill, using the mound it was on to boost it to exceptional heights. An array of towers sprung out of a central keep, a circular one that twisted and rose, almost like a spiral rising into the sky. The tallest towers were high above the rest of the castle, one ranging far above the other, the two of them clinging together for support, like a child leaning upon a parent to walk. The whole thing seemed like an unnatural mountain, rising alone above a flat earth.

The city that lay in the shadow of Vernadam was visible by that time; a town that had sprung up around the foot of the hill, with no tall buildings, only three-story shops and dwellings clustered around a central square and tightly packed streets. Cyrus estimated that no more than a hundred thousand might live there, perhaps more if they were not particular about the amount of space each family had.

Cyrus rode at the front of their procession, with Longwell at his side. They passed all manner of people, horses and carts, all moving aside so the army of Sanctuary could pass.

It was a mile outside of town that a rider on the back of a stallion approached them. His navy armor was almost a perfect match for Longwell's, down to the surcoat with the Lion insignia, though he was considerably wider than the dragoon in both shoulder and belly. A wide smile broke out on the man's face as he got close enough for them to see. "Hail, Sir Samwen Longwell," he said in a deep voice as he approached.

"Hail, Sir Odau Genner," Longwell said, lips curling into a smile. "What news from Vernadam?"

Sir Odau Genner brought his horse into the formation alongside Longwell's. "We sent Teodir to find you months ago. We'd begun to worry he was lost along the way."

"He is with us," Longwell said. "I came as soon as word reached me, and I have brought ..." Longwell raised an arm and gestured to the army behind him, "... a few friends with me to heed my father's call."

"Indeed you have," Odau said with a broad grin. "We had heard you were coming with a force weeks ago from our spies afield, that you had crossed the border with western magicians and knights and footmen, but I scarce believed it until I saw it with my own eyes through the spyglass atop the tower only an hour ago. Your timing could not be more fortuitous."

"It goes poorly, then, the fight against Syloreas?" Longwell's face drew up, muscles contracting.

"We are but days from defeat, total and wretched, like the conquests of old—though the Kingdom does not know it yet." Odau Genner pointed north, and Cyrus looked in the direction indicated. "The army of Syloreas is encamped a day's ride from here. We will meet them in battle the day after tomorrow, in a final defense." Odau looked at Longwell with undisguised relief. "Our defeat was virtually assured before your arrival. They have a knight with them, a westerner, and his power is fearsome. He and his compatriots have won every battle for Syloreas, their mere presence sends our dragoons and footmen onto edge and they retreat far more easily than they should given their numbers."

"This is poor news," Longwell said. "Odau, this is my general, Cyrus Davidon. It was through his offer of assistance I came to be joined by all these souls willing to traverse the divide between our lands. Cyrus, this is Odau Genner, a dear friend and knight of my father's."

"Pleased to make your acquaintance, Odau," Cyrus said. "How can we help? Do you need us at the front?"

"I am pleased to meet you as well," Odau said with a nod to Cyrus. "You are not needed at the front at this moment. It is essentially agreed between King Longwell and Briyce Unger that we will meet in battle on the day after tomorrow in the fields north of the Forest of Waigh. When we sighted you from the watchtower," Odau said with a smile, "your father gave immediate orders for a feast to be put on, with a banquet in the town for your men after their long journey. Your high officers are invited to break bread with the King in the castle, to discuss the battle, if you are amenable, and to be well taken care of after your long journey. He offers his full hospitality to both you and your army."

"A generous offer," Longwell said. "My father's full hospitality comes rarely, and I suspect his current predicament accounts for much of it. Lose the battle and his Kingdom is lost, so why not open the coffers and wine cellars wide in hopes that we can turn the tides of fortune back to his favor, eh?"

"I think that might have been his intention," Odau said with a grin. "He said something about 'showing your men such a time that they'll want to fight harder for this Kingdom than our own will.'"

"Goodness. Well, that should keep the doxies well paid," Longwell said. "Are you to ride back with us or are you here only to deliver his message?"

"I'll only need signal him to give your assent," Odau said, "and then I can guide you into town. Your men will be billeted in the village, each a bed of his own—"

"We have some women in our ranks as well," Cyrus interrupted, causing Odau to start. "I trust they'll be provided for as well."

"Uh … ah …" Odau stammered. "If they're of your army, I trust we can find a place for them as well, though obviously that is not our custom and it perhaps will take a bit of adjustment—"

"We'll try to make it easy on you," Cyrus said. "But if you could make sure they receive the same good treatment, that would be very helpful."

Cyrus could see the tension on Odau's face. "We will ... make every effort to accommodate them. I'm certain that we'll find them lodgings to their satisfaction. If you gentlemen will follow me ..."

They rode onto the city's main street to find cheering crowds on the corners. Curious children and adults pushed each other aside (more the adults pushing each other and the children trying to squeeze their way to the front for a better view) to get a look at the army of Sanctuary. Cyrus looked at the attire of the peasantry and found it much the same as he would have seen in Reikonos, though of different fabrics and styles.

They came to the main square of the city and halted, Odau holding up a hand to stop them. "This is where we leave your army. Our men are already working to clear accommodations for them, and they'll be working at it for some time. However, the lodgings for your officers are ready at the castle, and we have food and drink waiting for you. If you'd care to join me—"

"Give me a moment," Cyrus said and turned Windrider around. "Odellan," Cyrus said, and the elf made his way through the horse ranks to him. "You'll see to the army and make certain everyone gets food and lodging?"

"Aye, sir," Odellan said. "You can count on me; I'll not rest until they're taken care of, every one."

"Tell them to have fun," Cyrus said, "but make certain they understand that they'll need to keep themselves in line. I have no problems with them enjoying whatever sort of recreation they can find—honorably, of course—but I want no angry complaints from the local populace. That means keep the drinking to a manageable level, and make sure they're all in bed at a reasonable hour. We'll likely be marching by midday tomorrow, so let them know that."

Odellan hesitated, the slightest grimace on his face. "You don't wish to address the troops yourself, sir?"

Cyrus looked around the square; the noise was already overwhelming, and the army was strung out along the narrow boulevard halfway back to the town limits. "This isn't the best place for a speech, and I doubt they'd hear much of it anyway. Make sure they understand. I'm going to talk with the King and see if we can hammer out a strategy to beat this army that's coming."

"Aye, sir," Odellan said. "It will be as you say."

"I never doubted it for a minute," Cyrus said, bringing his horse around and looking to Odau. "How many of my officers does your King expect for this feast?"

"We could house several hundred comfortably," Odau said with a pleasant smile. "However, his Grace expects you would have twenty or so officers to lead your troops."

"I'm going to define officer a little more broadly then." He turned to look at the force on horseback behind him. "Ryin, Nyad, Curatio, Terian, J'anda—Longwell, of course—I'll also have the Baroness, Martaina and Aisling come with us." He glanced through their ranks and saw Mendicant sitting on his small pony next to the massive desert man, Scuddar In'shara. "Mendicant and Scuddar, too."

Mendicant, only about four feet tall, pointed a clawed finger at himself, and Cyrus saw his mouth open, sharp teeth visible within, though he only saw the goblin mouth the word, "Me?"

Aisling guided her horse from behind Odellan. "Why me?"

Cyrus shrugged, but his eyes never left hers. "I have my reasons. For all of you." He looked around. "All here?" He tossed a glance back to Odau. "Lead on."

There was a short road to the gates of the castle. The curtain wall took advantage of the steep slopes around the hill it was built upon—Cyrus estimated that a siege would be well nigh impossible by traditional means, as the only easy approach was up the winding path to the main gate. "It seems to me," he said to Odau, "your King could simply close up his wall and wait for this Briyce Unger to get bored of standing at the bottom of his hill, trying to rally forces to crash his gate. He'd never have to surrender if he didn't care to."

"Aye," Odau Genner said with a slow nod, "and the King might do that, yet. But his Kingdom would be lost, nonetheless, as with no one to defend the smallfolk, Briyce Unger could control every city without ever taking Vernadam." Odau smiled, but it was a bitter one. "If one controls all of a Kingdom but for the castle that governed it, has one not conquered that Kingdom?"

They made their way up the twisted path and Cyrus noted the curves and at least one unnecessary switchback in its construction—undoubtedly designed to make siege more difficult. He looked up at the stone behemoth that stretched into the sky above him and marveled at the single-minded effort it must have taken to construct such a gargantuan fortress. *How many slaves worked how many years to do this? Or was it simple workmen? Either way, this is nothing short of astounding; it's a wonder.*

Smooth walls gave way to ramparts that jutted out over the hillside below like an uneven lip sticks out from a face. *From the ramparts they can shower boiling oil or arrows onto anyone who tries to climb the hill.* The stone was all grey, dull, with some blocks taller than he and wider than three men laid end to end. *Where did they quarry all that stone? And how did they get it here?*

"Why did you pick me to come?" Cyrus looked over in surprise to see Aisling looking at him. He had not heard her ride up, so busy had he been staring at the castle. "I'm hardly an officer—or even one of your favorite people, of late." She frowned. "Or ever."

"I have no quarrel with you, Aisling," he said. "You have a unique perspective, and I'd be a fool to ignore it."

He watched her deflate slightly. "If my point of view is what you seek from me, then I will do my best not to fail you in that regard."

"Perhaps it's not all I seek," Cyrus said, smiling, then urged Windrider forward, "but it's all I have time for at the moment." He looked back to see her looking at him cautiously but with slight wonderment.

The path straightened as they reached the gate, guiding their horses under the portcullis to follow Odau Genner. Once through it, Cyrus found himself in a massive courtyard, twice the size of the entire castle at Green Hill. He could smell the stables to one side, saw the activity bustling ahead in the entrance to the keep, where a procession was already making its way down the steps to greet them.

Guards stood at attention in columns down either side of the steps, arranged to face the stairway. The procession came down, and at the head stood a man with the same build as Longwell—muscular, tall, dark haired, though grey was present, frosted in a patch on the top of his head. Cyrus saw no crown, though the cloak he wore was of finest velvet. He was flanked by ten men, all in armor like Longwell's, every one of them wearing the surcoat with the black lion on the front.

Cyrus followed Odau Genner across the courtyard, and he felt the Baroness brush against his side. He glanced at her and saw her look back, a nervous smile flitting across her face. "It'll be all right," he said. "You're here as part of my army."

She raised an eyebrow. "I have no ability with sword or shield or bow, nor any of the magical powers that many in your army possess." She looked down at herself and then back at him. "I look nothing like the women of your army."

"And yet you are, nonetheless," he said cheerfully. "So worry not."

"Why have you asked me to come along with you to the castle, rather than being lodged in town with the rest of your people?" Her voice betrayed the worry that her face concealed, along with something else, something more hopeful.

"You know the people of Luukessia," Cyrus said, whispering to her as they followed Genner toward the steps. "You have been the enemy of Galbadien for all your years. I'd be a fool to have you along and not ask your opinion of these men."

"Don't you trust these total strangers?" she asked, almost mocking.

"As a rule, I trust no strangers."

"But isn't this King the father of your man Longwell?" She regarded him carefully. "You trust him, do you not?"

"I do," Cyrus said. "Samwen Longwell is a man of honor. But he left this Kingdom for good reason, and he has yet to tell me what it is … so I keep my suspicions, and I keep watch."

"A sound plan," she whispered back. "But if I may be so bold as to make an observation …" she glanced at him out of the corner of her eyes, waiting for him to give her a subtle nod before she continued. "I am nearly a stranger to you. Do you trust me?"

"Mmmm," Cyrus let out a deep, guttural sound that reminded him of a purr. In his head, it was a simple stalling tactic, as he tried to find a way to phrase his reply so as not to offend her. "Not entirely," he said at last, drawing a small smile of response from her. "But neither do I distrust you."

The smile was cool, but her green eyes danced and gave life to it. "When it comes to the confidences of 'Cyrus the Unbroken,' I suppose I shall take what I can get, when I can get it." They arrived at the King before Cyrus could make his reply. "If you introduce me, remember to call me Cattrine," the Baroness said in a last whisper, drawing a smile. "Better not to tell them from whence I come."

"Your accent is rather distinctive," Cyrus mumbled as Odau Genner filled the air with a formal and lengthy announcement of the arrival of the Sanctuary officers.

"I can fix that," the Baroness said, sotto voce, her words now carrying the smooth, flat cadences of a Reikonosian born.

He raised an eyebrow at her. "How did you do that?"

She kept her eyes forward, on the King. "I've been listening to you."

"May I introduce Cyrus Davidon," Odau Genner said, "General of the army of Sanctuary."

Cyrus bowed low to the King, who, upon closer inspection, was thinner and more gaunt than Longwell. His eyes were slightly sunken and his flesh had settled oddly upon his bones, as though his build had once been powerful and was now diminished, the excess skin loose and ill at ease on his frame. The only exception was his belly, which was distended and paunchy, hanging over his belt.

"My cherished son," the King said, opening his arms wide to Longwell, who followed a pace behind Cyrus. The King's gaunt features lifted in a smile. "You have returned to us in Galbadien's darkest hour, and at the head of your own army from the west. This is more than I could have imagined was possible when last we parted."

Cyrus looked back to Longwell, who stood stock still, a pained smile pasted on his features. "Father," he said before making his way forward to embrace the man.

Cyrus watched, noting the dragoon's slow movement, the uncomfortable shuffle as he went to hug his father, as they fumbled to place hands, and a thought ran across the warrior's mind—*Do they even know each other?* After a moment, father and son parted, and as they withdrew, Cyrus noted the awkward space between them that lingered, even as the King put his hand upon his son's shoulder and tried to draw him close. Samwen went along with it, but the dragoon remained tensed.

"Greetings to all of you," the King said with the same, wide smile. "I welcome you as friends of my son and thank you for coming to the service of our Kingdom in this hour of need." His arms were spread in welcome, but his right hand remained on his son's shoulder, resting there, drawing Cyrus's attention from the King's words to his face. "If my son trusts you as allies and compatriots, you must surely be of the finest quality, and I look forward to getting to know you as we break bread together." He extended the hand that wasn't on Longwell's shoulder and gestured to the stairs and the open doors above them. "Come, my friends, and let us welcome you to the halls of Vernadam."

The King turned and began to make his way up the stairs, adjusting his hands so that he could wrap an arm around his son's shoulder and pull him close. Cyrus watched the King whisper to Samwen, unmistakable pride and emotion on the elder man's face.

"Does something seem a little odd there?" Cattrine asked him quietly.

"I didn't want to be the first to say it, but yes," Cyrus said, keeping his voice to a whisper. "We should probably wait to talk about it until later."

Cyrus followed, leading his party up the stairs. The door to the keep was an arched portal fifteen feet tall with wide, solid wooden doors, which were opened by the guards. They swung inward in a wide arc, and as Cyrus passed through them with the Baroness at his side, he caught a glimpse of others behind them, helping to pull them open. A grand hall lay ahead, with another staircase that led to a large landing that split in twain; the steps then veered left and right, to a balcony that wrapped around the entry foyer.

Cyrus paused on the marble tiles. They were checkered in black and white squares, with a craftsmanship that he hadn't seen outside of the Elven Kingdom. He looked at the Baroness but she remained cool; the palatial appearance of the keep was deeply at odds with Green Hill or any of the other keeps he had seen in all his days.

The King continued onward to a room to their left. Double doors, smaller than the entry, swung open at the hands of a servant and Cyrus found himself in a formal dining room. The checkered marble floor gave way entirely to white tiles, and a long dining table stretched the length of the room, culminating in a chair that was taller and more ornate than any of the others. "I'll bet you a gold coin that's where the King sits," he whispered to the Baroness.

"Not only is that a poor bet, but since someone sacked my home, I find I have no coins with which to gamble."

"Did I hear a note of complaint?" Cyrus asked as his eyes roamed the room.

"About losing my husband? Never," she said. "I do, however, wish I had been allowed to keep his fortune." She sighed. "It was hardly worth the trade, but if I could have had his money and been rid of him, I believe I might have been able to find some measure of happiness." She frowned. "Damn this land and their thorough dislike of women with any strength at all."

"I agree," Cyrus said. "You should find somewhere that they can appreciate you."

Her eyes narrowed. "Are you mocking me?"

"In this case, no." His eyes tracked around the room. "I might later, though, so be on your guard."

The balcony from the foyer extended into the dining hall, and a hearth sat behind the King's chair, though it was not in use. Paintings of knights, ladies, scenes from nature, and of castles dominated the decor. The walls were comprised of a faint white plaster, apparently spackled over the natural stone walls of the keep. The whole thing gave the room a more comfortable look to Cyrus's eyes, reminding him of the houses in Reikonos, wood structures, rather than the rock and stone that made some keeps feel like dim caves.

The smell of fresh-baked dough filled the room, along with other scents that he couldn't quite place. He thought he caught a hint of fish cooking, but it mingled with the smell of other meats and perhaps some vegetables as well. He heard a clatter in the next room and realized that it must be the kitchens. A door swung open and then closed again, confirming his suspicion as a line of servants walked into the room in perfect step, snaking their way around the table, each standing behind a chair. Cyrus lingered in the doorway as he watched the King make his way to the head seat and point his son to the chair to his right. The King stopped before sitting down and beckoned to Cyrus to come sit on his left. Cyrus exchanged a short look with the Baroness and came forward, placing himself in the seat that the King had indicated.

"I am very pleased to make your acquaintance, General Davidon," the King said as Cyrus took his place and stood in front of his chair. He waited as his other officers filtered in, each guided to their place at the table by one of the members of the King's armored procession.

"And I am pleased to be here and able to help, your Grace." He followed the King's example and sat after noting the other members of the King's procession beginning to do the same. Cyrus felt the servant standing behind his chair scoot it closer to the table as he did so and he nodded in thanks to the silent steward behind him, who did not so much as look at him. "May I ask some questions so that we can begin to formulate a strategy for the coming battle?"

The King waved his hand. "The battle is not until the day after tomorrow, and I feel confident that with your help, we can easily vanquish Briyce Unger's army and his mercenaries." The King's gaunt face tightened as he plucked a grape from his plate and put it into his mouth. He continued to speak, even as he chewed, causing the Baroness to cough lightly next to Cyrus. "Only a handful of these western mercenaries, that's all Unger has, but the demon one, the half-man, he carries power that is truly fearsome, to hear my generals tell of it."

"Half-man?" Cyrus asked.

"Yes," the King said, taking a bite from a plum and letting the juice run uninterrupted down his face. "He stands not more than half the height of a man, stout of build and bearded like a mountain man of Syloreas—"

"A dwarf," Cyrus said, locking eyes with Longwell, who nodded. "You say this dwarf casts spells?"

"He possesses western magic of a sort," the King said, his mouth turning down as his eyes grew narrower still. "The power to knock an entire legion to the ground, to send men from their feet without warning or ability to stop it. His prowess with a hammer has become the stuff of nightmares, the tales young recruits are told in the barracks to scare them at night when they learn the trade of war and battle."

"A paladin?" Cyrus asked. "That sounds like a paladin."

"I trust that won't present a problem for you?" The Baroness murmured in his ear as servants set a bowl of soup in front of him, a heavy one with rice and mushrooms.

The smell of cream in the soup was heavy in Cyrus's nose. "For me alone, perhaps," Cyrus said, trying to decide which spoon to use out of the dozen implements arranged around his place setting. "For our army, no."

"This half-man has been a dagger in our side during the whole campaign," The King said, his voice high in complaint. "His mercenaries get stabbed through the chest, fall to the ground, and minutes later they're whole again, back up and fighting."

"Sounds like they have a healer, too," Cyrus said. "We can fix that."

The King waved his hand in frustration. "Enough of this talk. Count Ranson can tell you more about this drudgery later." He brightened. "Let us move on to more gladsome topics." He turned to Longwell. "How was your journey, my son?"

"Long," the dragoon replied. "I had forgotten the distance between here and the bridge since last I trod the path."

"I see," the King said, slurping his soup, the broth dripping down his weathered and bony chin. "Did you have problems with those bandits from Actaluere?"

The Baroness was seized by a sudden fit of coughing, causing Cyrus to look at her in alarm. She stopped after a moment, hand in front of her mouth. "Terribly sorry," she croaked as the King and the others at their end of the table stared at her.

Cyrus felt the presence of eyes upon him, like prey in the night, being watched by a beast. He looked up and found a man across the table, seated next to Longwell, staring at him. The man's hair was light, his face ruddy and his eyes dark. His armor carried the same blue sheen in the steel as Longwell's, though his surcoat was different, a tiger on a white background. His eyes met Cyrus's and there was an instant jolt of hostility between the two men. The man was middle-aged, older than Cyrus by at least fifteen years, but with only a few signs of grey in his platinum hair to show it. "I beg your pardon, sir," Cyrus said, feeling slightly annoyed by the man's gaze, "but can I help you?"

The man stiffened in his seat, as though he had been insulted. "No," he said, his voice low and scratchy. "You cannot help me." His accent lilted in the same way as Longwell's and the King's, the end of his statement rising in pitch.

"Forgive me," Longwell said, "for not making introductions. General Cyrus Davidon, this is Count Ewen Ranson, of the castle Ridgeland to the southeast. He is the marshal of my father's armies."

"Ah, so it's you I'll be coordinating with," Cyrus said, letting the icy calm within take over his outward persona, frosting over the internal desire to scorch the man for his rudeness. "I am pleased to make your acquaintance, Ewen."

"You'll call me count or marshal," Ranson snapped, his pinched face causing him to look especially snotty.

"Very well," Cyrus said. "My full title is Lord Davidon of Perdamun, Warden of the Southern Plains and General of Sanctuary. You can go ahead and call me that. Every single time you address me, that is—and don't leave out the 'Warden' bit as it's very important."

Ranson's ruddy complexion went blood red. "What foolishness is this?"

"Why, Count Ranson," Cyrus said, his icy reserve melting quickly, "it's called custom and protocol, and it's the very thing you just threw in my face, so you should recognize it."

"What I recognize," Ranson said, still flushed scarlet, "is that sitting before me is the same sort of scum that's helping our enemies trounce us in battle after battle. The same cheeky bastards from a foreign land, come to lord it over us with your magics and fancy ways—well, I'll have none of it. You don't fool me—you're all the same."

Cyrus stared across the table at the count then looked to the King, who sipped another spoonful of soup with a slight smile, waiting to see what happened next. Cyrus turned his gaze back to the Count. "Do you really believe that?"

"I do," Ranson said, unmoving.

"I see," Cyrus said, feeling particularly wry. "I guess I shouldn't expect anything less from a treacherous Luukessian. After all, you're an easterner, the same as Baron Hoygraf of Actaluere, beaters and oppressors of women, rapists and—"

There was a crash of furniture as the chair that Count Ranson was sitting in fell back, splintering on the floor. The count's sword was in his hand and a look of purest rage was on his face. "You take that back, you filthy bastard, I've never laid a hand in anger on a woman in my life, let alone beaten and whipped them like that scum—"

"Oh, I'm sorry," Cyrus said, mock-offended, "perhaps I shouldn't have unfairly grouped all you easterners into the same lot." He picked up one of the six spoons gathered around his plate and dipped it in the soup, bringing it up to his mouth slowly and taking a long sip with one hand while keeping the other rested on Praelior under the table and well out of sight.

"Well said, sir," the King guffawed. "Count Ranson, surely you can tell that there are differences between our guests and these mercenaries. After all, I see no half-men here among our guests."

"We left our dwarves back at the village," Cyrus said. "But let's be plain," he looked to Count Ranson, who had resumed his seat with the aide of the servant lingering behind him, "there are several nations and powers in the west, just as there are here. To confuse the peoples of different nations and guilds with each other is as insulting to us, in some cases, as it would be for me to make the comparison here that I just did."

"I had said before that we should move to more felicitous topics of conversation," the King said with a sigh. "Perhaps we can do so now." With that, he picked up the remainder of his bowl and brought it to his lips, slurping the rest of his soup.

Cyrus sent a furtive look to the Baroness next to him. She was cringing even though she was trying to keep her eyes on her own soup, which she took dainty spoonfuls of. Past her were Ryin and Nyad, seated side by side and conversing pleasantly with Odau Genner. The rest of the Sanctuary members were sprinkled around the table, talking with their counterparts from Galbadien's army.

The only two notable exceptions were Martaina and Aisling, each of whom was only a few seats down from the Baroness, on the other side of Odau Genner. Martaina's hand was on her bow, which leaned against her chair, while she used the other to feed herself. Her eyes were slitted, watching the table coolly for any sign of trouble; if Cyrus had to guess, he would have bet that her bow had in fact been nocked with an arrow only moments before, when Count Ranson had been out of his chair.

Aisling sat a little further down than Martaina, a quiet spot in the gathering. The dark elf seemed to be watching everything with a furtive eye, and Cyrus noticed her turning her ears toward certain conversations under the guise of adjusting her hair. All the while, she was nursing her bowl of soup but had scarcely eaten any of it.

"What do you think of our predicament, General Davidon?" The stiff words drew Cyrus's attention back to Count Ranson, who was looking at him with eyes that were hard like stone, dark circles glaring at him out of the candlelit dim.

"I think we should march out tomorrow and meet your enemies," Cyrus said, taking another spoonful of the soup. It was rich and flavorful, and he found himself enjoying it much more than anything he'd had in months.

"The battle is set for the day after tomorrow," the King said from the head of the table as a loaf of bread was placed before him. He reached for it with both hands and tore off the end, handing it to a servant who slathered it with butter. "I see no reason why we should hurry into it recklessly, especially now that we have forces at our disposal with which to surprise Briyce Unger." The King's smile was broad and full as he took the bread from the servant and bit into it, crumbs falling upon his deep blue blouse.

"Sire," Count Ranson said, "we have danced to Unger's tune throughout this entire war and look what it has gotten us."

"I'm inclined to agree with the count," Cyrus said, drawing the King's attention. A very brief flash of ire was visible in the King's eyes but disappeared quickly. "Obviously, I have no idea what your strategy has been from the outset, but I know that in battle, if an enemy expects attack in two days, I prefer to hit him the day before, when he doesn't expect it."

"That sounds like base chicanery," the King said, lowering his head and biting deep into the bread in his hands. "Like something that would come from the Kingdom of Actaluere and not our own halls."

Cyrus heard another cough from the Baroness and saw her begin to open her mouth. He reached over and tried to drop a hand on hers and missed, sending his gauntlet to her thigh instead. He looked at her with chagrin and saw her mouth drop slightly open and her eyes widen in amusement. He began to stutter an apology, but the count started to speak again, drawing the Baroness's attention—and his own—back to the table.

"They have yet to treat us with the honor you speak of, Your Highness," Count Ranson said in measured tones. "They struck without warning, have burned and pillaged our lands, used outsiders with power that we could not match, and now stand at our gates, ready to send us into ignominious defeat. If your enemy strikes at you from behind, does it not make sense to do the same to him?"

The King chewed his bread thoughtfully. "Let them have their dishonor. We shall hold our heads high and defeat them nonetheless."

Cyrus could see the Count lock his jaw and lower his head, turning away from his liege. "Your Majesty," Cyrus said, "I understand your wish for your army to maintain their honor. However," he continued, feeling the tension rise in the room, "I'm afraid I'm going to have to march with my army on the morrow."

The King's face became slack, a grim mask at the defiance being aired in his hall. "You would do this without my leave?"

"I apologize, Your Highness," Cyrus said. "I intend no disrespect, nor do I wish to challenge the high standards with which you govern your realm and conduct your affairs. However, I led my army to this land with the intent of bringing every last one of them home again, and I will live up to that promise to the best of my ability. That means if I'm going to pit them against superior numbers and a force that contains spellcasters, I'm going to need every advantage I can get, even ones I make for myself. Which includes the element of surprise, something which has won more battles than any wizard."

The King watched him through half-lidded eyes, his mouth downturned. "I find your intransigence ... disconcerting. But I cannot find fault in your desire to protect your people." A lamb leg was placed in front of the King, and he picked it up. He took an enormous bite, chewing as he responded, words coming between movements of his jaw. "Very well, then. Let it be upon your honor. You will be at the head of our army and in nominal command of the battle. If anyone should ask, I will put the dishonor of surprise attacks upon you, not our Count Ranson." Ranson stiffened at that, but nodded his head somewhat reluctantly. "Would you be amenable to that, Lord Davidon?"

"Amenable to taking over your army?" Cyrus smiled. "I think I can manage that."

"To clarify," the King went on, "you will lead the battle, but Count Ranson will have full control over the movements of our army. If you wish for him to do something, you will have to convince him yourself."

Cyrus felt his hands clench and heard a sharp intake of breath from his left. He looked over to realize his gauntlet was still on the Baroness' thigh and hastily removed it, earning a pitying look from her. "Very well," Cyrus said.

The King's eyebrow rose. "Very good, then. Let us speak of these dull matters no more, and turn our attention instead to the entertainments of the evening." He lifted his hands as if to clap them, but before he could, a door opened at the far end of the room and a quartet of musicians with instruments came forth, situating themselves in the corner far to Cyrus's left, where the King could see them best. The lead musician was a singer, and his voice rang out over the room, a smooth, dulcet sound that echoed beautifully from the walls as heads turned to watch.

Cyrus looked from the singer to the Baroness as the rest of the members of the group began to play stringed instruments. The Baroness looked back at him with deep amusement, a sly smile on her face.

Cyrus leaned close to her ear. "I was reaching for your hand, earlier, to try and calm you down after what was said."

She pulled back to look at him, and her eyebrow raised, her smile widened before turning coy. "And you think taking my hand would calm me? Apparently we should change your nickname from Cyrus the Unbroken to Cyrus the Oblivious—to take into account the effects you have on women that you don't even notice."

Cyrus hemmed then hawed. "I doubt that my taking your hand would be cause for all that much excitement."

"Mmmm," the Baroness seemed to ponder his reply as she let out a humming sound that harmonized with the music. "I don't know. I think you might be underestimating your charisma and legendary reputation as a leader who keeps very strictly to himself—including his hands and all else."

"Ha ha," Cyrus said with a fake, low-key laugh. "I prefer to channel all my efforts into battle. It's less dangerous."

"Well, now," the Baroness said, "I suspect that has more to do with the women you've courted. Perhaps if you tried one who didn't carry a sword ..."

"Perhaps one who carried a dagger, instead?"

She put her hand on her chest in mock outrage, drawing his attention to her shirt, which had a high collar but reminded him for a beat of the low-cut dress she had worn when first they met and how it had displayed her ample bosoms. "That a lady would carry a weapon is such an outrageous proposition." Her feigned shock disappeared as she tossed a shoulder casually, then smiled. "However, when in the company of Arkarians, one can never be too well armed, especially if one is a woman."

Cyrus reached for his wine glass and took a deep drink as he pondered his reply. "And when in the company of beautiful women, regardless of origin, I find that blades are the least painful way that they can hurt you."

The Baroness reached for her wine glass and held it before her. "I'll drink to that truth, Lord Davidon, if you'll drink to mine—when it comes to men, being outmatched by them physically is quite a bit more painful and likely to happen than being outmatched by them mentally." She smiled broadly as she noted his pained reaction. "Present company excepted, perhaps."

"I'm not likely to do either if I keep drinking this excellent wine," Cyrus said, setting down his cup and watching the servant behind him rush forward to refill the glass.

"Oh my," the Baroness said in a quiet voice as the singer trilled in the corner. "Lord Cyrus Davidon, physically and mentally vulnerable? Quickly, grab for my hand—I may become very excitable."

He chuckled under his breath as she leaned in closer to him. "You're different than the women I've known, Cattrine." He stared at her and she stared back, her green eyes glinting at him.

"Have you met many Baronesses?" She said it with the amusement that she seemed to layer over everything, and he found himself chuckling again.

"No. But I doubt that's why I find you so intriguing."

"Oh?" He caught a glimmer of interest in her eyes, but the sound of chairs scraping against the marble floor drew his gaze back to the King's seat, where the King himself was now standing.

"If you'll all excuse me," the King said as the music died in the room, the last squeals of bows drawn across instruments ending abruptly. The entire table rose belatedly to pay him homage, but he walked from the room toward a nondescript door, three servants and two armored guards in tow, before they had all gotten to their feet.

"Did I just miss the end of the party?" Cyrus asked as they sat back down.

"You'll have to excuse the King," Odau Genner leaned over the table from several seats away to address him. "He's not feeling quite well right now—understandable, given what he's faced with at the moment."

"Lord Davidon," came the voice of Count Ranson across the table from him. "My army can be ready to leave by sunrise tomorrow. Would that be sufficiently early for you?"

"I'd like a chance to review maps of this area, if you have them," Cyrus said, watching the Count as the man nodded. "I don't want to leave and march off to battle without some hint of strategy." He smiled. "I'd like to catch them while they're sleeping tomorrow night, if we can."

"That should be possible," Ranson said, a hand on his clean-shaven chin. "They'll be camped in the northern reaches of the Fields of Gareme. It is half a day's march. It is a flat land, and if we can deal adequately with their scouts, we should be able to approach them without being seen." The count's face twisted into a half-grin. "Which is better than meeting them in the middle of the fields in broad daylight."

"Aye," Cyrus said and glanced at the leg of lamb waiting upon his plate. "Why don't we meet first thing in the morning with our officers to discuss the strategy? We can come to some agreement before we leave."

"Very well," Count Ranson nodded and stood, executing a short bow. "I will go and make preparations." The older man grimaced slightly. "If you would be willing to hear suggestions, I am very familiar with those lands and could likely help you to come up with a battle plan."

"I am eager to hear suggestions, Count," Cyrus said with a tight smile, "as I have no knowledge of these plains you speak of, nor of the Kingdom of Syloreas's army."

"Very good, Lord Davidon," the count said with a curt nod. "I'll have one of my men send for you at sunrise and we'll discuss preparations then." The count let a half-smile of obvious relief flood his face, then turned and walked around the table and from the room, through the double doors into the foyer.

The singer commenced with his song again shortly thereafter, and Cyrus had some more wine. He saw Samwen Longwell sitting across from him, but the younger man did not meet his gaze, picking at his food instead. *Did something happen between father and son when I wasn't paying attention?* He looked down the table, noted the others engaged in conversation and discussion save for Aisling, who seemed to almost disappear between two Galbadien men in armor, and Martaina, who was no longer seated but had instead removed herself to lean against the wall. Cyrus had to almost turn around in his chair to find her, but when he did, she nodded at him.

He shook his head and turned back to find the Baroness delicately picking at the meat on her plate with a fork and knife. "How do you do that?" he asked.

She glanced at him and went back to sawing off a small cut of meat no larger than Cyrus's pinky knuckle. She then delicately speared it with her fork and placed it into her mouth, chewing slowly and with a smile on her face the entire time. When she swallowed it, her smile grew more enigmatic. "It's called patience, Lord Davidon, and it's required when you're eating like a lady, else you might become exasperated with the miniscule bites that manners require you to take and try to gnaw the meat directly from the bone."

Cyrus held the leg bone in his hand, pondering the meat on it, then the five different forks and three knives that were set around his plate. "I hope you won't be offended if I don't subscribe to your dainty eating habits."

She chuckled. "I think I should be more offended if you did. I am eating like a lady, after all. If you did the same, I might wonder about you, to think that perhaps the reason that you're rumored to have gone so long without female companionship in your bed is something more basic than poor luck and good consideration."

He looked at her, stunned. "Wait. How did you know it's been …?" He sighed as the answer occurred to him. "Rumors."

"All flattering to your character, I assure you." She patted him on the arm. "A true gentleman and a man of strong discipline, one who has been in love for a long time and held himself in check during that period." She took another bite and her smile faded. "A man for whom rash intemperance is not even a consideration. I admire that about you, if what they say is true."

Cyrus managed a tight smile. "It's true enough, but I haven't felt like it was a mark of prestige, exactly."

"Be proud, Lord Davidon," the Baroness said. "You are very unlike the men I have known. And in my case, this is a very good thing, possibly the highest compliment I can pay."

Cyrus grasped for his cup and took a long drink of wine. "Thank you, I think."

"You're welcome—I think."

The Baroness became caught up in a conversation with Ryin and Nyad only moments later, and Cyrus was left to finish the last of his leg of lamb before a succulent slice of chocolate cake was placed in front of him. Feeling slight disquiet in his stomach from the richness of the food, he took a deep inhalation from the cake, then two small bites and decided that stopping was the wisest course. With a last look around the table, he stood, and the servant behind him quickly helped him move his chair.

The Baroness turned her head. "Calling it a night already?"

"I think so," he said. "I'm not quite sure what time it is, but I'm tired and I have an early morning meeting tomorrow."

"I should probably turn in as well," she said, aided by the servant behind her who darted in and helped her move the heavy wooden seat so that she could stand. The Baroness turned to Ryin and Nyad. "Good night, you two."

Cyrus didn't hear their replies, as he was already looking toward the door. Martaina waited beside it, and as Cyrus offered his arm to the Baroness out of politeness and she took it, he saw the elven woman's face crease with a smile that she hid by turning away and looking at the musicians at the other end of the room.

"Something funny, Martaina?" he asked her as he passed through the door.

"Not a thing, sir," she said, still amused when she turned back. "There's a steward in the foyer providing us escort to our rooms," she said. "I'm told the one that they have for you is quite palatial, fitting with your numerous and august titles."

He raised an eyebrow at her. "Now you're making fun of me."

Martaina smiled. "Not at all, sir. Shall I come get you at sunrise for your meeting?"

"The count said he'd send someone," Cyrus said and turned back to the Baroness. "Get some rest."

Cyrus walked into the foyer, the Baroness's arm tucked through his. A man waited in the middle of the room, with two others behind him. "Sir and Madam," the man said with a little bow, his silk crimson shirt moving delicately as he dipped low. He looked first to Cyrus. "I have a room for you, General. Will your companion be needing a room of her own?"

Cyrus felt a brief awkwardness before he looked at the Baroness, a slight smile on his face as he felt the rush of the wine, causing his head to swim. "I don't know," he said. "Do you?"

She tilted her head in surprise and looked back at him. "I don't know. Do I?"

Cyrus felt the moment slow down around him, looked at her, her green eyes locked on his. The smell of the lamp oil filled the hall and gave off an oddly intoxicating scent. Cyrus could feel his head swimming in a fog, the wine mixing with the fatigue to make him smile more than he should have. He saw the faintest hint of a flush on the Baroness's cheeks, and he smiled, the weight of other things on his mind gone, blown away in a carefree breeze for the first time in months. "No," he said. "Tonight, I don't think you do."

She smiled at him, then looked to the steward. "I won't be needing my own accommodations," she said. "But thank you for asking."

"Very well," the steward said, bowing again. "If you'll follow me." He led them up stairs, through corridors, winding around passages. The steward kept up a steady stream of commentary throughout, but Cyrus did not listen; his eyes and attention were fixed upon the Baroness, who had scarcely taken hers off of him. He could see the levity within her expression, mixed with more than a little amusement but tempered with the slightest bit of concern.

"Here we are," the steward said, ushering them through a set of double doors off a long, torchlit corridor with lamps hanging overhead for good measure.

As they entered the room, Cyrus stopped in mild surprise. It was indeed palatial; white marble floors filled the cavernous entry. Stuffed chairs and a long sofa made of cowhide and stuffed with down made up a sitting area in front of a fireplace. A luscious bearskin rug was in front of the hearth, where a fire blazed quietly. The walls were the same sort of plaster that had been present in the dining room, but the ceiling was far, far above them and three different chandeliers cast their light down upon the room.

Cyrus walked, the Baroness on his arm, to the center of the room. "Your bedroom is in there, sir," the steward said. "There is a garderobe—a toileting room—in a separate closet on the other side of it. Is there anything I can get for you?"

Cyrus looked at the Baroness, who shook her head. "You may leave," she said. "Thank you." The steward nodded his head, bowed, and made his exit, leaving Cyrus alone with her, a growing unease in his belly, a nervous sort of tension that caused him to taste bitterness in his mouth. "What's wrong?" she asked, hovering closer to him, close enough that he could feel her, feel his body ache for her to come closer.

Cyrus swallowed heavily. "Why are you doing this?"

She stepped closer, pressed against his armor, her cloth riding blouse giving him the strangest urge to run his hand across the fabric. She took hold of his gauntlet and pulled it slowly off; Cyrus felt his palms sweaty, sticky, and wished he could wipe them somewhere. He felt a tinge of embarrassment as she took his hand in hers and placed it on her back. "Because I want to," she breathed, whispered in his ear. She pulled back and looked at him, locked eyes, stared him down, and the animal urge within consumed him and he kissed her, deeply and heavily, breathing hard as he broke from her. "Because although it may have been a long time for you since your last lover, for me ..." her hand stroked his cheek, "I have never been with a man I have freely chosen."

She pressed her lips against him, again, and he felt the rising tide of his desire. His fingers went to the straps on his pauldrons and loosened them, then he lifted them over his head and dropped them to the floor where they landed with a fearsome clatter. His breastplate and backplate went next, along with the gorget that protected his neck, his lips firm against hers the whole time. He heard his remaining gauntlet hit the floor then the vambraces from his arms and bracers from his forearms, each making a clank of its own.

"I didn't know that it would be so easy to get you to agree to take off your armor," she said, breaking away from him, "but so hard to actually get it all off" She dived back in at him again, pressing her lips against his neck, kissing, suckling, causing a little thrill of sensation to run through him.

Her lips met his again and he thrust his tongue into her mouth, swirling it against hers as he kicked off each of his boots, one at a time. His greaves fell off next, and she helped him slide the chainmail that undergirded it all over his head, leaving him in only his cloth underclothes. She stepped back from him for a moment, her eyes on his, and he could feel all the heat between them as he pulled off his undershirt.

He reached for her, his fingers caressing the collar of her shirt, and he unlaced the front of it, starting to slip it over her head. Her hand came up quickly and found his, stopping him. "Please," she said, and he could hear a hint of pleading in her voice, "not out here." She turned her head toward the bedroom. "In there. In the dark."

"All right." He reached for her and lifted her up, and she squealed in pleasure as he cradled her in his arms and kissed her again. He carried her into the bedroom and laid her upon the bed, extinguishing the lamps, plunging the room into semi-darkness. He could see her face in the narrow shaft of light coming from the main room, saw her eyes as they flicked toward the door. He got up and drew it nearly closed, so that only a crack remained, shedding a narrow band of the luminescence as he returned to the bed—and to her embrace.

Chapter 15

When Cyrus awoke in the morning, it was just before sunrise. He felt a lazy smile on his face. The Baroness lay curled against his side; he had awoken in the night and they had made love again, madly, feverishly, and afterwards held each other until Cyrus faded into another deep, dreamless sleep. His fingers traced lines along the maddening number of scars that crisscrossed the skin of her back and belly, and he wondered at the sort of man who would do such a thing.

The morning light was shining into the main room of their suite, brightening the interior of the bedroom as well. Cyrus heard a faint knocking in the distance and paused, listening for it. It came again, a moment later, and he gently shifted the Baroness off his arm, laying her head upon a pillow, and rolled out of bed, grabbing a blanket and wrapping it around himself as he walked out into the main room.

There was another insistent rapping as he drew the bedroom door shut. His bare feet padded on the cool marble and when he reached the door, he opened it to find Martaina waiting outside with a young boy.

"Sir," Martaina said with a thin smile. "Count Ranson has sent a page for you—he is ready for you and the officers to meet to discuss the battle strategy."

"Oh," Cyrus said. "Right. I'll need a few minutes to get dressed and I'll be right along." The young boy nodded and ran off down the hall, while Martaina stood still. "I thought I told you to get some rest. Were you out here all night?"

"Yep," she said, backing herself against the wall opposite his door. "Aisling was with me at first but ..." The elf's face tightened and her eyebrow raised in amusement. "She left after your first round of ... nocturnal calisthenics."

Cyrus froze. "You heard ... She heard it too? Damn." He felt a sharp stab of guilt. "I suppose I'm going to have to deal with a scorned dark elf at some point."

"I doubt she's murderous about it," Martaina said. "But I would say she is disappointed. The Baroness, on the other hand, sounded very pleased—"

"Oh, stop it," Cyrus said. "Just because you've appointed yourself my bodyguard doesn't mean—"

"I'm your bodyguard?" Martaina laughed. "I'd be hard-pressed to protect you from all the threats you face, let alone the wife of an enemy you killed last month whom you just invited into your bed. I'll do my best to watch out for threats, but if I'm your bodyguard, I demand you make my job easier."

Cyrus pasted a fake smile on. "If you're not my bodyguard, why are you lurking outside my door at all hours? Are you some sort of gratuitous peeper?" He looked down at the door handle. "Should I hang something over the keyhole in order to get some privacy?"

Martaina let out a noise of faint amusement. "Unless you plan to stuff a sock in both your mouth and the Baroness's, I'll still hear you."

"Thanks," Cyrus said. He shut the door and paced back into the bedroom, snugging the blanket around his shoulders. He opened the door and found the Baroness waiting for him, a white sheet lying across her lower body. She jumped in surprise when she saw him, and he noted again the series of scars that ran across her arms and chest, rises in the flesh that looked as though skin had been torn in strips from her arms. Wide cuts crisscrossed the surface of her stomach, angry red lines that looked out of place on her pale belly.

"Was someone at the door?" she asked.

He let the blanket slip to the floor and slid into bed next to her. She remained sitting, giving him a full view of her back, which was wretched in its appearance—great patches of skin and meat seemed to be missing, as though parts of her flesh had been torn out, ripping the musculature from underneath as well. He ran a single finger down her spine and she stiffened, and he saw her shoulders shake as she exhaled. "Please," she said, "don't touch me there … don't look. It's horrible."

"Have you looked at mine?" He sat up and leaned forward to sit next to her, shoulder to shoulder. She turned her head to see him and he leaned forward further. "I've been in a fight or two in my life that left me with scars."

He felt her hand upon his back as it slid down below his shoulder blades. "These … what are these from?" she asked.

"From whippings," he said, and felt himself tense at the memory, "from when I was at the Society. It's how they disciplined you when you got out of line or defied orders." He reached out and took her other hand in his. "Or when you ran away."

"Ran away from what?"

"From battle." He stroked her hand with his, intertwined his fingers with hers. "From the Society. From anything, really."

"You ran away from the Society?" He felt the cool touch of her fingertips go lower, still brushing the thicker scar tissue. There was quite a lot of it.

"Once." He rubbed the palm of her hand with his fingers, felt the smoothness of it save for a few callouses that had formed in the last month. "The first year I was there. I got quite a few of these whipping scars that year."

"How old were you?" She leaned in and put her head on his shoulder.

He felt her warm breath on his neck and he wrapped his arm around her. "Six." She jerked her head away and looked up at him, pity in her eyes. "I was six when I went to the Society."

She leaned her head back down on him. "How long before your meeting?"

He ran his fingers down her side, causing her to shiver. "I could leave at any time."

She pulled her head off his shoulder, her long brown hair loose and framing her face, flowing down either side of it. He caught a sparkle from her green eyes. "Any time? Meaning in an hour?"

"I could wait an hour," he said, and caressed her again. "Easily an hour."

Her hand slipped below the sheets and he felt the heat, the pressure. "My, my," she said with a cluck of the tongue, "you do seem to be a man of infinite vigor." She kissed him again, briefly.

"It's been a while," he said. "I doubt I could keep going at this pace forever." She kissed him again, and he broke it off after a moment. "Although, I confess that I'm feeling enthusiastic enough to try. I had forgotten how much fun this could be."

"Mmmhmm," she said, tracing a line of kisses down his shoulder. "But if you never leave this bed, won't your army eventually leave without you?"

He felt a slow smile spread across his face. "I am the General, you know. My army doesn't move without me."

She leaned closer and kissed his lips gently. "And if the Count sends for you again?"

"Martaina will tell them to go away," Cyrus said, letting her kisses consume him, returning them with all the passion and intensity he'd had for her last night. He turned his shoulders and bore her gently to the mattress, letting his desire for her carry them both away again.

Chapter 16

"General Davidon," Count Ranson said brusquely as Cyrus walked into his war room an hour later. The Count stood behind a table in the center of the room, some of the other Sanctuary officers—Longwell, Curatio, Terian and J'anda—as well a few of the Count's lieutenants were scattered around him. "I hope you don't mind, but we did start without you." Cyrus noted just a hint of contrition in the Count's pronouncement.

"I don't mind at all," Cyrus said. "I apologize for my tardiness, but it has been a rather long ... uh ... journey." He shot a look at Martaina, who snickered behind him. "Anyway, why don't we get to it?" Cyrus walked to the massive table, a circular one that had a diameter greater than the height of a man and looked down at it. Painted on the surface was a map of the Kingdom of Galbadien, along with parts of Actaluere and Syloreas. The map ended at the beginning of the peninsula that contained the Endless Bridge back to Arkaria and also cut off the land of Syloreas above a mountain range. "Very impressive," Cyrus said. "I bet it would also be good for setting up a dollhouse in the middle and then playing—"

"If I may," the Count said tightly, bringing a long stick out to point to the open plains above Vernadam, which was marked on the map with a small, carved stone castle roughly three inches tall. It was a remarkable approximation for the size, even sitting on a small, green-painted rise on the table. "They are encamped approximately here. They will meet us in battle tomorrow, as it has been arranged," he swept the stick down an inch, "here. The whole of the plains is relatively flat ground, as such things go—some sloping hills but nothing too disagreeable for fighting."

"What kind of tactics have the Syloreans been using?" Longwell asked, his eyes focused on the map table.

"Less of the usual," Ranson said. "They haven't been engaging us on horseback nearly as much as they have in the past, preferring to use their footmen—infantry, I believe I heard your men call them," he said with a nod to Cyrus, "and leading with their bloody magical mercenaries."

"How has that played against our dragoons?" Longwell asked, the fingers of his right hand resting on his chin, deep in thought.

"Not well," Ranson went on, "thanks to that bloody half-man. He holds his hand out when the dragoons charge and half our number are blasted from the backs of their horses, and their animals tend to go into a rage, spooked into stomping their own riders when they recover."

"Sounds like a paladin, all right," Curatio said. He leaned both hands on the table. "We'll be needing to take him out of circulation first—him and their healer."

"Let's hope they don't get the same idea about you, yes?" J'anda smirked at Curatio, who shrugged in return. "I know," the dark elf went on, "we have more than one healer, but still—why tempt fate?"

"It's not fate I'm worried about," Cyrus said, staring down at the table, willing it to give him more information, a closer look at the battlefield. "It's those mercenaries. We don't know for sure how many there are or if they have more spellcasters in reserve. I don't care much for surprises, and we certainly seem to be facing our share of them."

"If we could catch them while they're sleeping," Ranson said, "with our dragoons on a full charge and your army dealing with the mercenaries, I feel confident the battle could be won easily."

"You're telling me that you can defeat the Sylorean army if we just take care of their mercenaries?" Cyrus raised an eyebrow at the count. "All right, but we're not going to plan on that. I will focus my army one hundred percent on dispatching the mercenaries, and then we'll rally and break the Syloreans. Are they mostly on horseback or footmen?"

"Footmen," Ranson said. "But they have a healthy contingent of mounted cavalry as well." The count drew himself up, swelling with pride. "They do decently well on horseback, but they're not as well trained as our dragoons."

"Let's plan to hit them in the night and catch them by surprise," Cyrus said, "preferably when they're sleeping. No reason to make things harder on ourselves. If that doesn't work, we'll have to improvise based on the ground we're on when the fight unfolds. No matter what, my army will target the mercenaries until we've removed that threat. Then we'll join you in breaking the rest of the Sylorean army."

"That seems to be as much as we can plan without knowing the landscape of where we'll be fighting," Ranson said. "When will you be ready to march?"

"Within the hour," Cyrus said then looked around at his officers. "We'll ride back to the village in fifteen minutes, so gather your things and meet in the courtyard." He heard Martaina clear her throat, and when he looked at her questioningly, she widened her eyes and stared him down, as though he were forgetting something. "Oh. Make that ... uh ... twenty minutes, I think." He caught a few stares and a raised eyebrow from Terian then nodded at them all and left, Martaina trailing behind him. "What?" he asked her when they had turned a corner.

"I just wanted to suggest you might allow enough time to say a farewell to the Baroness," she said, now walking alongside him again. "And I wasn't sure how much time you wanted to allot for that."

"I don't think I have enough energy for a long goodbye," he said, almost under his breath, drawing a chuckle from her. "But better to not rush it, right?"

"If you care about her?" She looked at him, waited for the slight nod, and went on. "Probably best not to rush it, no, sir."

"Right you are," he said, turning a corner. He thought of something then stopped in the corridor. Martaina's reflexes allowed her to stop with him, without missing so much as a step. She looked at him questioningly and he gave voice to his thought. "Do you have any more spare ventra'maq? I doubt very much that they have anything like it in this land, given their lack of magic."

She narrowed her eyes at him, annoyed. "I do need some for myself, you know."

"When?" Cyrus asked, amused. "Do you have someone that comes to join you at my door at night? Is it one of the guards, perhaps? The wall in the hallway—is it comfortable when your back is thrust against it?"

"Ha ha," Martaina said without humor. She reached into a pouch at her belt and withdrew a small vial of dark liquid, roughly the color of blood. "Warn her about the poor taste or she'll likely be quite upset with you afterward."

Cyrus held up the vial between his thumb and forefinger and stared at the liquid within. "How could I get more?" He caught a glare from her. "You know, if I needed it."

She let out an exasperated sigh. "If you keep up the same pace you've been going at, you'll need it. I can gather the herbs that go into the solution, but only an enchanter can add the mystical component to make it work."

Cyrus stared at her. "Can J'anda ...?"

"He's always done it for me."

"Thank you," he said. "Your diligent service does not go unnoticed, I hope you realize that."

"And I hope you realize," she said, somewhat irritably, "that that's a week's worth of protection—tell her to drink the whole thing, and she'll be safe from unintended quickening of your seed," she leered at him with a raised eyebrow, "or anyone else's, for that matter—for seven days. After that, she'll need another dose, even on the days when her month's blood is with her—I have heard of women becoming with child while thinking they were safely immune during those times."

"Noted," Cyrus said as they continued down the hallway. After a few seconds, he asked his next question. "Who else do you think she'll be getting seed from?"

Martaina sighed. "Her? I doubt anyone, but it's impossible to tell, isn't it?"

"I suppose," Cyrus said. "For example, I knew this woman who was married, presumably happily, yet there were hints that she might not be and might indeed find need for ventra'maq when she was far, far from her husband."

"Talking about anyone in particular?" Martaina's voice had gone cold, frosted even, enough to chill the hallway.

"I tend not to pass judgment," Cyrus said, keeping his tone even. "But it does make a body curious, especially someone who's—perhaps not a close friend, but more than an acquaintance, since this person tends to stand watch outside my room whenever I bed down in a strange keep."

"I also keep watch when you're by a campfire on your own, at the edge of the encampment." The bitter tinge in Martaina's voice was gone, replaced instead by something else, something with a mournful quality to it. "And when you ride toward the edge of the army, away from the others. Or when you steal away, hoping no one will see you, so you can be by yourself. I watch out for you then, too."

"Elven eyesight," Cyrus said under his breath.

"I put it to good use." Martaina's leather glove creaked as her hand reached behind her and ran down the length of her bow. "But I watch out for you because Thad asked me to, before we left. I would have anyway, though perhaps not as zealously."

There was a moment of quiet as they rounded a corner, and Cyrus spoke. "You keep his command faithfully, if he asked you to watch out for me."

She stopped. "But not the other, is that what you're saying?" Cyrus, not so quick as Martaina, stopped a step later and turned back, saw her statuesque face show strain, her eyes slightly glazed. "I keep faithful to the request he made of me to watch out for you, but not faithful to—" She choked back the words, fighting against emotion. "Damn it," she said at a whisper.

"I told you," Cyrus said. "I'm not judgmental. I won't say anything, but—"

"It's me." Martaina held her hand up in front of her, pointing her index finger into the leather armor that covered her chest. "It's me. I know who I am. I am a master archer, and an expert tracker, and a brilliant swordfighter, one of the very best rangers at hunting through woods and chasing down prey over any land, but when it comes to keeping a husband ..." She let her voice trail off. "We can't all be good at everything, can we?"

"No," Cyrus said. "No one is perfect. Not at everything."

"Then how can I be so good at everything else," she said, calm running over her, "but not ... I can follow your orders. I can be a good soldier. But when it comes to being a ... a faithful wife, or doing what ... what society says I should ... I come up short on every occasion. I can hunt down any prey on land, but I can't keep myself out of another man's arms when I'm away from my husband."

"That's uh ..." Cyrus blanched, unsure of what to say. "... I ... I don't know what's happened between you and Thad—"

"Nothing," she said, the emotion gone again. "Everything was ... fine ... when we left. We get along well. When we're together, everything seems to work, but the minute I knew I was coming on this expedition and he wasn't ..." She shrugged and another crack came through her facade, her face crumpled. "Why am I telling you this? This isn't your concern. You're about to lead an army into war ... I don't know," Martaina shook her head, "we've got a battle to attend to, though." She forced a weak smile. "My problems have been with me for a thousand years; I doubt they're going anywhere in the next few days while we save this Kingdom."

"Yeah," Cyrus said, rubbing his face, running his hair back over his ears. "They do seem to be in a spot of bother, don't they? I'd be less concerned about this fight if we knew how many of these Arkarian mercenaries are going to be in it."

"No predicting that until we're in it," she said. "But however many there are, we still have them outnumbered."

"True," Cyrus said, and continued the walk. "But do we have them overpowered? Knocking entire swaths of men and horses flat to the ground with a single spell? That sounds like something Alaric could do, but not many other paladins I've heard of."

"That is a mite puzzling," Martaina said, in step with him. "If this paladin is so powerful, he'd be wanted in every guild in Arkaria. So why come over here?"

Cyrus smiled, faintly. "Why would anyone from Arkaria come here?" he asked, a trace of irony in his voice as they reached the door to his chambers. "Running from something, I'd expect." His smile evaporated, replaced by a pensive expression. "The question is—what is he running from?"

Martaina did not answer, and Cyrus opened the door to the chambers, stepping inside to find the Baroness on a chair by the fire, a blanket covering her lower body, her riding clothes back on. "Hello," he said. When he reached her side he leaned down and kissed her, full and long, and when they broke he could see the wistful smile on her face. "Good morning."

She reached up and stroked his beard. "You already said a fine good morning to me before you left, but I'll take another, if you feel up to it."

"I'm afraid I don't at present," Cyrus said with genuine regret. "I have to leave."

"I see." Her fingers ran between the long hairs on this jaw. "Perhaps when you get back, if you've any energy left."

"It'll be a couple days," Cyrus said with a grin, "I suspect I'll be ready to repeat what we did last night by then. You may spoil me, getting me too used to this."

She kissed him, gently but quickly. "I could become quite used to it, though perhaps at a slower pace than last night."

He shrugged. "I have some lost time to make up for."

She withdrew her hand. "Perhaps when you get back, you'll let me shave your face?" She blushed when she saw him look down. "Not that I don't enjoy the beard, but I like your face. I should like to see more of it, to feel your cheek against mine."

"Perhaps you'd like to cut my hair as well?" He ran a hand through his long hair, to where it fell on his shoulders. "I've been letting it grow for near a year now, and I think I've grown quite tired of it being this long."

"No, I love your hair," she said, running her fingers through it. "Leave it as it is."

"As you wish," he said. She kissed him again, and he returned it, but it was different than those from last night—more affectionate, less passionate, as though they both were acutely aware of the little time they had. "I should go," he said once he broke from her.

"You don't want me to come with you, I take it?" No accusation, only acknowledgment.

"It's not very safe for a non-combatant on the battlefield," Cyrus said. "While I have no doubt you could be quite the fighter if you ever decided to dedicate yourself to the arts of war, I don't believe this is a time for teaching. It's a place where mistakes can have unforgiving consequences."

"Then I will stay here." She folded her hands on her lap, a look of peaceful contemplation serene on her face. "And await your return."

"Are you all right with that?" He stood, looking down on her with as much tenderness as he had.

"It is the way of the women of Luukessia," she said. "We wait for the men when they go off to war. I may not be in this land much longer, but for now, this is still my way. I cannot go with you, for all you say is true, so I will wait, and bide my time, and stay here until you return—on the day after tomorrow," she said pointedly, looking him in the eyes.

"I'll be back as quickly as I can."

"Be safe," she said in a whisper. "I don't think I could bear the thought of you dying."

"I wouldn't concern yourself with it overmuch; it's never stopped me before." Cyrus walked to the door and started to open it, then turned back to her. "Oh, I almost forgot." He slipped his hand beneath his armor and pulled out the vial. "Do you know what this is?"

She stared at it, an amused smile on her face. "Poison?"

"Ah, no," Cyrus said. "It's called ventra'maq."

Clouds drew in around her eyes and she adopted a wounded tone. "You mean after only one night with me, you don't want me to bear your children?" She broke into a smile, her shoulders shaking from silent laughter.

"I'd like to keep practicing," Cyrus said as she got up and joined him at the door, slipping the vial out of his hand as she kissed him. "As often as possible."

"You'll probably need quite a bit more of this, then." She popped the cork on the vial and drank it down. "Ugh." She made a face, her eyes closed and lips puckered. "Ugh, ugh, yuck. On second thought, perhaps bearing your offspring would be a preferable alternative." She opened her eyes but they remained squinted and she dabbed at the corner of her mouth with her sleeve. "That is vile."

He stared at her blankly. "All the women take it. How bad can it be?"

"Bad enough that I'm pondering whether it might be better to simply remain celibate, as you have these last years—"

"Bah!" Cyrus said, and leaned in and kissed her one last time before stepping out the door.

"Keep me in mind, while you're away?" She looked at him through the open door, serenity still hanging over her, a faint glow of contentment Cyrus hadn't seen from her before.

"Indeed I shall," he said, "and I'll be counting the hours until my return."

"You mean you'll be counting the hours until next we're in bed together?" She gave him a sly look.

"I also enjoy our conversations."

"Really? Perhaps we could have a long, enduring one the moment you get back, the kind that lasts all night, and that doesn't involve any touching at all." She smiled innocently. "How does that sound?"

"Painful," he said, drawing a laugh from her. "Can't we do both?"

"I think," she said as she took his hand and kissed the knuckle of his gauntlet, "that that is indeed what lovers do."

"I have to go," he said, bending in and kissing her again. "Truly, this time."

"Then go," she said, still wearing the same smile, "with my blessing, and my thoughts, and all else I have to give you."

Cyrus shut the door, slowly, watching her as he did so, letting the handle roll in his hand, the metal squeaking against metal. He turned and found Martaina standing there, looking quite put out. "Are you finished now? Truly finished?"

"I could go back in for a few more minutes if you'd prefer ..."

Martaina whirled, letting her traveling cloak billow outward in an even circle as she did so. She started walking down the hall, and Cyrus took two quick running steps to catch up to her. "I take it you don't like the long goodbyes?" He saw her look daggers at him. "That'd be a no."

"I don't mind a long goodbye, but, ugh," she said. "Young love is so filled with sap and sweetness, it makes me ill."

"I could go for a little sap and sweetness right now," Cyrus said. "I wonder if they can make flapjacks down in the kitchen?"

"Your orders stipulate that we leave immediately, General."

"I'm feeling a little peckish," he said. "I think I might have worked up an appetite, you know—" Before he could finish his sentence, Martaina soft-tossed him an apple and he caught it, fumbling it a little but recovering before it slipped away. "That'll do for now, I suppose. But I do wonder if the kitchen could send something with us—"

They traipsed downstairs, Cyrus thinking about food the whole way. As he passed through the foyer, one of the servants bowed and handed him a small package wrapped in canvas, with a string tied around it. "Provisions for your journey," the servant said and bowed again.

"What is with all this bowing?" Cyrus whispered as they walked out the front doors of Vernadam and descended the stairs. "You'd think there were gods wandering the halls around here."

"I've seen a god," Martaina said, taking the reins of her horse from the servant who waited below. "None of us looks much like him."

"Don't know how much bowing I'd do to him, anyway," Cyrus said as he put his foot in a stirrup on Windrider's saddle and hoisted himself up. "He was the ugliest sonofabitch I've ever seen."

Martaina raised an eyebrow at him as she righted herself in the saddle. "And Bellarum is a handsome fellow by comparison? Am I remembering perhaps a different God of War than you?"

"He's not as ugly as Mortus was," Cyrus said. "At least, he didn't look that ugly when I saw him."

"When you saw him?" Martaina's face contorted in consternation. "When did you see the God of War?"

Cyrus urged Windrider toward the gate, Martaina a few paces behind him. He ignored her question as Terian came alongside him. "Davidon," the dark knight said. "It's a fine day for battle, is it not?"

"The battle's going to be tonight," Cyrus said, gesturing to the Sanctuary members gathered at the gate to follow him. "We're meeting the count and his men in the village?" Cyrus waited until Longwell nodded at him, then started out of the gate and turned back to Terian, who was on one side of him while Martaina had taken up the other flank. "And, yes, it will be fine," he said, catching a glimpse of Aisling riding close to Mendicant, as far away from him as possible while remaining in the knot of Sanctuary forces. "I'm particularly looking forward to swinging my sword around; it's been a while."

Martaina snickered and looked at him, amusement on her features. "Interesting choice of words. I'm surprised you have enough energy to swing a sword after all the time you spent ... wagon racing with the Baroness on your bed last night."

Terian straightened. "Wagon racing? Is that supposed to mean something?" His brow furrowed. "Did you rut with her last night, Cyrus?"

Cyrus felt his cheeks burn with embarrassment. "A gentleman never tells."

"That'd maybe be of concern to me if I'd asked a gentleman, but instead I asked you. Did she bring the dagger to bed? Because after Vara, I can see that being the sort of thing you'd be into, pain and whatnot."

"I didn't hear a dagger come into play," Martaina said. "Although it may have on the fourth time; there was so much squealing it sounded like they were having a livestock auction in there."

"Aren't you bound by an oath of silence or something?" Cyrus asked.

"My gods, Cyrus," Terian said. "I knew you'd been deprived of female company all these years, but—four times? Have you not been taking matters into your own hands?" He looked down. "I suppose the gauntlets make it somewhat colder, but—" Terian shifted his gaze to look at Martaina, "Four times? You're not exaggerating?"

The elven ranger smirked and held up her hand, the four fingers extended, and she nodded.

"I guess it's too much, asking an elven woman to be quiet," Cyrus said, glaring at Martaina.

"I didn't *say* it," Martaina replied, her eyebrow raised. "And it sounds like you might be picking up some local color, sir—like their attitude toward women."

"Not true," Cyrus said. "I made sure my partner crossed the finish line each time. I even let her ride on top of the wagon once."

Terian smirked at him. "So is this the end of the dour and sour Cyrus? Have we finally banished the thoughts of Queen Frostheart to the nether realms of Mortus's tower?" Terian's smirk turned into a frown. "Or wherever that giant oddity went when he died."

"I don't know," Cyrus said soberly, the thoughts of the blond-haired elf returning for the first time that day, "but I think we're on our way."

"Good," Terian said, "because you were really insufferable—boring and whatnot—for the last couple months." The dark knight smiled, but there was a malicious edge in his voice. "I felt bad for you. Honestly, it made me a little sick inside. I almost felt like if you died, it'd be a mercy killing."

"It might have been," Cyrus said. "But we're moving past that now. And this is no time to think about ... her." He blinked. "Actually, either of them, for now. I need to focus on this battle. After that ... I guess we'll see."

"What happens after that?" Martaina asked.

"If we crush the Sylorean army, I suppose we go home," Cyrus said. "If we just splinter them, we'll probably have to pursue them north for a while, help break them so this doesn't happen again in the near future."

"And if we lose?" Terian's smirk had returned.

"Then I suspect we'll have bigger problems to worry about than whether I'm over Vara," Cyrus said with a smile of his own.

"Dealing with the odd smell that hangs on my chainmail is a bigger concern to me than whether you've embraced sanity and returned to the realm of normal womenfolk," Terian said. "But all the same, you were one sour bastard after she twisted on you."

"Look out there," Martaina said, pointing her finger down the hill, past the town. The army of Sanctuary was assembled in the streets, already facing in the direction they were set to march. Beyond them, out in the fields, another army waited. On one side of the pasture were thousands of men on foot, at least five-fold what Sanctuary had. Across the field, and not nearly so well ordered, were thousands more on horseback; so many that Cyrus could not hope to reasonably count them all.

"Where the hell were those guys when we came into town yesterday?" Terian asked.

"I'm guessing they were set up to the north," Cyrus said. "Probably positioned between where the enemy is coming from and Vernadam."

Curatio rode up as they started around the switchback, heading down the path. The sky overhead had taken on some clouds, and the sun seemed to be trying to shine through them, but dimly. Cyrus caught a hint of dust as the wind blew across his face, the dry, earthy smell of dirt that came off the hill behind them.

"You ready?" Curatio said as he slowed his horse to ride next to Terian. "Head clear? Prepared for battle?"

"Quite so," Cyrus said.

"And was the Baroness still aglow when you left her?" Curatio's usual infectious smile had been curiously absent of late, but Cyrus saw the tug of it on the elf's mouth, even as he looked straight ahead, giving Cyrus only a view of the healer's profile.

"Been doing a little eavesdropping, Curatio?" Cyrus cocked an eyebrow at him.

"It wouldn't take much eavesdropping to hear your conversation about 'wagon rides,' even if I hadn't been quartered next door to you last night."

They rode into the village. The army of Sanctuary was already assembled in formation, neatly ordered rows beginning at the square and leading all the way down the main avenue out of town. "I'll need to talk with Odellan and Longwell as we're riding," Cyrus said as he rode down the street, the musk of animals filling the air around them, the hooves clopping. "No need to delay our departure, especially since it appears Count Ranson is already waiting for us."

Cyrus rode down the line, the others falling in behind him, leading the procession past the rows of his army. He heard hundreds of greetings and acknowledgments of his presence, and smiled, trying to wave at as many of them as he could.

"You might want to cool it off with the excess enthusiasm," Martaina stage whispered behind him. "You're so damned happy this morning, they're bound to wonder where their real general has gone."

"I prefer going to war under the command of a testy general," Terian said as Longwell and Odellan fell in behind them. "There's something unseemly about storming into a fray of swords and arrows, blood and bile, with a guy who looks so damned happy."

Cyrus rolled his eyes and rode on, past the villagers lined up on both sides of the streets. *I wonder if they know how close their Kingdom is to defeat? I wonder if it matters?* His thoughts were dark as he rode to the end of the line and the edge of the village. *Where else could they go?*

The steady sound of hoofbeats carried him forward as Cyrus led the procession out of town; ahead, Count Ranson waited on horseback with Odau Genner and a few of the other familiar faces he'd seen back at the castle.

"Good day, Lord Davidon," Ranson said as they closed. "My army is assembled and ready to move."

"Well, then," Cyrus said, "let us not hesitate any longer."

"As you are the leader of this force," Ranson said, "you'll be proceeding ahead of us, I trust?"

"Aye," Cyrus said, and felt a stray droplet of rain splatter off his armor, touching his cheek as it splashed. "I trust Sir Longwell can guide us."

"I'll be accompanying you as well," Odau Genner said with a nod, "if that's all right with you, General."

"Always room at the front of battle, less so at the rear," Cyrus said, grinning at Genner in a manner that was not returned. He turned to the army following behind him. "All right, Sanctuary, let's move out!"

Chapter 17

The ride was long, and by sundown Cyrus was weary of the journey again. They passed into woods called the Forest of Waigh, and the ground become uneven around them as they followed a road north. The trees were bunched close together, moss hanging from the branches, blotting out the sky at the highest levels of the boughs. Raindrops still made their way through, however, and a steady drizzle kept the expedition cool as they made their march.

After the sun went down, the rain seemed to come in torrents, wave after wave of water sluicing down on them, reminding Cyrus of the time he'd been caught in a riverboat during a storm.

"Ha ha," Terian crowed as Cyrus passed him after inspecting the wet and weary column. "Not quite so happy now, are you, Mr. I-Just-Experienced-The-Long-Forgotten-Thrill-Of-My-Crotch-Last-Night-And-Can't-Wait-For-More!"

Cyrus ignored him and they plodded on through the gathering darkness. The storm went on into the night, a driving rain that threw sheets of water onto Cyrus's armor, the heaviest downpour that they had experienced since arriving in Luukessia.

"Our pace has slowed," Longwell said as he and Odellan rode next to Cyrus. "Unless the rain lets up soon, we won't be on the Fields of Gareme until long after midnight." The dragoon looked at Cyrus, almost cringing from the fury of the rain pounding his helm. "And we won't be in a position to hit their army until after sunrise."

Cyrus cursed. "I guess we should have left last night."

"I'm certain they'll have scouts, sir," Longwell said. "They'll see us long before we see them; we need lanterns to travel in this dark, but a single scout doesn't."

"We have pickets out as well," Cyrus said. "If we're lucky, perhaps they'll catch any enemy scouts before they get close enough to spot us."

"Doubtful, sir," Odellan said, raising his voice over the pouring rain battering their armor. "A scout could pass within yards of us without us noticing, but they're not likely to miss an entire army tromping by."

"I feel obligated to warn you in advance, sir," Longwell said, "the dragoons will not be nearly as effective fighting on the plains after this weather."

"What?" Cyrus stared at Longwell, questioning.

"The rain will turn the fields into mud," Longwell said. "The dragoons will be at poor advantage if the army of Syloreas holds true to their usual tactics and carries spears. In a full out charge, dragoons can break through lines of spears, though with some difficulty." He grimaced, his eyes hidden in the shadow his helm cast over them. "In this, it becomes unlikely they will be able to."

"Damn," Cyrus said. "What about bowmen? Surely they must have some."

"Bows are not nearly so well loved here as you'd find in Arkaria," Longwell said with regret. "They are neither as accurate nor as useful at range, and as such we have archers, but you'd be in a much better position relying on the Sanctuary rangers to fulfill any role you'd have in mind for my father's bowmen."

"That's to both our advantage and detriment, then," Cyrus said. "At least we won't have to advance under volleys of arrows, but it would be awfully nice to be able to shower them with a hail of them."

"With the accuracy of our rangers," Odellan said, "we could use our archers to target their officers, perhaps? And these magic-wielding mercenaries that are of such concern?"

"Yes," Cyrus said. "And we'll be turning loose some spellcasters of our own. I doubt that they have a wizard." He smiled grimly. "That bodes ill for them."

They rode on through the wet and the night, the rain coming down around them with all the fury of a sky's rage turned loose upon the earth. The ground turned to mud, the sky became black, and the lamps that were carried by the army forced Cyrus and the others on horseback to ride alongside the column, straining to see in the dark as the water that fell through the trees above continued ever on.

"The troops are cold," Odellan said, forcing Cyrus to turn around and look for the elf. He was a horse-length behind Cyrus, trying futilely to turn his face from the rain. "They could use a rest and they won't be of much use to us in a fight if they arrive fatigued."

Cyrus nodded. "Column, halt!" he called out, and heard his cry taken up by others down the stream of endless soldiers that vanished into the black behind him. Curatio and J'anda appeared out of the darkness on the other side of their troops, riding their horses to join Cyrus and Odellan.

"Can't see a thing," J'anda said, his hair soaked and his deep blue skin fading into the night. "The rain has cut our visibility to nothing."

"Remember that time in the Realm of Darkness," Cyrus said with a smile, "when Curatio lit up the sky?"

"I could do that here, I suppose," the healer said with a wry smile, "but we'd be giving away our position to anyone with eyes; and I can't be sure over the rain, but I suspect there's enemies about."

"There are," Martaina said, riding up with Terian behind her. Cyrus saw something in her hands, a rope, and she tugged on it as her horse slowed, and Cyrus saw it trail to something dragged behind her, something cutting a wake through the mud on the path. "I caught this one hiding in the trees."

Cyrus looked at the object at the end of the rope. It moaned, a low, plaintive cry, and he realized it was a muddy human, a man bound by the hands, stretched prone across the ground. He raised his face from where it had come to rest in the mud and groaned. Cyrus could see some blood dripping in the low light, mixing with the sopping wet dirt that coated him.

"Is he capable of speaking?" Cyrus asked.

"I can fix what ails him, if you'd like," Curatio said.

"Please," the man croaked. "Please ... it hurts, so much."

"Oh," Martaina said and dismounted. She bent over the man and reached down. He screamed, a long, agonized howl, and she came back up with an arrow. "Almost forgot about this. I had to hobble him so he wouldn't get away." She scowled. "Tracking is a real bitch with all this rain washing away footprints."

Cyrus guided Windrider over to the man, and peered down at his dirty face from horseback. It was impossible to see any detail of the man, only mud that covered his face and long hair. He appeared to be wearing a tattered cloak, and if his shirt and breeches had been new before Martaina dragged him along, it was now impossible to tell. "My name is Cyrus Davidon," he said. "Answer my questions and my healer will soothe all your pains."

"I ... I won't," the man breathed. "Torture me all you want, I'll never tell you a thing."

"I believe you wouldn't," Cyrus said, staring into the man's eyes; they were wide, but defiant. "You've got a good-sized hole in you, you've just been dragged a considerable ways, and you're still so full of spit and whiskey that you'd tell me to go to the hells eighteen times over, even if I cut off your leg. I admire your spirit. Curatio, heal this man."

"Uh ..." The healer sputtered. "All right." He muttered under his breath and Cyrus saw the glow of a healing spell encompass the wounded captive.

"Is that better?" Cyrus asked, soothing.

"Yes," the captive said, momentarily losing his defiant tone. "But I still won't talk."

"I didn't expect you to," Cyrus said. "I just wanted to make sure you didn't bleed to death while my enchanter cracks your mind open like a ripe gourd. J'anda?" Cyrus turned and looked at the dark elf, who nodded. "Take him."

J'anda closed his eyes and stretched his hand out at the man, who recoiled and turned from where he'd been sitting upright, and scrambled to crawl away. He made it almost a foot before a blue light swirled around his head and he went slack, on all fours in the mud. He swayed, then put a hand on the stirrup of Martaina's horse and pulled to his feet, turning to face Cyrus, a dazed look in his eyes.

"What's the word, J'anda?" Cyrus looked at the enchanter then to the captive, who stood stonefaced, staring straight ahead.

"He's a scout from their army, all right," J'anda said, his eyes closed. "Bad news. They've encamped at the edge of the forest. They've traversed the entire plains to be ready ..." The dark elf sighed. "They had planned to ambush us when we arrived tomorrow. They're already set up to hit us with a charge the moment we emerge from the forest."

"Dammit," Cyrus said. "The trees are too thick to allow us to move off the path in any numbers."

"That was the plan," J'anda said. "If they could lock down the army, keep it from getting mobile on the plains, the dragoons would lose their advantage." He shook his head sheepishly. "Hard to do much with an army of horseman all trapped in a line."

"Excellent strategy on their part," Odellan said. "It does rather complicate things for us."

"Ask him how many mercenaries they have and what types," Cyrus said, patting Windrider on the side of his neck. The horse's mane was soaked.

J'anda stared into the man's eyes, as though he were trying to sift the truth out. "Two warriors, two rangers ... a healer ... and a paladin." The dark elf turned back to Cyrus. "I had to pull that out of his memories; he didn't know what they were by name, but he's seen what they can do."

"Should be simple if we can get the healer first," Terian said, lingering behind Martaina. "He goes down and the paladin is vulnerable. Wiping out the rest of their army will be as easy as making a new recruit cry if we can sift out those two bastards first."

"I don't think we should discount the effectiveness of their trap," Odellan said. "They can pincer us, surrounding our forces as we emerge from the woods, making our numbers count for nearly nothing." He looked to Cyrus. "I believe you're somewhat familiar with the technique."

"I've always called it a choke point," Cyrus said. "Like when we employed it on the bridge in Termina, you're grabbing your enemy around the throat and slowing the flow of blood—their troops, in this case—until they falter."

"And falter we may," Odellan said, "unless we can break through their ambush."

"Could be tough in the rain," Longwell conceded. "Poor maneuverability, the numbers against us, our visibility cut to nothing and we're fighting on unfamiliar terrain. Perhaps we should wait until morning."

"I think not," Cyrus said, a grin on his face. "By then, they'll be up and waiting for us."

J'anda raised an eyebrow at him. "Perhaps you didn't hear me when I told you what I learned from this scout's mind—they are already waiting for us, and the minute we appear from the forest, they'll spring on us from three sides."

"I heard you," Cyrus said. "Which is why they'll be totally caught by surprise when our army marches into their rear flank at dawn."

There was silence save for the rain, which showed no sign of tapering, large droplets of water hammering down in the puddles all around them. "All right, *General*," Terian said, sarcasm dripping over Cyrus's title, "how do you propose to maneuver 2,000 dragoons, 5,000 footmen, 1,000 of our soldiers and fifty of our horsed veterans in a long, wide arc through the muddy woods so that we can flank them? Oh, and do it all in the next ... what, four hours? Five? Before dawn."

Cyrus didn't answer them, even though every last one of them was watching him. He only smiled.

Chapter 18

The sun's first rays had scarcely begun to show over the horizon and Cyrus was still riding. He could feel the fatigue edging on him. A river lay to his left, burbling against its bank, snaking out of sight. Less than a mile ahead was a bridge: large, made of stones stacked one on top of the other, grouted together to hold against all manner of traffic that would cross it. The river was not particularly wide or particularly deep but enough so to make traversing it wickedly difficult, even if the water hadn't been as high as it was.

"It is called the Fennterin River," Longwell said, his voice a low whisper. "The bridge ahead is called Harrow's Crossing. The Fennterin overruns its banks every spring, likely in a few weeks as the water seeps down from the highlands when the rains come. They built the bridge to aid travelers going to the northern towns, to help keep the trade routes open to Vernadam and southern Galbadien in times of flood."

Cyrus stared at the bridge in the distance and saw figures over the small ridge of stones that railed either side of it. "You're sure that the walls are only a few feet high?"

"Absolutely," Longwell said. "I've been on it countless times; it's low enough that an upset horse could easily jump over."

"Good." Cyrus peered ahead. "Martaina, what does it look like to you?"

The elf was to his left, and her eyes were trained on the bridge. "Men on horseback, some others dismounted, with bows." She turned to him and smiled. "I think that scout J'anda pulled the information out of had the right of it; it looks as though they've placed their entire cavalry and all their bowmen on the bridge to protect their retreat."

"Leaving a nice wide swath of open fields between them and their exit route," Terian said, his destrier carrying him along with them. "Imagine their surprise when they see an army at their backs and their retreat cut off."

"Let's keep it low," Cyrus said, dropping his voice. "We still need the element of surprise." He heard the soft release of an arrow to his left and turned to see Martaina, bow in hand. She shrugged and he followed her sightline to see a body up the incline of the riverbank, rolling down, lifeless, an arrow protruding from the face. "Good shot."

The riverbank sloped at a steep angle, obscuring their view of the fields and the flat ground above them. They had taken a long, circuitous route that Martaina had found for them through the woods, traversing rocky paths and uneven ground, taking care to eliminate the enemy's scouts and even one small line of pickets when they reached the edge of the forest. They had crossed from the wood's edge to the incline down by the river several miles west of where the Sylorean army waited in ambush. It had taken all night. *But it will be worth it, if we can pull this off.*

Every twig snap seemed to carry with it extra danger, and the long night's journey had taken its toll. Cyrus looked around at the ragtag officers on horseback: Terian's dark eyes darted back and forth, keeping careful watch for anything around them. Curatio looked relatively intact, but Cyrus caught a glimpse of the healer rubbing his face, as though he were trying to brush off the desire to sleep. Past him was the wizard, Mendicant, the goblin's green scales and facial ridges barely visible in the dawn's early light.

The bridge drew ever closer, and Cyrus beckoned for others to join him at the fore; Nyad, Ryin, Mendicant, and J'anda came forward, along with a few other spellcasters. The voices on the raised bridge were hushed, but occasional laughter came from the horsed cavalry.

Cyrus held up his hand, bringing them all to a stop a hundred feet from the bridge, partially obscured. "Remember," he whispered so that the spellcasters could hear him. "I want chaos. Fire. Lightning is acceptable, but only if it produces a hell of a thunderclap. Chaos is the word of the day, ladies, gentlemen, and goblin, so let's spread the word to the Sylorean army." Nods greeted him as the spellcasters turned their attention to the bridge. "Let's give 'em a sunrise they'll remember," Cyrus whispered.

"Their last?" Terian shrugged when Cyrus turned to look at him questioningly. "Well, it is."

"J'anda," Cyrus said, "are you ready to do your part?"

"I am ever ready to do my part," the enchanter said, "and, if needs be, the part of ten thousand others as well."

"Needs be," Cyrus said. "Get to it."

Cyrus waited, counting the seconds as they passed, the cool air coming off the river slipping through the joints of his armor, chilling him. He ran his hand over his helm, straightening it. *Damned hair,* he thought, shifting it back under his helm. *At least the beard will be gone soon.* He felt a stir of something within and smiled.

The first blast of flame exploded on the bridge only a moment later, a blast ten feet wide and ten feet tall, at the railing opposite them. Screams tore through the early morning silence, breaking it as another burst of fire landed on the bridge a moment later and shouts overcame the pre-dawn calm, dissolving it into the chaos Cyrus had sought. Three men tumbled over the side of the bridge in the first few seconds, along with their horses.

Cyrus heard a soft moan from Martaina. When he looked over at her, she wore a frown. "Couldn't we have found a way to rout them without hurting the horses?"

"Sorry," Cyrus said with a shake of the head. "I've got no love of harming animals, but we need to throw their rearguard into utter disarray."

Another dozen or more horses vaulted off the side of the bridge, flames covering their riders, wreathing the end of the bridge in a way that reminded Cyrus of another bridge, only months earlier, and a wizard who had sacrificed years from her life to bring twice as much fire as his whole corps of spellcasters were delivering now—and not nearly so sustained as what Chirenya had created.

Cyrus could feel the heat, as though a furnace door had opened in front of him. He could see bodies tumbling off as the men and horses sought to escape the fiery doom that awaited any who remained on the bridge. They fell, dropping off the side onto the rocks in the shallows below. Most remained unmoving, but a few still moaned or cried out. Cyrus saw one man trapped under a whinnying horse that could not stand, though it kept trying, and he cringed. "Martaina," he said. "For the gods' sakes, give them some mercy."

He heard the arrows begin to fly only a moment later, and he turned away from the destruction he had ordered as the last of the inferno faded away. The bridge was silent, but the ground and water below was a mass of moaning and whinnying, the survivors of the jump crying out for relief that would not come—at least not in the way they intended it.

"I'd say you'd suffer in Mortus's oil pits for that bit of cruelty," Martaina said as she loosed another arrow, "but I think we both know that at this point, that's not likely true."

"There were some folks suffering there, that's certain," Cyrus said, recalling the phantoms that had been loosed when Mortus died; souls crying out, screaming in pain for vengeance; they sounded much like the suffering souls under the bridge. "No time for recriminations now. J'anda?" Cyrus looked to the enchanter. "Are we set?"

"Set," J'anda said. "Excellent choice of words. They look like a matching set, in fact." He waved his hand toward figures that were lined up in even rows behind them, stretching over the riverbanks and onto the river, horsemen with the helms of Galbadien's dragoons, walking on water as though it were the greenest grass. "Let us hope that our enemies don't look too closely at their conformity and see through the illusion of it all."

"They've never seen an enchanter at work," Cyrus said. "And by the time they figure it out, hopefully it'll be too late." He drew his sword, Praelior, and urged Windrider up the bank. "Let's get out in front of this charging army of specters and get these Syloreans turned around." His horse stormed up the embankment as Cyrus held his sword aloft. He heard the others follow him in the morning gloom and saw the illusory dragoon army close behind as they crested the top of the ridge.

A flat, grassy plain stretched before him, running all the way to the edge of the Forest of Waigh. Cyrus saw the road that led from the bridge back to the forest, the one they had been following with the army until they caught the scout. Set up on either side of the road at the forest's edge were ranks of soldiers, footmen with pikes, polearms, and swords. Standard bearers waited at either end, each of which was divided into six armies, each with four or five ranks lined up one behind another. They were arranged in a half circle around the entrance to the woods, although now many of them had turned, heads looking toward the bridge to try and make sense of the flaming chaos.

When Cyrus crested the edge of the embankment he judged the distance to the nearest army at only a few hundred yards. He let Windrider carry him onward as he watched the armies before him panic, men turning, stunned at the appearance of a charging army on the rear flank. The Sylorean officers screamed at their men to turn in formation but Cyrus watched them hesitate before beginning to organize. *Too slow.*

Detached from the body of any of the six legions, dead in the center of the road back to the forest was another cluster, smaller, this one only a few men. Cyrus squinted, and saw that one of them appeared to be much shorter than the others, and had a long beard, one that reached nearly to his waist. The dwarf carried a hammer almost as tall as he was, holding it diagonally across his body with both hands. The small group of fighters was only about six strong, Cyrus noted. He pointed his sword at them and noticed Windrider had already altered his heading to charge the mercenaries. "Clever horse," he said faintly. "So, so clever."

The others changed course behind him, and Cyrus felt the wind rushing through his hair, blowing it out the bottom of his helm. His mouth was wide with a feral grin; he was going into battle, riding into danger from the fore, his forces behind him. The dwarf ahead of him was already running out to meet him, along with the others in his party, while the rest of the Sylorean army was still executing its turn and trying to shift their formations to deal with the threat at their flank. Cyrus saw horses beginning to stream out of the woods behind the backs of the Syloreans. The real Galbadien Dragoons were forming up to hit the unsuspecting Syloreans from behind while Cyrus distracted them.

"Watch out for the paladin's attack!" Cyrus shouted as they closed the distance to the mercenaries. He locked his eyes to the dwarf, watched him extend his hand, felt Windrider tense beneath him.

A blast of ice sent the dwarf staggering, his hand flying into the air as he loosed a massive burst of force that went sailing over Cyrus's head, barely brushing his helm but sending it flying. Cyrus could see the two mercenary warriors, armored at the fore, and the two rangers, their bows drawn and arrows ready to loose. Each of them was downed in the next moment; one caught an arrow in the face from Martaina, who smiled grimly as she drew another arrow. The other was blasted by a bolt of lightning that originated from Ryin Ayend, who sent the man spiraling through the air as though thrown.

"Spellcasters!" Cyrus yelled, "let loose on the armies! Keep them off us while we finish the mercenaries!" He watched another arrow sail forth, this one from Aisling, and it came to rest in the thigh of the mercenary healer, who let out a cry and fell to the ground.

Flames sparked up in a line along either side of their charge, isolating Cyrus and the Sanctuary forces from the Syloreans on either side; the lines blazed back toward the woods but stopped behind the mercenaries, sending the grass into conflagration as it looped around the four surviving mercenaries, cutting them off from Sylorean reinforcement.

Another arrow caught the healer in the face as he cast a spell, sitting on his haunches, his legs in front of him. His hand dropped, limp, into his lap, and he fell backward, dead, forcing Cyrus to smile. The dwarf had been knocked over by the ice spell, but was back on his feet now, hunched over, the two heavily armored warriors flanking him to either side. "Get the paladin!" Cyrus shouted as the dwarf's hand rose again, this time without warning. Cyrus was only ten feet away now—

The air around the paladin's hand rippled as his spell burst forth from his mailed hand. With the aid of Praelior's mystic enhancement to his speed and reflexes, time seemed to slow as the air folded around the force of the spell, the world distorting as the enchantment sped toward Cyrus. Windrider had already cut hard to the right before the blast landed, and the horse managed to dodge under the effects. Cyrus felt himself hit by the widening radius of power as the wave bloomed outward, like a wall had been picked up and slammed into him. He flew sideways off the horse, dragging his legs behind him as he flipped in midair, before coming to rest on his shoulder.

The impact knocked the air out of him, but he maintained his grip on his sword. He looked back and saw the paladin's attack wreaking havoc behind him; half of Cyrus's small force had been hit, and a trail of upturned earth ten feet wide marked the place where the paladin's incantation had wrought its effects. Those who hadn't been hit had dodged outside of the cone of destruction, trying to get their horses back under control. Cyrus saw Curatio among them, as well as Terian. "Come on!" Cyrus shouted and slung himself to his feet. "Terian, get over here!"

Cyrus turned and found the dwarf already upon him, hammer raised above his head. Cyrus brought Praelior up, turning aside the dwarf's first attack by landing a glancing blow on the head of the big, stone hammer that sent it reeling off to the side. The dwarf was fast, however, and used the momentum of the attack to pirouette, coming around with a spinning assault that Cyrus dodged, but only barely.

Cyrus brought Praelior around and landed the blade on the hammer's long handle; it was almost as long as the dwarf was tall, and when he hit the wood with his blade, it chipped only slightly. *His hammer is mystical. Praelior would cut through regular wood as easily as passing through flesh.*

"You're faster than most dwarves I've met," Cyrus said, feeling the hammer strike a glancing blow off his breastplate as he landed one home upon the dwarf's shoulder, leaving a thin line in the steel that drew the mercenary's attention.

"Oh, yah?" The dwarf smiled, his long, brown mustache and beard shaking. The beard was braided at the bottom, and his bushy hair was ponytailed in the back. He wore weathered armor, steel with a dirty sort of look, and his eyes carried little spots of brown in the middle of large white eyeballs. "Then I'll tell you that you move faster than most humans I've met."

"So long as we're forming this fine mutual admiration society," Cyrus said, meeting the hammer's head with Praelior again, blocking the dwarf's attempt to crush his skull, but at the cost of sending a jarring pain through both of Cyrus's arms, "I'll tell you that your hammer is quite impressive, even for a mystical weapon. Most of them I've met can't stand up to my sword."

"Big strapping fellow like you, dressed all in black? I'm surprised your foes don't all run away from you screaming in terror." The dwarf pivoted around and landed a blow under Cyrus's exposed armpit as he was stepping into a swing of his blade. Cyrus felt the armor hold but ram, hard, into his ribs. They cracked and felt the searing agony run through his side, gritting his teeth, trying to keep the pain from overwhelming him. The dwarf pressed forward, lifting his hammer over his head for a killing blow, but Cyrus used Praelior to deflect the strike, whirling away from the paladin.

"I believe you're mocking me, sir," Cyrus said, tasting blood in his mouth. A quick glance around the battlefield found the Syloreans in panic; they'd turned and engaged J'anda's army thinking it was real and had discovered too late it was not. The Galbadien dragoons were visible behind the dwarf, some already cutting through the Sylorean forces, their upper bodies visible over the heads of the writhing and panicked Sylorean army as the dragoons cut their way through on a charge. Shouts drowned out everything, screams of the defeated and the battle cries of those still standing and fighting. The only difference was in pitch, not volume.

"I believe you're right," the dwarf said without irony. "But it's nothing personal, even though you did just kill my comrades." He brought the hammer down furiously again and Cyrus felt the impact as he blocked it with his sword.

Being on the defensive is not a good strategy for this fight, Cyrus thought. *I need a healing spell.* "The Syloreans are faltering." Cyrus sidestepped another vertical attack from the dwarf. "Without you and your friends to save them, the Galbadien army will break them." Cyrus lunged forward as the dwarf was turning to swing his hammer around again. Cyrus's attack ran right along the seam of the dwarf's waist, and he felt it hit chainmail; the dwarf halted his attack and tried to back off, toddling backward on his short legs. "Where do you think you're going?"

"Away." The dwarf swung his hammer with one hand and Cyrus was forced to step back. The dwarf raised his other hand and white light coursed down his side, a small healing spell. The dwarf smirked at him. "Just for a second though, lad. I wouldn't want to step out on you before I've killed you, after all."

"Not much chance of that." Cyrus came at him again, ignoring the pain in his ribs, embracing the agony, letting it enrage him.

"Why?" The dwarf smiled, that irritating smile. "Do you think your friends'll be saving you? Because I don't."

"Oh, yeah?" Cyrus brought his blade down and it clanged against the head of the hammer, and he raised it and brought it down again, this time cutting centimeters into the handle. "Why's that?"

"Because ..." the dwarf said, bringing his hammer up and hitting Cyrus in the nose with the handle, "... Curatio there is far too busy trying to rally your spellcasters to keep the Sylorean army from turning around and stampeding through you lot on their retreat."

Cyrus staggered back, stunned by both the blow to his face and dimly aware that the dwarf had called Curatio by name. He glanced back, a quick turn of the head and saw that it was true; the healer was with the spellcasters, flames were rippling in careful lines across the plains, turning back the tide of screaming Syloreans as the Galbadien dragoons continued to cut through their ranks. Cyrus turned back to the dwarf and over the little man's shoulder he saw the Sanctuary army, the bulk of it, burrowing into the footmen in the center of the melee while the dragoons drove through the flanks of the Sylorean army.

"So you're from Sanctuary, eh?" The dwarf leered at him, little half-smile wicked upon his face. "You're a long way from the Plains of Perdamun, lad." He balanced the hammer in his hand, bouncing it with one hand and letting the handle slap his palm in the other as he advanced toward Cyrus slowly. "A long damned way you came just to try and kill me and mine."

"I killed yours," Cyrus said, trying to shake off the disorientation. Blood flowed freely from his nose down his lips and every word he spoke let more of it run into his mouth, the hard, metallic taste of it drowning out all else. "Now all that's left is to kill you."

The dwarf chuckled, his small frame gyrating slightly from the laugh. "Easier said than followed through with." He extended the hammer with one hand and pointed it at Cyrus. "But if you want to give it a try, now seems the opportune moment."

Cyrus clutched Praelior in both hands, holding it defensively. "I've been known to do dumb things," he said, staring the dwarf down, "but attacking a strong adversary to no purpose while I'm injured isn't one of them."

"Let me give you reason, then." The dwarf held up his palm and Cyrus nearly flinched as another blast of force hit him before he could dodge.

The spell made contact with his shoulder as it passed and jerked him around in a half-circle before leaving him to come to rest on the ground. He felt the numbness in his arm from the blast, and clenched his other fist to find he had, in fact, held onto his sword. He rolled to the side as the hammer landed in the mud where he had lain, splattering his armor from the force of impact. The hammer came down again as Cyrus rolled to a knee, this blow missing him by only inches.

Cyrus saw Terian, a half-dozen paces away, the flames from the spellcasters behind him, a wall of fire keeping the army of Syloreas from retreating. The dark knight stared at him, blade in hand. Smoke was everywhere, black clouds that drifted lazily around him. "Terian," Cyrus said. "Help me!"

Terian did not move, and Cyrus cocked his head at the dark elf, who stood still, watching. Cyrus started to call out to him again but the hammer hit him in the face, a short, fast stab that landed on Cyrus's already-wounded nose and caused a flash in his eyes. He blinked and realized he was on the ground and the dwarf was over him, brandishing the hammer.

"Friends, eh?" The dwarf said, shaking his head. "Guildmates, yah? Someday, lad, maybe if you grow wise, you'll realize that you really can't rely on anyone but yourself." The dwarf chuckled. "'Course, that'd mean living long enough to learn from your mistakes." He hefted the hammer on his shoulder. "Best of luck with that."

The dwarf raised the hammer above his head and brought it down on Cyrus, a full-force swing from on high. Cyrus watched it come down, the arc slow and graceful, and wondered what it would feel like when it—

Chapter 19

Vara

Four Months Later

There was a thundering sound, somewhere far above Vara, and one of the people across the foyer let out a shriek that overpowered the moans of the last few unhealed wounded. "Those damnable catapults," she said, meaning it. The smell of smoke drifted in from outside, so thick she could taste it. The weight of her armor felt heavy on her shoulders, and it was seldom ever a bother.

"What has happened here?" Ryin Ayend stared around the foyer, the stone that had burst the window only moments earlier was still sitting in the Great Hall, in the midst of splintered tables.

"We are under siege," Alaric answered him, crossing the distance between them and placing a hand on Ryin's shoulder. "I am most pleased to see you, my brother, but unfortunately the news you bear will have to wait, unless you have anything life-threatening to tell us?"

"Not exactly," Ryin said. "But I was sent back to let you know—"

Another thunderous roar filled the room as the entirety of Sanctuary quaked to the foundations. There was a moment's respite from the fury and then the earth shook again so violently Vara was only just able to keep her footing. Others were not so lucky and landed on the floor in a heap.

"If I am not mistaken, we have just lost the southwest tower to a bombardment," Alaric said, much more calmly than Vara felt.

"Lucky shot," Vaste said, pulling himself to his feet. "There's no way that was intentional, not with a catapult. Those things are hideously inaccurate."

"You don't have to be that accurate when you're firing a ton of stone." A voice whipped through the room and Vara saw Erith Frostmoor, a dark elven healer, cut down the stairs and take in the foyer in one glance. "I was on the battlements—we did lose the southwest tower, and it was a lucky shot, but the boulders they're firing at us are bigger than any I've seen heaved from a catapult before. Two lucky hits and the tower came down, along with whoever was in it at the time."

"Applicant quarters," Vaste said. "Gods, that'll be messy."

"Healers," Alaric said, looking to Erith and Vaste, "get to the wreckage of the tower and begin pulling the dead and wounded out. Any able-bodied warriors should join you. Rangers, I'll need with me," he said, voice tight, "along with anyone who can cast a spell. I believe it is time to give the dark elven host a taste of our fury."

"Taste of our fury?" Vaste said with a frown. "That sounds awfully cheesy, Alaric. Why don't you give them a taste of our bread and stew while you're at it?"

"Because at this point our bread and stew are in a puddle on the floor of the Great Hall," Larana whispered, so low only Vara heard her.

"Spellcasters," Alaric said, "with me. All others, to your duties."

Alaric was on the run, out the door and descending the great stone stairs that led to the grounds of Sanctuary. Green grasses of summer had grown in thick, and the sun was shining overhead as Vara ran across the grounds, a few steps behind her Guildmaster. It was a wide lawn, a massive open space in the land surrounded by Sanctuary's curtain wall, big enough that it protected the enormous stables, a garden out back, a cemetery, an archery range, and other outbuildings that were not part of Sanctuary's main structure.

The curtain wall was tall enough for them to repel a siege from, at least with archers and spellcasters and swords enough to fight off ladder-climbing invaders and siege towers. *But not as tall as I would have made it,* she thought. *For this I would have preferred walls that stretched halfway to the sky, as can be found in Pharesia. Or a moat around the whole thing would be a wonderful defense, rather than simply letting them roll their damnable siege engines up to the wall and have at it.* "What is our plan, Alaric?" she asked, wondering if she would catch the old knight's attention.

"Their army is of little threat to us at present," Alaric said. "But their catapults and siege towers present a slight problem. So we will deal with them."

"A 'slight problem'?" She looked at him in astonishment, but he did not turn back to acknowledge her, merely kept running toward the wall. A stream of others following his orders trailed closely behind and the smell of fire and smoke was strong the closer they got to the wall. "Alaric, they just sent the bloody southwest tower crashing to the ground! They launched a boulder into our foyer. If that is only a slight problem, then I fear the day that we face your definition of a major one."

"Yes," Alaric said, "I fear that day as well."

They reached the wall, slipping into the interior of the heavy stone structure by means of a tower door. The wall was miles long and had passages with rooms and accommodations inside the towers that were placed at intervals along the length of it. Its thickness, with a solid mass of stone at the front, was able to stop most projectiles, but toward the interior facing, it made way for a corridor that spanned between the towers. Alaric started up a spiral staircase inside the tower, striding out into the bright daylight when he reached the top. Throughout, Vara followed on his heels, as close as she could keep up to the Guildmaster, who moved faster than his venerable appearance would have indicated he could. But then, she had long ago learned she should not underestimate Alaric.

When she stepped out into the sunlight on top of the wall, the roar reached her ears again, filling them with the sounds of thousands of voices. It was a cacophony of anger and fury coming from the army outside the walls, their battle lines formed in neat rows that Vara could see from where she stood far above them. They filled the plains around Sanctuary, more numerous than she could count, an army arrayed around them for one purpose alone—to break down the walls, sack Sanctuary, and parade the survivors along a celebratory death march back to Saekaj Sovar for the pleasure of their Sovereign. *I'll be certain to be good and dead if Sanctuary falls,* she thought with a shudder. *Surviving would bring with it unpleasantries I'd just as soon not deal with.*

The wall was lined with bowmen, rangers who had strung their weapons and were loosing a tide of arrows down into the army below every few seconds while using the battlements for cover from the counter barrage of arrows. A shout made its way over the cry of the army below, and Thad, the castellan of Sanctuary, giving the orders to the defenders of the wall, cried out over the carnage, "Aim for the towers! Kill the dark elves pushing them!"

Vara came to the edge of the battlement and glanced out. Wooden towers built to the height of the curtain wall were sliding over the uneven ground, born along by the efforts of soldiers below. She looked left, toward the gate, and saw a battering ram working at the front as boiling oil was poured down upon it. A hundred catapults and trebuchets stood further back, behind the first ranks of the army, launching all manner of abuse into the air in addition to a rain of arrows that was being sent at the Sanctuary defenders. Vara ducked behind a rampart as an arrow missed her face by a matter of inches. "I do so love the weather we're having today," she said. "Pleasant enough temperature for summer, not overwhelmingly hot, not a cloud in the sky, unless you count the clouds of arrows—and I do."

Alaric remained standing, tall, above the battlements, and an arrow flew past him, followed by another. Before Vara could cry out, one shot through his head, passing through him as neatly as if it had gone through another stretch of empty air. The Ghost did not even seem to notice it, though Vara felt the cry of warning and alarm die on her lips. "Weather aside, I hope we have a healer upon these battlements for those who are not quite as ephemeral as myself."

"Ephemeral?" Vara stared at his receding back. "You just had an arrow fly through your head as though it weren't there."

"Which?" Alaric asked, halting to look back at her. "The arrow or my head? Because I've heard the latter mentioned to me before once or twice—in insult, usually."

"Bugger it," Vara said and charged to the next tooth in the wall, now only a few feet from where Alaric stood next to Thad, who was taking advantage of the cover offered by the crenellations. When a swarm of arrows landed around her, soaring through the gaps, she took to hands and knees, crawling the last few feet, shoving the bowmen out of the way as she passed.

"Lass," Alaric said as she crawled up to crouch behind the crenellation beside Thad, "it would seem you've found a somewhat undignified way of hiding from the arrows."

"Not all of us have insubstantial heads," she said in irritation. "And I don't want my quite substantial brains splattered all over the wall whilst I have no idea where the nearest healer may be."

"Right here," came a dull, accented voice from behind Thad. Vara leaned out, briefly, to see Andren, the scruffy elven healer, his back against a fortification, a flask in his hand as he calmly took a drink. A strong smell of booze reached her nostrils. Andren's long, dark hair was tangled even moreso than usual. His beard was thick and seemed to have grown thicker in the last months, as though he were unconcerned about keeping it groomed at all. The bushy beard and long, tangled hair coupled with his white, frayed and dirtied healer's robe, gave him the look of one of the vagrants found in human cities—*and not at all like an elf should look.*

"A sober healer," she said. "I'd like one competent enough to perform a spell."

"Oh, so that's how it is," Andren said mildly, sticking his fingers out and waving them in the general direction of a human a half dozen paces away who was screaming with an arrow sticking out of his palm. "I'm quite competent."

"I said competent and sober."

"Meh," Andren said with some indifference. "I'll pass on that last one; highly overrated, especially when you're being bombarded with arrows, projectiles, and some fairly wounding insults, in the case of you."

"Thad," Alaric said, cutting off any response Vara might have made, "it would appear they've begun the assault on our gate."

Thad smiled weakly. The younger warrior was human and clad in crimson armor, the steel bearing chipped paint that revealed the metal beneath. He had always reminded Vara of a younger, less adept and perhaps less handsome version of Cyrus. *And for that, especially now, I hate him.* "I guess you could say that. They started moving toward us with intent about fifteen minutes ago. Before that, they seemed quite comfortable to maintain their distance and keep us blockaded."

"They've clearly changed to a war footing," Vara said, watching one of the siege towers drawing close to the edge of the ramparts, "and I'd be fascinated to discuss how exactly that happened, but I'd rather do it after we've put these bastards to rest and repelled them."

"Indeed," Alaric said, and gestured behind himself. Vara turned to see a line of spellcasters—druids, wizards and a few enchanters making their way across the wall, taking positions of their own next to the bowmen at the ramparts. Larana was among them and truthfully the only one among them whose name Vara knew; all the rest were new people who had been recruited in the last few years. *New people that I have to get to know and remember the names of. Is there any more annoying bane anywhere in my existence?* The thought of the black-armored warrior flashed through her mind. *Oh yes. Well, in the scale of things, he's still rather new, I suppose.*

"Let us dispense with this bombardment, shall we?" Alaric stood in the gap between the crenellations as Vara exchanged a look with Thad. "When I signal, spellcasters, unleash hell upon those towers."

"What's the signal?" Thad asked then flushed under his helm as Vara sent him a searing look.

"I think this will do," Alaric said and extended his hand in the direction of the tower, which was creeping toward the wall only fifteen feet or so away from deploying its bridge to allow the troops within to storm the Sanctuary battlements.

Vara let out a scream of pure fury and stood in the gap next to Alaric. *Bombard my home from afar, will you? Send your mindless foot soldiers to knock down our wall and drag us out? I shall show you, oh Sovereign, you bastard of bastards, you terrible and daft ruler of mine enemies.* She threw out her hand and began to cast a spell of her own, just as Alaric's went off, an incantation leaving his palm that shook the ramparts and blasted the stray strands of hair out of Vara's face as it flew.

She watched the wave of force fly, distorting the air in a line following from Alaric's palm to the siege tower, where it impacted a third of the way up the structure. The impact was immediate and obvious; the wooden tower splintered, chips exploding outward and showering the army below with splinters as a fearsome groan of breaking logs preceded the awful listing of the whole structure, which began to tilt forward. Cries from behind the rectangular creation's wooden facade told her that the occupants of the thing knew what was coming and were perhaps powerless to stop it.

The whole contraption came crashing to the ground, the upper two-thirds tilting down, falling upon the army stacked up beneath it. Vara saw a wave of movement as the soldiers beneath it tried to flee, but it seemed unlikely that any of them made it through the panicked crowd; the crash of the tower splattered a hundred or more men beneath its shadow and pulped countless more who had been inside it.

With Alaric's blast, a wave of spells leapt forward from the Sanctuary battlements—fireballs and bolts of lightning seemed the most popular choices. Vara saw the pale flash of a few charms fly from the enchanter ranks and watched as they took possession of the biggest and strongest warriors below them in the field, turning them against their own allies, the swords and daggers of the Sovereign's own turning against their fellows. Vara saw Larana loose a particularly large blast of fire at a catapult that was several hundred feet back from the wall and it hit with the same force as Alaric's burst, if not more; an explosion seemed to follow, launching the operators of the contraption away in flames and turning the whole thing into a pyre that blazed thirty feet high.

Vara's own spell hit a bevy of soldiers below the wall, pushing them to the ground. She looked over to see Alaric had moved farther down the wall. His hand pointed at another tower as it burst, showering the army below with fragments of wooden refuse as it tilted and cracked, falling apart onto the dark elves in its shadow. She saw her Guildmaster begin his run down the wall, heading toward his next target, another siege tower.

"Has this been going on the entire time we've been gone?" Vara looked up to see Ryin Ayend, who had asked the question. He slid in beside her, behind the crenellation, as he loosed a fireball at a distant trebuchet, setting fire to the launch mechanism and sending its crew scurrying away. "You haven't been under siege the whole time, have you?" he asked.

"No," she said and fired another stunning blast at a thick cluster of archers, sending five of them to the ground, unconscious. "This army only showed up in the last few days, malingering at the edge of the horizon, interdicting travelers that came our way." She pointed at a tent in the distance. "They've been interrupting the flow of our applicants, however, and we were debating what to do about it."

"It's an army," Ryin said, shooting another fireball at the same trebuchet he had disabled a moment earlier. The flames from his burst began to lick at the contraption, and it caught fire after a moment's hesitation, causing the druid to smile. "They don't tend to spring forth out of nowhere, especially when the dark elves are already at war with the Human Confederation and the Elven Kingdom. What happened?"

"What indeed?" Vara muttered, so low she doubted he would have heard her. "The army comes from Aloakna, on the coast. The dark elves sacked the town a fortnight ago with a host of fifty thousand."

"What?" Ryin's eyes grew large; the human's face was almost innocent, awestruck. "Aloakna is a neutral city! Why would they destroy it? They were a major trading partner to the dark elves."

"And the elves, and the humans," Vara said. "They didn't have much of a standing army, relying on being neutral to protect them. By the accounts we heard, whatever mercenaries and guards they had on hand put up a spirited defense, but to little avail. The city was sacked inside of a week of siege, and the dark elves showed little mercy to the occupants, killing and raping in mass number, conscripting some of the surviving dark elven men into their army." She felt her expression harden. "Then they came here."

"But why here?" Ryin asked. "They have armies stalled in their advances against the elves in Termina and the humans in Reikonos still?" He waited for her to nod assent. "Why waste time on us now?"

A crashing sound interrupted her answer; in the distance, a catapult exploded as a result of Larana's attack and another siege tower crashed to pieces down the wall. Below them, the dark elven army was in chaos as their own soldiers randomly turned against them, guided by Sanctuary's enchanters. Vara watched as a hulking dark elf in heavy armor swung a mace through the heads of three of his comrades, splintering them, before he was brought down by a swarming attack of swords by several of his fellows.

"I daresay the Sovereign didn't think he was wasting time," Vara said with a slight smile. "After all, when you send a host of fifty thousand to attack something so small as Sanctuary, you likely think that your target will disappear from the map without difficulty."

"But he knows we have the power of magic," Ryin scoffed. "He's not stupid, is he?"

A bolt of lightning arced down from one of Sanctuary's wizards into the crowd below, crackling as it jumped from the metal armor of a whole platoon of men-at-arms, causing them all to fall, if not dead then at least unconscious. "I doubt it," Vara said. "He's been making some exceedingly shrewd moves thus far in the war, and they've been incredibly audacious ones at times, but we keep hoping he'll overreach." She let a grim smile come across her features. "Perhaps he finally has." She let the smile fade. "And you lot? You've been gone six months, longer than you had any right to be without letting us know anything. What the blazes happened to you?"

Ryin's expression turned pained, and for a moment they were both distracted by the explosion of another catapult in the distance. The armies at the foot of the wall were beginning to recede now, slowly pulling back, the lines breaking as the more fearful among them started to retreat. "They're leaving," Ryin said, watching, almost spellbound, as fire and lightning chased them away, a flurry of arrows felling whole lines of dark elves as they retreated in no formation at all while a few of their brethren remained behind, standing near the wall, motionless, still under the control of the Sanctuary enchanters.

"They'll be back," Alaric said, appearing behind them from within a fog, coalescing into his shape of armor and man, the expression on his face grim and unsatisfied. "Now that the Sovereign has an eye fixed on Sanctuary, he'll send more, make no mistake. They'll withdraw to a safe distance, interdict our new applicants, and bottle us up until their next hammerblow falls."

"Where are the rest of your number?" Vara asked, turning back to Ryin. "With them, we could make an attack, drive the enemy back. They could increase our ranks by a third again, and all blooded veterans now, yes?"

"Yes," Ryin said, "they've certainly seen battle. But ... they sent me to tell you what happened."

"Did you not go to aid Longwell's father?" Vara jumped in before Alaric could ask a question.

"We did," Ryin said, "and we succeeded in defeating his enemies—well, of a sort, anyway—"

"By all the gods, get on with it man," Vara said, drawing a look of severe irritation from Ryin. "What happened? Did you beat the army that was invading them or not?"

"We did," Ryin said with a sort of haunted quiet. He looked out over the wreckage of the battlefield and Vara's gaze followed his over the ramparts. There were bodies, countless, armored, cloth-clad, and filling the ground for several hundred yards away from the wall. "We fought a battle at a place called Harrow's Crossing, and we crushed the armies that were at the throats of Longwell's people."

"Very good," Vara said brusquely, "and yet I see no army here, save for you, so I must ask again—what ... happened?"

"Perhaps if you remained silent and let him explain," Alaric said, drawing Vara's searing irritation to her Guildmaster in the form of a glare.

I want to know where he is. Vara scowled. *The man's been gone for months, and when he finally sends a messenger, we get the bloody slowest of druids, a man who can't seem to form a non-contrarian thought to save his unblessed soul.* "Fine," she said. "I'm waiting, though. You beat them at this place ... this ... Harrow's Crossing? Defeated their enemies? Sent them scattering in utmost defeat?"

"We did," Ryin said, and the smell of the fires began to waft in off the battlefield, causing Vara to cough quite unexpectedly. "It was masterful. Cyrus came up with a brilliant strategy to defeat the superior odds that were waiting for us in ambush."

The druid smiled, and Vara wanted to slap him, to grasp him by the shoulders and shake him until the words she wanted to hear finally came out—*That he's alive and well. That they'll be teleporting in later tonight, or perhaps tomorrow, hardened, veteran, ready to help us get about the business of throwing back this siege.*

"But there was a problem after that," Ryin said, interrupting her thoughts. "They won't be back for quite a while."

Vara felt the sudden pain, felt it where she least wanted to, and knew it affected her the way she didn't care for it to, could tell in the sag of her face that she was exposing undesired emotion. *I won't ask about him. I won't. I'll wait, and he'll tell us, tell us all, and I won't have to ask. Because, after all, the general is with his troops, he couldn't leave without them, of course, he wouldn't ...* She tried to straighten her expression, tried to change it, but she was sure it ended up as a cringe.

Ryin went on, apparently oblivious to everything she knew was written over every inch of her face. "We ran into ... well ..." He hesitated. "We ran into a bit of a snag."

"A snag?" Alaric spoke in the nick of time, halting the inevitable and fast approaching scream that Vara felt building, the pressure ready to cause her to explode. "Perhaps you could be more specific, brother."

Ryin's head bowed slightly. "All right. Well. The thing is, we beat the Kingdom of Syloreas in the battle. But there was another problem after that."

"Oh for the gods' sakes, man!" Vara blurted out, drawing every eye on the battlements around them and causing Ryin to take a step back. "Will you stop bloody stalling and get right the hell on with it? Is he all right? Did Cyrus die?"

"Yes," Ryin said. "He died at Harrow's Crossing, but he's been resurrected from that." Vara felt some of the tightness in her chest subside, only to be replaced by a deeper, more painful sensation only a moment later as Ryin went on. "But to answer your other question ..." Ayend's face drew tight again, seemingly unready to part with the information, as though it pained him to do so. "... He is most certainly not all right."

Chapter 20

Cyrus
4 Months Earlier

"Get up," Cyrus heard the sound of joy in the voice as he stirred back to life. "We've won." He blinked his eyes, and there was a thin sheen of smoke and haze before them. Acrid burning smells filled his nostrils, and he choked on the sharp, sour taste of blood in his mouth. Nausea overcame him and he leaned over, vomiting up everything he had ever eaten, the acid and bile leaving him gagging, lying on one shoulder, face half-buried in the mud and vomit.

"It's not quite that easy to shake off," Cyrus heard but couldn't turn to look. The nausea returned and he tried to throw up again, but only spittle and base liquid came out, and he rested his cheek again in the mud. "Coming back to life isn't as easy as walking across a village street; it's death, and there's a price to be paid in vitality and body when you come back this way. It is not a cheap price, either." Cyrus recognized Curatio's voice as the one speaking; he was lost as to who the other might be.

"We've won a great victory here." The other speaker was talking again. The voice was damnably familiar, and Cyrus struggled to roll to his back so he could look up. "All thanks to you lot. Excellent strategy, and you did it perfectly, held them in place for us to hit them." Cyrus's vision cleared, and he recognized Count Ranson standing above him, smiling for the first time since they'd met. "He should be up and celebrating with us; we've routed the Sylorean army and sent them running north in disarray, their mercenaries gone."

"Give me a minute," Cyrus said, his voice hoarse.

"Take your time," Curatio said. "That was no gentle blow you took; Partus crushed your head before he went running off."

"Partus?" Cyrus asked. "That dwarf, that was his name, wasn't it?" Cyrus waited until Curatio nodded, a short, sharp jerk of his head. "Why does that name sound so familiar?"

The healer pursed his lips, his expression guarded. "Because he was the Guildmaster of the Daring once upon a time. He took their most experienced members and fled to Goliath around the time you joined us."

"Partus," Cyrus said. "I've heard Erith curse his name."

"As well she should," Terian's voice came from above him, and the dark elf's face appeared in view next to Ranson. "He's a strong paladin; maybe the most powerful I've ever met, save for Alaric."

"I could have used your help back there," Cyrus rasped, looking at the dark knight. "I called out to you."

"Sorry about that," Terian said. "I was about to be overrun by the Sylorean army, so I was watching my back because I knew the flames were about to die. Sure enough, they did." He ran a hand through his long, stringy black hair. "When I looked up again, he'd already killed you and escaped."

"Dammit." Cyrus tried to sit up and felt all his stomach muscles involuntarily contract, causing him to heave again. When he finished, he wiped his mouth on his gauntlet, feeling the mud from his hand stick to his face. "He got away?"

"He did," Curatio said. "We were badly disorganized after his first spell, the one that knocked half of us out of the fight. I managed to get our spellcasters in place to contain the armies, but there was no one left to stop him. He bounded off like a rabbit after he killed you, slipped over the bridge in the chaos."

"Did any of the Sylorean army get away?" Cyrus took Ranson and Curatio's proffered hands and let them pull him to his feet.

"Perhaps a quarter of them," Ranson said with the same smile. "I've got my army in pursuit, and messengers have already come back to tell me we've dispatched a good many of them. They've no horses, no provisions, and we managed to kill their generals." The count folded his arms in front of him. "I expect fewer than one man in ten who entered this battle on their side will ever see his homeland again."

"I suppose that's some sort of worthy accomplishment," Cyrus said without any enthusiasm. "Kingdom defended, mission accomplished." He felt the heart go out of his joy. "Now we can go home, I suppose."

"I wouldn't be so quick to leave," Curatio said. "Partus is still out there and he can be one devilish nuisance if he were to rejoin the

Syloreans." The healer looked to the Count. "Do they still have a functioning army up in the north?"

The count shrugged. "Aye, they do. I'll grant you, I still fear that half-man, but without an army at his back he stands much less chance of causing us ulcers."

"Dammit," Cyrus said. "Let's get a tracking party together. Does he have a horse?"

"I didn't see him take one," Terian said with a shrug. "Doesn't mean he didn't get one later, but I think he went over the bridge on foot."

"He won't have made it far on those stubby legs," Cyrus said. "We can run him down on horseback." He looked around. "Where's Windrider?" The horse appeared out of a cluster of mares a few feet away with a whinny, prompting Cyrus to smile. "Never far, that's for certain."

"I'll go with you," Terian said, sliding his blade out of his scabbard. "Should be easier to bring down a white knight if you've got a black knight alongside you."

"All right," Cyrus said with a nod. "Next time when I call for help, you'll be there, though, right?"

Terian rolled his eyes. "No. I'm going to let you die, purposefully and horribly, just like this time. What do you think?"

Cyrus stared at him blankly. "Well … okay, then. Where's Longwell?"

"Over here," came a weak voice, and Cyrus turned to see the dragoon sitting with his head between his legs a few feet away, also covered in mud. Longwell's head came up, also caked in mud, and he looked pale as a cloud. "Count me among those hit by that bastard's spell; I went flying and my horse landed on top of me with all the force of a tree falling on a mushroom." He put his hand over his mouth. "Ugh. Shouldn't have mentioned food."

"And Martaina?" Cyrus asked. "We'll need a tracker." A hand went up a few feet away from Longwell, and Cyrus barely recognized the elven woman; her garb was normally predisposed to blending in with the dirt and greenery of nature, but now it was caked in mud, along with her face and hair. "Did a horse land on you, too?"

"Not a horse," Martaina said. "I'm pretty sure it was an elephant.

At least that's what it felt like when it hit me, after a nice, long, lazy end-over-end flight through the air." She shook her head and looked at Curatio pityingly. "Did you resurrect my horse?"

"I did," Curatio said, "but you'll likely not want to be riding her for a bit. Keep in mind she probably feels as bad or worse than you do."

"I'll go with you," Martaina said, "but I don't know how well I'll be able to track at the moment. It's delicate, sensitive work, filled with subtlety and nuance." She hung her head. "Right now I feel like I just want to fill a bucket with everything I've ever eaten in my thousands of years of life." She retched. "Which would take quite a bit of force, and I feel it coming on."

"I'll go with you," came a soft voice from behind Cyrus. He turned to see a shapely leg, clad in smooth leather, make its way in front of him. He raised his head to see Aisling, her arms folded across her belly, as though she were trying to push up her small breasts. "I'm a fair tracker; not as good as Martaina at her best, but good enough to sift out some dwarf from a running army of men."

"You sure?" Cyrus asked as he hoisted himself up into the saddle. "I don't want there to be any tension—"

"What tension?" she asked with a forced smile.

"I recommend you wait a little longer," Curatio said, looking up at Cyrus on horseback. "Some of you are going to be feeling poorly for a while yet."

"I can feel poorly sitting here on the ground doing nothing," Cyrus said, "or on a horse, tracking down the miniaturized bastard who killed me. I pick the latter, if only because it dispels that ugly sensation that sitting on one's backside brings when there's unpleasant work to be done."

It took a few more minutes to get a hunting party saddled and ready to ride. Cyrus looked around the battlefield, beheld the smoke and carnage. The dragoons had hit the Sylorean lines hard. With their retreat cut off by the spellcasters' fire magic, the horsed riders had cut the unhorsed and lightly armored infantry to pieces. Even the men-at-war, wearing armor considerably heavier than Cyrus's (and much more constrictive, judging by its somewhat primitive design) had been struck down by the dragoons, who had used their lances to knock over the poorly balanced warriors and finished the job later or let the mud do it for them.

The hunting party rode out across the bridge, Cyrus noting how badly muddied the grasslands had become. Horse hooves had ripped the soil, leaving dark marks where greenery had been only hours before. The smell of upturned earth had a rich, deep aroma that reminded Cyrus of the gardens at Sanctuary. The sky held a grey tinge, clouds masking the sun from shining down. It seemed appropriate to Cyrus that the sun shouldn't shine down brightly, that the sky shouldn't be blue; after all, thousands of men had died only an hour earlier. *Nature could not find much cause for glory and celebration in that.*

"So this is it?"

It was Terian who spoke, jarring Cyrus out of his daze. He turned to see the dark elf keeping pace next to him. Martaina and Aisling rode in front, the former still looking as green as her usual clothing and the latter keeping a close watch on the muddy ground ahead of them. "We go home after this?"

"I suppose," Cyrus said. "So long as we get this dwarf, then the Kingdom is saved. And we're back to whiling away the days in the Plains of Perdamun, trying to find new targets to hit and places to explore for our own edification and whatever treasures we can pillory." He shrugged. "Or I suppose we could get involved in the war again, though I doubt there's much edification or gold to be had from walking that road."

"I doubt we'll avoid it," Terian said. "The Sovereign is doubtless upset with us, to make no mention of the fact that you killed countless of his soldiers while defending Termina. It seems likely that my people will seek revenge if they know who inflicted those losses upon them."

"I didn't invade their territory looking for a fight," Cyrus said. "The elves didn't even invade their lands. The dark elves decided to start a war of conquest against their neighbors, and I happened to be standing in the way. You can't tell me you wouldn't have been on that bridge with me, trying to keep your people from raping and pillaging the town."

Terian looked at him, hard, a strange burning in his eyes, and when he spoke, his voice was broken. "No. I can't say I wouldn't have been with you. After all, we are ... friends. Comrades at arms."

"And you wouldn't have done it yourself, even if I hadn't been there?" Cyrus didn't look at the dark elf. "You wouldn't have tried to protect those people yourself, just because it was the right thing to do?"

"I ..." Terian choked down whatever he was about to say, and Cyrus turned to look at the dark knight, who was strangely animated; his mouth opened and it looked as though he were trying to speak, but nothing came forth at first. When it did, it was low, hoarse, and barely understandable. Cyrus had to concentrate to hear him, tuning out the sound of hoof beats, of laughter from Ryin somewhere behind him, of someone else heaving from atop their horse. "Dark knights aren't quite as fond of hopeless causes or helping the defenseless as you are. I don't ... I mean, they were elves, and my people are enemies of the elves—"

"You work with elves every day," Cyrus cut him off. "You've saved their lives. You've fought for them. You're a member of Sanctuary, Terian. If you wanted solely to enrich yourself, the big three would gladly take you on. Hells, man, you could even make a fortune plundering in the dark elven army, like some others do." Cyrus noted Terian's face become stricken, but he went on. "But you're here with us. You could be anywhere, but you're with us. Not where you could become the wealthiest, not where you could seek the most power, but here in Sanctuary. Can you tell me why you'd voluntarily come back if not to 'help the defenseless' and fight for 'hopeless causes'?"

The dark knight's mouth opened and closed again several times, but no discernible noise came out that Cyrus heard. Terian's eyes blinked repeatedly, and he finally stopped trying, closing his mouth, turning to look straight ahead. After a long silence he finally said. "That's really an excellent question."

Cyrus waited for him to elaborate and when he did not, the warrior shrugged and continued riding. The dwarf's trail carried them over plains, lightly rolling hills that began to trend further and further downward, until they finally came to the edge of a swamp.

"Gods, it smells like troll town in there," Terian said, holding his nose.

"That's not very nice," Nyad scolded him. Her red cloak was stained with mud, and her usually relaxed expression was gone, replaced by one that was quite cross.

"Not nice but accurate," the dark knight said. "Have you ever been to Gren? No? Then shut up."

"Curb your tongue, dark knight," Ryin said darkly. "There's no cause for rudeness."

"There's no use in your bedchamber wench being offended for the whole troll race and snapping at me either, but she did." Terian pulled back on the reins of his horse, turning it around to face the druid. "Keep your bitch on her leash; even Vaste wouldn't have taken umbrage at such a simple observation."

"All of you—shut up." Aisling's voice cut through the argument, silencing all three officers at once. Cyrus raised an eyebrow as the dark elf dismounted her horse and crouched by the edge of the water. The swamp's edge was murky water, brown and shallow, a pool the size of the Sanctuary foyer, broken by small hummocks of trees and land that broke out of the mire. She stood and looked up to Martaina. "How long would you say?"

"Fifteen minutes at most," the ranger answered. "Probably more like ten. The water looks shallow enough that I may be able to keep up with his footprints." She straightened in her saddle. "Doubt the rest of you will be able to see them, though."

"I don't need to see them so long as you can," Cyrus said. "Let's keep going."

Their progress was slowed as Martaina stared into the muck. They went along at a slower pace, the elf squinting into the water, pausing every few minutes, trying to decipher the dwarf's path. "He's leaving heavy impressions in the mud beneath the surface. He's not running anymore, but he's still … jogging, I would say. Walking fast. He's also limping a little now, maybe from an injury or a cramp."

"That's amazing," Terian said, holding his horse back at a distance with the others while Martaina and Aisling tried to decipher the trail. "Can you tell what he had for breakfast this morning, too?"

"If we follow him long enough, we'll find some evidence of that," Martaina said, not breaking away from her staring contest with the water. "This way."

The water dried up ahead, and a set of tracks led them forward, cypress trees sticking out of the sodden ground around them. "It would appear we're experiencing a drought," Longwell said from behind Cyrus. "This swamp is usually considerably farther underwater, near impassable on horseback."

"Too bad for us," Mendicant said. "If the water were any higher, it might have stopped him from passing this way."

"Yeah, you short folk don't tend to like to get wet, do you?" Terian asked.

"It doesn't take much for us to get in over our heads," the goblin replied. "Rather like this fellow."

The ground got higher for a spell, and the brush around them got thicker as bushes sprang out of the wet ground, the undergrowth and trees slowing their progress. In some cases they were forced to go around; in most, Cyrus felt at least a few low-hanging boughs and branches clatter on his armor and felt a moment's pity for those not wearing any.

"I hear him," Martaina said a few moments later, a small smile turning up the corners of her mouth. "He's not far ahead now, and I don't think he knows we're here. He's slogging along, maybe a thousand feet ahead." She angled her horse slightly to the left. "This way." She pulled her bow out and notched an arrow.

They rode across a small patch of level ground, and when they crested a small hill, Martaina froze, holding up her hand to halt them. She listened intently as the rest of them remained quiet. "Do you hear that?" she asked, a look of intense concentration upon her face.

"I do," Curatio said. "Something in the underbrush ahead, in addition to our dwarven friend."

"What, he's got company?" Terian asked. "Or is there an animal nearby?"

Martaina continued to listen, and cocked her head, befuddlement showing through the mud and dirt on her face. "That doesn't sound like any animal I've ever heard."

Curatio shook his head. "Nor I. But he's not far, we should be able to overtake him now."

"Let's not be too hasty," Cyrus said. "I'd prefer to bring him down before he can throw out one of those spells that sends men and horses flying like kites in the wind. Rangers, ready your bows. Nyad, Mendicant," he turned to acknowledge the two of them, "I want you to cast a cessation spell on him, shut down his ability to cast spells. J'anda," he turned to the enchanter, "mesmerize or charm him if you can. Let's not take any chances on this. It's the last task we have before

us, then we can go back to Vernadam to ..." he cleared his throat, "...
celebrate."

Mild snickers filled the air from those around him, which Cyrus
ignored. "Good for you, sweetie," Nyad said. "I think it's a very healthy
thing you're doing with Cattrine, and you can ignore these naysayers.
They're just jealous because they're all going to back to lonely beds."
J'anda shot her a withering look. "Well, some of them are, anyway."

Cyrus turned back to the path and caught Aisling staring at him.
She looked away and spurred her horse forward. He followed along
with the rest over a hummock that rose to a small hill. When he reached
the top, he started to jerk back on Windrider's reins; Martaina and
Aisling had both stopped abruptly, trying to avoid sliding down the
slope. "What?" Cyrus asked. "The slope's not that bad."

"What is that?" Martaina asked, pointing ahead. The ground before
them dropped down to another patch of flat ground. Cyrus's eyes were
drawn to motion ahead, where something was struggling, and another
figure was on top of it, wrestling in the high grass.

"Looks like our dwarf got tangled up with the local wildlife,"
Cyrus said, urging Windrider ahead. The horse obeyed his gentle
command and galloped down the hill.

As they drew closer to the battle, Cyrus caught glimpses of Partus
struggling, flashes of the dwarf's face, panicked, as something rode his
back and dragged him down again and again. The thing was bizarrely
shaped, like a man crossed with a four-legged beast; its skin was pale,
wet, and slick. Clawed hands grasped at Partus, seizing him, jerking him
back down to the ground behind the high grass, and a face appeared,
something Cyrus caught only a glimpse of before it was gone.

He jerked on Windrider's reins about twenty feet from the
disturbance and the horse reared back, coming to a fast stop within a
few steps. Cyrus dismounted and ran; as he drew closer, the thrashing
between dwarf and the creature was more pronounced.

"Help me!" Partus screamed. He was lifted aloft, and the creature's
face was on his neck, buried, blood streaming down the white flesh.
"HELP!"

Cyrus lunged forward the last few feet. His sword was in his hand,
and he took care not to hit the dwarf as the writhing mass twisted on the
ground. Cyrus brought his sword down on one of the creature's forelegs

and Praelior bit deep into the ghost-white flesh, severing it. The creature halted, unbalanced, Partus still clutched in its mouth, the dwarf screaming, the beast's face hidden by the dwarf's body. It dropped Partus slightly, exposing the upper part of its face; white-grey skin thinly layered over a hairless, dome-like head, roughly human-shaped, but peering above the dwarf's figure were two eyes, black all the way to the edges, and protruding from the skull as though the creature had been choked.

"What the hell is that?" Cyrus heard Terian dismount behind him. Two arrows hit home in the creature's backside, the only part of its body that Partus wasn't shielding with his.

"GET IT OFF ME!" Partus shouted as it dangled him in its teeth, the dwarf hanging from its mouth.

Cyrus strode forward, feinting toward the creature as more arrows landed in its posterior. He took a swipe at it and it retreated. Cyrus took two more steps forward and lunged at the monster, trying to bury his sword in it. He missed the flank and fell, Praelior coming down with him. He hit his knees, catching himself with his palms, and he watched as the creature dropped Partus immediately and used its remaining three limbs to leap at him.

The teeth caught him on the armor, clamping firmly down upon his breastplate and backplate. He saw the creature's mouth, a wide, gaping void, countless teeth, the lips bending outward almost like a beak. Cyrus rolled, sending it writhing through the grass. He kept his grip on his sword, which he brought around in a wide arc and used to lop off the beast's hind leg. It struggled, biting down on him. His armor did not flex at its bite, the steel failing to yield to savage teeth even as the creature jerked its head back and forth on him. The weight of it pushed Cyrus to the ground, and he pulled it down with him.

Cyrus could feel the weight of the thing atop him as he pushed against it on the soft, muddy ground. His left arm was wrapped around the neck of the creature and his right was clutching Praelior. He pushed his blade up, into the stout body of the thing, felt the give as he pushed it through the skin. He felt the monster buck and squirm as it fought his hold, the desperate thrashing growing more maniacal.

After a few seconds, Cyrus felt an impact, and then the body went limp. He rolled it off and sat up, tossing the body aside, the putrid smell of rot in his nose. His hand came up and brushed his hair out of his eyes.

"You all right?" Martaina was at his side, her bow in her hand.

"I'm fine," Cyrus said. He looked to his left to see Longwell, spear in hand, the pointy end still buried in the creature's fat neck. It lay next to him, pressed to the ground. "What the hell was that?"

"I've never seen anything like it," Longwell said, wriggling the tip of his weapon in the creature's neck. "As far as I know it's not native to these parts."

It was upright, its skull and eyes staring blindly up at them. The eyes were still black but unmoving now, and lifeless as well. Cyrus leaned over and stared into them, and something prickled in the back of his mind. "This thing is …" he shuddered. "There's something very disturbing about this creature." He blinked. *And familiar,* he thought. *Something very familiar about it.* "Anyone ever seen anything like this before?"

"Not that I can recall," Curatio said, on his horse a few feet away. "But it seems … I don't know, there's something I can't quite put my finger on, but it seems like something I've run across at some point before."

"I was thinking the same thing," Longwell said, peering at it. "But I didn't want to say it, because I know damned well I've never fought one of them." He poked at it again, causing the body to wriggle with the motion. "I wonder if there are more?"

"It was a nasty bastard," Cyrus said, standing. "But pretty weak overall. If it hadn't gotten me off my feet, I don't think it would have been a huge challenge." He stooped and picked up his helm. "Speaking of challenges …" He turned his head and saw Partus a few feet away, Terian standing next to him with a sword across the dwarf's neck. "There you are, my half-sized, bearded nemesis."

"Here I am," Partus said, his eyes still staring at the creature. "Not planning on going much of anywhere, either. I don't care what you say, that thing damned near got me, and if there's any more, I'm not looking to face them alone, though I might have made a better show of it if your wizards hadn't cessated my damned spells. Anyhow," the dwarf said, hands up, "I suppose I'll be coming with you." He looked up at Terian. "Unless you're planning on being done with it right here and taking my head off."

"So very tempting," Terian said, and let the blade drift into Partus's neck.

"I think not," Cyrus said. "We're not executioners."

"Well, then," Partus began to stand, and Terian kicked the dwarf's legs out from under him, causing him to fall. He lay on his back, staring up. "Oh, so that's how it is, eh? Are you quite finished?"

"I could stand to do it a few more times," Terian said.

"I'll just bet you could, you blue-skinned sadist. Not a great surprise to me that a dark knight feels the need to poke at me when I'm unarmed and surrendering; it's not as though you'd stand a chance when I have my weapon in my hand," Partus said.

"I'm more than a match for you, Partus," Terian said coolly. "I just never did like you is all, so I'm taking this opportunity to get a few digs in for all the joy you gave me back when we were Alliance officers together."

"I hear a lot of talk from you, Lepos," Partus said, his ruddy complexion dark, "but I'm without my hammer, your sword's at my throat and your wizard's got a spell preventing me from sending you back to Arkaria in one good jump. Why don't you just be a good lad and hand me my weapon and I'll empty your head with it, just like I did your friend there." He pointed to Cyrus, his small eyes fixed on Terian.

"Enough," Cyrus said. "Bind him, gag him, and put a rock in there first so he can't move his tongue around. We don't need him hitting us with a spell if he can cast sublingually." Cyrus smiled. "Better still, strap his hands around his neck; if he wants to cast a spell he can take his own head off and solve our problem of what to do with him."

"What about this thing?" Aisling was on her hands and knees in the grass, next to the creature. Cyrus blinked in surprise. He hadn't even noticed her there.

"What about it?"

"Maybe we should bring it with us?" She ran a finger along the flesh of its arm. "I know there are some strange and fanciful creatures in the world, but this is unlike anything I've seen. Might be worth taking a closer look at with a dagger. Especially," her eyes flashed, "if there are any more of them out there."

"I don't see reason to concern ourselves overmuch," Cyrus said, "but better to be overprepared than under, I reckon. Bind it, too, just in case, and bring it along on the back of your horse."

"My horse?" Aisling said, looking at him with equal parts disbelief and offense. "Why mine?"

"Because as the brilliant originator of the plan," Cyrus said with a smile, "you get to carry it out." He sniffed. "Also? That thing smells."

"Great," Aisling muttered under her breath. "Because I need more reasons to help you find me unappealing."

Cyrus ignored her, whistling instead to Windrider, who came to a halt beside him. He patted the horse and climbed up in the saddle. "Mendicant," Cyrus said, and waited for the goblin to appear out of the clump of the Sanctuary party, which had gathered behind him, between where they stood and the hill that he had charged down, "do you think your horse can bear the weight of you and our prisoner?"

"If we don't run him too hard," the goblin warned. "It's been a long day, though, and we'll be needing to rest the horses soon."

"It's an hour or so back to the edge of the swamp and a little farther to the crossing," Cyrus said. "Let's make camp once we've met up with the rest of our army, give our horses a night of rest." He frowned, adjusting himself in the saddle and feeling a dozen aches and pains. "And ourselves as well. We'll make our way back to Vernadam tomorrow."

They took a few minutes to get situated and give the horses ample time to drink from a small stream of fresh water, and then started back. The journey took hours, and seemed slower than the trip in, the party mostly quiet from the fatigue of traveling through the night on the evening before.

Cyrus found himself riding next to Aisling and Martaina at one point, as the two trackers attempted to steer them clearly back toward the plains. "I never did get a chance to ask you," Cyrus said to Aisling, startling the dark elf, "what was your impression of the Galbadien rulers when we were at Vernadam?"

Her eyes became snakelike as she studied him. "I came to make my report and found you ... otherwise occupied."

"You say that like it's a curse," Cyrus said mildly. "You've been badgering me for two years to loosen up, and now I have. Perhaps it's a sour taste in your mouth, some envy that springs from deep within."

Aisling let out a sharp exhalation of breath, almost like a hiss, and rolled her eyes. "You presume too much. Just because I've been honest about my interest in you, don't assume that I'm so petty and insecure that I can't handle even the thought of you pleasuring yourself with another woman." She held her head high as she spoke to him. "I've offered in the past to bed you and another woman at the same time, though something tells me that the Baroness wouldn't be much interested in that."

"Fair assumption," Cyrus said. "But still, I point out, your reaction to this turn of events is rather ..." He thought about it, trying to find a diplomatic turn of phrase, "... sharp. Less than pleasant."

"I beg your pardon, my Lord of Perdamun," Aisling said, bending at the waist in a graceful bow that saw her nearly fold double yet not lose her balance on horseback. "My intention was not to be acute in my response to you. If I was, I apologize. Perhaps I was merely dismayed that after so many times offered, it seemed that you might finally be coming around—and you did, but with someone else." Her eyes flashed again as she stared at him, and he caught a flippant toss of her white hair. "Forgive me for not quickly adapting to the new state of things." Some of the acid was leeched out of her words, but enough remained that Cyrus felt the burn of it.

"I ... can't say I feel nothing for you. I am warming to you, but ..." he pulled back, not wanting to finish his sentence.

"You felt more for her?" Aisling did not bother to hide the bitterness; she wore it plainly. "I can't fault you for that; it's not as though you can control the direction of your feelings. But it does hurt."

"I have to ask," Cyrus said, feeling the pull of a question within. "What is it about me that draws you so? You tried to seduce me, even though you knew I was in love with Vara. Now I'm with another woman, and still ..." She blanched and he stopped speaking.

There was a pregnant pause before she spoke. "You asked, and in your question you have your answer."

He thought about it for a moment. "I don't understand."

"You're guileless," she said with a sigh. "There's no deception within you when it comes to personal matters. In battle you're cunning when need be, but you're straightforward in all else—you go right at what you want, no treachery, no trickery."

Cyrus raised an eyebrow at her. "What about Vara? I danced

around her for ages."

"Not exactly." She steadied herself on the horse. "That wasn't guile, that was a form of cowardice."

"I don't know whether I should be offended by that or not."

Aisling shrugged. "You didn't think you had a real chance with her. When it became obvious she'd warmed enough to you, you tried. Good effort, but it would appear she needed more time. That's not on you, that's on her. You threw yourself into the path of a god, ready to die for her. It's hardly your fault that she became fixated more on what she'd do after she lost you than what she'd get from being with you."

"That ... was sweetly poetic," Cyrus said. "But I think you give me too much credit."

"Nope," she said, voice flat. "Unless you didn't jump in front of Mortus's hand, the credit is yours. You were willing to die for her; she was unwilling to live past your death. Kind of a peculiar irony, but there it is. Not all that surprising, though; human and elven ideas about death are dramatically different. Probably has something to do with your lifespan."

"Not for me it doesn't," Cyrus said. "For me it's training and doctrine. The God of War doesn't suffer cowardice—at least, not on the battlefield," he said, face flushing at the recall of Aisling's earlier mention of his cowardice. "That means committing to the fight, above all else, including one's life."

"I don't hear you talk much about your religion," Aisling said, matter-of-factly. "One might conclude you're either not terribly faithful or you're just not much of an evangelist."

"Following the path of the God of War is who I am," Cyrus said, a little miffed. "I don't evangelize because no one wants to hear about the glory of battle, the sacrifice of blood on the altar of combat. Most Arkarians consider that savage behavior."

"I wouldn't mind hearing about it sometime," Aisling said, "but I doubt you'll get me to change my lacksadaisical worship of Terrgenden to a lacksadaisical worship of Bellarum."

Cyrus chuckled. "Now who's the unfaithful one?"

She smiled. "I never said I was faithful. But I would say I'm worth it."

He laughed again. "Well, I'm not sure I am."

"From what I heard the other night, you are," Aisling said, a little regretfully. "And what girl wouldn't want a man who's willing to die for them? What you did that day in the Realm of Death confirmed everything I'd felt about you from the beginning. Vara is more the fool for letting you slip away."

"It's kind of you to say." Cyrus steered Windrider out of the swamp as they reached the edge of the plain. The horse whinnied in gratitude when they reached dry land and Cyrus patted him on the back of the neck. "Soon, old boy. You'll get unsaddled and brushed out, and we'll get you taken care of. Just a little farther back to the crossing."

"Sir." Longwell drifted toward Cyrus, Partus trussed up and gagged on the back of his horse. "Now that we've won the battle, my father will want us to stay for a spell, to enjoy at least a moon of feasting and celebration for winning the war."

"Winning the war?" Cyrus looked at him in askance. "We broke one of Syloreas's armies, but surely they must have more manpower somewhere. This army was hardly the be-all, end-all."

"I suspect they do have more, yes," Longwell said. "It was a weak offering, and uncharacteristic of Unger not to have led the battle himself from the front. For him not to be present at all is simply bizarre."

Cyrus shook his head. "I can't imagine he thought that was wise strategy, sending only that many and no more. Unless perhaps Actaluere drew him away with an attack, I would have thought he'd throw everything he had at this fight; after all, he was inches from defeating your Kingdom. That's hardly the moment to pull back and be cautious." Cyrus thought about it. "Is it possible he brought another army around wide and flanked us, attacking Vernadam?"

Longwell thought about if for a moment and then shrugged. "I can't see what good it would do him. He might conquer the town, but in order to take the castle, he'd need time, which he wouldn't get if we beat his other army in the field. He'd get flanked while trying to mount a siege of the most impregnable fortress in the land." Longwell shrugged again. "Not the wisest course, and Briyce Unger is no fool. No, more likely he's into something else, though I can't imagine what."

A fearful wind was whipping across the plains now and it brushed through Cyrus's hair with all the enthusiasm of a cat at play with yarn. The green grasses came up to the knee of his horse, and the smell of the animals, wet with the travel through the swamp, followed them. He could hear the chatter behind him and the rustling of the grass in the breeze, as well as the occasional whinny. The plains lay uneven all the way to the horizon, and Cyrus could see the river ahead.

A thought occurred to him and he turned back to Longwell. "Your father greeted you with great enthusiasm when we arrived the day before yesterday."

Longwell's jaw tightened under his helm. "Aye. I expect he was quite pleased that I returned, especially seeing how I was at the head of an army that could save his realm. Even as ... distracted ... as he is nowadays, it had not escaped my father's notice that Syloreas was about to conquer his Kingdom."

"But you left," Cyrus said. "You're the heir to the throne, aren't you? But you went far, far away. You must have gone for a reason."

"I did," Longwell said. "My father and I had a great disagreement. My mother has been gone for many years, and she and I always got on better than my father and I did." The dragoon's tension was obvious even through his armor. "My father thought I'd come under unsavory influences."

"What?" Cyrus did a double take. "You've never acted with anything but honor for as long as I've known you."

Longwell gave Cyrus a slow, subtle nod of acknowledgment. "I've always tried to; but it led me to defiance of my father's will. In his eyes, there is no greater sin. It led me out of his house, out of his Kingdom, and out of this land, as I couldn't see myself fighting for Actaluere or Syloreas." He puckered his lips in distaste. "That much a traitor I am not. Now, in his hour of need, I return. Let us hope that buys me back into his good graces for longer than a fortnight." The dragoon shook his head as if to clear it. "It matters not. We shall find ourselves in good company and my father will throw an impressive feast."

"I could use some time to rest after this journey," Cyrus said. "Two months to get here, a nasty battle along the way, one big fight, and a little hunt for a dwarf," he waved toward Partus, whose wide-hipped rump was facing Cyrus off the back of Mendicant's horse, "and we're done. Some feasting and celebrating doesn't seem out of line. Our people have earned it—especially given how far they've walked," he said with a smile. Windrider whinnied. "And horses, too, of course."

The river appeared before them, broad and dark in the falling light, and within an hour they were crossing the bridge, the Galbadien army already encamped on the other side. Tents had been set up, large ones, and there was some manner of dinner being served from the fires. A wagon train had come with the army, giving them more sustenance than conjured bread and water. Cyrus saw Sanctuary army members, looking far different than the Galbadiens in their distinctive livery.

They rode into the camp in the gathering twilight, cheers from the men, cups hoisted into the air in their honor. The men of the Galbadien army, dragoons and footmen all, came forth to see the dwarven mercenary who had caused them such fear paraded along on the back of their prince's horse. That thought crackled across Cyrus's mind as they walked in a procession toward the area where it appeared Sanctuary's army had concentrated.

"You're the prince of this land, aren't you?" Cyrus asked Longwell, who was waving obligingly to the troops they passed, and receiving a great many toasts of hoisted mugs and shouted promises to buy him ale when they returned to town.

"Yes," the dragoon said bitterly. "Why do you ask?"

"It just occurred to me, that's all." Cyrus steadied himself as the crowd closed in on them, cheering louder. "I'd never thought of you as a prince before, and I didn't know if someday you were going to be ruler here, or if you had siblings."

"No siblings," he said glumly. "Just me. But as for ruling the Kingdom ... that remains to be seen. Blood will out, but my father designates his heir as he sees fit. I don't know that I want the crown," he said, keeping his voice low.

"I'd say you're favored for it right now." Cyrus took in the steady chant around them, a low but rising one of Longwell's last name. "Just going by the words of the fighting men."

Longwell let a smile slip through his glumness. "It's their respect I wanted all along; my father would have had me be a court lackey." He grasped the lance that stuck vertically out of the holder on the back of his saddle. "It was I who wanted to be on the battlefield. Just as he was, once."

They paraded about, on a slow path to where Cyrus saw Odellan in his distinctive armor. The elf waited for them, arms crossed, a smile upon his face as they approached. Count Ranson waited with him, along with Odau Genner and a few of the other members of the Galbadien war council Cyrus had seen at the dinner and strategy meeting. Cyrus dismounted and grabbed the gagged and bound Partus, lifting him off Mendicant's horse and setting him upon the ground. The dwarf's legs were tied together, allowing only shuffling steps. Cyrus nudged him to move foward toward Count Ranson.

"Well done," the Count said, delivering a slow but sincere clap that was picked up by the Sanctuary and Galbadien soldiers that surrounded them. Large tents were stationed in a rough circle around them, the biggest of them open to the air, with only a roof to cover the insides from the elements. A few tables were within, along with the remains of some dinner that reached Cyrus's nose; the smell of meat was unmistakable and made his mouth water after two days of salted pork and insubstantial bread. "Truly, you've done wonders here. Defeated the mercenaries, helped us break the Sylorean army in a crushing defeat. Wondrous," the count smiled. "Truly wondrous."

"And this was all their army?" Cyrus pushed Partus forward again.

"No," the count said. "They had another one that was moving south, a host more than double the size of this one, but according to our scouts and messengers, it's turned north, back to Syloreas." The count scratched his cheek. "We received word by carrier pigeon that they crossed back over their own border last night and that the royal convoy with Briyce Unger and his generals was riding hard to catch up. They've started to abandon some of the southernmost keeps that they'd taken in our territory." He shook his head. "They could have put up a much nastier fight here if they'd shown up with everything, but it seems something else is going on; it's not like Briyce Unger to stop fighting in the middle of a war."

"Sounds worrisome," Cyrus said. "I'd suggest you ask this one," he pointed to Partus, who leered at him out of the corner of his eyes, "but I don't know that he'd spill it."

"He'll tell you anything you want to know," Terian said, striding forward off his horse and clapping Partus on the back with such force that the dwarf was nearly knocked onto his face. "He's a mercenary now. All you have to do is pay him a fat sack of gold, and he'll do whatever you want, including betraying his former masters." Terian unslung his sword and rested it, edge down, on Partus's armor, the blade only inches from the side of his neck. "Or maybe just the thought of saving his skin will be enough to get the old dwarf talking."

"Terian," Cyrus said. "We'll be handing the prisoner over to Count Ranson. It'll be up to him how he wants to handle him."

"As I understand it," Ranson said, a look of concern upon his weathered features, "you'll need magic to contain this one." He waited for Cyrus to nod, then shook his head. "No, it won't do. You can keep him. Just get him off our shores; kill him or take him back with you, it makes no mind to me. If you mean to leave him, then let's kill him and be done with it now."

"Tempting," Terian said with a wide grin, looking down at Partus, whose eyes were slightly wider but spiteful, and who wasn't saying a word. "Very tempting. I could find myself enjoying an execution."

"Not today," Cyrus said. "Let's have a talk first. Nyad," he looked back to find the wizard behind him. "I'll need a cessation spell, if you could, please."

She nodded, and began to cast the spell. Her eyes rolled back in her head, a light green glow seemed to emanate from around her body, giving her red robe a peculiar aura. She nodded once at Cyrus and continued to speak low words under her breath, keeping the spell in effect.

Cyrus pulled the gag out of Partus's mouth, and the dwarf spat the last of the oversized rag out with a choked noise that turned into a cough. When he was finished, he glared at Terian. "After all we've been through, dark knight, I'd have expected a little more kindness from you when you stuffed that in."

"After all we've been through," Terian looked at the dwarf with a raised eyebrow, "you should have been grateful I didn't slit your throat before putting you on the horse."

"Enough niceties," Cyrus said, pushing Partus's shoulder enough to cause the dwarf to look up at him with a smoldering rage in his eyes. "Where's the rest of the Sylorean army heading?"

"North," Partus said, his eyes flicked down in uncaring. "What, you didn't hear him a minute ago?" He jerked his head toward the count. "Might wanna clean your ears out."

Terian lifted a knee and hit the dwarf perfectly in the back. Partus's armor had been removed before they had bound him, and the dwarf let out a sharp cry and fell to his knees; Terian's hit had perfectly landed on the tender spot above Partus's kidney. The dwarf sucked air in through gritted teeth, his hands still bound behind him.

"Terian, enough," Cyrus said, placing a hand on the dark elf's breastplate, barely touching him but prepared to hold him back. "He's a smartass; it's not as though we haven't dealt with those every day of our lives."

"He's a Goliath smartass," Terian seethed, "and you'd do well to remember it. They're treacherous, traitorous blighters who have no issue with sticking a blade in your exposed back the moment it's turned. If he sold out his own guild to Goliath for a few pieces of silver, you can imagine what he'd do to the likes of us for much less."

"I didn't sell out my own guild," Partus said, wrenching himself off his knees and back to his feet. "Time came that the Daring was too set against moving forward, I moved on. Hardly my fault others followed with me. It's not as though they came with me when I left Goliath, did they? Save for the few you lot just left rotting on the battlefield here."

"I can see you're real broken up about their deaths," Terian said, now leaning against Cyrus's placed hand. "If we left you to your overwhelming grief for just a few more years, we might even see a single tear."

"I'm not the excessively sentimental kind," Partus said sullenly. "Unlike some people I know, I deal in the real world; and I don't know if you've noticed, but sometimes in our line of work, things take an occasional wrong turn down a bad alley. Those blokes knew what they were into when we signed up for this. So did I. If you mean to take my head off for what we've done, I'd take it as a kindness if you'd get to it and spare me, please, this sanctimonious, holier-than-thou sermon from the dark knight." He straightened. "I think I've had quite enough of being lectured on virtue by you, Terian Lepos."

"What's that supposed to mean?" Terian asked, and Cyrus felt the very slight pressure against his hand from Terian's breastplate slacken.

"It means Aurastra," Partus said with a sneer.

Cyrus watched as Terian's pupils seemed to dilate before his eyes, like pinpricks of color lost in the light. He felt the subtle shift in the dark knight's footing through the plate armor, sensed something was amiss before it happened, and a shudder ran through his arm as Terian drew his sword and let out a shout, pulling the blade over his head.

Before the dark elf had a chance to get his balance, Cyrus lunged, kicking Terian's legs from underneath him. They landed with a clatter of armor as Cyrus seized the dark knight's sword hand by the wrist, holding it up as he crashed to the ground on top of Terian. Cyrus shoved down with his weight and strength, pinning the dark knight into place. "Enough! You're not killing him."

"Oh yes, I am," Terian said, not even bothering to strain against Cyrus. The dark knight glared at Cyrus with frosty eyes. "It may not happen today, or tomorrow, or even this month or year, but something you need to realize, Davidon—it will happen. If I mean to kill a man, he will die." Terian jerked his hand away from Cyrus, and slowly slid his sword back into the scabbard as Cyrus stood up and proffered a hand to help Terian up. "Nothing stops that. It's just a matter of timing, that's all. But you're right," Terian said, hauling himself back to his feet. "It's not today."

Cyrus watched Terian out of the corner of his eye but also saw the smug Partus send Terian a little wave. The dark knight didn't react, at least not visibly, though Cyrus could swear he felt Terian's glare burning a hole into his back. "I'm not even going to ask you what Aurastra means," Cyrus said, his attention back on Partus.

"You should, it's an interesting tale," the dwarf said.

"I want to know about the Sylorean army." Cyrus kept his gaze trained on the dwarf, though he spared a glance at Count Ranson, who watched the proceedings with cool disinterest mingled with a certain disdain. *He's not impressed with the discipline of my army right now, that's for sure. Neither am I, when you come to it. I just had a man try and slay a prisoner in front of me and I had to take him down myself. Not a great sign; at least I got the result they were looking for.*

"Yeah, it went north," Partus said. "We split far up the countryside from here. They were supposed to hit country towns, plunder and pillage and the like, lay siege to some keeps and then meet us at Harrow's Crossing for the battle with you lot, but a couple nights ago the King—Unger, the bloke who hired me—gets a messenger from his capital. Something happened up there, something bad. We're in the middle of dining on some spoils from a keep we'd broken down the night earlier, and he takes his officers and loads up and buggers off in the middle of a meal." Partus spat on the ground. "Left one of his lessers in charge, didn't say much of what it was about. Didn't much matter, neither, rolling over Vernadam was supposed to be a foregone conclusion, that we were going to crush your army at Harrow's Crossing even with our reduced numbers and waltz right in or blockade the place if necessary. War over." Partus let out a rough snort. "Promises not worth the warm air they're breathed into."

"So what was it about?" Cyrus spoke and Partus turned to look at him; previously the dwarf had been addressing his comments to the Count.

"Told you, I don't know." The dwarf shrugged his shoulders.

"You said he 'didn't say much of what it was about,'" Cyrus repeated. "Word for word."

The dwarf let a half-smile curl his lips, a snide one, as though he knew he'd been caught. "I did say that, didn't I? Well, he didn't say much, and what he did say didn't make a bit of sense, really, not to me at least. Then he and his band buggered off before he went and explained it."

Cyrus rolled his eyes. "Enough drama. What did he say?"

Partus met Cyrus's eyeroll with one of his own. "He said, 'they're coming.'" The dwarf held his bound hands in front of him. "That's it. And then he got on a horse and scampered off to the north with his little wagon train in tow, as though Mortus himself was following behind him."

Cyrus concentrated, looking at Count Ranson. "That mean anything to you?"

Ranson shrugged. "Nothing. I'm left with the obvious question of who 'they' are. Actaluere's army, possibly?"

"I doubt it," Partus said, with a slight snicker. "Because you see, you're missing it. It doesn't matter, the bit he said. Because that's not the news. It's *how* he said it that matters. That and what he did afterwards."

Count Ranson sighed heavily. "Very well. How did Briyce Unger say it, then?"

"Scared." Partus let it slip matter-of-factly, like he was letting loose something precious indeed. "He was scared, I'd stake my life on it."

Ranson's mouth opened slightly at the dwarf's words, as though he were weighing them in his mind, trying to calculate the value of them. "That is ... interesting. And, if true ... greatly disturbing."

"Disturbing?" Cyrus looked around at the officers behind him, and the men surrounding him, and found one face in particular—Longwell. The dragoon's mouth was slightly agape, his eyes wider than usual. "Longwell?" Cyrus asked. "What does it mean? Why does it matter?"

Longwell stepped forward, brushing past Terian to stand next to Cyrus. "Briyce Unger, the King of Syloreas, has led every single battle he's fought from the vanguard. He fights like a madman in personal combat; it's said no man can take him down. He carries a mace with a ball the size of a man's head, and the spikes on it are as long as my forearm. He's huge, taller maybe even than you," Longwell acknowledged Cyrus's height with a nod. "He is one of the mountain men of Syloreas, rocky and inhospitable. They don't fear many things. Briyce Unger is the most fearless of them all."

Longwell looked at the circle around Partus, and the dwarf looked at him and nodded. "So for this man—dwarf—whatever he is, to say that Briyce Unger took this news and was scared ..." The dragoon swallowed hard. "It doesn't sound terribly good for him."

Cyrus watched Longwell carefully then shifted his attention to the still-chuckling Partus. "Let me give you a helpful hint, mercenary," he said, stripping the smug look from the dwarf's face. "When the fearless man is afraid, it's not just bad for him, as a rule." Cyrus stared north, as though he could sense something was ahead of them, over the horizon. "It's bad for all of us."

Chapter 21

The rest of night was subdued; conversations hashed over and over again. Partus was gagged once more and bound hand and foot, tied to a cot and put under guard. He was allowed water before he went to sleep, but only with a cessation spell over him, then he was strapped down and left quiet with two guards and Mendicant to watch over him. The goblin was ordered by Cyrus to thoroughly cover the dwarf with a fire spell should he attempt to escape, a fact which was not lost on the wide-eyed Partus.

Cyrus sat in a circle around a fire with his officers, but the conversations lost his attention after only a short while. They discussed what Partus had talked about, but it meandered in circles. Terian was silent, almost as though he were pouting or lost in his own thoughts. After their conflict, Cyrus had not bothered to approach the dark knight. *Better to let him stew on it and talk with him in the morning. He's sore that I had to remonstrate with him in a public forum.* He frowned. *Well, he shouldn't have tried to kill the prisoner.*

Longwell contributed little to the conversation, only reiterating that Briyce Unger had little use for cowards, so the thought of him terrified was disquieting, at least. Ryin weighed in with his own observations, after which Nyad proceeded to dissect at length (interminably, to Cyrus's mind) every bit of what was said about the Sylorean army, Briyce Unger, and all other minutia. Shortly before midnight, Cyrus gave up and retreated to a tent that Ranson had indicated was for him.

Within, he found a wooden cot with a roll of furs to use as a mattress. Cyrus lay upon it, resting his head, hearing the sounds of the thousands of soldiers encamped around him. Though he knew the latrines were far from his tent, the smell of the battlefield was still present; the first hints of souring flesh, the real or perceived scent of blood on the air. He buried his face in the furs, sniffing at the clean, just-washed smell of them, the barest remains of soap still on them. He thought of the Baroness, of the morrow, and of how he would feel her against him again, and he slept.

The next day came similarly gloomy, and he woke to the sounds of the camp stirring. After stretching, Cyrus stepped outside the tent. Rain was in the air again, the heavy, humid feeling of a storm, ready to break. The clouds were grey and wended their way to both ends of the sky without break or interruption. Some patches were darker than others, but it was all a dark sky, and all a worrisome thing to have hanging over one's head, ready to break loose at any moment.

After a brief conversation with Count Ranson, who urged Cyrus to begin the journey back to Vernadam, which awaited them for celebrations, Cyrus rallied the Sanctuary army. They made their way out of the camp, the column being led once more by the riders on horseback. They had left behind their own wagons at Vernadam, and so made their way onto the rough road leading into the Forest of Waigh before the morning had entirely left.

The sky remained gloomy but did not deliver on the promised rain until nearing midday, when it came in short, staccato bursts. For ten minutes the skies would pour buckets and then stop, the clouds finally breaking to reveal sunlight. A few minutes later, another cloud would cover the sun, drench the army of Sanctuary as it tried to hide under the boughs of the forest, and then be onward in the sky, letting the sun shine down again. After the fourth rainstorm, Cyrus lost count, not worrying, already soaked and near uncaring about the chill. Although he felt bad for the soldiers in the column, he knew the only thing for them was to finish the march, which would take another six hours or so before they'd reach Vernadam.

Cyrus spent his time quiet, thinking of the Baroness, of her touch. He found to his surprise that even in the short time he'd been gone, he'd missed having her travel with them, that he'd wanted to comment on something to her. *Madness. That was fast.* He imagined her face, her smile, and lapsed once again into thinking of the night before he'd left, and felt his own anticipation for their arrival.

The journey passed quickly, especially after the rain, and the Forest of Waigh ended when they had only three hours of marching left to their destination. From the moment they left behind the tree-covered skies, Vernadam was visible in the distance, the towering top spire sticking above all else, a faintly shadowed pillar on the horizon that grew and grew as they marched closer. Sundown cast it in a shadow against the purple sky, a black outline of the tallest castle Cyrus had ever seen.

They reached the city not long after sundown to much jubilance and celebration in the street. Women leapt from the crowds and kissed the men in the column (some to great joy, some to great dismay) and Cyrus found himself pelted with flowers and the recipient of countless offered bottles, most of which he declined.

They halted in the square to cheers and adulation. The environment around them was stunning, excitement was rampant, and Cyrus could feel himself sucked into it, a heady feeling of being a part of something grand, once-in-a-lifetime. He dodged a group of Galbadien boys who chanted his name, "CY-RUS, CY-RUS, CY-RUS," and thought quietly that they looked to be of an age with some of the newest recruits in his army. The village was entirely turned out, and the smell of strong wine was already pervasive in the street, along with good ale and some urine as he rode past an alley or two.

He shouted to Odellan. "Keep them in line," he said, and saw the elf nod at him. Cyrus gestured to his officers to proceed, and they did, to muted cheers and a widening chant of Cyrus's name that seemed to grow even louder as they exited the square and the village, ringing out even as they made their way up the path to Vernadam.

"Figures," Terian said, muttering under his breath. "We all go out and fight the battle, and he's the one that gets the cheers."

"I don't remember seeing you get your brains dashed out by a hammer for this victory," Cyrus said.

"No great loss there," Terian replied. "You didn't have much in the way of them to start."

Cyrus chuckled as they made their way up the winding path. It was darker, now, and the gates to the castle were visible ahead. The switchback sent them winding around at a slow canter, and Cyrus felt the discomfort in his haunches from all the sitting over the last months. *A month without riding might be nice. Well, without horseback riding, anyway ...*

The gate of Vernadam was impossibly large, yawning, the portcullis up and inviting them in. Cyrus imagined trying to lay siege to this castle, to deal with the meandering path, to fight against the steep sides, or attempt to put a siege engine against the curtain wall. Even the thought of bringing a battering ram heavy enough to shatter the great wooden gates was laughable. *I pity whatever fool tries to take this place by force; assuming they were provisioned, it would be the effort of years.* His mind drifted again to within the walls, to the Baroness, to the bed in his chambers. He was tired, again, after a long day's ride, but not ready to sleep, not yet ...

They went through the tunnel of the portcullis, into the courtyard, and Cyrus looked up to the stairs that led to the front doors. The doors were open, and a procession was making its way down, following the King. He was almost to the bottom, and in the bevy of servants and house guards was another face, a shining one, resplendent, really—Cattrine, in a green dress of the most elegant silk, waiting for him only a few steps behind the King.

Cyrus dismounted and one of the servants from the stables came and took Windrider's reins from him. He waited until Longwell, Terian, and a few of the others joined him; Partus was paraded before them, looking murderously annoyed. Still gagged, the dwarf couldn't say anything, but he grunted in irritation every time Terian poked him to move forward.

The courtyard was insulated from the breezes that had run so infrequently outside, and Cyrus found himself a little warmer as he took his first steps toward the King. He could see the Baroness, a glow in her eyes and on her skin, as he smiled at her and came before the King, who nodded at him.

"King Aron," Cyrus said, "I present to you the dwarven mercenary who has caused you so many difficulties, as a sign, from us of the Sanctuary Army, that we hope your troubles with Syloreas are at an end after the battle of Harrow's Crossing."

The assembled servants and guards burst into spontaneous applause, encouraged by the benign smile upon the King's face. When they had quieted, the King spoke, not taking his eyes off the dwarf. "Your gift is much appreciated, as are your efforts in these dark days, made light by your victory over our enemies. When my only son left," he turned toward Samwen Longwell, who looked at his feet, "I feared the worst for my house, only to see the worst come after his departure. But what I thought would be our ruin became our salvation as he returned with you wonderful people of the west."

The King raised his hands above him. "I declare the next thirty days to be a time of celebration and feasting throughout the Kingdom of Galbadien. Let all who are fit raise their cups to Cyrus Davidon, Samwen Longwell, and the heroes of Sanctuary, who have delivered us from our ancient foes! Let all who have lips to speak praise their names, and let us dedicate this time to salving their weariness, resting them from their troubles, and feasting them upon the most succulent delicacies our lands have to offer." The King's thin face was positively radiant. "This in the name of those who have ventured so far to offer a hand of friendship. This is your time." He spread his arms wide, beckoning them forward to the castle. "We invite you to stay with us, and enjoy all we have to offer—in the name of our friendship."

Thunderous applause greeted them, echoing forth in the courtyard from every servant and guard, as loud as in the open air of the square in the village below. There would be feasts, and songs, and plenty of wine, Cyrus knew, but his eyes were fixed on a point past the King, on a face still glowing, still smiling at him, and thinking of a time long past dinner and dessert, when the hours were late and the darkness was nigh

...

... and he stayed awake long into the night, he and Cattrine, in each other's arms—and even when the knock came at their door the next morning summoning them for breakfast, they were not quickly to be stirred or parted.

Chapter 22

A month passed in an eye's blink, to Cyrus. He found himself in need of exercise beyond what the Baroness offered in their chambers in order to offset the rich delicacies that the King continued to feed them, and so he took up practicing with his sword in the courtyard every day before lunch and again before dinner. More often than not he was joined by the Baroness, clad not in her dress (nor in the much less formal attire she wore to their bed) but in the riding outfit she had donned during their journey from Green Hill, and he taught her the way of the sword, a day at a time, with a blade provided by the King's armory as a gift.

"Not quite like that," he said, behind her, pressed against her, steering her arm with his hand wrapped around hers. "Like this." He made a motion and then drew back his hand, watching for her to make the same motion. She did, and he spoke. "Very good."

"Such ample encouragement," she whispered as she made the motion again, a short strike with the light blade, enough to cut a throat, if need be. "Do you teach all your students from this position?" She looked up to him, catching his eye, and he saw the hint of wryness in her smile.

"Not quite," he said, rubbing himself against her, feeling her press back, and sensing the promise of something else later, something that would perhaps help defray the slow slide of lethargy that thirty days of idleness could bring a soldier. "But with you, I do prefer a hands-on approach."

"Indeed?" she said quietly. "And where would you prefer those hands to be?"

He started to answer her but stopped when a stableboy passed by them on his way into the castle. The sunny day shone down on them from above, the white stones of the castle gleaming in the light. Cyrus looked around and realized that only a few souls were out and about today, which was unusual for the courtyard. "I'd prefer them be in several places at once, if I had my druthers," he said once the stableboy passed from earshot. "But as I only have two, I can think of where I'd prefer they go first ..." He whispered in her ear and she laughed, giving him a kiss on the mouth for his suggestion.

"Had enough for today, then?" he asked her when they parted.

"Of swordplay? I think so, yes," she said with a smile and a glimmer in her eyes, sliding her weapon back into the scabbard. The blade was thin, more of a rapier than a proper broadsword, but quick and light enough that Cattrine, thin and lithe, could wield it lethally. "Of being physically maneuvered by you? No. Not even close."

He walked with an arm around her as they headed back up the steps into the foyer. "Hard to believe we've been here for a month." He frowned. "Even harder to believe we're leaving tomorrow."

"Ah, yes," she said with mild enthusiasm. "I finally get to see this mythical 'Sanctuary' I've heard so much about. And perhaps I'll finally meet this much-vaunted Vara, and see how much competition I have."

"That would be none." He stopped her in the stone foyer, delivering a long, passionate kiss that caused a nearby servant to cough politely. "She gave up the fight before we even met; the battle is ceded to you."

Cattrine stared at him, something vague and mysterious hiding in her expression. She reached up with a lone finger and pressed it to his lips. "I do enjoy hearing you talk about love in war metaphors."

"They're very similar, I've heard," he said with a wide grin. "Battles and fighting and all that. Even some bloodshed. Also, all is fair in both of them."

"All that aside," she said, serious, "what's to become of me when we arrive back in Arkaria? Am I to stay in Sanctuary, be your kept woman?"

"I would be perfectly fine with that." He wrapped his arms around her, but when he went to kiss her again, he got her cheek instead of her lips. "What's wrong?"

"I am not some broken woman, waiting for a man to save me." She looked momentarily embarrassed. "Which is why I took you up on your offer. So that I would never have to come before a man again and beg him to give me what I want—and that includes you."

"Just because you're with me doesn't mean you're bound to me," Cyrus said, letting her pull from him. "You can find some meaningful work, some endeavors to devote your time to." She did not look at him. "Baroness—"

"For heavens sakes, Cyrus," she snapped. "I am no longer a Baroness. Everyone else calls me Cattrine, and the least you can do as the man I am intimate with is afford me the same courtesy." She looked at him with rueful humor and the slightest amusement. "Please."

"I'm sorry." He found he meant it sincerely. "It must be difficult."

"Hm?" She looked at him in curiosity.

"Not knowing what to do next," he said. "Not knowing ... where you're going, or what you'll do when you get there. Being reliant on another person for food, for sustenance, for room and board, for everything. I apologize for having put you in that position."

She sighed. "You didn't. Being born a woman in Luukessia put me in that position. You're relieving me of it; but that doesn't mean it'll be easy. Many a bird has struggled before taking flight for the first time." She looked at him with great irony. "More than a few die trying to fly. I hope I'm not one of those."

"There are many kinds of work available for a woman in Arkaria," Cyrus said gently. "Even around Sanctuary we could surely find something to do that wouldn't involve fighting, if you wanted."

"I appreciate the offer," she said more quietly. "I would like to remain near you, so that we can continue to ... explore ... what our next step might be together."

"Ah, yes," he said. "Next steps ... well, I can think of one that tends to be a natural path."

Her eyes flashed. "Rings, ceremonies, commitments? As I recall, I already asked you to do me that service once and you denied me."

"I did. But had I known what I would be getting at the time," he said with a wide grin, "I might not have been so reluctant to commit to it."

She put on an offended look and smacked him on the arm. "You do me wrong, sir, to say such a crude thing to me." Her look softened. "Especially since I did offer at the time, and you declined that as well ..."

He sighed. "If only I'd known what I was missing. Why, I could have had another month's worth of your physical company in my bedroll on the way here."

"Is that all you keep me around for?" She kept her body at a slight distance, hovering just a few inches away.

"Not at all," Cyrus said. "I also find your insight excellent and your conversational skills top notch. But I can't say I haven't enjoyed the other."

She ran a hand through her brown hair, letting it fall out of the knot she'd styled it in before coming outside. He loved the way it lay, framing her face. "I confess that I've enjoyed this time with you as well—all parts of it, not having to worry, merely being ..." she steered around the words he expected her to use, the ones she hadn't yet—nor had he, either. "... together, without a care in the world," she finished but without her customary smile.

"It's something I'm rather unaccustomed to," Cyrus agreed, as they made their way up the main staircase. "Someone once suggested to me that I might consider taking a vacation, but really, for as long as I recall, battle has been my release, it's the way I spend myself when I get too harried and wound. But this, to slow down and take things easy," he slid a hand along her side as he said it, "has been nicer than I could have guessed it would be."

"You didn't think spending a month in the company of an insatiable woman," she slid her hands behind his back and grasped him, firmly, awakening him as she had by rubbing against him in the courtyard, "would be utterly exhausting and relaxing all at once?"

"I ... hmm ..."

They broke from another kiss with a grin and continued on their way. He watched the gleam in her eyes, the hunger, watched how she slowed her pace, to tease him, to make him wait. His long legs yearned to run, to scoop her up in his arms and carry her back to their bedroom, the place that they had made their own—he had seen her cry, watched her work through nights of pain and countless agonies from her past while he was there, waiting and watching and holding her. She had been there, too, for him, though he had never been as obvious about it. He had grieved in his own way, and she had rested his head upon her bosom, held him in her arms as he felt her warmth and let slip away a thousand dreams and memories of Vara, her golden hair and silver armor—

Cattrine let out a squeal of delight as Cyrus swept her up in his arms, just down the corridor from their room, carrying her at a light run. He opened the door with one hand and carried her in, his fingers eager to unbutton her shirt, to unlace her breeches, to throw her entire ensemble on the floor and get her to the bed, where he could feel her against him, to be with her ...

They were on the bed when the first knock came, and Cyrus paused, his clothes already off. He waited, still, listening as the same methodical knocking came again. He met Cattrine's eyes and she watched his impishly, waiting to hear if the sound persisted or went away. There was another knock moments later, and Cyrus exchanged a look with Cattrine, wrapped a blanket around himself, and walked across the cold floor to the door and opened it.

Martaina waited outside, along with Odau Genner, who wore a pained expression on his pinched face. Martaina was impassive, standing as though she were on guard.

"Yes?" Cyrus asked, looking between the two of them with slight irritation.

"My liege summons you, Lord Davidon," Genner said. "He requests your presence in the throne room immediately."

"Then I will be along—immediately," Cyrus said. "Provided he won't be offended if I dress myself first."

"I believe that he would consider that an acceptable delay," Genner said with a nod. "We await your company, sir." With that, he left, walking down the hall.

"What are you doing out here?" Cyrus asked Martaina.

"I've been here all along."

"You weren't here a few minutes ago when I came in." Cyrus snugged the blanket around himself, making certain that nothing undue was visible.

"No," Martaina agreed. "I went around the corner for as long as it took the two of you to go inside. But before that, I was out here."

"How did you know we were ... oh." He looked at her, annoyed. "Elven hearing."

She smiled faintly. "Get dressed, sir."

He closed the door, letting the grain of the wood slide against his palm as he pondered what the King might have to say that was so important it couldn't wait.

"Who was it?" Cattrine asked from behind him.

Cyrus jerked slightly from surprise. "Odau Genner. The King wants to see me immediately for some reason or another."

She wore a robe, dipping slightly over her shoulder to reveal some of the scars that she had tried to hide from him, at first. "It seems unlikely he would summon you urgently for mere triviality." She drew close, and reached under the blanket, drawing his attention to her. "We can finish our ... interlude ... later." She kissed him. "You should get dressed."

He grunted and retrieved his underclothes from the bedroom, pulling on his trousers and sliding into his shirt. "I wouldn't mind it, you know. Getting married to you. Now that I know you, I mean."

She stood next to his armor, ready to assist him in strapping it on, the chainmail already in her hands. Her back was turned to him, but he saw her freeze, halfway down, having stooped to pick it up.

"I would do right by you," he said, coming up behind her. "I said no before, back when I didn't know you, but I know you now, and I have no problem if you wanted to—"

"Not yet." She turned to him and smiled weakly. "It is custom in Luukessia for a short courtship, only a few days in many cases. What we have done, here, this last month is ... not unheard of, but rare. And I have enjoyed it, every day of it. As an unmarried woman, before I was the Baroness, it would have been impossible. My virtue was guarded carefully. Now that that particular castle has fallen, I find myself all the happier for it." She smiled. "I wish to continue enjoying our time together without worry or pressure. Having you here, without concern of marriage or imminent motherhood from our dealings—that ventra'maq is really quite the wonder—I find myself in the dubious position being able to tell you I am not ready, whereas before I would have welcomed your offer." She laid aside the chainmail and grasped both his hands, bringing them to her lips and kissing them. "Please don't be upset that I say no—it is not no forever but only for now."

"I'm not upset," Cyrus said. "Long courtships are common in Arkaria, as are short courtships. Everything is acceptable, depending on where you are. As are extended periods of ... well, what we've done here. I am not upset, and I understand." He smiled and didn't even have to try terribly hard to force it. "I trust you'll let me know if the day comes you'd want to take me up on my offer?"

"I ..." She started to answer but stopped, and he studied her as her small hands found his chainmail again and held it up for him, indicating he should lower his head to put it on. "I believe the day may come ... perhaps soon, even ... when that could happen." She smiled. "Be patient with me."

"But of course." He held still as she strapped his breastplate and backplate on. "I think I can wait. At least a little while." She slapped his backside in mock outrage and he laughed.

A few minutes later, he stepped out of their chambers and started down the long stone hallway. Martaina fell into step a pace behind him. "Any idea what this is about?" he asked her.

"As much as you do," she replied, her green cloak trailing on the ground.

"What, you couldn't hear it from across the castle when they sent Genner to summon me?"

"No," Martaina said with a thin smile, "it must have gotten drowned out by the sound of your suggestive banter with the Baroness."

Cyrus took a left turn coming down the steps in the foyer, walking to the massive double doors opposite the ones that led to the dining hall. Two guards in the livery of Galbadien soldiers opened the door, holding it for Cyrus to pass. Martaina halted outside the door, drawing up to the frame and stopping. Once within, the doors began to close behind him and Cyrus found himself in the throne room, a place he had been on only a few formal occasions since arriving at Vernadam. Once had been for a presentation ceremony in which he and the other officers of Sanctuary had been recognized for their good works, for their efforts in the battle.

It was a long chamber, the ceilings half a hundred feet high, with arches of stone and great columns to support them. The block was dark, grey, and cast a pallor in the room that even the row of stained glass windows to Cyrus's right could not break. Light shone in from outside, but not nearly enough to counter the gloomy atmosphere. The air seemed stale to Cyrus, as though it were not moving within the chamber. Ahead of him was the King, on a raised dais a few steps off the ground.

The King's lips were pursed, his eyes narrowed in disgust, and the small ring of courtiers that stood around him loosened as Cyrus approached the foot of the steps, creating a half-circle with the throne anchoring the center, allowing the King to look down on Cyrus with curled lips, his poorly settled skin wiggling with the motion.

"Your Majesty," Cyrus said, dipping slightly in a bow when he reached the bottom of the steps. Looking up, he tried to discern from the courtiers' expressions what might be going on; none of them were particularly helpful. Most looked dazed, surprised, and a few looked downright hostile. "You summoned and I answered your call. How may I be of service?"

"It should surprise you not that we have received letters of vital importance this morning through carrier pigeons," the King said, his expression still harsh, though guarded. "The first is of some note—the Kingdom of Syloreas asks us for peace and has summoned us to a moot at the ancient citadel of Enrant Monge, the place of meeting."

Cyrus listened and tried to decipher the unsaid message that had turned the room sour. "This is good news, is it not?"

"It is," the King said, puckering his lips. "Though to summon us to Enrant Monge is the unlikeliest of maneuvers for Briyce Unger; there has not been a moot there in fifteen years, and he speaks of putting aside the past to face new dangers that await us all. I wonder of what he might be speaking, if it might be a Western doom."

"Doom?" Cyrus asked. "I'm sorry, I don't understand."

"Perhaps I could endeavor to explain?" Odau Genner appeared from the line of courtiers; Cyrus hadn't even noticed the man absorbed among them. He was wearing clothing rather than armor. *And let's be honest, the man's as plain as bread when he's not being obsequious.* "Enrant Monge is an ancient castle in the middle of Luukessia," Genner began, "maintained to this day as the site of all discussions between the three Kingdoms."

"All right," Cyrus said. "So he's summoned you there ... and you suspect a trap?"

"No," Genner said with a smile. "You do not engage in hostilities of any kind at Enrant Monge. It is a place of peace, kept as a shrine to the days when our Kingdoms were united and all Luukessia was ruled from within its great halls. To fight at Enrant Monge is anathema, unheard of. To be summoned there by Briyce Unger is a shocking development. We expected to hear from him, but only in the form of a letter requesting terms to go back to our earlier borders."

Cyrus shrugged. "So he's got some other threat in mind?" There were nods from the courtiers. "Any idea what it is?"

"We are not receiving regular messengers," Genner said. "With our army moving north and Unger's forces still withdrawing from the keeps they've taken, we don't have a clear idea of what's going on." He cast a look at the King. "But this is all mere courtesy, to let you know about the conclusion to the war you helped us win. The King has summoned you here for a different purpose entirely."

Cyrus gave the King a polite nod, inwardly chafing. *I'll be old by the time these bastards get to their point.* He shifted in his armor, feeling the discomfort in his greaves from the thought and touch of Cattrine, still waiting in his bed ...

"We have received another message," Genner said, somewhat grave. "This one is also of some import."

"I appreciate a good sense for the dramatic as much as the next person," Cyrus said, "but would you mind just cutting to point? I'm a soldier, and we're not renowned for our patience or craftiness with words."

"Very well, General," the King said. "On your way to our land from the bridge, you laid siege to the keep at Green Hill in Actaluere."

"I did," Cyrus said calmly. "Though it wasn't much of a siege. It took less than an hour." The courtiers all shuffled uncomfortably. "Is this a problem? Your son told me conquests of that sort are common, and in fairness, Baron Hoygraf provoked us by kidnapping one of our scouting parties and holding them prisoner.

"It is all well and good to storm a keep, take some plunder," Odau Gennar said, "and young Longwell was correct, such skirmishes do happen regularly, and if not part of a sustained invasion, are generally overlooked." He hesitated. "However ..."

"However," the King interrupted Genner's dramatic pause, brandishing a letter, "this was not a normal instance. We have received *this* because of it." He unfolded the page, waving it from the throne. "A declaration of war! From Actaluere!"

"Excuse me?" Cyrus stared at the paper. "Actaluere has declared war on you? Or on Sanctuary?"

"On us," Genner said. "Because we are harboring you. They demand—"

"Look at this!" The King stood, holding the paper before him, waving it at Cyrus. "You come to my Kingdom and you bring war and despair. And now you would retreat back from whence you came and leave the wreckage behind!"

"Hold it," Cyrus said. "You were a night away from total defeat when we got here, let's not go forgetting that. Second, if it's as you say, I won't leave until I can resolve this situation with Actaluere." He watched the King's outrage subside, the waving of the letter stopped, and the page crumpled as the King's hand fell by his side. "So they're upset with us for raiding Green Hill?"

"Not exactly," Odau Genner said, stepping in. "The thing you have to understand is that Milos Tiernan, the King of Actaluere, is quite cunning, but not disposed to wanting a war. We suspect this declaration is his way of warning us of his dissatisfaction."

"So you don't think he means to prosecute a war against you?" Cyrus asked, confused.

"Oh, he will fight," the King said, "and he will roll across our western border with nothing to stop him, sacking everything in sight and leaving our land a smoking ruin. But he warns us first, so that first we may accede to his demands, and let the whole thing be taken back, put away, and never spoken of again. Honor satisfied, he will rescind his declaration of war and be done with it."

"Honor satisfied?" Cyrus looked at Genner, hoping for an explanation. "What does Tiernan want?"

"You took something from Green Hill when you sacked it," Genner began delicately. "Something important—vital, really. He wants it back."

"That's fine," Cyrus said. "None of the plunder we took was of vital importance to us. Some gemstones, silverware and the like. Whatever of it he wants, we'll give back, no issue." Cyrus looked around at the courtiers, some of whom seemed extremely discomfited. "So what is it? A jewel? A sword?"

"I do not believe you understand," said Odau Genner, looking at his boots.

"That much is plain," Cyrus snapped. "Because none of you are explaining this in anything other than a circuitous way. Be out with it, man! What the hells does he want?"

"Your lover," the King said, matching the fire in Cyrus's voice. "The Baroness Cattrine Hoygraf. He wants her returned immediately, to satisfy his honor."

"His honor?" Cyrus spat. "I took her rightly from a man I bested and killed, a man who tortured and abused her. What claim does he think he has to her?"

"No claim at all if you come to it," Genner said. "You are correct, you took her fairly from a vanquished foe, and by all the standards of Luukessia, he has no right to ask for her back. But nonetheless, he does ask—and if you do not return her, he will invade our western reaches."

"And I'll ride out to meet him, kill his army, cut off his head, and leave a smoking ruin of his Kingdom," Cyrus said, a feral savagery overriding his senses, anger hot in his veins. He felt himself shake, such was the fury that poured through him. "By what right does he imagine he can do this thing? What gives him the right to try and take her away?"

The King exchanged a look with Genner, who looked back at Cyrus. "By honor and blood, sir, does he demand her return. And it is honor that drives him, make no mistake. Your taking of the Baroness does make him look weak, a fool, and her return after a threat of war will soothe his pride, balm his wounded reputation." Genner let out a small smile, though the King returned to sit on his throne, hands resting on the arms of it. "After all," Genner said, "would you do any less if someone took your own blood?"

"Own blood?" Cyrus said, feeling as though the ground had dropped from beneath him. "Whose blood?"

The King leaned forward in his seat, his thin fingers caressing the arms of the throne. One of his hands darted up to stay Genner, who had begun to answer. "You don't know, then?" The King seemed to relish the thought, as though he were gaining sustenance from Cyrus's unknowing. "Your lover, Baroness Cattrine—before she was the Baroness Hoygraf of Green Hill, was someone else entirely. I suppose she never told you her maiden name?"

Cyrus waited, his jaw clenched, as the King savored his moment of triumph.

"Oh, yes," the King proclaimed, "she didn't. What a snakelike creature a woman is, how like a viper to envenom you, and without

even an exchange of the proper truths. I see how it is. Very well, then."
He smiled. "Before your lady Cattrine was Baroness Hoygraf, she was
Cattrine Tiernan, the Contessa of Caenalys, the capital of all Actaluere,
born to the title by blood.

"Because, you see, she is Milos Tiernan's own dear sister."

Chapter 23

"You're not going to hurt her, are you?" Martaina broke the silence between them on the walk back to Cyrus's quarters. The steady noise of his boots smacking against the marble with each step drummed a rhythm of fury, the walls seemed to blur as he passed. At Martaina's words his head snapped around at her.

"What?" He nearly recoiled away from her. "No, I'm not going to hurt her. What kind of a question is that?"

"A valid one," the ranger said, trying to keep pace with Cyrus's long footsteps as they chewed up the ground between him and his quarters. The meeting had ended shortly after the King had made his revelation—Cyrus thought of it as twisting the dagger, the King had seemed to enjoy his pain so—and Cyrus had left the chamber, not hearing anything else that had been said save for that the royal convoy would begin the month-long journey to Enrant Monge on the morrow. "You've been told something that augers badly for a woman you were—dare I say—beginning to fall in—"

"I was not," Cyrus snapped. "I trusted her, that's all. I invited her into my bed. I ... started to ... barely allow myself ... I had become comfortable with her," he finally allowed. "But she has lied to me. Everything about her approach to me from the start to now has been based on that lie."

"She never lied to you," Martaina said, breaking into a jog to keep alongside him. "Can you blame her for not wanting you to know that she was the sister of the King of Actaluere, being as they were the ones whose envoy had captured and harmed our people?"

"Yes, I can blame her," Cyrus said. "Very easily, in fact. If I wasn't shaken from taking her along with us by the fact that her husband kidnapped and raped some of my people, I likely wouldn't have been dissuaded had I known her brother was a royal prick who sold her into slavery to the baron. But she didn't give me the opportunity. She lied." He heard the words, and they sounded foreign to him, burned in his gullet.

"Be cautious, sir," Martaina warned him. "Don't do anything you'll regret later—"

"I won't regret a bit of it," Cyrus said, the words stinging his lips with a fire of their own. "What's with this sudden concern? Do you honestly think I'm going to ... what? Slap her around? I don't care how furious I am, I don't hit women." He paused. "When I'm not in combat. I mean, some lady brandishes a sword at me, my gentlemanly ways tend to go right out the window—"

"Just ..." Martaina stopped, tugging on Cyrus's arm. "You're angry, sir. Understandable. But you may make of things differently later. You may want to go easy."

"I don't expect I'm going to be seeing this betrayal differently in the evening's light," Cyrus said. "Nor in the light of the moon, nor tomorrow's, nor the next moon's, nor any day from here going forward til the end of all days. She ... lied to me. She betrayed me." He felt the emotions play across his face, felt it contort, the rage coloring the inflection of his words. "You think I'm likely to forget that? She's the sister of someone who's a declared enemy of ours. Whose servant did things—"

"She's the wife of said servant, and you got over that enough to pleasure yourself with her," Martaina replied, unfazed. "You took your armor off with her, sir—and that's not something you tend to do. You may be wearing it now, but she's already through it. You're stinging right now. Tread easy." Martaina withdrew, seeming to fade as she began to step backward. "Lest you find out how much more it can hurt."

Cyrus looked back at her, unflinching. "I'm a warrior. Taking pain is what I do. Gather the officers together, tell them I'll met with them in the dining hall in fifteen minutes." He straightened. "Truly fifteen minutes, this time. Let them know." He turned away, trying to keep an even pace on his journey through the halls until he reached his room. His urge was to throw the door open and storm in, but he restrained it, shutting it near-silently. He heard something stir in the bedroom, and Cattrine's head peeked around the doorframe, followed by the rest of her, shyly displaying her nude skin, the scars obvious and plentiful. She had done much the same for the last thirty days, and every time it enticed him, drew him in, the sight of her this way.

Now he saw only the scars, jagged, angry, marring the perfect skin, interrupting the smoothness of her flesh, things he barely noticed yesterday, but were now glaringly obvious, standing out, filling his vision. They were all he could see. "Get dressed," he said. "Your brother threatens war on Galbadien."

Cyrus watched her confidence crumple, the smooth, seductive look evaporating from her face like a mirage when one draws too close. One of her hands wrapped around her breasts while the other sank lower, as though she could cover herself with them. "He what? I'm sorry?"

"He threatens war. On Galbadien, for harboring the Sanctuary army." Cyrus's gaze was cold, unmerciful, and he could feel Cattrine wilt before it. "The King and his advisors seem to believe it's his way of salving his wounded honor, because he's embarrassed that a foreign army marched through his realm, slapped down one of his barons, and stole away his own flesh and blood without challenge."

"That ... does sound like him," she said. "But it's just the rattle of the sword, surely he can't mean to—"

"They think he does," Cyrus said. "They think he knows they're weak on the border and that he won't hesitate to exploit that to save himself some rich embarrassment."

Her eyes flicked down, even as she stood away from the doorframe, exposed, in the middle of the room. Her hands hovered near uselessly around her body, and she seemed to shiver, though the room felt warm to Cyrus's skin.

"I didn't mean ... I'm sorry," she said, still not meeting his eyes, "for not telling you."

"Yes," Cyrus said. "I'm sorry, too. Would it really have been that bad? I already took you on knowing what your husband was. Did you think having an ass of a brother would have stopped me?"

"I was afraid," she said, as her body jerked from an unseen chill, "that you might think something like this could happen, and you would change your mind. I thought that perhaps it would be dangerous to tell you, that you weren't as honorable or decent as you appeared to be. I had reasons," she said, finally looking up at him. "Very good ones, every single one, or at least they sounded so in my head."

"I trusted you." Cyrus stared at her, and she flinched away. "In a way I haven't ... with anyone ... in a long time. I understand your reasons, but as of about thirty days ago ... when you knew who I was and what I stood for ... they should have been null and you should have told me the truth."

"I'm sorry." She still did not look up, focusing instead on the floor, the marble, anything but him. "I'm sorry, Cyrus ..."

"Yeah." He heard the scrape of his boots on the floor as he turned back to the door. "I have to go meet with my officers. King Longwell is leaving tomorrow; they've been summoned to Enrant Monge by Briyce Unger."

"Will we be going as well?" she asked.

"I don't know yet," Cyrus said.

He heard her move across the floor, taking tentative steps, her feet making a slight sucking noise as they pulled from the marble floor with each step. "Will you hand me back over to my brother? As though I were a piece of property?"

Cyrus felt the answer within him, steeped in the rage he felt inside at her betrayal. *Yes! I'll hand you over to him, let him have you, be done with you and your lies, your deceits, with your ...* He nearly choked at the memory of her fingers tracing lines down his skin. "You should get dressed," he said simply, and walked out the door, careful to open it no more than was necessary to slip out, so as not to expose her to anyone who might be walking down the hall.

As he walked away from the closed door, he stopped, halted by some unseen feeling, something that ran through him, a ripple of strong emotion, and he tried to quiet it. *She lied. She betrayed you. Just like Vara. Just like Imina.* He felt his fist clench. Felt his mask of emotionlessness deteriorate, and he placed his hand on the stone wall of the hallway, as though he could draw some unseen strength from it. He imagined pebbles falling within him, into the giant void, the roiling maelstrom in his chest, the storm that threatened to break loose out of him and cause him to shed tears, something he had not done since ... He remembered, and then pushed it down, back into the depths, along with the storm, along with everything else.

One foot in front of another. Keep walking. I need to meet with the officers. I need to decide what we're going to do next. He took a breath, then another, slow, as though he could excise the venom within simply by breathing it out. He imagined the stones falling inside him again, rocks, boulders, dropping into his center, weighing down his heart, so that he couldn't feel the emotion within. He imagined ice, cold, frigid blocks of it, stacked all around his pain, cooling him, building a wall that it couldn't escape. He let it contain the emotion, bury it, push it far out of sight, behind the wall, where he could no longer taste the bitterness of it in his mouth, and the blood rushing through his ears subsided.

One foot in front of another, he told himself again, pulling his hand from the wall, letting his own strength hold him upright again. He stood up, trying to straighten his spine, as though standing as tall as possible could help somehow, disguise his weakness, put it to the back of him, where he wouldn't feel it and no one would see it. He resisted the urge to let his knees buckle, fought it, let the ice hold his emotions in check. *One foot in front of another. Keep walking.*

He took a step, then another, and the pace became quicker and quicker as his feet carried him away from the door, away from the handle he wanted to turn, the words he wanted to say, away from the feel of her skin against his—and back to his duty.

Chapter 24

"Did you know?" It was Ryin who asked the question, after Cyrus had laid out everything that King Longwell had told him. Reactions had ranged from shocked horror (Nyad, who had her hands covering her mouth, her eyes wider than usual) to calm acceptance (Curatio and J'anda, each of whom let only a single raised eyebrow appear on their faces—Curatio, the left and J'anda the right, the contrast of their light and dark skin and facial reactions making them appear as bizarre mirror images) to unflinching, uncaring emptiness (Terian). Only Ryin spoke, though Samwen Longwell had a question of sorts on his face.

"Of course he didn't," Nyad said, turning to slap Ryin across the arm with a backhand, drawing an annoyed look from the druid as he rubbed his shoulder. She turned back to Cyrus, and her expression changed to perplexed. "Wait, did you?"

"He didn't," Curatio said, studying Cyrus. "This is not the sort of thing our gGeneral would have hidden from us."

"I'd like to hear him say it," Ryin spoke up again, still massaging the place where Nyad had struck him. He looked at the faces around him, Curatio, J'anda and Nyad in particular, showing some irritation with him. "It's not as though it's the first time he's played games with the truth to get something he wanted. I just want to hear him say he didn't know."

"I didn't know," Cyrus said, his voice devoid of any emotion. "But now we have consequences to deal with."

"Actaluere's declaration of war isn't as problematic as one might think," Longwell said, drawing the officers' attention to him. "They'll have received a summons to Enrant Monge as well, and they'll be obligated to attend. We'll have a chance to smooth this over with Milos Tiernan himself."

"What if our esteemed General doesn't want to smooth it over?" Ryin asked. "I mean, we are talking about handing over his lover—"

"She's my nothing," Cyrus said, drawing a gasp from Nyad. "She is nothing to me, now." He didn't wait for the officers to react before plunging ahead. "She is, however, under the protection of Sanctuary, granted asylum because of the barbaric treatment of women in this land."

"Asylum she gained from you under false pretense," Ryin said. "She didn't mention she was the sister of the monarch, did she? That seems like material information that could have influenced our decision to allow her to come along."

"It wasn't 'our' decision," Cyrus said dully. "It was mine."

"Great," Ryin said sarcastically. "Because your stubborn decisions never lead us into war."

"Calm yourself," Curatio said to Ryin. "We do have a reputation to consider. Once we grant someone protection, do we lift it and throw her back to the same brother who willingly wedded her to that monster the moment it becomes inconvenient? That doesn't seem to be the Sanctuary way."

"And starting another war for Galbadien to contend with?" Ryin Ayend looked around the other officers. "Is that the Sanctuary way?"

"It is if we start and finish the war for them," Terian growled. "I'm no fan of the Baroness, but I could stand to have another few battles before we head home." He smiled coldly. "After all, we have troops that need seasoning. It'd be a shame if they marched all the way out here to take part in only one good fight before we turn around and go back to Sanctuary."

"Cyrus?" J'anda's cool voice seemed to demand a level of quiet from the others in the room. "What do you intend to do?"

"We go to Enrant Monge," Cyrus said. "We'll travel along with the Galbadien court, and I'll speak with Milos Tiernan, outline our position, and we'll see where we go from there. Maybe there'll be a war with them ..." He let his voice trail off before it returned, only slightly above a whisper, "... and maybe there won't."

"What position will you be outlining to him?" J'anda asked, looking around at the other officers.

Cyrus did not move, did not blink, and gave no hint of any emotion when he answered. "I don't know yet. But I've got a little less than a month to figure it out."

Chapter 25

They left the next day in a long procession, wending down the hillside from Vernadam, Cyrus, the officers and the other guests he had brought following the King's court. King Longwell was carried down on a litter to a horse-drawn carriage below. Unlike other carriages Cyrus had seen, this one was massive, almost a full living quarters in and of itself. When they reached the bottom of the hill, Cyrus saw his troops assembled for the first time in a month, though he knew Odellan had taken them through regular exercises.

"This looks like a fat and happy lot," Terian said as they rode along the length of the column of Sanctuary's army. "I'd gather that thirty days of rest has been good to them." A harlot in red exposed herself from a balcony above them, then gestured to Terian with a come-hither finger. "A little too good, maybe," the dark elf said. "Perhaps I should ask around and see if our boys have been behaving themselves."

"I don't care what you do," Cyrus said grimly, "so long as you're with us at Enrant Monge when we get there."

"Maybe you should come on this inspection tour with me," Terian said, slowing his horse. "It seems you have frustrations of your own to work out."

"I've worked out plenty of frustrations in the last month," Cyrus said, tense. "It seems to have left me with even more than when I started."

"Perhaps you're being too formal about things," the dark knight suggested as Cyrus brought his horse to a halt, watching as the column began to get underway, marching slowly, in time, toward the west road out of the village. "You're putting too much emphasis on feelings, and trust, and emotion and all these other ugly things that have no place in a bed."

Cyrus stared at the dark elf as Terian tied the reins of his destrier to the hitching post. "Occasionally, Terian, I find myself envying you for the simplistic approach you seem able to take to your emotions."

"Don't speak about things you know nothing about," Terian said darkly. "I am merely suggesting that you might be attaching too much significance to something that need not be so desperately complicated—or nearly so painful as you seem to be making it."

"And I was expressing my admiration for your ability to go unfettered by the messy entanglements that seem to be constantly drawing me down," Cyrus said. "I was quite sincere in what I said."

"You still don't know what you're talking about, Davidon," Terian replied, voice cold. "There's a difference between this and the people you care about."

"I wish there was, for me," Cyrus said. "Unfortunately, thus far, there hasn't been. Perhaps in the future."

Terian smiled, a half one. "Stay a while. With our horses, we can catch up to the army after we finish our business within. Start now. It gets easier every time you do it, just like battle, and your soul gets hardened to it after a while, and it becomes reflexive, as it should be. A glorious release, without that horrible, life-draining emotion you attach to it."

Cyrus's smile was fake, but he tried. "Perhaps some other time. After as long a break as we've had, I suspect our formation will need some practice, and I mean to be there to see it."

"As you wish," Terian said coolly. "But you know full well that Longwell and Odellan can handle that better than you can. If you want to make excuses for yourself, find better ones. If you want to make yourself immune to such pains as you feel now, best get started. Either way, stop fooling yourself." The dark knight turned and began to walk toward the door to the establishment, which was pushed open by a woman wearing a dress that exposed more supple, pink, flawless flesh than Cattrine possessed on her entire body. Cyrus's eyes were drawn to it, even as the woman wrapped an arm around Terian's waist, and let the door swing shut behind them.

Cyrus turned in his saddle to look down the column and caught sight of Cattrine toward the back of the formation with Ryin and Nyad, her horse shuffling along at a slow canter. His eyes took her in, her dark hair as well kempt as any time he had seen her, her riding clothes cleaned and in fine order. Her lips looked especially red, her scars well hidden now. She looked at the ground as she rode, despondent, though Nyad seemed to be chattering happily in her ear.

"The Baroness has an ill humor about her," Odellan said, startling Cyrus as he appeared next to Windrider on his own horse. "A cloud hangs over her, some grief unspoken, I think." He looked at Cyrus in curiosity. "As though Yartraak himself has settled darkness upon her heart."

Cyrus stared at Odellan, trying to decide what to say. He finally settled on, "Keep your eye on the formation. I want our march in perfect order, and after today I want weapons practice for every one of our fighters; we'll be ready if battle comes our way." After seeing Odellan's nod of acknowledgment, Cyrus spurred Windrider, who whinnied in anger at the rough treatment and took off at a run. "Sorry," Cyrus said to the horse after a moment. "I'm sorry."

"I'm sure the horse accepts your apology," Martaina said, coming alongside Cyrus. "Now perhaps you should turn those words in a different direction—"

"Perhaps you should keep yours to yourself," Cyrus snapped. "Because as it happens, I recall about a month ago you told me that even with all your vast experience, you didn't know what you were doing in relationships."

"I can see you're blinded in your pain," Martaina began slowly, after a pause, "but let me bring something forward in your mind. In spite of our similar ears," she said, pushing her hair back behind the points of her ears, "I'm not Vara. If you're looking for a sharp-tongued reply or an argument, look elsewhere. I'm a little too old to slap back at you just because you swing an emotional gauntlet or three my way."

"I only have two gauntlets," Cyrus replied.

"Then that must be something else you're swinging around," Martaina said, deadpan. "You might want to put it back in your pants before someone loses an eye—like you, yourself."

Cyrus bristled. "What are you trying to say? Be plain about it."

"I'm suggesting that you might stop swinging around your ..." she lowered her voice, "... pride, as though it were some sort of weapon to keep people at bay."

"My ..." Cyrus started to shout, but lowered his voice, "... pride ... doesn't seem to get me in anything but trouble of late, as I follow its lead from one woman who stabs me in the front to another who lies to me."

"I don't think we're talking about your pride anymore ... sir." Martaina said. "We're either talking about your groin or your heart, and you might want to differentiate. Because if it's your groin, it probably would have led you in the same direction as Terian went just now. If it's your heart, then you can't really fault it because you don't choose the direction it goes anymore than you could choose what direction you went in as an orphan, dropped off at the front door of the Society of Arms."

Cyrus felt the slap of her words, a surge of memory at the reminder of the first time he walked through the gates to the Society—and the first time he left after that, running through them in the snow, as fast as his six year-old legs could carry him. He felt a blinding flash of anger and the desire to lash out again, to get Martaina away from him—the sting from her knowing too much. The wall of ice dissolved and made cold fury in its stead. "Your counsel is not needed, ranger. And it occurs to me that your efforts at bodyguard haven't gone terribly well, either, considering not a month ago I got my brains dashed out by a dwarf with a hammer, and you did nothing to stop it. Be gone—I'd have you go back to what you were doing before, taking care of the animals, joining scouting parties, anything else."

"And who will watch your back in these unpredictable lands?" Martaina asked, cool, but her words carrying the unmistakable hint of venom.

"I'll watch my own, thank you very much," he said. "I can't do a much worse job of it than you have." He urged Windrider on, this time sparing the spurs. "Why don't you try keeping an eye on Partus as we travel?" he asked. "I don't much care if he lives or dies, after all."

As he rode away, he heard her say something, low, almost lost under the sound of hoofbeats, but there nonetheless. "How do you feel about you, yourself, dying?"

Cyrus felt his eyes narrow at her words, and he leaned forward to ride faster. "I don't much care if I live or die right now, either."

Chapter 26

The journey to Enrant Monge took over three weeks, during which time Cyrus was once again as he had been during the first leg of their trip from Sanctuary. He took his meals alone, gave orders only when he had to, and ignored the few accolades directed his way from soldiers in his army until the word had circulated that the general had sunken once more into a black mood at which point the army went silent whenever he would ride by.

The officers also left him to his own devices, supping without him when they made camp for the day. Cyrus was frequently invited to dine with the King in his own tent. He declined every occasion, often sending one of the other officers in his stead, wordlessly handing off the parchment invitations that seemed to be delivered to him every day in the morning, at the noon hour and when evening came.

The only people who didn't give him a wide berth were J'anda (who attempted a conversation composed of sheer surface-level pleasantries with him at least once per day), Curatio (who only disturbed him to discuss disciplinary matters or things of other import to the army approximately once a week), and Terian (who wandered by for conversation whenever he felt like it; Cyrus could discern no pattern to the dark knight's attempts).

The two people whom Cyrus actually wanted, in some deep place within him, to talk to said nothing to him. Both avoided him, going so far as to remain out of his sight whenever possible. Cattrine continued to ride with Nyad and Ryin, though he saw her speaking with almost all the officers at various points in time. She seemed to be trying to give him space, staying as far away from him as possible.

The other person he wanted to talk to had said nothing to him in a month; Aisling had taken to guarding Partus, who was forced to walk while tied to the back of a horse that cantered along. The dwarf looked somewhat ragged after the long journey. Though he was getting no more exercise than any of the other members of the Sanctuary army, he seemed worse the wear for it. He was ungagged only while the cessation spell was cast around him, he was never left unguarded, and his hands remained shackled at all times. The dwarf wore a perpetual scowl until such time as he became exhausted, which was almost always an hour or two into the walk for the day. Aisling seemed to be near him at all times, watching him through slitted eyes, a silent guardian. On the occasions when Cyrus had seen her, she had avoided any sort of eye contact, defying his prediction that when she heard about his falling out with the Baroness, that she would come directly to him. He tried not to read too much into it. *Once burned, twice shy. When burned many times ... well ... I can identify with that.*

Their path led them on a long, circuitous route, at first following the road that had led them to Vernadam. When they passed a massive lake, they turned north on a wide road; at the signpost Cyrus found he still couldn't read the Luukessian language, and worse, he found he did not care. North, south, east or west, they all seemed much the same to him. *We'll settle this war, and then ...* he thought of Vara, and it still stung, like a dagger picking at an old wound. He thought of Cattrine, and the pain was fresh, like a sword biting at his innards. He pictured the wall of ice again, building it within him block by block and it seemed to soothe the ache, although it did not go away. *I don't know what we'll do then.*

Cyrus's black misery did not seem to lessen as the days went by; if anything, time and isolation made it worse, like a festering wound. He went to sleep thinking of Vara and Cattrine, Cattrine and Vara, and he felt them trouble his dreams, the two of them, like predatory lionesses, circling him while wounded on a battlefield, each one striking in turn, taking a piece of him away until there was scarcely anything left.

Enrant Monge was on a plateau in the center of Luukessia. As they approached, the ground became hilly, the slope rising and falling as they navigated the hills. After a few days of this, it began to level, and Cyrus found himself looking upon the castle one evening as they were close to their end for the night.

"The King told me when I supped with him earlier that we'll leave the army nearby," J'anda said, stirring Cyrus from his silent reverie. "When we stop for the night, they'll encamp there for the time that the moot takes place. He's asked you and no more than five other officers to come along when he and the rest of the court goes to the moot."

"Fine," Cyrus said, his voice scratchy from disuse. "You, Longwell, Terian, and Curatio. We'll bring the Baroness as well, give her an opportunity to see her brother."

"I can't decide whether that will be a very good idea or a very bad one," J'anda said. "But I suspect it will be one of the two."

"Either Tiernan will be happy to see her or he won't," Cyrus said. "It doesn't much matter to me which it is."

"It would not much matter to you if you were being slowly picked apart by vultures on a battlefield, I suspect, " J'anda said, prompting Cyrus to send him a look of indifference. "Thank you for proving my point, I think."

"Impressive," Cyrus said without feeling. "You sussed that out without even having to reach into my mind." He laughed, a low, grim laugh that caused the enchanter to edge away almost nervously. "I wonder what you'd see if you cast a mesmerization spell on me now. What do you think my heart's desire is at this moment?"

"I ..." J'anda swallowed deeply, and Cyrus could hear the reluctance in his answer. "I don't think I would care to know, whatever it is. Your thoughts are not your own, they're the blackest sort of darkness. You look at a bright summer's sky like we've had for the last three weeks and it looks bleak and grey to your eyes. You are covered in it; it swallows you whole, infects you in a way I have only seen happen to you once before—and this time, it may actually be worse. And since last time involved a death of someone dear to you, I would have thought that that would be impossible."

"Well, doesn't that just make you all kinds of wrong," Cyrus said. "Before I just mourned the loss of a friend. Now I get to watch my faith in others gradually disappear."

"I don't think it's others you're losing faith in," J'anda said. "I don't think it's that at all. I think you're starting to lose belief in yourself, that that is what is really eating at you—your confidence is shaken because you feel betrayed. After all, how could this happen to you, twice in a row? You trusted them, you opened your heart to them, and they hurt you. You are wounded. You are licking those wounds. You may think it's your belief in others that is waning, but this is a problem of you, my friend. You are taking it too personally; these sort of things happen."

"What do you know?" Cyrus snapped. "I haven't seen you with a woman in three years."

"I wasn't talking about women," J'anda said coolly. "I was talking about you. Have you not seen me with you in the last three years? Because then I might be speaking of something I know not."

"Listen—"

"I'm going to ride off now," J'anda said. "I am not upset with you, though I expect you are with me; I just imagine that you're running a bit low on people to talk to and I don't want to make it easy for you to drive another away. We'll speak again later." With that, the enchanter rode off, leaving Cyrus staring at him in openmouthed irritation.

Within the hour, the army was beginning to set up camp in the shade of a forest in the hills. From atop one of them, Cyrus could see Enrant Monge in the distance and other armies, smaller ones, encamped to the north and the west, like the three points of a triangle.

Enrant Monge was a castle but not like Vernadam at all. The blocks that it was made of were smaller, yet the design was less ornate and more functional. A simple curtain wall with parapets extended in a perfect square around a courtyard with three towers in the keep. The towers looked to be of different construction than the outer wall, as though they had been added later; cracks in the wall also looked to have been patched with some sort of grout that was visible in the orange light of sunset as the towers cast shade over the whole scene and a cool breeze blew across them. The castle was only a mile or so away, he estimated.

The journey went all too quickly for Cyrus; a few minutes and it seemed to be over. He and the others—Curatio, J'anda, Longwell, Terian, and the Baroness, the latter two trading uneasy looks—rode along with the small delegation from Galbadien to the gates of Enrant Monge. Cyrus had noted that the castle's four walls each had a gate, one at each compass point. They entered through the eastern gate, and Cyrus looked back to make sure his delegation was still with him as he followed the King's over the drawbridge. He saw each of them in turn; Longwell, whose gaze was moving around, examining their surroundings with a little awe, Cattrine, who met Cyrus's look with indifference and turned away after staring him in the eyes for a few seconds. Curatio and J'anda seemed somewhat wary, and Terian was watching Cyrus when he caught the dark knight's stare. Terian did not look away, however, but continued to watch, Cyrus could feel, even after he had turned back to the path ahead.

The drawbridge was long, a hundred or more feet, and Cyrus pondered the age of the wood with every step Windrider took. It creaked and he looked down into the water. The dark moat rippled as the last vestiges of daylight sparkled across the surface, the orange sky reflected above the ramparts of the castle's mirror image in the water. As they crossed under the gate, Cyrus saw a few guards standing at attention on either side of them. They carried poleaxes and did not move, their livery something very different than what Cyrus had seen before, a kind of red and yellow surcoat with a coat of arms that had red diagonally at top right and bottom left and yellow at top left and bottom right, with Luukessian writing in the banner across the top. Their surcoats were flawless, their helms a shining metal that gave him a stabbing reminder of Vara. He cast another look back at Cattrine, but she was looking elsewhere, her gaze sliding off the guards at attention.

They passed through a bailey and into a smaller keep, between the guards standing at attention outside it. Once through the gate, there were no guards, only stewards, unarmed, waiting for them, bowing (*Again with the bowing,* thought Cyrus, *it's a wonder these people have spines left at all after so much of it*) as King Longwell brought his delegation to a halt and Cyrus stopped his just behind him.

"Welcome to Enrant Monge," the lead steward, a short man in flowing grey robes with long hair that matched them, said, "the heart of unity in Luukessia."

Cyrus heard Terian snort loud enough to attract the attention of everyone around him. "Sorry," the dark knight said, "I guess I must have failed to notice the unity in all the battles I've fought since I got here." Cyrus sent him a dirty look, which was matched by Curatio and J'anda. Terian shrugged, unfazed.

The steward ignored him and continued his clearly pre-practiced speech, hands in the air above him. "The delegations from Syloreas and Actaluere have already arrived, and we will begin with the traditional welcome ceremony of peace in the garden in half an hour." The steward nodded. "I would remind you that no weapons or armor are allowed in the garden of serenity, and that no violence is permitted within the walls of Enrant Monge under penalty of death."

"That's usually how my acts of violence turn out anyway," Terian said, prompting Curatio to shush him.

"Your tower quarters are prepared," the steward said. He bowed again, causing Cyrus to unwittingly roll his eyes. "Go forth in peace, brothers."

"But not sisters, eh?" Cyrus heard J'anda mutter to Cattrine, causing her to laugh airily.

"This way to the tower," Odau Genner said from his place next to Count Ranson, who looked back at the Sanctuary members in amusement. If the King thought anything that had been said was funny, he hid it well, riding atop his horse with only the thinnest hint of expression.

Cyrus dismounted in the courtyard and let a stableboy lead Windrider off with the other horses, back toward the first bailey that they had crossed. Cyrus looked around the inner keep—the three towers he had seen from the ridge above Enrant Monge were visible now, and ahead of him was another walled structure—not quite high enough to be a keep, but through a tunnel he could see trees.

"The Garden of Serenity," Cattrine said, brushing against him as she walked past. His eyes followed her, sinking lower, to her backside, her riding pants clinging to the lines of her figure after the last long hours on horseback. He blinked and looked up as she turned and caught him, her eyes flashing ... something. Before, Cyrus would have assumed lust coupled with amusement, but now it was mixed with coolness. "The center of the castle and the place where the old keep sat in ancient times, the seat of old Luukessia before the schism. Our entire land was ruled from here."

"I'm sure it was very impressive," Cyrus said with some tightness. "Did I hear him say we're not allowed weapons or armor within the walls?"

"Of the Garden of Serenity, yes," Cattrine said. "You'll be expected to leave them behind in your room in the tower."

He started toward the tower and leaned close to her as he passed, felt the brush of her hair against his, sensed her close and fought off the momentary, mad desire to take her in his arms and— He stopped and whispered in her ear, "and will you be leaving your dagger in your room in the tower?"

He leaned back to see her eyes, and when he did he saw ice, pure and cool, her green irises frosted over. "If I didn't," she said, "I'd be in violation of the laws of Luukessia and subject to death."

"That wasn't really an answer," Cyrus said, and followed the King and his party toward the tower built into the outer wall of the garden— one of three, but the only one on this side of the keep. Within, he found a dim entry chamber and thick stone walls. The place was lit with small windows, arched but only six inches or so across. Candles hung from the walls and the overhead chandeliers, giving the rooms and the stone within an orange glow, something flickering and dimmer by far than the bright, open-paned windows of Vernadam or even Green Hill. Sanctuary, by contrast, made the tower look even dimmer.

Cyrus waited as King Longwell and his party were escorted to chambers on the lower floors. Cyrus and his party were paired with another steward, a younger one, who led them up several spirals of the staircase, which ran up the center of the castle. Cyrus estimated they were on the fifth or sixth floor when the steward came to a stop and began assigning them rooms. Cyrus deferred to Cattrine, allowing her first choice. The steward opened a door and offered a smallish chamber, not even as large as the bedroom in the suite he and Cattrine had shared at Vernadam.

She nodded in acknowledgment, and the steward blushed. "There is no bath for the ladies in this tower, madam. If you'd like, we can bring up a wooden laundry tub and fill it any time you'd care for a bath."

"Thank you," she said. "That will be fine."

"Where's the garderobe?" Terian asked, peering into Cattrine's chambers, drawing a look of annoyance from the Baroness, whose passage through the door was blocked by the dark elf. "Or do you have a communal chamber for that?"

"Ah, no," said the steward with a hint of embarrassment. "Enrant Monge is an ancient keep, sir." The steward blushed further at Terian when the dark elf turned his full attention on the dumbstruck lad, who likely had never seen a dark elf before. "We do not have garderobes."

"Oh gods," Terian said in disgust. "Chamber pots? We're to use chamber pots? Why not just stay with the army? At least I could walk away from the latrine."

"We clean your quarters every morning, sir," the steward asserted, seeming to make a slight recovery. "I assure you, we take the utmost pride in—"

"Cleaning my shite?" Terian asked, darkly amused. "I'm sure you do." He took note of Cattrine, standing behind him and bowed in an exaggerated manner as he moved aside to allow her to pass. "A thousand pardons, my lady."

"You'll need a thousand and one, since you presumed to call me 'your' lady." Cattrine stepped past him as though he were no longer there.

"I apologize," Terian said, fake contrition oozing over his voice. "A thousand and one pardons to Lord Davidon's bedchamber wench, I apologize for—"

She slapped him hard; whether it was because he did not see her attack coming or because he chose to let her hit him, Cyrus could not say.

Terian rubbed his jaw where her hand had landed, a slight smile on his face, the skin already deepening to a darker shade of blue. "Is that not considered to be violence in this place of peace?" Terian asked the steward.

"I saw no violence, sir," the steward replied without emotion. "Even were it to happen again, I suspect I still would not see it as such. Enrant Monge is a place of peace, not a place of veiled insults or unkindness toward women."

"Well, isn't this a fine place to stay," Terian said acidly. "Perhaps you'll show me to my own room now, so that I may express my sentiments to my chamber pot."

The steward led them on, and Cyrus saw Cattrine disappear behind the door of her room, giving one last look at him before she shuttered herself within.

Cyrus was the last to get his room, a floor above the Baroness's, and not next to anyone but Terian, who had entered his own without comment. Cyrus found his accommodations small but did not complain nor say anything but a brief thanks to the steward, who closed the door and left Cyrus in his room.

Cyrus stared at the walls, the small, rectangular space reminding him of the dungeon room he had taken for a brief time at Sanctuary over a year ago. With a sigh and some reluctance, he began by unstrapping his belt, grasping the scabbard of Praelior, holding it in his hands while he studied it. *Avenger's Rest,* he thought, remembering the name of the scabbard. *I just came from a month of rest, and already I am weary again.*

He placed the sword with care upon the bed then eased himself down on the frame, careful to not land too heavily upon it for fear of breaking it. *I find myself again rampant with desire.* He removed his helm and laid it upon a nearby table. *I had a month of free expression of that as well; after such a long time of lacking, it now feels strange to go without the touch of a woman.* He grimaced, feeling his desire blossom inadvertently once more. *This needs to stop if I'm to be attired in cloth during my stay here, lest my embarrassment become a constant.*

He tugged at his boot, felt the first of them give, sliding around his heel and off, as he set it upon the stone floor with a quiet clang. *I could have been back at Sanctuary now. Back among the others ... Vaste, Andren ... Alaric.* The Guildmaster's name brought a slight tremor of unease; he remembered Alaric's anger, his rage at Cyrus, the night before they had left. *How is it that I can take wrath and anger from creatures as tall as a building that want to kill me—from a god, enraged, ready to smite me—but that of a man smaller than I, a simple paladin and Guildmaster, terrifies me?* He felt a burning heat under his collar and slid the gloves from his hands, one by one, placing them upon the dresser. *All he did was raise his voice, and I cowered before him, as though I were a child again, listening to the thundercrack of my father's voice.* Cyrus paused. *I don't even remember my father's voice.*

He worked loose the pauldrons from his shoulders, and laid them at the foot of the bed. *We killed a god. I had saved Vara. It was a moment of triumph, and he ... merely yelled at me.* Cyrus slid off his vambraces, one at a time, working them free to expose the sleeves of his undershirt. He tossed them upon the bed next to the pauldrons. *I had scarcely thought of that, since five minutes later I was neatly gutted and tossed aside by Vara but ... that might prove tense, if Alaric is still upset with me when I return.*

His eyes ran across the room, searching for something familiar but finding only his own armor and darkened surroundings, the single portal window shedding light. *It's been months now, doubtless he'll have forgotten whatever irritation he held for me by the time I return. He was fine, after all, when we spoke a few minutes later. He even rallied the army for me to take along.* Cyrus's greaves came off and slid down, and he laid them at the foot of the bed on the stone floor, careful not to let them drop for fear of the awful clangor they would make when they hit.

What awaits me at Sanctuary when I return? Possibly a still-angry Guildmaster. A woman who has rejected my advances, who has rejected me ... He stopped and pictured her, Vara, as he had seen her once in the garden behind Sanctuary on a sunny day, her hair glowing in the light. He felt the stab again. *She is unlikely to have changed her mind; she is more stubborn than anyone I've ever met.* He unfastened his breastplate and backplate, and took them off, lowering them to rest on top of his greaves. *So I'll have at least her to contend with.* A light blanket of misery settled upon him. *Which might not be so bad, save for the fact that ...* He rubbed his eyes, as though by blotting out the world he could change it to suit his liking. *... I don't know that I feel any differently about her than I did when I left.*

Cyrus lifted his chainmail over his head in a single motion, slipping it off and depositing it with the other armor he had left on the bed. He paused, noting a few new holes in the links where blades had slipped through since he'd last had it mended, and shook his head. *All this heavy armor and I'm still vulnerable to all manner of attacks.* He smiled ruefully. *Perhaps the secret is to not get hit. That might be a better solution than armor. But I suppose it's rather like not falling in love*—and he felt the searing pain of Vara and now Cattrine—*if only it were possible to prevent.*

He looked at the full-length mirror in the corner, at the stained and messy cloth undershirt and sighed. *What the hell am I supposed to wear to this ceremony?* His eyes fell upon the dresser, a tall armoire next to it. He opened the dresser first, finding cloth shirts within of varying sizes, even one large enough to fit him, and then pants as well, with laces for the front.

Upon opening the armoir he blinked. Long robes of green cloth occupied the interior, the same style and cut as had been worn by the stewards that had greeted them upon arrival, but the green was far deeper and more lively than the dull grey worn by the brethren who seemed to maintain the castle. Cyrus wondered at them, at their origin.

Do they come from one of the Kingdoms? Or are they set apart and stay here? I should ask Cattrine— The thought cropped into 'his mind before he could quell it, a remnant of the month they had spent together at Vernadam. He felt the bitterness of the thought; it had occurred to him infrequently on the journey, creeping up on him when he least expected it, when he forgot the argument, forgot her betrayal.

A gonging in the hallway drew his attention as he finished slipping into the robe. It fit over his head, thick and heavy like burlap, and his new underclothes protected him from the roughness of the cloth. He glanced into the bottom of the armoire where several sizes of boots awaited, and he immediately knew that all of them were far too small for his needs. He sighed and tried on the largest of them, stopping once he had crammed his foot far enough in to know they would never fit. He replaced the footcovers he wore under his boots instead and made his way out of the room.

Cyrus found the others milling about in the hallway, down the spiral of the stairs, and the deep, resonant gonging continued, ringing forth once every thirty seconds as the tower continued to empty. Cyrus led the way, finding Curatio and J'anda still in their own robes. Longwell and Terian had similarly changed into garb resembling his. Longwell appeared to be at peace with his robes while Terian fussed at his, muttering mild curses in the dark elven language that Cyrus knew only because of how foul they were.

Cattrine waited on the landing below, still clad in her riding outfit. The others followed Cyrus, and when he paused to acknowledge her, looking her riding outfit up and down with a flick of his eyes, she spoke. "Women don't wear the robes of the brethren." She drew up and folded her arms. "Women are to be clad in dresses at all times and not to adopt the accouterments of men." He raised an eyebrow at her, letting the unasked question hang between them. She smiled, but there was none of the sweetness or promise it carried a month earlier. "This ought to leave my brother with a certain sting."

"Yes," Cyrus agreed, "I know from experience you're quite good at that." He didn't wait for her to respond, instead leading the way down the stairs to the bottom.

When they reached the bottom he followed the grey-clad stewards in a column out into the courtyard, where they joined a long line outside the gates to the Garden of Serenity. They stopped in the small tunnel, as each of the members entering was called forward, their full rank and titles being yelled out into the garden.

Cyrus heard an echoing voice as they waited in a line, moving forward as one person from each Kingdom was admitted at a time. There were heralds stationed at each entrance to the garden and they took up the call of their fellows whenever a name and title were called out, making certain that everyone in the garden and waiting in the tunnel heard it as well. The herald shouted in front of him and Cyrus found himself cupping one hand to his ear as he did so.

Odau Genner was in front of him and leaned back to speak. "Our King will have you go before him, so that he may enter last. I suspect Actaluere will do the same."

"What about Syloreas?" Cyrus asked.

"Master of Scylax Hall, the Grand Duke of the Erres Fjords, conqueror of Viras Tellus, victor at the battle of Argoss Swamp and master of the north, the King of Syloreas, Briyce Unger!" The shout carried down the tunnel and drew a sharp sigh of reprobation from Genner.

"The northmen always do things differently," Genner complained. "Uncivilized blighters, aren't they? Focused on war and destruction, conquest and battle. Bloody savages if you ask me." Another name was called, this one from Actaluere's rolls. "Don't get me wrong, we've been known to engage in a war or two ourselves. But the business of Galbadien is not in war, it's in the good, green land. We'll fight, when necessary, but the Syloreans ... they'll fight simply because they want to fight."

"It's of great interest to me," Cyrus began, folding his arms over his green robes, "how many times I've been to lands when people are at war. You know what's funny about that? It's always the other party that seems to have started it. No one ever wants to admit that they might be at fault for a war beginning, but everyone damned sure wants to win once it's begun."

"Yes, I see," Genner said. "How peculiar."

A succession of names went on as servants of King Longwell passed him in the line, going forth into the garden. Count Ranson was called shortly thereafter, with a litany of titles. By now, Cyrus was near the front, and when one of them in particular was called—"Victor of the Battle of Harrow's Crossing!"—he saw Ranson stiffen and turn, appalled, his mouth agape, until his eyes locked onto Cyrus's and he shook his head in apology. Cyrus watched and shrugged, feeling a strange mix of despondence and indifference that he couldn't quite attribute to any one thing.

When Cyrus drew near to the front of the line, the herald stopped him, asking him quickly for a title and listing, finding nothing about him on the parchment he held in front of him. Cyrus obliged, quickly, between the herald's repeated shouts of the titles and names given by his opposite numbers on Actaluere and Syloreas's sides of the courtyard.

"General Cyrus Davidon of Sanctuary," the herald began after completing the call for the Baron who had just entered from Actaluere. "Warden of the Southern Plains, Lord of Perdamun, conqueror of Green Hill, victor of the battle of the Mountains of Nartanis, defender of the Grand Span in Termina, and vanquisher of the Goblin Imperium!"

Cyrus took the cue from the herald and walked forward, out of the tunnel and into the garden. Though slightly smaller than the foyer at Sanctuary, it was filled near to brimming with trees and plants of all kinds, as well as flowers in planters. Four paths led down into the center of the garden, which was a sort of small-scale amphitheater. Three of the four sections had already begun to fill, with green robes seated to his left, nearest him, and opposite them, blue robes that he suspected represented Actaluere's delegation. Across the center of the amphitheater and to his right was the Sylorean delegation, clad in white robes. To his right was an empty section, bereft of any occupants. Tempted though he was, Cyrus avoided sitting within those seats, veering instead into the Galbadiens'.

He found a clear segment of benches not far from Odau Genner and listened to the next two names called, waiting to hear Samwen Longwell announced to follow him. Instead, he heard something quite unexpected.

"The Baroness Cattrine Tiernan Hoygraf, late of castle Green Hill, free woman and advisor to the guild of Sanctuary." A buzz of conversation and muted outrage came from the Actaluere delegation, men in blue robes muttering and casting glares toward the Galbadiens, a few choice epithets making their way across the aisle. For their part, the men of Galbadien seemed muted in their response; Odau Genner's eyes would not meet Cyrus's and were centered entirely on his leather footwear.

He turned to see Cattrine come down the aisle, seating herself on the empty bench behind him.

Cyrus stared at her. "I thought Longwell was next."

She didn't emote when she answered, keeping neutral. "He was behind you, but his father asked that he be announced just before the King, and Samwen acceded to his wishes." She made a face, a very slight one, of triumph. "The King also asked that I step forward, I think hoping that it might prompt a reaction from the Actaluere delegation." She wore a bitter smile. "I believe it has."

Another was called from Syloreas, a mountainous man whom Cyrus took note of as he strode down the aisle and took his seat with the rest. All of the men of Syloreas seemed larger to Cyrus's eyes than the Actaluere or Galbadien delegations, closer to his own height. He spoke to the Baroness, but did not turn to look at her as he did so. "I'd be a bit careful of how hard you provoke your brother looking for a reaction. You might find one you're not liable to enjoy."

"He pledged me to a man who beat and tortured me for a year," she said, her voice like iron. "I'd worry if you hadn't killed my husband because then I might have something to fear. But even if you send me back to Actaluere with my brother, what is the worst that can happen?"

"You never ask that," Cyrus said. "It's just bad form."

Cattrine almost seemed to chuckle, and for just a moment the distance between them faded until Cyrus remembered that they were not at Vernadam any longer. "Why is that?" Cattrine asked when her reserve had returned. "Do you subscribe to the western superstition of believing that your gods will inflict such things upon you as some sort of punishment?"

"I don't subscribe to much," Cyrus said, "but I've seen gods, and they're not why I fear to say something like that. It's almost as though you're tempting it to come true, as though you're seeking pain." He shook his head. "I've got enough pain already, I don't need to seek any more."

The herald's call was jarring, dragging Cyrus's attention away from Cattrine and back to the matter at hand. "Oh gods," she whispered behind him.

"The victor of the clash at the Dun Crossroad, the Blade of Actaluere, Baron of Green Hill, and now Grand Duke of all Forrestshire—Tematy Hoygraf!"

He walked with the aid of a stick, leaning heavily with every step, fighting the pull of gravity with his upper body, and warring against legs that almost didn't seem to want to carry him. His hair was still black, his beard still unkempt and patchy, but long where it grew, and his pale blue eyes were filled with just as much spite as when last Cyrus had seen them, glaring at him from the floor of the man's own living quarters. Baron—now Grand Duke—Hoygraf worked his way down the aisle and seated himself with great effort, glaring all the while at Cyrus and Cattrine.

"That," Cyrus said, a little chill running down him, "is why you never ask what the worst that can happen is."

Chapter 27

"What the hells, Cyrus?" Terian hissed at him a few minutes later, after he was announced and had taken his seat. "You getting so weak and soft in your old age that you don't remember how to properly kill a man anymore?"

"Why don't you test me and find out?" Cyrus answered him in a calm voice. *Grand Duke. I gutted him and he got a new title. Imagine what his King will reward him with when I kill him for real next time.*

"What now?" Terian asked. "We kill him, right?"

"Not here," Cyrus said. He glanced back and saw Cattrine frozen, staring across the distance at the Grand Duke. "Hey," he said, snapping her attention back to him. "Whatever our differences, you will not be going back with him, understand?"

"Thank you," she whispered. "You are ..." She swallowed heavily, "... a man of the finest quality. A woman would be lucky to possess you, even for so short a while as I did."

"Your mush is making me nauseous," Terian said as J'anda seated himself next to them. "And I'm already homicidal thanks to Hoygraf's sudden appearance, so let's not push it, all right?"

"Your sword is usually far better aimed than this, my friend," J'anda said to Cyrus without a hint of admonition.

"I'm sorry," Cyrus snapped, "I can't recall ever stabbing someone in the stomach with the intention to make the wound painful yet mortal. I'll try harder next time to maximize his suffering while minimizing his chances of survival." Cyrus's expression hardened. "Or maybe I'll just get back to what I do best, which is killing on the spot and leaving no chance of survival."

"That's the spirit, play to your strengths," J'anda said without enthusiasm. "We still may have to deal with this bastard."

"Not here," Curatio said as he seated himself with them. "If you truly mean to revenge yourself upon this man, it at least needs to wait until we're clear of Enrant Monge. Assuming our general doesn't disagree," he said with a nod to Cyrus, "I don't think we should be causing any more hell for our hosts to deal with. We did come here to help them, after all."

"To the blazes with our hosts," Terian said, his eyes afire, "in case you haven't noticed, King Longwell is using us as the spear to keep his enemies at bay while he tries to decide how best to pluck their Kingdoms. He'll have us sacking their castles 'ere long, sending us all around this land making us keep his damned peace."

"You ready to leave?" Cyrus asked Terian, challenge infusing every word. "I'd say Alaric's about due for a messenger, and you could go right along with them—"

"I'm no coward," Terian said, sullen. "I'll stay until the end of the fight. But I don't like being used, especially not to build someone's empire. We came here to save Longwell's father's Kingdom, and we did that. Now he's just using us to prop up his army."

"No doubt," Samwen Longwell slid onto the bench in front of Cyrus, alongside Curatio, and leaned back. "He will keep us here as long as possible and use whatever pretense he can to extend our stay. The timing of this trip and Actaluere's declaration was so fortuitous I don't wonder if there weren't missives exchanged before the declaration arrived."

"Usually not a fantastic sign when a man's own son accuses him of sinister motives," J'anda said with a shake of the head. "What do we do, then?"

"We wait," Cyrus said as Actaluere's King was announced. "We sit here and we watch the whole summit, and we decide where we go from there."

At that moment, the King of Actaluere was announced with great pomp and circumstance, and a title that took almost two minutes for the herald to fully read. When he came out, Cyrus watched along with the others. Milos Tiernan was a younger man than Aron Longwell, or Briyce Unger, for that matter. His hair was long and black, but straight, and his high cheekbones and cold eyes surveyed everything carefully as he entered from the tunnel, a slow, steady gait to his walk, no crown upon his head. He had no crow's feet at the edges of his eyes, no obvious wrinkles. His eyes moved slickly, smoothly, and they were smaller than most, Cyrus judged, as though they were always watching everything around him.

When Tiernan reached the amphitheater, he seated himself in the front row, his gaze focused on a mountain of a man in the front row of the Sylorean delegation. Cyrus had noted the Sylorean when he entered; the man appeared to be nearly as tall as Cyrus himself or possibly taller, and he shifted uncomfortably in his robe, as though he chafed under it as some sort of weight upon him. Long, jet-black hair belied a face that bore a couple of choice scars—one under the man's right eye that stitched several inches down to his jaw. Another ran the length of his forehead, as though it were just another furrow in his brow. *If that's not Briyce Unger,* Cyrus thought, *I'm a gnome.* The entire Sylorean delegation seemed ill at ease, and Cyrus could see, almost instinctively, that every last one of them was watching Unger for a cue, trying to decide how to act, and shifting aimlessly in their seats as though eager to leave.

"And finally," the last herald announced, launching into a two minute recital of titles before concluding with, "King of Galbadien, Aron Longwell!"

"As a point of literal correctness," J'anda said with a sigh, "he should have saved the, 'and finally' for after the recitation of titles." The enchanter looked pointedly at Cyrus. "And I thought you were overly impressed with your accolades. You are a rank amateur compared to these shameless self-gratifying professionals."

"What are you talking about?" Terian said with a malicious grin. "He's very much in the realm of professional when it comes to self-gratification." The dark elf cast his wicked smile at Cattrine. "Especially of late."

Cyrus did not volley back at Terian, instead shifting to watch King Longwell make his way slowly down to the front bench in their segment of the amphitheater. For the first time, Cyrus noted that a few of the grey-robed stewards were lurking behind each set of benches, as though they were waiting for something, standing still, arms crossed behind their backs.

One of the heralds spoke, not echoed by the other two. "Now I introduce to you Brother Grenwald Ivess, the patron of our order, the Brotherhood of the Broken Blade." A portly, balding man with the last vestiges of grey hair ringing the sides and back of his head made his way down to the empty set of benches on the fourth side of the circle, the unoccupied set to Cyrus's right.

"The Brotherhood of the Broken Blade has cared for Enrant Monge for thousands of years," Cattrine said quietly, drawing the attention of all the Sanctuary delegation save for Samwen Longwell, who was leaning over, face resting in his hands, watching the proceedings below unfold as Grenwald Ivess took his seat. "They keep and maintain it as a place of regard for our ancestors who were united in ruling Luukessia. Their mission is to keep it ready for the day when Luukessia will unite again under the banner of old and we will become as great as our fathers before us, equal and worthy to carry on their proud tradition of unity." She pointed to a fourth tunnel, the one that Grenwald Ivess had come into the garden through. "Out that tunnel is the fourth gate of Enrant Monge, the south gate—also called the Unity Gate. If the day comes that the Kings forge the final peace, those who have attended here will walk out of that gate; it has not been used since Enrant Monge was the seat of all the land."

"What happened here?" J'anda asked. "What caused the Kingdoms to fragment?"

"I do not know," Cattrine said. "We have no real records from those days. Our writings have all been lost to the ravages of age, and no one lives who has more than a tale passed down through the millennia, weakened and twisted by the passage of time." She shrugged. "I doubt you could get an accurate accounting from anyone who wasn't there themselves to see it—ten thousand years ago."

Cyrus's head swiveled slowly along with Longwell's, Terian's and J'anda's, and all four sets of their eyes came to rest on Curatio, who looked back at them impassively, almost disinterested. "Curatio?" J'anda asked.

"Yes, J'anda?" Curatio wore an almost patronizing smile plastered on his face.

"Do tell."

"Tell what?" Curatio said, maintaining his overly friendly smile as below them Grenwald Ivess stood and launched into a florid greeting that Cyrus didn't catch a word of. "Oh, I'm sorry," the healer said, voice slightly above a whisper. "Are you under the impression that I know something about what happened here ten thousand years ago?"

"Ten thousand years ago?" Cyrus asked. "Kind of a funny number.

Been coming up a lot lately."

"A few times in the space of months could be considered hardly more than a coincidence," Curatio said.

"But it's not, is it?" J'anda asked. "The War of the Gods, ten thousand years ago? It spilled over here, didn't it?"

"Not really," Curatio said. "There were certainly expeditions, but when the war began, I firmly believe it constrained itself to Arkaria. What happened here, I believe, happened shortly before the war. I haven't heard much more than rumors, secondhand, keep in mind—but to understand even those, you must realize that humans do not originate on Arkaria.

"I'm sorry, what is he talking about?" Cattrine asked.

"He's over twenty thousand years old," Cyrus said. "He lived through your land's schism." Cyrus watched Cattrine's jaw drop then watched her eyes flick to Curatio, appraising him, looking for some sign of the age he didn't show.

"That sounds ridiculous, Curatio," J'anda said. "Humans are likely the most populous race in Arkaria. They certainly have more in numbers than the dwarves, the gnomes, the elves or the trolls."

"Very true, but it was not always so. The rise of the Confederation and their power is very recent, remember. In fact, I recall the days when there were no humans." He sighed. "Not fondly, exactly, but ... uh ... well." He paused, slightly pained. "It was simpler back then, you understand."

"So if humans don't come from Arkaria ...?" Cyrus let his words trail off.

"They are from Luukessia," Curatio said, "and from inauspicious beginnings did they come to Arkaria—the ancients sent expeditions to Luukessia for purposes of slaving, bringing back tens of thousands of humans to their capital—where Reikonos sits today—as labor for their empire. The expeditions stopped after the ancients were destroyed, obviously, but humanity on Arkaria sprung from the ashes of the empire and took root in their lands."

"A fascinating history lesson," Longwell said, skeptical. "But I have a hard time believing that, if you'll forgive me."

Curatio shrugged. "I saw enough of it myself to be sure it's true, humans marched into the coliseum to fight for the entertainment of the ancients. I saw them tending the houses, working in the fields. I've never been to Luukessia myself until now, so all I'd heard is what those on the expeditions told me."

"You knew the ancients?" Cyrus asked.

"Some of them," Curatio said. "I was in their capital for a time."

"Interesting story. Will you play Alaric and refuse to tell us any more of it if we ask later?" J'anda watched the healer with a coy smile.

"I'd rather not remember some of those days," Curatio said darkly. "But I'm willing to discuss parts of it. Back to the point, though—the last time the ancients came here, Luukessia was already in chaos and the land was dividing into what I presume became the Kingdoms you have today." He shrugged. "That is all I recall of it."

"Fascinating," J'anda said as the volume rose down on the floor, drowning out any further whispering.

King Longwell was standing now as was Milos Tiernan and a few of their aides as well. "I have done nothing to you," King Longwell said, his voice comically raised. "Did I ransack one of your castles? Did my army? No."

"It was your vassals," Milos Tiernan said, his voice calm, much calmer than Longwell's. "I see them, even now, sitting with my sister, as though to taunt me with her as an affront to my honor." Cyrus looked at the man carefully, watching his facial movements, and decided that if there was any sign of effrontery there, it was well hidden. "Your mercenaries came through my lands and caused great harm to my people."

"Your Baron kidnapped my people and brought great harm to your own lands," Cyrus said, standing, and drawing a gasp from the crowds on Actaluere's and Galbadien's benches. "Had he simply let us pass, none of what you're upset over would have happened, and he'd still be a baron," Cyrus pointed to Hoygraf, who glared at him, hunched over on his seat, "with all his equipment still functioning, and not a Grand Duke who lacks any grandiosity."

"You have no standing to speak here, sir," Milos Tiernan said, still unexpressive.

"And yet I'm standing and I'm speaking," Cyrus said. "How 'bout that."

Cyrus felt the tug of Odau Genner pulling on his sleeve, so he sat and Genner whispered to him, "Interrupting the debate of Kings is not considered to be appropriate."

Cyrus stared at the clearly disturbed Genner, whose face seemed to be twitching from thought of the infraction of the rules. "I'll do it sparingly in the future," Cyrus said, causing Genner to twitch anew.

They returned their attention to the floor, where King Longwell was reading a list of grievances to Briyce Unger of Syloreas, who stared at his feet in utter boredom. When Aron Longwell finished, he asked, "What say you, Unger?"

Briyce Unger stirred, slowly, as though awakening from a sleep. He got to his feet, unfolding his massive frame. He was muscled like Cyrus, though he was older, and his physique bulged even through the sleeves of the robe. "It's all true," Unger said. "I won't deny a bit of it, though some of those injuries don't sound like things my men did, especially a few of those villages you claim were damaged. Seems they're a mite further south than my armies got, at least to my understanding, but I'll not quibble with your accounting."

A buzz ran through the garden, one of amused joy in the Galbadien ranks, slight shock in Actaluere's, and mutinous rumblings from Syloreas. "What's that about?" Cyrus asked Genner, who watched agape.

"Briyce Unger has just accepted the King's reportage of grievances," Genner said, his mouth flapping in shock. "That means he'll agree to pay reparations for the damages. Such things are never agreed upon this quickly in the moot, and certainly not wholly—I mean, we included villages in the listing that suffered no damage, so we would be able to cede some out from the final figures. That's how it works, you see, you profess a list of damages, they deny it totally, then you give them a smaller list, they acknowledge one, maybe two, and it goes on—no one accepts a list of grievances wholly, not ever!"

"Why would he do that?" Cyrus asked.

"How much will he be paying?" Terian asked, a glimmer in his eyes.

"I don't know on either count," Genner said. "It's all to be decided later, in smaller sessions. This first session is for the points of major contention, when all the grievances are reported; the mediations come later and are handled by underlings, not the Kings."

"Briyce Unger," Grenwald Ivess spoke, as King Longwell took his seat. "Now has come the time for your first grievance to be brought."

Unger took his feet once more, and motioned up the steps behind him. "I have a grievance mightier than anyone else, one that concerns everyone in this room, eventually, one which will destroy us all if left unchecked."

"You fear my mercenaries?" King Longwell was already on his feet. "You bring your own, wreck my Kingdom, and now you wish to warn of the dangers of westerners, now that a group of them is poised at your neck?" Cyrus watched the King, and from the side profile he could see veins standing out on the man's temple, his ire either real or well feigned.

Unger waved his hand in utter dismissal. "Were your western mercenaries camped outside my hall in Scylax even now, I would be unworried. I have greater concerns." He waved his hand up the stairs, and four of his men came down, carrying a large bundle between them, wrapped in cloth as though it were a funeral shroud being borne by the four warriors, one at each corner. "Things have happened between us, battles," he nodded at King Longwell, "wars, takings of women and sisters," he nodded at Tiernan. "But what is waiting for us right now is a threat graver than any of our petty concerns."

"I doubt he'd feel the same had he taken Vernadam a moon ago," Genner said under his breath. Cyrus heard grunts of agreement from the benches in front of him.

Unger ignored whatever comments were made and focused on his oratory. "In the last month and a half, my Kingdom has been invaded."

Milos Tiernan sat up in interest, as did Aron Longwell, Cyrus saw. "I didn't think Count Ranson's armies had made it into Syloreas's territories yet?" he asked Genner under his breath.

"They haven't. It must be Tiernan, that bastard opportunist. He always strikes when a back is turned." Genner guffawed. "Better Unger than us."

"What accusation are you making here?" Milos Tiernan asked.

"I'm not accusing anyone here," Briyce Unger said, holding up his arms. "I've lost the northern mountain reaches of my Kingdom to an invasion. No man is responsible, not as near as I can tell. It's this," he kicked out with his toe, pointed at the bundle his soldiers had laid at his feet. "These ... things."

With that, his men pulled back the cloth. A smell of rot wafted over the crowd, causing a few weak stomachs to gag. Cyrus's eyes were fixed on the black cloth, on the creature within. It was pale of skin, without a hair to be seen. Decomposition had set in and the flesh had begun to decay, maggots crawling over it, but the figure was still visible, and Cyrus stood to get a better look.

It walked on four legs, even with a roughly man-shaped body. A hideously disfigured mouth was still visible, though the edges of it had begun to decay. Had he not seen one recently, it still would have looked familiar, though Cyrus could not place the thing, could not decide where he had ever seen one before, or even if—

"It's the ..." J'anda was the one who spoke. "From the swamp, when we captured Partus, it's the ... ghoulish thing that was attacking him. It's just like it." The enchanter covered his nose. "But I think it might smell worse than the other one."

"These things," Briyce Unger said, "have cut to the heart of my Kingdom. They come by the thousands, out of the mountains to the north, the impassable lands of snow, and even now they are sweeping south toward Scylax." The big King drew himself up, and a look of utter calm descended upon him. "And soon enough, if we don't act together, they'll keep coming south, until they cover all Luukessia."

Chapter 28

"What in the blazes is that?" King Longwell cried out, half-laughing. "A rotted goat?"

Briyce Unger looked down at the festering corpse then back at Aron Longwell, who was still chortling. "Does that look like a goat to you, Longwell? Is your vision so poor and your wits so dulled from sitting your throne these last years, not feeling the song of blades in your bones, that you don't know something unearthly when you see it?"

Aron Longwell stiffened. "You insult me, sir."

Briyce Unger drew up short. "I suppose I did, at that. It was not my intention when I started, but I got there, sure enough. I apologize. But surely you must see that this is no man, no beast that we've ever seen."

"I've seen one before," Cyrus said, standing. He looked down the benches toward the center of the amphitheater as faces turned toward him. "One of them attacked us after the battle of Harrow's Crossing. They're fast, they're mean, not too tough, but enough that it gave us a fight."

"I've never seen such a thing," Aron Longwell said with a shake of his head. "Ridiculous creature."

"Sire," Count Ranson spoke from next to him. "I told you of this when I returned. Lord Davidon brought the body of one of these things back to us at the crossing, but I scarcely believed it was real. I have heard reports of similar creatures, sporadic, herds being culled, disappearances throughout the Kingdom, and a few indescribable ... things ... found responsible."

"I still do not believe it to be real," King Longwell. "That could be some other sort of creature, a farm animal, dressed up to look like something ..." He stared at it, as though trying to discern its nature, "... something else entirely. This is a distraction, meant to muddy the issues before us at a time when we should be addressing grievances."

Briyce Unger let out a bellowing sigh that turned into a grunt. "Once you're quite finished reporting your grievances, then will you be willing to listen to me about these creatures?"

"I disbelieve that this threat you name even exists." King Longwell shook his hand in the direction of the corpse. "You are playing at something, Briyce Unger, but I know not what."

Unger's eyes narrowed and the man seemed to grow another foot as he swelled with anger, dark clouds gathering across his countenance. "You and I have known each other for a great amount of time, Aron Longwell, and you know full well that I am not one to move about treacherously. If I want something, I go straight at it until I get it or I'm too badly beaten to go onward. I am telling you that something is devouring my Kingdom whole. A pestilence—a scourge of these things, is sweeping down out of the mountains of the north, taking whole villages and leaving only the survivors who can outrun their grasp before they move again. If you choose not to believe me, that's your prerogative, but understand this—they are coming, and I doubt seriously that once they've run across all the lands of Syloreas they'll simply stop at your borders, bow to your greatness, and hold their line."

"I am of a mind to listen to King Briyce," said Milos Tiernan. "At least insofar as maneuvering goes, he shows little of the taste for it that you and I have, King Aron." Tiernan raised a goblet at Longwell, who seethed. "Perhaps there might be something to his claim; I have my doubts that he would wait until this late stage in his life to develop a knack for treachery."

"I think I might have heard an echo of an 'old man' joke in there somewhere," Briyce Unger said, voice dripping with irony, "and yet I don't care. What will it take to convince you that we need action?"

"There have been reports from the northern reaches of my Kingdom as well," Tiernan said shrewdly, "strange news, strange occurrences, odd creatures blamed, but not in such numbers as you claim. I would like to send an observer to see these things with his own eyes and report back to me with the veracity of your assertions." Milos Tiernan finished, taking another sip from the goblet that was held by one of his courtiers. "If what you say is true, there should be no shortage of places where they could witness your Kingdom under siege from these creatures."

"Aye," Unger said, "no shortage. We can do that, arrange for someone to come north with us, see some of the carnage these things leave. But we'll need to hurry."

"What is the great hurry, Unger?" Aron Longwell sneered with disdain. "Afraid that your mystery creatures will vanish by the time his observer gets there?"

"No, you great dolt," Unger said, bitterness dripping from his words, "I'm afraid that by the time they see the truth of my words, we return and your man motivates your slow-spinning arse into action that my Kingdom will be naught but ashes and blood." He drew himself up again. "Every Sylorean, we men of the north, know battle in our souls, quest for it in our lives, but this scourge that sweeps across our lands spares not women nor children, and is unmerciful in every way." He looked around. "I see in these things the death of all I hold dear, of my lands, of my people ..." he seemed to grind out the last words, "... even of the rest of Luukessia. And I don't mean to have it happen while I'm lying about. Give me your observers and I'll take them north, I'll show them the right of it, and we'll come back—but when we do, I want your word that you'll move your armies to action, because if you don't—if you don't mean to do anything—then I'll be leading all my armies in a last charge. Something, anything to stem the tide of these creatures," he spat onto the grey skinned rotting body at his feet, "and try to save my people."

Chapter 29

The moot went on for a bit after that, a few more grievances aired (by King Longwell only—every time he was offered the opportunity to speak, Unger demurred and Tiernan did the same), petty concerns, mostly, dealing with small matters.

Cyrus turned to Odau Genner as Grenwald Ivess took to his feet once more. "What about Cattrine?" Cyrus asked. "I must have missed the resolution of what was to happen with regard to her."

Genner shook his head. "There was little argument because the discussion was tabled as unresolved, destined to be debated further in the coming days. The reporting of grievances can only end with accession or dispute; in larger matters, accession is the rarer course." Genner smiled faintly. "I suspect it will be hotly debated on the morrow in session."

"The King wants me to turn her over, doesn't he?" Cyrus asked, prompting Genner to hem and haw. "I won't. I will not send her back to the arms of that coward so she can be whipped and beaten."

Genner's face became slack. "Then you'll need to fight for her, else you'll be placing our Kingdom in the midst of another war, one I have doubts we could win at present." He looked away. "It's not something we need to worry about yet, anyway."

"Who will the King send north?" Cyrus asked, causing Genner to cough.

"I suspect Count Ranson will be our envoy," Genner said. "If I had to guess."

"I want to go with him," Cyrus said, feeling a stir inside. The moon shone down overhead; long ago the sun had set and it was deep in the night. The stars were barely visible against the blue-black of the sky, and the torches burning on sconces around them lent the garden a smoky scent, reminding Cyrus once again that he was not in Sanctuary, with her smokeless torches and bright hallways. "I want to go north, to see this threat for myself."

Genner nodded. "You are in charge of your own army. I can't see the King refusing you, especially while we are still encamped here at Enrant Monge—and it seems unlikely we will be leaving until this expedition returns from the north."

The benches cleared a few at a time; some of the delegates remained to chat with others in their own party, and in a few cases, with other delegates. "There looks to be some crossover," Cyrus said. "Some of them know each other?"

"Oh, yes," Genner said. "It has been over a decade since the last moot, but the older among us know each other. Between you and me," he said with a smile, "this is how the diplomacy gets done, the deals worked out. It's not presented in session, but haggled by lower level intermediaries, argued back and forth, until something amenable comes to be discussed in the garden." Genner shifted his weight from one foot to the other. "We have discussions, surely, but all the real work is done when the session ends or on a break. In these meetings all we do is shout our position at the top of our lungs, never changing it until we've privately agreed with the other side on concessions. With Actaluere, anyway," Genner amended. "Briyce Unger is usually not so subtle in his negotiations."

"Sounds like a lot of bullshit to me," Cyrus said. "I think I prefer Unger's method."

"There is no finesse, no subtlety to it," Genner said. "He is a brute, a man who leads with his sword and follows with whatever is left."

"Aye," Cyrus said with a smile. "I like him already."

"Eh?" Genner looked at Cyrus, mystified. "I'll communicate your desire to go north with Count Ranson, old boy. I wouldn't presume to tell you exactly how it has to be, but if they're in as great a hurry as Unger appears, they'll likely leave tonight or early on the morrow, and you'll be restricted to taking only horsed men with you. I doubt they'll want to wait for men on foot given the urgency of this mission."

"That shouldn't be a problem," Cyrus said, and turned to look at the others, now folded into a group behind him. "I mean to go north with Unger," he told them. "We'll only take those on horseback, and I need a good, solid corps of veterans—somewhere between twenty and thirty, but not so many that the army is crippled without us." He nodded at Curatio. "You and J'anda, for certain. Longwell, I'd like you to be your father's eyes on this, in case he doesn't trust Ranson." Cyrus turned to Terian. "You, I think will need to stay and keep an eye on things around here."

"No," Terian said. "I'll be coming with you; send for Odellan to keep an eye on things in the castle here if you must, but I'm coming along."

Cyrus raised an eyebrow at him. "Is that so? All right. I'll need you three to go to the army. I don't want Odellan to leave them; he's proven himself far too apt at commanding them to pull him away from that now. Have Ryin and Nyad come here to watch the proceedings for us. I'll want Mendicant and Aisling going north with us as well as a druid or two as can be spared. Make sure you leave at least a couple healers behind."

"You'll be needing to send a messenger to Alaric," Curatio said. "We've been gone for over four months now."

"We're about to split our forces rather dramatically," Cyrus said. "Let's wait until we get back to send word. I don't want anyone to have to anchor their soul here on Luukessia just yet; they may need the return spell to carry them back to Sanctuary at an inconvenient moment."

"Very well," Curatio said shrewdly, but Cyrus could see the argument in his eyes that the healer was saving for later. "If you'll excuse me, I'll start culling a force out of our army to go north."

Cyrus nodded, and watched J'anda and Terian follow the healer. "I'll confer with my father, if it pleases you," Longwell said, still somewhat despondent. "Make certain he doesn't take our desire to go north the wrong way."

"I could certainly use some help in that department, young Longwell," Genner said. "Between you and me, King Aron seems quite changed from the days when he rode at the fore of the dragoons. More quick to anger, less quick to listen."

"Aye," Longwell said. "My mother's effect on him is sorely missed. Let us go." He gestured to Genner, who followed him. Aron Longwell was already making his way toward the tunnel which they had entered through hours earlier, leaving Cyrus alone with Cattrine and a few remaining delegates. Briyce Unger waited too, speaking with two of his men at the bench he had been sitting upon during the moot, his white robe colored orange by the tint of the torchlight.

Cyrus glanced at Cattrine and then walked away from her, stepping over the benches in front of him in a clumsy descent, avoiding the stairs and the line of people filing up them toward Actaluere and Galbadien's gates. He stepped over the last and looked at Cattrine again; she was frozen, all but her eyes, standing in the place where he had left her, looking from him to where the Grand Duke Hoygraf watched her, standing with his walking stick, his face twisted in a smile that made Cyrus want to snatch away the cane and batter him with it until the man moved no more.

Instead, Cyrus continued on across the center of the amphitheater until he reached Briyce Unger, who had watched him during his approach. The smell from the corpse of the thing that waited at Unger's feet permeated the air. The King stood at Cyrus's eye level, and when Cyrus approached, the big man stopped speaking with his subordinates, eyeing Cyrus with cold brown eyes.

"Briyce Unger?" Cyrus asked. "My name is—"

"Cyrus Davidon of the guild Sanctuary," the King of Syloreas said, unmoved. "I heard your name announced when you came in. My men who survived tell me it's you that's the hero of Harrow's Crossing, not Ranson."

"It was me," Cyrus said. "Does that gall you, sir?"

"Can't pretend it tickles me overmuch," Unger said, still not registering much in the way of emotions on his bearded face. "Six months ago—hell, even three months ago—if Harrow's Crossing had happened, I would have come after you with everything to avenge my men. Nothing personal, you understand—well, as impersonal as the heat of battle gets—but no one does that to my army and gets away with it." The big man shrugged. "Now, with all this," he nudged the remains of the creature wrapped in cloth at his feet, "I find myself hoping you and your army of western magicians will be on our side."

"I'd like to be," Cyrus said. "I want to go north with you, get a look at these things for myself."

"I thought you said you already saw one," Unger said, regarding Cyrus with some suspicion.

"I did," Cyrus said. "When we went out to capture Partus after Harrow's Crossing, we found him being attacked by one of them. If there's more," he leaned in closer to Unger, "I want to see them for myself."

"There's more," Unger said. "Plenty more. You're more than welcome to come along; especially if you bring your western magics." Unger cocked his head, and Cyrus saw the regret channel through the man." We could use more than a little of it in Syloreas right now."

"I take it you'll be leaving soon?" Cyrus asked.

"Right now, if I could swing it," Unger said with a laugh that sounded like a bark. "Most likely at first light."

"I've already got my people assembling a force to ride out with you," Cyrus said. "About thirty or so, all veterans."

"Good enough," Unger said, nodding. "And your King won't be providing a problem?"

"He's not my King," Cyrus said. "I came to render aid because his son is my friend and an officer of my guild."

"Heh," Unger said with something that didn't sound anything like a laugh. "Honor bound, is that it? To a fellow warrior?"

"Something like that," Cyrus said. "Honor is pretty important in my guild."

"Feh!" Unger waved him off. "Honor. I don't begrudge anyone their honor, but I hear it come from the mouths of the dishonorable more often than those who truly show it. Victory is what's important now, and I'd trade all my honor if it kept my Kingdom from falling to these beasts. Show me a man who's obsessed with only his honor and I'll show you a man who'll be defeated time after time. Honor! Tell me about honor on the day you see your enemies marching into your towns, slaughtering your people."

"Defending your people is a kind of honor," Cyrus said. "These things are beasts, so the only honor here is protecting those who can't protect themselves from these things."

"Fair enough," Unger said. "I suppose I was still thinking of it the way Aron Longwell cries about it. Wraps himself up in the word as though it could shield you from a thousand swords. But it doesn't shield you from the reality of war, we're seeing that now." He nodded at Cyrus. "I'm going to go get myself an hour or so of sleep before I start having to make preparations again. Come to the north gate with your people at sunrise, and we'll be off."

"Count on it," Cyrus said.

"Oh, I will," Briyce Unger said with a toothy grin as he began to ascend the amphitheater stairs behind him. "I'm already planning my strategy around having some of your mystics to help save us from our troubles."

Cyrus gave the man a nod as he left with the rest of his delegation, and watched him disappear from sight into the tunnel. When he turned, he saw that the amphitheater was empty, and the garden around him was quiet, save for the buzz of crickets in the night air. There was a very slight movement across from him and he realized that the last person in the amphitheater besides him was Cattrine. She sat on the bench in the same place she had been throughout the ceremony, watching him, as gravely as if someone had died.

Her skin held a certain flush in the torchlight, a warm, browned hue from all the travel of the last months. Her auburn hair was perfectly matched to the lighting, and he saw the slightest flicker of her eyes as he crossed the center of the amphitheater, heading toward the tunnel through which he had entered. "Going to stay here all night?" he asked her, pausing at the end of her row.

"Perhaps," she said, quiet, calm. "I … can't believe he's still alive."

Cyrus felt a sharp pain within. "I'm sorry." She looked up at him in surprise. "Whatever else has happened between us, I'm sorry I didn't free you from him. I may not care for the fact that you lied to me," he felt his body tense as the anger came back to him, "about your brother and who you were, but I wouldn't wish being married to him upon you, no matter what."

"I don't wish to go with him," she said, and lowered her head. "I don't wish to ever be subject to … to that man, ever again."

"You won't have to," Cyrus said. "I won't let him take you."

"You would fight your way through the whole Kingdom of Actaluere to spare me?" she asked with a subtle smile. "You would go into the heart of the sea country, into the city of Caenalys and fight your way through the streets and over the bridges, and do so on my behalf?"

Cyrus felt the clench of his jaw and hated it. "If I have to, I will."

She stood, then, and turned to him, watching him, her green eyes hard like emeralds and unrelenting in their pursuit of him. "Even though I didn't tell you who I was?" She took a step closer to him. "Even though I lied by omission, as you say? Even still?" She stepped closer yet, and was now only a few feet away from him.

"I would." He nodded. "All the way to their capital if necessary, all the way to their throne room, I would fight my way to your brother himself, crush all his guards and pry a promise from his lips to never pursue you or attempt to make war to honor his own name, under penalty of my return."

She stared at him, still as a statue. "What a man are you, Cyrus Davidon. How deep must your conviction run, that you would do that for a near-stranger?"

He flushed, and swallowed hard. "You're not a stranger, we've been—"

"I know," she said, and took another step toward him, reaching out and running a palm down his cheek. "I almost thought you had forgotten, in your anger, as though you wanted to disavow ever knowing me, ever holding me ..."

"What happened, happened," Cyrus said, feeling the touch of her hand on his face. He could feel the roughness, where once it had been soft and smooth, now calloused from the ride and practice with her blade. "But it's done now." He felt a great pressure in his chest, a warmth within him at her touch, at the remembrance of nights and days in Vernadam. "You saw to that when you didn't tell me the honest truth."

"I didn't lie," she said, coming closer, her forehead nearly on his. "I wouldn't have lied to you. But I feared that you would not fight that hard for me, for a near-stranger, or even for a lover, had you known who my brother was and what complications it would bring. How was I to know?"

"Because you know me now. Because you got to know me, the real me." He couldn't look at her. "You could have told me at Vernadam. Any time in the days we spent together, the infinity of blissful days that we held together."

"I was afraid," she said, holding her hand awkwardly, still touching his face. He leaned into her as she stroked his cheek. His breathing became suddenly slightly heavier, his heart thumped in his ears. "Afraid you'd be ... upset. A fear that turned out to be accurate, I would point out."

"But it wouldn't have been," he said, his voice low, his eyes now on hers, gazing into them. "Not if you'd told the truth before all the hell broke loose. Before there was threat of war. I wouldn't have been angry if you'd told me then. If you'd been honest and not tried to hide forever—and we could have ..." He took a breath, felt a pulse within him, the deep thrum of his desire. *How can it have been less than a month? I wasn't so on fire with need after years, but now ...*

"We still could," she said, slipping closer, drawing her forehead to his with her hands then slipping her arms around him. "I still want you. I've missed you ... the touch of you, the feel of you against me in the cold night air ..." Her hands ran down his robes, clung tight to him, pulled him against her. "I want you," she whispered in his ear, and her mouth found his earlobe and sucked on it gently, her soft breath against the side of his neck causing Cyrus's entire mind to blot out any thought but her ...

He was both acutely aware of every moment and yet it blurred around him as though he were in a stupor of tiredness. She pulled him down, onto the nearest bench, and he felt her hands lifting the hem of his robe, felt the rustle of cloth as she tugged her breeches down and he heard the sound of her leather boots echo on the floor of the amphitheater. Her kisses were tender yet forceful, and every one of them seemed to awaken some beast within him that had been locked away for the last month, clamoring quietly to get out, chambered in a room of bleakness and despair but now afforded a view of the sky and charging toward it with all its strength.

He kissed her back, roughly, and it was just as it had been at Vernadam. He craved her, kissed her on the side of her neck, sucked on the sweet skin there and heard her moan as he unlaced her cloth shirt's collar and slid it up. She kicked off her breeches underneath him and it turned loose his animal excitement. Something froze him, for just a beat. "Won't somebody see us?"

"They're all gone," she said. "Off to bed, and won't be back to the garden until tomorrow afternoon."

"But ..." He sat there, feeling foolish but still wanting her, held back by an invisible tether. "You're still a married woman."

Her eyes were on his, and he could see that she wanted it too, wanted him. "That never stopped you before."

"I thought you were a widow before."

"So did I," she said, pulling him closer, "but so little is my regard for the man that this almost seems more delicious than before." She pulled him close and kissed him, and they melted together into action and activity, the cold night air made warmer by Cyrus's skin pressed against hers, held by her embrace until they had finished.

"You're a man of commendable vigor," she said, her voice muffled from her face being pressed against his chest. She reached a hand up and brushed her hair back so he could see her face, glowing, almost resplendent. Her shirt had been lost in the moments between her initiation of their second lovemaking and his arrival on the floor. He felt the stone chill against his back and bottom, but it seemed to soothe his hot flesh. "The Baron could never manage to satiate me in such a way as you have."

"Don't talk about him when you're with me," Cyrus said, but it came off snappish, and he saw her flinch from his words. "It's been a month; of course I'd have some pent-up desire."

"You have years of desire, my love," she said with a sigh. "And your vigor is hardly something new; how many times did we engage in such things at Vernadam? I'm only pleased that you haven't grown tired of me quite yet." One of her hands slipped down as she smiled.

"Stop," he whispered, imploring her. "Not here. Not again."

"Why not?" she asked. "I used to come here as a child, you know. With Milos and my father, whenever a convocation was held. We had three of them, two within a year of each other. This is a sacred place to us, here in Luukessia, because of the connection Enrant Monge has to our ancestors." She lifted herself off him, exposing her upper body, and causing him to bristle as she got to her knees, causing him to tremble at the sight of her nakedness, the scars that crisscrossed her body still visible to him now, obvious, inescapable signs of her torment, almost as though they were marks of her guilt. "I used to wonder if the man I would marry was in the crowd of nobles who would come with us to the moots." She became ashen as she tucked her hair behind her shoulders. "As it turned out, he was—though not the man I would have picked for myself."

"You're talking about him again," Cyrus said, sitting upright. Now the stone underneath his buttocks simply felt cold, uncomfortable to his touch. Cattrine remained on her knees, leaning back to rest her haunches on his thighs.

"I'm sorry," she said gently. "I meant to say that I hoped back then that I would meet a man like you—strong, brave, noble and true, one that would treat me decently, more decently than many of the ladies I knew in court were treated by their husbands."

"So were you looking for a man to take care of you?" He eyed her warily.

"I was taught to take care of a man and he'll take care of you— something of a lie, I realize now, but at the time it seemed reasonable enough."

He felt bile rise in his throat, heat on his face, and he recoiled from her, pulling himself free of her grasp. The sweat and the smell made him feel only dirty now, as though any clothing he touched would be soiled, ruined, unusable at any time in the future. The stickiness of his skin as it pulled away from the stones that he had sat upon felt as though his flesh had to be peeled from it the way the skin of an apple is removed, and the grittiness remained as he rose to his knees and clutched at the robes that lay only a few feet away.

"Did I not please you, m'lord?" Cattrine's eyes were upon him, but the slight mocking undertone in her voice made him ill, made him feel dirtier still. "Is your tireless drive such that I need convince you of my affections once more?" She pressed close to him again, laying her head upon his shoulder from behind as he leaned over.

She still felt good against his skin as she pressed herself to his back, and he felt a momentary urge to turn, to hold her, but he pulled away instead, the fight won at last by that nagging sense of disgust that had welled up within him. It overcame the last of his desire, spent finally from all her efforts, and he felt the monster within's clutches let loose of him, and a fearful anger took hold. "Get off me," he said, and let his robe cover him and his shame.

Her face was a mask. There was no kindness upon it as there had been in the past, but some fear or anger crept out in slow measure, revealing itself subtly through the tilt of her eyes, the thinness of her lips as she regarded him. "Did I do something to make you angry?" she asked with the subtlest hint of insincerity. "Do you wish to hurt me now? Because if so, I do request you keep it below the collar and above the sleeves." Her fingers traced lines over the flawless skin just above her neckline down to the jagged scars that ran across her breasts and along her arms, and down to her left thigh where a particularly heinous wound had left a half-inch indentation in her inner thigh where the skin was simply missing, as though someone had gouged a small cube of it out.

"I'm not going to hurt you," he said, almost spitting the words at her. "You're still the same woman who came before the man who she thought killed her husband and immediately offered herself to him." The deep disgust welled within him. "Have you been manipulating me all along? Taking advantage of my ... desperation, my heartbreak, my naivete?"

He saw the flicker of hurt in her eyes at his words, and her skin reddened around her neck, turning the same fiery red as it always had post-coitus, little blotches, like fall leaves on the palest parts of her flesh. "I wouldn't call you naive. You're a man grown, and you've known the touch and seduction of a woman before. I came to you in your hour of need in Vernadam, willingly, as you aided me in mine by taking me away from Green Hill. I see nothing to be ashamed of in that. You offered your help to my escape, but gave me no guarantee that such aid would continue forever. I took what you gave, and drew closer to you—but do not ascribe my motives to selfishness, Cyrus. That would be unkind. I did nothing with you that I did not want to, that I did not wish to do wholeheartedly."

"Funny," Cyrus said, slipping his feet back into his footcovers. "You just used my body—my appetites—to try and sway me back to you," he said, the rage filling him. "Is this nothing but a game to you? Like your brother plays with Luukessia? Am I just a piece to move around the board to your best advantage?"

He saw her face tighten, harden, as though the mask had solidified in stone and there was nothing left but it. "My best advantage would be to rule Actaluere, but alas, even as the eldest child, I am a daughter, and thus ineligible to be in the line of succession. The best I can do is to get out of this forsaken land, where being born a girl gives you less chance than a mutt of finding a man who won't beat you or lord his power over you. You offered that. Don't fault me for accepting it."

"And everything else?" Cyrus asked, staring at her pinched expression. "That was all ... what? Sugar on top? A gift to me for making good my promise and freeing you?"

"It was ..." her voice cut out, but the coolness of her gaze remained, "... whatever you wish to think it was."

"I think it was manipulation," Cyrus said. "I think behind your eyes is a fearsome calculator, someone as subtle and wicked as Milos Tiernan ever has been. I think you saw a chance to solidify your power, and you saw me as a chance to do it, so you took it. I think you saw a man at the head of an army who had the ability to give you what you wanted and you went for it, clumsily at first, then recovered and came about it a different way, and in my moment of weakness you found your opportunity."

"See it however you like," she said. "But remember, it was you who invited me into your bed, not vice versa."

"Oh, I see it now," Cyrus said, quelling the anger within. "I see it all, now, all you've hidden." He reached down and took hold of her riding breeches from the ground and the shirt next to them and tossed them to her. She caught them, flinching as her hands curled around the cloth and pulled the shirt over her head. He watched the scars disappear beneath it, along with all else. "I think your scars are your excuse; that there are other things that mar you far worse than anything so surface-level as those. I think you are cunning, far more cunning than I would have given you credit for."

"My goodness," she said, "all this thinking will come to a bitter end for you." She remained fixed, unexpressive, save for the coldness that radiated off her in waves, reminding Cyrus of the Northlands of Arkaria, the frozen tundra that even in summer remained frosted. "You'll spin about for quite a bit longer I suspect, weaving more and more suspicions." She tugged on her pants, sliding into them and lacing them tight. He watched as the drawstring dug against her flesh, biting into her skin, leaving a red line where it hugged her waist before disappearing under her shirt. "Draw whatever conclusion you'd like, Lord Davidon," she said coldly. "But tell me this—what do you mean to do with me now? Would you still defend me to the death? Would you march your armies into the land of Actaluere to save me from having to go back to my husband? Or do you hold me in such low regard that you would throw me back to him, as a plains cat would toss aside the remains of a meal it is finished with?"

"As tempting as that would be, discarding you back to the tender hands of the Grand Duke Hoygraf," he said spitefully, watching her stiffen as he said it, "I am not so cruel as you and would not use that bastard merely to hurt you as you have hurt me." He shook his head. "Even after all else, I'll honor my pledge." He looked away from her. "I suppose it's the least I can do, as payment for what you've done to—and for—me."

Her eyes flared. "You think me a doxy, now?" He watched, waiting to see if she would strike at him. "You consider me a whore because I gave myself to you? More the fool you are, Cyrus Davidon." She tied the neck of her shirt together, but he could still see the redness at her collarbones. "Have it your own way, then. I'll take your safe passage from this land as payment. And I'll thank you, once it's all over, for teaching me once again a lesson I should have learned before."

"Oh?" Cyrus asked, as she turned from him, grabbing her boots and starting up the stairs. "What's that?"

"That no man can be trusted," she said, looking back at him, eyes flashing in the light of the torch next to her. "Not even the one who appears as a hero—a knight, shining—who says he will save you. All men are the same, with their own barbs, and swords, and their own ways of inflicting scars." Her flush carried all the way to her face this time, and she left, her bare feet slapping on the stone up the steps, and when she reached the flat ground at the top he heard her stride turn to a run until she was gone.

Chapter 30

The dawn found him sleepless, in his tower room, with his armor already strapped on. He left as the first rays came over the horizon. The stableboy, a red-haired, freckled lad, yawned and handed over the reins to Windrider. Cyrus took them and mounted up, riding the long way around the castle, through the southern courtyard and the western one, until he reached the northern one and its gate, taking particular note of the southern gate as he passed it, the portcullis down and rusted, ominous in the silence pouring forth from beyond it.

Cyrus rode out the north gate of Enrant Monge, and found an assemblage waiting. Curatio and J'anda, Terian and Longwell, along with Aisling, who rode next to Mendicant. Not far from them waited another figure, smaller, and Cyrus called out when he saw him.

"What is he doing unbound?" Cyrus asked, pointing at Partus, who sat upon his horse, his warhammer slung behind him.

"It seemed the thing to do," Curatio said, drawing Cyrus's attention.

"The suicidal thing to do, you mean," Cyrus said. "He killed me."

"Now, now," J'anda said, "you've died several times. What's the harm in one more?"

"I don't know," Cyrus said, irritable. "What was your name again? I'm having trouble remembering."

The enchanter shrugged and smiled, then loosed an illusion upon himself that made him look like Cyrus, armor and all. "Do you think you could remember my name now, you handsome devil?"

"That's pretty damned disturbing," Terian said, trying not to look at the two of them. "If the two of you touch each other, will you become one massive Cyrus, like, twelve feet tall?"

"No," J'anda-Cyrus said, "we would simply touch, just as would happen with anyone else."

"Are you sure?" Aisling said, staring at the two of them with undisguised amusement. "Try giving each other a hug and a kiss, just to be certain."

"That's revolting," Terian said.

"I could stand to watch it a little while," Aisling said with a coy smile. "And then maybe participate—"

"Ugh, ugh, ugh," Terian said, shaking his head and speaking so loudly that it drowned out the rest of Aisling's sentence.

"You know," J'anda said with a raised eyebrow at Cyrus, "if you wanted to really disturb Terian—"

"No," Cyrus said, and then looked his doppelganger up and down. "It's not that you're not pretty enough," he said with more lightness than he actually felt, "but I find that this morning I'm simply not in the mood."

"Hah," J'anda-Cy said as Terian gagged in the background. "The way you say that would seem to indicate that later you would—"

"No." Cyrus shook his head. "But you do look good like that."

Cyrus looked over the space before them. They were on a dusty road, assembling with a few others. Cyrus saw Count Ranson and another man, clad in the surcoat Cyrus had seen on the men of Actaluere, speaking with Briyce Unger, who seemed to be watching them both with little interest. A guard posse of thirty or so was assembled near Unger, and Cyrus urged Windrider forward toward the King of Syloreas, catching Unger's attention when he neared.

"We'll be riding at a fair clip," Briyce Unger said with a nod of acknowledgment to Cyrus. "Not so hard as to kill the horses, but we'll be pushing them. Likely need some time to rest and care for them between rides, but I hope your animals are up to a hard pace, because we'll be traveling north for at least the next month to get to Scylax." The King looked at them soberly.

Without another word, Unger turned his horse around and yelled while spurring it, causing the horse to whinny and charge ahead at a gallop. Unger's guard began to trot forward as well, following their King. Cyrus waited for Count Ranson and the Actaluere envoy to fall in and he waved a hand directing the Sanctuary force, numbering somewhere around twenty-five, he estimated, to fall in behind them.

They rode hard for the rest of the day, taking breaks every few hours to care for the horses and feed the men. Unger marveled when Cyrus had Mendicant conjure oats for the animals, shaking his massive, shaggy head. "You westerners and your magicians," he said as his horse fed, "our ancestors had the right of it; your land is one in which our men do not belong."

"I'm a man," Cyrus said, raising his eyebrow at Unger. "And I have no magic. You saying I don't belong?"

"Don't know," Unger said. "Can you fight those fellows that use it?"

"I've fought a few," Cyrus said. "Killed a few, too."

"All the better for you," Unger said with a smirk. "Perhaps I'll get the chance one of these days." The King's smirk faded. "Not anytime soon, though, I hope. We need all the help we can get now, magical and otherwise."

"What's it been like?" Cyrus asked as he ran a brush along Windrider's side.

Briyce Unger didn't answer for a moment. They stood under a tree that was ten times the height of a man, and Cyrus could see the sun shine through the boughs, casting leaf-shaped shadows on the King of Syloreas's face which moved subtly as the leaves swayed in the wind. The shadows moved, the shifting patches of darkness giving Unger's face the tint of a man uncertain, greyed out, cast in shadow. "They come in great numbers. One or two of them is no challenge; like fighting any man or perhaps a cunning bear or mountain lion."

A very slight smile crept over his lips. "I rode back from Galbadien, from the war, when I got the message from one of my nobles in the mountains saying his hall and the villages around him had been overrun by beasts he could scarce describe—that it was like things out of our old mountain legends, the things that would bring about the end of all men. This man was brave and old and rode with my father in wars that could only be described as fearful. I went home, as fast as I could, and made it only in time to fight one battle with this scourge, this plague.

"I've fought battles," Unger said, his face haunted. "You know, I can tell by your face you've been in a melee or twelve. You don't fear the battle, you thrill to it. I do, anyway. But this battle was different. I've been overmatched before, no shame in that. Being outnumbered is a northman's lot, it's the way of Syloreas. We fight harder because we have fewer men, that's the way of things.

"But these ... creatures," he pronounced with disgust, "they keep coming. We met them in a village in a pass. They came at us, and the battle was good at first; I was up to my knees in their dead by the end of the first hour, as it should be. The second hour, I was up to my chest in a pile of my own dead, and still they came. They do not bend with the chaos, they do not ebb with loss; they are implacable, unstoppable, insatiable in their desire to destroy all around them, and they gave me a taste of fear, I am not ashamed to say." The King of Syloreas stopped, and looked at Cyrus, shaking his head. "My first taste in a long, long while. I have never, not in battles where my men were outnumbered ten to one, not even on the day I found myself alone in a pack of wolves, ever felt so afraid and surrounded by the odds arrayed against me."

The King of Syloreas swallowed hard. "I confess I thought myself a coward after that. Retreat against poor odds is acceptable; sometimes a strategic retreat is the only way you can win a war later, or preserve a Kingdom to fight through another day. But when I ran from that village, I did not do it strategically or in the name of preserving anything but my own arse against a foe that seemed unstoppable, a scourge that looked to take everything, and fill the land from end to end with my dead and theirs until I could see no more ground."

Cyrus listened and watched the King as he shook his head once more in amazement, or consternation at his own story, and walked away from Cyrus still shaking his head.

The next days were long and hard on the horses. Cyrus, for his part, had been riding on horseback so heavily for the last few months that it seemed almost as though he would live the rest of his life there. It was almost as if he had known no other life but this, save for a brief spell in the castle of Vernadam, when he slept in a bed and received all the blessings of civilization, and all the affections a woman could give.

By the time the second week of their ride had rolled around, the days were long again for riding, and Cyrus found his mind weary. Sleep did not come easily at night, and his restless slumber was punctuated by evenings when he thought of Cattrine, of their encounter at Enrant Monge, and he tossed and turned in his bedroll near the fire, unable to find any relief.

His eyes wandered frequently during the ride, as the fatigue conspired to wear him down. Aisling always seemed to be about, though she kept her distance from him. He found himself looking for her, especially when he rode near the back of the group. He watched her on her horse, his eyes drinking in the curves of her body, and he let his mind drift, thinking of her and Cattrine and Vara, interchanging the three of them in his mind and memory, imagining himself in bed in his quarters at Vernadam with Aisling, her blue skin pressed against him. Then it was Vara, her blond hair glistening in the light cast by the fire in the hearth, scars on her back and legs reminding him that it was in fact Cattrine that had been there with him, satiating his hunger, not Vara or Aisling.

He tried to shake the thoughts out of his mind, but neither the water he splashed on his face nor the rest he tried to take at night could keep them at bay for long. He spent long days thinking, not of what waited for him ahead nor of his companion travelers (save for when they spoke to him, which was more than they had in the last few months when he had a constant black cloud around him) but of Vara and her betrayal, and of Cattrine and her betrayal, and of Aisling, and the three of them, and all the things that he and Cattrine had done, all the little pleasures, of how he wanted to feel them again.

They journeyed across flat lands, plains, through forests that grew more lush and leafy as they went north. Summer was beginning to set in hard upon them, the sun beating down and warming the land. A week of vicious heat after leaving Enrant Monge became milder as they went on, easing into beautiful traveling weather.

Cyrus could see mountains in the distance after three weeks, foothills just ahead that made him remember Fertiss and the halls of the dwarven capital back in Arkaria. He could see snow-capped peaks, something that looked singularly out of place after the heat they had experienced only scant weeks earlier. The plains became greener as they went, nursed by flowing streams that came from the mountains. The land was verdant, reminding Cyrus of everything that Vernadam had been when they arrived, and even, vaguely, of the Plains of Perdamun, where he was certain it was now hot, hotter than what they had experienced at Enrant Monge or after it as they headed north.

The foothills became steeper as the mountains drew closer. Women remained the only thing on Cyrus's mind, and in rapid succession they came and went in his head, Aisling, Vara, Cattrine. He wondered why Aisling would fit into his thoughts, and realized that she was one of the only women on the expedition with him, and the only one he truly knew other than in passing. At last he realized with a shock one night while staring at her as she sat at another fire, her back to him, that she was the only woman with them that he found remotely attractive. She had made suggestions to him in the past, things that made him warm in the night when he recalled the words. Now she said nothing to him, as though he were not even there.

I feel like a teenage boy, he admitted to himself one night by the fire, long after the others had gone to sleep, and he had tossed in his bedroll for hours. *Just as confused and alone as I did back at the Society, unsure of anything, and even more conflicted.* He shook his head, as though he could somehow jar loose contemplations of either Vara or Cattrine, both of whom dominated his thoughts. *I am a warrior. I need battle, I need the clarity of it. To go this long without combat is a drain, and I obsess over these ... lustful, useless thoughts.*

"You may be setting some sort of record for sleeplessness." The dry voice of Terian came from behind him and he turned to see the dark elf, sitting once more with his sword across his lap, a rag polishing the edge of the blade. "I remain amazed that you don't fall unconscious on your horse each day as we ride."

"And you?" Cyrus asked. "Do you linger, sleepless each night as I do? You must, if you see how little rest I get."

"Aye," Terian said. "I suspect I get a bit more sleep than you do, but perhaps not by much."

"And what's on your mind that keeps you from rest?" Cyrus asked, trying to turn aside the dark knight's inevitable inquiry before it was made. "What halts the repose of the great Terian Lepos, isolates him from the nocturnal peace he craves?"

"Perhaps I worry about you," Terian said with a wicked smile. "After all, the wheel has turned for you, my friend. After Harrow's Crossing you seemed to be at an apex of happiness, such a contrast to the horror that was your glum state of mind on our journey leading up to that point. Then, with one little revelation, all your happiness was swept into the gutter like all the other rubbish and you were in the darkness of Yartraak's despair again. One could almost feel sorry for you." He shrugged. "If one didn't know better, one might think that you were beginning to get as jaded as I am, as you've started to stare at our roguish ranger somewhat hungrily," he nodded his head in the direction of Aisling's bedroll, and Cyrus saw a shock of her white hair sticking out of the top of it. "You have the look of a man on a diet of barley corn who hungers desperately for meat. Or are you merely switching your affections once more?"

"I am ..." Cyrus let his voice trail off, "... not certain of much of anything, but I doubt I have any genuine affection left in me at this point."

"So rampant lust, then?" Terian said coolly. "I understand that all too well. I hope to find a soothing balm for that at the whorehouse in Scylax." He rubbed the pommel of his sword. "I'm told they have quite a good one, at least according to a couple of the Syloreans I spoke with."

"How lovely," Cyrus said with only a dash of sarcasm.

"Don't be so high and mighty with me, Lord Davidon," Terian said, his face falling into shadow. "Now that you've awakened to what you've been missing all these years, I sense a craven desperation in you. Give you a few more days of staring at the dark elf girl and soon enough you'll be thinking that a brothel would seem a sweet release."

"I certainly hope not," Cyrus said. "I don't care what you do, Terian, but I'm not you. I don't begrudge you your entertainments, but don't fall into the trap of thinking that I'll make the same decisions you do simply because I'm feeling unsatisfied."

"You'll see, soon enough," Terian said with a small smile, a bitter one. "You could ignore it before, when you channeled everything into battle and into your idiotic feelings for Vara. Now that that's all done, the Baroness opened your eyes. Sure, she stabbed you good, in the heart, but now you're awake. You know people will betray you, that women will betray you, but you know what you want from them—at least part of it. She did you a favor, helping you get out of your chains and reminding you that you have a ... pulse," he said with a salacious grin. "Give you a month more of suffering in silence, bedding in common areas and you'll either go crawling off into the woods to take hold of your own release or you'll get smart and realize that the coin of the realm will buy you the same relief, and it'll be that much better for being real."

"I doubt there's much 'real' about what you do in a whorehouse,"

Cyrus said. "Other than feel really, truly cheated afterward."

"Ah, there's that sanctimoniousness again," Terian said. "You think you're better than me, I know, but you're not, and the sooner you realize it the better off you'll be. I've never had a whore betray me nor lie to me in a way that could hurt my feelings, bruise my ego, or stab me in the heart. I've never had a harlot turn down my coin nor send me running dejected to fight another man's war in another man's land, and I've certainly not had it happen twice in a row. If you lie down with dogs, you get fleas." His smile disappeared, replaced by a thin look of malice coupled with warning. "And when you lie down with a woman and give her your heart, you get swallowed up, lost. You've seen it, you've felt it, you've lived it—what? Three times now?—yet still you ignore the lessons of your own experience. That makes you more a fool than any fool I've met, motley or otherwise."

"Such a friend you are to me, Terian," Cyrus said, "and so wise is your counsel. I won't deny that after my time with the Baroness, I am … awakened … to possibilities again, as you put it. But I'm a man, not a beast, and my wounds are my own concern, as is satisfying my cravings, whatever they might be. I'd rather have some feeling to go along with that satisfaction, as a man, so I don't simply rut in the dark with a stranger, like a beast."

"Push comes to shove," Terian said, "when you're cold and alone after this long ride and the warmth of a friendly bed beckons to you, you'll go to it, unquestioning, stranger or not, gold exchanging hands or not. I know you, even more so now, and I know what you'll do."

"You don't know me, Terian," Cyrus said as he settled back onto his bedroll. "You may think you do, but you don't—not a thing about me, really. And I'm beginning to wonder if you ever did."

Chapter 31

The ride got harder as the mountains rose before them. They cut across winding trails, over rough ground, and their pace slowed. Cyrus was thankful for Windrider's sure footing, especially after one of his own warriors went plummeting over an embankment by accident two days from Scylax. With the aid of the druid spell Falcon's Essence, the body was retrieved and revived, but extra care was taken from then on. The fall drew the scorn of the experienced Syloreans, until a small rockslide sent two of their own to death, and Briyce Unger admitted, while Cyrus and he retrieved the bodies, that many a visitor to their city fell victim to the mountain roads.

"It's a good defense," Unger said. "Scylax has never been laid siege to, not in the six thousand years it's stood." He and Cyrus each carried a body over their shoulders, walking on air back up a steep embankment to where their party waited above. "But it's rubbish for travel. My father's grandfather had walked this path a thousand times but died to a rockslide on a summer day without even seeing it coming. Got him and his whole hunting party in a good slide, carried his corpse halfway down a mountain. They found the horses sticking out by their feet."

"Not a good death," Cyrus said, letting the curious sensation of his feet on solid ground carry him up, even though he knew his feet were neither on something solid, nor strictly speaking, were they on the ground at all.

"Not for a warrior like him," Unger agreed. "A death in battle, that's the way we go in Syloreas. An axe to the face, a chop to the neck, a greatsword through the belly, a dagger to the throat, all fine ways to go. A landslide? In your bed with a cough?" The big man spit, as they began to crest the edge of the road. "I'd sooner die of my heart collapsing in my old age, a woman rocking atop me." The King seemed to consider that one for a long moment. "Actually, that one doesn't sound too bad."

They both laughed, and Cyrus gently put down the body on the ground before Curatio. The expedition was spread out along the road, a few of the Syloreans already working to push the fallen rocks from the slide over the edge of the mountain. Cyrus watched them roll, one by one, stirring a few more and then looked up. Snow capped peaks were above him some great distance, too far for him to fairly judge. The white was striking against the blue skies, almost looking like clouds that crowned the mountain, merging with the sky where the two kissed.

Cyrus caught sight of Aisling leaning against one of the rocks, giving it a hearty shove. He could see the sinews of her arm muscles straining, displayed by her sleeveless shirt, to push as a few of the Sylorean warriors stood back and watched, seemingly in awe of the blue-skinned girl who was less than half their mass and at least two feet shorter than they rolling a boulder by herself, albeit somewhat slowly. He watched her boots dig into the path as she put her bare shoulder to the rock and pushed. He saw her pants tighten as she bent to give it all her strength and he felt the heat within him and turned away as she launched it over the edge to a muted cheer of those observing. He turned away not quite in time, though, as she looked over, flushed with the triumph of her efforts, her skin a darker hue, and caught him looking for just a beat before he managed to turn away. Her look only changed a little, cooling slightly when she locked eyes with him, as though she knew the very thoughts within him and wished she didn't.

He felt the scarlet of embarrassment on his face and grabbed his helm off Windrider, snugging it onto his head, letting the metal hide part of his cheeks as they blushed. The road was cleared moments later, and after the two dead were raised, he climbed back into the saddle, trying to focus his thoughts on the ride, on the road, on the perils of mountain travel.

After an hour of reflecting on the way the dark elven woman looked when exerting herself, moaning as she pushed the rock over the edge, he had to concede that somewhere, deep inside, Terian may have had something of a point. It was as though the Baroness had introduced a poison into his system. Fever and delirium were following it, a heat under his skin that Cyrus could scarcely control as it overran his thoughts and drove them from Vara to Cattrine to the nearest woman at hand. *Aisling is pleasant enough to the eyes. And fit, gods know. Dexterous, agile, and amusing in her way ...* He shook his head again, rattling it inside his helm. *And has lusted after you for nearly two years, only to turn cold in the last months. You could have had her freely any time, yet you have desire for her now, when she is the only woman of interest in view, and after being spurned and betrayed by two other women. This is petty lust, the basest of emotions, and unworthy of her, as a true and skilled guildmate who has saved your life more than once.*

Yet thoughts of her lingered, interspersed once more with Vara and Cattrine, tormenting him, robbing him of sleep, causing him agonizing bouts that did not subside quickly or without pain. By the time the gates of Scylax were in sight he was grateful and deeply considering Terian's advice, wondering if by a simple exchange of coins he could somehow purge the poison from his system, even if only for a few days or a week, and be done with it, clear-headed once more and ready for battle. *I don't remember it being this bad after Imina. But then, Imina never did anything quite like what Cattrine did, and certainly not with as much enthusiasm ... nor as often ...*

They came around a bend in the road to see Scylax laid out before them. It was carved into the mountainside like villages he had seen when visiting the Dwarven Alliance but larger in scale than anything he could imagine dwarves building and less reliant on caves. There were multiple streets built into the mountain, some fifteen or twenty levels that were joined by stair-like rises in place of cross streets. It was as though someone had laid out a city map into the side of a mountain and turned the houses and notched the buildings into the mountain's side. Cyrus could see houses exposed to the elements out front, on the face of the cliff, but they were carved into the rock toward the back of each level. There was even some greenery on the streets, from trees that could weather dry, frigid winters. Farther around the sheer surface of the mountain were paddocks for animals, huge numbers of them, and granaries carved into place on one of the levels.

Above it all, toward the peak, was the castle Scylax, squat and constructed on the edge of a plateau that looked down upon the city and up to the mountain behind it. It lacked the towering spires of Vernadam, instead using rounded construction for the masonry, bending with the curves of the cliff, the half dozen or so structures within the massive curtain wall being broad and circular, reminding Cyrus just slightly of a temple he had visited years earlier in the bandit land southeast of the

Endless Bridge, back in Arkaria.

"You got something against building on level ground?" Terian asked Briyce Unger as they took in the city.

"Too easy to attack on flat ground, as our ancestors discovered," Unger said with a wide grin. "When we Syloreans make an enemy, we tend to make it a good one. This town and castle can be defended by our women and children while the men are away, if need be, and can be held against a siege of ten thousand by only a few hundred."

"Great, so why are we here to help you again?" Terian asked with a smirk. "Get all your people together, crowd them inside the damned castle and keep killing these creatures until they stop coming."

"Doesn't work that way," Unger said with a shake of the head. "We could hold off a siege here for a few years, maybe, if need be, but not with the whole city in our gates. If it were men at our gates, I would consider it. Men can be beaten back, they weary, they fall to death and eventually wisen to the notion that holding a siege in a place like this is a poor idea. It's not as though there's an abundance of food or water to feed an army just lying about in the hills, especially not over a long period. But these things ..." He shook his head. "I don't know that they need food and water, they don't seem to weary or fatigue, they just keep coming—relentless—when you kill them by the hundred. Lock ourselves in tight, even if we lasted five years, I think they'd still be waiting when we came back out. They're beasts, not men."

The road straightened along the cliff's edge until they eventually reached the gates of the city. The path led them through into the middle of the town, where they were greeted by curious children, clapping at the approach of their King, and joined by washerwomen and men with pickaxes, covered in dust. Cyrus watched the men, and realized that whatever they were doing must involve digging into the mountain, as they were, every one of them, caked in earth.

"Miners," Partus said, drawing Cyrus's startled attention to the dwarf, whom he had not realized was by his side. "I didn't know you humans had it in you before I came here."

"There aren't a lot of men who do it, that's for certain," Cyrus agreed. "Not many have a taste for rooting about in the guts of the earth the way dwarves do."

"Not me," Partus proclaimed. "I left Fertiss when I came of age, happy to get out of the dark. Never would have liked to go back to anything like it, if I could have avoided it."

"What brought you here?" Cyrus asked. "To Scylax? Your hammer is more powerful than almost any I've fought, able to stand up to my blade. You know how to fight, at least well enough to get into one of the big three. So why Luukessia?"

"Because I didn't want to be in Arkaria anymore," Partus said with a grim shrug. "Shouldn't come as a surprise to you. After all, you loaded up your horses and traveled for months on a roundabout course to get here—why wouldn't somebody else do the same? And for money, no less, rather than the simple nobility you preach."

"There were plenty of places to make money in Arkaria," Cyrus said. "A dwarf with your skills could have had a place in any army—the Elven Kingdom, the Human Confederation, the Dark Elven Sovereignty, even your people in the Dwarven Alliance would have fallen over themselves to add your power to their cause, and they would have paid, too." Cyrus waved vaguely toward Briyce Unger. "More than you'd know you were getting out of Unger, wandering blindly over here."

"Who said anything about blindly or wandering?" Partus asked with a scowl. "One of my associates, one of the ones your lot killed, he was from here originally, came to Arkaria on a trading expedition a few years ago. He knew that Unger would pay good gold for help from Western mercenaries, so I came."

"Mercenaries," Cyrus said. "You used to be the leader of the Daring. They had ideals, beliefs, at least the ones of them I knew—Erith, Cass, Elisabeth—you're telling me you wanted to give that up for mercenary work in another land?" Cyrus shook his head. "Smells like bullshit to me, Partus. What happened with you and Goliath that sent you scrambling? Did you get caught up in the exile?"

"I was gone long before that," he said with a shake of his craggy head. "I heard about it, though. I was in the Gnomish Dominions, gathering moss on a garrison detail that had gotten quite a bit easier once your crew," he waved at the Sanctuary force around them, "wiped out the Goblin Imperium. My busy guard duty, escorting convoys and whatnot, got pretty simple after that." The dwarf seemed almost upset about it. "Only got to kill a few highwaymen, and that got old quickly."

"So why leave Goliath?" Cyrus watched the dwarf for his reaction.

Partus played it cool, returning Cyrus a grin. "I had something of a ... personality conflict with Malpravus and another of his officers. Caused us to go our separate ways not long after that clash in the Mountains of Nartanis with the Dragonlord."

"You were there for that?" Cyrus asked.

"Hah! I was, but I'm not surprised you didn't see me, covered as you were in the glory of the kill. I was there the day you killed Kalam, too, and the day you went into the Realm of Death with the allies and we all got caught up by the skeleton." Partus smirked. "Course you wouldn't notice, would you? I'm not exactly of a height that'd catch your eye. Besides," he said, slightly surly, "I'm told all my people look alike to you tallfolk. Same gripe the gnomes got."

"My best friend was a dwarf," Cyrus said. "I've got no problem telling one dwarf from another. Besides, you're bald, kind of fat, and you've got a braided beard." He shrugged. "Hard to miss."

"You had a friend who was a dwarf?" Partus watched him. "All right, I'll bite. Who was it?"

"What, do all you dwarves know each other?"

"Yeah, we're all members of the same club," Partus snapped. "What was his name?"

Cyrus looked back to the road, watching the townsfolk watch him as they rode past. "His name was Narstron."

"Oh, him," Partus said with a nod. "Yeah, I knew him."

"What?" Cyrus cast a look at him, and the way he said it was almost mocking. "You did not. There are millions of dwarves, and you're telling me you know Narstron? Don't lie."

"No, it's true," Partus said. "I didn't know him well, but I knew him in passing. He was my mother's youngest sister's fourth son. Went to the Society of Arms in Fertiss, and he died down in the depths of Enterra."

"I didn't see you at his funeral," Cyrus said coldly.

"I've got a lot of cousins," Partus said with a shrug. "One hundred and twelve, I think? A hundred and twenty by now, for all I know. I said I knew him in passing. It's not like we were best of friends. I could pick him out of a crowd and he could likely do the same for me. I remember when he died, and you're right, I didn't go to the funeral. I thought, 'what a shame for his mother,' and then I went on living my life." He shrugged again. "No reason to get all fussed about a near-stranger shuffling off; if I did, I'd spend all my days in mourning, because I know a lot of strangers that got kicked loose just a month ago as your army rode right through them—"

"Yeah, all right," Cyrus said, "so you don't have to get broken up by every person you've ever met that's died. Still, he's your blood, you might have shown a little compassion."

"Perhaps you missed that number," Partus said. "One hundred and twelve first cousins. Ten brothers and sisters. 'Course they're all still living back home, but me, I'm out. If I was to worry about attending funerals for people just one generation back from me and those related to me like your friend, I'd be forever going to funerals." The dwarf straightened in his saddle. "And get damn near nothing else done, like folk back home do."

"Wow," Cyrus said. "You're a real wellspring of humanity."

"I sense your sarcasm," Partus said with unconcern, "but you should hardly be surprised. After all," the dwarf said with a glint in his eyes, "I'm not human at all."

They came to a crossroad. To Cyrus's right, the cliff's edge loomed. When Cyrus looked over it he saw the next level down carved into the mountain, only fifty or so feet below, and the next below that. *It looks much steeper from this perspective than it did on the approach.* Cyrus followed Briyce Unger's lead as the road sloped steeply, and a herd of goats was moved out of their way by a shepherd who drove them down a side street. The road rose at a steep grade, and Cyrus worried he would fall out of the saddle, or worse still, that his horse would buck slightly and they would both tumble end over end off the mountain, but somehow he hung on, as did Windrider.

"Unforgiving avenue," Mendicant said from somewhere behind him. "What happens if someone slips on this?"

"They fall," Terian said. "All the way down."

"All the way?" Mendicant looked over his shoulder, and his green scales seemed to dim in color. "Oh."

They made their way up the hill to the front gates of the castle Scylax, and Briyce Unger waved them forward. "We'll stay here for the night, enjoy my hospitality, and tomorrow we'll be on our way north again."

"How far are we going?" Cyrus asked.

Unger's smile faded slightly. "Not as far as I'd like. It seems that this scourge has moved south rather quickly. They're only a week north now. Seem to have stopped their forward movement for a bit, for whatever reason."

"Consolidating power?" Longwell asked, looking around from horseback down the hill. "Awaiting reinforcements of some kind?"

"Hard to know if they're awaiting reinforcements when we don't have a bloody clue where these things are coming from," Unger said with a shrug. "Perhaps if we can drive them back, far enough north, we'll find the source of their numbers."

"How far north does your territory stretch?" Cyrus asked.

"A good ways," Unger said. "All the way until the land gets too inhospitable, where the weather is bitter cold, even in the summertime. Our farthest town north used to be a village called Mountaintop, nestled in the last valley before a terribly tall peak with sheer slopes. There were trails where you could go farther from there, but between the wolves and all else, if you struck out to go farther your odds of coming back became exceedingly poor."

"So the real wonder," Cyrus said, "is if these creatures came from north of there."

They followed Unger up to the castle Scylax, which was even more impressive upon Cyrus's inspection. A steward offered a tour, taking them through the grand entry (which was not so grand as Vernadam's) and around. The curtain wall extended around the cliff's edge, providing a fine look off the side of the mountain below. The only direction one could assault the castle from, Cyrus conceded, was the town of Scylax below, and even that would be a disastrous feat to attempt for any army. Any assault up a steep road would come under an approach covered by bowmen as the gates to the castle were surrounded on both sides by two long protrusions of the wall. The last fifty yards in particular were totally exposed to arrow fire from both sides of the approach.

Within the keep Cyrus found the towers to his liking. They were more wood than stone, and furs were used for decoration far more than cloth. Instead of blankets on Cyrus's bed, he found a bearskin, big, shaggy, and comfortable. Wood floors, wood furnishings and a chest decorated the room. He sat on the bed after being showed to his quarters and reflected that although it wasn't nearly as comfortable as the one at Vernadam, it was good and somehow reminded him of the Society of Arms.

Dinner was a raucous affair, with mead and ale flowing far more generously than they ever had at any of the other, more formal meals that Cyrus had taken. The Syloreans laughed and bellowed, all activity in the room stopping when a fight broke out. Briyce Unger presided over two young men as they proceeded to punch the snot out of each other to the cheers of the crowd. When one of them finally stayed down from a blow that made Cyrus's jaw hurt to watch it, Unger raised the young man's hand in victory to the cheers of the crowd.

Terian had left, Cyrus knew, after dinner, disappearing out of the room, heading toward the town, he suspected, and the brothel somewhere below. A raw, aching sensation bothered Cyrus, something unsettled about Terian, about women, about everything, but he ignored it by taking frequent drinks from his flagon of mead, which was constantly refilled by a serving woman, a middle-aged one who began to look better and better as the drinking continued. Which was to say she was passable by the time Cyrus found the motivation to get back to his bedchamber—alone.

Cyrus drifted off that night under the influence of too much mead, too much ale, and too many thoughts of Cattrine and Vara. They became some sort of demonic swirl in his head, the two of them, and were joined by a third before he finally fell asleep, the vision of the three women in his mind spinning with the room around him.

Chapter 32

The next day dawned with a knock on his door, and when Cyrus stumbled out of bed to answer it, he found a steward waiting, a young boy no more than twelve. "Hot bath, sir?"

"What?" Cyrus asked, squinting his eyes.

"Would you like me to lead you to the hot springs under the castle so you can have a bath, sir?"

Cyrus felt the throbbing under his forehead and wondered if a bath would even be a good idea at the moment. "No, thank you, I'd rather sleep for a while longer."

"Very good, sir," the boy said, his mousy brown-haired head bobbing up and down. "I'll wake you for breakfast, then. The King gave orders that the expedition will leave an hour after that."

"Good enough," Cyrus said, and meant it. "Just fetch me some bread or a chicken leg or something, right before we go." He rubbed his eyes. "Let me sleep as long as possible, I'll eat on the run."

And he did so, as the boy returned to him an hour later with a mutton leg, and Cyrus ate it on his way out of the keep. His horse was saddled, cleaned, and waiting for him when he arrived, Briyce Unger himself holding the reins.

"Hello, Windrider," Cyrus said with a burp, running a hand along the horse's flank as he approached.

"Windrider?" Unger asked. "What kind of name is that for a horse? A bit girly, wouldn't you say?"

"I don't know," Cyrus said, uncaring. "I didn't name him."

"Let's be off, then, shall we?" Unger said, starting his horse toward the gate. "I trust you rested well."

"I have a hangover," Cyrus said, "but the sleep was fine."

"No complaints with the hospitality?"

"I wish your servants had brought me less mead and ale," Cyrus said, feeling a vein pulsing in his temple. "But that's less a hospitality complaint and more one related to your servants helping me to curb my own bad instincts."

Unger laughed, a deep bellowing one that grew deeper as they went out of the gate and found Terian working his way gingerly up the slope, looking incredibly uncomfortable in the saddle. "You look like you're going to have a long day of riding ahead of you, lad."

Terian grimaced, shifting himself awkwardly. "What happened to you?" Cyrus asked, drawing a pained expression from the dark knight.

"Let me tell you something about Sylorean women," Terian said, bringing his horse into line next to Briyce Unger's. "You may think this looks like a small town, and that perhaps their whores would be ignorant mountain wenches, unsure of which direction to ride a man. And you'd be wrong." He shifted again in his saddle. "I have never in my life met a woman who did to me what that woman did to me last night. I hurt in places I didn't know could hurt, was bent into positions I didn't know I could be contorted into, like a braid of hair." He shook his head. "And I'd love to go back, but I'm not sure I'd survive the experience."

Unger let out another bellow of laughter. "You met Muna, did you?"

"Was that her name?" the dark knight asked mildly. "I didn't hear it over the sound of my own screaming."

Unger laughed again, and reached over to slap Terian on the back. "If you think she's rough," Unger said, "you should avoid Ashini. Muna takes it gentle on you folk from out of town as a rule."

"The word gentle is not in her vocabulary," Terian said with a cringe, "and not because she's some ignorant mountain wench, but because she actually used a riding crop on me."

"I've heard enough," Cyrus said, blanching. "Keep your experiences to yourself."

"Why?" Terian wore a nasty grin. "You starting to regret not coming with me?"

"I regret a lot of things in my life," Cyrus said, "but not going with you last night doesn't look to be one of them. I mean, it looks like you're going to be walking bow-legged for a few days, which ... maybe I'm old fashioned, but I thought it was supposed to be the woman who walks like that afterward, not the man."

They rode down the mountain and out another gate, this one on the opposite end of town from the one that they entered the day before.

Cyrus rode next to Briyce Unger, and they traveled in a companionable silence for almost an hour before Unger broke it. "You've come a long way to get here."

Cyrus shook himself out of the daze of thought he had been in. "Aye. This is ... five months? I think five months since we left home."

"That's not only what I meant," Unger said. "You came here for your own reasons, but it was a long trek. At least I understood Partus's motives. He wanted coin, and it was easy enough to part with gold for the sake of his use. But you? You come all this way for your friend," he gestured to Longwell. "You help his Kingdom out—yeah, I know it's his father's, but that old buzzard will die some day and your friend will take the throne—but then you stick around and come north with us?" Unger shrugged. "Bit strange, you ask me."

"I caused another problem for Aron Longwell," Cyrus said. "I stayed to sort it out, came to Enrant Monge to help fix it. But when this ..." he thought about it, and was unable to come up with a suitable word of his own to describe the creatures they were riding to find, "... scourge, came up, I suppose I ..." He thought about it. "I don't know, I felt obligated to come for some reason."

"Are you a crusader of some sort?" Unger asked him, reserved. "Did you come here to spread the message of your gods? Because we've had that kind come through here before, trying to evangelize, get us to worship your western deities, and it doesn't hold much interest for us in Luukessia. Our ancestors didn't buy into it, and we don't buy it either."

"No," Cyrus said. "I follow the God of War, but I don't tend to do much evangelizing."

"God of War?" Unger said, thoughtful. "Bellarum. That was his name, wasn't it?"

"Yeah," Cyrus said with a nod. "That is his name."

"That one I could understand," Unger said. "God of War makes sense to me. But the others? Goddess of Love? Mischief? Earth, Air, Water and Fire? Feh!" He made a motion with his hand as though he were brushing them all away. "Don't need gods for those things. I've got my father, and his father, and the line of their fathers all the way back to the beginning. They watch over us, keep the stars in the night sky, and the sun up in the day. Who needs your cold, uncaring gods when you've got your ancestors, people who strained in their lives along a line so far back it's impossible to see to the end of it. All of them looking out for you, because you're the one who'll carry their legacy forward. No, I'll take my ancestors to your gods any day. Gods don't give a damn for you; with ancestors, you're what they've left to the world."

"What if they've got more than just you to worry about?" Cyrus asked, with wry amusement. "What if your father has several kids? Wouldn't he be limited on how much time he can spend helping you?"

"No," Unger said with a broad grin, giving Cyrus the feeling he was part of an inside joke by the King's grace. "He's dead, stupid. He's got all the time he needs, it's not like when you're living." He let out a barking laugh. "This is why I don't discuss religion with westerners. Someone always comes out looking the arse." Unger straightened up, turned serious. "So you didn't come here to be a crusader for your gods. Did you come for the glory, then, to further the greatness of your name?"

"No," Cyrus said. "There's a war going on back home. If that interested me, I could make a hell of a name for myself in Arkaria about now."

"Ah," Unger said, nodding sagely. "It's the other thing, then."

"What?"

"When a man leaves his home behind to travel a world away—as far as yours is from Luukessia—he's either running to something or running from something. For you, it'd be the latter, it seems."

"Where I come from," Cyrus said, feeling the shame creep across his cheeks, "a man doesn't run from anything. Not a warrior, at least."

"Where I come from," Unger said, "it doesn't matter if you run away for a bit, retreat, you know? Stay in every fight and lose, and what does it get you if you get ground under and lose the war? But a strategic retreat," Unger's eyes lit up, "that's saved an army or two. But that's not you, I'd wager. Not coming at the head of an army. So what are you running from?"

There was a pause, a long one, before Cyrus answered. "A woman."

"Couldn't have been anything else, I suppose," Unger said with a chuckle. "Only thing that can make a man run this far."

"I don't like to run," Cyrus said. "I'd rather not have."

"I'd rather not have an army of beasts ripping apart my Kingdom and its peoples," Unger said darkly. "So if it's all the same to you, I'm rather glad you ran and ran here. It may end up doing me more good in the long run than that army you wiped out at Harrow's Crossing would have in your stead."

They rode north for another few days, the ground getting higher and the air colder. Snow-capped peaks became more and more commonplace, and they passed through villages built on the sides of mountains, where people greeted them with all the fanfare due an allied army on the march. Cyrus looked into their faces, the men dressed in the garb of farmers and goat herders, the women drab, wearing skins that were faded and worn, and the children dirty from their day of activity. He looked upon them all and saw himself somewhere else, with a woman of his own, and children, and he wondered where that could possibly be, the place he saw.

On fourth day after they left Scylax, they passed through a village with gates of wood, each post carved into a spike as a fortification. "This is the village of Shaheer," Unger told him. Over their days of travel they'd spoken at some length, and Cyrus had managed to keep his emotions at bay thanks to Unger, who kept his mind focused on other things. "It's the next village ahead that we're going to. This scourge seems to have stopped in the valley over the next mountain; they only took four or five villages, one keep that we know of." Unger's face darkened. "Of course there are other towns north that we can't hear from; likely as not, they all fell first—if these things came from the north."

Deep in the mountains, they had reached a point where going outside at night, the temperature would fall enough for Cyrus to see his breath. During the days, the air had picked up a chill that Cyrus knew had nothing to do with the season—summer was in full bloom back at Enrant Monge, after all. The altitude and the cold together conspired to remind Cyrus of times long ago—*and best forgotten,* he thought.

The ride got harder. They went north again, this time over a pass that was relatively clear, a contrast to the times when they'd trudged their animals up hills and winding roads. When they reached the crest of the pass, they stopped. To either side of them were mountains, one double peak to Cyrus's left, and a particularly tall mountain to his right, one that seemed miles high. Looking ahead of them, he could see hints of snow still patchy on the ground in the valley below, some of it obvious and hiding in the shadows of little forests that dotted the valley. The smell of pine needles was strong in the air.

"There," Unger said, his finger extended, pointing to a collection of houses in the distance, miles away and nestled in an uneven fold of green ground next to one of the patches of woods. "That's the village that's held by this scourge. It's called Pinrade, and it used to have about five hundred people living in and around it."

"Do you think they're all dead?" Cyrus asked. "That these monsters killed them all?"

"My instincts from fighting these beasts when we clashed with them tells me yes," Unger said with a nod, "every man, woman, child and animal that remained in that village is dead." He kept an even expression. "But I'd surely like to be proven wrong."

"You intend us to move directly toward it?" Cyrus asked. "Or perhaps have something more subtle in mind?"

"We have an army in place in the valley east of here," Unger said. "Not the full force available to me—that's lurking a little south of Scylax, gathering along with additional conscripts we're pulling from the reaches of the Kingdom—but a decent-sized force of five thousand or so that is battle-hardened. We'll meet up with them and probe north a little, see how firmly dug in these blighters are."

"They didn't look capable of doing much digging," Cyrus said wryly.

"Aye, but they come in force, making digging in irrelevant. They overwhelm you with numbers, crush you under the weight of so many of them." Unger shook his head. "I have my doubts about doing this with five thousand, but it's a fraction of what we've thrown at them so far."

"How many men have died thus far?" Cyrus asked.

"I fought them with ten thousand men," Unger said. "We met them on bad ground—for them, not us. They kept coming until I called the retreat, and never once did they show hesitation, even when the ground was covered with their dead."

They moved east once out of the pass, down to some even ground, using a forest for cover as they left the road, the pace slowing as they made their way along a line avoiding the village by giving it a wide berth.

"Our men will be encamped a few miles from here," Unger said.

"Are you sure they're still there?" Cyrus asked. "I mean, if these things are as bad as you say they are, what's to stop them from sortieing out and slaughtering your men?"

Unger chuckled. "Nothing, I suppose, but they won't have gotten this army without a fight. So far they don't seem to do much sortieing; they come in force, move in on a town, and swarm it. They sit there for a while after, like nothing's happening ... if you look at the town from a distance, you'll see them ... not exactly making merry, because these things don't ever look happy, but they wander the streets, almost as though they're strutting around their new conquest." Unger bared his teeth in a feral grimace. "Bastards."

They came up over a rise and stopped, all in a line, and Cyrus's eyes widened in shock. Unger cursed, again, louder this time, and Cyrus made a gesture for him to shut up, which the King of Syloreas did, oddly enough. "Bastards," Unger said quietly. "Bloody bastards. It would appear you were right."

"I don't want to be right," Cyrus said. "I want to be wrong."

The rise led down to an empty, flat plain, hidden from the sight of the village of Pinrade, still several miles away. A full-fledged camp had been set up in the area—and it was completely, utterly destroyed. Tents were shredded, pieces of their occupants strewn over bloody ground. Bodies were scattered all over the site, both humans and the creatures that Unger called the scourge, their grey, pallid and naked flesh obvious against the clothed and more pink human bodies.

"No campfires," Terian said from next to Cyrus.

"They were told not to build any," Unger said, still seething. "These were experienced men. They knew how to keep out of sight."

"If that was a village of men in the distance," Cyrus said, "you wouldn't have thought it possible to keep an army out of their sight, not for weeks at a time. What made you think you could do it with these creatures?"

"Because they're animals!" Unger shouted, his words echoing across the slaughter below. "They're not men, these things, they're less than criminals, they're beasts, fit to be harnessed to a plow and forced to rip the ground of our fields. They're mindless, thoughtless animals, lower in mean intelligence than a dog, and worth less in value of life than fifty mutts."

"And apparently possessed of the same instincts," Terian said, "if they tracked your people down and wiped them out."

"Aye," Unger said. "And I'll kill them like a rabid one, without mercy or emotion."

They wandered down the hill among the dead. Cyrus watched as the horses snorted, their exhalations sending little clouds of breath into the cold air. *That's life, the surest sign in this chill, someone's breath fogging the air around them.* He looked at the destruction around them. *And there's none here.* "Curatio?" Cyrus called.

"I will try," the healer said as they reached the bottom of the hill, "but don't hold out much hope; it looks as if they've been dead for some time."

"Answer me this question, then," Terian said, "without an army at our backs, what's the likelihood we'll be able to take on whatever horde of beasts did this to them?"

"Not as good as if we had an army at our backs," Cyrus said as Windrider picked his way around the debris and bodies. "Why do you ask questions that you already know the answer to?"

"Rhetorical," Terian said. "Well, rhetorical and practical. Because, you see, those things," and the dark knight raised his hand and pointed to the ridgeline above them, "they seem to be watching us."

Cyrus cursed and drew his sword, dismounting from Windrider and slapping the horse on the backside after aiming him in a direction where there were no visible signs of the scourge. "Oldest trick in the book, isn't it? They set a trap for us."

"Stupid creatures," Bryce Unger said, unslinging a mighty spiked mace from his back, so grand in scale that it looked to Cyrus almost as tall as the man himself and with spikes longer than a child's forearm, "they're not smart enough to do anything so sinister. They must have heard us approach."

"You keep denigrating their intelligence," Cyrus said, "but we're the fools, the hundred of us, up against however many of them."

They were situated in a neat bowl-shaped depression in the ground, with hills surrounding them and the mountain rising behind them. The only avenue of retreat was the way they had come. To their left was an oppressive rise, a hill that backed to a steep series of cliffs, behind them was the north slope of the mountain they had just avoided by taking the pass back to the east. Before them, strung along the hillside for a mile or more, was a waiting line of the scourge, the creatures on all fours, moving only slightly, in position, watching from the top of the hill. *They could be here in thirty seconds, fall upon us in great number and force a conflict,* Cyrus thought. "Why do they wait?"

"They fear us," Unger said, clutching his mace and remaining atop his steed. "And they rightly should. Their numbers look small, weak. Perhaps they're all that remains after my men destroyed many of them."

"You seem far too sharp a battlefield commander to be taken in by bluster," Cyrus said, trying to keep any recrimination or reproach from his tone. "Why don't we assume the worst, and if it's better than we think, we'll be no worse off?"

Unger cursed behind him, and Cyrus heard the King of Syloreas let out a grim hiss. "Too right. Assume the worst. Perhaps they're surrounding us? Setting us up for another hammer to fall?"

"They could be trying to draw us in," Longwell said from beside Cyrus, still atop his horse, spear in hand. "You might do better fighting from horseback, especially with their disadvantage in height."

"I've always been rubbish at fighting on horseback," Cyrus said, "and with Praelior, believe me when I say you want me on the ground. I'm more dexterous and maneuverable than Windrider and faster to boot."

"You're also more vulnerable," Terian said, "but that's really more your issue than mine."

"I will try to keep you all healed and protected," Curatio said, "but against these numbers and with only one other healer to aid me, this could get fairly dirty, fairly fast."

Cyrus twirled Praelior in a circle from his hand, catching hold of it and pointing it toward the hilltop where the scourge still waited, making little noise and moving even less. "I didn't think keeping it clean was going to be an option."

Cyrus felt movement behind him and turned to see Aisling dismounted, standing just behind his shoulder. "I'm not much use on horseback, either."

"We could use a wizard or five right now," Cyrus said, and then saw Mendicant's pony step into line next to Curatio, the goblin's scaly skin glistening in the cold morning light. "I suspect you'll do well enough, Mendicant."

"As well as I can," the small goblin said, his claws looking particularly pointed. "I can put up a wall of flame twenty feet across when they charge, but I won't be able to maintain it for more than thirty seconds or so; after that, I'll be forced to engage one on one—or perhaps heave some fireballs into dense concentrations of the enemy."

"Do what you can," Cyrus said, feeling the tension flood him. "It seems they're waiting for something, and that concerns me."

"Another wave to flank us?" Terian asked, "reinforcements from the village? I wish they'd get to it."

The sun was too bright, Cyrus thought, seeing the light shine off the armor in the formation around him. Only a few had chosen to dismount; Briyce Unger's men remained on horseback, and besides Aisling, two veteran warriors of Sanctuary as well as Scuddar In'shara were the only others who had chosen to fight on foot. Scuddar looked particularly lethal, his robes a crimson red, his scimitar spinning in his hands in a display of swordsmanship that Cyrus never found less than impressive.

A wind kicked up around them as they stared across the hilly no man's land between them and the scourge on the hill. Cyrus kept his eyes moving, looking left to the ridgeline, then behind him again, for any sign of another attack, for any idea of what might be delaying the creatures charge.

"Will anyone feel bad if we just charge them and get it over with?" Briyce Unger asked.

"I'll feel bad if we do it and they sideswipe us with a flanking attack we ran voluntarily into," Terian said.

"I'll feel worse if we die of old age while waiting for their attack," Curatio said, "and for me, that's saying something."

"J'anda," Cyrus said, "I suspect you're about to have to find out if these things can be mesmerized."

"I was planning to try," the enchanter said. "Failing that, perhaps I can take charge of a few and disturb their formation to start things off?"

"Can a spell even reach them out there?" Terian asked.

"For most, it would be impossible," J'anda said, closing his eyes and raising a hand. "For me, it is merely another day." A glow wrapped his fingers, a greenish-blue hue that encompassed him, and his eyes snapped open. "Oh. My. Oh, gods. This is … they are not mindless beasts. Not at all." J'anda's eyes widened and the enchanter let out a long, gasping exhale that clouded the air in front of him. "This … unfathomable … they … ahhhh …" His eyes rolled back in his head, he shuddered and shook in the saddle as Cyrus ran between the horses that separated them while the animals began to snort, shuffling back and forth on their hooves. The sounds of the horses took on an eerie quality, being the only noise audible other than the crackling voice of the flailing enchanter.

Cyrus reached J'anda's side and grabbed him by the robes, jarring the dark elf. His eyes snapped open and looked down at Cyrus, wide, the enchanter's usually unflappable calm gone. His breaths came in deep, rattling bursts, as though he were cold and winded, ragged in his breathing as his thin shoulders rose and fell in poor time. His eyes locked on Cyrus and they were wild, filled with undefinable emotion, as though the enchanter's mind were overwhelmed.

"J'anda?" Cyrus asked, dragging the dark elf's eyes to him. Cyrus could see the bloodshot element to them, the red, strained look that they carried. "Are you all right?"

"Yes," J'anda breathed, "and no. Not all right at all. They're … you would not believe what they are." He reached down and clutched Cyrus's shoulder. "*Who* they are." J'anda pushed off, balancing back on his horse and moving away from Cyrus. "They are not fools. They are not beasts. And they are not mindless."

"Who are they?" Cyrus asked, spellbound by the enchanter's seeming breakdown.

"Not now," J'anda breathed. "Not now … I cannot even explain it, not now."

"Why not?" Terian interrupted, and the dark knight's eyes and voice burned with impatience. "What's got you so addled?"

"Addled?" J'anda asked with a laugh, a loud, high, demented one. "You don't know. Of course you don't, you couldn't. And it doesn't matter right now, anyway, because we have to run." The crazed amusement fled his face and he looked Cyrus straight in the eye. "We have to run, we have to leave now. We might stand a chance if we hurry, if we fly back to the pass."

"What the blazes is going on here, J'anda?" Cyrus asked. "What are you talking about? What are these things? What is wrong with you?"

"I saw," J'anda whispered. "I looked into the mind of one of them when I charmed him and I saw—what they are. Who they were. What they've been through. And I know," he said hoarsely, "I know. And something else, too—" He looked away, stunned, frightened, back to the hill where they waited, still, staring down at the expedition.

"That more of them are coming—enough to destroy us all. And they'll be here in moments."

Chapter 33

"Start moving," Cyrus said in a tone of low dread. "Everybody start heading back the way we came." No one moved, and Cyrus felt the pressure building internally, and it exploded out of him in a shout. "What are you waiting for? He told us they're coming, MOVE!"

With that, some of the Syloreans broke ranks and began a run up the hill from whence they had come, a few of the reluctant Sanctuary members following just behind. Curatio hesitated, as did Longwell, and Cyrus waved them in the direction of the hill as he tried to find Windrider in the chaos that was breaking around them. "This isn't a moment to stand here and die, get moving!"

"Not leaving you here until you're saddled and going, sir," Longwell said, and Curatio nodded as well. Terian, too, lurked with them, along with Mendicant. "This isn't a time to be leaving anybody behind."

Cyrus watched the others who had dismounted with him, climbing up into their saddles, and he looked for Windrider. Cyrus was surrounded, the Syloreans breaking around him, cutting him off from the direction he knew the horse had run. He heard a familiar whinny from behind the line of retreating Sylorean horses, but to cross them now would mean trampling, injury, unintentional death. He waited until the last of them stampeded past, and Windrider thundered to him. He slung a foot in the stirrup and jumped, sliding onto the saddle as his horse took off, trying to lead the way for the others.

"They're moving now," Longwell shouted.

Cyrus turned to see it was true, that the beasts on the hill—the scourge, as he'd come to think of them—were coming down in great numbers. "J'anda looks to have been right," Cyrus said. "They got some reinforcements."

A flood of them came as Cyrus and the others galloped, hugging the trail and following the Syloreans ahead of them as they hurried their way back toward the pass. The creatures of the scourge were behind him, Cyrus saw, waiting for trouble to descend, but it seemed as though they were losing them. The creatures, unable to keep up with the speed of the horses, were falling back as Cyrus and the others were pressing ahead.

Cyrus kept to the rear of the column, a little distance between him and the others in front of him. He felt a sudden cold, clammy chill run over his body but ignored it, continuing to hold tight to Windrider's reins as the horse raced along, fast enough to keep up with those in front of him but keeping an eye on the enemies coming from behind.

"Cyrus," Terian's voice came from beside him, low, hushed, barely audible over the hoofbeats. Cyrus turned and the dark knight was there, riding next to him, the nearest person ahead of him by at least ten feet. Behind Terian, to Cyrus's left, another swarm of the scourge was emerging from the woodline a few hundred feet behind the dark knight. Cyrus made to exclaim, already pointing, but Terian said, "I know. I saw them coming. We can outrun them on horseback. But I need to tell you something."

"What?" Cyrus asked, and he realized that he was sweating, an unusual feeling for such a cool day. His mouth was dry, papery, as though someone had poured sand into it, and his voice came out scratchy, so low he could barely hear it himself.

"You've been afflicted with a curse," Terian said as Cyrus felt at his throat, trying to discern the nature of his own malady. "You'll feel the fever in a moment, and the seering pain will start shortly thereafter. You may scream," Terian said, eyes cold, "but because of your throat, no one's going to hear you. I want you to know that this isn't personal, not really." Cyrus stared at him blankly, disbelieving, as Terian continued. "You killed my father on that bridge in Termina, and for a dark elf, that means vengeance. It has to be taken. I swore a vow and performed a soul sacrifice to become who I am, and I can't just let it go, not that easily. I do want to thank you, though," Terian said, drawing his sword. "I doubt I would have ever gotten this back if you hadn't brought it to me." Terian's eyes flicked forward, and his sword darted out and hit Windrider across the neck.

The geyser of blood from the horse hit Cyrus in the face, a slap of wetness so quick and brutal that he didn't even realize it had happened until it had. The next strike was even more brutal as Terian slapped him across the face with the dull edge of the blade. Windrider was already falling, skidding in the dirt and Cyrus felt himself lift off upon impact, cartwheeling end over end in the dirt and grass, his head hitting, then dull impacts along his shoulders and back as he rolled. The horse's weight settled on his leg and he felt the bone break, but the pain was muted, somewhere far in the back of his head, beyond the pain in his face, his body, and the desire to just sleep.

Cyrus coughed, and he felt the warm blood flow out of his mouth, onto the ground, turning the dirt red. He watched the little grains of sand float inside it. He felt something else, then, too, something around him—grey flesh, grey faces, horrible teeth, pointed and vicious, a bloody, disgusting spectacle that lingered in front of him, snapping at him, at his face, even as his vision faded into nothingness and he felt nothingness—save for the pointed, far off sensation of his flesh being torn by a thousand hungry mouths.

Chapter 34

"GET OFF!" A shriek echoed through Cyrus's ears as a chill sensation returned to his limbs and he saw a flash of movement in front of his now-opening eyes. Aisling moved above him, her blades a dance of motion as she cut through three of the scourge beasts and kicked another so hard it flew through the air and into its fellows. Cyrus felt blood dripping out of his armor but realized his skin was intact, his flesh renewed, and looked up to see Curatio, far in the distance, beyond a solid wall of the scourge, a hundred of them separating him from the healer and the others. He jumped to his feet in a well-practiced move and his blade was already out.

Cyrus heard the familiar whinny behind him and saw Windrider lift up and kick, stomping three of the creatures to death with rapidity, then back away from them to form a tight circle with Cyrus and Aisling. A wave of flame was burning through the flank of the scourge, the wall of beasts separating Cyrus and Aisling from the rest of the Sanctuary force.

"There seem to be an awful lot of them," Cyrus said, clutching Praelior and raking a circle around him, killing a half-dozen of the creatures as they began to surge in on all sides. "Not sure we can fight this many."

"Just you and I against the world?" Aisling asked with a hint of amusement. "I pity the world." Windrider whinnied, drawing Cyrus's attention to his neck, where stains of blood remained on his hide. "All right," Aisling conceded, "us four." She turned her head and attacked three of the beasts that came at her, her daggers a blur of motion, and there was a shriek as her horse was pulled to the ground, the creatures swarming over it, tearing it apart while Cyrus and Aisling fought off their advance. "Us three," she amended. "But they'll pay for that. That was the best horse I've ever stolen."

Cyrus flicked Praelior out in a defensive line around him as three of the scourge jumped at him, and he cleaved them neatly in two before taking the heads off two more that came at him. "Remind me to remonstrate you for thieving later."

"I might forget," she said with a smirk. "I've never been much for sermons, especially from a man whose life I just saved. That was some damnably clumsy riding on your part. Why'd you pick now to fall off your horse?"

"That was no accident," Cyrus said. "Terian cut Windrider's throat and cursed me."

"What?" she cried as one of the scourge leapt for her. Cyrus swung his sword and clipped the beast, sending it to the ground in a heap. They stood side by side, Windrider behind them, still stomping in a frenzy, keeping the creatures from pulling him down as they had Aisling's horse. Cyrus watched the hooves land on another one of the scourge and cringed at the sight of its skull caving in, no blood oozing from it, instead a thick, black liquid puddled underneath the unmoving creature. "Why would he do something like that?"

"You remember that sword you brought me? From that dark knight I killed on the bridge in Termina?" Cyrus's gauntlet caught the bite of a scourge, and he twisted it, breaking the creature's teeth as he jammed his sword down its throat then threw the corpse away.

"Yeah? Oh. Oh! OH! That was his father? The dark knight?"

"Apparently."

"Oh, wow." Aisling slung her blades in a perfect arc, catching another one of the beasts as it attacked her. Her dagger ended up buried in its head, and her hand moved like lightning, catching it with three more thrusts along the neck and flank as it dropped. "Whoops."

"That doesn't quite cover it."

"It'll have to do until we get out of here." Aisling's back bumped against his, and Cyrus felt her push against him as the circle around them tightened. Cyrus looked to the side and saw Curatio and the others falling back, the numbers overwhelming them. Mendicant cast another spell, and a fireball flew toward them as Cyrus ducked out of instinct. It flew past and landed in a thick knot of scourge, exploding and sending bodies and limbs flying in all directions.

"What the hell was that?" Aisling cried. "Is that goblin trying to add us to the corpse pile?"

"No," Cyrus said and pointed to where the fireball had impacted, "look!" He pointed, and only a few feet—and twenty or so scourge away—Mendicant had cleared a path for them. Beyond was open ground to the west, heading toward a mountain in the distance, but it was a long ways off, with plenty of room to outrun the scourge—

"Windrider," Cyrus said, but the horse was already kicking and bucking, making his way toward the open ground. "We'll only have a moment here," Cyrus said to Aisling, "you need to get on the horse first."

"Fine," she said tightly and was gone, already slipping into the saddle, "but get your sweet ass moving, will you?"

"I will," he said, and tensed himself. With a deep breath that lasted only a second, he let out a bellowing warcry that echoed through the mountain pass and charged forward, blade in motion, clearing the way for Windrider and Aisling to pass. His sword moved with the fluid grace he had come to expect after so many battles with it at his side. The scourge seemed to move slowly, unable to keep up with his speed but overwhelming in numbers. His blade found target after target, casting the bodies aside, damaged or dead. He kept going, heard the horse at his back, until he cut the last of them down and broke free to open ground and he felt Windrider thunder along beside him. He hoisted himself up, sliding onto the back of the horse behind Aisling and they galloped away, thousands of the creatures following in their wake.

Chapter 35

The mass of the scourge moved in a fluid line, not interfering much with each other as they ran, more slowly, behind Windrider as he carried Cyrus and Aisling toward the top of the hill. Far, far behind them, Cyrus could see the line of the Sanctuary formation falling back, Terian watching him from a far distance, along with Curatio. "They don't know that Terian tried to kill me, do they?"

"I don't think so," Aisling said, "unless one of them was paying more attention than I was, and I doubt it because I was the first one to start back for you."

"Then he's with them now," Cyrus said. "Hopefully he doesn't have any righteous vengeance he'd like to inflict on anyone else."

"It seems to me," Aisling said, the wind blowing her white hair into his face, "he's known for quite some time that you killed his father. I've seen him carrying that blade since before we left Sanctuary. So why did he wait until now to strike you down?"

"I don't think he did," Cyrus said. "He let Partus kill me before, at Harrow's Crossing."

"But he must have known you'd get resurrected," she said, her hands clutching the reins, holding on tight as they continued forward. "He can't have thought that would kill you."

"I don't know what he's thinking," Cyrus said. "Maybe he didn't want to get caught and waited for a moment he thought he could get away with it."

Aisling seemed to think about that. "He very nearly did; this was the perfect time. No one could have recovered your body from that onslaught, not with the numbers we were against."

Cyrus waited a beat before he answered her. "You did."

She kept facing away from him, looking straight ahead, the wind brushing past both of them as he realized for the first time that his hands were snug on her hips. "I'm no one," she said. "At least to you I have been." They reached the top of the hill and Windrider went on, west, toward the mountains in the distance. The mountain to the south of them was high, and a series of cliffs and gullies was visible to block them from passage. "Can't go south, can't go north because these little bastards are pretty heavy thataway ... same with east, since we just came from that direction."

"West it is," Cyrus said, and Windrider galloped on, not waiting for any other word on the matter. They plunged into a copse of withered pines as the land slumped down, and Cyrus kept an eye on the ground above them on the hill. It remained empty for quite some time, until finally he saw the first of the scourge crest it, a mile or so behind them. "They're pursuing," he said. "Not very quickly, but they are coming for us."

"That's of some consolation," she said, "because I'm not planning to stop to let them catch up anytime soon. And I doubt your horse is going to stop for water until he has to, unless I miss my guess." A breathy snort greeted her words. "Clever one, aren't you?"

They continued downward, along a loping plateau, still moving toward a mountain in the distance. "I'm hoping there's a pass somewhere around here," Cyrus said, "and maybe we can move ourselves around this mountain and join up with the expedition as they head south." He shook his head. "I daresay they've shown the envoys enough evidence to bring armies back to help combat this threat."

"What is it with you and the word 'daresay'?" Aisling asked. "You say it all the time. 'I daresay' this and 'I daresay' that. What does it even mean?"

"It's just a way of saying, 'I think.'"

"Then why don't you just say 'I think'?" She looked back at him, a little smile showing.

"Because I'm being pretentious," Cyrus said. "And you should allow me a little pretention in my life." He felt a dark humor settle over him. "After all, I've been betrayed by a good friend recently, as well as by two women I cared for."

"I'll allow you just about anything you want," Aisling said. "It matters not to me, I was just curious what it meant." She waited a moment further before she spoke again. "And it was 'loved,' not 'cared for,' if you want to be accurate about it, Mr. Pretentious." She leaned her head forward, bowing it slightly. "You loved them, both of them, whether you want to admit it or not."

Cyrus swallowed, hard, felt the pain rise in his throat, the bile that told him she was right. "Yes," he whispered. "I did. But at least they didn't try to kill me, as my friend just did."

"Rough year," she said. "Perhaps it's the company you keep."

"I was beginning to think maybe it was me."

The skies began to darken after midday. Clouds rolled in and a light snow began to fall scant hours later. The woods became thicker, and the snow blew with the wind, causing Cyrus to remove his helm in order to see. They kept going, but had long since lost sight of the horde behind them. The last hilltop that Cyrus had sighted them from was now hours behind them, and visibility was so poor that even when they reached a high vantage point they could see only a little ways.

"I don't see them," Aisling said, staring behind them. "When we find water, we should stop briefly before we continue."

"Agreed," Cyrus said.

They continued until past nightfall, and came out of the woods in a dark encroachment of rocks, leading a steep, impassable embankment. Windrider let loose a quiet whinny upon approaching it, scaring Cyrus for the implications.

"It would appear that our journey west is at an end," Aisling said. "And if we go south, I suspect that this ravine is the same one that kept us from making for the pass south earlier. Any suggestions?"

"North or east," Cyrus said. "We know for fact that they're east, so the only alternative is north."

"The problem with that idea," she groused, "is that we suspect that they're north as well."

"Go with what's suspected or what's known?" Cyrus asked. "I know which I pick."

"Not fair. Not sound, either. It's a choice between certain death and uncertain death, and I want to pick 'neither.'"

His smile disappeared. "Then you probably should have retreated with the others and left me behind."

The snow came down harder now, blowing in their faces as they headed north, across the hills. They crested another rise and Cyrus looked east, and in the distance, he wondered if the village that they had seen from the pass that morning was nearby, if it was somewhere out there, teeming with the scourge. "Do they eat people?" he wondered aloud.

"Morbid thought," Aisling said. "But I can't say I haven't had it myself. It seemed as though J'anda had something on them, had figured something out that he wanted to tell us, but the whole lot of them stopped it." She held her breath for a moment. "Can't pretend I'm not curious about what that was about."

"Nor I," Cyrus said. "This snow is getting worse."

"It's not even sticking to the ground," Aisling complained, "but it's turning everything to mud." Windrider made a noise that sounded to Cyrus's ears like assent. "This is going to slow us."

"I know Windrider can handle a long ride," Cyrus said, "but it's been months of walking, hell, almost a whole month now with only a day or two here or there for a break. This hard escape can't have been easy on him." The horse was stoic but turned his head to favor them with one eye.

"What are you suggesting?" Aisling said, the coolness in her voice just covering the dread beneath.

"I'm suggesting that if we keep heading north in this, we're likely to blunder into the enemy. I'm suggesting that we find somewhere that looks safe to hole up for the night, and we take it." He blinked the snow flurries out of his eyes. "We try and sleep in shifts, so as not to be surprised if these things track us like bloodhounds do."

"I don't love the sound of that," Aisling said. "Resting while we're being hunted seems like a bad idea."

"And getting lost and falling in a ravine or having Windrider die from exhaustion seems like a better one?" Cyrus looked around. "We don't even have any oats for him to eat, since the wizards are all gone and we're isolated on our own."

"Perhaps some field grass?" Aisling suggested. "He could try and find it under the layers of mud."

"We need a rest," Cyrus said. "Not so much for us as for him." He let out a breath. "Maybe a little for us."

"I can't imagine the conditions under which I'd feel I could rest right now," Aisling said, and Cyrus felt the tension in her, pressed as he was against her back. "But I'd imagine that some reprieve is better than none. And," she grudgingly admitted, "you're right about seeing ahead. We're more likely to stumble over the edge of a cliff in this mess than to be able to see clear forward on a decent path."

"Right," Cyrus said. "There's likely a place where that ravine shallows, and we might be able to cross it to get to the flatter ground on the other side, but we'll miss it if we keep going in this." He looked back behind them. "Also, we're leaving tracks right now. It might be best to find a place to lie low, so we can give them a chance to cover over." He shrugged. "Not that these things are trackers, but you can never be too careful when you're surrounded by the enemy."

They kept on for a while longer, as the terrain got rockier. They came upon another sheer cliff face, having wandered to a point where the ground rose to the east forcing them along a path parallel to the ravine. They went along, now boxed in by a cliff face on one side and a ravine on the other, forced along a steadily inclining grade, the ground carrying them upward almost against their will.

"I don't like this," Aisling said, so low that Cyrus almost missed it.

"What's that?"

"Being trapped," she said, pointing to the face of the rock to their right. "It's too sheer. If they come at us from behind we have to run ahead blindly, we can't even swerve right or left."

"Story of my life," Cyrus said, and when she shot him a confused look, he went on, "Running blindly."

"Ah," she said with a nod, "I thought you meant not being able to swerve left or right."

He thought about it for a moment. "That too, actually."

The skies were a deep grey, laced with swirls of clouds that stretched to either end of the horizon, punctuated by light streaming through the gaps between formations. The gaps between the clouds started to darken as the sun set. The cold air blew through Cyrus's armor and he felt it all the way through, even over the sense of weary tension that had him in its grasp.

Aisling's breathing was something he could feel even through his armor, and the tension was noticeable from her as well. Her shoulders were upright, and when Windrider would occasionally take a jarring step, Cyrus felt her go taut in his grasp. He tried not to wrap his arms around her waist, but every now and again he was left with no choice as he leaned, sitting as he was off the saddle. Her hair blew in his face constantly, the white mane possessed of a smell that reminded him of herbs, for some reason, as though she had some sort of greenery in it even now.

The howling of the wind was the only thing that surrounded them, blowing past, dampening all other sound. The canyon channeled it toward them, and Cyrus felt the razor claws of it, so shocking for a summer's day, and he reached to the saddlebags for his cloak, tucking it around himself and Aisling as best he could. He heard her murmur her thanks as he drew closer to her, the night air gradually growing colder and colder.

"Up there," Aisling murmured, and her finger came up to point. "There's something against the cliff face."

They drew closer and Cyrus saw it too. It was wooden, carved, and set up on small pillars, though broken and crumbling. "An old mine?" Cyrus asked.

"Looks like," she answered as they came upon it. It was square, two posts on either side and a lintel over the top, a beam to keep the roof from collapsing. It jutted only a little out of the rock, just enough to be noticeable if someone was traveling along the ravine.

Cyrus carefully dismounted and ducked into the entrance. The cave was dark, and his eyes couldn't adjust to the low light.

"You blind fool," Aisling said, appearing at his side. "Here." She pulled something out of a pack on her belt, and grabbed an old discarded stick out of the ground at their side. She ripped the sleeve under her armor, pulling a layer of cloth out and wrapping the old branch with it. When she was done she opened the small container she had pulled from her pack, then ran it along the blade of her knife. Sparks came, and the cloth caught, the stick becoming a torch, burning brightly and lighting the cave.

It turned ahead of them, twisting off to their right. Cyrus heard Windrider snort behind him, then felt the horse put his face on the back of Cyrus's head and push him forward. "You know," Cyrus said, looking back at him, "every day I'm with you, you become less a horse and more of a comic sidekick, I hope you realize." Windrider whickered and shuffled off beside Aisling, who idly stroked his face as they stared into the darkness ahead of them, contemplating it.

"If we don't look around and make sure the cave is secure," he said, staring into the distance, "we're probably not going to have a lot of luck sleeping tonight."

"Agreed," she said. "You first."

He sighed, and drew his sword. "A comic sidekick for a horse and a skittish ranger as a traveling companion, miles from a friendly face, surrounded by savage creatures that want to eat us alive." He frowned. "Why does this always happen to me?"

"You wanted to be an adventurer," Aisling said, with a little snap, "now you are. And oh, what an adventure we're having today, eh?"

Cyrus prowled forward, sword in hand, Aisling and Windrider behind him. Three branches of the main chamber turned into dead ends, and a fourth led to a narrow passage. When Cyrus thrust the torch into it to shed some light, it stretched through a narrow gap in the rock that was only just large enough for him to squeeze into.

"I think we're okay," he said, "though I suspect we'll be in some manner of trouble if the light from our fire or the smoke is seen outside." They walked back to the entrance, and as they approached the mouth of the cave, Cyrus realized that was no concern. Outside, the snow fluttered down in heavy waves, and had begun to stick to the ground and the rock face opposite them.

"Midsummer snow storm?" Aisling asked. "Perhaps the gods are with us after all."

"The Luukessians say the gods do not know these lands," Cyrus said. "And I doubt the God of Storms is much of a fan of our work anyway."

"Speak for yourself," Aisling said, doing a little pirouette that caught Cyrus's attention. "Everyone's a fan of my work."

"Oh?" Cyrus asked dryly. "Do you do a great deal of public exhibition of that sort of thing?"

She shrugged airily. "Only when I have a partner I really want to work with. Otherwise I tend to perform in private—and on privates—"

"Okay," Cyrus said, brushing past her, "you've found the edge of my comfort zone again." He took the torch and gathered a few more pieces of wood, setting them in a small pile further into the cave, just out of sight of the entrance. "Let's make a fire, then maybe we can take turns getting some rest." He looked to the mouth of the cave. "Seems like this will be far enough back to avoid any suspicion or anyone seeing the light of our fire."

"You know," she hunched next to him as he worked to start the fire, "most men might find themselves grateful if they'd had their life saved by a beautiful, mischievous, young woman—flexible in all the right ways, if you catch my drift—and might find some way to repay her for such a kindness, perhaps in a way she had long been asking for."

Cyrus stopped what he was doing, and a piece of wood slipped out of his hand and almost put out the kindling he had been trying to start. "Now? We're surrounded by enemies, in the middle of their territory," he waved at the walls around him as though they were under open sky, "and now you come back to propositioning me?" He sighed.

"Is it really such a bad thing?" She was hushed, deflated, all the air out of her.

"No, it's not. And if you had done so almost anytime in the last thirty days—at the right moment, at least—I would have given in to you without question." She brightened as he said it. "But." He watched her pause, uncertain again. "I would have been using you," he said. "You were right; I was in love with Vara. Completely, utterly, soul-consumingly, if that's even a word. I wanted her more than anything, and when she cast me out of her graces, I moved to Cattrine." He felt a grimace. "When she hurt me, it was only after she had ... accustomed me again to something I hadn't realized I had been missing. It's left me ... somewhat confused, full of sensation and emotion and urges that I honestly thought I had well and truly suppressed." He looked back toward the little fire, placed a few small sticks onto it and watched it begin to catch.

"But it's not suppressed anymore, is it?" She eased next to him, took a small piece of tinder and put it on the burgeoning flame. "You're loosed, and you feel it now, the blood in your veins, and ..." Her hand reached down, under his armor, through the gap in the chainmail, and he felt her warm touch on his side, on his skin, and somehow it lit a fire of its own in him. "You're not cold to me like you were before."

"I'm not," he admitted. "I was in love. I had no room in my mind, my heart, for anyone but her. But then I started to feel something for another woman, and it changed things. She changed things," he corrected. "But she's gone now, and I'm empty, Aisling, empty all the way to the bottom of me. Whatever is left is only desire, there's no emotion behind it." He looked into her eyes, warning her with everything he had. *Turn back, understand how burned up I am inside, how cut up and bled out, there's no feeling left, nothing for you* ...

"I want it," she said quickly, urgently, and she kissed him on the lips, a kiss he did not return. "I don't care how empty it is, I want it. I've wanted it all along." She kissed him again.

"I feel nothing," he said, stopping her. "There's nothing in me, now. Whatever I had, the two of them took. It's not fair—not to you, anyway—"

"I'll decide what's fair for me," she said, kissing him again, pushing herself into his arms. "I'll decide what's good for me, what I want."

"This ..." Cyrus kissed her, felt her kiss back, let her hands run over him, taking his armor off, "... this is all you get, you realize? No emotion, no heart, just ... the physical. It's all I have left."

His armor dropped off, piece by piece, and her dark blue hands ran across his pale, hairy chest. She tugged him closer, letting her leather armor slip off over her head, exposing herself to him and pushing close. He could see the contrast now, the dark navy skin against his winter white; the night and day, the difference between her and the other women. "I want it," she said again, and she helped him out of his pants. "I want it. To hell with the rest."

The fire had taken on a life of its own and burned, quietly, a slow roar next to them while the snow and wind howled outside the cave, and the warmth within took on a life of its own.

Chapter 36

Cyrus awoke to a long beam of light reaching across the dirt floor of the cave. He started to sit up and realized there was something on his arm; after a moment he acclimated to his surroundings and remembered why Aisling was lying across his body, her hair tickling his shoulder and her soft, steady breathing rising and falling against him. A forceful whinny behind him caused him to look over at Windrider, who glared at him accusingly. "I have no oats," he said. "Maybe some grass." A snort from the horse caused Aisling to stir, then sit up, allowing his arm to be free.

"Good morning," she said, blinking the sleep from her eyes. She pushed the stray strands of white hair off her face, tucking them behind her in a ponytail that she made by tying her hair with a string. "Did you sleep well?" she asked with a mischievous grin.

"I did," Cyrus said, trying to keep his expression carefully neutral, even as she let the blanket fall away from her chest, and the cold air became obvious. "Which is surprising, given that we're in a somewhat sticky predicament."

"Mmm," she said, stretching. "Were you talking about our escape and flight from the scourge or what happened last night?" She lay back across his chest for a moment, teasing him with a gentle bite to the ribs that caused him to jerk in surprise. She sat back up and laughed, looking at him with undisguised mirth. "Still so sensitive. We'll work on that."

"You sure?" Cyrus asked. "I mean, what I said last night stands ..."

"I heard you then," she said coolly. "I'm a big girl. I told you what I wanted all along, and if what you want from me is just the thrilling realm of a physical relationship," she swung a leg over him, climbed on top and straddled him over the blanket, "then I promise, I can thrill you more than those other ladies could."

"Oh?" Cyrus said, leaning back on his arms. "As much as I'd love to test that assumption this morning, it's going to have to wait. We need to get moving."

"Couldn't it wait just a little while?" she asked, teasing one of his chest hairs by twirling it on her finger. "It wouldn't take long at all ... at least for me. You might take a little longer, based on what I've seen so far." Her face split with a wicked grin, her eyes shining even in the light of the faded fire, burnt down to embers.

"Later," Cyrus said, and indicated for her to move. "I'm not immune to your charms, but I am possessed of a sense of self-preservation, and we have no idea how many of those things are out there nor where they are. We need to start hoofing it." He looked to Windrider. "Literally, in your case."

They dressed quietly, Cyrus eating some bread from his saddlebag, giving some to Aisling, and then feeding the rest to a semi-appreciative Windrider, who still seemed to be glaring at him. Once they were done, Cyrus started toward the entrance to the cave but felt a subtle tug on his arm. He looked back to see Aisling, shaking her head at him. "Let me look," she said. "You're absolutely terrible at any kind of stealth. You'll give us away if they're out there."

He shrugged and stood back, extending his arm toward the entrance in invitation. Aisling crept to the side of the cave, hugged it, and seemed to blend into the shadows. He could see her move, slightly, every now and again, but only because he knew she was there and where to look. She crept to the entrance of the cave over the course of five minutes and looked out, avoiding the sunlight that was coming in. After a minute, she turned and slipped back toward him, taking another couple minutes to make it over to him.

"Nope," she said, her voice hushed "this is bad."

"Bad? Bad how?"

"They're out there," she said. "About eighty, by my count, in a line, moving through the ravine below us, just over the ledge that goes past our cave. If we go out, they'll see us. We need to wait."

"I don't love that idea. What if they circle around and come check this place out? It's not as though the entrance is well hidden."

"Agreed," she said. "I was thinking ... how about the narrow passage at the back of the cave? It might lead to another exit."

"And it might lead to us getting trapped in a tight space when they overrun us," Cyrus said. "Plus, Windrider is gonna have a hell of a time fitting through there."

"So you'd rather go the way that we know includes scouts for the enemy?" She shrugged expansively, her white hair highlighted by the darkness. "Have it your way."

"No," Cyrus said. "The other option is that we can sit here and wait for them. They may just pass by. Or," he said with more of a smile, "we could fight. Though I'm not exactly sanguine about our odds, especially without a healer. Eighty of them is a lot, and I wouldn't be surprised if there were more."

"So we wait?" She had her arms folded, looking at him with a sly expression, waiting to see what he said.

"Hell, no. I'm terrible at waiting." He sighed. "To the narrow passage. We can at least take a look around."

Despite a slight argument from Windrider in the form of resisting Cyrus's attempts to pull him along gently by the reins, the horse did give in and follow. Aisling slipped into the narrow passage first, having to make little accommodation to enter, given her slight figure and short stature. "You want to go next?" Cyrus asked Windrider, who just stared at him. "Fine. I'll do it." He slid in, having to turn sideways to avoid an edge of rock that jutted out, but once past it, he found he could walk comfortably. Windrider followed, stepping over the obstruction, but the wide-bodied horse's progress was slow, taking time and brushing against the walls of the passage. When it began to widen again, Cyrus checked and found a few places where the jagged rocks had broken the horse's hide. "Sorry," Cyrus said, patting Windrider's neck. "But it looks superficial."

"Cyrus," Aisling hissed at him, a low noise that caught his attention. He trudged along the widening path of the cave, and realized for the first time that there was light ahead of them, coming from around a corner. Aisling was against the wall, he finally realized, blending with the shadows. He saw a dark blue hand beckon him forward, and he left Windrider's reins behind, creeping up behind her. When he got close, she grasped him firmly, pushing him slowly against the wall, her arm across his chest. She held a single finger up to her mouth, then slid out from cover and inched around the corner.

Cyrus edged up and looked around. Ahead was a slight drop, some form of embankment. He frowned; the horse would have some difficulty getting down that. He froze and caught his breath. Aisling was creeping ahead, and something was moving below. Two somethings, he realized, with grey, pallid flesh, and jagged teeth, rounded heads. A long, thick tongue came out of one of their mouths as it appeared to say something to the scourge next to it, a high, throaty screech from deep within that sounded like nothing Cyrus had ever heard before.

Aisling jumped off the embankment just then, as Cyrus drew his sword, ready to join her. She hit both the creatures moments after reaching the ground, daggers sliding into the base of their necks, and both went limp without so much as a sound, falling from all fours to flat on the ground, overlarge tongues spread out on the dirt. Aisling looked back and beckoned him forward, and he grasped Windrider's reins and began to gingerly make his way ahead. "Ais," he whispered, "if there's two, there's more—maybe we should turn around."

She either didn't hear him or ignored him, going forward more quickly than he could stealthily catch her. He followed, cursing her silently the entire time, watching every step, the low light from ahead the only illumination since Aisling had put out their torch after they emerged from the narrow passage. The light grew brighter as they went around another corner, and Cyrus found himself on the edge of a large chamber, an enormous, roughly circular room that had a sequence of stones that leveled down to the floor, a few feet below the cave opening that Cyrus stood upon. Aisling had already descended, her feet moving so quietly that Cyrus couldn't have heard them even if he hadn't been awestruck by the sight before him.

In the center of the chamber was something very familiar; a portal, of exactly the same kind that dotted the landscape of Arkaria. Ovoid, standing lengthwise above the ground, like a door turned sideways, it was massive enough for ten people to walk through shoulder to shoulder, even if they were Cyrus's size. His jaw fell open, and he stared at it; it glowed, the source of the light he had wondered at. Beyond it was another exit, a wider one, much larger than the tunnels they had just come from.

"Ais," Cyrus said, keeping his voice low even though he saw no sign of the scourge, "we need to get out of here. What if there are more?"

She halted, but only after she had crossed the thirty or so steps to reach the portal. She ran a hand along the edge of it, as though she were feeling the runes carved along the side to make certain it was real. "Where do you think this leads?"

A dark glow came from within the portal, something like mist with light shining through it; like clouds with the sun behind them. "I don't know," Cyrus said, "every time I've gone through one of these things when it's active like this, I've ended up in the realm of one of the gods."

"Might be worth a look, don't you think?" She looked at him, vaguely mischievous, and he suddenly found her deeply annoying.

"No," he said, "it isn't. We have somewhere else to be getting to, in case you forgot. There are enemies all around us—"

"Yes, they have this valley pretty well sewn shut at this point," she said, letting her fingers trace the lines of one of the runes. What do you suppose our odds are of managing to slip through and get away from the hordes of these scourge that fill this place?"

"They're good if we face them on open ground—" Cyrus began.

"They're bad, because we're outnumbered by a ridiculous amount and if we lose Windrider, we're done." She smiled again. "Now we have another option. Virtually certain death out there, or the *possibility* of death in here." She gestured to the portal with a hand extending out to it, as though it were something she were revealing to him for the first time. "I know which one I pick."

"We only go to the realms of gods when we know they're not home," Cyrus said, his voice rising. "If this leads into one of those places, it's virtual suicide."

"So is going out there," Aisling said, and the smile faded from her face. "They're hunting us and they will find us sooner or later if we stay out there. I know a hunter when I see one and those things are tracking us down. They'll come, and they'll overwhelm us and we'll die a horrible death out here where no one will ever find our bodies." She looked back to the portal. "If it's down to that or being smashed by a god, I know which one I choose." Before he could react, she turned, took one step away and looked back at him. "I guess you'll just have to decide whether you're willing to jump in front of a god's hand for me." Her smile twisted into something else, something sad, and she stepped into the portal and disappeared behind the misty light.

Chapter 37

Cyrus followed her only a moment later, after a pause and a curse, and he yanked Windrider's reins to lead the horse through the portal. He felt the air distort as he stepped through, the world seeming to upend and twist around him, light blinding him, until his feet settled on solid ground and he bumped into something ahead of him, and realized it was Aisling.

"Why does this look so familiar?" she asked, and Cyrus looked around the room they stood in.

It was a massive chamber that drew off into the distance, a room longer than it was wide, with torches burning in sconces on all the walls. Cyrus could smell something, a faint dustiness, and display cases lined every wall, while others sat in the middle of the floor. A tingle ran through Cyrus as he stepped forward, pushing Aisling behind him. "Because we've been here before." He looked around again, saw the balcony in the distance with the stairs leading up to either side of it, and felt a shudder. "This is Mortus's treasure room." He took a step forward and laid his hand on one of the pedestals. "We're in the Realm of Death."

"Nice to see they left the lamps on for us," Aisling said as she stepped up to join him. "But wasn't this place filled with howling death when last we were here? Spirits of the damned, loosed upon the demise of their master?"

"Yes, that's true—" Cyrus said, and stopped. There was a faint rattle, something clicking slowly against something else, as the torchlight flickered around them as though stirred by a wind he couldn't feel.

"What?" Aisling asked, then froze at attention, listening. "Oh, gods."

The rattle got louder, and a howling torrent of fury burst through the door at the top of the balcony. Souls, the damned, the trapped remnants of the God of Death's collection filled the air around them, a tornado of spirits, circling lower and lower.

"Time to move," Cyrus said, scooping up Aisling in one arm and pulling her back to the portal. Windrider was already turned and galloping through. Cyrus followed, letting the world distort around him as he stepped inside, and a moment later found himself back in the cave, in the circular chamber, and it was still empty. "That was lovely. If you ever leave me to jump into idiocy like that again, I'll let you die."

"You should really save that kind of sweet nothing for pillow talk, darling." Aisling's ears perked up and she turned, backing away from the portal as flickers of light flashed from within it. "Can those things follow us here?"

"I daresay we're about to find out."

"Oh," she said sarcastically, "is that what you *think*?"

They backed away from the portal as shapes started to coalesce in the light, black shadows, and something began to emerge. A horrific screeching preceded it, as though something had taken to tormenting an animal and refused to let it go. The first shape came through the portal and a shock of horror ran through Cyrus from top to bottom; claws and a four-legged appearance became obvious first, then the rounded head and vicious teeth, followed by the black, glassy eyes that had no feeling behind them. It skittered out, one of the scourge, followed immediately by more.

"That's—" Aisling said, her voice jerking to get the words out, "—the souls of the damned, from the Realm of Death, they turned into—is that—how is that possible?"

"They're taking physical form." Cyrus's voice was a low growl, and it came from a part of his throat that wanted to scream, something he never did. "They can't come through as spirits, so they're taking form, and ..." He turned, and saw others coming through the big entrance. "We'll never make it out through the narrow passage." He tightened his grip on Praelior. "Charge the big tunnel—NOW!" His last word came as a shout and he ran, sword swinging as he did so, his blade striking out as his legs pumped, chewing up the ground between him and the opening that seemed to lead out of the cavern.

The first of the scourge looked as though it was slithering toward him. He struck with his sword before it had time to react. More followed, countless, and he struck at them, too, using the speed Praelior granted him to stay a step ahead, clearing the tunnel, which although larger than the narrow passage, was only a few feet wide. They came at him a few at a time, but he moved on, driven, emotion bubbling over as he swung his sword. Daylight was ahead, and he kept on toward it—

They broke out into the sunlight and Cyrus's eyes fought to adjust to the brightness. The sky was clouded over, but still somewhere above the sun shone, behind a cloud, and he tried not to blink from it as he sliced through three more scourge. He could smell rotting flesh, it filled his nose and the still air around him, even as the cold and the snow were obvious, the ground covered with white for miles all around. He looked down from the abutment he was on, a craggy trail of rocks, and below was a path leading to a village, teeming with the scourge, thousands of them, making the thirty or so he had cut through in the flight from the cavern look like a miniscule number by comparison.

"Come on!" he heard Aisling shout, and he turned after striking a few more down to see her already on Windrider's back. The horse lunged forward and Cyrus jumped, catching a foot in a stirrup as Windrider passed and jerking himself onto the horse through sheer rote practice. They galloped down the hill and through the center of the town as the streets began to fill with the monsters, streaming out of buildings. As they rode by an open door, Cyrus could see bodies inside, a cloth dress that had been dull grey, stained now with blood and horror.

Windrider did not spare the speed as he ran, carrying them along the path out of town, galloping along a snowy road toward the pass they had come through only the day before. They did not meet any resistance, and the horse kept up the speed for as long as possible, until they were beyond the valley and into the pass, leaving behind everything that they had seen save for the horror which they carried with them in their minds.

Chapter 38

They found mountain springs and places for Windrider to graze after they cleared the snowy valley, and they stopped occasionally, long enough for Cyrus to rest and tend to his horse, which he did mechanically, at best. After a day's ride wherein they had barely exchanged a word, Aisling said to Cyrus, "Let me do it," and took care of Windrider herself before they retired for the night.

Cyrus lay down on the bedroll, the only one they had. His thoughts had been a swirling fury all day during the ride, racing so fast that he could scarcely even grasp them. He ate only a little, finding he had no appetite, and when Aisling came to join him on the bedroll, curiously, he found something he did have an appetite for, but he did that mechanically as well, though she did not seem to notice. She fell asleep immediately thereafter, and to his surprise, he did as well.

They arose early, before dawn, and were riding again minutes later, following the path south. The horse's hoofprints left a deep impression in the thin snow that coated the ground, and Cyrus felt every one of them resonate through him. His mind was stirred, unclear, but the same thought kept bubbling to the surface over and over again. *This is my fault. This is all my fault.*

After another day and night, another perfunctory evening spent with Aisling, who either did not notice or did not care that Cyrus was vacant and unable to look at her with his eyes open whilst they were together on the bedroll, he still found himself able to go through at least the motions there. It was a curious thing: he couldn't seem to think straight, couldn't manage more than a few bites of bread until he was starving, but she moaned in pleasure at his touch and enjoyed his company for as long as it lasted, but it left him even more hollow, empty inside, and lost in thought.

On the third day they arose and dressed in silence once more. She did not seem to feel any need to bring conversation out of him, but let her body speak, and he drank in the sweaty stickiness of her, and he found he didn't care. Something primal urged him on, gave him solace with her, allowed him to put aside all the thoughts that drew him down and silenced him during the day.

On the fourth day they reached lower ground and at a high point they looked out over the greener fields, where the snow had not fallen this far south, and saw a caravan ahead.

"That's them," Aisling said. "They're moving at a decent speed, about a half day's ride ahead. We can probably catch them by nightfall tomorrow if we hurry."

"Let's hurry, then," Cyrus said, the void in him now filling with something else, a gut-deep thought of satisfaction at a confrontation that loomed large ahead of him like the mountains that filled the horizon. "I've got some talking to do when we get there. We'll need to keep to cover so they don't see our approach." Cyrus's voice hardened. "I don't want Terian to know we're coming."

They spent another night alone under the stars, Windrider keeping silent vigil for their night's watch, while beneath the blanket on the bedroll other things occurred that sent the horse shying away into a thicket beyond their camp. They rode the next day again in silence and Cyrus tried to focus his thoughts on keeping to the path, on avoiding being seen by the column ahead. They kept to the trees as often as possible, moving openly only when there was no high ground ahead that they might be seen from. When nightfall came they took a break. Cyrus laid the bedroll on the ground. Aisling came to him, and when they were done they rolled it up again by silent accord and continued the ride, heading onward toward campfires they could see just over the horizon.

The wind was more subtle here but still carried a bite that left Cyrus's armor icy cold. The night had come down around them like a black shroud pulled over one's eyes, and the chill left Cyrus with a sense like ice melting on his tongue. Howls of distant wolves in the mountains brought to Cyrus's mind the image of lonely hunters, separated from their pack, and brought Terian to the forefront of his thoughts again. *Soon.*

They reached the camp around midnight. Sentries called out, two warriors of Sanctuary whom Cyrus knew in passing, and when he rode into the light, the shock on their faces was sweet to him. He admonished them to be quiet, gave over the reins to Windrider to one of them, and was pointed in the direction of a small figure when he asked his question. Cyrus crept along, not half so stealthily as Aisling, to one of the nearby fires, and found the sleeping figure he was looking for. When he reached down, it stirred, then sat up, eyes widening at the sight of him.

"Lord Davi—!" Mendicant began to cry, but Cyrus put a hand over the goblin's mouth. After holding a single finger over his own to quiet the wizard, he took his hand away and Mendicant spoke unhampered. "Lord Cyrus," he said, his voice a whisper. "You have returned to us."

"You didn't think a little thing like ten thousand of those beasts would be the death of me, did you?" Cyrus asked, not harshly but not kindly, either. "I need a small service of you."

"Anything, m'lord," Mendicant said. "All my spells are you at your command."

"I only need one of them. Come with me."

They made their way to the other side of the camp in the pervasive quiet. Cyrus heard a few bodies stir as he passed, and one of them made to cry out, but Aisling quieted him with a quick hand. Cyrus went on, Mendicant just behind him, until they reached a fire at the edge of the camp. Cyrus held up a hand to stay Mendicant, who stopped, and with a nod from Cyrus, began to cast a spell.

Cyrus walked forward, not bothering to be silent any longer. He could see Terian, asleep, clutching the long, red sword that Cyrus had given him, snug against his body, cradled as though it were a lover. It remained in its scabbard, something that no doubt carried none of the majesty of the one that his father had used—it had remained with his body on the bridge, after all. Cyrus looked at the blade as Terian held it and thought of the words again—*It will drink the blood of my enemies. All of them.* He drew Praelior, and let the sound of the steel against the scabbard awaken his target.

Terian's eyes fluttered open, and Cyrus saw his hand tense around the hilt of the sword. After a moment of widening in shock, they returned to normal, and Terian lay there, staring up at his general, and nodded once in complete and utter disinterest. "Hello, Cyrus."

"Hello, old friend." Cyrus pointed his sword at Terian. "I trust you've had a satisfying few nights of sleep?"

"For the first time in a while, I would have thought," Terian replied. "But not really. Been a little fitful, if we're being honest."

"'*If* we're being honest'?" Cyrus snorted. "That'd be a first, at least in recent memory. Honesty would break you, dark knight. Honesty would have meant that instead of playing a treacherous dog and trying to feed me to those rotted beasts, you'd challenge me in open combat and let the dice roll what they may."

"I could have taken you in open combat," Terian said. "There wouldn't have been much challenge in that. The only challenge would have been your allies and guildmates, who wouldn't have let me approach within a mile of you with sword in hand to ask for a duel."

"You think not?" Cyrus asked, pushing the blade toward Terian's throat, causing the dark knight to blanch not one bit. "You think they wouldn't have let me cross swords with you in honest dispute?"

"No," Terian said, "because they'd know you would die. You can't match a dark knight, Cyrus, and no one but you is fool enough to trifle with magics when they have only a blade to do it with. Stab me five times and I'll cast a spell that takes away my wounds and visits them upon you in return, restoring me and cursing you to a self-inflicted death. Anyone with sense would not let you face me in a duel. So it was treachery, a surprise, the quick and dirty, and off you went to die at hands other than my own—yet still I would be revenged."

"This from a man who told me once that he despised those who weren't what they appeared to be," Cyrus said, and saw the flicker in Terian's eyes. "Well, it would appear your boundless hypocrisy has come back to visit you. Get up."

Terian shuffled his feet out of his blanket and stood before Cyrus, leaving his sword to lie on the ground. "Pick it up," Cyrus said, nodding at the sword. "If you wanted to have a go at me, now you'll get one—a legitimate one."

"You think so?" Terian said, and his hand flew up in a quick motion, as though he were flinging something at Cyrus with it.

Cyrus stood back smiling grimly as Terian blinked then thrust his hand at Cyrus again. "Pick up your sword, dark knight," Cyrus said, "and let's truly see who will win this battle of blades."

Terian looked around as he stooped to retrieve his blade. "Mendicant," he said, seeing the goblin standing a distance away. "You've had him place a cessation spell over us."

"Over us and everything nearby," Cyrus said, noting that several of the bundles on the ground, officers of Sanctuary who had been sleeping were stirring now, sitting up in their bedrolls with tired eyes. He saw J'anda look at him with an openmouthed astonishment that turned into a smile. Cyrus nodded his head at the enchanter and turned back to Terian. "You tried to kill me dishonorably and failed. I give you one chance to do it in a duel and perhaps save that shredded rag you call your honor." Cyrus held his sword upright, in front of his face. "I wish you the best of luck, because I suspect you'll need it."

"Luck," Terian said with unmistakable sorrow. "Never did seem to have much of that." He hoisted his sword above his head in a high guard, waiting for Cyrus. When Cyrus beckoned him forward, Terian attacked without warning, striking with his blade as Cyrus blocked it, knocking the red sword aside.

The camp was awakening now, the sounds of a battle echoing through the night. Cyrus heard the cries of surprise, of alarm, of his name, and he felt the warm flush that battle brought to his skin, coupled with the chill of sweat that had long since settled and grown cold from the mountain air. He tasted the embers in his mouth, the ashen desire to strike back at Terian for knocking him asunder and cursing him, and it was the bitterest thing he had ever eaten. From out of the darkness, figures strode closer, whispers were exchanged by those who knew what was happening, and Cyrus could smell fear in the air, mingled with the metal of his blade as he set it against Terian's again and again as the dark knight raged against him.

"What's the matter, warrior?" Terian said with fury, bringing his sword down for another attack that Cyrus blocked. "You're not attacking me. Am I too fast for you? Were you too arrogant for your own good?" He clashed with Praelior and then drew the blades close to look at Cyrus between the locked swords. "Was this how it was with my father? Did he overmatch you until someone else had to save you?"

Cyrus pushed him back, sending Terian staggering, and then brought Praelior back to a defensive position in front of his face. "No. Your father attacked me when I was wounded and near dead. When Vara kept him from killing me," he said, circling the dark knight as Terian watched him with smoldering eyes, "they fought for a spell, and before he could land the coup de grace on her, I stabbed him through the back." Cyrus spun Praelior in a neat circle in front of his face. "Your father was a coward, like you, and I ended him like a coward—"

"LIAR!" Terian lunged at Cyrus, his weapon high over his head, coming down in a furious attack that sent reverberations through Cyrus's armor from his gauntlets to his boots. "My father was a hero of the Sovereignty!" He brought the blade down again and again against Praelior, and still Cyrus repelled each blow and turned it aside. "He was the most powerful dark knight in all Arkaria! He could kill you and Vara a hundred times over!"

Cyrus batted another thrust aside and finally attacked with the speed that his sword granted him; each of Terian's blows was slow and telegraphed, the dark knight's rage keeping him from intelligent action. Cyrus brought his sword across Terian's body in a slash that caught him under the pauldrons, in the armpit, and the dark knight cringed and staggered back as Cyrus pursued him. The warrior's next attack caught him across the arm, went through the niche at his elbow, and Cyrus saw blood fountain out of the gap and splatter the ground in large drops.

"Your father was a coward and a plunderer," Cyrus said as Terian backed away from him. "He came to Termina at the head of an army bent on destroying the city, harming her occupants, and doing so without an army to stand up for them. He did it after burning Santir, an undefended human settlement, and cutting a swath across Confederation territory without mercy or care for who they killed or whose lives they wrecked in the process."

Cyrus brought his sword down in an overhand strike that caught Terian across the wrist that held his sword. The blade hit the dirt and fell out of his hand. Cyrus brought Praelior down again and Terian's hand was severed, his armor broken, shattered and sundered metal over a stump that drained dark blood onto the ground as Terian clutched it with his other hand.

"Your father was a coward," Cyrus said again, holding Praelior at Terian's throat. Terian's face dissolved from agony into rage as he tried to stand. Cyrus's blade stabbed down, into the gap in his greaves and laid his knee open. Cyrus felt Praelior cut through the chain beneath and Terian screamed, writhing as Cyrus forced the tip of the sword into his leg. "He lived as a coward and died as coward, as a man who followed the orders of a coward, without regard for those he inflicted pain upon. It would appear," Cyrus twisted his sword in Terian's knee and the dark knight screamed in a voice loud enough to echo through the mountains, "that his character bred true in you. That Alaric—and all of the rest of us—were wrong about you. Thou art a dark knight. And thou never didst crawl out of thy father's shadow."

Terian was breathing heavy, but he managed to gasp out a response. "And what are you, warrior? A man who follows Alaric's every suggestion like a lapdog? Who doesn't think for himself but snaps to attention when someone calls you, asking for help, regardless of the rightness of their cause? At least I believed in something, in someone. You professed to be of Sanctuary too, but you left Baron Hoygraf to bleed to death in agony. So which is it, Cyrus Davidon?" Terian managed a wicked grin. "Are you the virtuous knight? Or are you like me and don't care what it takes to get the job done, even if that means getting a little blood on your hands? What do you believe, Cyrus?"

"I believe," Cyrus said, and leaned down, taking a knee, but keeping his sword pointed at Terian's uncovered throat, "that I just beat you in a duel." Terian writhed, chafing at the edge of Praelior pressed against his skin. "I believe that makes your life forfeit." He gripped tighter at the hilt, felt the power of the sword run through him, and he hesitated. The wind picked up again and a chill ran through him. In the great emptiness within him he heard a call for him to stop—heard it, and ignored it. Cyrus could smell the blood now, the sweat running down his face, could taste it as he licked his lips, and as Terian's eyes widened, he drove his sword into the dark knight's throat and watched the light fade from his friend's eyes.

Chapter 39

"That was unnecessary, Cyrus," Curatio said, stepping out of the circle that had grown to surround them and pausing by Terian's side. "He was humbled, defeated." Curatio thought about it for a moment. "Well, he was defeated anyway." A glow encompassed his hand, and he brought it down to Terian's face. Cyrus watched the dark knight stir back to life. Blood proceeded to geyser out of his open throat until Curatio's healing spell took hold and the wounds were mended, new skin stretching to fill the gaps rent by Cyrus's blade as his hand was joined back to his arm. "Terian," Curatio said, "you know what's to happen now."

"I won't go," Terian said, his eyes dull as he retched, his hand reaching up to his neck and wiping the blood from the newly knit flesh found there. "Let me loose here, in the wilderness, and I'll make my own way."

"And a month or a year from now, I find a blade in my back?" Cyrus turned Praelior back to rest above Terian's face. "I think not."

"You'll be bound," Curatio said to Terian. "Tied, gagged, and put ahorse, allowed to eat only under the watch of the cessation spell—"

"I am seriously enjoying the irony of this," Partus called from somewhere in the circle. "It's quite delightful, Terian—you'll come to enjoy the taste of having a rock on your tongue at all times, and having to have someone unbind you to make water."

"I won't," Terian said, eyes blazing. His hand came up at Cyrus and the warrior brought Praelior up to slash it off again—

"Enough," Curatio said, and turned the blade aside then watched Terian, whose hand went limp in front of him as the dark knight's face fell. He looked to Aisling, who was standing off to the side, a thick coil of rope in her hands. "Bind him."

"No—" Terian said, but Longwell and Scuddar came forward and restrained him, turning him over and grinding his face into the dirt as Aisling wrapped the ropes around his hands and feet then gagged him with a rock, a cloth, and a rope for good measure. The dark knight writhed on the ground when they were done, his hands and feet bound separately, securing each wrist to the other, each leg to its match at the ankle and a coil tied the two together, inadvertently putting Terian into an seated position. Silence pervaded the circle around him, as though everyone was afraid that speaking might make them complicit in whatever crime the dark knight had committed.

"Terian Lepos," Curatio began, "you have been accused of attempting to murder your general. You will be returned to Sanctuary at our earliest convenience to be judged by a tribunal of your fellow officers, and we'll decide from there what's meant to be done with you." He stared at the dark knight, who refused to meet the healer's gaze. "And I, for one, am greatly disappointed in you."

Cyrus could see the glare of contempt that Terian leveled at the ground, not turning it anywhere near Curatio. The healer crossed the space between them and placed a gentle hand on Cyrus's shoulder, leading him away from where Terian sat, silent, not bothering to struggle against his bonds. "You didn't have to kill him, you know. I thought you'd learned your lesson about revenge."

"That wasn't revenge," Cyrus said. "That was warning. I knew you'd bring him back, that he'd be dragged along with us. I need him to be afraid, to think I'd kill him if he got out of line."

Curatio stopped, his hand still on Cyrus's shoulder. "It is good to have you back." The healer's eyes flicked from Cyrus to away, in the distance. "I confess, I had thought we had seen your certain end when we saw you ride off to the west."

"Nothing is certain as regards my end," Cyrus said, "save for that it is not yet here." Something flared in his mind, the memory of where the journey had taken Aisling and him. "Curatio, those things—they come from—"

"The Realm of Death," Curatio said quietly. "Yes, we know. J'anda saw into one of their minds, remember? He saw that they were the spirits unleashed when Mortus died, that they have come through a portal and been made substantial. How did you know?"

"We found the portal," Cyrus said. "It was in the back of a cave we took refuge in on the first night, during the snow. We went inside, thinking it might be an avenue of escape." He looked down in anguish. "There are more of them, Curatio. Countless more. Think about when those things broke loose from the Eusian Tower, there were enough of them to blot out the red sky of the entire realm."

"I know," Curatio said. "More than I'd care to count, that's for certain. All Mortus's prisoners, his damned souls, and all they need do to receive physical form—albeit a horrific one—is to step through a portal, and a faded shadow of life becomes theirs once more."

"But how is it possible?" Cyrus asked. "Those ... things ... are they alive?"

"Close enough," J'anda said, slipping up to join them. "They were dead, all of them, in torment from Mortus's efforts to keep them imprisoned, enslaved ... now they are loosed, and after arriving through the portal they have form and substance. Not life, as you or I would define it, with need and want and reason. But they have desire. They have hunger. They crave flesh and pain, and would visit it upon whomever they encounter." He shook his head. "They are not mindless beasts; they will coordinate, attack, and they aim to harvest and kill every piece of idle flesh on this continent, to have every soul they can rest between their teeth to join them—in death."

"So you're saying that thousands of years of torment have left them slightly bitter and resentful of us living folk?" Cyrus asked. "Oh, joy." He took a breath. "How many have made it over thus far?"

J'anda shrugged. "Numbers are meaningless to them. They're smarter than beasts, but all the torment has left them lacking in will. They move in packs, in herds, and finding fresh prey seems to be their only concern. More will come, as they continue to seek new flesh. I sense that others have tried to explore the other portal—the one that leads to the Island of Mortus in the Bay of Lost Souls—but that their efforts there are fruitless, and they have turned all their focus to this one, with the promise of flesh both tantalizing and near. The one that came down to us, to the swamps? I suspect it was a newer soul, one less paralyzed into group action." J'anda shrugged. "That is but a theory, though. Who knows what they will do, how many will come?"

"But you have a suspicion, right?" Cyrus asked. "You were inside one of their minds, you looked around. What do you think they'll do?"

J'anda was slow to respond. "I have already told the others this. I suspect they will go in the direction of flesh. If there is no prey north or east or west, then they will come south. They can sense life at a great distance and desire to extinguish it. It is a predatory need for them, a relentless hunger, a jealousy that crosses to obsession. They will keep coming as long as there is life in front of them." J'anda became withdrawn, his voice quiet, hollow, and he stared past Cyrus as he spoke. "Until there is no more life left."

Chapter 40

The ride back to Enrant Monge took a month, a month during which the expedition was quiet. Cyrus spoke at length with Count Ranson on the day after his return, and with the envoy from Actaluere; all were agreed that the scourge was serious, and a threat to every Kingdom in Luukessia.

"Those creatures are beasts," the envoy from Actaluere, a pompous snot named Reygner, sniffed, "and their numbers are vast, but there is a very clear danger in what they can do to us, to our land. I intend to press my King to send immediate aid north. There will be plenty of time to make war amongst ourselves after these foreign creatures are expelled from Luukessia." Cyrus did not bother to dispel the man's perception of the scourge's intellect.

Ranson had been less forthcoming. "I intend to tell the King what I have seen," the count told Cyrus later, away from the rest of expedition, "but I do not expect he will listen. I mean—ancestors, man! We saw an army of Syloreas torn to pieces, a host of these beasts, but not so many that a firm defense wouldn't sway them or cause them to go down in defeat." He shook his head in frustration. "I will urge him to action, especially as you say there are numerous more of these things, but I expect he'll take my counsel and pick out only the parts that appeal to him."

"Oh?" Cyrus asked. "What parts are those?"

Ranson hesitated before answering. "Sylorean Army, torn to pieces."

"What will you do, Count?"

"I will do nothing I am not ordered to," Ranson snapped. "To do otherwise is treason of the highest order, and I have no desire to oppose my Sovereign and sign my own death order when I could avoid it."

"And if your treason could save your people?" Cyrus watched Ranson, whose face fell.

"I doubt it could," Ranson said. "We have not seen the full force of these things, in any case. You say there are more, but I ask you how you know this? Yes, yes," he waved off Cyrus, "I have heard your explanation, of gods and tormented souls released, but such thoughts seem ridiculous to me, just as they will to any other in Luukessia that you tell. Ancestor worship is our philosophy, not mythical gods or all-powerful beings."

"Fine," Cyrus said, "then call them your tormented ancestors, returning to visit their pain and anguish upon you for all their sins past."

"Ancestors!" Ranson cursed. "It makes it sound all the more ridiculous when you say it that way."

After Ranson had ridden away, off to the other side of the procession, Curatio brought his horse alongside Cyrus. "It does sound ridiculous, you know."

"That an army of tormented dead that we unleashed is visiting all manner of hell upon the northern reaches of a land most of us had never even heard of until a few months ago?" Cyrus looked at Curatio, and found a certain irony that allowed him to smile rather than weep. "I can't imagine why any part of that statement would strain the credibility of the person who spoke it and professed to believe it."

"Nor can I," Curatio said, with only a little irony of his own. "Yet all levity aside, this is the truth that we are faced with. We are culpable for whatever happens here, because we were the ones who killed Mortus."

"I don't want to think about it that way," Cyrus said, and looked away from the healer abruptly.

"You may not want to," Curatio said, "but I suspect that your wants are unlikely to stop your mind from wandering in that direction."

"Aye," Cyrus said in a whisper, "there has indeed been some wandering. But it's not all that is on my mind."

"Hmmm," Curatio said, "betrayal, backstabbing, deception, abandonment, duels to the death, arguments with women, deeply conflicted feelings, and an army unlike any we've ever seen on the march toward the civilizations of this land. I can't imagine what else you might be thinking about." After a moment's pause, the healer said something else, more conciliatory. "Try not to let it all weigh you down." Without another word, he urged his horse forward and left Cyrus riding alone.

But he was not alone that night, later, when he found a spring in the woods near the site of their camp. When his clothes and armor came off, the sound in the brush made him reach for his sword. His fingers dangled on the hilt when a single twig snapping turned him in the direction of the presence.

Aisling stepped out of the shadows, and wordlessly removed her clothing, slipping into the spring with him. There was more passion in her kisses than usual, and Cyrus returned them, every one, with just as much, craving her, wanting to feel the sweet bliss of forgetfulness. He found he wanted the tender moments of peace that only she could give him, where everything else was by the wayside.

When they were done, they did not exchange a word, but she aided him in washing himself and he did the same for her. She quietly stole off toward the camp by herself. He followed moments later. She had not come to his bedroll at night, not since they had returned to the expedition, but along the trail she would find him sometimes in an unguarded moment, against a tree, or in a soft patch of grass, and he would be able to ease his mind, to forget about all else for just a few precious minutes.

They passed Scylax without stopping for more than a few hours, allowing the horses to rest and for fresh provisions. They entered through the gates, were entertained on the main avenue, and rode out through the gate down the mountain only a few hours later. Some of the Syloreans changed horses; Cyrus did not have the luxury, and Windrider seemed to bear it better than the other animals anyhow. Occasional days of rest were required, or more often, half-days. They moved as quickly as the animals allowed, not giving much thought to the pains of the men, which were healed by Curatio whenever they asked.

Only a week south of Scylax they found themselves loping over open plains again, the mountains receding far behind them, distant, cloudy, with a darkness hanging over them, a wintery gloom that was nothing like the summer suns still kissing the plains around them. It was late summer, in fact, Cyrus realized, and some of the wild flowers had begun to turn brown where they had been purple, blue and yellow only weeks before when they passed through. A cool day manifested unexpectedly; the sky was dull grey like in the mountains, and the wind had the slightest kiss of bitterness to it.

The last night they camped on a grassy, windblown plain, and Briyce Unger called together Cyrus and his officers with Count Ranson and the envoy from Actaluere. They'd had plenty of discussions along the road, but this was to be their last. Cyrus listened, somewhat dully, as Unger confirmed for the hundredth time what the others would tell their respective leaders. Cyrus stayed silent; he had nothing to contribute, and Ranson was still skeptical of how his King would react while the Actaluere envoy was unrelenting in his belief that Milos Tiernan would immediately see reason. Cyrus, for his part, was not so sure.

"What do you think their next move will be?" Briyce Unger had asked Cyrus, after he had confirmed what he wanted to hear from the envoys. Cyrus blinked at him, in a daze. "The Scourge," he said, as they had taken to calling the damned souls given flesh, "what will their next move be?"

"I don't know," Cyrus said. "J'anda says they'll come south, looking for flesh and blood, eager to destroy life. When that will happen, I don't know. Maybe it already has."

"They'll butt up hard against Scylax," Unger said. "I've already ordered an army to reinforce the town, and they'll evacuate the townsfolk into the keep if it gets especially ugly. Fighting in the pass will be a nasty business, though, if we get Longwell and Tiernan to send armies. We may have to draw them out in order to crush them."

"The best thing we could do is march back into the valley where Pinrade is and destroy the portal," Cyrus said. "But that's going to be a hell of an undertaking."

"Could you destroy it?" Unger asked. "Could your people with their spells and whatnot knock it down?"

"Maybe," Cyrus said. "The only wizard I have with me is somewhat unexperienced in such matters."

"It can be done," Curatio said, speaking up for the first time since the meeting started. "But it will be neither easy nor a short process. More spellcasters would be better, and I'll need to uh ..." He looked around, but J'anda and Longwell were the only other Sanctuary officers present. "Let's just say that we'll have to do more than a little heresy in order to get it done. Which I don't have a problem with, but I've been around since before such things were considered heretical."

J'anda blinked. "Wait ... what?"

"It can be done," Curatio said, "and that's the important part. But I'll have to be there for some time, preferably not interrupted, in order to strip the enchantments off the portal. After that, you should be able to use enchanted weapons to break it to pieces and guarantee it never re-opens."

"There's something else we need to be concerned about," Cyrus said. "If these things come from the Realm of Death, then there's another portal that opens onto the Island of Mortus. J'anda, you said their efforts there have been fruitless but we don't know what that means. They could be massing there right now, ready to swim the miles to shore in order to stage an invasion of Arkaria like they're doing to Luukessia."

J'anda cursed and ran a hand over his smooth face. "We'll need to send a messenger to Sanctuary."

"Yeah," Cyrus said. "We'll wait until we're at Enrant Monge tomorrow and we've met with the other Sanctuary officers, then we'll figure out who we can send. We need help if we're going to make a push for that portal. I doubt the thousand we have is going to get the job done." Cyrus looked to Briyce Unger. "No offense to your people, but we're talking about using a coordinated army to thrust through the enemy rather than fighting toe to toe with them while they try and bleed us to death and vice versa."

"I got the gist of your strategy," Unger said. "You're talking about using mobility and speed against them, the two things they lack against a horsed army. The problem is, your thousand don't all have horses, and your speed advantage is less in the mountain passes between Scylax and that valley. So first of all, you need Longwell's dragoons, and second, you need flatter ground, or you'll be driving them back over those same damned roads that collapse in landslides and send people to a long fall and a quick stop at the bottom."

"What would you suggest?" Cyrus asked. "Draw them onto the plains and have a bloody free-for-all there?"

"It may come to that," Unger said, "if they decide Scylax is too tightly buttoned up to bother with, and they're truly hungry for blood, they ought to head south. If we can come at them with the three armies—Galbadien, Actaluere and Syloreas, we can probably match them, put them down, and all the while you take your army another couple weeks north through the passes and into that valley, and put the crushing blow on their reinforcements." Unger nodded. "That'd sort them out on our end, leave us to mop up whatever they had left over here, but they wouldn't be getting that constant stream of endless numbers like they apparently can now." Unger had a strange light in his eyes. "I'd fight like all hell, too, way past the close if I had an army of raging souls behind me who had no fear of death and no care for numbers."

"There's something we're missing here," Cyrus said. "If they're more than beasts, then there has to be more to them than just a simple hunger. There's something driving them besides rage if they're coordinating their attacks. J'anda, did you sense any sort of leadership structure to these things?"

"Just because I didn't sense it doesn't mean it isn't there," J'anda cautioned. "I got the picture of the creature's mind, but it was not like reading a map or even like absorbing the thought of a normal person— not that there necessarily is such a thing as normal. But this is how it is—humans think a certain way, as do dark elves, elves, gnomes, dwarves and so on. Within every species is a certain way of thought, and I understand all of them—except trolls. Well, with the exception of Vaste. Within each species there are also variations of their manner of thinking, some radical, some bizarre, but none as different as the jump between species. The point is, I understand all of them, can read all of them, can know all of them. This creature ... I could not know given a year or two or ten in its mind. It is angrier by far than a troll, more guarded than a dark elf and more bizarre than any mind I have ever seen into. I get flashes, enough to understand the origin, but only pieces of the whole. I could read a man's mind and feel confident in telling you everything of the man," he blushed and looked away from Cyrus as he said it. "This thing, I would not feel confident telling you I know anything of it but the facts I outlined. They are ... bizarrre. Truly bizarre. They could well have a leadership and a hierarchy driving them and I would not know it."

"Marvelous," Cyrus said, running his hands over his eyes and then through his hair, brushing it over his shoulders. "We have an enemy that appears countless in number, unknowable in intent—other than that they want blood and death—we have no way of judging their movements, their desire, how far they will take this, and even though we now know their origin, we don't know if they have a leader of any sort or if there is any motivation for them to be doing what they're doing. We're completely blind, facing a numberless enemy." He sighed. "At least we have a plan."

"And our plan involves slipping behind the lines of this enemy and trying to cut off their entry point to this realm," J'anda said. "This doesn't sound like our best plan ever, if I may say so."

"When have you ever hesitated to say so?" Cyrus asked, holding his head. "But you're right. This ... will not be pretty."

Unger smiled, an unsettling one. Ranson and the envoy from Actaluere had left moments earlier. "The fight ahead or the moot?"

"Either one," Cyrus said. "I wonder if King Aron has at the least soothed Milos Tiernan over the Baroness Cattrine?"

"I doubt it," Unger said. "It's not Tiernan who's truly upset by that anyhow; my spies say he's most displeased with what Grand Duke Hoygraf has done to his sister. It's Hoygraf himself who is driving that issue. Milos Tiernan would just as soon have his sister away from Hoygraf forever, but Hoygraf holds too many favors in his Kingdom, too many strings of powerful people."

"How?" Cyrus asked. "The man's a sadist."

"Aye," Unger said, "but sadism can have its uses when you run a Kingdom. And the man was a dog of war, until you perforated his belly. Now he's unlikely to walk straight upright ever again, but he has allies in Actaluere. He controls easily a third of their armies, and King Tiernan's a clever bastard. He knows it, he knows Hoygraf knows it, and he's playing it entirely cool in order to keep Hoygraf from acting on it."

"I crushed Hoygraf's army," Cyrus said, waving off Unger. "I broke his keep, killed his men. What the hell else has he got?"

"You did not break his army," Unger said. "His army was two days march behind you when you hit Green Hill. You killed his attendants, you killed many of his close advisors, but not his army. He intended to delay you until they could crush you, and it would have been a rather clever stratagem if he'd been facing traditional forces. Unfortunately for him, you were more magical and somewhat cleverer than he might have given you credit for." Unger chuckled and shook his head. "Still, bedding his wife before the man was dead? I admit, I have no respect for Hoygraf and his woman-beating ways, but cuckolding the man after you opened his belly and left him to die? The Grand Duke will be upset with you for the rest of his life, shortened though it might be by the grievous wounding you gave him."

"I don't give a damn about Grand Duke Hoygraf," Cyrus said. "I can handle him if the time comes."

"Oh, the time will come," Unger said. "I mean, did you not think that word would get out about your escapades in the Garden of Serenity before we left?"

Cyrus froze, and caught the look of confusion from both Curatio and J'anda. "You heard about that?" Cyrus asked Unger.

"Oh, yes," Unger said with a laugh. "That was all the talk of the moot the night before we left. You have a set of brass ones, Cyrus Davidon. Everyone knew about that."

"I didn't hear about that," J'anda said, slightly miffed.

"Everyone who was of the three Kingdoms," Unger amended. "The Garden of Serenity is not exactly a holy place, but it's as near as we get in Luukessia. My goodness, lad ... taking the wife of a man whose grievance was that you had taken his wife, and doing it there? Sort of defeats the idea of suing for peace, doesn't it? I mean, you're adding fresh grievances by the bucketload. You're quite fortunate you didn't speak with King Longwell before you left, I'm certain he would have given you an earful for that last insult."

Cyrus looked to Samwen Longwell, whose face was drawn. "Yes, that's something of an insult," Longwell said. "And yes, it likely made my father's negotiations after we left somewhat more protracted, if you did in fact do ..." he coughed, "what he said you did."

"I did," Cyrus said, unrepentant. "Twice."

Longwell was overcome by a fit of coughing. "Ahem ... uh ... the Baroness would have known how great an insult this would be. I'm surprised she still ... ah ... acceded to your ... charms." The dragoon looked uncomfortable at every word, and when done, settled into a silence in which he would not meet Cyrus's eyes.

"She was the one who started it," Cyrus said, drawing another coughing fit from Longwell, a wide grin from Unger, tired disinterest from J'anda and practiced neutrality from Curatio. "I didn't start it, she did. So if she knew what she was doing was insulting, she did it on purpose."

"Aye," Unger said, "I can't imagine why she would choose that moment to insult the man who beat her. If the man were one of my barons, I'd have him flogged in the streets of Scylax for pulling even a tenth of what that bloke has. What a load of goat dung he is."

"We seem to have wandered afield from our original topic of discussion," Curatio said with a weak smile. "We have a meeting—or moot, I should say—tomorrow, yes?"

"Yes," Unger said. "It may already be in progress when we arrive. If so, they'll move directly to our topic, and Ranson and what's-his-name from Actaluere will have their moment to speak, but nothing will be decided until after the Kings have a chance to talk with their men in private. We'll go to any other business then adjourn. Should be a short session."

"Thus was said about every long meeting I have ever attended," Curatio said dryly, "and I've attended one or two very long meetings in my life."

"So, we have a war to begin," Cyrus said, "a land to unite," he nodded at Briyce Unger, who nodded back, "a guild to inform, troops to rally, reinforcements to summon ..." Cyrus folded his arms, and settled his eyes on Longwell, Curatio, J'anda, and finally on the darkness beyond the campfires where he knew, in the distance, Enrant Monge lay just ahead on the horizon, beyond the black skies, "... and I don't know which of those things will be hardest to do. I really don't."

He left them, then, without word, deep in his own thoughts, and paced through the campfires, looking for Aisling. *She's never around when I have need of her, not immediately, anyway.* He went beyond the last fire, and edged into the woods. *Yet when I go far enough away ...* he heard a rustling in the bushes.

He felt her hand around his shoulders, felt her tongue in his ear, gentle, caressing, smelled the cinnamon on her breath. "Productive meeting?" she whispered.

"Not really," he said, and turned to her, backing her against a tree. "What about you?"

"Been waiting for you," she said as she let her fingers brush through his hair, then kissed him again, and he felt his head swirl as he lifted her gently off the ground and pinned her against the tree as their passion consumed them.

"Put me down," she said after they were done, and he did, leaning against the tree for support, his weight resting heavily on his left arm. "I'll see you back at the camp." He heard her words, sensed her pull her breeches back up, then heard her footsteps disappear, as they always did, quiet to the point where he couldn't hear them, and he was left alone, again, in the woods, in the dark, and he stayed there for quite some time.

Chapter 41

It was midafternoon when they rode into Enrant Monge through the northern gate of the Syloreans. After the second gate, the stewards of the Brotherhood of the Broken Blade greeted them and quietly informed them that there was a session underway at present in the Garden of Serenity. They would be expected within the half-hour, then the debate would shift to hear their reports. Briyce Unger nodded and was on about his business, heading toward the tower nearby, while the Actaluere envoy headed west through a keeping gate and Cyrus and the others followed Ranson to the eastern bailey.

The sun was still high in the sky as Cyrus made his way out of the tower set aside for the Galbadien delegation a half-hour later. The stewards had shown him to the communal bath, and he'd washed the dirt of travel from him, felt the cool water rinsing the dust and grime of long days of travel from his skin, along with something else which was becoming familiar, the smell of Aisling, her sweat and the tangy aroma of cinnamon. He caught a peculiar look from one of the stewards, who thereafter tried to avoid making eye contact with him. When he looked in the mirror, he realized his neck was covered with bruises from bites; not small ones, either, but ones that were obvious and exposed above his armor. Fiddling with his collar was of no assistance; they stood out against the green of his robe. With a sigh, he left, joining Curatio, J'anda, Longwell and Ranson in the courtyard before the Garden of Serenity. Aisling and the others had gone to rejoin the Sanctuary army, still encamped in the eastern woods outside the castle.

They were called into the garden, the walls bathed in orange by the light of noon. Clouds were on the horizon, but as yet the breeze was soft, the sun was unobscured, and the weather pleasant enough, if a little hot. They were not announced, not this time, save for Briyce Unger, who went first and with little fanfare. Cyrus watched from the tunnel as Unger strode out to take his place in the amphitheater, and Cyrus and his delegation were ushered out moments later, as a quiet settled upon the proceedings, and he took a place on an empty bench, conspicuously far to the back of the Galbadien delegation. Count Ranson went forward, invited to a place of honor nearer to Aron Longwell, though not as near as it had been before the expedition; Ranson took a seat in the third row rather than the first.

Cyrus scanned the audience until he found Ryin Ayend and Nyad, sitting a few rows closer and upon the aisle opposite the one Cyrus had entered by. The soft breeze stirred Nyad's hair as he looked upon her, and Ayend next to her looked especially drab in the dull green robes provided by the Brotherhood of the Broken Blade. Seated to the left of the two of them was Cattrine, her dark hair shining, her face less so, reserved, and focused on him but for a few seconds before she broke eye contact, impassive, hesitant, almost fearful.

The greenery around them almost faded into the backdrop as the meeting began. The assemblage was quiet, and there was a sense of restlessness in the audience made all the worse by the breeze, stirring as it was every few moments. Cyrus could feel it in the air, a desire to move, to run, and as he looked down at Cattrine he felt it grow stronger. He longed for touch, for hers or Aisling's, and wished desperately he were elsewhere, though he could not define why.

"I offer a welcome to our brothers who have returned from the north," Grenwald Ivess looked somewhat haggard, a little pallid, and the lighting helped not a whit. "Would that you had come at a more auspicious time, when we had more ... pleasing news to report." Cyrus looked to Unger, who sat isolated in the front row of the Sylorean bench by himself, and watched the King look to the men behind him, his brow furrowed. *Why is the King sitting alone? What is going on here?*

"I take it there was little progress whilst we were away?" Unger asked, drawing his attention back to the assembly. "No forward momentum on making amends between our august Kingdoms?" The King of Syloreas was loud, restless, and his hair moved as he turned to look back once more at the row of men behind him, none of whom would look him in the eye. Cyrus watched as he slapped one of them on the knee, enough to jar the man to attention but not to compel him to look at his King for more than a few seconds before lapsing back to staring at his feet.

"I take it by your rather enthusiastic demeanor," King Aron Longwell stood, commanding the attention at the center of the room, "that no one from your delegation has told you the news yet?"

"I haven't seen anyone from my delegation since I got here," Unger said, wary. Cyrus could not see King Longwell's face, but the relish was evident in the man's voice, and it gave Cyrus no comfort, none at all. "Since they all appear to be too craven to tell me whatever ill news you all have, and since you seem all too eager to do it, Aron, why don't you just go ahead and be on with it?"

"You do me insult, sir," Aron Longwell said, his hand springing to his chest as though Briyce Unger had just plunged a dagger into it. "I do not take any pleasure in your pain, and to suggest otherwise—"

"Tiernan?" Unger interrupted King Longwell, and Cyrus looked to the King of Actaluere, who was actually somewhat pale himself, not nearly as well composed as he had been two months earlier, the last time Cyrus had laid eyes on him. He reminded him much of his sister now, as she looked when Cyrus had seen her at her worst, when she realized her husband was still alive. "Would you do me the courtesy," Unger strained at the last word, "of breaking the news to me before I'm dead of old age, as it appears King Longwell is going to be too busy feigning umbrage for the next fortnight."

"Scylax has fallen," Tiernan said without preamble, and the silence was overwhelming enough that Cyrus had to relive the words in his mind to be sure he'd heard what he thought he did. "We received the carrier pigeons only hours ago."

"I'm sorry," Unger said, as though Tiernan had not said a thing. "You mean to tell me that the village has been taken and they've fallen back to the castle for a siege?"

"No," Tiernan said, "the message came to us with very clear wording—the village was overrun yesterday, and the pigeons were the last to fly from the castle." Tiernan pulled himself up and faced the King of Syloreas. "'They are inside the walls. Castle Scylax is lost. Their numbers ... '" Tiernan swallowed, deep, and his eyes fell away from Unger as the King of Syloreas sat down, heavy, felled like a tree in the forest, "'... their numbers are overwhelming. None will survive.'"

Chapter 42

There was a still quiet in the garden for several moments after Tiernan delivered the news. Unger sat on the bench in his row, stunned into disbelief, staring at the ground in front of him. Even King Longwell had reseated himself. "Scylax was a city of fifty thousand," Unger said at last. "Fifty thousand people, and none survive?"

"We do not know, your grace," Grenwald Ivess said, a peculiar quiet settled over his words. "Perhaps some fled through the mountains before this ... this—"

"Scourge," Cyrus said, loud enough to be heard. "It's a damned scourge."

"Before this scourge ... arrived at their gates," Ivess finished. "They would not have had pigeons to tell us, in all likelihood, and thus we do not know. All of this happened days ago, that much is certain, for the pigeons to have reached us here at Enrant Monge. Obviously, if Scylax has fallen, this is a matter of gravest concern—"

"That might be understating it," Unger said, quiet, shaking, his head bowed. When he raised his face, determination had settled in his eyes. "When these things move from Scylax, they'll be hard pressed to travel fast until they're out of the foothills. But that won't take long, even for them. They'll be out on level ground and moving south as pretty as you please, and we need to meet them with an army big enough to crush them, now, and with a plan to seal them off from taking Luukessia, immediately."

"Such a plan," Tiernan said, a slight flush coming back to his face, "would be monumental in scale. I have been to your city of Scylax once, and to take it would require more effort than any two armies in Luukessia could muster."

"So you see the threat we face," Unger said. "We need an army, we need forces to stand against these things, we need to meet them with blood and blade, sword and fire, and we need to drive them back. We have a plan," he said, gesturing to Cyrus, "and people with experience who can carry it out, who know the origin of these creatures—"

"The origin of these creatures?" Aron Longwell scoffed. "Assuming you have actually been invaded, and this isn't some elaborate farce cooked up by you to distract from Galbadien's inevitable conquest of your armies and your lands," a few eyes were rolled, including, to Cyrus's surprise, those of Samwen Longwell, "then these invaders are probably but savage men from beyond the northern reaches of your Kingdom, not some mythical beasts that are unlike anything approaching that which we deal with in everyday life."

"Your own man has seen these creatures in action," Unger said, gesturing to Ranson. "Your own son has seen them, enough to know that this is no charade, no farce scheduled to hew me out of comeuppance for my invasion of your lands, Longwell. If you mean to press your victory, by all means, press your victory—send your army north, to the foothills of Scylax," Unger's lips twisted in a sneer, "and take my capital by force of your arms. You won't get complaint from me—by all means, if you can take it, you can have it, and I'll be all the more thankful for your help in beating back this threat."

"I have no desire to sit on the throne in your mountain hall," Aron Longwell brushed Unger's statement aside, but even at a distance of several rows, Cyrus saw the gleam of perfidy in Longwell's eye, the hint of hesitation as he said it, and heard the lie through every bit of it. "I have a Kingdom to rebuild after you plundered your way through the middle of it."

"Sir," Cyrus heard Count Ranson say from behind King Longwell.

"Not now," the King replied, and held up his hand to silence Ranson. "This seems like some crass deception that only you could have come up with, Unger, and I want no part of it."

"Will you not at least listen to your own man before becoming an intractable prick?" Unger fired back. "He saw what we're facing—what you'll be facing soon enough, if you don't band together with us." Unger turned to Tiernan. "What about you, Milos, you seem the reasonable sort, at least enough to save your own skin. What say you?"

Milos Tiernan stood, slowly, like a broken thing, or a puppet that was jerked by its strings to its feet. "At this time, I am unable to pledge you any support. Our grievances with Galbadien are unresolved and look to be unable to be resolved. As such, my army will be going to war as soon as we leave this place. They are already moving." He looked to

Aron Longwell and shook his head. "Fair warning. We will crush you."

"And when my western army," Aron Longwell's hand came up and indicated Cyrus, "uses their magics to demolish every one of your horseman, footmen, and bowmen, then takes your war and makes it in the streets of Caenalys, you may say I warned you as well."

"Good luck with that," Cyrus said, and stood. "You have no western army, no magics at your disposal. The army of Sanctuary will move north to assist Syloreas." He jutted his finger at Aron Longwell, whose face had degenerated into utter contempt. "You'll be twice damned, sir. First, when Actaluere destroys your western Kingdom, and again when these beasts sweep down from the north and eat the remainder of your realm alive, dooming your people to death."

"You dare talk to me in such a way?" Aron Longwell pointed his finger back at Cyrus, and the garden fairly exploded in shouting; Unger was yelling at Milos Tiernan, who remained silent but whose delegation was on their feet, shouting at Unger in return. The Galbadien delegation had become a fury of its own, turning inward, and Cyrus was being shouted down by a dozen of the King's military advisors, including Odau Genner, whose red cheeks were especially puffy and his eyes were slitted with rage.

"ENOUGH!" The booming voice of Grenwald Ivess crackled through the warm, breezy midday garden like a thunderbolt had landed in their midst. "We hereby adjourn for a cooling off period until such time as there is a reason to meet again." Ivess looked saddened, his pudgy face locked in a semi-scowl. "As you know, if there is no call from any party for a meeting within twenty-four hours, then the negotiations are over, and this summit will be dissolved." He held his hands up. "I urge you not to do that, gentlemen. Find common ground, find a reason to negotiate, and talk amongst yourselves so as to discover a purpose to keep talking rather than going your separate ways—and into war with each other." With that, Ivess, turned and left without another word.

Cyrus half-expected the cacophony to resume, but it didn't. The delegates filed out through their tunnels. Cyrus waited for the Galbadiens to pass him by, and they did, some with muttered curses, others with simply dirty looks. "What now?" J'anda asked when they were nearly alone; very few of the delegates had stayed to speak with their counterparts in the other governments, far fewer than last time.

"We have an officer meeting," Cyrus said, looking over each of them in turn—Nyad, Ryin, Longwell, Curatio and J'anda. He did not see Cattrine, who had been seated by Nyad and Ryin, and wondered what had become of her. "Right now, back at the tower."

He didn't wait for any of them to acknowledge before walking toward the tunnel. He strode through the half-light cast by the torches as he passed under the wall, the sunlight behind him and torches within the only signs of light in the long structure. The shadow cast by the whole thing was enormous, and spanned a great distance.

As he emerged, he caught movement to his right and reached for the sword that wasn't there. It was Cattrine, and her green eyes were what he saw first, and it reminded him of the summer, of all he had seen since leaving Sanctuary all those months ago. He felt a pronounced drop inside but quickly walled off. "Lord Davidon?" she asked, her voice quiet.

"Yes," he answered, barely above a whisper himself.

"I need to know the truth of what you've seen." She held her distance, a few feet from him. "I need to know about these things. Are they truly as bad as Briyce Unger says they are?" She hesitated. "Do you believe that they will cover our land in a darkness?"

He hesitated, staring into her green eyes before blinking away. "I believe they will cover Luukessia in death, yes. Absolute, total death to everything they come across. They will sweep from the mountains to the seas and leave only blood and decay behind them," Cyrus said, letting the fervency of his thoughts seep out of him, mingling with the undercurrent of feeling he experienced from seeing her, hearing her speak. "I believe they will be the end of Luukessia to the last person here, that they won't quit coming until that happens." He closed his eyes, just for a moment. "And I believe that without help, that's doomed to be the fate of this land, regardless of how much blood those of us who will fight are willing to shed."

She looked in his eyes, stared into them, and Cyrus was reminded of nights and days at Vernadam, but he did not look away. "I believe you," she said simply and turned, walking in the opposite direction of the tower.

Cyrus opened the door to his room back at the tower and put his armor back on while the other officers trailed in behind him over the next few minutes. "I love what you've done with the place," Ryin said as he shut the door behind him, the last to enter. Nyad sat on the bed, where Ryin joined her. Cyrus looked out the window, and far below he could see over the wall into the Garden of Serenity, empty, the trees and plants around the edges a marked contrast to the stone benches and amphitheater at its center. He turned to face the room and found J'anda and Curatio each occupying one of the chairs, while Samwen Longwell leaned against the wall. Longwell looked as though he were relying more on his armor than his strength to keep him upright. He had looked like that quite a bit lately, Cyrus reflected, though he had no motivation to ask the dragoon what weighed on him.

"We found out where this scourge comes from," Cyrus said, drawing the attention of everyone in the room.

"Yes, we surmised as much since it was stated in the assembly," Ryin said, unconcerned. "From where do they hail? The far north of this country?"

"You're a little off," J'anda answered. "Try the Realm of Death."

Silence gripped Ryin and Nyad. Cyrus watched the slow tick of emotions run over both of their faces—confusion, disbelief—Nyad turned scarlet after a moment, and Ryin grew still. "From where?" Nyad asked.

"The Realm of Death," Cyrus said, subdued. "They're the reconstituted spirits of the souls Mortus had imprisoned, given flesh by the journey through the portal from his realm." Nyad sat openmouthed, and Ryin did not speak, merely shook his head slowly. Cyrus looked at him, and gave him a slow smile after catching his gaze. "This would probably be a fine time to say, 'I told you so.'"

Ryin looked at him almost perplexed, lips slightly parted. "What?"

"You were the only one who argued against invading Mortus's realm before we ended up killing him," Cyrus said. "You were the sole voice that suggested against going."

"I voted for it in the end," Ryin said. "I was only opposed to the concern of heresy being committed in the process. I had not considered any … other consequences." He rubbed his eyes. "Certainly nothing like this. Does this …" He halted, and a look like guilt weathered the human, turning his visage from that of a young man to a much older one in a second's time, "… this means we're responsible, doesn't it?"

Cyrus let the silence endure for almost a minute. "Yes. It does."

It became uncomfortable after that, a low, drudging toil of quiet, as though everyone were fighting hard not to say anything. Ryin spoke at last. "We can't just leave them to it, then."

"It was never my intention to leave them to it," Cyrus said, "even before I knew we were the cause of this particular calamity." He looked at the druid. "I suppose I am a little surprised not to hear you argue against it, though. I mean, you haven't been renowned for wanting to get involved in other peoples' wars."

"I'm a bit of a contrarian, but this isn't their war," Ryin said, "it's ours, spilled over here. If what you say is true, then the only thing that has spared Arkaria from the fate of these creatures falling on us is that our portal is in the middle of the Bay of Lost Souls." He frowned. "These things can't swim, then?"

"It would seem that the distance to shore is a problem," J'anda said, indifferent. "It is quite far from the portal on the Island of Mortus to Arkaria, several hours sail by boat."

Nyad frowned and looked around the room. "Where's Terian? Shouldn't he be here?"

This time the silence was pained, and Cyrus felt a particularly sharp dagger in his heart. "We'll need to mobilize the army to get them ready to march north. I'll ride out and give orders to Odellan while the rest of you …" Cyrus ground his teeth slightly, "explain what's become of our illustrious dark knight. I doubt I could come up with anything that would make sense at this point. After that, one of you," he pointed a finger between Nyad and Ryin, "needs to return to Sanctuary and deliver the news of our predicament—and to ask for aid." He looked them all over once, then went for the door, and shut it behind him as he heard the quiet tones of Curatio explaining something matter-of-factly, too low for Cyrus to hear.

"HE DID WHAT?" Nyad's voice was loud enough to be heard in the hallway as Cyrus descended the ramp, down to the bottom of the tower.

The air was warm as he walked out, across the courtyard. The nearby stable was open to the air, a single line of stalls under a cover that afforded only a little protection from the elements. Windrider waited, standing above a spread of oats lying on the ground next to a watering trough. He gave Cyrus a steady gaze as the warrior approached, and Cyrus pulled his gauntlet off to stroke the horse's face as he took hold of the reins. "You've done well," Cyrus said in a breath, and caught motion from his side, a stableboy moving in his peripheral vision. He patted Windrider as the stableboy, a red-haired, freckled lad no older than twelve edged closer, staring at Cyrus.

"Are you him?" the boy asked.

"Yeah," Cyrus said, patting Windrider, "this is my horse."

"No," the boy replied, edging slightly closer to Cyrus. "Are you ... him? Lord Garrick?"

Cyrus paused, uncertain of what to say. "I am Cyrus Davidon, of Sanctuary," he answered after a moment. "I know not this Lord Garrick of whom you speak."

The stableboy was quiet, his eyes staring out of the shade cast by the barn's flimsy straw roof. "He's legend, Lord Garrick of Enrant Monge. He was of the last generation of rulers of the castle before the fall and the fracture of Luukessia. He's our greatest ancestor, watches over us from above." The boy eased closer and ran a careful hand, stroking Windrider's flank. "They say he keeps his eyes on us, here in Luukessia, from above, from the halls of all our ancestors in the land of Gredenyde." The boy's eyes blinked at Cyrus innocently. "They say he'll come back to us—to save us—in our darkest hour of need."

Cyrus's hand paused on Windrider's neck, and he froze, his blood running cold. "I'm not your Lord Garrick, believe that. And I wouldn't put much stock in prophecy if I were you."

There was a pause as the boy studied him. "Are you sure?

Cyrus took the reins and started to lead Windrider out of the cover under the barn, felt the warm sunlight stream down on him as he stepped from under the cover of the stables. "I've never been more sure of anything in my life." He slung the saddle over the horse and bound it, then slipped a foot in a stirrup and heaved himself up. "But I will do my best to save your land from what's coming."

The stableboy followed him out, covering his eyes with a freckled hand, that of a lad who had been working long hours in the sun. "I've heard the rumors, since the pigeons came. They say Scylax has fallen. They say something is coming from the mountains of the north, something terrible, something that wants to devour the souls of every man in Luukessia." Cyrus didn't say anything as he steadied himself in the saddle. "Is it true?" the boy asked. "Is it true that they're coming, these things, to kill us all?"

"Aye," Cyrus answered finally.

"But you're going to stop them?" The boy looked uncertain, and Cyrus tried not to look too hard on him; he knew there were boys only a couple years older in the Sanctuary army. *Only a couple years older physically but worlds older in maturity, having seen blood, and bile and battle.* "Then that makes you Lord Garrick, doesn't it? Come to save us?"

"It's not your darkest hour yet, kid," Cyrus said, and started Windrider forward. "Save some fear and legends to pass on to your grandkids." The clip-clop of the horseshoes on the stone echoed as Cyrus steered his horse out the eastern gate and into the second courtyard, across it, then out of Enrant Monge and down the road.

The world opened up before him when he left the second gate, the forests a mile or so in the distance smoking with pillars of wafting black coming from the fires of his army, his and Galbadien's. The road crooked into a forest path as Windrider went along, the branches cut high enough that even though they formed a thick canopy over him, reducing the sunlight, none of them threatened his face as he rode.

The breeze was soft, even as Windrider galloped along, at a higher speed than normal. "Just a little farther," he whispered to the horse. The warm sun tried to peek through the boughs overhead, but the shade was cooling, late summer's wrath spent on the trees overhead, long before it got to him. He could smell the fresh air, the same air he'd been breathing for months, the pine almost blended behind everything else, the tinge of the horse's smell, though it wasn't as heavy now as when he was stationary. *Terian. The latest in a long line of people to betray me, to harm me. What is it about them? About me?* His eyes fell downward. *Vara ... why did you—*

The arrow hit him in the shoulder, glancing off his armor but causing him to jerk in surprise. Windrider whinnied and shied involuntarily, trying to compensate for Cyrus's abrupt change of balance. Cyrus gripped the reins and tensed his abdomen, trying to right himself on the horse. The second arrow, however, hit him in the neck, putting to sunder any idea of maintaining his grip. The shock of the arrow caused Cyrus's fingers to loosen, and he felt himself fall, the heavy impact of his body and all that armor hitting the ground caused his head to wash, as though he were floating on an ocean all his own. His fingers came up without thought, found the round shaft of the arrow protruding just above his gorget, tracing it back to the place where it was lodged in his neck.

"Isn't this fortunate?" A low voice scratched into his consciousness. Cyrus turned his head and saw a man in a dark cloak hobbling in the midst of a party of other men. Cyrus's vision was blurred, his head felt heavy, but he knew that voice. Clarity struck his eyes, and the man came into focus for a moment: black beard that was thin, very thin and patchy, his pale skin even paler. "Now I can thank you properly for crippling me," Grand Duke Hoygraf said, and Cyrus saw figures all around, beginning to circle him.

Praelior. Cyrus's hand moved to his sword, felt the rush of strength it gave him. He drew the blade and pulled to his feet, still feeling as though he were moving underwater. The men around him seemed to move at regular speed, and Cyrus blocked one of them who came at him with a polearm, cutting the man's head from his shoulders, covering his blue livery and surcoat with blood.

"Well, look at you," Hoygraf said, maintaining his distance from Cyrus, watching him with a spiteful smile. "I suppose I'm not the only one of my wife's lovers who refuses to die on command." Hoygraf's face twisted into spite. "The difference is, you'll stay dead when I kill you."

"Didn't ... kill you," Cyrus said, and felt blood bubbling out of his mouth as he spoke, the sour taste coating his tongue. "Stabbed you ... bad enough you wished you were dead. Planning to do it ... again ... in a few minutes, but now I'll do it so many times you'll have to die when I'm done."

"You're bleeding like a cow with a cut throat," Hoygraf said with a sneer. "I don't think you'll last a minute the way you're going now."

Cyrus felt a slow smile spread across his bloody lips. "I'll only need thirty seconds." Cyrus flung himself backward, sword first, sensing the presence of Hoygraf's men behind him. He hit the first with a hard stroke between the eyes, the blade running down the man's forehead and stopping after cutting out the mouth. The man dropped as Cyrus freed his blade and brought it around to the next attacker, catching him across the chest and cutting through the breastplate of his armor. The bottom of the man's blue surcoat fluttered to the ground and Cyrus watched as he stepped on it, as he finished his stroke and blood spattered across the dirt and the surcoat. *Two left,* he thought, *and they're right over—*

The arrow hit him in the lower back and cut through the chainmail where he'd exposed it while in his attack. Cyrus felt a curious punching sensation and force, each in twine, arcing along his spine as he fell. Even the might of Praelior was unable to mask the pain or give him enough strength to fight off his knees. He sat there, wobbling, as a man with a sword shuffled, hesitant, over to him. Cyrus jammed Praelior upward with all the speed and strength he had left, and saw the sword enter the bottom of the man's jaw as his mouth opened in surprise, and watched it flash through the man's tongue, visible through his gaping maw, blood running down the blade it.

A sharp pain in the back of his neck threw Cyrus facedown in the dirt, and he felt something hit him on the sword hand, hard. The world faded as Praelior was knocked away and Cyrus felt his body rolled onto his back. The branches above him were swaying, whether from the breeze of the late summer's day or the swimming of his head from the wounding, he could not be sure. He tried to draw a breath but struggled, his chest heavy, every attempt so labored that it felt as though he were trying to lift a mountain to even partially fill his lungs.

Grand Duke Hoygraf appeared at the edge of his vision, filling his eyes, another man next to him with a bow and arrow, a nameless, armored man in the Grand Duke's livery. "You killed my men," Hoygraf said flatly. Cyrus tried to reply but felt only the bubbling of blood on his lips. "You had your way with my wife," the Grand Duke went on, "destroyed my home, left me an invalid, unable to walk straight." The Grand Duke's cane came down on Cyrus's face, and another dull pain made its way through Cyrus's consciousness.

Curatio. He'll find me. Aisling will help him. Martaina will …

"You think you've hurt me," Hoygraf said, kneeling in front of Cyrus's face. "You think you've beaten me? Humiliated me? Did you think I would let that stand unanswered?" He spat, and curiously Cyrus could feel the warm spittle make its way down his cheek, and he tried to move a hand, go for the Grand Duke's throat, just as he'd been taught—

"No," Hoygraf said, and Cyrus saw a dagger in his hand, saw Hoygraf catch his arm and rip the gauntlet off, throwing it away. Cyrus watched as Hoygraf lifted the exposed arm and stabbed the dagger through Cyrus's wrist. The sharp pain was there, in the background, but Cyrus barely felt it. "Did you think I would simply let you have my wife, wreck my keep, leave me to die and merely forget about you? Let it pass?"

J'anda. Mendicant. Odellan. Longwell. I need ... help. The names ran through his mind one by one as though by thought he could appeal to them directly to come to him. Weariness settled upon him like a heavy blanket, dulling the pain.

"I know your western magic," Hoygraf said, and twirled the dagger in his fingers. "If I leave you here, as you are, they'll find you. They'll bring you back to life." Hoygraf's lips pursed and he shook his head. "I can't have that. I need everyone—everyone—to know that you don't trifle with me, not this way. And I'll make sure ... that you won't come back."

Alaric ... Cyrus's thoughts were drifting now. Was Alaric even around?

The knife flashed in front of Cyrus's eyes, and then he felt a sharp pain in his neck, the blade's edge against his flesh, sawing down.

"They'll have a hard time reviving you, I'd wager," he heard the Baron's voice say, "without a head."

The last thought through Cyrus's mind before the flash was uncontrolled, unanswerable, and unexpected.

Vara ...

Chapter 43

Vara

The Council Chambers seemed to briefly twist around her, the torches a blur of light in her peripheral vision as she honed in on the druid's face as he spoke, a dull, tanned mass of flat nose and pale lips that she wanted to hit with the palm of her hand as she would slap an overripe melon to get it to crack open. Instead she pressed her armored fingers into the table and pushed, hearing a splintering sound that caused her to draw back her hand self-consciously. She looked up and saw Vaste staring at her with his pointy-toothed grin, and she gave him venom in return.

"… so, of course, he's keeping the army in Luukessia and marching them north, to meet and battle the scourge as it continues to come south," Ryin Ayend finished with a nod of his head, perched atop that implausibly thin neck.

"Oh, of course," Vara said, letting sarcasm drip from every syllable. "Because the problems of another continent are so much larger than the enemies storming down our own gates."

Ryin's jaw worked open and then shut, a quick motion that caused his lips to purse. "Of course we didn't know over there what you were experiencing here, else we might have come back a bit quicker. However—"

"This scourge," Alaric said, interrupting. "You have mentioned the danger they pose, but you did not speak to the origin of these creatures."

Ayend's face went ashen. "Ah, yes. Well, you see, that's the other part of the problem and the reason Cyrus sent me back. He wants you to send reinforcements—"

"Then he's just as daft as ever he's been," Vara said, and she felt the twitch and contraction of the muscles at the corners of her eyes. "Unsurprising, given that he's been operating out of contact for so long, but the idea that the war here would just run a pleasing and gentle course is ridiculous, and a supposed 'master strategist' such as Cyrus

Davidon should damned well have known that the Sovereign of Saekaj wouldn't be sitting idly by while he grew fat in his black armor, feasting beyond the eastern sea."

"You don't understand," Ayend said with a shake of the head. "He's not just fighting the good fight for the sake of it over there—"

"Because he's never gotten involved in an ill-advised fight before?" Vara said, cutting across Ayend's words.

"To your advantage, I believe, not his," Ryin said.

"Yay, verbal fisticuffs," Vaste said, "I have so missed the arguments in these chambers over the last months."

"I haven't," Alaric said, dark circles under his eyes now that his helm was removed. "Vara, if you might, please allow our esteemed brother Ryin to finish his train of thought without interruption ... About the origin of this scourge ...?"

"Ah," Ryin said, all contrition. "That is the sticky part, as I said."

"Something on the order of five times now you've said it was a sticky part," Vara said, her fingers now on her face and ready to dig into the skin in lieu of anything else to squeeze her frustration out on. "Some of us grow weary of being sticky—"

"Not I," Vaste said. "I could do with more of it. Though not with any of you."

"Perhaps you might cut to the point of it and be done," Vara continued, ignoring the interruption, "so that those of us who have other things to do—say, seeing to the defense of Sanctuary—could get back to that."

"Would you allow me," Ryin said, irritation infusing his tone, "sixty uninterrupted seconds without the extreme pleasure," he put emphasis on pleasure, as though it were the foulest curse, "of your sweet and indulgent voice, and I might complete a full sentence and thus end the story I am trying to tell." His jaw worked as though he were chewing something heavy. "J'anda read the minds of these creatures and saw their monstrous origin, and then Cyrus and Aisling confirmed their creation by seeing—"

"What a wondrous pairing, those two," Vara said, and her hand dropped from her face to the table again, where she dug her fingers into the edge once more.

Ryin ignored her. "—seeing how they were created. There is a portal, and it leads to Mortus's chambers. The creatures are the souls turned loose after the God of Death's—well, his death," Ayend said, after struggling with the phrase. "They are the legacy of what we released when we killed Mortus." A heavy silence covered the room before Ryin began to speak again. "Cyrus says he will stay until the end to defeat them to, ah …" Ayend pursed his lips, "… atone for his part in their release."

Vara's eyes met Alaric's, which were cool indifference, but she caught a glint in them that she ignored. "Well," she said, suppressing the internal desire to scream, "isn't that … noble … of him."

"He's quite the honorable chap," Ayend said coolly.

"Interesting to hear you speak so favorably of him," Vaste said with amusement, "seeing as you've always been his harshest critic."

"I'm everyone's harshest critic," Ryin said, sitting up straight in his chair, "because I don't believe in letting ideas pass unless they've some virtue and until they've been considered carefully. Perhaps we made a mistake in killing Mortus, perhaps we erred in defending Termina for the evacuation, perhaps not on one or both counts; either way, there are plainly consequences that need to be dealt with by someone, both here and abroad. Whatever our prior decisions, we are stuck with the fallout from them now, and I see Cyrus trying as best he can to cope with his part. Luukessia is at war, these things are numerous, the land is fragmented and the coming war will likely be disastrous. Cyrus could use additional forces to drive these things back and finish them in order to have Curatio destroy the portal."

There was a long pause, and Alaric stared at Ryin from his place at the head of the table, the grey skies highlighted out the small windows behind him to the balcony. It might have been Vara's imagination, but the sky seemed to dim further as Alaric wrapped a hand around his mouth as if trying to suppress any sound that might escape. "No," he said at last. "His cause is, of course, just, and worthy, but the army we broke is not the last of what we will see of the dark elves. We cannot move to assist our comrades in Luukessia unless we know for fact that the dark elves have moved all their armies against other objectives." He bowed his head. "I do not see us coming into an abundance of news in that regard, not anytime soon, not more than idle rumors."

Vara stared at him, at the specter of quiet and defeat that hunched the Ghost's shoulders. *We should protect our own gates, take care to watch our backs now. What has happened to these people of Luukessia is unfortunate, all the moreso because of our part in setting loose this scourge, but to send more of our army to aid them would be to sentence those remaining behind to defend Sanctuary to a terrible and bloody death, especially now that the Sovereign has learned how to breach our very foyer and send his troops in directly. No, further excursions would be a terrible idea, awful in its application and idiotic in the stripping of more forces from our own walls ...*

Even still, she spoke. "Perhaps ..." she said, "... if I went to the front south of Reikonos and spoke with my sister, who helps head the defense of human territory, we might gather some idea of how goes the war in general, and the disposition of forces. With that insight, we might know if it were safe to send another expedition to assist our beleaguered forces in Luukessia." She clamped her mouth shut after it was said, and wanted to scream. *Where the hell did THAT come from?*

"An interesting idea," Vaste said. "And here I thought you were firmly against committing any more troops outside of our walls. I wonder what might possibly have shifted the weight in your mind against that idea."

"An outpouring of concern for our army across the sea, no doubt," she said icily.

"Because you spend a vast majority of your time concerned about the plight of our new recruits," Vaste replied with a barb and a raised eyebrow.

"I spend my time as an officer concerned about our entire guild, you miscreant."

"Of course," he said contritely.

The doors opened to the hall behind them, a slow creak of the hinges as Erith Frostmoor entered the chamber, her white hair bound behind her in a long braid, her robes tattered, the white thread now brown and smudged. "The hour is over," she said as she took her seat, as though it were an explanation of itself.

"The hour is ... what?" Vara asked her with a cocked eyebrow.

"Is over," Erith said, her usual mischief faded, her eyes weighed down in hard lines, lips tight, the purple flesh that made them stand out from the blue skin of her face tightly compacted in a line that wavered.

"The hour we have to resurrect people who might have been killed in the tower collapse is up, and they were still pulling bodies out of the stone when I left a few minutes ago." She lowered her eyes. "It looks like a quarry where it came down, piles of block everywhere, and you can still hear moans and cries from inside, so all hope is not lost, but ..."

"A terrible day," Alaric pronounced. "To see so many of our brethren fall in a battle that we didn't even truly partake in. How many unaccounted for?"

"Eighteen," Erith said, her head hanging. "Some yet live, and our strongest are working to unearth them, but some are certainly lost. Then there are the consequences of the collapse. It looks like someone took the corner of the building and dragged it down, exposing all the lower floors to the air and elements. You'll have to have someone more familiar with design tell you how that will affect things. We've lost a good many quarters, though, I can tell you that much."

"We have empty housing enough," Vaste said. "Not to marginalize the loss of the tower or the deaths, which are unpleasant, no doubt, but we will make do. The bigger concern is if the dark elves come again, with more men, more war machines."

"The Sovereign is unpredictable yet spiteful," Alaric said, still holding himself to his seat, pensive. "Yes, I think it might be wise to have you speak to your sister about the war's progress," he said with a nod to Vara. "We need to know what to expect, what will be coming and how it will hit us." He brought his hands around to steeple in front of his face. "You will go immediately, and return as soon as possible."

"Very well," Vara said, and began to stand.

"Hold," Ryin said. "I will take you to Reikonos, but there is one last thing I have to report."

"Oh, good," Vara said, lowering herself back into her chair. "Because you weren't overly dramatic enough with any of the other information you brought us. What pointless drivel have you left to—"

"Terian," Ryin said, and Vara stopped speaking, a knifeblade cutting into her under the armor, as though something unseen had stabbed her.

"What about him?" Alaric said, stiff, shifting in his seat to focus attention on Ryin.

"He attempted to kill Cyrus while they were on the northern expedition."

"Attempted to kill him?" Erith said with mild surprise. "What, did he cook his infamous vek'tag casserole again? Because that isn't technically an attempt to kill, though your digestive tract won't know the difference."

"It goes somewhat beyond cooking," Ryin said archly.

"Not many non-dark elven palates can handle that spider-meat your people consume like some of us eat chicken," Vaste said, chiming in, "though I've always found vek'tag to be something of a delight."

"Shut up," Vara said, her voice only a whisper. *How could he have known?*

"What?" Vaste said, watching her. "You can't seriously mean that Terian would actually try to kill Cyrus? This must surely be some sort of—"

"It is no mistake," Ayend said. "It was deliberate, plotted. He cursed Cyrus and slit the throat of his horse while he was on the run from the scourge. Save for the efforts of Aisling and Mendicant, he would have died."

"They saved him?" Vara said, and her voice cracked slightly.

If Ryin noticed, he did not call attention to it. "It was how Cyrus and Aisling discovered the origin of the scourge. They became entrapped behind enemy lines together for several days after their retreat was cut off."

"How ... fortuitous that she was able to save him," Vara managed to choke out.

"Yes, you sound extremely pleased that she was able to risk her life in order to spare him from our guildmate's treachery," Vaste said. "But if I may observe, you and Alaric seem unsurprised that Terian would try such a thing. Whereas I am shocked, and there is little that shocks me, aside from the smell that comes from Erith's quarters."

Erith flushed a deeper blue. "I'm not much of a housekeeper."

Vaste snorted. "And they say that trolls smell. But that is neither here nor there. The point remains that our esteemed Guildmaster and fellow officer seem to know something of this that the rest of us do not."

"While in Termina, defending the bridge," Vara began, "Cyrus killed a dark knight. He was Terian's father."

"Oh, dear," Vaste said, his green face wiped clear of amusement for once, and his mouth open into an 'o' that was distorted by his ungainly teeth. "The sword."

"What sword?" Alaric said, leaning forward now.

"Aisling brought the sword of that dark knight back to Sanctuary," Vaste said, and shifted to one side in the chair. "She carried it with her in the escape and presented it to Cyrus as a trophy of his accomplishment."

"His accomplishment?" Vara leaned onto the table. "I fought the bloody bastard almost to the death before Cyrus stabbed him in the back—"

"Let us keep sight of what has happened here," Alaric said gravely. "Terian discovered a truth we hoped he would not find out until we could comfortably present it to him here, in carefully controlled circumstances."

"It would appear the circumstances have spiralled far, far out of your control," Erith said with a furrowed brow.

"Yes, and your predictive powers are usually spot-on," Vaste said mildly. "I suppose we're all allowed a failure of judgment every now and again."

"It was not a failure of judgment," Alaric whispered, "it was a failure of communication. I saw no way for him to know that his father had died, and so I worried not about it but of the myriad of other things we have to deal with. Had I known, I could have predicted his response, the slyness of it, the wait, the consideration. Terian is many things— conflicted, devious, somewhat cold—but revenge is not out of the question for him. If he knew what had happened, I would have assumed vengeance could follow, in its own time, and that it would be in a manner of his choosing."

"Am I the only one wondering why you brought him back after he left the guild, then?" Ryin asked. "If you knew he was this dangerous?"

There was a pause, stark and quiet. "Because danger is not all there is to Terian," Alaric said, "and there is good in him, enough to outweigh the baser desires, should he have the right … outlet."

"He's a menace," Vara said, and the words surprised her, "and now a murderer, it seems."

"It seems," Alaric said. "But there are no innocents at this table, remember that. Our profession is the sword and shield, but I note that none of you choose to use a shield."

"I use a shield all the time," Vaste said, "but I call it Vara, and it squirms when I force it to absorb the blows of my angry enemies. Also, it speaks harshly to me sometimes."

Vara felt the snap of heat across her cheeks. "This is hardly the time for humor, you fool. We have too many problems for you to sit here and make light of every one of them!"

"I've got the time," Vaste said. "What else would I be doing? Trying to solve them? They're a world away! Silly idea, that."

"Enough," Alaric said quietly and turned back to Ryin. "Why did Cyrus not send Terian back with you?"

Ryin started to speak, then stopped. "I don't know. He was in something of a hurry to go meet with the army and prepare them to move. I'm certain it slipped his mind."

"It slipped his mind to send a dangerous prisoner who wants him dead back to a place where he could be held with some modicum of security in our dungeons?" Vara asked, incredulous. "I shouldn't be surprised, his head as full of pudding as it is, but here we are, nonetheless ..."

Erith's eyes narrowed. "It doesn't sound as though Cyrus is functioning at a terribly high level to have overlooked something so elementary as that, even after a few months away. And to remain out of contact for as long as he has with all this going on ..." She shook her head. "He's under duress, I'm sure."

"Vara," Alaric said, "if you could speak with your sister, that would be helpful to us in planning our next move."

"Yes," she said, "very well," and stood up. Ryin matched her across the table. "Do warn the army guarding the foyer that we will return, likely in the middle of the night at this point, and so if they could be generous and give us a moment's hesitation before trying to impale us, it would be appreciated."

"You're not capable of anything so mild as appreciation," Vaste said, "only lesser stages of ire and woe."

"You know nothing of my lesser stages of ire and woe, not being a recipient of anything but the higher stages yourself."

"Once they get past a certain point," Vaste said with a shrug, "they're more like fury and misery, but really, who's keeping track?"

"You are, you green—"

"Enough already!" Alaric said and brought his fist down upon the table with a clatter that sent the empty metal cup sitting in front of him over and sideways, spilling the little remaining liquid therein on the old finish of the Council table. "Our guildmates are in danger, we are under siege, we have unleashed a plague upon another land and lack the resources to help them effectively. Yet still the four of you that remain argue like small children over who got the greater portion of the sweetroll. Well, let me say this, children—" He whipped his head around to favor each of them with a glare from where he stood now, looking down at them, "there is little sweet about our current predicament. If you want to bicker and whine, resign your position as officers, leave Sanctuary for a safe place, like Fertiss, and pick at each other for the better part of every day while the world continues to descend into chaos safely out of your sight."

Alaric stiffened in his battered armor, the dark green tinge to it looking almost black in the cloudy light filtering in from behind him. "But if you mean to make a difference and live up to the mission of this guild, put your humor aside and let us work to end this siege, so we can make good on repairing the consequences of our error in killing Mortus." With that, Alaric grabbed his helm and put it on his head, straightening it so that the slits where his eyes were visible were shadowed and Vara could see only the hint that he was behind them. "The time for light-hearted fun is over; these are dark times, perhaps darker than we can safely bear. This is a time for adults, for the things of grown-ups, for battles, a time to leave the simpering humor behind as we struggle with our burdens. The hour grows late, and for the young, it is past your bedtime. Leave us, if you want no part of serious things. But for those who remain ... go to work."

With that, he became insubstantial, a fog that rolled toward the doors behind him and out of the balcony, disappearing over the edge in a fine mist, as though the air outside were reabsorbing him.

"So ..." Vaste said, as the four of them stared out the window at the exit of their Guildmaster. "Who put the caltrops in Alaric's chair today?"

Vara turned from the table, casting a look at Ryin, who nodded and followed her to the space in front of the door. "Perhaps it was something you said," she told Vaste, who remained in his chair with a look of quiet unconcern. "Or perhaps it was everything you say." The winds began to pick up around them, stirring the stuffy air in the Council Chambers. Vaste said nothing as the maelstrom of the teleportation spell caused the walls to dissolve around her, and the last thing of Sanctuary she saw was the troll's green face, a second's hesitation showing in the puckered brow and downturned lips as the whirlwind carried her far, far away from him.

Chapter 44

Reikonos was a town astir, the streets quiet and yet frenzied, the long stretches of thatched-roof homes canceled out by the bigger buildings with wooden beams making up their construction. It was a hodgepodge of old and new, of stone buildings and wood shacks, and the streets were both calm and chaotic in alternating segments. Vara walked along with Ryin trailing a few steps behind her as they headed toward the southern central gate through the city's walls. The sun seemed to be higher in the sky here than it had been at Sanctuary, and there were few enough clouds that the late afternoon warmth was still present and cooked her in her armor as she moved through the quiet then the chaos.

"Lines," Ryin said, "for the communal ovens." The druid was right, though she didn't want to acknowledge it. There were clusters of people, women mostly, around the places where there were ovens for public use. *Not everyone has their own, after all, as this is not Termina.* A rueful thought occurred. *Even Termina is unlikely to have those things, now.* "In time of war, meat must surely be limited, so daily bread is likely the cornerstone of their diet at this point."

"If they're just getting to the ovens at this time of day, it's going to be a late supper," she said.

"True enough." He came alongside her, trying to match her pace. "But I suspect that the grain shipments put them at the mercy of whichever merchant has some that day—there's likely a line for that as well. Rationing, shortages, all that."

"What fun," was all she said and tightly at that.

The street vendors who were normally set up on this, the busiest thoroughfare in the city, were noticeably absent this day, giving the streets an even more abandoned feel, quieter than she had seen even in the years she had lived in the city. *Cyrus would not like this, not at all,* came the thought, as unbidden as it was frustrating. She increased her speed, pumping her legs to a faster walk, as though she could somehow leave that line of thinking behind if she were to just walk fast enough to outpace it.

Ryin kept up, his superior height his only saving grace. The walk was long, and the walls of the city came into sight after a while, tall, grey stone that rose up in a curtain wall around the buildings nestled within. It was nowhere near as high as the one built around the elven capital of Pharesia, but it still stuck a hundred and fifty feet in the air and circled for miles in either direction, a monumental effort of stonework that gave the city a washed, sandstone look that was out of place in the more northern environs where one expected darker stone— for some reason she couldn't define.

The southern gate was open, enormous, wide enough for fifty men to walk astride through it and even for a few elephants to be carted out simultaneously on each other's shoulders, as Vara had seen once in a magic circus when she was younger. There was little enough traffic on the road by this point; the ovens were all well back in the city, and the houses closest to the gate became more of the ramshackle variety and less of the carefully orchestrated stone, the roofs declining in average height precipitously and the woodwork growing older and older as they went. *Who lives here?* she wondered. *The guards that man the walls, likely, if they're not housed in barracks. Farmers who work just outside the gates, perhaps? Working people, not merchants, who would be near the markets and shops. Not quite the poor, but not the wealthy or aristocratic.*

They passed beneath the gates and under the wall, which stretched almost a hundred feet from entry to exit. She stared up into the faces of guards who looked down on them, bows at the ready in case some trick was attempted, some effort at siege tried. Guards milled about in the passage under the gate as well, picking at the wagons and people trying to pass through. She and Ayend, on their way out, garnered nothing but a few suspicious looks from the men in armor and pointed helms, their spears and swords aimed at those trying to gain entry into the city and unconcerned with those attempting exit.

The horizon was darkening in blue as they emerged from under the portcullis and the whole world opened up around them. There had been shanty houses creeping toward the outer walls for some time, but some enterprising soul—*probably that bastard Pretnam Urides and his laughable Council of Twelve*—had had them burned, and all that remained was twisted wreckage, scorched wood and little else, a graveyard of destroyed hovels for hundreds of yards around the walls of the city. They followed the dirt path onward, the vegetation sparse in this well-trodden area, with all the trees and grass that had grown nearby charred by the flames.

The walk was over an hour, and the road grew more congested toward the end. There were tents about, plenty of them, old, billowing, lined neatly along the rolling hills of the city outskirts. There were farmhouses, too, older ones that had been commandeered by the army, and troops marched in formations up and down the road. Vara stopped and asked the captain of one of them about the guild Endeavor and was pointed down the road. "Another mile, perhaps two. They're toward the front, but there's several miles between us and the enemy positions," the captain said, weeks of beard growth on his tanned face. "Been like that for a few months, staring across at them, but they're not moving right now."

"Thank you," Vara said simply and went on, Ryin in tow. When they passed the last ranks of horsemen and began to see the armor take on a fancier sheen and the weapons carry the glow of mystical power, she knew they were close. The tents were less weathered and between the combatants being better attired and the presence of attendants whose sole purpose appeared to be serving the fighters rather than engaging in any sort of battle themselves, she veered from the road and asked only one skeptical warrior for direction before she was pointed to the largest tent in view, one with a flag out front on a pike.

Vara approached with a slow, steady walk, eyeing the troll guards as they stared back at her, assessing. "My name is Vara," she said, holding her position a good twenty feet from the front flap entry of the tent. The tent was enormous, at least fifteen feet high at the center, circular, and large enough to house thirty men under it. "I am here to speak with Isabelle of Endeavor."

The troll on her left grunted, his armor a poor fit for his oversized bulk. He was close to twice her height, and his grunt brought with it a foul odor, even at the distance she had maintained. She curled her nose and held a hand in front of it. *Trolls. I forget sometimes how civilized Vaste is compared to some of their number.*

"No see," said the troll on her right, marginally shorter than the other, but with eyes that burned with slightly more intelligence. "Miss

Isabelle not to be disturbed."

"I can see from your grasp of the human language that we're about to reach a tragic impasse in this discussion," Vara said, narrowly avoiding folding her arms in front of her, instead keeping her hand at a little distance from the hilt of her sword where it rested on her belt. "Let me state this again, for those of us in this conversation whose brains are not quite the equal of their bulk—I am here to see Isabelle. Is she inside?"

The troll on the left reached for his sword and had it drawn quicker than she thought would be possible, though his feet had yet to move into any sort of offensive posture. The one on the right made no such move, did not change expression, but held his ground. "She no see you—"

"I'll see her," came a voice as the tent flap was raised. A blond elf emerged into the daylight with a blinking countenance marking her otherwise smooth and timeless features. Her robes were flawless white, she was perfectly groomed and would not have been at all out of place in a ballroom. *Even here, on the battlefield, Isabelle has an unflappable air about her, as though she weren't presently standing on ground trodden by soldiers and surrounded by armies but instead was far away, at a society party. She even wears a tiara,* Vara thought, looking at the simple golden circlet atop her sister's blond locks, rubies and sapphires crowning it. "Come in, dear sister," Isabelle said, holding the flap, "and your guest too, if he'd like."

"Wait here," Vara said to Ryin without looking back at him. She made her way between the towering trolls, who both moved aside, their dull, steel-plated armor catching the glint of the sun's light as she passed. She grasped the tent flap herself and indicated to Isabelle to step back inside with a simple hand gesture. Isabelle smiled in amusement and did so without any comment, as Vara followed her in and let the flap fall behind her.

"You pick an interesting time to visit," Isabelle said, making her way into the open area at the center of the tent. "But then, you always did have a sense for timing."

"Good or ill?" Vara asked, letting the smell of the tent overwhelm her. It carried a whiff of incense; not too heavy, but present, enough to overwhelm the smells of the encampment around them and all the waste that came with it. A simple bed lay in the corner, a mattress with heavy pillows on it, all in good order. A table was deployed in the middle of the tent with folding chairs around it. A few stands littered the perimeter of the tent, and a blanket lined the floor, clean and neat, and padded enough to take the hardness out of each step. Vara felt the impact softened within her armored boots and tried to brush off the irritation at her sister's accomodations. *I can't recall ever traveling in quite this high a style, not even when I was an officer in Amarath's Raiders.*

"Good timing," Isabelle said, reaching toward a bowl of apples set upon the center table. "Hungry?"

"No."

"You don't approve of my accouterments," Isabelle said, and that damnable amusement was still there, the faint tug at the corners of her mouth and the sparkle in her eye. "The little luxuries I'm afforded as an officer of Endeavor."

"Oh, yes, you live in grand style for someone at the front line of the greatest war Arkaria has seen in centuries," Vara said, brusque. "Very fine, indeed."

"This bothers you … why?" If Isabelle was annoyed by her sister's attitude, she showed it little or none, and Vara was quite used to the subtlety of her older sister's emotions. *Glacier-cool, she is. Which is why she is so annoying.*

"I care not at all *how* you live while at war," Vara said, "only that you continue to do so."

"Concern, sister dear?" Isabelle picked the apple off the top of the pile and took a bite, a long, satisfying crunch. "Has the loss of our parents mellowed you at last?"

Vara bristled. "I have always cared for my family."

"And always been exceptionally poor at showing it," Isabelle said around a mouthful of apple. "Not that I haven't appreciated the years of scorn through my attempts to cultivate a relationship with you."

Well, I'm here now, you spotted cow, Vara thought, but did not say. Instead, she said, "I appreciate your forbearance during my more difficult periods of interaction."

"That would be your whole life, dear," Isabelle said gently, "but nevermind that, I suppose. What brings you to me now? Not a sense of familial loneliness, I suspect."

"The war," Vara said.

"Of course." There was a flicker in Isabelle's eyes, tired, and the smile faded as she held the apple in her hand then gave it a look as though it had lost its appeal. "This war consumes everything, and the attention of all. So what of it? What do you need?"

"News more than anything," Vara said and let herself take a step closer to Isabelle. "How goes the front here? Is the Sovereign pushing his troops forward?"

Isabelle surveyed her sister with a demeanor almost more stoic than Vara herself could manage. "No. Not at present. Why do you ask?"

Vara considered for just the briefest space of time lying. To say something other than the truth might be preferable to letting Isabelle know, after all. But for Isabelle, it mattered little because—*she always knew anyway.* "We've been besieged. They surrounded our walls and threw an army at us—"

"The one that sacked Aloakna," Isabelle said wisely. All two-hundred-plus years of her sister's sageness were on display now, and Vara felt more than a rush of irritation. "Yes, that makes sense, revenge for Termina."

"Thank you for your insightful analysis," Vara said. "We broke them, of course—"

"Of course," Isabelle said with the trace of a smile.

"Oh, stop going on about it as though it were some sort of foregone conclusion," Vara said. "There were some fifty thousand of them, and our number is much reduced of late—"

"Why?" Isabelle asked, and took a walk sideways, eyes facing on a perpendicular line, as though she didn't even care to look at Vara. "Why are your numbers reduced while your star is on the rise? Even here, the talk is of Sanctuary, and your slaughter of Mortus. Killing a god?" She cocked her head at Vara, and smiled slyly. "No one even thought it was possible, let alone that you would be strong enough to attempt it and crazy enough to try."

"This is irrelevant," Vara said, stubborn irritation clawing at her. "Yes, our recruiting numbers were up, until the blockade a week ago, and yes, people had been streaming to us in record number for protection and to join us, but—"

"But Cyrus Davidon left," Isabelle said, stopping at a fold in the tent and pulling aside the fabric to look out, "taking an army with him, and vanishing over the Endless Bridge with both a strong corps of your best veterans and possibly your heart, should such an object exist."

There was a quiet in the tent, a silence and chill unadmitted by the opening of the side to the air. "You bitch," Vara said.

Isabelle let the fabric fold back on itself and fall free of her hands, letting the side of the tent close. "You have a quite the grasp of the human language, sister. There was a time when you were content to swear at me in elvish."

"I'm expanding my horizons," Vara said.

"You're in love with a human," Isabelle replied. "And you are not even willing to admit it to yourself."

"This is all off the table for discussion," Vara said. "Yes, Cyrus Davidon went on a mission to aid one of our guildmates across the Sea of Carmas. Yes, he's been gone for several months. I need to know if the Sovereign is moving because he—Cyrus, I mean—is in need of aid in Luukessia and we can't strip anything from Sanctuary's defense unless we're certain that the Sovereign's armies are fully engaged elsewhere—"

"They're not," Isabelle said quietly. "This front has been quiet for nigh on a month and not from any stinging defeats we've dealt to the dark elves, that I can assure you. Our contacts with the Elven Kingdom—on a daily basis, in case you wonder—indicate no serious offensives along the Perda, either, not at Termina or anywhere else. The Sovereign waits and has removed some of his forces from both of these fronts, reshuffling them elsewhere." She gave a little shrug. "Perhaps he directs them to the east, toward the Riverlands." Her face darkened in the shadow of the tent. "But I would suspect not."

Vara waited, just for a beat, before she asked the question that tore at her. "What do you suspect?"

"That the vek'tag herds in Saekaj that have supplied the meat that has filled the bellies of the dark elven army are running thin enough that they may not be viable if the herds continue to be killed at this aggressive pace," Isabelle said, without a trace of care, "and that the mushrooms and roots and other crops that grow in the gardens of those caves are insufficient to feed the war machine that the Sovereign is grinding out at present. That the supply lines run thin and he has turned an eye toward an easy, almost-undefended prize to remedy that problem—and its name is the Plains of Perdamun." She didn't smile, exactly, but gave her sister an almost-cringe, as though the knowledge caused her pain. "It is the opinion of the Confederation's government—and the Elven Kingdom's as well—that the Sovereign is moving troops into place to take the southern plains, to destroy anything that stands between him and the rich crop lands that could feed his empire and his armies, as we move now closer to the harvest."

"And Sanctuary is what stands between him and that resource?" Vara let the air hiss out of her, not really surprised but neither pleased.

"The fact that he can claim revenge for the action in Termina will be no small bonus," Isabelle said, "and there are countless dark knights in his army who had allegiance to Mortus, which might motivate them in some measure."

Vara tried to think through the swirl of new information filling her mind. "I have not nearly enough available—Sanctuary has not nearly enough available to counter this threat to the Plains. But you—" She took a step toward her sister. "If you and the Human Confederation attacked now, struck back at the Sovereignty's army here, it would force them to—"

"A good stratagem," Isabelle cut her off. "A worthy idea. Were I in charge, I would pursue that strategy, though not just to try and help my sister but to deny the Sovereignty something they need to continue the war." She drew up short. "However, I am not in charge of the war effort. Indeed, I am not even consulted. My guild remains at the mercy of the Council of Twelve, though," she drew a short smile, "thanks to other events, that power wanes by the day."

Vara felt the air go out of her, all her energy in one giant exhalation. "You tell me the Sovereign is marshalling his forces, pulling them away from the fronts he has pressed since the beginning. Well, they do not go north and they do not go west, nor do they appear to be heading east. My guild is south, is all that remains in the south. What am I to do, Isabelle? They hold the majority of the Plains already, uncontested because we lack the power to project our forces north to drive them back, and because no other army exists that could or would do so. I sit in the middle of the territory that he wants, this Sovereign, this gutless bastard who sits on the throne in Saekaj," she watched Isabelle's eye lashes bat a little at that, "and you tell me he's coming, and what am I to do?"

"I have seen your guildhall," Isabelle said carefully and took a step toward Vara, holding herself just slightly out of arm's reach. "With some ingenuity, with some effort, I believe you could hold out against any magic and any army that the Sovereign might throw at you. Especially with the numbers you describe, you could hold it indefinitely with supplies of conjured bread and water—"

"And we'll have nothing to help Cyrus with, and he'll die across the sea fighting some unholy scourge that will devour his stubborn arse whole and choke on it!" Vara felt the words come rushing out. "Of course it will end up gagging on such a large and ridiculously stupid morsel, but he'll be dead nonetheless." She felt it expelled, the hot flush it brought to her cheeks to have said it, and when Isabelle pulled out a chair and slid it invitingly toward her she sat down on it, heavily, and leaned her elbow on the table. Isabelle took the seat next to her, sitting almost knee to knee with her, the incense in the tent reaching an almost overpowering level, even though it had changed not at all since she arrived.

"So we come to the truth at last," Isabelle's steady blue eyes flashed at Vara; they were cooler than her own, more reflective of Isabelle's deliberative personality. "You worry about the safety of your guild, but you worry more about the fate of your—"

"Do not say it." Vara felt her hands come to her face automatically, as though she could hide her shame by covering her cheeks and closing her eyes. "I don't need to hear it aloud. Again."

"You fear for him." The words were calm and yet infuriating, as though they contained a slap to the face buried within. "You're afraid he'll—"

"Die, yes," Vara said, and the effusive heat came back, "that he'll die in that foreign land, that he'll be ripped apart by these creatures they sent word about, these things that were unleashed from the Realm of Death. I'm afraid that he'll stay in the fight long past the time when reason should tell him to bow out, because he feels guilty about letting them loose. Because of—oh, dammit!—because of me. Because he saved me, and because I sent him over there, practically drove him over there." She felt the burning of the words in her mouth. "Well damn it, damn them, damn him, and damn me, too." She looked up and caught only the faintest glint of amusement in Isabelle's face. "I don't wish to discuss this any further."

"No, I imagine you wouldn't." Isabelle averted her eyes for a moment and looked to the bowl of apples. "It hasn't been easy, has it? With Father and Mother gone?"

"I rarely went home," Vara said. "I barely notice, with all the things going on—"

"Oh?"

"Don't be irritating." Vara let the words come out seething. "I shouldn't say I don't notice. I might phrase it differently. There are many distractions, especially of late. When I think of them, I feel—" Vara rolled her eyes at her own weakness. "Guilty. I feel guilty for not paying homage to their memory. For not weeping in a corner. For feeling more distressed about the departure of some lunkhead warrior who will die in a mere century versus the loss of ..." A warm gasp came loose then. "They lived for thousands of years, and to come to such an abrupt—especially for mother—untimely, unexpected—"

"She fought for Termina," Isabelle said quietly. "She fought for you."

"She died for me," Vara said, meeting her sister's gaze. "It's becoming a pattern, people dying for me, killing for me, and consequences I don't care for spinning out of these actions. I should like it to end."

"There is only one end," Isabelle said, "and that has some rather definite consequences of its own that I don't think you'd care for, either. Those dead are passed, and only one of these people remains to be saved, and that is Cyrus Davidon."

"I can't save Cyrus Davidon," Vara said, and then felt her teeth grit themselves, her jaw tensing. "I can't send anyone to help Cyrus, not with the Sovereign making his move all around Sanctuary. If it is as you say it is," she shook her head. "My course is clear. I must defend Sanctuary. It is the higher duty to which I owe my allegiance. More than venturing overseas on some fool's errand to throw myself into another war." She straightened up in her chair and heard the creak of her armor plating as she did so. "I have enough war to cope with here in Arkaria."

"And if he dies?" Isabelle asked, and her fingers delicately touched the candle that rested on the table, letting the hot wax fall across her finger.

"Then he dies," Vara said, and ignored the screaming voice deep within, the one that wanted to throw her body to the ground and rail against it being so. "It will happen sooner or later anyway, there is little I can do to prevent that."

"You haven't asked my opinion," Isabelle said, rubbing a little wax between her thumb and forefinger, "but my prerogative now as head of the family is that I will give it, and it is thus—"

"Oh, good," Vara said under her breath.

"You should go to Luukessia. You will regret it if something happens to him and you are not there. It will haunt you all the rest of your days. You may not want to admit that your heart goes with the man, but it does, and I know you well enough to say with certainty that this torment will not end, not for you, not truly, if the worst comes to pass. It will only fade in time, perhaps, and become the ghost of a memory, rather than the full-blooded, all-consuming horror that it presently is, asserting itself all over your will."

"Your opinion is noted," Vara said, and stood, controlling herself enough not to knock over the chair with her ascent. "But I'm afraid that I cannot do what you suggest."

"Which is the greater fear?" Isabelle asked, and rose to stand as well. "That Sanctuary will fall to defeat and destruction by the dark elves? That Arkaria will fall under the heel of the great menace whose tendrils even now stretch out of the blackness of the caves of Saekaj Sovar and are entangling the rest of the world? Or that you, Vara, not only the last but the stubbornest of all the elves ever born, will lose someone that you value most in a place that you may never even laid eyes on?"

Vara did not speak, giving both ideas a moment to weigh in her mind, like heavy stones on scales, tipping the balance one way or another. *Cyrus or duty, duty or Cyrus?* She thought of her mother, and there was reassurance there, in the last words that she had said before she died, when they had talked. "I am elf, and my life is long, my sorrows great. I will hold to my duty because that will see me through all other pain. When all else falters, fails and fades away, my duty will not. I am paladin, the white knight. My life is a crusade, and my sworn duty is all that matters." She felt her hilt for reassurance, and watched

Isabelle's eyes follow the motion of her hands. "I'm not going to draw a sword on you, it's merely an action for emphasis."

"Oh, good," Isabelle said dryly, "though with you, it is hard to tell sometimes." Isabelle ran her hands over the white robes that she wore, still a pure color even here at the front of the battle lines. "Very well, you hold to your duty then, your crusade, as it were. Though I did think most paladins chose a more spiritual crusade, something nobler and more aligned with grandeur and changing the world—like evangelism, or serving the poor, or defending the weak. Something to inspire the soul and fill it with a billowing, all-consuming purpose—"

"All piffle," Vara said, and took the two steps to the entry of the tent. "Be as grand as you want in your inspirations, but most paladins fall short because they are all grandeur and nobility and little action on the ground. They say they want to free the slaves or evangelize or other rubbish, but then they do things on a daily basis that have little in common with their overarching goal. No, I glory in the small. Duty is a small thing and yet the largest. Every act on a daily basis that I use to serve my guild is a reward in itself, and leads me on to the biggest of goals—to serve my guild by defending it from harm. My crusade is the simplest, lowest, and yet highest and most manageable of all of them. No bombast, no bold proclamation, just simple service, day in, day out. And it is simple. All I need to do is get up and point my sword in the direction of the nearest threat, or pick up a shovel and begin whatever work need be done." She knew her eyes flashed but didn't care. *It is all that matters, the littlest things. The big ones can only be attended to after the small.*

"You've developed into a very reasonable person," Isabelle said, but she didn't smile.

"I strive for reason in all things," Vara said, and ducked to exit the tent. "Take care, sister of mine."

"I didn't say that was a good attribute," Isabelle said, and Vara froze at the flap, her back arched. She almost stood up, but the brush of the canvas ceiling against her hair was already ever-present. "You might try being a bit unreasonable in your thinking from time to time."

Vara turned back. "I might have been accused of being unreasonable from time to time, you needn't worry about that."

"Not an unreasonable pain in the backside," Isabelle said.

"Unreasonable in the sense of making a decision with your soft, yet-walled off and vulnerable heart rather than your thickly protected and indestructible head. There is a clear difference between the two."

"If there is," Vara said, and pushed open the flap to let the smell of the army camp outside wash over her, the faint foulness of the cooking and the latrines and all the bodies pushed together in this space, along with the warm evening air, "I can't afford to discover what the former might be saying and still expect to hold to my duty. And that, really, is the essence of the crusade right there, isn't it? A simple choice, and one that is already made."

"Take care," Isabelle said, "you and your choice. Take care that you don't regret that choice later."

"I am elf," Vara said, as she left the tent, and let the flap fall behind her. "My life is long, and my sorrow is great—and what is the weight of one more regret on the top of that pile in the grand scale?" She knew Isabelle heard her, even though there was no answer from within the tent. She ignored the trolls that flanked her on either side as she crossed back over to Ryin, who waited by a fire. She ignored the thought of that weight, too, consciously at first, but by the time the return spell took hold and carried her back to Sanctuary, she had forgotten it entirely.

Chapter 45

Martaina

There was something wrong in the air, something she couldn't quite narrow down. It was as if the breeze had shifted direction, and it carried with it an ill smell, something far away, something like death. She sniffed again, and it was faint, something dead, some blood, and it was too early and the woods too sparse for the camp to be getting fresh meat tonight. *And if we were, odds are better than good that I'd be the one providing it,* Martaina thought.

There was a stir as the expedition returned, Aisling at the fore with Terian, bound and gagged on a horse that she led. Martaina caught sight of Partus, further down the line, untethered, riding a horse of his own. "Before you left," Martaina called out to Aisling, who looked at her in return, "the dwarf was bound hand and foot, and Terian was loosed upon the world. You return and the dark knight is the one restrained."

"Does that make you curious about what happened?" Aisling asked, a sly smile perched on her blue lips.

Martaina sniffed the air again, trying to tune out the dull, pungent scent of people and focus on what she was scenting from upwind. "Not really."

"It's quite the tale," Aisling said, handing off her reins to one of the other rangers that Martaina had set to taking care of the animals. Mendicant hopped off his pony and took up the rope that was tied around Terian's bindings as he started to lead him off. "Filled with adventure and derring-do."

Martaina looked at the dark elf as she approached, the usual measure of thistles caught in her white hair. With another sniff, something else became obvious as well, something that was beyond the usual faint hint of cinnamon that Aisling used to freshen her breath, something primal and sweaty on her blue skin, something that wasn't usually there, in spite of the dark elf's self-proclaimed reputation. Martaina watched her evenly, not giving her much expression, though she knew that scent, would know it anywhere, as pronounced as it was. "And also," Martaina said, "filled with much sex with your General, it would seem."

Aisling's face didn't fall as expected, it almost flushed, near-aglow. "You can tell?"

"I can smell it," Martaina said, and went back to her quiver, checking each arrow in turn for splintering on the shaft, and fussing about every fletching.

"Smell what?" Aisling stared back at her.

"Him," Martaina replied, "on you. Every man in this guild has a unique smell when they sweat. His is faint most of the time, but after a long ride and strenuous activity, it gets more pronounced. It took me a minute to sort it out, because it smells like he might have been in a hot springs recently, and that sulphur really covers it over well, but no, it's there, it's obvious—oh, and his horse, too. Very different smell than other horses, and it clings to him like that thistle in your hair." She watched with some minor satisfaction as Aisling's face purpled about the cheeks, her race's version of blushing. "Don't fear; I won't tell."

"Much appreciated," Aisling said tightly, "I doubt our esteemed general would much like it if this ..." She searched for a word but admitted defeat after only a few seconds, "... this were to get out among the guild."

"Because his last two relationships were something he actively tried to hide?" Martaina raised an eyebrow at her and watched Aisling flinch away, the fingers of one hand touching her lips almost self-consciously.

"Ah, good to see you've returned," Odellan said, wandering in from the opposite direction. His smell was straightforward, clean whenever possible, just like him. *Not bad looking, either, for one so young,* Martaina thought. "Where are the officers?" he asked Aisling.

"Back at Enrant Monge," Aisling said, all trace of her embarrassment gone. "I believe the general will be along shortly."

The smell from the woods was stronger now, Martaina thought, something obvious about it, the blood. She hadn't heard anything, but that was hardly an indicator given that the camp noise was so prevalent. *I wouldn't smell anything either, but I'm here at the fringe, and the wind is just right.* "Somebody died," she said.

"Beg pardon?" Odellan looked away from Aisling, to her, and Martaina realized now she'd said it out loud.

"There's blood in the air, a lot of it," Martaina said with some chagrin. "I can track based on many factors, and that is one of them— one I don't talk about much, obviously. It's faint, but there, and it's a ways off, so that means there's a lot of it."

"You're saying—" Odellan began.

"Someone died?" Aisling asked. "No ... someone was killed, if there's that much blood." Martaina could hear the young dark elf, and the slow line of reasoning as she drew it out in her head.

"How close by?" Odellan asked. "After all, there are armies encamped to our east, north and west—"

"Somewhere between here and Enrant Monge, I think," Martaina said, sifting through it.

"Let's go take a look." Aisling's hand went to her dagger, resting on the hilt, palming it. "After all, it could be—"

Odellan whistled, and a few nearby warriors came trotting over. "Short march. I'll need a couple of rangers as well, as runners if need be. And a healer, so someone fetch one and bring them to catch up." He looked to Martaina. "Lead on?"

"Yes," Martaina said, and let her bow find her hand, and an arrow nocked itself. "Follow."

She didn't run through the trees, not exactly, but followed the path, the one that Aisling and the others from the northern expedition had come in on just moments earlier. The wind had shifted directions, now, and was blowing from the east. *I hope what we're looking for is on the path, because wandering afield on a search like this will be like trying to hit an apple at forty yards with a black hood on.* She smiled. *I can do it, but it'll strain me.*

The wind was fair but shifted again as they got closer down the path. It was all woods around them now, slight bluffs and rises on one side of the road. She ran along, her feet on the uneven path, the suggestion of rocks through the leather soles of her shoes. Hers gave flexibility but not as much support or protection. But neither were they as weighty as what the warriors wore, either, and she had to slow down to keep from outrunning the escort behind her.

The wind shifted again, and the smell was obvious now, close, a bend or two ahead in the road. Too many scents, mingled together to make a distinction about what she was smelling other than blood. The leaves whipped by her on either side, the string of her bow bit into her fingers the way it always had, the elven twine. It wasn't a problem and hadn't been in the thousand years since she first started to use it, but it was there, the pull of the string, just another feeling, a reminder to her that she was alive.

She came around the corner, a hard twist in the road just beyond a rise that blocked the view and there it was; blood, plenty of it, oozed out all over the road. The bodies were gone, dragged off, save one, the black armor so familiar that she knew the scent then, at least one of them. Martaina heard a hiss behind her as Aisling came around the berm, and she too saw what was there in the road.

The body was laid out, defaced in the cruelest ways possible, the head missing. The sword was still there, amazingly enough, and stuck in the body, which had been stripped naked, the armor left off to the side. It was still obvious, even so, whose body it was, being so tall and muscled as it was. She dropped next to it, felt the slide on the dirt road against her knees, as her fingers ran over the shoulder, as though she could offer the corpse some reassurance.

Aisling was across from her now, kneeling, not saying anything. There was a pall and quiet, the warriors who had followed them speaking only in hushed voices. It was obvious to them, too, who it was, and the rage and tension in the air was palpable. The words "The General" were bandied about, over and over, and she heard one of the rangers that had followed along running back to camp even as another ran down the road toward Enrant Monge.

"How long?" Aisling asked, jarring Martaina out of the long stare she had given the uneven cut around the throat, the place where the lifeblood was draining out onto the sand even now, aided more by gravity than the beating of a heart that had ceased minutes ago. Martaina looked up at the dark elf, who stared her down, and in the red eyes there was a fierce flame, as though the gates of the Realm of Fire had opened and all blazes had spilled loose into the dark elf's soul. "How long?"

"He's been dead ten, perhaps fifteen minutes," Martaina said as she felt the arm again. It wasn't cool to the touch, not yet, and wouldn't exactly cool in the warm summer sun. "It's possible that the head is around here, somewhere—"

"Unlikely," Odellan said, and he was standing over them. "If someone takes a head, it's either meant as spite to deprive them of resurrection or it's a trophy. It's not meant to be done just to kick it around a clearing." The elf grew thoughtful, his helm held in the crook of his arm, his usually dark, sun-kissed skin a bit white. "Not in an orchestrated attack like this."

"Hoygraf, then," Aisling said, and she stood. "Actaluere."

"That would seem the most likely." Martaina stood, the wind blowing a few grains of sand from the road across her face along with a few stray strands of hair.

"This is not an opportune time or place for us to make war on Actaluere," Odellan said, responding more to the sudden rumble that ran through the thirty or so warriors, armored and armed, standing behind him arrayed along the road and even up on the embankment. "Calm yourselves."

"I don't wish to calm myself," Aisling said, though she kept her pitch well under control. "I wish to find the bastards responsible and collect their heads for myself while returning his to where it belongs."

"This is not a moment for rash action," Odellan said.

"This is not a moment when we can afford to wait and NOT act, either," Aisling said. "We have less than forty minutes to find his head and have a healer reattach it or else he will not be coming back to life. I would have to guess that will put at least some kink in our efforts to defend Luukessia."

"We cannot simply charge into the midst of the army of Actaluere," Odellan said, "regardless of how strong our suspicions might be. What if this is some feint by Galbadien, some political game by the Syloreans? Or a simple, ill-timed and gruesome bandit attack?"

"This is about as likely to be a bandit attack as you are to sprout gills and start swimming about in the wellsprings under Saekaj Sovar," came a voice from the embankment. Martaina looked up, but not far; Partus stood there, a few feet above them, along with others now arriving, trickling in from the encampment as the news spread. The clink of chains heralded the arrival of Mendicant, Terian in tow. The dark knight's eyes flashed as he saw the body, but his mouth was covered by the gag and his expression muted by the cloth that covered half his face.

"What's he doing here?" Martaina asked Mendicant. She saw the goblin start in surprise at being addressed.

"I couldn't just leave him at the campsite," Mendicant said. "They're all heading over here, now. So I brought him along."

"He's probably getting a deep feeling of joy from seeing this," Aisling said, leering at Terian. The dark knight shrugged then shook his head. "No? Must be because you wanted the joy of doing it for yourself." She waited, and Terian looked at her knowingly then nodded once. "A finer friend I doubt he's ever known," she said, and touched the headless body with the toe of her shoe, delicate, almost a caress. "At least when he killed your father, he didn't know what he was doing, that he was harming you. His excuse was duty; what's yours? Spite?"

"Enough of this," Odellan said. "We need the officers, and we need them now."

"They won't be here for twenty more minutes," Aisling said, wheeling about on him. "By then it'll be too late to act. Do whatever you will, but I'm going to the Actaluere encampment. I'm likely to stir some trouble, and anyone who wants to come with me—"

"No," Martaina said. "You know he wouldn't want it. Not like this. Not a war without any proof, not a fight to no purpose. Odellan is right; we don't know for fact it is Actaluere."

"You're a fool if you think it's otherwise," Aisling said, her eyes narrowed. "But since you make mention of it, there were other bodies here and now they're gone. Why don't we simply follow the trail, oh skillful ranger?" She indicated the drag marks in the dirt of the road that led off the embankment, back up into the woods, with a sweeping gesture that was as much sarcasm as grandiloquence. "You know ... while we wait for the officers to appear and make their august rulings and decisions and whatnot."

Martaina wanted to slap her own forehead. *Of course. Follow the trail.* She didn't waste time agreeing or disagreeing, but instead sprang into motion, her feet finding purchase on the embankment as she followed the drag marks. It was a short jaunt, only a few feet, as the bodies were tucked into the underbrush, covered by a few pine needles and a couple of fallen branches. Their livery was obvious, and the smell of the fish and sea that was so dominant in the soldiers of Actaluere that she had met was present.

"The most obvious conclusion is most often the right one," Aisling said, and her daggers were in her hands now. "Actaluere soldiers, dead at the edge of Praelior."

"How can you tell?" Partus shuffled through the brush next to them, his head peeking out from just behind Martaina.

"Because some of these wounds look like something cut through them in impossible ways," Martaina answered, turning her head to look at him. "This one, for example—through the bottom of the jaw and out. You see many non-mystical swords do that?"

"Gold coin for the pretty she-elf," Partus said. "Looks like you got your culprits, you got your general fighting with them, and ... you've still got no head. You gonna ride out into their camp and raise havoc, or what?"

"Or what," came a voice from behind them, and the surface noise that was filling the air, all the soldiers, the low hum of conversations, was interrupted with the sweep of Curatio into the woods, silhouetted against the light coming from the break in the trees where the sun shone down closer to the road. His white cloak billowed as he walked, reminding her of the priests of Nessalima back in Pharesia, their robes just as loose as the healer's. "Windrider rode back to Enrant Monge in such a fit that the lad who tends the stables swore to me he had been possessed by powers of darkness heretofore unseen in Luukessia." The healer took a deep breath and his nostrils flared. "We have a dead general, we have no head, we have assailants from Actaluere, and we have more problems than we can safely count without an abacus." Nyad, J'anda and Longwell followed in his wake; the younger Longwell was flushed, his helm carried in the crook of his arm as well and his lance not with him.

"These are Hoygraf's men," Longwell said, heavy boots crunching in the greenery as he came to stand next to Odellan, staring down at the bodies. "Let there be no doubt."

"So now we know who took the head," Curatio said, "but we can't prove it beyond doubt, and that's a flimsy premise to start a war on now, when we least need to be ensnared in other conflicts."

"We already had a conflict with Hoygraf," Aisling snapped, "that's plain. We just haven't seen the end of it, yet." She spun one of her daggers, twisting it fast in her grip. "I mean to see it through though, even if the rest of you don't—"

"This will be fruitless," Curatio said, holding a hand up to forestall her. "Even if we rallied the army and ran down the entire Actaluere force, which—given their size and ours, would be quite the endeavor given the time constraint—there's still no guarantee his head is there, in their camp. They'd be foolish to be caught with it, after all—"

"He never was all that bright," Longwell said, "but proud, though." Heads swiveled to him. "Hoygraf, I mean. If Cyrus did take the Baroness's charms in the Garden again before we left," no one noticed the slight flinch from Aisling save for Martaina, "then that is the last in a long line of insults and woundings that our general has inflicted on the man. It's more than his pride can bear. He'll keep the head, and it'll be dipped in tar and put in a place of special favor so that he can keep it together for as long as possible."

"Well, that's the sort of fixation that's not grotesque and disturbing at all," J'anda muttered so low that no one else heard him.

"I'm not hearing solutions, and the clock is winding down," Aisling said. "So let me propose one—you don't want to send a whole army into the Actaluere camp because you don't think we should start a war now, fine. I'll go, and I'll sneak my way—kill my way to Hoygraf, if necessary—and retrieve the head." There was a dangerous glint in her eyes. "And I can do it, too."

"Far be it from me to suggest otherwise," J'anda said, "but we might benefit from a bit of guile instead. An illusion, perhaps, to ease your passage. Less sneaking, more walking through the middle of the camp without any questions."

"Then what?" Curatio asked. "Go to the grand duke's tent and ask politetly to see him? Ask for the head back?"

"Threaten him with the loss of his own as well as his manhood," Aisling said, still twirling her daggers. "I think he'll see the wisdom in parting with it." She paused. "The head, not his manhood."

"I don't wish to be crude—" Longwell said.

"That hasn't stopped anyone else," J'anda said under his breath.

"But at this point, the grand duke's manhood is inextricably tied to the head," Longwell went on, grimly, "though I know that your

Arkarian sense probably doesn't understand or wish to acknowledge it. Cyrus has castrated Hoygraf—not literally, I would hope, but in a figurative sense, through everything he's done, and the Grand Duke's actions are absolutely in line with trying to regain his power and pride, as it were."

"This is disturbing on so many levels I can't even count them all," Martaina said. "We have little time. You think he won't give up the head?"

"I think he'd rather die," Longwell said, "given the humiliations he's been subjected to by our general. Stealing the man's wife and having his way with her is well beyond the realm of embarrassment to be sure, especially since we all know—as he probably does—that she was with Cyrus more than happily." Longwell shook his head. "If you want the head back, he won't surrender it willingly; you'll have to kill or cripple him further."

"Done and done," Aisling said, and turned west, disappearing into the brush.

"Dammit," Curatio breathed, and Martaina cast him a look. "Go with her," the healer said, "J'anda, you too. Find the head, bring it back. I'll rally the army in case you fail."

"You're going to start a war over this, Curatio?" Partus said with muted excitement. "Ill-timed, but I admire that."

"To hell with your admiration," Curatio said. "I don't care what time it is; if our general dies permanently, I will make an example of the Kingdom of Actaluere that even the scourge won't find palatable." He waved his hand at Martaina. "Go."

She was off then and heard J'anda following behind, slower. She tried to match his pace, but the enchanter's sandaled feet didn't make for very fast travel and after a short distance, he said so. "I apologize, but this is going to be difficult." They ran along the southern wall of Enrant Monge, the castle's guards looking down on them from above on the battlements.

"It's not far now," she replied, and kept moving. "Just over that rise." She pointed to a crest of the rough territory ahead.

"You know these woods already?" J'anda asked, keeping up with her.

"I've been hunting," Martaina said. "What do you think the

likelihood is that Aisling will wait for us?"

"Low. Lower than that, even, maybe. What's lower than ground level?"

"Saekaj Sovar, as I understand it." She met his weak smile, and they kept on, her quietly slipping through the woods and him crunching in the underbrush as though he were unaware of the noise he was causing.

They came to the top of an overlook, and down below was a camp. Not quite as simplistic as the Sanctuary encampment, this one had clearly been used many times over the years. It was open ground, with latrines clearly dug, tents set up in lines and in a careful order. "Looks like the same type of site that the Galbadien army uses," Martaina said as the two of them hunched over in the bushes, looking down.

"Here," J'anda said, and his hand moved over her. The light around them shifted, and J'anda became a human, wrapped in the same helm and armor as the guards they had found dead in the woods. The enchanter regarded her carefully for a moment. "The illusion is perfect; you look like a man."

"Which is rather dramatically different for her," came Aisling's voice from behind them. Martaina looked to see the dark elf crouched only inches away, "Since that would doubtless scare off any of the five men she's slept with since coming on this sojourn."

Martaina felt her face redden, the heat coming to it. "You sound envious."

"Not at all," Aisling said, her face a mask, only the slightest edge of spite creeping out of her words. "I'm quite content with what I've got, and I'll continue to be content with it if we manage to finish this out."

Martaina shot a look at J'anda, whose hand was extended toward Aisling. A moment later, the illusion took hold and the dark elf was replaced with a dull-looking man of Actaluere, slack-jawed under his helm with its over-exaggerated nose guard. Aisling was off, down the slope with a cloud of dust trailing behind her. Martaina kept a careful eye on J'anda, who looked to her with a gentle shrug. "Five men?" The enchanter asked. "I'm envious."

"Because you weren't one of them?" Martaina asked, and felt the dryness in her mouth as she said it, the humiliation of her exposure.

"No," J'anda said with a dismissive wave, "because you could have been sporting and saved one of the men for me, at least. Two if you were feeling charitable."

She blinked at him, and he was gone down the slope in the moment after that before she had a chance to respond. She followed after, hoping the illusion worked hand in hand with the stir of dirt she was causing on the slope. She came to the end of it, the red dust of her descent caught up with her and overtook her for a minute, but she kept moving until it was cleared and she entered the edge of the tent city of Actaluere's encampment. She saw the man who she knew was J'anda, just ahead of her, but could only tell him by the dust of the slide on his illusory surcoat. Aisling, ahead, was not only dusty but walked with a slight, almost unnoticeable sway.

"Playing games, soldier?" One of the men she passed, stirring a pot of stew over a fire, shook his head at her. "This is how you know you've been too long idle; men start playing like bloody children."

She didn't answer, afraid of what the response would sound like, feminine or not. Instead, she followed J'anda, the trailing blue of his stained surcoat, and they walked on past the small tents of the army, toward the larger ones ahead, the tents of the commanders and even one, the largest—*for the King, surely*—which stood higher than all the rest and was crowned with a circle of pennants atop it.

The smell of food was present, all manner of it, and the latrines, too, as she snaked her way through the camp. Her bow was still on her shoulder, she could feel it with a touch, but it was invisible, no sign that it was there at all. She felt the weight of it too, though, slung where it was. The aisles between tents were clear enough, though men lingered outside in the summer sun, laughing, slouching, aimless in most cases.

The ground between tents grew wider as they drew closer to the King's tent. The gaps grew between them, the tents got bigger, and the spaces where men sat around fires were broader. *Fewer men around these fires,* she thought. *More elite.* There were no fires burning now, though, and few men, now that she thought about it. There was sound in the distance, though the sound of cheers or jeers, she couldn't tell.

Aisling had slowed her pace, and now Martaina and J'anda caught her, walking as a triad down the quiet, abandoned pathways between tents. "Where did they all go?" J'anda asked, casting his gaze left, then right.

"To wherever that cheering comes from," Aisling said, and the tension bled in her voice. "And likely where the head of our illustrious general is, too."

They came out of a cluster of tents and the sound grew louder. There was a gathering in front of the King's tent, where a wide space was cleared. Their view was obstructed though, and only the top of the massive tent was visible behind the last few large tents in the way. "Think they're having a party around it?" J'anda asked.

"If so, the celebration will be short-lived," Martaina said, and ran her hand onto her bow, checking to be sure it was still there even though she couldn't see it. There was blood in the air again, fighting now to be scented over the camp smells.

They emerged from between two tents and found the source of the cheering and catcalls. There was a courtyard of sorts constructed before the King's tent. A throne sat to one side, unoccupied, all done in brass but with places for poles to be threaded through so it could be carried on the shoulders of strong men, or placed atop a wagon.

It was not the empty throne that the crowd of soldiers of Actaluere were cheering, Martaina realized quickly. It was the woman stripped naked and tied to a post in the middle of it all, and the head on the top of the post. A flash of brown hair was obvious and visible, though it had been cut short, roughly—by a sword, she suspected—and the back was lashed and red with fresh blood from the shoulders to the buttocks and down the back of her thighs. The woman was on her knees, and the only proof Martaina could find that she was still alive was the steady, slow heave of her shoulders up and down with each breath, the rise and fall of her shoulder blades that put the lie to the idea that a human body could not take the punishment revealed on her skin.

"The head," J'anda said under his breath. "It's atop that pillar, where that woman is being ... ugh." He made a sound in the back of his throat, such utter disgust professed that aligned perfectly with Martaina's sentiments. She had seen worse tortures but few enough. Crimson stained the dirt all around the post, the ground ran red with the woman's blood.

"She's still alive, whoever she is," Aisling said. "Look at her—"

"I see," Martaina said tightly. "They've cut her hair, but you can see the old scarring; it's Baroness Hoygraf."

"Dear gods," J'anda said, staring as the woman turned her shorn scalp and revealed a face battered and bruised but still recognizable. "She was safe at Enrant Monge; how did they—"

"It matters not," Aisling said, and her tone was hard and uninviting for further talk. "We need the head."

"While we're here, we might consider freeing her as a kindness," Martaina said. "I, for one, wouldn't wish to experience another moment of what she's endured, not any of it."

"Where is—" J'anda started but cut himself off. "There he is."

From behind the crowd to their left, where he had been obscured from their view, came Grand Duke Hoygraf, his face waxy pale, and his limp pronounced with the cane he leaned on for guidance. His every step looked as though his abdomen caused him pain, though his face was already cut cruel enough into a scowl that it might not have mattered to his expression. He limped his way across the dirt, back to the pillar and his wife, the head of Cyrus perched atop, the lifeless eyes of their general bearing silent witness to everything that happened around them.

"If he starts to launch into a soliloquy, I'm begging you to send an arrow through his eye," Aisling said.

"If he does," J'anda said, "I might send an arrow to his eye myself. Hell, I might do it without him speaking. This is an atrocity. How a man could do such a thing to an enemy is beyond me, but his own wife?"

"Love and war are a thin line," Aisling said, "and thinner here in Luukessia than anywhere else I've seen." They stood at a distant edge of the crowd where it was less populous, but there were at least a hundred in attendance around the spectacle, and all armed with swords. "Can we win this fight?"

"Not by numbers," J'anda said, "nor by easy deception. My spells would be of limited use with this large of a crowd. I could sow discord, perhaps by charming some of them, having them attack others, but it would be a small few, say fifty or so. There is no chance I could mesmerize this many of them, nor that I could divert all their attention from the center long enough or with enough guarantee that we wouldn't be caught." He shrugged. "I don't think even an army marching into their midst right now would guarantee we wouldn't be discovered while freeing her, gathering the head and making our escape." He shook his head. "By the numbers, we need our army to finish this. Unless we all want to die in the process, in which case we might as well go now as later."

"No deaths," Aisling said. "Defeats the purpose. There has to be another way, and we only have a few minutes left, now. We need an opening, something to give us an out." The grand duke hefted a whip in his hand and lashed his wife twice across the back in quick succession, opening fresh lines just above her buttocks. "Killing him before we die would be awfully satisfying, though."

There was a stir in the crowd, something other than the ordinary jeers, and the grand duke stopped, and spoke. "See what happens? See what comes your way when you are wicked, deceptive, conniving, deceitful, and treat with our enemies?" He opened his arms wide in grand gesture, as if encompassing all with his motion, though he was careful to shift his weight so much of it still rested on the cane he leaned on with his left hand. "Be assured, we are a faithful enemy, and repayment of what is owed comes to all who give us cause." He gestured to the head on the pole with his right hand, and the sneer on his face might have been mistaken for happiness in another man, Martaina thought, but not on his.

"You ... promised ..." Martaina heard Cattrine speak, low, low enough that she was likely the only one other than the Grand Duke who heard. She caught the look on Hoygraf's face that told her she had assumed correctly, as the man hobbled over to where his wife lay on her knees, still bound to the pole, totally exposed, bleeding. The Grand Duke leaned down, as if to listen. "You promised," Cattrine said, gasping the words out in a low, guttural whisper, "if I submitted ... you would return his ... remains to his guildmates ..."

"So I did," the Grand Duke said, sotto voce; Martaina strained to listen, though the crowd had grown quieter, watching the Grand Duke in a seeming conversation with his battered and humiliated wife. "And so I shall." A knife appeared from the leather of his belt and cut her bonds. Cattrine dropped to all fours when released, unable to hold her own weight. The Grand Duke reached up and grasped Cyrus's head by the hair and lifted it off the pole, suspending it slightly over her, appearing to look it in the eyes for a moment before he dropped it onto her ravaged back, causing her to cry out from the pain of the impact. It rolled off and came to rest by her side. "Go on, then. I return him to you now, and you may carry him back to his fellows." Martaina could see the grin form on Hoygraf's face, beneath the dark, scraggly beard. "I think you have a few minutes left, so you might wish to hurry. If you can." He stood and the grin on his face told Martaina everything she needed to know. *He thinks there's no chance for her to make it in time.*

"He's letting her go," Martaina said, "with the head, to return it to Sanctuary."

"Why?" J'anda breathed.

"Some sort of bargain between them," Martaina said, and her fingers twitched, desirous to hold her bow, to feel the arrow knotted between her fingers, to let it fly and see it run through Hoygraf's skull. "Doesn't seem likely he intends her to actually be able to save him, though, does it?"

"We have minutes," Aisling said. "Barely time enough, if that. Every moment we wait brings him closer to permanent death."

"There is mercy in us, though, is there not?" Grand Duke Hoygraf had begun to speak again. "For a man of Actaluere, our superiority is nothing but obvious, and we can find it in ourselves to allow the fallen enemies to go back to their brethren, can we not?" He placed a boot on Cattrine's cut and bleeding rump and rested his weight on it, causing her to cry out. "Once we show someone their place, and they are convinced of it, is there any reason not to be a little generous? When they know the price of betrayal, can we do any less than reassure them of their place in the order of things?"

He pressed on her again with his hard-soled leather shoe, and Cattrine, who had been trying to get to all fours to crawl was forced to the ground again, and her screams of pain were almost too much for Martaina to bear; the bow was in her hand and an arrow ready to fly before she felt J'anda's hand on her wrist. "Hold," J'anda said.

"No time," Aisling said, and Martaina could hear the agitation in her voice. "He means to let the sands run through the hourglass before he lets her go, if even he does so then."

"WHAT IS THE MEANING OF THIS?" A voice crackled through the air as though a thunder spell had been unleashed into the midst of the gathering, and all the heads turned. A phalanx of soldiers emerged to their right from the main road through the camp, their armored boots slapping the dirt into a cloud, their deep-blue armor and surcoats those of Actaluere, but different than the Grand Duke's livery. In their midst was a man Martaina had not seen before, yet whose station was obvious by the amount of bodyguards surrounding him—

"Milos Tiernan," J'anda said, "the King of Actaluere."

"I figured that one out all by myself," Martaina said, and let the bow dip downward; the illusion made it look as though she were doing nothing more than holding a sword over her shoulder.

Tiernan made his way through his crowd of bodyguards to Hoygraf, who waited with an air of patient expectation, seemingly unworried. In truth, Martaina could smell the fear on him; the man had begun to perspire the moment Tiernan had spoken. Tiernan closed to feet from Hoygraf, who stood between the King and Cattrine, who was now up on all fours, one of her hands clutching Cyrus's hair tightly. "You mean to force us into a war?" Tiernan said under his breath, standing only two feet from Hoygraf now.

"No war," Hoygraf said. "You heard them; the Westerners mean to go to Syloreas's aid. And no war with Galbadien, either; my dear wife has pledged to return to me and has accepted her punishment—and more to come."

"Has she now?" Martaina heard a distinct frosting on Tiernan's inflection as it cooled. "I am certain she enjoyed your lash with all enthusiasm; but tell me, Hoygraf, what possessed her to accept your punishment, seeing that she was well free of your loving touch?"

"You would have to ask her," Hoygraf said, with a minimal shrug. "Love of her husband, perhaps."

"Trying to save my homeland, more like," Cattrine said from her hands and knees.

"We all have our own reasons," Hoygraf said with a further shrug. "She has received what she was promised and shall receive more in the bargain. Now she will return the head of Sanctuary's General to them, then come back to me, and war will be averted with Galbadien because of it." Hoygraf's teeth showed, evenly, far too polished for Martaina's taste, too white for the blackness of the man's soul. "And you can send your forces north to Syloreas to counter this threat that has everyone so worried."

"You know very damned well that western magic works to revive the dead for only so long after they've been killed." Milos Tiernan appeared to shake with this pronouncement, as he stared down Hoygraf, but still he kept his voice low enough that none of the crowd could hear. "You have killed him, which I would suspect would be an act of war in the view of the westerners, and stripped him of his head, and now you sit here, torturing my sister and letting time pass idly by. How long ago did he die, Hoygraf?"

"I hardly know," Hoygraf said. "An hour, perhaps? Perhaps less, perhaps a little more. It is hard to be worried about such things when you are striving to enforce richly deserved justice." He broke a little smile again toothily and pretended to wipe a bead of perspiration from his brow that was not even there.

"Now you expect my sister to return him to his people, in the condition you have rendered her to, before the allotted time runs out?" Tiernan's voice was steady, surprising Martaina. There was an edge of restrained fury in it, she could hear, but it was not raised at all. "You want this war, want to fight the westerners, want your revenge, do you?"

"I fear no westerner," Hoygraf said, and leaned heavier, both hands on his cane, but the smile was gone. "And certainly no silliness of the north from the Syloreans. Let them come, and we will break these western fools. Let Syloreas fall to whatever chews at it, and the army of Actaluere will deal with that as well."

"I need a courier." Milos Tiernan raised his voice now, so that the entire crowd could hear. Martaina had set foot forward before she even realized she had, stepping out of the circle of observers, crossing the ground between her and the post, where Tiernan stood facing Hoygraf and Cattrine. The voice went low again, but Martaina followed it as she approached them, the lone person who did so. "You are a fool, Tematy, and your war is direly timed. You are twice the fool if you think that whatever afflicts Syloreas will be easier to defeat without their aid as with it. You may have dominion over my sister now—to my eternal shame and dismay—but you do not rule my Kingdom. You do not declare war for me or take action that will cause me to have to fight after you provoke others into them." Martaina arrived at his side, then, and the King of Actaluere looked to her without any sign of recognition.

"Please take my sister and her … accompanying package … to the Sanctuary camp to the southeast. Ensure that she is able to return their general's head to them, but give them no further message." His face twitched. "Stay with her while she is there, and perhaps one of their healers will find it in them to ease her pain. Do you understand?" Martaina nodded, and Tiernan waved her off. "Be on with it, then, with all alacrity. Hurry."

Martaina knelt next to the Baroness, whose head snapped back at her approach and again as she wrapped an arm around Cattrine and pulled her to her feet. The Baroness's legs did not work, not at all, and she was dead weight as Martaina carried her along, half-dragging her to the edge of the crowd, which watched her. There was silence from behind her as Tiernan and Hoygraf continued to stare at each other, or possibly at her, and she could almost taste the bitter conflict between the men, burning hotter than the summer day around them, and with none of the occasional idle breeze to break it up. The quiet was oppressive in its own way, and every step she could feel the Baroness sag against her and the slippery, bloody, naked skin of Cattrine was slick within her grasp.

They made their way past the circled crowd, and J'anda and Aisling joined them as they passed. "I'll take this," Aisling said, and laid a hand on Cyrus's head. "I'll run ahead."

"No," Cattrine said, halting, her words choked with pain. "I need to get it to … Curatio. To the Sanctuary guild members."

"You have," Aisling said quietly, and Cattrine cocked her head. Her eyelids fluttered. "Let me take it, so that I can get it there in time."

"All right," Cattrine said, weakly, and relinquished her hold. Aisling, for her part, did not waste a moment—she ran, no stealth, no guile, and faster than Martaina would have thought the little dark elf could have moved, disappearing between the tents ahead of them in a flat-out sprint in the direction of the Sanctuary camp.

"I'm going to get you to Curatio," Martaina said to Cattrine. She could feel J'anda hovering next to her. "We need to get something to cover you, and we'll make certain you're healed."

"I'll give her my robes when we're out of the camp," J'anda said. "Take care with her, those wounds are …" The enchanter cursed, a word that Martaina had heard before, something in the dark elven language that was so foul it left a bitter taste in the air. "Barbarians."

"No doubt," Martaina said, hurrying along as fast as she could side-carry the Baroness. The tents around them passed in slowest speed. The soles of Cattrine's feet were red with blood and covered with dirt, which stuck to the crimson in flecks, dust holding in place from the stickiness. Every time Martaina tried to readjust her grip, Cattrine cried out; there was nowhere to hold the woman that wasn't hurt, oozing blood with her every motion. "I'm not certain she's going to survive the walk to camp," she whispered to J'anda and hoped he caught it.

"I will endure," Cattrine said. "This is not the worst of my husband's affections I have experienced, not by a very lot. I have saved him, and with him, this land, and that is all that matters." With that, her head drooped, and she fell into unconsciousness, yet no more of a weight on Martaina's shoulder than she was before.

Martaina exchanged a look with J'anda, and they hurried on, the trail left by the Baroness's feet dragging a line of red through the pale dust that followed them all the way back to the Sanctuary camp.

Chapter 46

Vara

"So they circle," Alaric said from the head of the Council table, Vara, Vaste, Erith and Ryin there with him. "The Sovereign needs food for his legions, and he turns his eye toward the Plains of Perdamun." The Ghost rested a hand on his helm, the peculiar, almost bucket-shaped helm. "They will not let us rest long, if their objective is to hold the plains for themselves. We would be like a knife perched at the small of their back, ever ready to strike at our leisure, destroying their caravans and tearing asunder their lines of supply."

"Not that we would do such a thing, attacking caravans and whatnot," Vaste said with a sense of irony.

"You're damned right we would," Ryin said, frowning at the troll. "This is a war, the dark elves are our enemies, and we would be fools not to toss as much chaos as possible into their camp."

"I was making a joke," Vaste said, straitlaced. "Bear with me, as I know it was the first I've ever made, so it may be hard to discern given my usual tendency toward the serious—"

"The Sovereign is right to fear us in this way," Alaric said. "As Ryin points out, our loyalties in this war were long ago revealed by our actions, and if they were to begin running shipments of grain to the dark elven armies in the north and west, we would be ill-brained not to cost them as much as we could, especially now that he has tipped his hand to reveal that he wants us destroyed." The Ghost shook his head. "And so we enter a period of consolidation and licking wounds on the Termina and Reikonos fronts; all that remains to supply his army for the next hundred years is to put his boot on our guildhall and apply the pressure until we are finished."

"Or so he thinks," Vaste said then shot a look around the table. "Right?" He looked to Erith. "Right?"

"Why are you looking at me?" Erith snapped. "Because I'm the only dark elf at the table?"

"Yes," Vaste said, nonplussed, "the same as if we were discussing something to do with trolls, I'd probably be the reference point."

"Well, I don't know what the Sovereign intends," Erith said with little restraint. "He doesn't run his plans by me, nor I by him. I left Saekaj when they opened the gates and allowed the exodus, and I haven't been back since. From what I know, he's vicious enough that yes, he would stomp us down if he thought we were even a slight threat. Just look what he did in Termina, and the elves were doing nothing more than passively supplying food and weapons to the humans."

"Not the happiest thought," Ryin said, "but what do we do? Can we take on whatever he sends our way?"

"Yes," Alaric said.

"No," Vara said after the moment's pause that followed her Guildmaster's statement. "Alaric, the dark elven army at full force must number in the hundreds of thousands, of which there are quite a few magic users. Not as many as we possess, to be certain, but a considerable number. We have something on the order of four thousand at our disposal, and even with the somewhat gross mismatch of our spellcasters to theirs, we are desperately outnumbered."

"Were we fighting on open ground in a great melee, that would be of greater concern," Alaric answered. "But we fight behind the walls of Sanctuary, which cannot be breached by magical means, and which we can hold nearly indefinitely against traditional methods of siege, as we have already proven." The Guildmaster drummed his fingers against the table. "We need only keep careful watch in the foyer and on the wall, so that any catapults, trebuchets, or siege towers are destroyed before they come close enough, and we will be fine."

"And if they breach the wall?" Vara asked.

"They will not."

"Your confidence is unfounded," Vara said, and she felt her blood go up. "They have magics, the same as ours, and they can be detrimental to rock and stone—"

"Which will be nullified by the enchantments that surround the wall," Alaric said with calm, his hand now at rest. "Should they heave a great exploding fireball at us, it will disappear before it hits anything."

There was a silence for a beat. "Well, that seems like the sort of thing each of us should be wearing on our persons," Vaste said. "All the time, you know, in case you're standing at a privy somewhere and a mean-spirited wizard hurls a lightning bolt at you."

Heads turned to him slowly. "Happened to you often, has it?" Ryin asked.

"Really, when you're handling your delicate parts, being struck by a lightning spell even once is quite enough to be getting along with."

"It is not the sort of enchantment that is easily carried with you," Alaric said. "It is rather more permanent, in much the same way as the alarm spell protects the grounds. It also has the ability to stop curative magics as well, which would be detrimental if you were, for example, stabbed by a blade and then someone tried to heal you." The Ghost shrugged, a motion that was, like the man himself, subtle.

"So what do we do?" Erith asked.

"We wait," Alaric said.

"But if you're that firmly convinced that Sanctuary is unbreachable," Ryin said, leaning forward with a passion that was not uncommon in the druid, "shouldn't we send another army into Luukessia to aid Cyrus? Isn't our duty to them?"

"Perhaps I have overstated my position," Alaric said. "I do not believe that they will be able to breach the wall or overwhelm us through an assault on our foyer at present with the numbers we have to guard the wall and our sanctum. To send another army to Luukessia, along with the number of spellcasters and leadership it would take to make any significant difference over there would leave us in a weakened condition here. Our defense would be tenable but also inflexible. The less force we have available, the greater my concern. As it is, we may be able to begin offensive moves against the dark elves should we find ourselves able to confront their smaller armies and do so piecemeal. Sending away another two thousand, which would be the minimum in order to be of any sort of assistance to Cyrus, would leave our cupboard rather bare." He shook his head. "In the event that they were to break our internal defenses or open the gates, that is not enough to mount a firm defense without resorting to ..." He drew quiet for a moment. "... measures that do not bear thinking about."

"Ooh," Vaste said with a childlike delight. "Tantalizing! Another mystery with no hope for resolution at any time soon."

Alaric favored the troll with a carefully measured gaze. "There is more to this place than stone and brick, my friend, and there is more to our guild than a simple roster of warriors, rangers, enchanters, healers, wizards, druids, paladins and that lone dark knight."

"We do have that rock giant," Vaste said. "Did we ever get him back?"

Alaric sighed. "I sent a druid after him; he should be back by tomorrow. But over-reliance on Fortin is a folly of its own sort. He can be killed; he is not invincible after all."

"Neither are we," Vara said. "Our defense should bear that in mind."

"Which is why I am not sending away another two thousand of our number," Alaric said with a deep sigh, "much as I might wish to aid our comrades. No, I am afraid they will have to make do with what they have, and we will re-evaluate should things turn worse." Alaric raised his hand to his cheek and leaned against it, his dark, weathered gauntlets pressing his tanned flesh white where the fingers lay. "And I have a feeling, given what our friends are up against, that even with our illustrious General at the fore, things will indeed get worse."

Chapter 47

Martaina

The walk was long and painful, even with J'anda to help her shoulder some of Cattrine's dead weight. Though she didn't wish to say it, she could plainly tell the enchanter was not nearly as strong as she, not nearly so capable of feats of strength, and so she suffered under as much of the woman's burden as she could carry. *At least she is only a healthy woman, not excessively weighty, as some are. Though now I wish she were Aisling; the woman is a twi, and would surely be much easier to carry than the Baroness, who was certainly well-fed if not well-treated ...*

The birds were chirping in the trees above her; they had hurried on, avoiding the slope that had required them to slide down before entering the camp. They took a half-mile detour that had them on the road, watching for any sort of traffic. Not far, by Martaina's estimate, was the place where Cyrus's body had been found. *Hopefully Aisling got his head back to them and in time ...*

They came upon the very bend, the place where it had happened. There was nothing there but a bloody mess to mark the passage of events, nothing to show but the disturbed dirt that was as readable to her as any book was to a priest—perhaps moreso, depending on the dialect of the ground. She could see footprints, the places where the Sanctuary warriors had trod, dragging something with them back toward camp. There were other tracks, too, fresher ones, smaller, more dainty, leading out of the woods. "Aisling brought the head back here," she said. "From here, I think they dragged his body back to camp. Though," she conceded, "with or without the head, I cannot say."

J'anda made no reply. The enchanter was thin, dangerously so. *Between her and me, we would be able to carry him along easier than J'anda and I laboring under just her weight.* To the enchanter, who was shouldering as much of the burden as his lean frame allowed, she said nothing.

The camp was in motion when they arrived, armored men moving about, the shine of the late afternoon sun catching on their armor, which was dull and unpolished after the long marches and recent idleness. She could smell the camp scent again. There was a quiet in the air, too. It was not as a meadow at midday to her ears (which was still quite loud) but neither was it as active as the camp had been before. The weight of the leather on her shoulders was nothing compared to the numbness setting in on her right arm where the Baroness had been perched for the last twenty minutes. Her mouth was dry and she craved water, but had feared to set Cattrine down not only for the woman's own health but because she wondered if she would be able to get her up and moving again should she stop.

"Ahoy!" The call took her by surprise, even as she walked past the sentries, one of whom was Odellan, whom she noticed late.

"Ahoy?" J'anda called back, struggling under the Baroness's weight, "have you gone nautical?"

"What?" Odellan said, approaching them. He reached out and took up Cattrine's weight, picking her up. She was wrapped in J'anda's outer robes, and the dark elf looked odd with only his tunic and pants underneath, both simple cloth and as close to the opposite of his rich red garb as possible. Odellan lifted the Baroness, cradling her in his arms. "I served on a galley on the River Perda early in my career."

"Oh, good," J'anda said, "for a moment I thought perhaps a career in piracy was in the offing."

"An Endrenshan of the Elven Kingdom would not stoop to such a low," Odellan said, adjusting the Baroness in his arms as he started through the small tent city of the encampment, Martaina and J'anda following behind. "Though another two months encamped here and this soldier might consider a pirate's life."

"Are you taking us to Curatio?" Martaina asked. Her mind was racing, her body fatigued, and she wondered how far away the healer was. *He can still fix her wounds, make her whole again ... physically, at least ....* "Did they manage to resurrect Cyrus?"

"I remain uncertain," Odellan said, carrying Cattrine against his mystical, shining armor, still polished even now, the carving in the breastplate filling the lines with blood from the Baroness. "I would assume a call would go up over the camp when the news made its way out, but I have heard nothing as yet." Odellan's already unexpressive face took a further downward turn. "Which, as you know, for an elf, is disquieting to say the least."

"It means there's likely nothing to be heard as yet," Martaina said.

"Aye." Odellan circuited the last campfire as they came upon a tent that Martaina knew had been used by the few healers who had come along on the expedition as a communal quarters. *Warriors bunk with warriors, for whatever reason, rangers with rangers, and wielders of magic flock together as surely as any fowl of the waters.* He didn't even duck as he pushed his way through the tent flap, Martaina only a step behind him.

The smell in the tent was horrible, blood overwhelming, more of it possibly than even at the scene of the attack, though it wasn't as confined a space. There was a lamp burning, too, and the oil helped cover it only a bit. The tent was long, at least twenty feet, and ten wide. There were three healers all huddled in the corner, and Martaina could see Curatio on his knees, between the others, who stood with their backs to the flap.

"We have another who needs help here," Odellan announced, and one of the healers, a human, sprang toward him immediately, leading the elf to the corner where he laid the Baroness down upon a flat bedroll covered in a thin white sheet. Martaina watched for just a moment and knew that however the sheet had started, it was no longer white.

"Did you manage in time?" J'anda asked, stealing Martaina's question before she could ask it. She held her tongue out of habit, realizing only now that she was the only non-officer, non-healer in the room save for those being healed. Ignoring the pain in her shoulder from carrying Cattrine at the distance she had, she was in fine condition—*especially compared to the man who lost his head only an hour ago. Oh, Vidara, let it have been less than an hour ago.*

Curatio's face was lined by the shadow of the tent, lit by the faint orange glow of the lamp. "It was in time." He ran a hand along his forehead, one drenched in blood that left markings in the lines of his brow. "Only just, I think, and because his head has been separated for some time, our healing efforts have been unable to fully repair the damage. Still," he took a breath and blew it out through his lips, which seemed to have lost all their color in the darkness of the tent, "he is alive, and well enough for now, though unconscious. I would not be surprised if he developed a fever over this, though."

"But he'll live?" Martaina let her breath hang in her lungs, as though she dare not chance to believe she had heard it correctly.

"He'll live," Curatio said, "but with a scar across his neck, I'd expect. A thin one but there, from what we weren't able to heal. It appears minimal, almost superficial, as I can heal somewhat more powerfully than most, but ... it is there. He'll need to travel in the wagon as we begin our journey north."

I saved him, Thad, Martaina thought. *I was faithful to my word ... in this way.* "Why are we moving the army north?" Martaina's surprise at the question coming from her was genuine; she had not realized she asked it until it was out. A feeling of giddiness had flooded her, blotting out the pain of her arm.

"The scourge is sweeping through these lands," J'anda said in answer. "It is ... a problem we must deal with for several reasons. Especially since Sanctuary and Syloreas will be the only ones to stand between it and the balance of Luukessia."

"You are wrong," came a voice from the corner. It was faint, but stronger than when last Martaina had heard it. She turned, and Cattrine was sitting up on the bedroll, Odellan and the human healer at her side. "Actaluere will send its army north to aid you. I have seen to it." Her face was still pale, white, and her eyes were sunken, as though she were already dead. *I have not seen a more haunted and beleaguered look on a face since the night Termina fell.*

"You were under the protection of Sanctuary, m'lady," Curatio said, standing from where he had been at Cyrus's bedroll. Martaina caught her first glimpse of the warrior; he looked almost normal, though his chest was bare and there was an accumulation of congealed blood about his throat. His chest rose and fell in a normal rhythm, though, and she felt her breathing return to normal and her focus shift back to Curatio.

"I no longer require it," Cattrine said and, clutching the fabric of the robes closer to her figure, she stood tentatively, reminding Martaina of a foal get to its feet for the first time. *Phantom pain, the searing agony that stays even after the flesh is knitted together. She is no doubt feeling it harshly now.* "I'll be making my way back to the Actaluere camp to rejoin my husband. Because of that, Actaluere will not go to war with Galbadien and my brother will be freed to send his troops north with Briyce Unger."

"What a complicated little web we find ourselves in," J'anda said.

"M'lady," Curatio said, with a faint, almost patriarchial smile, "there will be no healer for you next time, you realize this, yes?" His hand swept the length of her. "No one will be able to save you from your husband when next he puts the whip to you, and none of us will be close at hand to soothe the damage afterward."

Cattrine stared at him dully, then turned her back to him and let the robe slip to just above the small of her back. The other healers, humans, young—gasped at the scars, but Curatio managed to hold any reaction to himself. "I have never before had the luxury of protection from my husband, sir." She paused, and Martaina could read the regret and fear in equal measure hidden underneath the bravery on the Baroness's face. "And for the benefit of my people, that is a burden I will have to accept again."

Chapter 48

Cyrus

The world swirled about him, to and fro, and he caught glimpses of darkness and light in twain, lamps and the sun. Everything hurt from the neck down, and other times everything hurt from the neck up, but the divide was there, at the neck, and consciousness was a fleeting thing.

His mouth was dry, appallingly so, like someone had opened it and poured sand in until it ran over his lips and out, down his face and off his chest, leaving everything scratchy and dusty. He could smell old, dried blood, that more than anything, but oil was in the air, too, and fire, and other smells, familiar ones, like plants or an ointment, and moldering flesh. Faces blurred in front of him, forcing him to thrash about. He felt pressure on his arms, saw Martaina before him, and Aisling, Curatio at least once, but they were gone again a moment later.

"He has a fever," Curatio's disembodied head told him. The words echoed through the dark space he was in, like booming words lit out of the clouds and born on thunder.

"Searing hot to the touch," Aisling said, but she was not disembodied at all, he could see her plainly, see her naked, her dark blue curves hidden in the shadows around him, suggestive, and he took a deep, gasping breath as he looked at her.

"Is he awake?" That was Martaina, and he saw her as well, but she was headless, just the green cloak and attire of the ranger was visible, only a flash or two of a head being where it was—*where it SHOULD be, dammit.* "His eyes are open."

Cyrus could feel his eyes, too, and they were crusty, like someone had dropped stones in the corners of them, and no matter how much he blinked or rolled them, he couldn't get them out. "... pebbles ..." There was no answer from any of the three of them to that, even though it made perfect sense to him somehow, just that one word. Wasn't it a perfect way to describe everything that was happening?

It felt like a day passed, or possibly an age, or maybe only a few minutes. It was brighter now, a lamp overhead shining. The sand was everywhere, the dust, encroaching, filling his eyes and face. It was just like the last time, exactly like it, and Cyrus was suddenly six again, and very, very far from home, if ever there had been such a thing ....

"The Arena is where you will learn to fight," the Society of Arms Guildmaster told him, him and a half a hundred other strays and orphans, all his own age. Most were smaller than him, he thought as he looked over the crowd. A few roughly the same size. None bigger. "Where you will face your fears and put them to death. Where you will learn to serve Bellarum and the needs of war." He was a big man, the Guildmaster, and he spoke from the far entrance. The entire thing was sand, sand around the feet, all the way to the edges. One might have expected something like the coliseum, a place he had been once with Mother, but it wasn't; no stands around the edges for spectators, just a single, boxed enclosure where the Guildmaster stood with the other adults—a man in a white robe, and two others in armor.

"Fear is weakness," the Guildmaster said, his face knit with scars on each cheek and rough skin on his forehead. He looked older than Mother, older than the man who had brought him to the Society, but beyond that, Cyrus couldn't tell his age. "Weakness is the sum total of all your flaws, all your faults, all the things that can get you killed in battle. We purge weakness here; we don't coddle it. If you fear something, face it down. Run it to the ground. Beat it out of you." The Guildmaster looked them all over, and there was nary a flinch from him, though Cyrus heard the sobs from some of the others. "If you fear to be hit, then you'll need to face it. Many of you wish to go back to your comfortable places, even if those places are the streets. You won't find comfort here, because comfort is weakness."

With that, the Guildmaster left the enclosure and walked into the arena; some of the crying subsided, and Cyrus could hear the soft crunch of the sand against the Guildmaster's metal boots, his steel armor scuffed with age. Cyrus wanted to cry, could feel it, but his tears were already gone. More than half when Father died, all the rest when Mother went. He was as dry in the eyes as the arena floor, dusty but wracked with emptiness. He'd gone along when the big man—Belkan was his name—had led him here; after all, with Mother gone, what else was there?

Cyrus looked to the boy next to him, who wore rags, browned and barely covering him. It was winter now, and cold outside. How could one not be cold out on the streets, wearing something such as that? The boy's eyes flashed at him; he was one of the ones that was Cyrus's size, one of the very few, and his brown hair was over his eyes, long, unlike Cyrus's short cropped bangs that barely touched his forehead where his mother kissed him every night—or had, before—

"Fear is weakness," the Guildmaster said again. "It is in your nature to be weak. We will make you men—or women, as the case may be," he said with a nod toward two girls who were in the front of the crowd of children. They weren't crying, Cyrus thought, oddly, though he heard other girls crying among all the boys sobbing around him. "Breaking fear is nothing more than looking it in the eye and spitting in its face, finding your courage, and daring it over and over again. Pain is nothing to fear. Pain only hurts. Battle is nothing to fear, because it brings only pain. Commitment to your cause will draw out your fear, excise it, take it away. You must subsume yourself in the cause of war in the light of battle, and learn to love the draw of combat. The crack of bone and hand, the slash of sword and steel, the rending of flesh with axe, these will be your daily prayers, the things that you commit yourself to, to draw out the fear. I can make you fearless."

The crying didn't stop at that, it seemed to get worse, but Cyrus felt the little flecks of dust fall out of his eyes and he realized for the first time that *that* was what he wanted, what the Guildmaster had offered. He had cried when he had learned that Father died, cried hard, and even worse after Mother, though for a shorter time. He had stayed with the neighbors, though not for long, until Belkan had come for him. All that time he had felt the gnaw of fear, felt it chip at his bones, awaken him in the night when the tears had come, felt it eat him at him like it would someday come and take him whole, drag him off into the night where he would never be seen again.

"Who among you," the Guildmaster said, "wants to be fearless?" The words echoed in the arena, over the sand pit, and there was silence apart from the sobs, a quiet that settled among the crying children, all so far from home, wherever that was to them.

Cyrus felt his hand go up, as though it were out of his control. It went up above the others, the first, a silent flag to mark his surrender—and his desire to be free of the fear—once and for all.

Chapter 49

Vara

The Council Chamber had emptied quickly after the meeting, as though everyone had other things to deal with, other urgencies to be handled. Erith and Vaste, she knew, were both balancing the responsibilities of the Halls of Healing, keeping it running while Curatio was away. She wondered if Ryin had even set foot in his own quarters since returning to Sanctuary to find it under attack. Alaric, however, remained in his seat, as though carved out of the same material as the chair, not a Ghost at all but a mountain lain down in the middle of the room, growing out of the stone floor. His head was bowed and his helm lay upon the table, as it always did. A kind of darkness enshrouded him, like the clouds that hang over a peak at midday, hiding it from the view of the world, and she could tell naught about his mood or intentions save that they were present and as hidden as the man's face usually was.

"You have something on your mind," Alaric said, breaking the silence between them, his eyes not finding hers but remaining fixed on the edge of the table.

"Always," Vara said, not sure where she found it within her to be even slightly smartass. "It's the peril of thinking, you know."

Alaric did not smile, did not return hers because she did not have one to return. "What is on your mind, lass?"

"You've proven to have an uncanny knack at guessing what sort of things might be on the minds of others." She shifted her hands to her lap, letting the steel gauntlets clink against the metal of her greaves. They were like a second skin by now, she had worn them for so long, but in moments such as this, they found ways to remind her, subtly, that she was different than even many of the women of Sanctuary. "So why don't you tell me ... what is on my mind?"

Alaric let a long sigh, his head settling back down to look at the edge of the table rather than her. "Your mind is on Cyrus, in Luukessia—"

"My mind is on our guildmates," she said hotly, "facing the consequences of our mistakes, in a foreign land—"

"One of whom is our General," Alaric said calmly, "a man with whom you are developing a somewhat tangled history, even if you don't wish to admit to it." She didn't bother to interrupt him again, but she felt the burn all the way up to the tops of her ears, which was enough to tell her that her pale face was, by necessity, flushed. "You needn't bother denying it, and nor do I care. I did not allow Cyrus to casually disentwine himself from admitting his feelings for you, even when he didn't want to, and if you want me to speak your mind for you, don't pretend to be offended when I speak to you what is truly on it. Yes, you worry about our troops, and our guildhall, and Sanctuary, but your emotions sweep you, old friend, and your emotions—the ones you don't care to admit—are so loudly proclaiming your thoughts for the man in black that I cannot ignore them in favor of anything you might say."

"It is my fault, Alaric." She heard the echo of the words in the silence, even though they were no more than a whisper. "We went to the Realm of Death for my people—to save my people, to find out why Mortus wanted me dead. And he killed the God of Death—"

"I killed the God of Death," Alaric said, and there was menace in his voice, "lest you forget."

"But Cyrus threw himself in the path of Mortus." Vara's head was up now, and she stared down the Ghost. "I should have died there, and none of this would have happened. But he threw himself in front of Mortus and cut the hand, and we fell upon the God of Death like crows upon a piece of carrion. If he were still alive, Luukessia would be ... I don't know, not being overrun by these creatures. We're responsible ... I'm responsible, Alaric! It's my fault." She felt the strong emotion, and it caused her to shut her eyes, to cover her face with her hand. "It's all my fault."

"Because you made him love you?" Alaric's voice was oddly distant, and Vara looked through her fingers to see him on his feet, back to her now, facing the window and looking out across the plains. "Because you forced him to defend you in your time of need, follow you when Mortus's assassins pursued you, and try to save you when you had lost all hope?" Alaric still did not look at her. "Yes, I can see how this is entirely your fault."

"I know it sounds absurd." She rose from her place at the table but did not move closer to him, merely stood, as though she were a child in the Holy Brethren again, answering an instructor's question. "But it is so, that his …" she struggled with the word, "… feelings for me, they caused him to act, to set things in motion, and what I did afterward sent him over there, where our people face … whatever those things are."

"A scourge, I believe they call them. And a scourge I believe they are."

"How do you reconcile a thought like that?" She let the words hang before asking her next question. "You said you killed Mortus, and I suppose you did, struck the final blow. But we all killed him together, all of us, and you may have struck the last, but Cyrus struck the first, and he did it in my name, for me, binding us all together in some grand pact that has unleashed untold hell upon people who I had never even heard of until this last year. How do you … handle that? How do you not let it weigh upon your thoughts every waking moment of the day? How do you live with the idea that someone so dear and frustrating and annoying and noble and fearless is facing the consequences of what you've wrought, that they could die so far from home, and never return to …" She almost coughed, overcome with annoying emotion. "How do manage that, Alaric? How do you bury that and get on with things?"

The Ghost was quiet, his broad shoulders almost unmoving beneath his armor, his silhouette against the shadows of the evening sun outside. "I don't know that you can, lass. What I would advise … is that you recognize that what is past is past, and that no amount of agonizing or wishing will change the outcome of that day in Death's Realm, and that no excess of cogitation will change what happened that night in your quarters. No matter how much you think and dwell and wonder, no other outcome will make itself known but what has happened." Alaric's hand reached out to the window and he touched it, the fingers of his metal gauntlets clicking against the glass, as though he were trying to touch the orange sky beyond. "You can scarce change the past or what has gone before. All you can do is dwell in the moment, and work to change the course of things from here on." He turned his head to look at her. "That is what I would advise."

"Is it?" Vara asked, and she let her fingers clench inside her gauntlets. "Then why is there a pall over you, Lord Garaunt? Why does it seem that darkness has settled on the Ghost of Sanctuary, and that the ephemeral Guildmaster seems weighted down even more than he has ever been before? If dwelling in the past does not change the course of things then why are you still there, every day, every night, and letting it own you, become you?"

Alaric made no reply at first. "It would seem that I am not the only one for whom an uncanny knack for guessing the minds of others has become a standard. I said that the advice I gave you is what I would advise. I did not suggest that it was in any way what I, myself, was doing."

"You think about it, too, don't you?" She left the table behind carefully, walking toward him, halting a few paces away. "It is on your mind, always, what has happened, what we allowed to happen, by our actions and inaction—"

"Yes," Alaric said, and his head went back to the window, which his hand had never left, still touching the glass. "It is a ... difficult thing to lose guildmates. When we lost Niamh, I was once again torn with indecision. We have lost several in the last few years, and that is to be expected, normal attrition for a guild of our size and the way that we run things. But Niamh ... was precious. She had been here almost since the beginning of Sanctuary, twenty-odd years ago. To see her lost, not to some raid but to a deliberate attack by an assassin, was wrenching. I questioned myself in ways that I had not in years. Not since ..." he shook his head, "... Raifa. For everything that followed, that led you and Cyrus into peril at Termina, that took you into war—every single thing that happened—I questioned my choices, my thoughts, the distance that I had allowed you to operate at. And even though there was not a single thing I would have done differently than either of you, from the moments before Niamh died to the night on the bridge when you held off an empire, I still questioned. Even in Death's Realm, when I tried to bargain with Mortus, I wondered in the moment if sacrificing one guildmate in order to save the rest was the right choice." He bowed his head and his hand came free of the window.

"The truth is ... I was relieved when Cyrus jumped in front of Mortus's hand. I wished I had had the courage to do it myself, to die so that none of the rest of you would have to. I was relieved because his courage spared me from the cowardice of consigning one of you to death, to making the impossible decision of entering battle with a god or letting one person die as a sacrifice. Cyrus made the choice I couldn't find it in myself to disagree with. He spared your life, and ..." Alaric's eyes found her then, "... and I was glad, glad that the God of Death died that day, because the alternative would be to lose you, and that would be ..." He did not finish.

"So it weighs on you, too," Vara said, though she did not touch him, did not so much as place a hand on his shoulder. It would be unseemly, somehow, between the two of them. There was always much unsaid, and Alaric was no more profligate with his touch than she was; *two distant people, so bizarrely different than someone such as ... say, Niamh.*

"It weighs on me," he said. "But it need not weigh on you if you should follow the advice I give you—"

"Rather than the example you set for me?" Vara felt the taste of the irony on her tongue, and it was not to her liking. "That should be the first time, I would think."

"I rather suspected you would not listen, preferring instead in your infinite stubbornness to do things your own way," Alaric said with a note of melancholy. "Or my own way, if you prefer."

"Stubbornness is hardly a quality reserved for the officers of Sanctuary," Vara said, "but if I may boast, I think we bring it to such a level that few could ever hope to master it in the way we have."

"True enough. But my counsel is sound; if you would heed it, you would agonize less."

"And you would agonize just the same," she said. "And I would still ..." She shook her head as though the mere action could cleanse the bitterness from her palate, "... worry. About—"

"Him." The Ghost's crisp use of the word sounded like a shock in the quiet. "As do I. I worry for all of them, but should the General fall, Curatio will surely evacuate the rest. He is reasonable in that way. Cyrus, on the other hand ... does stubbornness with a skill and effort that even I can admire." He looked back at her, sidelong, with a hint of a smile. "You truly do know how to pick them. You and he are matched horses, unbroken animals that are unlikely to ever be cut loose of your maddening habits of pride and—"

"Yes, that will do, thank you." She eased closer, and took up her place next to him, on the other side of the double doors to the balcony, at the window opposite. She looked out across the sunlit plains, the grasses set to fire by the sunset, the horizon showing the first sign of purple. "So we wait. And dwell on our every previous bad move."

"We wait," Alaric said. "Because we all have a duty—he to his part, us to ours." He let the quiet infuse the air, the stillness of the coming dusk settled over the Council Chambers, and the sun dropped a few degrees in the sky before he broke the silence again. "They'll be coming, you know."

"I know," she said. "When?"

"Soon," Alaric promised. "The Sovereign will not wait. And for all my bravado in Council, you should know—they may yet break us. He will send ... almost everything at us, here, because the future of his war depends on it."

"Then I suppose we'll have to break him. His army. His war." She said it more certainly than she thought it, as though Alaric's confidence had made its way to her, and they had reversed their roles in the minutes since the meeting ended.

"I suppose we shall," he said, and lapsed into a silence that carried them well past the time when the sun sank below the horizon, and the room's torches and hearths lit themselves, and they could no longer see anything out the windows but darkness and the reflections of themselves in the glass.

Chapter 50

Cyrus

"So you want to learn to be fearless?" The Guildmaster smelled of sweat and leather, as Cyrus's own father had. "You want to know what it feels like to be empty of all dread, to be free from worry, to unconcern yourself with that gut-ripping, heart-rending sensation they call fear?"

Cyrus's hand wavered in the air, his six-year-old, thin arm quivering from being in this strange place. "Yes," he said, quietly.

"What was that?" The Guildmaster asked again.

"Yes, Guildmaster," Cyrus said, louder this time, adding the honorific because adults liked that. He knew they liked that. Belkan had told him so.

The Guildmaster towered over him, his six-year-old self, Cyrus realized, dimly aware that this was not him now but years ago, a strange divide in his consciousness between the awareness of memory of how he thought then and how he thought now, whenever NOW was. The man's armor was scuffed from use, yet the polish was there, impressive in its way, and his gauntlets were stiff, as though his fingers were locked into position all in a line. "What do you fear, Cyrus Davidon?"

Cyrus blinked, uncertain. How did one know what they feared? There were so many things, so very many … they hung out there, a thousand ideas just below the surface of his mind, things that he could snatch at but that wisped like vapor when he made to grab at them, to seize them and put them into the light where all could see. "I … I don't know, Guildmaster." *Maybe if I add the title he won't be mad at me for not knowing …*

The Guildmaster's face honed in on him, watched him, but there was no malice there, Cyrus thought, no anger. "It would be hard indeed to eliminate fear when you cannot even say what it is that you are afraid of."

"My father," came the voice to Cyrus's right. He turned his head, and saw the boy with the brown hair, the unkempt and bushy hair that grew long, and his hand was raised too, though for how long Cyrus was uncertain. "I fear my father. When he had too much to drink, he always came after me—"

"Good enough," the Guildmaster said. "You fear your father, Cass Ward?" The man took a step toward the boy named Cass, and Cyrus watched him go, turning away, and he felt regret for not knowing the right answer straight away, felt the burn of shame for being too embarrassed to name his fear, to shout it out loud and look it in the eye the way the boy named Cass had. "You fear your father because he hit you?" Cass nodded, eyes disappearing under the mass of hair. "Because it hurt?" Cyrus watched the Guildmaster, wondered if he was going to hit Cass, as though there were some lesson in that. "A reasonable fear for a normal person. Pain causes fear. You fear pain, it paralyzes you, holds you back, keeps you from giving it your all in fight. You feared your father because he was bigger than you, stronger than you, could hurt you and cause you pain." The Guildmaster stood over Cass now, and Cyrus saw the man's hand come down on Cass's head, not to hurt him, but to rest in the boy's hair, and the Guildmaster gave him a slight mussing, as though in affection. "Good on you, boy, for admitting it. Fathers can frighten, no doubt. But you fear them because of the phantom of pain. I will teach you not to fear pain. I will teach you to make the pain your own, to live in it, to turn it against those who would use it on you, who would seek to make you fearful—and to make them fearful instead. There are worse things in life than pain."

The Guildmaster looked over the crowd. "This is the Society of Arms. I teach the art of war to those who want to learn. I will teach you how beat your enemies, to make them fear you. I will teach you to purge this weakness, to exploit it in others. I will make you brave and fearless—at least those who want to learn. Some of you are fearful even at the prospect of what I have said, of living in pain to overcome it. You won't last very long." The Guildmaster walked back to the enclosure at the far end of the arena, where a healer waited for him, the white robes the brightest color in the room. "This is the path of the bold, the brave, the strong. This is the path for those who will fight fear to its natural death, who will pass through the fire and come out fearless." The Guildmaster looked over them again, the half a hundred. "And we will start to determine who those among you are … right now." He clapped his hands together, gauntlets ringing their metal chime, discordant, across the pack of children who waited. "This is your first test. Are you ready?"

There was still muffled crying in the crowd, a few sobs here and there, but most of it had ceased in the course of the Guildmaster's speech. He looked at the boy called Cass, saw Cass looking back at him from beneath his mop of hair, and felt his voice join a very small chorus of "Yesses." He knew, instinctively, that Cass's voice was in there, too, even as he saw the boy's head nod and his lips move.

"Very well, then," the Guildmaster said, and then raised his voice, the low guttural, reassuring sound turning harsh and discordant. "Then you will fight amongst yourselves until there is only one of you standing ... and we will judge which of you will remain, will learn to be fearless ... and which of you will spend the rest of your lives living like an ordinary person ... in all the requisite fear that brings with it."

Chapter 51

Cyrus found himself moving before the Guildmaster had even finished speaking. He heard the words, absorbed them, but after the command to fight, nothing else needed to be said. Belkan had told him what the Society was, after all—it was to learn to fight, like his father had fought the thrice-damned trolls. That meant hitting, it meant swords, it meant fists. He'd fought his father—wrestled, more like—trying to knock the man down to little effect. But his father was big, tall, muscled, could lay him out with a single swat—not that he ever would do that, but he could, and Cyrus could feel it. He'd fought with other boys his age, too, though, clumsy, uncoordinated fights, miming the things he'd seen the drunks do in the alley outside the Rotten Fish, the tavern just down from his home. Punches, kicks, biting—he'd seen a dark elf lose an ear that way, once, seen blood come down the face of another man and seen a dwarf kicked so hard in the groin that it looked as though his pants came up to his chest.

Cyrus head-butted the boy next to him, remembering what his father had told him about using his skull against the soft part of a face. His father had meant it as advice in case he'd been about the market and someone other than a guard had tried to take hold of him, but he used it now and watched the blond boy next to him, who was already near to tears, fall to the ground, his hands on his face and his low sobs turned to a high whine. Cyrus moved on, but the boy was already still. The child next to him was not as tall as Cyrus, and Cyrus jabbed the heel of his hand into the boy's nose and felt pain shoot through his wrist from the impact. This was near to a punch, and his father had taught him how to throw a punch, a good one, straight on and with his weight behind it. The boy on the receiving end fell to the ground sobbing, too, just like the last, and Cyrus wondered if he was doing well, if the Guildmaster would teach him how to be unafraid if he knocked them all down. *And if they get up, I'll knock them down again until they don't.*

He kept on, the sobs and wails growing louder and more persistent. He saw other boys, too, making their way through, knocking down the ones who stood dumbfounded, almost as though they were prey. It wasn't just the larger ones, either; Cyrus saw the two girls at the front, the ones the Guildmaster had nodded to, and he watched them both tear into a larger boy with a flurry of kicks that brought him to his knees.

Cyrus saw two come at him, both just a shade smaller than him, and he dodged the first and put a fist in his face. Blood trickled down the boy's lip, but he only flinched a little. Cyrus hit him again, then again, and felt a heavy blow land on the back of his head, with enough impact to send him sideways. He staggered, came back up with his hands in front of his face, and lashed out with a foot to the nearest one's leg. He tripped him sideways, leaving Cyrus to look at the other one, the one with a bloody nose. Cyrus leapt after him, caught him with another punch, then another, until the boy curled into a ball and Cyrus moved on, back to the first, whom he hit twice before the boy yielded, shaking where he lay.

"Enough!" came the voice, the call, over them, and what motion there was halted, all save one—Cass, the boy had been called, and he was pummeling another, hitting him in the face over and over. "I said enough, Ward," the Guildmaster called again, and Cass stopped his assault.

The Guildmaster and the others came out of the enclosure now, down the five steps to the arena's dirt floor. There was a wide gate opposite them, and it opened now, and a few men came out, waiting in a huddle behind the battleground, where at least forty of the fifty that had started lay on the ground, a few unmoving. "This was a good showing by some of you," the Guildmaster said. "A good showing indeed. Some of you have the seeds of fearlessness within you, the roots to grow mighty and strong in the sight of the God of War. Others ..." he touched one boy who was curled up with the toe of his boot, not hard, but the boy whimpered anyway, "... others of you will find paths more suited to your ... tendencies, shall we say?" He pointed to a few of the fallen, including the two boys Cyrus had just downed, and whispered to one of the armored men at his side, a painfully thin one. The other, a dwarf with a face that was all jaw and beard, shook his head a few times during the conversation. Their healer was already moving about the children on the floor, using his magic, mending wounds, sending some of them on their way, out the gates, where Cyrus could see other men waiting for them, herding them like the cattle he'd seen run through the streets of Reikonos in the past.

"Fifteen," the Guildmaster said, finished with his talk with the dwarf and the thin man. "Out of fifty-four, I'll have you know. That's how many of you will be inducted today. Twelve years from now, when your training is complete, perhaps five of you will remain. That is the way of things here in the Society of Arms. But don't think you'll be safe simply because you are one of the top in your form; there have been plenty of forms that haven't graduated a single warrior." The Guildmaster gave them a grin, one that highlighted that his smile was missing at least three teeth. "That's how we like it. Toughness will become a second skin to you, fearlessness is earned, not given freely, it's a confidence that comes with knowing that you will be able to deal with anything and anyone you meet or else you'll die with a sword in hand, and that will be fine, too. We will take … everything," his voice became throaty when he said this, "from you. You have no past. You have no future but war, weapons, and service. You will exist only in the present, in the moment, with your weapon in your hand, and conviction in your heart that whoever stands opposed to you will die by your hand."

He made his way through those still standing, as he said this. Cyrus cast a sidelong look at Cass Ward and got one in return. *He's trouble,* Cyrus thought. *Not the others, just him. He's the only threat in this room, the only serious one.*

"Cyrus Davidon," the Guildmaster said, and Cyrus looked up to find him lingering overhead. "Do you still wish to be a warrior, to lose your fear and look into the face of death unflinching?"

Cyrus heard the moans of those still fallen, the ones the healer was working his way around to, one at a time. The smell of sweat and sand was heavy in the room; *fear,* Cyrus thought with his six-year-old mind. "Yes," he said. "Guildmaster." He remembered the honorific at the last. *Adults like that.*

The Guildmaster studied him shrewdly, and Cyrus could smell the leather of the man, could see the scars where a blade had worked long cuts across the man's forehead in a diagonal slash, an X above his eyebrows. His cheeks were pitted worse, and when he smiled at Cyrus only half his face lifted. "That's good talk." His hand came down on

Cyrus's head, gave it a tousle, then came back to his belt, where Cyrus heard a noise of metal on leather and steel, a screech of a blade running out of a scabbard, then it was in his face, in his hands, pressed into his palms by the Guildmaster, a blade longer than his forearm. "But let's see if good action follows it. Take this …" The Guildmaster squatted, and pressed the weapon into his grasp then turned his eyes left, where Cyrus followed his gaze to a boy at his right, whom Cyrus had headbutted only moments before. Cyrus's look flitted back to the Guildmaster, and he felt the first stir of uncertainty as the Guildmaster looked back at him, watching, assessing, judging. "… and kill him."

Chapter 52

The weight was heavy on Cyrus's shoulder, the hand of the Guildmaster resting there, and Cyrus looked at it, looked at the metal gauntlet on the soft cloth of his shirt. That smell of leather was persistent, the other smell, too, that reminded him of the time he wrestled with his father and hit his nose, hard, and it wouldn't stop bleeding ... that was here as well, but it wasn't his nose that was bloody, not this time ...

The dagger had weight, too. He knew it was dagger. His father had showed him all manner of weapons, from short swords and axes to polearms, when he had gone to the militia house for a day. There were even a few hanging above the mantle in his house, he had seen them all his life. But when his father was clad in the black armor, he wore a sword. "A dagger is just a shorter sword, son," his father had told him. "You'll know it when you see it."

And he saw it now, the blade, it fit in his hand but the hilt bulged out on the ends. "Like this," the Guildmaster said, and pushed the guard up against his hand so that more of the hilt stuck out of the bottom of his fist. "Hold it like this."

Cyrus did, and he felt the Guildmaster steer him toward the boy, the one he had hurt so badly that the child hadn't bothered to get up yet. *And he is a child, not even a boy because he wasn't ready, couldn't handle it, folded and lay down when the call came over us—*

"Do it," the Guildmaster said. There was a silence in the arena that Cyrus reckoned had fallen in the last few minutes. "Go on."

Cyrus took another step toward the boy; he was over him now, hovering, and looked down over the patch of blond hair, where two grubby hands, smeared with dirt were held against the boy's face. He was writhing, sobbing quietly, no older than Cyrus. Younger even, perhaps. It was so hard to tell.

"Go on," the said Guildmaster again. "You want to be fearless? Be a warrior; do what a warrior does. Kill him."

Cyrus swallowed, as though he could drown his fears inside him. He stared down at the boy and felt only pity, looking at the ragged cloth, at the shoes that were no more than foot covers with holes in them. "They're orphans, all," Belkan had said when he brought Cyrus to the Society. "Like you."

Cyrus stepped closer, toward the lad, who was looking up at him now, eyes half-closed, curled up like a baby Cyrus had once seen sleeping at a neighbor's house. The boy was still, though, breathing steady, watching Cyrus closely, but with a far-off look in his eyes.

"Go on," the Guildmaster said from behind him. "Have at it."

There was a still in the arena and the place was dark, lit only by the lamps all around them, a thousand of them, perhaps, and Cyrus wondered idly who took the time to light them all. The boy waited for him, unresisting, crying softly, and Cyrus saw the little droplets of water that ran down the boy's cheeks, remembered the feel of his own before he ran out from overuse. *Pitiful. He's not there yet but close. Then he'll be like me.*

The air was quiet, everyone watching him, even the men at the door. Beyond them he could see snow falling outside, damp, and even more quiet out on the streets than it was in here, with the men watching and waiting. The fear bit at him, and he knew he was failing the test, hesitating, and he stared down at the boy again. The smell of urine was strong now, and he could not tell whether it was from the boy or from himself. He looked again at the boy, then at the gate to the world outside the arena, so small, and getting ever so much smaller by the minute, the quiet, snow-covered streets. The sand beneath his feet was crimson, red with blood.

Cyrus felt a weight on his shoulder, the Guildmaster's gauntlet resting on him. "Are you afraid to do it? Afraid to end him?"

Cyrus thought about it for a minute, looked again at the boy, and realized with utter clarity that he was not afraid at all, for once, that he really just felt sorry for him—

The dagger came around and plunged into the Guildmaster's belly without Cyrus even being truly aware of what he was doing. There was a sharp grunt from the man and his gauntlet squeezed Cyrus's unarmored shoulder tighter for a moment before he broke away, falling to his back, his hands clutching his midsection. There was a stunned, continued silence in the arena, and before the Guildmaster could speak, could proclaim, could say anything, Cyrus was off, running, dodging past the men at the gate, and his feet were slapping against the cobblestone street, stirring the wet snow and mud. He heard one of his pursuers slip and fall behind him as he dodged into an alleyway and past an open door where the smell of eggs wafted into the cold evening air.

The streets were twisted, and there were shouts behind him, a great clamor, but he ran, and when he came to the markets the noise was all but gone, buried in the sound of Reikonos by evening. There was still noise, in the distance, but Cyrus kept to the shadows. He saw guards in their armaments, patrolling, he saw men in heavy cloaks, and a few women wearing little enough beneath their robes, talking to every man who passed. He went unnoticed by them all, following the signs, the monuments, the things he knew and was familiar with. The stall in the corner of the market where the big man with bad teeth always gave him an apple. The house on the corner where the boy his age watched from the high window, never allowed to play in the street with the other lads. The spot where the man stood and called the news of the day, made announcements and proclamations from the Council of Twelve. He went slowly, carefully, but the streets were quiet and he had little to worry about. The evening shadows grew stronger as he went, and he could hear the torchlighters making their rounds in the distance. They had already passed here and the lamps shed a little light for him, enough to see as the snow came down harder, clumps of white that covered his shirt and turned it wet. He had no cloak, no coat, and his soft footcovers were soaked through.

The smell of the frigid air caused his nose to run, and he felt it freeze on his upper lip as he clasped his hands over his chest, rubbing them against the skin, trying to find warmth. His belly growled, roaring at him like the feisty cat that had lived in the alley behind his house but with more verve, more feeling. He shivered and felt the shake of his limbs, the chill that crept through the skin and went bone-deep. *Only a little farther,* he thought, and then he saw it.

It was a little house, to be sure, only a one story, but stone, good and strong. The roof was thatched, but he could see from here it had already begun to fail, caved in on one side. *The corner where Mother and Father sleep. It'll be all wet by now, then ...* The stones were still there, though, still strong.

He slipped from the shadows across the street and came to the door, his feet now slushing in the low places on the road. He could hardly avoid them all, his legs only so long, after all. He didn't knock at the door, which was slightly cracked, he just pushed his way in. *Warmth. A fire, sitting beside the hearth with mother like I used to—*

The house was quiet, a dread silence hanging in the air. The corner where the roof had failed was wet indeed, snow piling up in the place where Mother and Father's bed had been. The hearth was not warm, there was no fire, and it was chill inside. The only change was that the light wind was no longer present, though he could hear it stirring the roof now and again. The place was dark too, shadow consuming the entirety of it, only a little light coming in through the windows from the street and in the corner where the snow was gathering.

Cyrus let the silence hold, let his lips stick together, even as he felt the chatter of his teeth. When he spoke it was quiet, the last ounce of hope running out. "Mother?"

There was a quiet that lasted only one second.

"She is not here," came the voice from the darkness behind him, and he felt the fear again, the horror of it, and recoiled, backing toward the corner where the snow fell, even as a figure made its way out of the shadows. "Don't be afraid," the man said, and Cyrus could see the light catch his face. One of his eyes was squinted completely closed, and he wore a heavy cloak that extended from his neck to below his knees. "Don't be afraid, Cyrus."

"Who are you?" Cyrus asked, and shivered.

"A friend," the man said simply, and he took off his cloak with a simple flourish. He took tentative steps toward Cyrus, who could see now that the man wore armor, though of a different look than Cyrus had seen in the Society; this was older, he thought, more scuffed, and all metal, like his Father's. He offered the cloak, and Cyrus looked at it for only a half second before snatching it and draping it around his own shoulders, shivering into it, feeling the moisture from his skin absorbed into the cloth, but he also felt the chill reduce a little.

"I don't know you," Cyrus said, and looked away, to the hearth again. There was only darkness in it. The pot his mother had used to cook was gone, and the hearth seemed to leer at him, taunting. "Where's my mother?" He asked it plaintively, though he knew almost certainly what he'd hear.

"Surely you must know that she is gone." The voice was quiet, subtle, and the drifting sound the snow made as it landed in the corner was almost louder than the stranger's words. "Belkan told you, did he not?"

"He told me." Cyrus wanted to keep his distance, recoil, but he didn't. "I want to see her."

"I'm afraid that ..." the man hesitated, "is quite impossible, now. She is dead."

Cyrus heard but didn't hear, listened but didn't absorb. He shut his eyes tightly, and tried to remember the house when it was warm, when the smell of meat pies cooking over the fire filled the air, when he could feel her arms wrapped around him, and when he would tussle with his father on the bearskin rug—

"Cyrus," the voice came again, and Cyrus opened his eyes. "I know this must be difficult for you, this ... horrible change. But you must ... endure. Do you know what that word means? Endure?"

"I know what it means." His voice didn't sound like his own. It was huskier, like one of the boys who was sobbing in the arena.

"You must endure ... what is to come." The man went on, and Cyrus listened—but did not hear, the older Cyrus thought, watching it all, watching this man, this familiar man, give him instruction. "There will come a better day, when you are out of this storm. You must believe in that, hold tight to that conviction, because what will happen between now and then will not be easy on you."

"I don't wish to go back to the Society of Arms," Cyrus said, and the emotion flowed out of him. "I don't want to be there."

"You have no choice," the man said quietly. "If there were any other way, I would find it, but—they—are watching you closely, and there is no avoiding their gaze. You must follow this path, do this, stay within the bounds of the Society, to be safe. Do you understand?"

"But I don't wish to—"

There was a draft then, but the man's words overcame it and interrupted Cyrus in the gentlest way. "The mark of a man is his willingness to do things that he must do but doesn't wish to. You were a boy only months ago, yet now you are forced into the role of a man, forced to look out for yourself because no one else watches out for you, because all who did so are now gone." The man's hand landed on

Cyrus's shoulder, but it was different than the Guildmaster of the Society's, lighter somehow. "If you are to endure, you must do the things you don't wish to. You are afraid. I know this. Were I in your place, I would be afraid too, to feel so alone. But I tell you now, be not afraid, Cyrus Davidon, because you are not alone, however it might appear. Don't fear." The man's hand came across Cyrus's cheek and the soft touch of his thumb, even in the gauntlet, smeared away the wet droplet that had fallen.

He felt the world wrench, then the man's armor against his face, and he cried the tears he thought he had no more of, felt the strength and unyielding of the armor against his skin, even as the cloak wrapped around him. The wetness of his tears ran slick against the man's breastplate, and Cyrus felt himself lifted, cradled, carried along, as he quietly wept. There were reassuring words, he could hear them, but the ones that stuck out was the constant admonishment: "Don't be afraid."

They were outside the gates of the Society when next he looked up. The stranger's eye was puckered shut, as though it were too cold for him to open it. "Be brave," the man told him, and Cyrus saw another man just inside the gates, the dwarf from the arena. "Erkhardt," the man said to the dwarf and gently handed Cyrus over.

The dwarf gripped him firm under the armpits and laid his feet back on the ground as Cyrus took up his own weight again. He was tall, already up to the dwarf's chin. "Made quite an impression earlier, this one did," the dwarf said with a sort of grim amusement. "Wouldn't play along with the test. Stabbed the Guildmaster in the belly." He lowered his voice but Cyrus heard it nonetheless. "They'll not go easy on him for that, you know. Not that they were going to before, but ..."

"He will endure," came the stony voice from the man in armor. "And you will ensure that no harm comes to him."

"As ordered," the dwarf said. "Come on then, lad," he said to Cyrus, "let's get you in and see about making amends where we can." The dwarf saluted the man. "Safe journey to you."

"You are not alone, Cyrus," the man said as Cyrus walked the stone path through the gates and toward the old, darkened building of the Society of Arms. "Never alone. You are strong, show them that. And be not afraid."

Cyrus watched him, looking over his shoulder with regret, longing, really, even as the dwarf named Erkhardt was at his side. *After all,* the older Cyrus thought, as he watched it all play before his eyes like theater, *how could a child forget the last time he felt like he had a friend?*

Or a father.

Chapter 53

There was a rough bump, and the darkness swirled around Cyrus, lit now by daylight somewhere in the distance. It was above him at an angle, but it washed through the air and shone in beams that rested all over the space around him. His eyes were bleary, and no matter how many times he blinked, they did not clear quickly. He began to wonder if they would clear at all.

The smell of horses permeated his consciousness, filled his nose, and he heard the sounds of them, of people talking somewhere outside his field of vision. There was a pain around his neck as he turned his head, but the pain was only a dull ache, a long-ago reminder of some agony, he supposed.

"Would you care for some water?" The voice was soft, feminine, and cut over the clack-clack he heard every few seconds.

Cyrus coughed then cleared his throat. "Yes," he said, but his voice was hoarse, and his throat scratchy. A skin of water was thrust to his lips and tilted, just so a little ran out on his tongue and down his mouth, as though he had forgotten how to capture the liquid that was coming to him. It felt cool as it fell over his cheeks, and he realized the air was hot, and he had a blanket weighing him down.

He swiveled his head and saw the face that went with the voice that had spoken to him. "You," he said. "I ... I don't remember ..."

"If the next words out of your mouth are 'your name,' then you'd best prepare yourself for a thrashing." She sounded serious.

"Calm yourself, Aisling," he said with a wicked grin, and saw the flash of irritation crest her tanned, elven features. "Kidding, Martaina," he said, laboring to get her name out. "Your name is Martaina Proelius."

"Good to know you still recall the important things," she said, and pulled back the skin, capping it. "You gave us quite a stir, you know."

"Didn't intend to," he said with a cough. "As I recall, I was just going along, minding my business, when someone shot me with an arrow and proceeded to lop my head off." His hand came to his throat, felt the slight ridge along the middle of it, a scar that seemed unlikely to ever heal. "Hoygraf said he'd take it in order to keep me dead. His revenge."

"Yes, well," Martaina said and shifted, sitting against the canvas backing of the wagon, looking over him, "it didn't happen, obviously."

"Obviously. What did happen?"

"We managed to retrieve that empty gourd you used to think—you know, before you switched to using your groin—and reunited it with your body," Martaina said.

He ignored her jibe. "We're at war with Actaluere?" He felt the tautness in his muscles, surprising given how out of sorts he felt.

"No," she said with a shake of her head. "In fact, Milos Tiernan has brought his army north with us."

Cyrus felt himself stop, as though everything ceased moving all at once around him. "Tiernan did? He's not attacking Galbadien?"

"No," Martaina said, and Cyrus could see her face go masklike. The ranger was good, no doubt experienced at hiding herself; but he had known her long enough to see through it.

"What happened?" Cyrus asked and put enough of a commanding voice into the question that it cut through the rasp. Martaina's eyes turned rearward over Cyrus's head. "How long was I out?"

"Over a week," she said at last, and her hand disturbed the flap of canvas enough to let some light in, which caused Cyrus to blanch and close his eyes. "Curatio kept you well-medicated with opiates from the local poppy fields during your ... ailment. He had some difficulty reattaching your head because of the time that elapsed between when it was severed and when we received it. It was a very near thing, and your arrow wound and other injuries had to heal naturally because they missed the window to be cured through magical means."

"What happened while I was recovering?" Cyrus asked and tried to sit up. Martaina's boot landed upon his chest, keeping him down. His armor was absent, and he felt no desire to fight her attempt to keep him flat, letting his head sink back to the padded, moving floor of the wagon.

"Actaluere joined with Syloreas and sent the forces they had on hand at Enrant Monge north with us." She kept a canny eye on him, but her reaction was still closely guarded, he knew. "They mean to help fight against the scourge and have sent for more forces to come north while the first army moves up with us."

"Are we close to battle?" Cyrus asked. "If we're only a week out of Enrant Monge? Have the scourge reached this far south already?"

"It would be best if you didn't concern yourself overmuch," she said calmly. "We're holding at a line south of the mountains, here in Syloreas's southern flatlands, waiting for one of Actaluere's northern armies to meet up with us. After that, we've a week's march north to the rallying place where we'll be fighting them."

"Flat plains," Cyrus said, pondering. "Let them come at us?"

"That seems to be the consensus," Martaina said, looking down at him once more. "With Actaluere joining the remainder of Syloreas's armies, we have as many troops as we'll be able to muster and can fight them on as near to even footing as possible. Besides, remember these creatures thrive on broken ground. They took Scylax without much effort, after all."

"I haven't forgotten that, either," Cyrus said, "and apparently they scaled a mountain to do it. No, flat ground does work best for us, for our mounted cavalry. I find it a bit mystifying that Actaluere would choose to join with us, seeing as the Baroness was such a sticking point for them—" He stopped, having caught the waver in Martaina's expression, the subtle move of the muscles around her right eye. "She was returned to them, wasn't she? Back to the Grand Duke?"

"She went back to Actaluere, yes," Martaina said carefully.

"They took her?" Cyrus asked, and started to sit up again, only to feel the strength of Martaina's foot hold him down once more. "Took her back to him?"

"She went back to him voluntarily," Martaina said.

There was a silence that filled Cyrus's ears, as though the sounds of the horses and men outside had ceased. All talk and chatter and the smell of infirmity that filled the wagon was gone. "To save her people, then. To free the army of Actaluere to action against the scourge." He felt himself relax, his body limp against the padding that separated him from the wood floor of the wagon, and the deep dissatisfaction grew within even as he tried to shut it up. "And *they* let her." He said it with such casual disdain that it lit a fire in Martaina's eyes.

"Let her? No," the ranger said. "She argued forcefully to be allowed to. Forcefully enough that Curatio did not oppose it nor did any of the other officers."

Cyrus was quiet for minutes, the wheels bumping him along every few seconds as the wagon hit ruts in the road it traveled. "I can't decide whether I deem her incredibly brave or deeply stupid. Perhaps some combination of both."

"She went into it knowing what she was doing to herself," Martaina said, and he saw the restraint again, the mask, keeping her emotions in check. It was a mask made of thousands of years of experience at keeping others from her thoughts. "I don't believe you could ascribe stupidity to any part of her judgment process save one, perhaps." Her eyes narrowed at the last.

"And that part would be?"

"I decline to say." Martaina's head swiveled again to the back of the wagon, to the flap, and remained fixed there as they bumped along in silence.

Chapter 54

Vara

The horn sounded in the early morning hours as Vara lay in her quarters, the fire going low across from the foot of her bed, the crackle not disturbing the sleep she wasn't getting anyway. Her thoughts were far away, as usual, which was why she wasn't sleeping. The soft pops from the fire were soothing in their way, and when the horn reached her ears it took a moment to realize that it wasn't that far off—from the wall, it seemed, though she was dazed enough that she believed at first that it came from over the plains.

When it was sounded again, this time inside the halls of Sanctuary with the guards taking up the call of alarm, it was enough to stir her from her reverie.

Her bare feet hit the cold floor as she disentangled herself from the blankets that covered her bed. *Damn,* she thought, the urgency rising in her with the cacophony of horns and voices outside, *I would not have believed they would move against us again so soon. I assumed they would at least wait for the reinforcements to get here ....*

Her footcovers and underclothes went on first, followed by the armor, which took a while to strap on. The last thing she placed was her helm, which she detested and usually preferred not to wear. It was a shiny thing, like the rest of her ensemble, and covered the top of her head, leaving only part of her face exposed. It strapped tightly under her chin, and carried a movable crossbar that folded down over her nose for use during battle. She folded it down now after tucking her ponytail out the back, and made certain that the metal girding the strap was properly placed to defend against glancing blows under her chin. It met up with the gorget that protected her throat, and left only the space from her chin to her eyes unprotected.

She swung open the door and almost collided with the bulk of Vaste as she did so. The troll stopped himself in mid-stride, and Vara threw out an arm to his ribs, smacking him with her mailed palm as she tried to come to a stop before running into him. She looked up to his face and found him looking down at her. "Watch where you're going, troll."

"I was," Vaste said, "which was why I stopped when you threw yourself into my path. You, on the other hand, I wonder about. Can you even see with that monstrosity fastened to your head?" He waved a hand in front of her face, as though she were blind.

Vara felt a surge of irritation. "I have always possessed a helm to go with my armor, you rancid goat bladder."

"Perhaps," Vaste said without umbrage, "but I don't believe I've ever seen you wear it before. You typically go hatless, the better to allow your flowing golden locks to distract your enemies, I presumed. Much the same reason your breastplate is molded to be aptly named— another way to keep them focused on—"

"Ye gods! Will you ever cease your damnable vexing of me?" She didn't wait for a response, instead turning to head for the stairs, back in full flight as her feet tramped along the stones, issuing a loud clang with every step.

"I don't foresee a time when I'll stop making wry observations about the situation around me, no." Vaste's words were dry though loud enough to be heard behind her over the sound of her steps. The staircase further down was swarming with people, the members of Sanctuary turning out, the alarms still ringing in the air over the raised voices below. "Perhaps when I'm dead, which, hmm, maybe you'll get your wish—"

"Don't jest about that," she snapped, turning to face him. "I may be thoroughly irritated at you a majority of the time, but don't confuse that with genuinely wanting you dead. If I genuinely wanted you dead, I would have smote you down myself, long ago. We are in dire times, and if this alarm means what I think it does—"

"I believe there might have been a word of caring in that fusillade," Vaste said, halting only for a moment before sliding past her on the staircase with surprising agility. "Buried deep, perhaps, but I caught a grain of it hidden in the depths of the vitriol. Could it be you are fond of me, Shelas'akur? That my wit amuses you—"

"You annoy me on a near-constant basis," Vara said, now trailing behind Vaste's wide strides as they came down the staircase. "But—"

"Oh, fear not," Vaste said, "I've always known that you're not quite the demon you pretend to be. However, if I'm not much mistaken, this sudden softening of your armored persona has less to do with this siege and perhaps more to do with a certain General's absence—"

"Shut your slack-jawed mouth," Vara hissed, and Vaste did not turn nor stop on the stairs to answer her. He did, indeed, shut his mouth, and they began to slow as the crowds clogged the stairwell, members rushing down to the foyer below. She resisted the temptation to hit the person in front of her with a hard shoulder check in order to send them all collapsing like dominos down the stairs. Dominos she could run over in a dash to get there faster. *Resist.*

"Apparently we need wider staircases," came a voice from behind her, almost as acerbic as her own. She did not need to turn to know that the speaker was Erith Frostmoor. "Or smaller trolls."

"As though I'm the problem here rather than the dark elves that won't leave us be," Vaste said, turning his head to give Erith a blank look. "You know, those hideous creatures that seem to have it in for the whole world, starting wars and unleashing aggression on everything and everybody—"

"Fine, fine," Erith said, squeezing up against Vara in a way that made the paladin yearn to thrust an elbow into Erith's nose to get her to back up and leave some space between them. "It's not just you, then— it's the disorganized way in which we're all scrambling to get into defensive positions."

"And the fact that we're having to go to defensive positions to protect ourselves against the dark elven hordes," Vaste said lightly. After a moment, he sighed jauntily. "Is this how everyone feels about the trolls all the time? Because I think I finally get it, you know, after having been the brunt of it for so long. Kill them!" He raised his voice. "Kill the aggressors!" He lowered his voice again. "You know, it feels good not to be one of 'them,' for once. You should have had your people make war against the entire civilized world years ago."

"I hardly had anything to do with it," Erith said with as much frost as her name indicated.

"Oh, now, do give yourself some credit. You probably at least inspired one or two soldiers to pleasure themselves at the latrines."

Erith let out a hissing sound and Vara ignored it. The foyer was visible now, the stream of people that filled the stairwell breaking loose and running across the foyer floor. "At least it doesn't look like they've teleported in an attack force this time," Erith said, all trace of her irritation gone.

"Yet," Vara and Vaste said in a chorus. The troll raised an eyebrow at her, and she gave him a scorching glare that affected him little to none.

"Such happy thoughts you two share," Erith said. "Remind me not to come to either of you when next I experience a down day and need some optimism."

"Were you really ever going to visit Vara for such a thing?" Vaste asked, vaulting over the edge of the steps about fifteen from the bottom as the spiral opened up. He didn't wait for either of them to reply nor to reach the bottom; the healer ran for the door and was out onto the Sanctuary grounds before Vara even cleared the stairs. Taking the step Vaste had was not possible for someone of her height, certainly not without breaking a leg.

She was out the door moments later, having passed through the foyer, which was still guarded by a force headed by Belkan. The day was grey, the skies hanging, clouds overhead that muted the sun, wherever it might have been hiding. The green, well-trod grasses of the Sanctuary lawn were particularly dark today, the late summer having come to them. *Only a month or so from harvest and the Sovereign begins his move. Of course.*

She climbed the wall, the same place she had on the day when they broke the siege, and wondered how many towers there would be this time. Last time it had been a host of fifty thousand, a fairly thin line that came at them from one direction, head on. This time would surely be different; there would be at least another twenty-five thousand, perhaps even another fifty. They might attempt a direct assault again or attempt to encircle and direct their main attack at the walls rather than the gate.

When she took the last step off the ladder and stepped out of the stale air inside of the wall, she found herself overlooking the fields in front of the wall, all empty. The place where the battle had been done last time was open ground, though the smell of death still lingered as there had been only a small detail to deal with the fallen from the last battle, and they had been instructed to leave some of the bodies. Many corpses were still where they had fallen, left as a reminder for the next army that came along. The remains of the siege towers had been burned, though, and only blackened husks remained there.

Vara's eyes came up to the horizon, and she peered toward the place where she knew the portal was, north of the wall several minutes walk. It was there, but beyond it there were shapes, assorted figures that looked no larger than ants on the hill. The grey clouds did them no favors, and only through her elven eyesight could she even see that they were there.

"I don't see them," Thad said, drawing her attention. The warrior was at the edge of the wall, staring over. "But I know they're there, because the elves in my detail tell me so. How many would you estimate?"

Vara did not speak at first, not for a long, long moment, as she tried to count and failed. Part of the army that waited ahead was obscured, not visible at this great a distance. "Many," she said at last. "More than last time. More than I can count at this range." She felt the dryness in her mouth as she said it. "But more. Many more than before. At least double their number, visible from here." She blinked, and stared at the horizon, her picture of the dark elf force incomplete. "More than we can see. And that means ..." she tasted the dryness again, even as she said it, "likely more than we can easily handle."

Chapter 55

Cyrus

The days had grown long, Cyrus noted, even as the jarring motion of the wagon carried them on. The third day after he had awakened, Curatio gave him lease to leave the wagon. They had stopped, finally, having reached the open plains that were the rendezvous point for their meeting with Actaluere's northern armies.

"Don't nod your head too much," Curatio said as Cyrus stood, feeling somewhat weak as his head got light. He started to shake it to see if he could clear the feeling, but the healer grasped him by the face, capturing his chin and part of his cheeks between his thumb and forefinger. "Don't shake it, either."

"Why?" Cyrus asked. "Is it going to fall off?"

"Unlikely," Curatio said, "I'm just annoyed by how often you do that. Try speaking more."

"My throat feels raw, as though someone poured Reikonosian whiskey down it while I was asleep." Cyrus rubbed his neck.

"We gave you as much water as we could," Martaina said, standing with him now, in the wagon. She had not left for more than a few hours since he had awakened. "But it's surprisingly difficult to make a man who's hallucinating drink and eat."

Cyrus stood between the two of them, ducking his head to avoid hitting it against the canvas top of the wagon. "I would think after the last few days I'd never want to sleep again." He yawned. "Somehow I'm still tired."

"Get some sunlight," Curatio said. "It'll do wonders for you, that and walking around for a spell. Not an actual spell," he clarified, "because that's impossible and also heresy, but walk for a while."

"Yes, sir," Cyrus said as Martaina pulled back the tent flap for him. The air in the wagon had grown stale to him, the smell of healed wounds and sweated flesh was near-unbearable. He had put his armor on with Martaina's assistance, after saying flatly that he'd rather be able to walk ten feet with it on than thirty feet without it. She'd snorted her impatience with his attitude but ultimately helped him. He rested his hand on the hilt of Praelior and felt energized. *Thank Bellarum that Hoygraf didn't know the worth of my blade, or it'd surely no longer be with me.*

The air outside came in with a subtle breeze, a coolness, a tinge of winter on the wind even though the sun was shining its warmth down. Cyrus squinted away from it, looking back into the darkness of the wagon to either side, gradually turning his face toward the light. After a minute had passed, then another, he took a step forward unaided, sat down at the end of the wagon and slid himself off the carriage. His feet crunched against the ground where the wagon sat, made soft by a rain he had heard in the night. He sniffed, and realized that in addition to the smell of the campsite, he smelled himself, the odor of the tent and of sweated flesh, healed wounds, and he wondered if there was a river nearby or a pond that would be suitable for bathing.

His first steps were funny things, as though he were regaining the habit of balance, of walking. Martaina stood to the side of him, well clear, but he knew her reflexes were such that she could catch him should he stumble. Her speed was also such that he did not worry about it. The first steps were hardest, but his legs seemed to regain their use as he walked, the whole of the campsite laid out before him, the massive army more than he might have imagined when first he'd heard that Actaluere had joined with them at Enrant Monge. He could not see it all from where he stood, but he knew by what little he had glimpsed of it from the back of the wagon that it was massive.

"Where are Actaluere's northern armies?" Cyrus asked Curatio, who hovered only a bit behind him, just out of arm's reach, as though he were hiding the fact that like Martaina, he was lingering to save Cyrus from falling.

"A week's march, by the accounts we've heard," the elf replied, not stepping any closer to Cyrus. "They're making haste, and Briyce Unger and Milos Tiernan have been planning the coming battle. Their intent is to throw everything at the enemy, with Sanctuary at the center and our healers in use to help stem the bloodshed and fall of their people. Once we've broken the scourge, we'll march north through the passes to get to the cave where the portal sits."

"Forgive me, Curatio," Cyrus said, "but do I detect a hint of gloom in your voice?" He watched the elf's normally sunny disposition change not a shade.

"No gloom," Curatio said, "but perhaps some tempered expectations. I have been in many battles in my life, and I have yet to see a single one go precisely to plan. Things go wrong in war, and this enemy is even less predictable than most. I hope with all that is in me that we will crush them and drive them back as predicted. However, I would hope that our General might bring his own insight into our foes to the battle plan before we go into the fight, so that any troubles unseen by the esteemed leaders of Actaluere and Syloreas might be anticipated before we march headlong into the teeth of these beasts."

"I doubt Briyce Unger would be foolish enough to lock me out of the discussions," Cyrus said and coughed weakly. "Unless for some reason Milos Tiernan holds a grudge against me for what difficulties I've handed him."

"None that I've seen during the planning sessions," Curatio answered. "He's been courteous and careful to listen to all our advice thus far. Unger has asked after you and when you'll be able to meet with them, so I suspect that won't be an issue."

"Oh, good," Cyrus said, feeling his loping steps lack some of the bounce that they had before he had been felled outside Enrant Monge. After a moment's thought, he had to concede that any bounce had been gone long before that, probably before even leaving Vernadam. "The last thing we need is a turf war. Especially as we're facing the ghosts of our past sins."

There was no response from either Martaina or Curatio that he heard, but they carried on, the cool breeze encouraging him, the warm sun alternating with it, giving its heat when the wind would die down. It was a perfect sort of early fall experience, and the air held only the slightest hint of what winter might be like in this new land. At a normal time, Cyrus might have found it invigorating; now, it kept him going in spite of all that was on his mind. "You said that J'anda and Aisling helped retrieve me," Cyrus said, turning to look at Martaina. "I haven't seen either of them to thank them properly since I've recovered."

"J'anda is quite busy," Curatio said. "Odellan may run the troops, but J'anda keeps careful track of our spellcasters. He's been helping them in pushing their boundaries—especially the newer ones—to build their capacity for magical energy."

Cyrus blinked at that. "What?"

"Magical energy," Curatio said. "The finite amount of power we have for casting spells? You are familiar with this concept?"

"Yes," Cyrus said, "having seen a woman bleed part of her life energy out last year to go past the limit, I am familiar with it."

"It can be grown over time and with mastery of our craft," Curatio said. "J'anda is working to grow that ability before we go into the battle, especially with our healers."

"How does one … go about such a thing?" Cyrus asked.

Curatio sighed. "It would be difficult to explain to someone who has not cast spells before. Probably the easiest explanation is to say that we go about it very much the same as you go about building muscle with which to swing your sword—repetition, effort, practice. Exercises can be done."

Cyrus shrugged. "If you say so. Where is Aisling, then?" He waited for a response from either of them but got none. "Never mind. I forgot she doesn't do well at being kept track of."

Martaina gave him a slight smile as they made their way around some tents that had been brought by the Luukessians. As always, the army of Sanctuary seemed to prefer bedrolls for lighter travel and keeping the need for wagons to a minimum. Cyrus paused for a moment and stretched, taking his hand off Praelior. The lightheadedness came back, and he fought it, let it wash over him, tried to keep his bearings as it caused his head to dip and bob, as though he were floating in water. He let his hand return to Praelior and the feeling subsided. *Probably not the best sign, but at least I can still manage without falling over.*

"Perhaps we should begin to walk back to the wagon?" Martaina suggested. Cyrus turned to look at Curatio, but the healer was quiet.

"Not yet," Cyrus said. He felt a strange call within him, a hollowness and a need coupled together that were like an itch beneath his skin. "I need to bathe. I can no longer stand the smell of myself or of the wagon."

Martaina raised an eyebrow at him. "You can barely stand without the aid of your sword. Are you certain that this is the proper moment to go searching for somewhere to wash yourself?"

"It's either that or I go out of my skull from the stink," Cyrus said. "I'm rather amazed that the two of you can even tolerate being within a hundred feet of me; I know how well attuned elven senses are."

"You get used to it after a while," Martaina said with a slight smile. "You haven't descended to the depths I've come to expect from most dark elven men, so I wouldn't worry about it yet."

"I'm not worried for your sake," Cyrus said, "I can hardly stand it for mine. I've been in battles where I've been covered in blood and smell less offensive than now. All I want is a bath; where can I go to immerse myself in water?"

Martaina exchanged a look with Curatio, who shrugged. "There's a river a quarter of a mile away. I doubt you'll be able to walk there under your own power."

"I can," he said. "I will. I'll be fine so long as I have my sword in hand."

"I do hope you're talking about your blade and not—" Martaina gave him a crooked smile.

"Thank you for that," he said dryly. "Let me walk for a bit, get used to my legs beneath me again. If I'm not back by nightfall, I'm sure you'll come looking for me."

"You were assassinated a mere three weeks ago," Martaina said, "and that was hardly the first attempt. Are you certain you want to go about without guard?"

Cyrus shrugged. "You can follow, I don't care. Just let me test my strength."

"If you've got this quite under control," Curatio said to Martaina, "I have things to attend to before this day is done."

"Yes, I suspect I can keep a dozen or two of Actaluere's finest away from him if need be," Martaina said, with a vague and dismissive wave. "He could probably take one or two more."

Cyrus did not argue with her, instead pulling his hand off his hilt for another brief spell; the vertigo had lessened but muscle fatigue had set in. *She might not be far wrong.*

"Very well then," Curatio said and produced the most infinitesimal nod of the head, which reminded Cyrus of a bow for some reason. "I'll inform Briyce Unger and Milos Tiernan that you'll be ready to join their strategy talks tomorrow, if you'd like?"

"I'd like," Cyrus said. "Very much so."

With a final nod, Curatio turned, the hems of his white robes trailing behind him as the healer threaded his way behind a tent and out of sight. "He's a worrier, that one," Martaina said as he disappeared. "With good cause, obviously, but still a worrier." She turned to fix him with a gaze, after a cool survey of the area around them. They were at the edge of the encampment now, and Cyrus could see the open fields, unspoilt by men as far as the eye could see. "So what's this really about, this desire to bathe yourself? Because I have my suspicions."

"Oh?" Cyrus asked. "And what are those?"

"More than mere curiosities, less than full-blooded accusations."

"Yes, very clever," he said, letting his legs carry him on. The river was obvious in the distance, a thin blue line cutting jagged strokes across the uneven, loping plain, the early fall grasses already turning a golden yellow. "Why don't you go ahead and share your suspicions with me, so I'll be better able to gauge the truth of them."

Martaina snorted. "When it comes to assessing yourself, I suspect you are no more able to see the truth of things now than a titan would be capable of discerning the individual toes on a gnome's foot."

Cyrus didn't pause, didn't slow down, and in fact increased his stride. He felt a little stir of irritation to couple with the feeling already boiling inside him, that restless stir. "Oh? You think I've become myopic now?"

"I think you have. I think you've run from one pain into another, and now you're just going for the sake of going because the alternative is too much to bear." She said it matter-of-factly, and he listened for some insult or harshness, but it wasn't there.

"What's the alternative?" He kept his eyes on the river in the distance. *If I can just make it there, get clean for a bit, feel better ...*

"To stand your ground and face the pain, the fear that's crept over you of late." That held accusation, he heard, especially the note of her wording for fear.

Cyrus turned, and his hand fell away from Praelior's grip. There was no lightheadedness now, no spin to his thoughts, just a simple, knife-edged focus on Martaina, her brown hair spilling into the green hood of her cowl, banded behind her to keep it out of her face, as it always was. Her tanned skin was slightly more flushed than usual, though she did not appear indignant to his eyes. He saw one of her fists clenched shut, and he wondered if it meant she was angry or if she intended to hit him.

"Throwing the word 'fear' at a warrior of Bellarum is not something to be done lightly," Cyrus said, and he felt the cold edge creep into his words, frostier than the north winds by more than a matter of degrees.

"Yet I have done it, just now."

"And I so recently apologized to you for my mistrust of your motives and actions," Cyrus said, and his eyes narrowed of their own accord. "Is there some reason you throw this insult into my face on the eve of my return to the planning of this battle? A battle in which we'll be facing this implacable foe, this ceaseless enemy? Is there some detail of my actions that you've witnessed that would lead you to believe me unfit to lead an army? When you accuse me of fear, do you suspect I'll be cowering at the back of the fight, waiting for my soldiers to win the day for me?"

"I suspect you'll be at the fore, slinging your sword with the rest of them, and that you'll fight to the death—again—even if it means losing your body and never being able to come back from it." Her nostrils flared at this. "The fear came and went, as far as I'm concerned, came and went like a wildfire in the forests of old, gutting the underbrush and leaving no trees standing. That is you, near as I can tell—the fear of losing Vara, the pain of what she did, it covered you, burned out your insides, left you hollow. New growth started with the Baroness, but soon enough that was scorched through as well. I wish you still feared, feared to lose what you've already lost. Because now you're so empty there's nothing left for you to fear. The fear's already had its way, no taking that back now."

"You make it sound like there's nothing left of my own mind. I'm what? An empty vessel, waiting to be filled with whatever comes along?"

"What of this cause you've latched yourself on to?" Martaina said. "Defending the Syloreans?"

"You think I wouldn't have done this if Vara had—" he stuttered, "if she hadn't— hadn't—"

"If she were with you, your lover or your wife," she said it plainly, but the words twisted like a knife all the same, "I think you would still be here to fight for Luukessia, but I think you would do it for a cause and for obligation, for the repayment of a debt or the cessation of a consequence we caused. I don't think you'd be doing it half-hearted, empty-hearted, as though you have to drag yourself along to the next place we're fighting—"

"I did just recover from a fairly injurious wound—"

"And that's another thing," she said, the full force of her rolling downhill now, the momentum behind her words. "You did just spend weeks on your back, surely enough, no doubt. If you want to go and have your way with Aisling in order to relieve your strain and empty some more of your soul, by all means, do so—"

"Excuse me?" He asked her frostily, but it came out strained.

"—without making elaborate excuses about why you need to bathe yourself. Do you think me a fool? Do you think Curatio some sort of idiot? We know what you are doing, it's as plain as the head atop your neck, now." She glared at him.

"You think I need to hide my desires?" He glared back, and wondered why he'd felt so sorry for sending her away before. "As though I have some secret shame to hide?"

"Yes," she said. "And it does you no favors, nor Aisling either. You keep running from pain to pain, and now there's nothing left to feel, nothing left to fear, nothing left to lose. You've come to the point of bottom in your journey, and yet still you won't admit it, perhaps even to yourself."

"Bottomed out, have I?" Cyrus asked with tart amusement. "Oh, good. Here I was worried I still had farther to fall." He let his hand play across his forehead, felt the lines underneath his fingers. "Can I not … just … have some small solace?"

"Not from what you're intending, no." He could hear her speaking behind his hand, though he had no desire to look upon her now. "You are empty. There is no hope for a future left in you, do you realize that? No belief, no heart, no real desire to live. How else can you explain your decision to come back to the camp at Enrant Monge without escort—"

"A slip of the mind," Cyrus said and let his hand fall away. He kept his face straight as he looked upon her. "I have much weighing on it, and I assure you, my first thought was not that Grand Duke Hoygraf would be waiting at the side of the road between our encampment and the keep to ambush me and take my head."

"At one point, I think you would have thought of it." She kept her tone even, her expression flat but accusing.

"Possibly. Surely you don't think I went out on that ride thinking I'd be killed and decapitated? That I did it on purpose?"

"No," she said, "but my concern is that you've become reckless. That you've had your hope and belief burned out of you, and that uncaring is replacing all. Once upon a time, you strode for excellence in all things, you desired to be the best warrior in all Arkaria. I heard rumors you even desired to pursue the best equipment, the best of everything to help you do the task at hand better than anyone. That was tempered by the desire to hold fast to the bonds of loyalty in Sanctuary, but tell me now—what do you want, Cyrus Davidon?" She gestured to the river in the distance. "What do you want, beyond a bath and release?"

"I don't know," he said after a pause. "Victory, of course. To vanquish this scourge."

"And then?" Quietly. Accusingly.

"To go home, I suppose," he said, but now his voice was hollow.

"You suppose," she said, with a quiet all her own. "You've lost hope of a future. You've lost belief in a better day ahead, belief in what drove you, once upon a time. You were the most certain of us, a warrior with a rock-hard conviction in what he did, what he said, in his abilities. Thad told me that you were forged in the hottest fires of the Society of Arms, that you were the man who walked out of their gates after the graduation with nothing to prove to anyone." She threw a hand up to indicate him. "Where is that man now? What is left of him in front of me? You've let them strip it all away from you—"

"I let nobody do anything," Cyrus said in a low growl. "Some things happened, things I can't undo."

"And do you believe you'll return from that? That you'll pass the eye of the storm and come back to your old self unchanged?"

"I have no desire to return to my old self," Cyrus said, turning away from her and resuming his walk, the river ahead in his sight.

"Oh?" He heard her soft footsteps behind him; her distress with him was clear not only in her voice but in the fact that he could hear the ranger walk. "What is your ambition now? To slake the thirst of your desire with a dark elf whom you care not one whit for? To lose yourself in the pleasure moment over and over with a woman whom you have avoided for two years? To throw yourself into cataclysmic battle after battle until you no longer come back?"

"My ambition right now lies in recovering from my injuries, bathing, and yes, perhaps exerting some excess energies with Aisling, who has shown no small energy of her own to dispense with. Would you prefer I simply sit about, silent as a stone, pondering the best course of action to get me to better weapons, or a more serviceable guild, or perhaps thrilling to thoughts of the journey home and how much I might like to be among the towers and stone of Sanctuary now rather than fighting a foe of my own making a world away?"

"What I would prefer," she said, and grasped at his shoulder, turning him about, "is that you show some sign of life beyond speaking, walking, consuming and dispensing your seed." Her face was animated in a way that it never was. "Show me some sign of how you were before, before Termina, before Mortus's realm, or at least some small sight of what you were like in the interlude at Vernadam after Harrow's Crossing. Give me a sign that you still believe in something, that you hold some hope to your soul, that you have something to—" She expelled her breath, and her head went to the side, as if she were searching for something that she could not find in him. "That you have something to live for, for gods' sakes." Her eyes softened and the corners crinkled, and for a moment she was a thousand years old. "For our sakes."

The sun was not against the far horizon, not yet. It hung in the sky at an angle that told Cyrus it was one, perhaps two hours until sundown. He looked at it then back to the encampment, not so far distant, and then to the river. "Sometimes life is not about desire, or belief. Sometimes it's about crossing the void between big moments, about putting one foot before the other as you navigate the spare areas where nothing remains in a blighted heart. The only thing I can do for now is to keep going, to hold to my duty of fighting the battles placed before me, seeing to the tasks appointed me. You want me to believe? You want me to hope? This is hardly the first time in my life that I've been hollowed out, not the first by far that I've lost hope. In those moments, I've learned to keep walking, to keep going, to hold not to hope, but to whatever I can. I won't be the same man I was before, but I won't be like this forever, either, I doubt." He let show the faintest, most rueful smile. "The thought that I would … doesn't bear consideration."

"When will we see this new Cyrus?" she asked as he resumed his course toward the river, the smell of the grasses carrying over him, the light whipping of the wind at his armor a pleasant distraction.

"Whenever I get to him," Cyrus said, and he heard her footsteps cease. He did not look back, but he knew she was not following him any longer. "Whenever I meet him."

Chapter 56

The river was not fast moving, nor was it much of a river at all. It was somewhere between a creek and a river, a halfway between thing, not deep enough for Cyrus to worry much about wading across if he so desired, but deep enough for him to stick to the riverbank. He undressed himself and then sat upon the bank and let go of his sword. There was no one around, though he could see Martaina in the distance, between him and the encampment. A split from the river was visible, something that wended much closer to the camp, indeed almost through it, and he wondered why she had suggested this place for him before the reason of privacy dawned upon him.

He sat upon the bank and let the sun crawl lower in the sky, unconcerned. His head no longer swam, and his breathing was deep and steady, taking in the plains air. The grasses here were different than those around Sanctuary, fuller—more oats, he thought, less tamed. The Plains of Perdamun were broken and dotted with farms; these grounds were spotted only occasionally with settlement. He dipped his feet in the water and felt the coolness run over his toes. He looked to the direction of the light current and realized it came from the north, from the mountains in the far distance, where the enemy lay.

He stood and slid into the water, wading in on his knees, as it covered him to the waist. His knees touched the thousand pebbles on the bottom of the stream, and he let the current run over him, let himself fall back, let his hair submerge, long black locks clinging to his head as they dampened. He kept his face above the water then dipped it under for a moment, felt it run into his nose and he broke the surface sputtering, snorting it out.

"Finally reached the point of trying to drown yourself?" There was a quiet voice nearby, and he looked up to see her watching him, squatting near his armor.

"No," he said, ignoring the levity in her voice. "Just trying to remove the accumulation of weeks of sweat and sick smell."

"Not a bad plan, as such plans go." Her clothing hung loose, no cloak or armor visible from where he sat. She was down to the barest essentials, the daggers on her hips staring at him like they had eyes of their own. Her curves were smooth, and the shirt she wore had enough of a gap at the top that he was left not needing to imagine the breasts he had seen so many times of late. "Did you have any reason for it besides just the feeling of uncleanliness?"

"Yes." He nodded slowly.

"Must I inquire why?"

He stared back at her, waiting, with her head cocked, her slightly pointed incisors hanging out of her deep blue lips. "Must I say it?"

She squatted there, and he wondered if she was visible to Martaina, as low as her profile was, with the grass swaying and almost touching her cheeks. "Before, I've been content to let it pass. But now, yes. I want to hear you say it."

"Because I want you," Cyrus said. "Because I crave you and the relief you bring."

"Relief?" She unknotted the strings at the front of her shirt and shrugged out of it there in front of him, let her dark blue skin show to the world. She stepped out of a boot with a half-step, not ever leaving the ground but coming to her hands and knees. The other boot came off with ease, as she crawled toward the bank of the stream on all fours, naked to the waist. Her cloth breeches came unlaced with only a minimal effort from her, and slid off just as her hand reached the rocky edge of the water.

He waited for her, felt the rising tide within him, and when he felt her first kiss, it was as though the call within him were answered, the raging tide rising was dismissed. They were there for quite some time, the splashing of the water around them the evidence of a particularly noisy bath. Cyrus neither knew nor cared whether Martaina saw; she doubtless knew anyway. *It matters not,* he thought in the midst of it. But in truth, he knew otherwise.

They lay on the grassy bank for a while afterward, her head on his shoulder, not speaking. "Why?" Cyrus asked, into the silence of the setting sun.

"Why what?" Aisling's voice came back to him, jaded, wary.

"Why do you think I'm doing this?" he asked, spent, not even close to sure about what answer he would get. "Do you think it's because I—"

"I try not to look a gift horse in the mouth," Aisling said, and she rolled over, grasping at her shirt and pulling it on. "Though, I do occasionally put a gift *in* my—"

"There's the Aisling of old," Cyrus said, not moving, feeling the hard dirt against his back. "I had thought that perhaps finally getting what you wanted would rid you of your desire to be crass."

He saw the subtle shrug of her shoulders as she knotted the strings that knit up her shirt. "Have I gotten what I wanted?" She didn't look back at him. "I did get you, I suppose, and I did always say I wanted this, so I suppose in that way I got what I wanted."

"You were perhaps expecting me to be more … enthusiastic?" He rolled onto his side to watch her as she dressed, still squatting low and keeping her body down, out of sight of camp.

"I could hardly ask for a more enthusiastic partner, at least on a purely physical level." Her legs folded around in front of her like a gymnast and she slid into her pants, taking care to knot them back up. "Especially so soon after being an invalid."

"I'm not the same, am I?" He didn't watch her now, he let himself lean back to the ground, felt his wet hair slop into the dirt.

"No," she said, but her voice seemed cavalier and uncaring about the whole thing. "But who of us stays the same for our whole lives?"

"What would you have of me, then?" Cyrus looked up at the sky, the deepening shades of evening coming out now.

"Nothing that I think you would be capable of giving at present," she said, and he watched her put her boots on, one at a time, her white hair bound over her shoulder and leaving water marks on her tan shirt. "Which is why I don't ask."

"Do you think me fragile?" He couldn't seem to muster any umbrage for his question.

"I think you're already broken," she said, and stood, looking down at him. "But that's all right. We all break some time; and I'm here, willing to take what you're willing to give and willing to give what you need right now. Your spirals don't concern me; you're a big boy, and you'll work it out in time."

"Will I now?" He let a faint amusement creep into his voice, and he saw a whirl of white clouds tinged orange by the coming sunset. "That's reassuring."

"Be reassured, then," she straddled him, her cloth pants against his abdomen, and she leaned over to kiss him, deep and full on the mouth. He felt her passion behind it, the force, but he had none of his own to match it with, just the slight stir of something detached, and far away, a physical reaction that told him that if she stayed where she was, her clothing would need to be removed again …

As if she could sense his line of thought, she broke from him. "See?" She gave him a faint smile, and the long incisors poked out of her lips again. Time was he would have thought them predatory, but now he saw the hurt, the edge behind her eyes, the strain that she didn't intend to loose. She stood, and with a whirring of the grass, she took the first steps away.

He lay there by the stream, trying to gather enough energy to bring himself back to the water the clean off the grit accumulated during his and Aisling's lovemaking. He couldn't find it, though, and remained there, staring at the sky, until the first body came drifting down the current only a few minutes later.

Chapter 57

Vara

Day 1 of the Siege of Sanctuary

There were no catapults hurling rock through the air, no siege towers making their way over the plains, no arrows filling the skies above the wall. There was nothing but the sound of an army outside, the raucous cheers, the battle hymns, the shouts and glee of the invaders poised less than a mile from the Sanctuary walls, waiting, as though they would come across the open distance and split the walls wide.

"They sit, they wait," Thad said, addressing the officers, who were gathered around the Council Chambers. "Of course they stop the flow of convoys along the major roads nearby, but that's to be expected. We can't see them, of course, but you know they'll have taken all the grain that's being shipped through the crossroad north of here."

Alaric watched Thad from behind templed hands, as always. This time was different, Vara thought, in that the Ghost's brow was stitched together like storm clouds on the horizon, as though thunderheads were bound to streak down his face and unleash fury on the first poor bastard to cross before him. "Every day they hold the crossroads is another day they hold the Plains of Perdamun in their grip, another day closer to the harvest, another day closer to the eventual starving of Reikonos."

"Are we actively rooting for Reikonos now?" Erith said, causing everyone to turn and look at her. "I mean, I know we're sympathetic to the humans, but the Confederation and the Council of Twelve? Bumbling idiots. They did want this war, after all."

"The city of Reikonos is the largest in Arkaria with over two million people," Alaric said. "Should the dark elves take it, they will not be merciful to the occupants—or the human race."

"Oh, so we are rooting for the Council of Twelve," Erith said, not chagrined. "Okay, well, that's good to know."

"Personally, I'm more worried about me, then the rest of you, then our members, then the applicants, and somewhere down the list, the flower garden," Vaste said. "I'll worry about Reikonos and the rest of the human race when the destruction of all of the above is not hanging over my head. Especially the flowers because they're so pretty."

"What chance do we have to push them back?" Ryin asked, turning his question to Thad. "A hundred thousand or more, yes? How do we break an army of that size? How many would we need to do it?"

"More than we have," Alaric said. "I suspect that they will not be driven away as easily as they were the first time now that they have reinforcements. We can defend the walls against that number by keeping them at bay, but by bottling us up, they achieve their directive—they hold total control over the plains. There is no way we can effectively guard against the predations of their soldiers against the farms without being able to move our army to do so."

"Perhaps we cannot control the Plains of Perdamun while they have us cornered so," Vara said, speaking at last, "but we can give them pause and keep them from extending that control."

Alaric's eyebrow came up behind his hands. "You mean to fight a small war, to distract them, to split their forces."

"Yes," she said. "I mean to take a small force and do what they accused us of two years ago—find their convoys of stolen goods and strike them, then teleport back here with the spoils. They'll be forced to move soldiers off the line of siege to escort the convoys, and as we move closer to harvest time that will be a larger and larger group necessary to keep them safe. With a druid and a wizard we'll be able to teleport out of trouble before any army can reach us, and we can cause enough trouble and discord north of here to force them to keep splitting their forces."

"I like it," Vaste said, nodding his head at a sideways angle. "It almost sounds like something that could really work, as though perhaps it had been done at some point in the recent past."

"It seems a shame to let our enemies have all the fun," Vara said archly, "seeing as when Goliath and the goblins tried it, it worked very effectively at keeping all parties concerned fully off balance."

"Yes, and also prompted every power in the area to send in more troops," Ryin said. "What's to stop the Sovereign from doing so again?"

"Just package up another division or five and throw them into the Plains of Perdamun?" Thad asked. "The Sovereign has to be reaching a limit at some point. There are only so many able-bodied dark elven men still living in Saekaj. Sooner or later, the Sovereign will run dry of forces. He can't maintain any semblance of a line south of Reikonos, keep armies on the eastern frontiers with the Northlands and the Riverlands to keep them from interfering with his siege of Reikonos, and still keep the River Perda buttoned up the way he does while sending fifty or a hundred thousand more troops to the Plains of Perdamun. Something will give."

"And let us hope it is not our walls, and our forces, and our flowers," Vaste said.

"So we send a force?" Ryin asked, looking around, as though gauging the response around the table. "We do what the goblins did to us, raid the transports of the dark elves, wreck their convoys and cause them to spread out their forces, pull them from here?"

"It does seem somehow fitting," Alaric said from behind his hands, "that the war started in that very way, and now we return to the beginning for our own purposes. Vara, since it is your idea, I would ask you to spearhead this attack force. No more than a hundred at any given time are to go with you, and no fewer than three spellcasters with the ability to cast a teleportation spell to return you here. I will not have us lose people to mere accidents. Keep a wary eye around you, even if you travel at night, and be certain to be doubly careful so as to avoid ambushes. The dark elves will not long tolerate us raiding the fruits of their thievery." Alaric smiled and the hands came down. "I do appreciate the irony, though; they steal from local farmers, and we proceed to steal it back for our own purposes."

"Yes, it is somewhat delicious, isn't it?" Vaste asked. "It's like pounding your enemies as if they were mutton and then licking the tears off of their faces." There was an uncomfortable silence. "Oh, as though none of *you* have ever done that."

"Where are you going to begin?" Erith asked, looking to Vara. "The Plains of Perdamun are huge, and traversing the whole thing, even with all the portals available to you—I mean, the Sovereign will have sent out wagons by the hundreds to collect the bounty of the plains."

"We start in the north," Vara said, and she felt her mind harden in resolution. "Near Prehorta, the closest to their home and where they'll be paying the least attention. Then we'll move west, toward the river and then …" She felt a thin, malicious smile crease her lips, and she wondered idly if it stole the color from them when she did it. "If we do this right, we'll keep them rather busy …"

Chapter 58

Cyrus

The tent was stuffed, filled to the brimming with servants and clingers-on for both Syloreas and Actaluere. The men from Syloreas were big, of course, the rough and marked sort whom Cyrus had come to expect, with their beards and long hair and fierce looks. There were not many useless, effete ones surrounding Briyce Unger, but the few there were made up for the lack with annoying precision.

The men from Actaluere, on the other hand, were swarthier, smaller on the whole, and reminded Cyrus of the men who worked the docks in Reikonos before the dark elves had moved in and taken over the labor force there. Their hair was short, the fighters were easy to tell from the talkers—and there were talkers aplenty who had come with Milos Tiernan.

Cyrus sat on a cloth stool that had been provided for him by one of the talkers of the Actaluere delegation. It was a small thing, annoying in its way, and it made him yearn to stand, especially now that the most troubling aftereffects of his injury had passed. Every eye in the tent was on him, and he had just finished speaking about the bodies, the ones that had come down the stream while he had been there beside it only the night before.

"You'll forgive me, Lord Davidon," Milos Tiernan said, a slight grimace on his face, as though the very news pained him, "but … how many bodies were there?"

"More than I care to count," Cyrus said. "I stopped trying after thirty."

"And they were men of Syloreas?" Tiernan asked, couching his words in a tone that sounded uncomfortable to Cyrus.

"So it would seem," Unger said. "I looked them over when Lord Davidon's people came for me. They look like village folk from the foothills, judging by the goatskin clothing. I would presume that they washed down after their village had been wiped out."

"Fair to say." Cyrus stood, hearing the clink of his armor, unable to bear sitting any longer, not on the tiny stool. "The scourge is sweeping out of the mountains it seems, coming south now, just as we expected."

"Have you been informed of our battle plan?" Briyce Unger asked, the smell of sweat thick in the tent, the breeze of yesterday gone and replaced by the hot sun overhead, which turned the tent into a makeshift oven. The mountain men around Unger were shifting, listless, even though most of them remained seated.

"Seems simple enough," Cyrus said. "Form a line in the middle of the plains north of here when we know they're coming, sit and wait, and let them fall on us like wave after wave on the rocks."

"There's a bit more to it than that," Tiernan said, with that same slight grimace. "Though not much, admittedly. Every suggestion I put forward with the idea of a flanking maneuver was roundly rejected."

"If they come in as great numbers as we suspect," Cyrus said, "we'll be too busy protecting our own flanks to launch a counterthrust. With our healers at work, this seems like the best solution. If they come at us in a small number, we can get elaborate and envelop them. If they're going to mass and swarm at us with the ridiculous amount of them that we think are lurking in the north, then we're better off keeping it simple and defensive."

"Yet," Tiernan said, and stood, "if we allow our army to become pinned down, will it not mean our defeat? Will we not be pushed back, lose ground and lose heart?"

"Losing ground is an acceptable trade-off in this situation," Cyrus said as he watched Briyce Unger nod his head. "We have hundreds of miles of open ground to lose before we butt up against a forest and have nowhere else to fall back. Losing heart would be foolish so long as we keep them from breaking through. If they flank us, we're in trouble. If we can keep them in front of us rather than behind and continue to hammer them, we stand a chance. This battle is as much about standing toe to toe with them and bleeding them through attrition as it is about land and position. Let them have the whole plains," Cyrus said with a wave of his hand to indicate the land around them. "So long as we can bleed them dry in the process and lose few enough of our own, we win."

Tiernan conceded with a slight nod of his head. "Very well. This has been explained to me more than once, but the way you say it seems to make more sense than the others." He nodded in deference to Briyce Unger. "I hope you'll forgive me for saying so." Unger waved him off, and Tiernan went on. "Can you guarantee that your healers will be able to hold our lines together against the death and serious injury that these beasts bring with them?"

"I guarantee nothing in a battle save for bloodshed and death," Cyrus said, looking at Tiernan, a smaller man than he, as most were. He saw a hint of Cattrine in the King of Actaluere's cheekbones. "You will lose men, no doubt, even if my healers were to perform miraculous feats. The army is too large and my healers too few to effectively protect the entirety. They will do their best, especially since your army will be holding the left flank, and I have no desire to see you take casualties that will weaken my defenses in that area."

"Fair enough," Tiernan said, and his voice was graver than Cyrus had heard it at Enrant Monge. "Then I suppose we have our plan, we have our roles, and all that is left to do is to wait for my army, and then move north into the jaws of the enemy."

"Aye," Briyce Unger said, "and let us hope that this time, we bring a morsel too large for them to digest, a bone that they might finally choke upon." With that, the King of Syloreas stood, and as though his nervous energy was in need of a release of its own, walked briskly out of the tent without another word.

Cyrus watched him go, and saw the members of the Actaluere delegation begin to file out as well, save for a few—Milos Tiernan and two of his closest advisors, men Cyrus had seen at Enrant Monge. Tiernan caught Cyrus's eye, and the meaning was clear—*Wait a moment.*

Cyrus did as he was bade by the King's gaze, and after only another moment, Tiernan's advisors nodded in turn and left the tent, the flap closing behind them. The air was still now, and Cyrus stared at Tiernan, his piercing green eyes staring into Cyrus's own. The King held a brass cup that had been resting at his side during the convocation and he drank from it now, his eyes never leaving Cyrus. "So, you're the general of Sanctuary," Tiernan said when the cup had just barely left his lips. "You've caused quite the stir since you came to our land."

"None of it was intended to harm your realm, I hope you understand." Cyrus did not bend as he spoke, kept the deference he might otherwise have offered well out of his words. He said it harsh and firm, keeping it from being any sort of offering or concession.

"I do understand," Milos Tiernan said, though he kept his distance. "You trespassed, and I would have been content to let you do so, because there was little margin in me keeping you from crushing Syloreas so long as you didn't turn against me afterward." The King of Actaluere let out a bitter laugh. "Hell, even if you had, I would have been better off than opposing you while you were in the middle of my territory; having you come at us from the border with Galbadien would have been less sensitive than letting you sack Green Hill. That was a black eye for us."

"Yet you don't seem that upset by it." Cyrus watched Tiernan's reaction; there was a subtle tightening of the man's jaw as it slid to the side and his lips drew tight together, wrinkling as they pursed in an almost-smile.

"I don't have to live in Green Hill," Tiernan said, and took a small sip from his cup again. "Nor was I the one who gave the order to muster forces against you. That was your friend Hoygraf. Obviously, I don't care to see any part of my realm destroyed, but as I said—I would have let you pass, if for no other reason than it benefitted us greatly to not stop you."

"How does it benefit you to have us save Galbadien?" Cyrus asked, watching Tiernan carefully.

"How would it have benefitted Actaluere to go from two enemies to one?" Tiernan shrugged. "Luukessia has a delicate balance of power, one that none of the Arkarians I've met seem to fully appreciate, coming from so fragmented a land. If there comes a war to Luukessia— and there always does—it rarely involves all three parties. Alliances last a year, perhaps two, enough to firmly shellack one of the powers and to allow the other two to remember their disdain for each other, and then they dissolve." He touched his chest with a single finger. "I like the balance. I like knowing who my enemies are, always. I prefer to know that I can't trust anyone on my borders and that my best bet is to always keep a wary eye on both of them." His expression turned sober. "And I always liked to think that if an outside threat came from over the bridge, our three Kingdoms would band together and toss them back without a second thought."

"Second thoughts seem to be abounding in this situation," Cyrus said, catching Tiernan's eye after the King had seemed to go pensive. "Your whole land was almost in an uproar; you barely made it to this conflict yourself, and whatever is coming down from those mountains is looking to me a whole lot worse than most of the things that might have come across the Endless Bridge."

"Perhaps," Tiernan said with a ghostly smile. "But part of that was your doing—your interference. No one but an outsider would have caused the fragmentation that you did when you took my sister away from Hoygraf. No Luukessian, at least."

"I didn't know she was your sister when I did it," Cyrus said.

Tiernan gave a small chuckle. "If you had, would that have swayed you?"

"Doubtful."

"Then it matters little enough, doesn't it?" Tiernan started toward a pitcher of water that rested on a table near the side of the tent. "Your attack on the Baron—I'm sorry, it's Grand Duke now, isn't it?—on his castle and your subsequent actions forced me to guide my land toward a war I never asked for. That would be the only reason we wouldn't have rendered aid to Syloreas given what's happening, at least after my scout saw with his own eyes what we faced."

"You seem to like the idea of fragmentation in the land of Luukessia as a whole," Cyrus said. "But I note you don't seem quite so fond of it when it happens in your own Kingdom."

"No man enjoys having his own house thrown into chaos," Tiernan said, his back to Cyrus while he hefted the water pitcher and poured it into his cup. "Make no mistake, Hoygraf has enough power to throw my house into a good deal of chaos."

"You're very frank about that," Cyrus said. "I would have expected you'd do more to hide it, given your reputation for maneuvering and canniness. There doesn't seem to be much advantage to be gained from telling me you've elevated a man to Grand Duke who is poised to tear your Kingdom apart should he so desire."

Tiernan didn't stiffen, not exactly, though his expression was masked from Cyrus, with his back turned as it was. The King took another sip of water without turning, and the warrior wondered if perhaps it was because Tiernan was taking the time to compose his reply. "There is little advantage in lying about the troubled state of my Kingdom to an outsider." Tiernan pivoted and gave Cyrus a twisted smile. "Let us not be coy; you were my sister's lover not so very long ago. I might not speak as freely with a complete stranger, but if she did not tell you at least a majority of the things I've 'admitted' to you in the last moments, I'll eat my own horse for dinner."

"She did tell me quite a bit about the goings-on of Actaluere," Cyrus said, arms still folded. "But I assumed that it was from the perspective of the Baroness Hoygraf, not the ... whatever her title was ... Tiernan."

"Her primary title would be 'Princess,'" Tiernan said with a nod and a pained expression.

"Sounds oddly condescending," Cyrus replied. "So your Kingdom is in trouble, what of it? Why are we discussing this?"

"We're discussing it," Tiernan said with a slightly raised eyebrow, "because you began with an admission that you intended my Kingdom no harm, and I responded by offering a similar statement which we then proceeded to descend into until we reached the current point of conversation." He took a sip of the water, lightly, almost daintily, then pulled it away from his lips with a flourish. "I assumed that like my conversations with Unger, you preferred to remove all the guile from the subtext by throwing everything onto the table first, so that then we could proceed with our talk unfettered by the political silliness which I, incidentally, excel at."

"Putting aside your strengths in a conversation with me doesn't seem to be to your greatest advantage, either," Cyrus said.

"It's a strength; it's hardly the only one I possess," Tiernan said. "Speaking in circles around men like you and Unger nets me little when it's only the two of us; you may discern what I'm going about but it profits me nothing when I'm merely trying to make a point."

"What is your point?" Cyrus asked, not feeling half as overwhelmed as he thought he should given the waves of admissions and dizzying maneuvers that seemed already to have been employed. *Is he being genuine or trying to muddle the issue? Damnation and hell if I can tell. Then again, his sister was quite good at misdirection as well ...*

"I've yet to approach it," Tiernan said. "But here, let me say it without mincing the words—leave my sister be."

Cyrus didn't respond, not for a long, silent minute. "I have no more intention toward your sister."

"Oh?" Tiernan stared him down, a smoky-eyed gaze. "You swore you'd protect her, go to war for her, but now you're content to leave her to the hands of her loving husband?"

Cyrus felt a tightness all over his face. "Doesn't it make it easier for you if that's the case?"

Tiernan stared back at him. "As the King of Actaluere, yes."

"And as her brother?"

Tiernan's face twisted, his eyes narrower, little specks of green visible between the eyelids. "I don't have the luxury of being her brother right now. I'm trying to keep a Kingdom from a bloody civil war at the hands of a sadistic madman while laboring to help save Luukessia from something we've never seen before."

"I have no intention of making your job any harder as King," Cyrus said. "She made her choice, for her own reasons. She went back to him, and this after lying to me about who she was and doing everything in her power to insult and provoke him." He shrugged, dismissing the rumbling within him that wanted to argue. "I've done all I can for her at this point. My responsibility lies with helping to destroy this scourge that afflicts your land."

"And after that?" Tiernan asked.

Cyrus laughed. "After that ..." He let his words fade. "I suppose it'll be time for me to go home, won't it?"

"As the King of Actaluere, I would find great relief if you did." Tiernan set aside the cup, and started toward the flap of the tent. "After all, there's nothing so dangerous to a land that thrives on having a balance of power as something that could upset that balance, say, an army with more ability than anyone else's. So, as King, I would heartily support your leaving after you finish your duty here."

Cyrus shook his head in deep amusement. "To the hells with what you'd want as King. What you're not saying is at least ten feet deeper than any of the shallow platitudes you're throwing at me about what you'd desire and support as King. You want me to rescue her before I leave, don't you?"

Tiernan held still, his body facing away from Cyrus, but he slowly pivoted on a foot, his cloak swaying at his feet. "As the King, you know

I could never ask such a thing."

"Well, all I'm looking at right now is a King and not much else," Cyrus said. "Not much of a man, that's for certain—"

"Easy to say without the responsibility," Tiernan said. "I hear that when I walk among the people in Caenalys, sometimes, when I don a cowl and go out to hear what word on the street is. 'If I were King, I'd ...' followed by a suggestion of such gut-wrenching stupidity that it would annihilate my entire Kingdom with more certainty than disbanding the army and sending written invitations to Galbadien and Syloreas to come visit and bring all their soldiers." Tiernan took slow, striding steps toward Cyrus, his every word filled with emotion that Cyrus hadn't caught even a hint of in any of the meetings he'd been in with Tiernan. "To be a statesman is to do what is best for the land you rule and to do that first. Family comes second, and your own concerns come later, if at all. So I'm quite content if I've measured up in the first way, and forgive me if I give less than a damn how much of a man or a brother I look like to you."

"You sold your sister in marriage to a monster who whips her, naked, in front of crowds," Cyrus said with barely controlled disgust. "Better hold to that Kingly air you're sporting as tightly as you can. Did you know what he was when you gave her to him? Did you know what kind of man he was when you elevated him to Grand Duke?"

"I knew what kind of power he held when I did all those things," Tiernan said with little other reaction. "I knew what my Kingdom's peril was when I did it. I knew what the danger was if I didn't hand her off or elevate him for his service. And by service I mean his stupidity in becoming entangled with an army from the west." Tiernan spun, keeping his face away from Cyrus again. "I knew what I did as a King and I ask for no forgiveness. I made hard choices that others might not have. You may believe that or not. What I ask is that if you are going to leave these shores, take my sister with you so that she might have the opportunity to escape the horror of Hoygraf's charms."

"And thus allow you to salve the conscience of the brother so the King may continue to happily rule without one of his own." Cyrus shook his head, the disgust welling up within him. "It must take courage indeed to ask a stranger to make right by his own risk what you refuse to make right with yours."

"One life or a million," Tiernan said quietly. "I rule a million, and I gave over one to smoothe the passage of all of them. Find me another man who would not make the same choice in the same situation, and I'll show you a better man than I, one who perhaps enjoys a quieter mind and less concern for the far-reaching consequences of his acts."

"It's funny how a man can have such a long vision, to be so farsighted as to see all the problems of his land," Cyrus said, "but shortsighted enough to miss the ones that happen in his own house. I believe that could be called a form of blindness—or perhaps uncaring."

This time, Tiernan bristled. "I will see you at the battle and likely not before then. When we speak again, as surely we shall over the course of these events, I shall not make mention of this." Tiernan reached for the flap of the tent.

"Just as well," Cyrus said. "We wouldn't want to inflame that long-buried conscience of Cattrine's brother, after all. It might interfere with the plottings of the King of Actaluere."

"I did what I had to do, and I thought that perhaps you, as one who I had heard held some affection in your heart for Cattrine, might do me some small service and allow her a measure of happiness. I apologize, sir, for confusing you with someone who cared for her." He pulled the tent open and let it flap shut behind him.

Cyrus sat there in the empty tent for a long time after that, pondering what reply he might have made. Ultimately, he said nothing to the empty tent, though much to himself on the inside.

Chapter 59

Vara

Day 5 of the Siege of Sanctuary

The northern Plains of Perdamun were sun-kissed, the late-summer light bounding over them just as the horses of Vara's expeditionary party did. It was nearing daybreak, and the shadows were diminishing as the light increased. A fresh smell was in the air, the aura of dew and horse, of farm and field, and Vara steered her animal across the flat ground, the hoofbeats of a hundred following close behind her.

"This is such a clever idea," Vaste's voice grated at her from her right. "I really love the thought of the hundred of us being out here, all alone, in the middle of a territory crawling with dark elves. It's a smart idea, too, running out of our safely defended keep in order to sow discord among our enemies' supply lines, in hopes they won't capture and kill us. Very clever."

"It was exceedingly clever," Ryin Ayend said without a trace of irony. "Though I know you're being sarcastic, Vaste, it really was a good idea."

"Me?" Vaste asked, his expression clouded with a sour look. "Be sarcastic? Surely not. But if I were, perhaps it's not so much that I dislike the idea as I dislike the fact that I'm forced to rise before dawn to help execute the idea."

"I had just assumed that riding the horse as you were," Vara said, "you were experiencing some early saddle soreness that was making you complain in an infantile manner. Either that, or the conjured bread we've been eating of late is causing you some mild colic."

"I am not experiencing colic or any sort of saddle soreness—yet," Vaste replied. "I do expect that once we've engaged the enemy a few times and they begin to reinforce their convoys with extra soldiers, I'll begin to experience some digestive disturbances, though."

"I'm certain that will be to no one's advantage," Ryin muttered as they came over a slight rise in the plains. "Up there." He pointed to a line visible in the far distance.

"That'd be our first convoy, I suppose," Vaste said. "Can you tell if it's the dark elves from here?"

"It is," Vara replied. "At least ten wagons, no visible column of soldiers marching with it." She let herself smile then stopped when she remembered that there were others with her. "I believe it is time to show these dark elves the error of their ways."

"You make it sound as though we're going to hand them a list of table manner faux pas they committed at a dinner party," Vaste said. "And if that's the case, I would like to add that drinking directly from the soup bowl is considered bad form, though not nearly so much as scratching yourself in inappropriate places with your dessert fork." After drawing a long, uncomfortable look from both Ryin and Vara, he hastened to add, "I learned that one from hard experience myself."

"Let us have at them, then," Vara said, and urged her horse into a gallop. "No survivors in military garb. Let any civilians have the opportunity to flee but don't hesitate to kill. We can always resurrect any casualties later."

"Says the one who doesn't have to drain her magical energy to bring them back," Vaste murmured.

"Keep your wits about you," she ordered and then glanced at Vaste. "Oh, it's you. I forgot. Never mind, then."

"I'm actually very witty," Vaste said, "though you'd need to loosen up by a considerable margin to appreciate it."

"Oh, I appreciate it," Vara said, her horse already hard at work, running full out. "If only I could be as amusing as you."

"I read once that brevity is the key to wit," Vaste said, his voice barely audible over the hoofbeats of the entire raiding party. "Perhaps you should talk less."

They rode hard across the plains, the steady pace carrying them toward the slow-moving wagon train on the road ahead. It was only when they were a few hundred yards away that the convoy began to realize that there was danger afoot, and they hurried to move the wagons along but by then it was far too late.

The wagons were all flat-bedded, stacked high with barrels and crates. Dark elves sat up front in ones and twos, Vara noted as she assessed the threat. There were a half-dozen horsed soldiers with them, their armor of the boiled leather variety. *Not a spellcaster among them and woefully underdefended, prepared only for angry farmers upset at the theft of their crops. That will change after today.*

She raised her blade above her head and let loose a warcry. It annoyed her a second after she did it; it was far too close to something Cyrus Davidon would have done. *Loud warfare is the province of the savage and unskilled. I have other means at my disposal.*

She extended her blade as the dark elven soldiers lined up on horseback in a rank two wide, forming a spear as though to charge into the Sanctuary force. She let the tip point just between the first two, and then whispered the incantation she had learned shortly after she turned sixteen. A ripple of air flew forth, channeled from her hand down her blade, her spell sending a burst of concussive force at the riders.

Her blast hit the first of them as the horses made to swerve; they did not make it in time, and the riders were thrown, coming hard to the ground in a crunch of breaking bones and falling animals. Her spell carried through them and smashed the next in the rank, and the next, all the way to the fourth row. *Only four remaining now,* Vara thought as she sent her horse onward over the fallen enemies. She raised her blade and jerked her horse left, dodging the attack aimed at her by the first of her remaining opponents. She caught him flush against the gap between his leather armor and steel helm, and there was a gasping noise as he hit the ground. She readied her sword again and struck back at the final horseman still in the line, dealing him a glancing blow.

Once she passed, she pulled on the reins with her free hand and brought her horse into a quick turn. Her army of a hundred had finished the last of the dark elves. She turned to see the convoy trying to get away still and sent her horse galloping after it. She pulled aside the first wagon and aimed her sword at the dark elf sitting atop it. His hands came up in front of him, shaking, and Vara could see the age on his lined blue skin, the corners of his eyes with the crow's feet radiating from them. She did not say a word, merely maintained pace with the wagon and the man brought it to a stop. A few of the wagons behind his tried to escape off the road, and she watched them fail, one of them even losing a wheel trying to break right over a bumpy field. The Sanctuary raiding party was around them in force and they were outmatched.

"Step down," she said to the man atop the wagon she had stopped.

"I won't harm you or your people, so long as you make no threatening moves. There was the crack of a lightning spell heard several wagons back, and she rolled her eyes. "As I said." She pointed toward the field to her left. "Go stand over there. Run in fear for your life if you must, but don't come near the wagons."

The older dark elf nodded as he climbed down and then turned and sprinted across the field with more speed than she would have given him credit for, given his skin and the salt-and-pepper coloration of his hair. She shrugged and walked around the back of the wagon, where Vaste had already hoisted himself up and had opened a barrel. "Wheat," the troll said, "grains, oats, all manner of excellent suchness."

"Oh, good," she said, and found herself leaning against the side, "and I was somewhat worried we're ambushing a train filled with women's clothing or something of the sort."

"Why, are you looking for another dress?" Vaste asked, not looking up from the crates that he was inspecting. "All in all, not a terrible harvest if we managed to get eight wagons of this stuff. Not enough to bring the Sovereign's army to his knees, but if we did this regularly it'd be enough to keep us in the fresh foodstuffs for a while." He gave a long look around, surveying the damage they had wrought. "Well, it worked."

"Of course it worked," she said, looking over the ill-gotten gains. "And this is but the first of many. We need to hit them with such force and so often that they are compelled to send hundreds of troops with every wagon for fear it will disappear from the road as though swallowed up by the very earth itself." Something in the way she said it made Vara's own scalp tingle, and an idea worked its way in, just a passing one at first, framed from a memory. *We could ...* She shook her head, as if to rid herself of it. *No, ridiculous. Absolutely ridiculous ...*

But it stayed with her just the same.

Chapter 60

Cyrus

The days passed slowly after Cyrus's meeting with Tiernan. Cyrus remained in an agitated state; the river nearby was now clogged with bodies, so many of them falling downstream that he wondered how there could have been that many people in the north for so many to have washed downward.

"There are several major villages on this stream," Unger said to him as they stood nearby, watching the water source turn more and more tainted as the days passed. "It bodes ill for Syloreas that so many of our sons and daughters are feeling the teeth of these beasts."

It bodes ill for our army as well, if every source of fresh water is given over to being filled with rotting corpses, Cyrus thought, but he did not say it. Somewhere in the back of his mind was the thought of bathing as well, though that scarcely seemed to matter to Aisling. She had come to his tent in silence every night since their first rendezvous by the river, and she said not a word, no conversation, nothing. He did not want to break the quiet that she imposed to bring about any of the questions she might have that he cared not to answer. So he said nothing, but instead buried his lips in hers, pressing his face against her cheek, her neck, in her bosom. The silence was like water to him, just as vital to his survival, and he needed what she gave him so desperately now that he wondered how he had survived without it for so many years.

The camp had been quiet until the second army from Actaluere arrived. Cyrus watched them stream into the camp, at least thrice the size of the host that Milos Tiernan had brought with him to Enrant Monge. Other armies streamed in, too, from the east and west of Syloreas. "They've been turned out by riders," Unger had said to him as they watched a steady line of men in furs and skins come into camp day after day, few enough of them possessing any armor at all. A few genuine armies of Syloreas came as well, more of them bearing at least some protection for battle but not nearly as many as came in cloth and with rusty swords and spears.

They moved north the day after the Actaluereans joined them, striking out across the plain, following a road that seemed familiar to Cyrus. When the wind blew out of the north it smelled of rot and decay and carried a chill that ill-fitted late summer. When it came out of the south it was enough to remind Cyrus of the harvest and brought warmth aplenty. The memory of the Plains of Perdamun was still strong with him, and though the grains looked marginally different, he was reminded of home nonetheless as the days grew shorter a few minutes at a time. The ride north was slower than when last he had done it, the mountains in the distance still capped with snow.

Cyrus kept his own counsel as the days went on, meeting with his officers only when needed. They were well enough instructed that he didn't worry, and Odellan had a firm handle on the warriors and rangers who made up the front ranks of battle. He watched them drill at the elf's commands and tried to feel fortunate at having come across the Endrenshan from Termina. *I doubt he would feel quite the same. All things being equal, I rather suspect he'd prefer to still be there, in his city, were it still standing. Hell, perhaps even now that it's not.*

The last day of their ride carried them to a small town on the edge of the river, where the folk they found turned out en masse when Briyce Unger led the march through their village. Cyrus looked over the village, which was no more than a collection of hovels with thatched roofs and stone walls, perhaps two dozen at most, all grouped together around a mill with a waterwheel that turned. There was a sound within that Cyrus presumed was the sound of rocks grinding grist.

Cyrus listened as the townsfolk pelted Unger with questions, their worry bleeding into their voices. What about the dead bodies? Should we go south and find safety? What comes for us? What killed those people? Will it kill us as well? Has Scylax truly fallen?

The voices were overwhelming, and Cyrus watched as Unger held up his hands for quiet. The last of the cacophony died away, leaving an eerie calm settled over the village as the people waited to hear Unger's pronouncement. "Good people," Unger began, still atop his horse, looking like nothing so much as a mountain astride his destrier, "I bring with me sad tidings of news you've already heard. A vile enemy comes out of the mountains, and yes, it has taken Scylax and slaughtered the people there. This is done, and no amount of wishing will make it undone. But I bring with me allies—magicians from beyond the western shores of our land, the full army of Actaluere and all the men Syloreas can spare. You've heard the rumors and heralds and the messengers. Now hear me—we will fight our enemies back. We will drive them from here, whip them before us with sword and shield and send them scurrying back to their mountain den where we will crush them and ensure they never return to haunt our mountain home again."

Cyrus listened as the King of Syloreas said his piece. There was a certain magic in the way he did it, weaving his words together, causing the crowd to stay silent. Unger was not much of a wordsmith, but his ability to speak in front of the villagers came out and there was a calm in the midst of what was coming, a reassurance from their own King that they would be safe. Cyrus took it all in, unsurprised, and when they met at the inn that night, Cyrus said as much to Curatio, J'anda and Longwell.

"Unger's long been a thorn in my father's side," Longwell said, chewing on the moist bones of a chicken. "Unger's father was a dreadful King, to hear it told. The people were in an uproar all the time, there was a famine that he dealt with poorly or somesuch, I can't recall. Briyce, though, has been skillful, especially for a man so focused on battle. What he managed to do—striking into the heart of Galbadien—was shocking, considering that a generation ago Syloreas had lost a quarter of its territory just to our predations. Briyce can persuade and he can fight. He took back all that lost ground and then some." Longwell shook his head. "I wasn't looking forward to ever staring across our northern border at him."

"You were to be a King here," J'anda said, his delicate hands cradling a battered brass goblet of wine that looked so out of place in the refined enchanter's grasp as to nearly be alien. "What happened to make you leave?"

"Long story," Longwell said, and gnawed on a leg bone without enthusiasm.

"It would seem we have time," Cyrus said, glancing around the candle-lit room. It was dim, and reminded him of a bar he'd been to in Reikonos with Terian at his side. He tried to push that thought away;

he'd last seen Terian being walked along behind Mendicant's pony.

"I suppose," Samwen grudgingly admitted. "You've met my father. You got a sense for what he's like."

"More than a sense," J'anda said, looking sidelong at another table, where Briyce Unger sat with several of his men, drinking mead and speaking in boisterous tones; Cyrus could hear some braggadocio, something about a battle on a western shore.

"He wasn't always that way," Longwell said, carefully licking the grease from each of his fingers. His gauntlets lay on the table beside him, and his steel blue armor looked dark, almost black, in the candlelight. "He used to be a warrior himself, a dragoon, like me. He had courage, little fear—they said he won a battle against the old King of Syloreas by riding him down in a charge. Which would be unremarkable except that my father had only himself and the King of Syloreas had a hundred guards following him into the fight."

Cyrus raised an eyebrow. "I presume the Syloreans backed off after your father struck down their King?"

"You presume correctly," Longwell said, his head down, voice still clear. "They're fierce warriors, and they would have been glad to take revenge, but he fought him singly and won. When my father's army— smaller than the Sylorean one by half—rejoined him after the charge, they formed a line and held against the rage of the Syloreans for a full day without breaking. That was forty years ago or more, I suppose. That was the battle that made Briyce Unger King of Syloreas. My father had only been on the throne of Galbadien five years or so by that point."

"Briyce had no thanks for the gift of his crown?" J'anda sipped delicately from the cup again, then set it upon the table.

"No," Longwell said with a shake of the head. "As soon as his coronation was over he rode out at the head of their army and started to take back territory. They gained a half dozen towns and a major seaport by the end of his first week of fighting. Sent my father into a rage. Of course, I wasn't born yet when this happened, but my mother told me. By the time I came along, she said he was a different man than the one she'd known when he began. He only got worse after that, raging at the wrong people, fearful of losing so much as an inch of his Kingdom. He didn't lead battles anymore, no reckless charges. He was afraid to take a risk for fear of what it might cost him." Longwell brought his own goblet up. "And we lost territory after territory, and he got more calculating as time went on. Since the day I was born, Galbadien is a hundred miles shorter across the top than it was. Not much lost to the west, but still." He shrugged. "Father hasn't taken it very well, but he's yet to make an aggressive move to stop it, other than when he tried to invade Syloreas while Unger's back was turned."

"Fear of loss does funny things to a man," Curatio said, speaking for the first time since they'd sat down. The healer's eyes were firmly rooted in his own wine, though he hadn't had more than a few sips since they'd arrived, Cyrus knew. "It quickens the blood, slows action, paralyzes you. A man could have everything he wanted and be truly happy, but if you take away only the smallest thing, he becomes angry, resentful, and his happiness rots like a deshfruit left in the midday sun." Curatio took a finger and dipped it into his glass, then brought it out and let it drip on the table. "It only gets worse as you age, you know. The older you are, the more you see what you have to lose, and the more you fear what that loss might mean."

"I've heard he's not even the same since I left," Longwell said. "He dwells in his chambers, doesn't see anyone for days at a time, that not even the maidens they send him can lift his spirits for more than an hour or so at a go. He's fearful, all right, though I didn't see it when we quarreled before I left. He argued me right out of Vernadam, without so much as a notice that it might be anything other than petty anger driving him."

"A father and a son arguing?" J'anda said with a quiet chuckle. "Hard to believe."

"Oh, yes," Longwell said. "There was stubborn pride on display enough to choke the both of us. He rooted in his conviction, and I in mine."

"What did you argue about?" Curatio asked, ever the sage, implacable, all-knowing.

Longwell thought about it, and Cyrus watched the dragoon's face as it squinted in consideration. "I don't rightly know," Longwell said. "It seemed of vital importance at the time, some minor trifle about how the army ran that felt like the most important thing in the world, but upon reflection ..." Longwell let out a quiet, mirthless laugh, "I'll be damned if I can remember."

"Pettiness is hardly an exclusively human trait," Curatio said. "I recall—just barely, you understand—arguing with my own father. Though obviously this was some time ago."

"How did your father die, Curatio?" Cyrus asked.

The healer stared into space, his face blank. "It was a long time ago."

"Does that mean you don't recall?" Longwell asked, his attention turned to the elf. "Or that you don't want to?"

Curatio didn't change expression, and continued to stare straight ahead. "It was a long time ago."

"It would appear we've brought some of Alaric's 'vague and mysterious' along with us to this new land," J'anda said, prompting a chuckle from Longwell, and even a smile from Curatio, one that lasted far past all the other smiles at the table.

That night, when Cyrus lay down in his bed, the sounds of the inn alive around him, he tried not to think about what was to come. There was a fire in the hearth beside him, and the Syloreans were still drinking downstairs and telling stories, though Milos Tiernan and his few aides had left even before Cyrus and his party had called it a night. There was a quiet creaking as Cyrus shifted in the bed, which was old and made a corresponding amount of noise every time he moved in it. It gave a squeak of protest, the wood in the old frame taking umbrage to his motion on top of the thin mattress. There was still the smell of chicken in the air, and the aroma of the pickled eggs that had been kept in a barrel in the corner which the innkeep left open all night, as though the smell were of no consideration. The smoke of the fire did all it could to overcome it, yet still failed. The nub of a feather was sticking out of the mattress and poking into Cyrus's back, and when he shifted, another took its place.

There was a very quiet sound of a door opening, and a thin shaft of light flooded into the room, running across his bed for only a second before a shadow blocked it, then one more second before the door closed quietly again. He saw the figure, unmistakable in her curves and careful, quiet walk. "Aisling?" he whispered, and he felt a finger cross his lips as she silently slipped into the bed.

Her lips pressed onto to his, and the swarm of thoughts in his mind faded blissfully. The bed frame continued to squeak, building to a fever pitch of motion, and then subsided. She left as quietly as she came in, and once she was gone, his thoughts plagued him no more.

Chapter 61

Vara

Day 18 of the Siege of Sanctuary

The alarms sounded in the middle of the night, along with the customary calls of "Alarum! Alarum!" that set her teeth to rattling. *Why call out the elongated version of the damned word? Why not just say "alarm" and be done with it?*

She had slept once more in her armor and was down the stairs quickly enough to avoid the pileup that had seemed to occur with every alarm of late. Her only consolation was knowing that the members were taking every attack seriously. Except perhaps now, in the dead of the night, the slowness of things coming to awakeness. *Of course they would attack us now, draw us out weary and exhausted after I've just spent another day preying on their convoys and shipments.* She let slip a feral smile. *I'd strike them that way, just the same. No mercy.*

There were only two heralds in the foyer, two warriors shouting the alarm. Rather than correct them (*or slap them,* she thought uncharitably) she instead followed their outstretched hands, pointing to the front doors. She ran past the ranks of guards stationed around the portal in the foyer, swords, spears and axes pointed at the center of the room and she fled down the steps at a run, only a few others with her. She had heard the sounds up the stairwell and on the other floors as she passed them; *They'll all be awake and turned out soon enough.*

The night air was cool as she crossed the distance of the yard to the wall. The slap of her boots on the steps was lost to her breathing this time, steady, determined. She burst out onto the parapet and found a surprisingly quiet scene—a crowd of people circled down the wall a space, no one watching the fields below. She stole a glance over the edge, and by the light of the crescent moon she could see no army close by, no immediate threat, the grounds below still wafting the stench of the dead from the last battle, their bones now picked clean by the carrion birds, rats, worms, and maggots.

"What the bloody hell was that?" she asked as she shoulder checked her way through the crowd standing on the wall. Most moved aside when her voice was heard. *It is nice to know that some move aside not only because I am the shelas'akur but because I'm bound to knock them aside if they don't.* She burst through into the open space on the other side of the wall and there found Alaric, standing with his arms folded next to Thad, surveying the scene.

There were a dozen bodies lying splattered atop the wall, all dark elves she could see by the complexion of the ruined flesh, every one of them in armor of some sort. One of them was obviously a dark knight, fully covered from head to toe in plate mail, a stream of blood oozing out of the cracks and clefts. "What the hell is this?" Vara asked again, and this time Alaric turned to face her, registering no surprise.

"Hello, lass," the Ghost said. "It would appear that our enemies intended to launch a surprise attack to open our gates."

"I presume it failed," she said, kicking one of the bodies with her toe and finding it mushier than she expected.

"Indeed," Thad said, his amusement unhidden. "They tried to use Falcon's Essence to sneak over the wall a few hundred feet over our head. It worked, we didn't even see them coming until they hit the magical barrier at the perimeter and it stripped the enchantment right off of them, sending them plummeting to their deaths." He nodded over the wall toward the army in the distance. "My guess is that they're watching the gate, wondering why it hasn't opened yet. Could be a long night for the poor bastard behind those spyglasses."

"It could be a long night for those of us who were rousted for an alarm when there is plainly nothing to be alarmed about yet," she said, grinding her teeth together. "And also those of us who have an early morning sortie planned at daybreak."

"Sorry," Thad said with a shrug, "but it's the standard response to a surprise attack. We should be on our guard for the next few hours in case they try and storm the gates anyway."

Vara steamed for a moment, staring at the castellan in sheerest irritation. "You were at the Society of Arms in Reikonos, were you not?"

He blinked at her in surprise. "I was."

"Then I presume you were no Swift Sword."

Thad seemed to wobble as if not sure how to answer. "No, I was. I was most assuredly not one of the cursed Able Axes."

"I certainly believe that you might be swift but not able, based on what I've seen of your performance this night," Vara said bitingly. "I will be returning to my bed, and I trust *if* there is another alarm raised, it will be done only when an actual dark elf threat, complete with a still-beating hearts, is imminent."

Thad started to protest but was overcome by Alaric. "Do have a good night, Lady Vara."

"Lady Vara?" she spun at the Ghost of Sanctuary. "And shall I begin addressing you as Lord Garaunt?"

Alaric's gaze was steady and even, though there was a wearier bent to the man, she thought. "You may address me however you see fit, within the bounds of our mutual respect for each other." He favored her with a smile that was shot through with fatigue but made no move to return to Sanctuary or his own bed, and after a moment of watching him, she turned and made her way back inside, threading through the steady flow of people that were coming to join in the defense of their home.

Chapter 62

Cyrus

They were formed up in a line along the plain, north of the village he had heard the others refer to as Filsharron. It was at least two miles north of the place they had been staying in for the past few nights, the humble inn with the squeaking bed and the rapidly diminishing supply of pickled eggs. Cyrus could still taste one of them on his beard, a messy thing, and filled with the foulness of vinegar, nothing like the fresh ones he was accustomed to at Sanctuary. The line was surprisingly quiet, the anticipation running across the men in it. Cyrus was at the fore, and the Sanctuary forces were stacked four deep in rows behind him. The spellcasters were behind that in a loose formation, and to his right, at the end of the Sanctuary line, was the ragged, motley assortment of the men and armies of Syloreas. To the left was the more neatly ordered rows of Actaluere's forces, Milos Tiernan at the head with a few of his aides.

"Tiernan doesn't seem the sort that would lead his army into battle," Cyrus heard a rumbling voice say from behind him. He turned and saw Partus at the front of the line, his head well below the next person in the row.

"Appearances can be deceiving, I'm told," Cyrus said with a slight barb to his voice. He watched Partus fail to react and tried to decide whether the dwarf had missed the point or was merely uninterested in it.

"He doesn't look like he's led a battle from the front in his entire life," Partus said after Cyrus turned around. "Looks like he's enjoyed life at the back of the fray—not that there's anything wrong with that. I'd gladly take ruling a Kingdom over tangling with an army any day."

Cyrus tilted his head to look at the dwarf, which was easier since they remained on foot, all the horses well to the rear of the battle lines save for cavalry reserves on either flank. Longwell, Cyrus knew, was with the Syloreans, and had taught them a few basic maneuvers in the last few days to increase their effectiveness in battle ahorse. "Why are you still here, Partus? Did we turn you loose or something?"

"Aye, Curatio cut me a deal," Partus said, turning to loose a great wad of spit upon the dusty ground. "I'm to take part in this fight, and I can come back to Arkaria with the rest of you lot when it's all over and done."

"Couldn't you just have gone back to Arkaria on your own, over the bridge?" Cyrus asked.

"And walk months to get there, then have to travel five days over the bridge on foot and gods knows how many months after that just to make my way to the nearest settlement? I think I'd rather take my chances with you lot and these beasties. After all, I've seen what they can do and we're coming at them with a shite ton of men and swords." Partus hefted his hammer. "I like our odds better than I like the idea of the walk."

Cyrus shook his head. "Of course, you care about what happens to this land and it's people too, right?" He said it with all due sarcasm.

"I could give a pickled fig what happens to this land and its people," Partus said with another great slop of brown spit; Cyrus realized now that it was filled with tobacco juice. "I've seen enough of Luukessia to choke me out for seven lifetimes. I'll be heading back to the Dwarven Alliance after this, perhaps hire on as a mercenary to take up some nice, quiet picket duty watching the humans go about their business in the Northlands from atop a hill, or guarding the caverns and streets of Fertiss against drunken mischief-makers. All I want to do is get drunk every night on wine and ale, find myself in a bed with a woman every morning and work as little as possible at making a living."

"You're really quite the inspiration," Cyrus said, and turned back to the northern horizon.

"I don't see you sticking your neck out here under the axeman's blade any longer than you have to," the dwarf replied. "Or am I wrong and you'll just hang around here being jolly in the hinterlands with these tribes of squabbling men and children who sit around the campfires at night trying to engineer up new ways to fornicate with their animals."

"I don't see them fornicating with animals," Cyrus said, "but perhaps I spend my time in different places than you do."

"This whole land reeks of backwardness," Partus went on, undeterred by Cyrus's jibe. "Their women are like property, they've got no magical ability at all, not enough to cast a light in early evening, and their finest hovels don't even possess running water." Another gob of spit made the same squirting noise, though this time Cyrus didn't watch it. "This was a good lesson, thinking that things couldn't get any worse than they had for me in Arkaria before I left; they can. They did. And I can't bloody wait to get back."

"You're a charming fellow, Partus, don't let anyone tell you differently," Cyrus said and strode off down the front line, away from the dwarf. He didn't say anything until he reached Odellan, who stood at ease but still more at attention than most of the men around him. "What do you say, Odellan? Are we ready?"

"Having not seen what you've seen about these enemies," Odellan said, a little stiffly at first, "I don't quite know what to expect. That said, I'm confident that we're more up to the challenge than our companions from Syloreas and Actaluere."

"You mean battle discipline?" Cyrus asked.

"Compared to the men who compose more than half of Syloreas's fighting force, yes, I speak of discipline," Odellan said. "But when comparing us to Actaluere, I mean belief. I think the men of Syloreas who came here of their own volition will fight harder than the professional army of Actaluere," he said with a nod to the left. "I've looked in the eyes of some of those men dressed in skins and furs, with their swords and wooden shields handed down through generations. They're here to fight for their homeland, for revenge in some cases if they made it out of the towns that fell. They won't break for lack of courage and will fight so long as someone keeps leading them. Actaluere's army, on the other hand, seems to know which way the wind is blowing. They've done this before—not this, specifically, but they've been in battles. Their men will keep an awareness, and if things turn unfavorable, I suspect their officers will be the first to order a careful retreat."

"You think we'll have a concern with our left flank?" Cyrus asked.

"I think I'd have a care with both flanks, if I were you, General," Odellan said lightly. "But I wouldn't concern myself overly much with the left. Theirs will be an orderly retreat if it comes, and they'll warn us first so we can compensate. If the right breaks it will be quite a different story. They've got the volunteers sandwiched between us and the army regulars, so we may need to work harder to relieve the press on them if things get rough, may need to alter our line to cover their ground as the Syloreans fold toward us."

Cyrus let a smile show, one he did not remotely feel but knew was necessary. "You've given this a great deal of thought."

"As I should, General," Odellan said. "As well I should."

"Enemy on the horizon!" The shout came over them from the left, and Cyrus instinctively looked ahead, toward the mountains in the distance, trying to find the place where the fields met the lines of the mountains. There was movement there, to be sure, something too small to quite make out. *If I had elven eyes, I might be able to see.* His mind wandered. *If I had elven ...* She flashed through his mind so quickly and subtly that he didn't even know from whence she came. *Dammit. Not now.*

They waited in a tense formation as the movement went on, miles away, but edging closer. Cyrus had no spyglass like the kind he had seen in use on the top of the wall at Sanctuary from time to time. There was tension in the air, and the scent of the makeshift latrines blew from behind him, not so heavily it was overwhelming but enough to distract. *I would hope that it shifts directions, but coming from the north might not be any better than the present option, given the smell of death that these things carry with them ...*

The wait was long, an hour or more before they were fully in sight, a few hundred feet away now. They became clearer as they got closer, and by the time that clarity was obvious, it was also clear that there were more of them than he had seen at any time previous. The ground crawled, a solid mass of grey flesh as far as his human eye could see, all the way back to the horizon and coming along the plains in a wedge that pointed directly at him, at his army.

There was no fear to be had for Cyrus. It was a cool sort of uncaring that filled him. Those around him made little enough noise, a few prayers offered up from some of the men as the enemy closed on them. There were shouts down the line in the ragged army of Sylorean volunteers, and little else but battle orders and invocations for calm coming from the officers at the front of Actaluere's forces. In the distance, Briyce Unger was giving a speech to the Sylorean army, but Cyrus was too far away to catch any of it. Milos Tiernan quietly disappeared into the ranks of his force just moments before the first of the scourge closed the distance with them. Cyrus watched them draw nearer, shuffling across the plains in a loping run, their four-legged gait unlike that of any animal he had seen before.

Their flesh was still pallid, the nearest thing to the rotting dead he could imagine without taking a trip to a graveyard with a shovel. In a flash, he recalled the wendigos of Mortus's realm and realized that these were just a touch like those horrors but different somehow. Wendigos could speak, he knew, possessed some measure of conscious thought, though it was buried below the battle frenzy almost every time he had encountered them. These things were as dead inside as the worst criminal offenders he had ever encountered.

Their bleak eyes stared at him, black holes in their grey-skinned visages, their teeth pointed fangs. And how they ran: faster than a man, but slower than a horse, their gait akin to a three-legged animal but faster than one would expect of such a creature. They kept coming, Cyrus knew, and they would bunch up at the front line as the first of them started to fall. They were close now, only fifty feet away ... thirty ... ten ...

He swung Praelior with brutal force in a short stab as the first of them leapt at him. All along the line he saw similar movement, heard the cries of battle joined, and he killed the first of them with a solid impalement that it ran headlong into. He kicked the body from his sword and brought it up just in time to catch the next one, his speed enhanced by the weapon's enchantments enough that he could counter them faster than they could attack. He dodged out of the way of the next to come at him, letting the man behind him strike his first blow; he heard the sound of an axe driving home but was too busy dealing a killing blow of his own to shout congratulations. It was irrelevant, anyway; the front line was already beginning to muddle as the fight turned into a melee within seconds of contact with the enemy.

Cyrus waded through them, trying to keep his back to the men in the line behind him and letting through only what he could not stop personally, which was little. His sword moved in a flash of light, a dance of elegance. There was a bellow to his right and Partus unleashed a blast of force that tunneled through their foes and sent several hundred skyward as it flung them in its wake. The line of power cut through them for several hundred feet before it reached its end, but all along that line it appeared as though the earth had been shredded, all the grass cleared, the dirt upturned and every one of the scourge within that space had been tossed clear. That empty ground refilled only moments later, however, as the grey-skinned enemy flooded back into it, still surging forward toward the waiting armies.

The ground was full all the way to the horizon, the scourge lining the grasslands. *Battle. It was the be-all, end-all for me once upon a time.* He swung his sword, cutting the head from one of the scourge, and black blood sprayed out as another of the beasts used its decapitated fellow as a springboard to launch at him. Cyrus stepped aside and drove his blade deep into the flank of the creature as it passed; if it screamed, he did not hear it over the sounds of battle that filled his ears. *I used to thrive in the heart of the battle, used to glory in the destruction of my foes. Titans. Dragons. Goblins,* he thought darkly, and saw three of his own goblin soldiers down the line tear apart a cluster of the grey scourge-beasts with nothing more than their claws. *What happened? When did I go from believing in the glory of battle as an end of itself to thinking of it as a means to an end—to protecting people from it rather than bringing it to the foes most worthy of it?*

He racked one of the attacking demons with a sharp downswing that split it to the shoulder then plunged his next attack into the face of another enemy. His blows killed with each strike; he gave no mercy, severing heads and stabbing through hearts. *There can be no room for mercy with these creatures; they will fight on after losing a limb, keep dragging themselves toward you with any life left in their bodies, hoping to sink their teeth into you.* His next swipe killed three. *It would appear that being merciless is not something that I've lost with time and age. I lived for battle once. Now it's become merely a profession.* His blade cut into four more enemies in rapid succession, tearing throats, severing heads, and bisecting one of them. *A profession I'm good at, to be sure, but not the obsession, the glory that it was when I worshipped Bellarum with a faith that burned brighter than the flames of a brazier.*

Did I get soft? His sword moved of its own accord, cutting and slashing. *Did I buy into Alaric's ideals of honor and nobility and put aside the glory of combat? Did I do it because of him? Or for her?* The blond ponytail flashed into his sight again, as though he could see her dancing out there in the mass of the scourge, her own blade in hand, though he knew she was as far removed from this place and this battle as one could be.

No answer was forthcoming. Still, he worked his profession, Praelior in his hand, as the midday sun moved deeper into the sky above him, and night began to fall. Still the enemy came, on and on, wave after wave—and he slaughtered all of them that he could.

Chapter 63

Vara

Day 29 of the Siege of Sanctuary

The convoys had armed escorts now, almost a hundred soldiers of the dark elven army led by officers on horseback, their troops following behind them in their leather armor that was as easy to punch through with a mystical sword as unguarded flesh. Vara stared down at them, Vaste next to her squinting through a gnomish spyglass.

"This will likely only work once in this place, you realize that?" The troll asked, not breaking away from the spyglass.

"Not being an idiot, I do recognize that." She considered some form of physical reaction, like hitting him on the shoulder to let him know what she thought of him, but decided against it. *Too much like Cyrus.* "Although if we covered our tracks exceptionally well, we might be able to pull it off twice before the Sovereignty becomes wise."

"Perhaps," Vaste said. Below them lay a caravan, making its way into a short canyon where the road dipped into the plains to follow an old riverbed. "You seem to have no shortage of ideas to help us wage this little war of ours, but it's disturbing to me how many of them have been borrowed from Goliath."

"We go with what works," she said. "How did they manage it? Casting fire at either end of the canyon to spook the horses and then riding through?"

"Something along those lines," Vaste said, and she caught the unease in the way he replied. "They managed to turn it into a perfect ambush, save for the fact that Cyrus got inside the perimeter of their fire and played merry hell with the goblins until they retreated. I must suggest we do not allow something similar."

"As I saw it," Vara said, trying to remain patient, "he was only able to do that because of that wondrous horse of his. Any other horse would have been frightened away from jumping over a wall of fire. Soldiers would similarly know better than to try it in most instances. Besides, my intent is to merely contain the convoy while we eliminate their escort." She stood and dusted off the plains dirt that clung to her armored greaves. "As always, the drivers are free to go."

"As you say," Vaste agreed, but the unease was still there; she knew him well enough to hear it.

She whistled to the others and took up position on her horse. The Sanctuary raiding party was already disguised on either side of the road before the gulch; half a hundred rangers hiding in the brush with bows and arrows, and helping to conceal three wizards and four druids. Vara watched from the ridge above, some fifty warriors behind her ready to ride on her command. *A neat pincer maneuver if ever there was one. With their escort wearing little in the way of armor, the arrows will do their bit while the wagons are contained by the fire. We sweep down and mop up their resistance, and leave them mourning the disappearance of their ill-gotten gains.* She let her hand drift to her sword hilt then stopped herself. *I am not Cyrus Davidon, and I need not adopt his more obvious mannerisms.* She pondered for a moment, then wondered idly: *Does he touch the hilt of his sword not only out of nervous habit but to enjoy the faster reflex it offers? If so, that might explain a choice riposte or two he managed to get out when verbally cornered ...*

"Shall we go?" Vaste asked, now back on his horse.

"Too soon and we risk being seen, thus spoiling the ambush," Vara said, holding up her hand to keep the raiding party halted. There were another fifty or more horses with them, those belonging to the rangers and spellcasters below, and the smell of horse was strong here. "Too late and we're of little use—though I suspect we'll be of little enough use anyhow, given how well set-up this ambush is."

"Well set-up is not well executed," Vaste said, and there was a rumble of disquiet from the troll.

"What is your difficulty?" Vara asked under her breath, moving her horse close enough to him that only he could hear her whisper.

"Hard to explain," Vaste said, quieter still. "I recognize that we're in a bit of box here, and that what we're doing is necessary to draw pressure away from the siege, but there is something about using strategies that were first employed by Goliath while trying to sully our honor that I find damned disquieting in general."

"So it's a silly moral issue, is it?" she asked, and found she had drawn a frown from him.

"I have no moral objection to what we're doing here," he said. "We're attacking convoys of dark elves who are blockading us and stealing the goods that they've plundered from the farmers of the plains. If I have any objection, it's that I wish we had thought of the idea ourselves instead of having to steal it from the most loathsome sacks of treacherous flesh that are still strolling the land of Arkaria." He blinked, and looked pensive. "Speaking of which, where is Goliath strolling nowadays? You can't tell me there's a war consuming the land without them trying to get a piece of it."

"I bloody well wish they were strolling into the Realm of Death, enjoying the lovely taste of those fiends that our army is facing on the other side of the world," Vara said, no longer bothering to constrain her loathing. "I suspect they're still where they were when last we heard about them—hiding under the Sovereign's considerable skirt, doing whatever bidding he has for them."

"Does it not disturb you to think about what he might be bidding them do?" Vaste's angular face was filled with curiosity. "They're amoral, desperate, and quite powerful. Hardly one of the big three, but still strong enough to cause enormous problems for whoever crosses their path. And if they're in the service of the Sovereign, and his eye is fixed upon us—"

"No time to discuss that now," Vara said, and started her horse along the ridge. "The ambush is about to begin."

"I understand," Vaste said, "of course you're incapable of discussing something like this when you're riding a horse toward battle. You probably have to mentally prepare to eviscerate a dark elf or something. Don't let me interrupt that level of deep thought with something as frighteningly trifling as one of the largest and most powerful guilds in the land being deployed by our enemies to aid in our destruction. It's really not worth giving much consideration to, come to think of it."

She rolled her eyes, though he could not see it. "I don't see much that we're able to do about it at present," she said, allowing her steed to take her at a gallop toward the gulch far ahead as the first wagon in the convoy disappeared into it. "Perhaps if you'd care to raise it in Council later ..."

"I'd really rather annoy you with the thought," Vaste said. "I suspect the others will find it just as disquieting, but it's much more fun to watch you squirm and pretend you want to think about killing people rather than consider it."

"You're an arse," she said simply. But after a moment, she conceded, "And quite correct."

"Thank you."

The last wagon of the caravan rolled into the gulch and a wall of flame leapt up under the belly of the officers of the escort force, causing their horses to throw them. Vara could hear the sound of the armored lieutenants hitting the ground even from a few hundred feet away and over the first exclamations of the soldiers lined up in ranks. The sound of their cries took a turn for the more desperate and pained only minutes later, however, as the first arrows found their targets. She estimated something approaching a third of the soldiers fell with the first volley; half again as many fell with the second, leaving the escort in disarray, the back ranks breaking and even causing a few of them to run back down the road.

As if that would save you, she thought as she swept into the first of the runners. Her sword came down on him, hard; he had been looking back, not even seeing her until she was upon him. Blood spattered her horse's hair and was joined by more as she rained down death upon the second runner. She did not stop, riding her horse into the dark elven soldiers who still maintained their lines, after the third volley of arrows had landed. She cut a bloody swath through them as the rangers emerged from hiding at either side of the road and joined the melee.

Is this how you would have done it, General? She cut loose on another unsuspecting dark elf from horseback. He had been distracted by the rangers coming out of hiding, uncertain of where to turn. He lost his head for his transgression—*not that he would have kept it had he been paying full attention, but still. Is this how you would do it, Cyrus, were you here? Would you run our enemies to ground, ambush them, and drag them in different directions the way I am? Or would you have a different strategy, something so brilliant that it would take my breath away at the knowledge you came up with it yourself?*

She let out an audible curse, an elvish one that came from no particular setback in the battle but from a very deep place of dissatisfaction within her. Her blade came down on another dark elf, this one prepared with his sword waiting to block it. Her blade broke his weapon, went through his skull, and well into his torso before she pulled it back. *Damn you, Cyrus. Damn you for leaving me to do these things, to become what you were supposed to be. Damn you for—*

She stopped before she brought down her sword again, this time almost striking another dark elf, but this one not wearing the leather and seal of the Sovereign, but a hood and cloak that denoted a ranger, one dressed like a member of Sanctuary. "Sorry," she muttered in apology upon seeing his face. "I didn't mean to ... sorry." She looked around from the Sanctuary rangers on foot, their knives and short blades glistening with the dark blood of their enemies, then back to the warriors who had ridden into their enemies ranks on horseback; there was no sign of injury, though plenty enough of them had blood on their horses and selves. There was no crying left, no sobbing of the wounded or wailing of the dying. She looked to Vaste, but he merely shrugged, as if to say, *We're done.*

"Secure the convoy," she said loudly to one of the warriors nearest her, a capable human named Jet Tindar. "Don't kill them unless you have to." With a nod, Jet rode on, the warriors on horseback following him as the flames that blocked the gulch diminished at their approach. "The rest of you—let us try to clear the signs of our attack as best we can, and take the bodies with us so as to not give away our tactics." She felt the dull clack of her jaw. "Perhaps we can do this very same maneuver again in a week or two, to the same effect."

She pulled the reins and guided her horse away as the rangers moved into action, pulling the bodies together for transport. She didn't watch, unworried that the job would be done correctly, the blood would be covered over by a second group after the first had teleported out with the wagons, the corpses and the majority of their force. *Would you have done it this way, Cyrus? How would it have been different if you were here, instead of fighting over there?* She felt an involuntary twinge in her cheek; as small as even it was, it was more emotion than she would have preferred to be displayed on her face. *... and how would it be different for me ... if you were here ...?*

Chapter 64

Cyrus

Nightfall came upon the steppes—as Cyrus had heard the locals call the plains they fought upon—and still, the enemy came. The scourge filled the horizon as far as Cyrus could see, but as the light drained out of the day and the crescent moon cast its luminescence, there was no end in sight to the enemies that came upon them, filling the battlefield with their dead. His line of sight diminished to only thirty feet or so in front of him, Cyrus watched for the flashes of spells to give him guidance. The sounds of battle still rang around him, and the height of war was taking place on three sides. The smells that filled the air were all of the scourge, the decaying scent of dead flesh and nothing else.

They were overwhelming, so much so that Cyrus knew the army had been falling back all day, not out of a genuine pressure put upon them by the enemy but from a general weight of numbers pressing against the armies. The bodies piled up, too, and while it didn't seem to bother their enemy, as the creatures merely crawled over and avoided their own dead, for Cyrus they became a hazard after a short time, stacking three and four deep and providing an excellent ambush point for a live enemy to jump from behind their own dead and attack. He had seen a few of his guildmates attacked that way.

"It's nice to know we're at least running free of casualties," Odellan said between the clashes of weapons cutting into flesh.

A bellow sounded to Cyrus's right and another shockwave burst forth from Partus, blasting aside a line of the scourge, sending bodies into the air once more. "We're taking them out in great numbers, no doubt," Cyrus said. "But we've been swapping out people along the line all day as though this was some sort of sporting event where you can bow out any time you please. Our people are exhausted and there's still no sign that the enemy is coming close to running low on more bodies to throw at us. It makes me wonder just how many souls Mortus kept in his lands, if it's all of them, all the way back to the beginning of time, or if somewhere we'll eventually reach the end.

A cry and hue came from farther down the line, to the right. "Not a good sound," Cyrus said under his breath. "Do you think that means ...?"

There was no need for him to finish, as Martaina appeared out of the darkness to his right, firing two arrows in rapid succession, both hitting one of their foes in the face and causing them to cease all motion. She slid to a stop in front of Cyrus, slung her bow over her shoulder and drew blades, slipping into the formation next to him. "Bad news from the Sylorean lines, sir."

"Let me guess," Cyrus said, cleaving another head as one of their enemy slid past him in a foiled attack, "the Syloreans broke in the middle."

"Solid guess." She buried a dagger in a grey face and another in a stout, four-legged body. "Our healers did their best, but they ran short of magical energy about ten minutes ago. Mendicant is about to try something to drive them back, but we're running low on things we can throw into the breach."

"What about the cavalry reserve?" Cyrus asked. "Longwell was waiting for the right moment to turn them loose, and this sounds like it."

"He moved into action to shore up the left flank and give some relief to the army of Actaluere about two hours ago," she said, and her smooth motions with the blade prompted him to wonder how long she had been using them, she did it with such fluid grace. "They're still committed over there; I guess the enemy moved fast and doggedly, because from what I can see from here, it looks like they're barely holding, even with the cavalry reinforcement."

"Okay," Cyrus said, and motioned for two warriors in the line behind him to move up. "Let's you and I head over there, see if we can help. What's Mendicant planning to—"

There was a blast of fire that lit the night sky, a circle of flame that turned the whole field of battle orange with fury then red with its intensity as it burned brighter still. Cyrus watched as it slid around a widening hole in the line that he hadn't even been able to see without the fire. It pushed back, back toward the scourge, and Cyrus watched the four-legged creatures run from it in a way they hadn't run from anything he'd seen thus far.

"It would appear they're afraid of fire," Cyrus said, pushing through the line and making for the place where the flame glowed. "Nice to know; kinda wonder why we haven't figured that out before."

"You're the one who wanted the spellcasters kept in reserve in case we had to fall back," she said, leading him. Her bow was unslung now, and she fired it three times as she ran, picking off targets as she brushed by Sanctuary members locked in combat along the front. "Not such a bad strategy, actually, because we'd been doing well enough before now that they didn't need to intervene."

"We may yet need them to cover our retreat," Cyrus said as they reached the end of the Sanctuary line; he passed a few men of Syloreas who were in battle with the scourge, and Cyrus aided them with a few well-placed slashes as he did so. "I don't know if you've noticed, but we've easily killed ten thousand of these things and they've yet to blink at throwing another ten thousand at us."

"Being not quite as blind as you in the dark, I have noticed," she said. "I have also noticed that their number continues to extend beyond the horizon, which is a mite worrisome seeing as we're supposed to kill them all and then continue north to destroy the portal. I believe we may have the order wrong on that; we may need to destroy the portal before we can go north."

"A fine contradiction, isn't it?" Cyrus brought his sword around and slashed a foe that charged hard at him, killing it with one well-placed stroke. "I, for one, wish there were another way to do it, but as I don't possess a single flying mount with which to carry myself over these enemies, let alone a bevy of them to carry an entire army to the portal without fighting them, I'm afraid we may just have to do it the hard way."

"I don't know that you could define this as the hard way, sir," Martaina said, and her short blade was out again, working in a flash of metal against two of the scourge at once, "I believe this may in fact be the impossible way."

"I don't believe in the impossible," Cyrus said, greeting a jumping enemy with a kick that knocked it back to its fellows.

"Then I'd like to see you try and give birth to a child yourself, sir."

Cyrus shot her a sideways look and got one in return, only a hint of a smile as Martaina stabbed into another one of the beasts as it jumped at her. The fire of Mendicant's spell had died out, finally, and Cyrus wondered idly if the goblin had sacrificed any life energy to make it last as long as it did. The two of them were now firmly in the middle of the sagging Sylorean line, and they had, as predicted, failed squarely in the middle of the amateurs who were carrying hand-me-down weapons and wore no armor. *It's not from lack of courage that they're breaking, because none of them are running; they're literally being killed here in the center at too high of a rate to keep the line solid.* He looked back and saw holes that stretched clear through the middle, no reinforcement to seal them; the Syloreans had run out of men to throw at the problem.

"I believe that if you were looking in a dictionary," Martaina said through gritted teeth as she dropped to her back and let two of the enemy run headlong into each other while she executed a backward to roll to get to her feet again, "this might fall under the word 'untenable.'" Cyrus gave her a blank look for only a moment before he was forced back to attention on the battle as a foe went for his knee with glistening teeth. "It means—"

"I know what it means," he snapped, driving the tip of his blade through a skull and then whipping it out sideways to intercept another running foe's forehead. A slap of black blood hit his armor, where it blended with the metal and the night and a thousand other splotches that had already landed there in the day-long battle. "I don't like to retreat."

"Perhaps you should think of it as an opportunity to find some reinforcements and re-commence the battle on more favorable ground, then," she said. "Because we're only about five more minutes from ending up in the middle of that village, Filsharron, if we keep having to fall back like we are."

Cyrus cast a backwards glance and realized she was right, that the village was just behind them now, only a few hundred feet away. There were torches burning, and he could see motion in the streets; the back rank of the Sanctuary reserve of spellcasters were already standing in the outskirts. "Dammit." He turned to say something to her and watched as she landed two blades in a rampaging enemy's shoulder and neck, keeping it from attacking him, and he shook off his surprise. "Sorry. Didn't mean to get distracted."

"I'm here to watch your back," she said, the slight tension evident in her voice as she threw the body back at its fellows, bowling over another one of them.

"And what a fantastic view that must be," Cyrus said as he waded back into the fight.

"I've seen considerably better, even lately," she said, fending off three of the scourge at the same time.

"I'll try not to be insulted by that."

"Nothing personal, sir."

Cyrus waved at the Sanctuary line, motioning for several of the warriors toward the back to move to them, which they began to do, filtering in. "How long do you think we can keep this up?"

"When we hit the village, we'll fold," she said. "We don't possess the ability to continue falling back the way we are, especially not with that stream and all those houses providing obstacles." He didn't say anything, and she continued after a pause in which she dispatched three enemies with her blades. "The obstacles don't work to our advantage because we have to dodge around them, but it makes holes in our lines that they can exploit, because I think they can jump onto the roof of the houses in town and use it to leap over our lines. We of Sanctuary might be able to pull that sort of a retreat off, but the Syloreans are going to break. When they do, it's going to be near-impossible for us to form a survivable order of battle with all the enemies crushing in on us from our right."

Cyrus gave it a moment's thought. "Fair assessment." He let that seep over him as he dealt the deathblow to three enemies in rapid succession. "So, it's time to retreat, is it?"

He caught the motion of a shrug from her. "You could try and reform south of Filsharron, but I doubt the men of Actaluere are going to go for that, and I even more seriously doubt you could get the Syloreans to pull it off." She puffed as she struck again and again. "We've been fighting for a day; the Syloreans have lost half their number. We need more men to be able to beat them." There was skepticism from her now. "If we can."

"We retreat, they'll come after us," Cyrus said. "They'll keep coming, too, unless we can outrun them. Any suggestions on that?"

"Plan for it ahead of the battle next time?" Martaina asked, still fighting. "Falcon's Essence. If you can get a couple of the druids to spread it around the entire army, we can not only fly high enough to avoid them but it also gives you the ability to run faster. Couple it with a few wizards dropping some flame spells as we go, and you can pull off an orderly retreat."

"Not bad," Cyrus said. He looked back at the village. "Now seems the moment." He raised his voice, loud enough to overcome the battle and the crashing of the fight. "RETREAT! RETREAT!" He heard others take up the call, but he knew his own voice was heard in the back of the Sanctuary line, and that was all that mattered.

Like a flame moving across spilled kerosene, the fire spread across the ground in front of them. It stitched a line before the front rank of the army, a wall as tall as two men, and it lit the night with a flickering orange glow that reminded him of a night spent around a campfire. There was no smoke, only the smell of the fire at work on the grasses, and then on flesh as a few howls cut through the night, the bellows of their enemy as the flames licked at the grey rot. Cyrus watched a pair of black eyes through the wall of fire; they stared back at him, glaring, leering, jagged teeth held at bay by the flame.

The gentle sweep of magic ran across him, and he felt himself float off the ground. He turned to look at Martaina, and saw the Syloreans already moving behind her, well into the retreat, each of them floating, flying, and moving faster at a run than would normally be possible.

"You already had it planned, didn't you?" she asked, watching him warily.

"Of course," Cyrus said, and nodded his head as he sheathed Praelior and ran for the back of the lines, where he saw the horses all saddled and waiting. "Do you think me so arrogant that I wouldn't consider the possibility of retreat?"

She raised an eyebrow at him, and he caught it out of the corner of his eye as he ran. "Normally, no. In your current state, however, I have seen you make one or two errors of judgment, in my estimation."

"Touche."

He climbed onto Windrider, who ran out to meet him at his approach. The flames were burning behind him, a steady wall of fire that kept the enemy at bay. "Our wizards will give us about a five-minute head start," Cyrus said. "After that, I've got them riding in groups to cover the retreat, taking turns protecting us and burning them back."

"That may keep them off of us," Martaina said with a tight jaw as she brought her horse alongside, "but you know that won't stop them. There are villages along the way, and if we're not going to fight, and we're going to retreat, they'll be caught in the path of—"

"I know," Cyrus said. "We'll warn them, get them to flee, but ..." He shook his head. "You know they won't all listen. They won't all be able to run." He felt the tightness in his own jaw, the slight swell of emotion. "They'll be overrun. Just like Termina."

"We won't stand and fight for them?" Odellan rode up and joined them, now, then Curatio and J'anda. "You know what these things will do to the land, what they'll do to the people as they come down across the plains."

"I do," Cyrus said. "But we just threw everything we presently have at them and they chewed it up and spat it back at us." The Sanctuary army was already in formation and moving, Cyrus saw. Actaluere's was in motion also, even faster than Sanctuary's, and they were on the march south. It was the Syloreans who were the slowest to move, some of them still looking back through the fire at the demons on the other side that were pacing there, waiting to get through. "We could make a stand like this on every bit of open ground between here and Enrant Monge and we'd only succeed in slowly bleeding ourselves dry. We need to stage a slow retreat. We need to trade land for time."

"Time for what?" Odellan asked; Cyrus could see the ripple of emotions on the elf's young-looking face. "You just said there's no hope to beat them with what we have, and I can't see where you're far wrong about that. What could we possibly do with more time other than throw more of these men's lives down their jaws?" He gestured at the armies of Actaluere and Syloreas in turn, a sliding wave of the hand that came down in disgust.

"Simple enough," Cyrus said, grimly, as he urged Windrider forward, following the last rank of the Sanctuary army. The wizards and druids were riding at the rear, ready to hold the retreat against the overwhelming numbers of the scourge that waited just beyond the wall of fire, their black eyes shining with orange firelight as they paced, their number growing, crawling and scrabbling over each other now, waiting for the fire to subside. Cyrus watched them, stared back at them, at death, at fear itself, so overwhelming in its scope that it could eat whole armies and never even taste them, ready to devour them whole. *The maw of death,* he thought. "There's only one thing we can do, now.

"We get a bigger army."

Chapter 65

Vara

Day 35 of the Siege of Sanctuary

The dark elven wizard had appeared in a flash, in the middle of the night and had brought with him over a hundred dark elves, right into the foyer. The sounds of blades clanging against one another made for dreadful noise, but the fighting had spilled out onto the front steps this time, bodies fallen here, there and everywhere as battle raged on. Vara was in the midst of it, on the threshold of the entrance to Sanctuary, and there was war all about. There was no noise from beyond the wall, *at least—not this time, thankfully.* Her weapon was at a high guard, and it landed squarely between the eyes of a dark elf with all the armor one might expect from a well-trained and equipped warrior.

The smell of smoke was in the air, smoke and sweat, as she moved her sword in a defensive position. They had come in fast and the stairs were packed, the guard force that had been stationed in the foyer was there, prepared to attack and catch them as they teleported in, but the dark elves were too many to dispatch in a quick moment of frenzied attack.

"How are there this many?" Vara whispered under her breath as she parried the attack of another dark elf, capturing his blade under her arm and twisting to yank it free of his hand as she kicked his legs from beneath him. She plunged her sword into the weak spot where his armor met his gorget, heard the satisfying gurgling that ensued, and turned to attack the next.

She felt the dozen cuts she had picked up dispersed as the healing spell ran over her, a light glowing on her flesh. "They're elites," Erith said from behind her. "The Sovereign has sent his best in an effort to get that portcullis up so his troops can come running in."

"A clever strategem." Ryin fired off a blast of ice that frosted three dark elves who were at a dead run across the yard, having broken free of the melee at the door and were trying for the wall. "But he can't possibly believe that a mere hundred or so could break our defenses."

Vara frowned and ran through another soldier with her blade. "No, he surely wouldn't think that after the last time." She raised her weapon to take on the next comer, but a sound filled the air, a rushing of energy and magic, and she could feel the tingle of power on her skin as the light formed in the foyer, filling the gaps between the combatants with bursts of energy coalescing into figures who flashed into being, another wave of dark elven enemies. "SECOND WAVE!" she cried out and launched herself into a flying leap, coming down with her metal boots on the back of one dark elf while slashing her sword across two more, sending them spinning to the ground in a wash of blood.

The foyer was packed, flooding into the lounge, out the doors, as more shoving was taking place than blades being swung. She saw the wizard, the one who had brought this flood of enemies, and she leapt for him, dodging a half-dozen strikes from enemies as she passed overhead, but he winked out existence into a blotting of light as she landed, accidentally downing a Sanctuary ranger who had been standing almost on top of the wizard.

"One more cycle of this and he'll be delivering the next wave to stand on our shoulders," Andren said as he stepped out of the shadows under the stairs to the balcony, catching a dark elf by surprise with a dagger, dragging it across the warrior's throat as he spoke. The dark elf looked immensely shocked, hands clawing at his own neck. Andren, for his part, shoved his foe to the ground where the man bled and twitched.

Vara kept a wary eye on the healer as she swiped hard, using the space created by the wizard's escape to bring her sword around. She killed and maimed five dark elves in five seconds and then yanked a Sanctuary warrior out of the way to spear a sixth with her blade. "There won't be another cycle," she said, "he knows he's being targeted now. If he comes back, he'll be the first to die. The element of surprise is lost, and only a fool would continue to pack bodies into this room, knowing that we have reinforcements flooding down even now that will break them before they have a chance to open our gates."

"To hear you tell it, there's nothing but fools in this world, so I find it hard to believe you write off the assumption they wouldn't do something foolish without giving it a moment's pause." Andren stayed behind her, well back as she began to work her way through the mess of dark elves in front of her. They'd begun to pivot to her now that there was space to move again.

"You make a surprisingly cogent point for a drunkard," she said.

"I'm just going to pretend I only heard the complimentary part of that," Andren said, and she saw him tip his flask up to his lips as she pirouetted to strike another foe. "It could take a while, clearing this room."

She didn't have to labor to hear him over the sounds of battle. "We're surrounded on all sides by our enemies. We have nothing but time to fill—no expeditions, no operations, no tourism—and speaking only for myself, I rather enjoy turning aside every attempt by the Sovereign to break us down." She gritted her teeth as a dark elf with an axe rained down a blow that rattled her arm and she replied with a spell that sent the man flying across the room and into the fireplace, where he screamed and struggled to get out.

"I can see that," Andren said. "Working out a little of that unstated tension you've been feeling for the last few months?"

"I have no reason to be tense," she said, gritting her teeth again and burying her sword into another dark elf's shoulder. The man screamed and she promptly finished him off by grasping his hair, whirling him around, and running her blade in a sawing motion over his neck. "Unless you're referring to our present situation."

"Oh, yeah," Andren said, and she heard the click of the flask opening again. "That's what I was referring to, certainly."

"I can almost hear your eyes rolling."

"Would you like to try and convince me that what I'm thinking isn't true?" He leaned against the wall now, safely under the stairs, using her still as protection from the dark elves bearing down on her in twos and threes. "That you're not a little out of sorts because of Cy—"

"I wouldn't presume to believe you're actually doing any thinking," she said and her sword took on a life of its own, cutting through a rank of dark elves with maddening speed. "After all, your wine-sodden assumptions are worth less than the rotgut you fill your mouth and your days with." She raised an elbow as a dark elf closed on her. She rammed her armored joint into the side of his head, twice; the first blow knocked his helm asunder and the second caved the side of his head in. He fell to the ground, bleeding from the ear and skull and she went on, impaling the next one to cross her weapon.

"That'd be denial I hear," Andren said.

"You'd know the sound of that better than I, I rather suspect."

"Why would I deny what I am?" She caught a flash of him again out of the corner of her eye; two dark elves had stormed her and she was pressed against them, they were pushing her back and one was raising his mace to bring it down on her. "I'm a drunk, true enough, but that doesn't mean I let a good drink get in the way of what I do. You, on the other hand—" The mace descended and she batted it aside, freeing her arm from where her armor had locked against one of the dark elves. The ball of the weapon landed on her shoulder, unspeakable pain followed as the force of the blow ran through the metal, then the padding, and she felt her shoulder break. Her sword fell from her hand and the other dark elf pushed her back.

The mace came up again and she tried to raise her hand to block it but her arm would not respond. She dove low, at the legs of the two dark elves assaulting her, and felt their knees buckle even as she cried out in pain from the resulting blow to her shoulder as it struck an armored thigh. The dark elves were knocked off their feet and she felt them land heavily on her back. She rolled, already kicking them off her and got to her feet, reaching under her armor and sliding loose the extra blade she kept under her backplate.

"See, now that right there," Andren said, now in front of her after her move to counter the two dark elves, "that weapon you're carrying looks very familiar and the place you're carrying it looks familiar as well—I'm fair certain that Cyrus does just that exact thing, keeping an extra blade in just such a place in case he gets his sword stripped away from him."

She lunged at the first dark elf and buried the curved blade up to the hilt in his throat. She ignored his surprise and spun it loose, plunging it into the second one's gullet, up through the jaw. She followed him to the floor and grasped the blade of her sword and picked it up, turning back to the melee ongoing in the foyer. "Perhaps he acquired the idea from me, did you ever consider that?"

Andren's hand reached out, and she felt the soothing balm of his healing spell as the bones in her shoulder knitted together. "Perhaps, but I think it would be nothing but small recompense compared to that broken heart he acquired from you."

She stood, frozen, watching the fight going on for a few seconds as the tide shifted in favor of the Sanctuary forces and no one seemed to pay her any mind. She let out a howl of fury and leapt forward at the nearest dark elf, using both blades in tandem to hack the startled warrior to death with swift, sure strokes, then the next, then the next.

To finish the battle took less than thirty minutes, and when it was done she was soaked, disgusting, her own sweat and dark elven blood dripping all over her, the smell of steel and gore heavy in the air. She wiped her face and found it wet, slick from the work she'd done.

"I believe there are some that would say you look like a bride of Bellarum right now, drenched as you are in the blood of your enemies." Andren's voice held a sarcastic edge and she turned on him to find him still there, malingering beneath the staircase, shadowed in the gloom with his beard and flask, the lecherous—

"Who would say that, exactly?" she asked, taking steps toward him in a raw fury. "Who would say that to my face right now, would think it of interest, would dare to mention it to me?" She cast aside her secondary blade to the floor with a throw that caused it to lodge in a body. She watched Andren's eyes widen as she reached out a bloody hand and grasped his white healer's robes, leaving red on them, and dragged him forward and down to look her in the eye. "Are you a follower of Bellarum yourself?"

"Nope," Andren said, and took a long pull from his flask, even though his face was only inches from hers. He did not fight her grip, and the smell of strong gin came off him in waves. "But, you see, I know a fella who is. And he had this … all-consuming love for a girl much like yourself. Scary love, really, too scary to even admit to anyone, maybe even himself for the longest time, but it was there. It kept him away from others who might have wanted him, kept him isolated, alone … for years. When he finally went for her and got cut down … I think it hit him harder than anything, harder than losing his wife," she blanched as he said it, "than losing his best friend. Yeah, I think that pretty much did it for him. But hey," he took another swig, "what do I know?" Her grip on him slackened, and he pulled gradually away from her. "It's been a few months now. He's probably right as rain at this point. Moved along." Andred shrugged, and uncrumpled the stained cloth of his robe where her hands had clutched him. "After all, it's not like he spent years pining after that lady."

With a last shrug, the healer pulled loose of her, and she stood there, sword in her hand as the sound of horns blew in the distance, somewhere far over the wall, and she did everything she could to keep her face straight.

Chapter 66

Cyrus

The retreat was long, aided by the wizards and druids. Fires burned through the night behind them, giving them a rear guard as they retreated, long flaming rows that stretched out along the plain in an infinite line, with only a gap for the river, as the flames burned in a curve to follow the bank. Cyrus didn't feel the heat, not at the distance he was at; he watched a haggard Nyad keeping her eyes on the fire as they rode into the distance, trying for escape. After a few hours, the dim, distant noises of the scourge army faded, not to reoccur when the fire line came down. By morning, they were not even in sight as the sun came up.

"Where do you reckon they are?" Partus asked Cyrus, atop a small horse that Cyrus believed had been Ryin Ayend's.

"Spread out along the plains," Cyrus said, numb. The wind came from the north today, and it was all rot and death, cold and chill. *The end of summer is most assuredly at hand and winter is well on its way.* "Giving up on us to hit all the ripe, tender villages that are east and west of here. Gone to give some other poor bastards hell."

"Those things ..." Partus said, shaking his craggy, bearded head, "those things are the legends of torment come to life. They truly are Mortus's works. I've been in his Realm, many times, but these ... these are staggering, those things. Monstrous works. They look like—"

"Wendigos, a little bit," Cyrus said. "But four legged, no arms. No hair. I've met wendigos that could talk, that seemed like they had a soul. None of that here, just a raw, feral savagery you don't even see in wild wolves."

"Aye," Partus said. "So many, they cover the whole ground and could cover the land like locusts in the harvest. They'll eat Luukessia whole and everything on it."

"No," Cyrus said with a fierce shake of the head. "No, they won't." He urged Windrider forward, toward the front of the column, and they rode on until midday.

At midday they stopped by a stream; the armies of Actaluere and Syloreas had marched with them, their darker armor and distinctive flourishes marking them clearly—the Actaluereans had livery and surcoats, like Longwell's, though they almost all were dirty and stained with the black blood of the scourge. The Syloreans, on the other hand, wore no such livery but their armors carried fur padding that stuck out of the neck and at the shoulders, to give it a different appearance than most kinds of armor Cyrus had seen, and a distinct look that fit the northmen well. There was no tent pitched, and Cyrus knew it was because this was to be a fast convocation. Somewhere to the north, he knew, somewhere below the mountains that stared down from the horizon, was an army that was as relentless as it was unmerciful.

Cyrus took the cloth seat that was offered him again, his officers at his back. Tiernan was quiet, fingers caressing his unshaven chin, the first time Cyrus had seen a hint the man could grow whiskers. In Tiernan's hangdog look, Cyrus caught just a hint of Cattrine, but he brushed that thought away with all the ease of scouring the remains of baking from a pan. Unger, on the other hand, stared straight ahead, his eyes flicking to and fro from the small, quiet circle to the horizon, as though at any moment the enemy would burst over it and he might have his revenge.

"They're going to keep coming," Cyrus said after a moment of silence. Tiernan looked up at him as though Cyrus had drawn a sword; the King of Actaluere's eyes were wide yet vacant, watching as though he were a child, bereft of understanding for what was transpiring. "We lack the numbers to stop them. We lack the punch."

"We killed at least ten thousand of them last night," Briyce Unger said. The King of Syloreas appeared to have no desire to exit his seat, the usual twitch of his left leg muted, exhaustion heavy on the King's frame. "And more still came. More than could be imagined, I think, though it would be hard to tell in the dark."

"Yes," Cyrus said. "My elves tell me that they still filled the ground to the horizon, even after all we did. But there cannot be an endless supply of them."

"Whether there is an endless supply of them or not is wholly irrelevant," Tiernan said with an exasperated chuckle that lacked any humor at all, "what matters is whether there are enough to block us from sealing that damnable gate through which they invade our land. There seems no way to be able to pull that one off, as they don't break or back off even when confronted with overwhelming losses. As he said," Tiernan raised a hand and gestured to Unger, "we killed numbers of them so staggering it would make any of our armies break and scatter from the loss. We lost few enough ourselves, and yet we were the ones who broke. Still they came on and would have kept pressing on us until we were finished had it not been for the western magic that saved us. Ancestors!" Tiernan said it as though it were a curse. "How do you fight an enemy that will stand before you and let you pound on his face and not even blanch whilst you do so?"

"You pound away at him until he does blanch," Cyrus said.

"That might hearten me, if we were by some chance facing a human adversary with a human reaction," Tiernan said. Unger watched, silent, while the King of Actaluere spoke. "These things show no sign that we may ever push them back, that we might ever reach the end of their will." Tiernan threw up his hands. "They're purest evil. There is no soul, no essence in these things, just an all-consuming hunger to take life."

"Aye," Briyce Unger said at last, "and that is why we must face them again. Why we must hit them until we find their breaking point. You say yourself, you know—they are evil. They are consuming my Kingdom, eating it whole. Yours will be next, and Longwell's, until there is nothing left of Luukessia." Unger shook his head. "At this point, even if we went into the teeth of these beasts again, we stand only the chance to hold them back, not to win. We need more, Tiernan. We need more men. We need every man in the land with an able body. We need every army, every soldier, every farmboy who can wield a pitchfork and stand in a line." Unger waved a hand toward the mountains. "This isn't a fight to save Syloreas anymore, not that you were here for that anyway, but I say it because Syloreas is lost. It's gone. I'm sending my soldiers right now, today, to the corners of my Kingdom and I'm telling them to let everyone know—*Get out.* Go south. Come to Enrant Monge, flee to Galbadien or Actaluere. Buy time because anyone who stays in the north is lost. They'll all die, every last one."

"You paint a grim picture," Tiernan said, his complexion ashen.

"Yet you speak the whole truth, no exaggeration. So you would leave your lands behind, have your people flee into the south. What then? Not that they'll be greeted unkindly by mine own or Aron Longwell's—"

"They'll not be greeted at all by Aron Longwell's armies," came the voice of Samwen Longwell, and Cyrus turned to see him standing just at his shoulder. Longwell was tall enough already, but he seemed to have gained a solid five inches of height. "I am riding today for Vernadam." His jaw was squared, straightened, and he spoke from a well deep within. Cyrus could feel the emotion crackling off the man he had known for over two years now but never in this way. "I will ride to Vernadam, right now, today, and I will bring back all the army I can to oppose these beasts. I will turn out every man who is able, and I will come back at the head of them to stand with you in beating back this threat to our land."

Unger traded a look with Tiernan then cautiously looked back to Longwell. "And if ... when ... your father opposes you?"

Cyrus watched Longwell's face carefully, saw the slight trace that came and went before the younger Longwell let slip a slight smile, a false one, to be sure. "Then he will be the King of Galbadien no longer. I will see to it."

There was a quiet that settled over the convocation. "Well," Milos Tiernan said, breaking the silence that had settled on them as surely as the first snow, "this shall certainly be a winter for the ages."

"Aye," Briyce Unger said, "and perhaps the last one the men of Luukessia will ever see."

Chapter 67

After the meeting broke a few minutes later, Cyrus found himself walking beside Longwell back to the Sanctuary army. The lines of march had dissolved and men and women were lying about, scattered, some asleep and some not, all of them grizzled veterans now. *How unlike they were when we left out the Sanctuary gates ... when was that? Nine months ago? Ten?* He shook his head in disbelief. *How different were they when we left? Like newborns. Now they're not new anymore, and they've seen more of war in this time than even most guilds have.*

"Sir." Longwell spoke, jarring Cyrus out of his meditation. "I'll need to be leaving soon, as soon as possible."

"I won't have you go alone," Cyrus said. "You're talking about deposing your father. You'll need some help."

"And I'll have it," Longwell said, tense, "but it must be from within Galbadien, not without. If I come to Vernadam at the head of the Sanctuary army, it won't have the proper effect. It'll be seen as an invasion. It will be an invasion, the west to the east, the conquering lord of Arkaria come to destroy the peaceful traditions of Luukessia. Of power over peace, of domination and control rather than what this is supposed to be—me taking my birthright to save the land that I love."

"You cannot possibly expect me to let you do this alone," Cyrus said. "To go into the heart of the Kingdom of Galbadien as you are, without a single person to aid you? You'll take an escort—not an army, an escort, so that you'll at least have a healer and a wizard in case things become truly sticky. An enchanter seems useless against the scourge, so we'll bring J'anda with us." Cyrus gave it a moment's thought. "Nyad, Martaina, Aisling and I will accompany you also, along with a healer and a couple warriors and rangers. Less than ten, total. That could hardly be mistaken for an army by most eyes."

"Yet to the eyes who know," Longwell said, narrowing his, "that is more army than most of Luukessia could put together."

"Yeah, well, not everyone has to know that," Cyrus said. "It's a war of perception, not of force. Coming to Vernadam at the head of a foreign army doesn't sit well with me, either. It's when you come out that you need to be at the head of an army."

"Aye," Longwell said. "What are your intentions for the Sanctuary army, then, while we're away?"

"Odellan will lead them," Cyrus said, "and Curatio will take overall command. They'll move with the armies of Actaluere and Syloreas as they continue a fighting retreat across the steppes trying to winnow down the scourge's numbers while we're absent. Perhaps they'll get lucky and strike the great victory we're looking for."

"Sir," Longwell stopped his walk and laid a gauntleted hand on Cyrus's shoulder. "You need not come with me. You are an army unto yourself, and more valuable here at the front than as an escort to me."

"I doubt it," Cyrus said and felt a sharp pain within. "The army will fight here to hold back the tide, but they won't actually be able to do it, not without more men. Actaluere is sending more, but having me at the center of the line is useful insofar as I can hold it better than perhaps anyone else, can kill more than any other soldier, but I can't win the battle by myself, and I can't make up for the weakness inherent in this army. We lack men. We lack mobility. We needed ten thousand of your dragoons in that last fight, and a wider front to press up against without the weak men that Syloreas stretched to shore up our formation. We need soldiers, real soldiers, not farmers and field hands. We need men who can swing a blade and throw an axe, and the men who can't, who don't have the experience, are nothing but chaff."

"Why, then, do you come to Vernadam?" Longwell asked. "Even if it is as you say, and you believe that there is no hope to beat them here, only to delay them, what possible greater good could you do at Vernadam that you could not do more effectively here?"

Cyrus let out a long breath, and with it felt the emotions ground up within pass, as if he could expunge a plague of doubt all at once. "Your father is obtuse, we both know that. He won't come around, he won't listen to reason. But there is one man in that castle that will, one man who could command the legions of Galbadien with or without your father's blessing."

"Count Ranson," Longwell said with cool acknowledgment.

"Ewen Ranson is no fool," Cyrus said. "If both of us come to tell him what he already knows, then I think we can convince him to move the army. No coup necessary, because your father's will is irrelevant without an army to back it. Let him have Vernadam because we'll have the army, and that is what we need to beat these enemies back." Cyrus took another breath, and this one felt as though all his doubts and fears came back unto him, like he inhaled a lungful of death. "If we can beat these enemies back."

"I thank you," Longwell said, and bowed his head. "This was never your fight, not when we came here to battle the Syloreans, not when we ran afoul of Baron Hoygraf, not when we had to adjust and face the possibility of war with Actaluere. You have never once tried to bow out when things became more difficult than we had anticipated, and I think that would have been the first thought of most men, to run from such an unstoppable and implacable a foe as we now face."

"Implacable foes are the only kind I've ever known," Cyrus said without mirth.

Longwell nodded, but there was confusion hinted at on his young face, the lines that had just started to show expressing those emotions. "I thank you, regardless. I owe you more than I can possibly repay, yet still I shall endeavor to square the debt at some point."

"I wouldn't consider you too indebted to me," Cyrus said, "after all, we did unleash this scourge by our own actions—by my own actions."

"No one could have predicted that," Longwell said quickly. Too quickly. "We need to leave soon. Perhaps after a short rest?"

"Early evening, I think," Cyrus said. "A few hours of sleep if possible, and then we'll be on our way. Tell the others, will you? I'll speak with Curatio and gather us a healer." He looked around. "They're pitching tents," he pointed to a few of Actaluere's men, already hammering the first stakes into the ground, and the Syloreans across the camp were doing the same, "We'll rest, then we'll leave. I'll need to send a wizard to Sanctuary to request aid again, if they haven't already sent it. If they have, I'll still request more."

"Aye, sir," Longwell said. "I'll inform the others."

"Don't worry about Aisling," Cyrus said carefully, drawing Longwell to turn back to him, just as a cool gust blew through. "I'll tell her myself."

"Aye," Longwell said with care of his own, not revealing anything he might be thinking, masklike.

Cyrus watched the dragoon walk away. *Does he know? Everyone knew about Cattrine, at least everyone in the castle. I wonder if my soldiers knew? Rumors spread faster than wildfire, faster than the scourge. Even if the others didn't care, it's still ... unseemly. Isn't it?* He felt the urge fill him, even as he thought about her. *Two days of battle? You'd think that would have drained me ...*

He walked across the campsite, the smell of weary and war all around him. He could hear faint snores from some of the men, light talking from others but in hushed voices, the quiet maintained, as though any sound above a whisper might bring the dread monsters down upon them again. He could feel the light touch of the north wind again that told him winter was coming, was not as far off as he wanted it to be, here at the end of summer. Autumn would surely come first but would be the only buffer between them and the snows that would likely bury these plains in only a few months. The taste of snowflakes on Cyrus's tongue was something he could almost sense now, and he longed for water to wash it off, as there were another taste he could remember, one from the last retreat he'd ordered, not quite a year ago, in Termina, where the ash fell from the burning city across the river.

Cyrus's feet carried him along, a short walk to a tree that rested in the middle of the plains. There were men all around, in every direction, and horses beyond them. Even in the quiet of the camp there was activity, though subtle, understated. He could see Windrider where he'd left him, working on conjured oats that a wizard had made for him and the rest of the animals. Cyrus looked over the small knot of Sanctuary officers nearby and then to Mendicant, who sat next to Terian, still bound in chains and watching him.

Cyrus edged closer to the dark knight and the goblin wizard; Mendicant's back was turned, paying him no mind, but Terian kept an eye on Cyrus, his mouth covered by a rag that was tied in a thick knot. Cyrus could see that there was a rock stuffed between his lips by the tilt of the dark elf's jaw. His eyes blazed as he watched Cyrus approach, and when the warrior was only steps away, Mendicant stirred and turned to see him there.

"Lord Davidon, sir," Mendicant said, rushing to his short legs. The goblin came only to mid-chest on Cyrus and seemed nervous in his presence.

"I need you to cast the cessation spell, Mendicant," Cyrus said. "I need to talk to Terian."

"Of course, sir," Mendicant said, and shut his eyes, letting his hand rise as though to cast the power of his spell in the direction he was pointed. His eyes rolled under the thick, scaly lids as Cyrus heard the faintest mumblings under the goblin's breath. When his eyes opened, Cyrus saw a faint movement around his hands, the barest hint of the air rippling like water, not with the strength of a paladin's spell but enough to create a disturbance around them, causing the nature of the world to blur within the bounds of the spell in a way Cyrus had never noticed before.

Cyrus squatted down to where Terian sat, legs in front of him. No one had bothered to strip the dark elf of his armor and so he still wore parts of it, dark-tinged metal protection from battle. Normally it was spiked in a way that Cyrus had never seen in armor. Terian's pauldrons were gone, though, the most lethal piece of pointed armor he possessed, as was the helm, and the jagged additions to his elbows and knees, as well as the dark elf's boots. He wore a motley assortment of armor and leather, his footcovers now worn, holes in them from all the walking.

Cyrus tugged the gag out of Terian's mouth, and the dark elf spat out the rock, though not with any particular violence. Cyrus had been ready for him to launch it, but he didn't. He stared at Cyrus, and Cyrus stared back, but the hostility was all one sided. "I'm leaving," Cyrus said at last, wondering if Terian would speak at all.

"How nice." Terian's tone was cold and flat, and he lifted his hands, still bound. "Finally decided to get out while you can?"

"I'm going to Vernadam to try and involve Galbadien in this war," Cyrus said, and watched Terian's expression change not a whit. "I'm taking Longwell and a few others, and I'm going to see if we can tip the scales, because if we don't it's going to end very badly. You saw the battle?"

"I saw," Terian said at last, almost reluctant. "Looks like you're overmatched."

"Indeed," Cyrus said. "This whole land is overmatched by those things."

Terian shrugged his shoulders; without the spiked pauldrons he was much less intimidating and shorter than Cyrus had noticed before. "They're all going to die, one town at a time, until this whole damned land is wiped clean. And you get to live with the knowledge that you're responsible, Cyrus." Terian broke into a hollow smile. "How's that feel?"

"I don't know, Terian," Cyrus said with more calm than he was feeling, "how does it feel? Because I believe you were right there with me when we killed Mortus."

"I didn't make the choice," Terian snarled back. "I didn't lunge in front of the God of Death as he was about to strike down a willing sacrifice. I damned sure didn't cut him or finish striking him down when it was all said and done. I didn't do it, you did. So, the consequences are yours. Just like my father. I know you didn't know what it was going to cause you, but the consequences for that are yours, too." The dark knight let a bitter smile curl his lips. "And aren't they a real bitch, too?"

"I didn't know he was your father, you're right," Cyrus said, feeling the pressure on his knees as he squatted there next to Terian, "but I would have killed him even if I had." He watched Terian stiffen. "He was going to kill me, for sure. I know that doesn't bother you, but I don't just lie down and die when someone means to have at me."

"Really?" Terian asked, and it was a cold fury grimace that he wore. "Because I heard you did just that, and Vara had to save you."

"Maybe she did," Cyrus said, "but I wasn't going to let her fall, not at the hands of your father, not at the hands of the God of Death, not by anyone, not then."

"I dunno, Cyrus," Terian said, still wearing his smile, "your elf-bitch sounds like more trouble than she's worth. She seems to have landed you in all manner of shit. You're in deep now, old friend, near to over your head, if you're not already."

"She's not mine," Cyrus said. "Not anymore, if she ever was."

There was a silence for a beat, only the sound of Mendicant's continued incantation behind them. "You realize, of course," Terian said, "that if you'd only let my father kill her, none of this would have happened. Not any of the deaths here in Luukessia, not you and I—"

"Somehow, I think if you'd been there on the bridge, you might have seen it differently," Cyrus said. "Your father, a man you talk about when you're drunk as though he's the second coming of Yartraak—" Cyrus watched Terian blanch, "—and yet when he's dead you lionize him. You're willing to throw away your entire life to for a man who you couldn't stand while he was alive. Would you have let Vara die, standing on that bridge? Do you have so little regard for your guildmates that you would have switched sides right there, shifted your allegiance to the Sovereignty without care for the words you swore to Alaric, to the loyalties you pledged to me, to our fellows?" Cyrus gave a wide sweep of the arm to take in all of the people around them. "Or would you have just ... abandoned your duty? Let him hammer her down with a sword until she died, let him go through the rest of us one by one until he'd killed us all and taken Termina for the Sovereign?" Cyrus watched Terian with cool loathing, saw the doubt buried deep in the dark elf. "Did you love him? Was his path the one you envied, or did you have prickle of conscience somewhere inside that was as quiet as an ember snuffed out of a dead fire? Which was it, Terian? Did you leave him or did he cast you out? Was he the one you wanted to be? Or was he everything you hated about yourself?"

Cyrus stood, and looked down on the dark elf, who kept his head low, his lips a thin, drawn line, near-purple. "If you're the sort who would abandon your loyalties the moment any trouble came your way, then I will send you with Mendicant right now, today, when he goes to ask Alaric for more aid. He can decide what's to be done with you—but as far as I'm concerned, I'd rather see you exiled from Sanctuary if that's the sort of loyalty you carry."

"I'm ... no ... traitor," Terian said, and he bent his face upward toward Cyrus, contorted in fury. "I would have had my revenge on you and been done with it and quietly, so no one would ever have to know."

"Well then, it seems you're in a state of dissonance, Terian," Cyrus said, and stared down at him, "because you want to maintain loyal ties to Sanctuary and all that entails, but you want to kill a man who upheld the ideals you at least pretend you hold to. Faithfulness, fidelity, loyalty—these aren't just things we pay lip service to—"

"I ... never ... just paid lip service to what we do," Terian said. "I was there in the Mountains of Nartanis, in Enterra, remember? I've been there, in the places where we've spilled blood, and I never took the craven's way out, not once. You can call me a lot of things, Cyrus, and I am a lot of things, but I'm not a—"

"Coward?" Cyrus said. "You're not an ... Orion, only in it for yourself?"

A look of loathing came over the dark knight's features and he leaned forward. "Say that again ... and give me another reason to want to kill you."

"Why wouldn't I say it? You were there when he betrayed me, tried to kill me—like you did." Terian struggled against the bonds that held him as though he could break the chains. After a moment, the rattling stopped, the sound of him fighting against the inevitable. "But I tell you what. I'll give you a chance to prove yourself a loyal guildmate and not a treacherous killer."

"Oh, this should be good." The rage broke over Terian's features and he shook his head. "What would you have of me? To run suicidally into the open jaws of those beasts?"

"I would have you stand at the front of our army and help to lead them, help to hold the line, like you said you would when Alaric allowed you back to our guild," Cyrus said. "I'm leaving to summon help. We need more of it here. Make a choice, Terian. You can either go back to Sanctuary with Mendicant when he goes to request aid and go wherever the wind and your will takes you after that, or you can stay here, help the Sanctuary army, and try to prove that you still do have some honor—some loyalty—left. That you're not just some shadow of your father's, trying to strike a last blow out of an empty sense of revenge that will cost you all that you have left."

There was a shuffle to Cyrus's left, and he saw Aisling not far away. She made just enough noise that he knew it was intentional, trying to gather his interest. "Think it over, Terian," Cyrus said. "Either way, once I'm gone, you'll be on your way—either back to Sanctuary or turned loose here. Decide what you want to be, dark knight. A defender of those who need it or the avenger of someone who you loathed so much in life that you couldn't bring yourself to be anything like him or even serve the same master as he."

"And what are you?" Terian said, and Cyrus heard the clinking of chains as Terian willed himself up, dragged himself to his feet with perfect balance and hard effort. "Some champion of the downtrodden, ready to fight your way to the death to impress a woman who doesn't want you? Do you think she'll still be yours if you die here trying to save these people? Do you think it'll undo all the damage you did, if you just fight for them a little harder? What do you believe in, Cyrus? Protecting people? Rushing headlong into things, hoping to do good? Because it seems like your best intentions are doing more harm than good of late. Maybe you should stop trying to help people."

"Go back to Sanctuary," Cyrus said with a wave, and began to walk away. "Go back to them and listen while Mendicant tells them what a coward you were, if Ryin hasn't already. Be on your way, dark knight. For all your talk, you don't believe in anything but petty, shallow revenge—"

"You don't know a damned thing, Cyrus Davidon!" Terian's roar was loud, and he came at Cyrus in a charge, shoulder tucked low. Cyrus parried and kicked Terian's legs from underneath him, and the dark knight fell to his face in the dirt, the long grass sticking up all around him like towers hanging over him, the little lines of their shadows stretching across his dark armor as they waved in the breeze. "Of course you wouldn't, you don't even know what it's like to have a father—"

Cyrus landed a kick on Terian's ribs without even realizing he was going to do it, the white-hot blinding flash of rage subsiding after he heard the grunt of pain from the dark elf. "Now who's talking about something they know nothing of?" Cyrus asked, taking long, slow breaths. "Make your choice, Terian. I don't care which it is, but figure out who you want to be."

"I'll stay," Terian said, looking up from the dirt, cradling his arm against his side where Cyrus kicked him. "I'll help. I'll help protect the people. But I want you to know—"

"We're not done," Cyrus said. "I'm well aware that you've still got your axe to grind—though I suppose it's a sword, now." He turned to face Mendicant. "Pass the word that when I'm gone later tonight, he can be freed. Until then ..." Cyrus knelt down and grabbed the stone off the ground along with the gag, "... back to blessed silence." Terian glared at him but opened his mouth, accepting the stone, and then Cyrus tied off the gag behind him. The eyes watched Cyrus, though, the hatred burned, and he felt it, it coursed through his veins like a poison as he stared into the eyes of his friend—and gagged him so tightly he couldn't make a sound.

Chapter 68

"That was awkward," Aisling said as he slipped past her, not bothering to conceal his motions. The sun was creeping lower in the sky, now afternoon, and the wind was steady out of the north, not intermittent as it had been. "Are you sure letting him loose is the best of ideas? What if he follows you?"

"You know we're going, right?" He watched her, taking long steps over a sleeping body to stand beside her. She nodded, and he realized he was standing closer to her now than he had ever before in camp. "He'll be of use to them. Let him have his chance to redeem himself."

"And if he doesn't?" She played with her hair as he watched, twisting it around her finger, the white blending with the dark blue, a bright contrast, as though both were painted, so different from his own skin and hair. "If he tracks you, and kills you?"

"That's why I'm taking you with me," Cyrus said with an easy smile that he felt not at all. He was getting better at it, he realized with only a slight discomfort. "This way, you'll be there to watch my back. If you're not too busy with my front, that is ..." He leaned toward her, let his armor rest against her, and then took a long, slow kiss, right there in front of the entire camp.

She pulled away from him leisurely, opening her eyes slowly after the kiss. "You realize you just did that in front of ..."

"Everyone, yes," Cyrus said and kissed her again. "I don't care who knows, who sees. I've seen some of them do it as well, the soldiers. They crawl into their bedrolls together at night and everyone pretends to give them the illusion of privacy, like a silent law we all follow. Well, I want it too, to stop hiding, to stop worrying about it, to have you when I want you instead of always worrying I'll be found out." His hand slipped around her hip and pulled her waist close to him. "I don't want to hide anymore. I just want to have you whenever I want."

She watched him cannily, with a slight smile. "That might prove awkward in the midst of a battle."

"Try to pretend you wouldn't find it incredibly arousing."

She took a moment of slow inhale to pretend as though she were thinking about it. "Perhaps. But as we are not presently in a battle, there's no need to consider it. If you want to have me as a soldier has his lover, you need only lay out a bedroll and crawl in it with me and let the rest take its course. There's no danger but the idea that others will see their General having an immensely good time."

He let himself smile again, fake but with a foundation in the grim reality that he wanted to unburden himself, to claim that relief she gave him. "Well, there is another danger," he said, as he slid a hand around her waist to lead her off to where his pack lay, near his saddle, across the camp, "... after all, you do tend to bite when you're overly excited ..."

She slapped him in mock offense as he led her away, and they put down the bedroll on the ground and climbed into it. Everyone saw, but no one watched, and they remained beneath it until they were both well and truly sated.

Chapter 69

The dark elven army held its distance, she knew, though she rarely went to the wall to see for herself. It was a quiet night, all things considered, after another long day of riding the Plains of Perdamun looking for caravans to raid. This morning they had caught a fat one, killing almost two hundred dark elven soldiers in the process. In the afternoon they'd managed to spring a trap on another, sending some hundred and fifty more soldiers to their deaths and securing almost twenty wagons laden with goods and riches. Vara stared at her hand, which clutched an inlaid silver bracelet with a soft clasp that snapped gently when she pushed it closed. There was a light circle of the precious metal that parted, a decent-sized ruby encrusted within. Not the possession of a noble, she knew, not locked up as it was in one of the caravans. It was something owned by a farmer, given to his wife after a particularly good harvest. It lacked polish, but the ruby still shone, and she wondered which poor sod had lost his valuables in addition to his crop. *And likely his life as well and the life of his family, knowing how these dark elves operate.*

The lounge was muted around her. Ever since the guard had taken up in the foyer every hour of every day, fewer and fewer people seemed to enjoy conversations, exchanges, and ale within the bounds of the lounge. *I suppose it's rather difficult to make merry when there's a visible reminder that we're under siege only a few feet away. Perhaps I'd be happier in my room as well, were I one of them.* She had a book across her lap, but it lay unopened. *The Champion and the Crusader,* something she'd read dozens of times, the words as familiar to her now as any expression her mother had ever used. It was usually a good distraction. Usually.

Without warning, or even a clear idea of what she was doing, she stood and let her feet carry her. *In times of peace I'd wear cloth and leather. Now we live in times of war, and I go nowhere without my armor and my sword.* She let her fingers touch the hilt and guard and then mentally slapped herself for again acting like Cyrus.

The front doors of Sanctuary swung wide from her effort; they were not nearly as heavy as they appeared, which prompted her to wonder for the thousandth time if they had an enchantment on them. She had always meant to ask Alaric, but whenever she came into his presence there were always more consequential matters to discuss. The crickets were chirping in the warm night air, and she took each step slowly, drawing her pace so slow that she could feel the resonance of her every step clacking on the stone of the Sanctuary steps, each sound ringing out like the noise of the catapult's firing through the glass window atop the foyer. She glanced back; it had been repaired, oddly enough, and quickly.

When she reached the dirt path, she stepped off it, letting her feet sink into the soft grass. Even though she couldn't feel it, she drew some odd reassurance from the green, springy vegetation. It was the nearest sort of affirmation she could find, something that harkened her back to her childhood lessons in the Temple of Life, where the Priestesses of Vidara spoke to her for hours about the Goddess and all Her wonders. *She chooses the lengths of all the grasses, they said, and the seasons of their growth, and all that they become. She chooses the ones that live, and the ones that die as seedlings, and all the trees of the forest.* She took one step after another, letting her feet settle in the grass, while overhead the stars gleamed down at her, an endless field of them.

Does he see them, where he is? Is he under the stars tonight? Or staying in some great castle, or a quiet wayside inn? Is he at peace or war right now? Did he find a way to best this scourge that plagues those lands or ... She left that thought unfinished by the words in her mind; the unspoken unease that it reflected was not similarly dismissed so easily.

"What does an Ice Princess care for stars?" The quiet rumbling of the rock giant did not cause her to turn, even when she heard and felt his heavy footsteps behind her. "Do they remind her of the glisten of the light on the snow, where each bit shines as though it were fallen from the heavens?"

"As far as poets go," Vara said, stifling much of her annoyance, "you leave much to be desired, Fortin."

"I am not a poet," Fortin said, stepping into place beside her and looking up, his towering frame almost double her height, "merely an observer. Here, I observe an Ice Princess, one who doesn't care for such things, and she's seemingly transfixed. An odd occurrence, surely worthy of some note."

"Hardly worthy of any note, I would think." She gave him the barest turn. "You are standing watch?"

"Between the wall and the foyer," the rock giant said. "Though I am not of much use in a melee where others might be harmed by being in close combat around me, I do function well as a line of defense against any dark elves who decide to try and run for the wall, as though they could overwhelm our forces there and open the gates and portcullis in a hurry."

"Seems a foolish notion," she said, "with you between them."

"I agree," Fortin said in his hearty rumble. "But what brings the Ice Princess out here on such a night, I wonder? And she's trying to distract me from that question."

She rolled her eyes. "I hardly need to distract you from the simple fact that I decided to take a stroll under the summer sky."

"It is almost autumn now," Fortin said, "or so I'm told by those who keep track of such things."

"Ah, yes," Vara said. "Midsummer's eve passed with but a whisper, and now it is ..." She blinked. "Goddess, that was quick. It seems only yesterday it was the beginning of spring."

"The time does go quickly, does it not?" Fortin's low rumble was louder now, as he looked down at her, his eyes glistening red in the dark. "How long has it been since he left now?"

"Ten months ..." She said before she realized she'd even done it. She blinked, and turned to favor the rock giant with a glare. "That was craftier than I would have given you credit for."

The red eyes seemed to dance. "Which was why I could manage it when no other could. You simply assume I wander around eating rocks and bashing my head into things, as though I were some peon, like a troll. I am not."

"Yes, well, I shan't make that mistake again."

There was a movement of the rock giant's torso that was as expressive as one might expect from a creature who appeared to be made of living stone. "Why is it a mistake? You confessed your feelings for him, and he plainly felt the same for you. To make all these tiresome games, to accept, then to deny, then to reject him when you obviously still care, it's all very disagreeable to the constitution." Fortin clacked his jaw together and caused Vara to flinch from the noise of rock grinding on rock. "He was plain with you, but you can't find it in yourself to be plain with him?"

"I was very plain with him," Vara said quietly. "Plain enough with my intent, with my reasons. But that was between him and me, not him and me and the entire guild, which is why I don't discuss it."

"Oh, yes, I forgot," Fortin said with a heavy nodding motion, "fleshlings have their notions of privacy and decorum. Well, perhaps 'forgot' might be a strong word. 'Chose not to remember because your ideas are silly and irrelevant' better captures it, I'd say. If I were to act as coyly as you people do, I don't think I would ever find a partner to raise hatchlings with."

She blinked. "Is that how ...?" There was a noise in the foyer, and Vara heard it, her ears perking up. "Something is amiss."

"Come along," Fortin said, but he was already running, the ground shaking under his feet with every shuddering step. When he hit the front steps, the sound became worse, the stone floor hitting against the rock giant's bare skin, reminding Vara of the noise of bricks being slapped together. Fortin flung open the door and there stood the guard contingent, weapons pointing into the middle of the foyer as Vara slipped around Fortin's leg when the rock giant stopped, giving her free view of the room.

The alarm was silent, no one speaking or calling out for any manner of assistance. Still, the swords remained down, the spears remained pointed. Standing at the middle of the room on the great seal was a goblin, Mendicant, his scaly skin reflecting in the torchlight and his bright robe catching her eye. Behind him was another figure, however, only a little taller than he, with a beard that was braided all the way down to his waist, and a hammer slung across his back.

"Well, damnation," Belkan Stillhet said from his place beside a pillar, his sword held in his ancient hand.

"Or as near as one can get to seeing it from here," came the voice of Alaric Garaunt, as a faint mist subsided in the corner next to Vara.

She fell into step behind him as the Master of Sanctuary strode across the foyer toward the seal, gesturing to Mendicant, who was nervously looking around, to move away from the stranger in the middle of the room. "Partus," Alaric said, staring down at the dwarf who remained indifferent, examining his surroundings as though they mattered little, "how unpleasant it is to see you again."

Chapter 70

"Well, Alaric," Partus said from where he sat in the Council Chambers (in Cyrus's seat, which he had selected entirely at random, and oh, how it chafed at her) "it would appear you're in a bit of a bind here." Vara kept her eyes fixed on the dwarf as he spoke. *It's as though I fear to take them off him, as though I suspect he would begin stealing things were I to stop watching him for a moment.* She ran her tongue over her teeth nervously. *For all know, he might do just that.*

"So it would seem," Alaric said, looking over his steepled fingers at the dwarf. "I presume you had no idea that we were under siege when you jumped onto Mendicant's back as he cast his return spell?"

"Had I known," Partus said with a slightly sour frown, "I might still have done it, because being surrounded by the dark elven army here is still likely safer than what your blighting guildmates are planning over in Luukessia. They're going to fight a slow retreat across the northern steppes trying to buy time for Syloreas to empty—as in for all the people to leave the lands." The dwarf snorted in derision. "How well do you think that one's likely to turn out?"

"Mendicant," Alaric said, looking to the goblin, "you are here to make Cyrus's report, yes?"

The goblin had been still throughout the meeting thus far, as though he were awed by the surroundings; the Council Chambers and their stone walls, slow, quiet hearths that radiated warmth through the room. It was dark outside the windows out on the balcony, but within the chambers it was light, with torches aplenty burning on sconces on the walls in such close proximity that one could comfortably read in the room despite the hour.

"Mendicant?" Alaric asked again.

The goblin seemed to shake himself out of a stupor of sorts. "Oh, yes. Partus speaks correctly, the bulk of the Sanctuary army is presently engaged in a long holding action on the Filsharron Steppes, north of Enrant Monge." Alaric stirred, but the rest of the table was quiet and still, save for Partus, who shot a wicked grin at Vara. She held the urge to let fly a force blast but only just. "Cyrus, Longwell and a few others are making their way to Vernadam to try and sway them to enter the war with their army, and Actaluere is presently calling up the remainder of its forces to meet them at Enrant Monge in an effort to effect a counterthrust north and destroy the portal in the cave that is allowing them to flood Luukessia with these dead souls." Mendicant's eyes glistened as he spoke matter-of-factly. "Lord Davidon—"

"Lord of damned near nothing, if you ask me," Partus said with a chortle below his breath.

"He's Lord of Perdamun and Warden of the Southern Plains," Vara snapped without thinking then tempered the widening of her eyes out of sheer reflex. *Why in the blazes did I say that?* Partus made no reply but feigned being impressed by flattening his lips, then pursing them, holding a hand over his mouth as though amazed.

"Lord Davidon requests aid," Mendicant said after a momentary stumble, "for you to send another army to reinforce him and allow him to better fight back in the impending battle, assuming you have not already sent such an army."

Alaric sighed, while Ryin laid his head on the high back of his chair. Vara expected Erith to shift her gaze around the table, but her sight was firmly fixed on Partus at her right, the dark elf's icy glare beyond any sort of loathing Vara had come to expect even from the mercurial healer. "Can we teleport him into Saekaj?" Erith asked, indicating Partus with a nod of her head. "I think he'd do well there, in the vek'tag pens, eating their dung with the rest of the mushrooms—"

"How I've missed you as well, Erith," Partus said with a crooked grin. "I don't suppose we've spoken since the day I left the Daring—"

"You mean the day when you stripped our guild of most our members and left for Goliath?" Her arms were folded in front of her, and her teeth were bared in a snarl. "Gee, Partus, I can't really think of any reason why I might not have spoken to you since then. Oh, wait, because you're a traitorous, lecherous ass."

Partus feigned innocence and looked around the table as if for support. "Lecherous? Just because we had a singular night of passion—"

"It wasn't a night," Erith said. "It wasn't even a minute. Though I can see why you might have thought so; judgment is the first thing to go when drunk—"

"Aye," Partus agreed sadly, "which is why I was in your bed to begin with—"

"ENOUGH!" Alaric said, loud enough to draw the attention of all in the chamber.

There was a squeak at the door and it opened; Andren slid in as Vara stared at the healer, perplexed. Vaste followed a moment later and shut the door behind him, his staff in hand, and the troll stared at the table and those around it.

There was the sound of a chair sliding back and Partus was on his feet, his hammer unslung. "My gods, it's a troll."

Vaste blinked at the dwarven interloper who had been sitting with his back to the door and was now standing, weapon in hand. "Well spotted. What gave it away—that I'm seven feet tall or the green skin and big teeth?"

Partus hesitated, keeping his eyes on Vaste. He turned his head to speak to Alaric out of the corner of his mouth. "Did you always have a troll, Alaric? They're savages, you know."

Vaste's heavy frame swelled with a deep breath and then a long sigh followed. "Yes, I know, uncivilized I may be, standing here without a weapon drawn while you're clearly about to challenge me to a duel, but what can I say? I abhor civilized society. I'd rather just sneak up behind you when you're unable to defend yourself and mash you into a fine paste with my bare hands."

Partus pointed his hammer at Vaste. "You'll find me a greater challenge than you think if you mean to attack me when I'm not expecting it."

"I doubt I'll find you much at all, unless I'm crawling around on my hands and knees," Vaste said, and promptly walked past Partus to his seat, turning his hammer aside and toward the hearth with a gentle push of his staff. "Thanks to the rest of you for speaking up for me when he called me a savage, by the way."

"It was unworthy of answer," Alaric said, at the head of the table, his helm still on. His eye was piercing through the slight gloom that inhabited the room; not because of the darkness, Vara realized, but because of her mood. *He should have come back as well, not this miniaturized jackass.* "Andren," Alaric said, turning to the healer, who was in Nyad's usual seat next to Vara, "thank you for joining us."

"Aye," Andren said, then twitched as though he were reaching for something near his belt, hesitated, and thought the better of it. "Can't pretend I know what this is all about, though."

"I am taking things into consideration," Alaric said. "Mendicant, finish your report, if you please? Cyrus requests aid, I believe you said?"

"In most strenuous terms, sir," the goblin said. "We need assistance, desperately, to be able to finish this fight and destroy the portal. These things, this scourge, they are beyond number."

"As you may be able to tell," Alaric said quietly, "we have some minor problems of our own; the dark elves have left an army in place around Sanctuary to cut us off from the outside world while they attempt to starve us out and break us."

"How's it all going so far?" Partus asked snidely.

"Poorly on the starving us out," Vaste answered him with a grin, "even more poorly on the breaking us. Spirits are high. We're planning a dance recital for next week."

"How exciting," Partus said without enthusiasm.

"While I do not believe we could spare the army Cyrus has called for," Alaric said, "I believe sending a messenger—or two, as the case may be—would be both wise and prudent. Thus I am considering sending you," he nodded to Andren, "and Mendicant, to deliver the message to Cyrus that help will not be arriving."

"Well, won't that be a fun message to deliver," Andren muttered.

Mendicant straightened in his chair, and spoke, slowly. "I do not believe sending only two people to deliver that message would be wise."

Alaric frowned. "Why not?"

"Because to get to Cyrus and the rest of the army," Ryin said, "the messengers would have to travel through the Kingdom of Actaluere by themselves."

"I thought you said that Actaluere was now allied with our army's cause?" Erith asked, frowning. "Why would they deny our messengers free passage?"

"They wouldn't," Ryin said, speaking over Mendicant, "but you said Milos Tiernan was at the front with the army?" Mendicant nodded.

"Did he leave Hoygraf in place along the route?" The goblin nodded again. "There's your trouble; we ran afoul of this Baron Hoygraf on the journey in."

"You didn't think to mention this?" Vara asked, her irritation rising.

"We've been a little busy with our own problems here," Ryin said calmly. "Far too busy for me to mention the prosaic details of our trip, especially unrelated as they were to the crisis we were experiencing as I left Luukessia."

"So you presume that this ... Hoygraf," Alaric tested the word, as though he were tasting it and found he disliked it immensely, "would interrupt their passage out of some grudge?"

Mendicant's gaze shot immediately to Ryin, who kept calm—and yet Vara saw the hint of unease within him. "Yes," Ayend said, "if he caught a hint that we had messengers passing through—which he would—they would not make through his territory alive, even though the King of Actaluere is now allied with us."

"What the hell did Cyrus do to him?" Vaste said, low, almost too low to be heard.

"As I heard it," Partus said with a wide grin, ignoring the look of frozen horror on Ryin Ayend's face, "he stormed the man's castle, sacked the place, stabbed the man through the guts and left him to die— which he did not, by the way—then stole the man's wife and proceeded to cuckold him." Partus let a hearty guffaw. "I like your General. He's got style."

Vara felt the ice pump through her veins, freezing her expression at some bizarre in-between of shock and horror.

"So," Erith said into the quiet around the table, where every face was split between looking at Vara or looking away to spare her shame, "he took the man's wife and made her his lover? That does carry something of a sting." She cast a sidelong glare at Ryin. "I suppose you thought we were too busy for you to mention that Cyrus was taking a taste of the local flavor? And a Baroness, no less."

"Well," Mendicant said, his voice coming back to him now in the quiet horror that no one else would speak into, "they had some sort of falling out, you see. The Baroness went back to her husband." Vara felt the cold ratchet down a few notches. "Cyrus is sleeping with Aisling now."

There was a dead calm, a quiet so unnatural as to border on the surreal. Vara felt no motion in her face at all, nothing in her head but a screaming void, an interminable desire to cry out but her mouth, strangely enough, stayed well shut, fortunately. She caught Ryin's face covered out of the corner of her eye and saw Vaste bow his head. Erith tried to give her a smile of support but it was wasted. All that was there was what she saw, the screaming void in her head the loudest silence she'd ever known.

It was into that silence that Andren spoke at last. "Well done, Cyrus," the healer said, his face a smile of grudging admiration. He looked at Vara and his grin faded. "Uh ... I mean ... how dare he not spend these last months pining for a woman who rejected him so harshly that he fled the continent afterward." Andren turned to Alaric, faux outrage on the healer's bearded face. "I thought you sent him there to fight, not f—"

"Enough." Alaric was quiet this time, exhaustion seeping through every syllable. "This is no time for levity; our brethren are cut off from us, we remain surrounded. I have no time for petty concerns of who is sleeping with whom, outside of how it affects our lines of communication." He bowed his head, helm still blocking the view of his eyes. "They will have to remain without assistance and without warning. I see no way to return a messenger to them."

"If J'anda were still here," Vaste said, "he would be able to. But none of our remaining enchanters are nearly skilled enough to pull off the illusory treachery it would take to cross that territory, nor would any of our rangers be a particularly good risk."

"Then we remain on the same course as before," Alaric said, sweeping his chair back and standing abruptly. "Ryin, organize quarters for our guest, Partus."

Ryin blinked. "He's staying?"

Erith's jaw dropped in disbelief. "He's staying?"

Vaste clapped his hands together in faux joy. "He's staying? Oh goody, we can finally have that dwarven sleepover I've always dreamed of, the naughty one where the beard gets—"

"You stay away from me, you filthy beast," Partus said, brow furrowed at Vaste. "I'll have no part of what ever unnatural plans you're making with me at the center of them.''

"Can we please come back to why he's staying?" Erith asked in a hoarse voice. "Sending a wizard or druid to deliver him to Fertiss or wherever he wants to go seems a small price to pay for not having to deal with him anymore."

"I don't care to spare anyone at the moment," Alaric said quietly, and drew up to his full height. "He is our guest until the next time we send out a druid or wizard to somewhere suitably civilized. Until then, he can stay with us."

"Well," Partus said, as though trying to reconcile what he was hearing, "surely being under embargo as you are, you'll be needing to send someone to gather a daily ration of food from a major city—Pharesia, Reikonos—any of them will do."

"Actually, we're stealing our food from convoys that the dark elves have purloined from local farmers," Vaste said. "It's all very efficient, and saves us from having to—you know, being a former member of Goliath and thus well versed in all manner of banditry—*pay* for any of it."

"So," Partus said, "you could drop me off on one of your raiding expeditions. I could cross the Plains of Perdamun on horse."

"Do you have a horse?" Alaric asked—*with some small trace of satisfaction,* Vara thought.

"Well, no—"

"You could always walk your way across the Plains of Perdamun," Vaste suggested in an oh-so-helpful tone. "After all, they're only swarming with dark elves at the moment. I'm sure they'd love to have a conversation with such a charming fellow as yourself."

Partus's face fell. "I ... uh ... don't really think I'm on very good terms with the dark elves. I wouldn't care to run across them. Are you certain you couldn't lend me a horse?"

"I'm afraid we're rather in need of all the horses we have at the moment," Alaric said smugly. "But worry not, I'm certain we'll have a wizard heading toward a safe city in the next six months or so."

Vara watched him carefully and tried to guess at his game; as usual, the man they dubbed the Ghost was beyond explanation. *Keeping the dwarf here is pointless. He's no more use to us than a weight around our necks; best be rid of him.*

"That seems to be enough for now," Alaric said, and his armor began to fade. He turned insubstantial, into the faint fog, and rolled under the door to the stairs, disappearing faster than he usually did.

"A houseguest," Vaste said, now sarcastic. "I couldn't be more thrilled! I'll bring you the good linens, the ones with small pebbles crushed into them for your comfort and our amusement."

"If you'll come with me," Ryin said, gesturing to Partus, "we'll find you some accomodations."

"The dungeons have some particularly lovely quarters," Erith suggested. "Put him in the one next to the rock giant."

"You have a rock giant, too?" Partus asked. "Gods, do you have anyone normal?"

Vara didn't wait for the repartee nor any sort of reply; she was out the door and going, her feet heavy on the stairs up to her quarters. It was evening, after all—*time to sleep,* she told herself. *Or at least try and pretend to.*

"Hey," came the quiet voice behind her, the low baritone of Vaste.

"What do you want?" she snapped at him, unaware of how much raw emotion she was putting into her voice until she heard it.

Vaste came up behind her, a slow walk, his feet making soft footfalls on every stone. "He's not dead, you know."

"I bloody well know that," she said, lashing out again with her voice. "Not that I care. I don't, actually. I don't bloody well care."

Vaste gave her a subtle nod. "You're a liar and a thief."

"What?" She stared at him, perplexed and irritable. "I am not a thief!"

"So you admit to being a liar?"

"I admit to nothing," she said, "save for that you are a baffling, exasperating sort of fool whose flabby green arse is ripe for a good thumping."

Vaste raised an eyebrow at her then turned around, sticking out his backside and looking down as though to inspect it. "It does look wonderful, doesn't it? Ripe for thumping indeed. The way you say it makes it sound so kinky and appealing."

She let out a harsh breath, as though it could contain some magic that might strike him dead on the spot. "I am in no mood—"

"You've been in no mood for quite some time," Vaste said. "I don't expect the news that he's sleeping with other women will do much to improve it."

She let out a mirthless laugh. "If it is as you say it is, why would you bother to put yourself in my path when you know that I'll be ready to spray whoever annoys me with nothing but the sharpest acid?"

Vaste didn't grin, didn't smile at all, for once. "Because somebody should be there to take it."

"What?" She didn't quite boggle at him but was only just shy of it.

"I expect you'd think I would argue for Cyrus, or something of the sort," Vaste said, straitlaced. "But I'm not. Cyrus did what Cyrus did, I won't defend or condone it. But neither is he my concern at this moment. My concern is you."

"I'm fine," Vara said, letting her mouth stretch into a thin line, like the bricks in the wall. *Just like the bricks, unbreakable, standing strong.*

"With as much lying as you're doing, I can't imagine it will be much longer before you cross into the domain of thieving simply from sheer boredom at having mastered the lying." He raised an eyebrow again. "Would you say you're also getting better at lying to yourself with all the practice you're getting?"

"What do you want from me?" She felt a great wall of overwhelm, of fatigue, and suddenly going to her bed didn't seem so outrageous.

"I would like to see," Vaste said, "my favorite paladin stop taking it on the chin and start being honest with everyone." He shrugged. "But since Alaric is probably going to continue to be mysterious—"

"A joke," she said quietly, and felt the push of the emotions within her. "So excellently timed, too."

"I'll settle for getting you to admit that you're in love with Cyrus and that with every bit of word from Luukessia you die a little inside, and every month without word from them kills you a little more." Vaste stared down at her, and the humor was gone. "The truth is probably the hardest part to admit; especially for someone as …"

"Reserved?" She said, her voice brittle. She stared into his eyes, which were immense and brown, warm, something that she had always found favorable about him. *Perhaps the only thing.*

"I was going to say tragically repressed, but why don't we meet in the middle and say stoic?" He awkwardly put a large hand on her shoulder and rested it there lightly on her armor. "I know that you must be going through some sort of mental obstacle course of epic proportions, and that with the death of your father, and before that your mother, that you must be—"

"She warned me away," Vara said at a whisper. "Before she died, the last conversation we had, we were yelling and screaming at a fever pitch. I told her I loved him, and that I didn't care about my responsibilities as the shelas'akur, and she threw it back in my face. I said some very unkind things, some very crude things meant to shock her. She warned me away, told me that he would die before me and that I would mourn him all the rest of my life." She clenched her eyes tightly shut, as though doing so would mean all the emotion she was feeling would vanish like the world when they were shut, "and I listened to to her. I knew she was right, and so I told him goodbye, that it would never work ..." She heard her voice break a little, "and I sent him into the arms of her—that harlot."

"I would try not to think of it that way if I were you," Vaste said. "You attempted to make the best decision you could at that moment. Sure, it turned out to be monumentally shortsighted on an emotional level," he grimaced when she looked at him, disbelief at what he had said. "Sorry. But your mother had the right of it, if we were only looking at the long-term ramifications. Everything she told you is true, on a purely logical level." The troll looked strangely sage as he spoke. "But the problem is that love and logic are the poorest of bedfellows. Not unlike you and Cyrus."

"How am I supposed to comport myself in this circumstance?" She shuffled two steps to the right and put her back to the wall, between two sconces. The clink of her armor against the stone was enough to remind her that she wore it to protect herself from harm. *But there was no protection from Cyrus Davidon, he got under my damned armor as surely as though I weren't wearing any at all.* "How am I to handle the thought of him ... over there ... with her ... while I'm here, trying to keep the only home I have left from being ground under the boot of the greatest tyrant in Arkaria?" She brushed a hand along her smooth face, felt it run up to her eyes and cover them, blotting out the light. "How am I supposed to ... Vaste ... how do I ...?"

She dissolved, then, and he caught her in his massive arms, enfolded her in them, and she sobbed into his white robes, felt the tears trickle down her cheeks in a way that was still foreign to her. She felt safe and warm, wrapped up with him there, and she held onto him for quite some time, just like that, in the middle of the hallway.

Chapter 71

Cyrus

They rode south for more than a month, and the autumn hounded them the whole way as though they were the prey and it was a predator. The steppes near Filsharron were low, and the yellowed grass went green for a time as they rode west to avoid the swamps southeast of Enrant Monge. It was a long, drawn out course, but they saw no sign of scourge as they went, and after a week's travel, Longwell looked ahead upon the apex of a small hill and pointed; ahead of them was a short wall, and tucked behind it was a stone house.

"Guard house," Longwell said. "At least a couple men manning it. They should have seen us already; though they may report to a larger watch, which would be ..." he held a hand above his eyes to shield them from the sun, "over there." He pointed to a nearby hill that was taller, covered with trees. Cyrus could see man-made structures breaking up the symmetry of the woods atop it, but it wasn't easily defined. "We're at the crossing for Gundrun; they'll be wanting to know who we are and for what purpose we're coming to Galbadien there at that house."

"Might I suggest we not tell them we're here to overthrow the King?" J'anda said it with a wry smile, but it caused a pallor to settle over them all.

The smell of autumn was in the air; the wind came from the east, the stink of the scourge was gone for at least now, and the leaves were turning all along the road. Reds and golds were full fledged, and the shock of them together was something Cyrus couldn't quite recall. The air was crisp, like the first bite of an apple, and the briskness spread across his skin, the sweat from riding giving him the chills. The woods had been quiet around them, this intermittent sea of trees and fields that was something much less desolate than the steppes had been.

"Are you ready for this?" Cyrus asked Longwell, as they trod along the road on horseback. It was only the ten of them; Cyrus, Aisling, Longwell, Martaina, J'anda, Nyad, Scuddar, and Calene Raverle, along with a healer whose name Cyrus had yet to catch, a human who said little to nothing. Raverle had made a fairly quick recovery after Green Hill and had made no mention of what had happened, though Cyrus knew there was a stillness about her that hinted at things, things going on in her depths that he preferred to not inquire about.

"Ready to either usurp my father's throne or claim my birthright, depending on how things go?" Longwell did not look at him, merely kept his gauntletted hands on the reins as they went. "I suppose I'm as ready for that as I'll ever get."

"Glad you're keeping it in perspective," Cyrus said, and they went on in silence.

The border crossing was a simple thing. The guards said nothing to them, merely nodded assent as they approached the shack. When they had gone a few hundred feet past it along the path into the woods, Cyrus turned back to Longwell. "That was easy."

"They see ten people, one of them wearing a surcoat of the Galbadien dragoons," Longwell said without emotion, "they probably assume we're not going to invade the Kingdom as we are."

"That makes them all the more foolish, then, doesn't it?" J'anda asked from behind them.

"Not in the context of Luukessia," Longwell said. "A man with a spell may do much damage in Arkaria, but very few spellcasters would care to brave the bridge simply to come to Luukessia for the joy of it."

The weather over the next days was pleasing to Cyrus, who had not missed the hot, listless days of summer, even after the few he had spent waiting at the camp near Filsharron for the battle to come to them. The nights he spent under the bedroll with Aisling, separated slightly from the others. She was the only thing that allowed him to sleep soundly at night; her activity, her vigor. He lay down at night spent not only from the ride but from her, letting himself rest in her.

His dreams were clear, surprisingly so, considering the scourge and all that it meant for Luukessia. They rode on at a fast pace but at one which allowed for proper care of the horses. He watched Martaina at night when she looked after them, picking out their feet, using Nyad's ability to conjure grains and oats for them when they stayed in the wilderness instead of an inn. Some nights they did stay in towns and ate hot food made in the taverns instead of the hard cheese they carried with them. Occasionally Martaina would bring down an animal on an evening when they took extra rest and would make a stew or something similar. Occasionally it was long into the night before she was done cleaning and preparing the animal, but when Cyrus had the first taste, he knew the wait was worth it, even tempered as it was with the pickled eggs and conjured bread that they had to cut the hunger pangs.

They crossed through canyons and foothills, came down through wide forests choked with game. Those nights were bounteous with their harvests, and the nights spent in roadside inns where the fare was little more than warmer bread and the barest stew were ill enjoyed by comparison. Cyrus began to feel the slightest of his life's blood come back to him one night sitting by a fire, in a circle with the others, his patera—a cooking pot, cup and bowl all in one—filled to the brim in front of him with something Martaina had created from some animals she had snared and the spices she carried with her.

"This is really quite magnificent," J'anda said, supping it straight from his patera. "Where did you learn to do all these things—hunting, fishing, cooking, tracking?"

"My father," Martaina said, stirring the small cauldron that she carried on the back of her horse. "He was one of the last of the breed of elves who lived their lives in the Iliarad'ouran Woods outside Pharesia. That forest is rich with wildlife, and a small band of our people chose to live outside the city gates, off the land rather than within the walls, herding, domesticating animals. It was a simpler life, a subsistence life, rather than one focused on creating excess and serving the monarchy, with their demand for as much of your grain and livestock as they could lay hands on."

She stirred the spoon slowly in the cauldron, a small one, only slightly larger than Cyrus's helm. "He taught me how to fire an arrow as quickly as you can pluck it, how to follow tracks, and skin a beast fast, get it over the fire and roast it on spit." She blinked. "It was all we did, all day long, and the sooner we finished those chores the sooner we could get to the idle fun of the things we wanted to do." She smiled. "So we got very good at it."

"I take it he's passed on now?" Nyad asked quietly. "If he was one of the Iliarad'ouran woodsmen, I know the last of their number was—"

"Yes," Martaina said simply, cutting her off. "About a milennia ago. He was the last. I chose not to follow in his footsteps to carry it on."

Nyad nodded without saying much else; it occurred to Cyrus after a space of seconds that the tension was heavy, which was probably due to the fact that Nyad's father *was* the monarchy that Martaina's father resented. "So," he said, trying to break the silence, "what do you think they're doing back home right now?" He felt a peculiar twinge at the words, especially the thought of Sanctuary as home. *It's been nearing a year since we've been away ...*

"It's fall now," Calene Raverle spoke up. "Apples would be coming into season in the Northlands." Her voice was soft but strained, as though it had been poured through a sifter and all that was left was smoothness. It could barely be heard it over the sound of the crickets though everyone listened intently. "Have you ever walked through an orchard on a fall day and picked apples as you went?" Her eyes were far off now, thinking about it. "Felt the cool grass beneath your feet, like a thousand tickling kisses?" She let a small smile crop up on her petite face. "You take the first bite of one, hear the crunch, feel it crackle in your mouth, the tartness of the yellow ones." She took a breath. "They make cider with some of the excess, you know, and if you can get some cinnamon for it ..." She breathed again and a sadness crept over her. "I don't suppose they have much in the way of apple orchards around Sanctuary though, do they?"

"I believe there is one across the river Perda, to the south," J'anda said. "I miss fall nights at Sanctuary, when the barest chill cancels out the warm sun. You know that two-week period after summer ends and we get our first chill, but then the warm weather comes back before it turns a little blustery? I like that. It's like the last kiss of summer before it leaves. Not that it gets desperately wintery in the Plains of Perdamun, like it does outside Saekaj, anyway, but I like that last ... that last goodbye. A fond farewell, if you will."

"The gardens around the palace have a certain kind of vegetation that only blooms in fall," Nyad said. "Pharesia is far enough south that winter's touch is not that painful, but when they prepare the gardens for winter, it is an impressive sight ... for the few days when it freezes, they make ice sculptures and fill the grounds with them. And at the smaller palace outside Termina, they used to—" Nyad's broad face carried a smile that faded as she looked around and settled on Martaina, who stared evenly back at her. "Well, it was beautiful. Though I suppose that's gone now," she said with a touch of sadness.

"Longwell?" Cyrus asked, and the dragoon seemed to settle into deep thought.

"Vernadam sits so low in the land that summer lasts longer for us than it does for most of Arkaria," he said. "Winter is a short affair, a few months only of lower temperatures, and a very quick autumn to bridge between the two." He shrugged. "I spent time in my youth at Enrant Monge and in the northern parts of Galbadien and found them to be very different than life at Vernadam. Autumn in the north is like winter at home."

"What about you?" Aisling spoke up, dragging Cyrus out of his quiet. "What do you miss most about autumn at home?"

Cyrus pondered that for a moment. "I don't, I suppose. I mean, Sanctuary's been home for the last couple years. Before that I was living in the slums of Reikonos, where every day is the same, even the ones where the snow goes to your knees. Before that ..." he shrugged. "Still in Reikonos, all the way back to when I was at the Society of Arms."

"So," Nyad asked, "you don't have any distinct memories of autumn? Nothing?"

After a moment's thought, Cyrus shrugged. "We went on a training exercise to the Northlands once in the fall, the year after I joined the Society. It was almost as much a camping trip as anything, to get us familiar with staying out overnight, sleeping under the stars. But they took us away from the city for this one, on a long hike, aided by a wizard for transport. I remember seeing the leaves change. You don't see much of that in Reikonos, because it's not like Termina; there aren't many trees in the city itself, it's mostly houses and buildings. I remember that pretty well, the hues of the leaves, how different they were from the green ones I was used to seeing. Trees all down the road and beyond." He hesitated. "I think that was the training exercise where I finally got the Able Axes to leave me the hell alone."

"Able Axes?" Nyad said, her brow puckered with confusion.

"Blood Family," Cyrus said. "The Society of Arms splits its trainees into two separate classes, the Able Axes and the Swift Swords."

"Ah," she said, with a subtle nod. "They were bullying you, then?"

Cyrus shrugged, felt the cool breeze. "They had their reasons. It's all very competitive, very 'us vs. them' in the Society's structure. They saw me as an easy target, so they took their turns trying to break me." He shrugged again. "It didn't work."

"What did you do?" J'anda asked. Cyrus looked around; every eye was on him, even Martaina's, which was decidedly knowing.

Cyrus waited before answering, sifted through his emotions to see if he could find it, a thread of regret for what had happened. It was strangely absent. "I killed their leader."

Nyad choked on a spoonful of stew, and a little of it sluiced out of her upper lip, dribbling down her pale chin and along the cleft. "I'm sorry ... you killed him?" She waited for the nod, then looked around, wide-eyed, to the others sitting around the fire before she came back to him. "How old were you?"

"Seven, I think," Cyrus answered, racking his memory.

"My gods," Nyad said, holding her bowl apart from her as though it contained something appalling. "How old was he?"

Cyrus gave it some thought. "He was about ... oh, I don't know, sixteen or so? Perhaps seventeen."

Nyad stared at him, gaping. The look was not held by anyone else, though Longwell watched him sidelong, wary, and J'anda seemed disquieted, his teeth visible in a grimace. "Why did you kill him?" Nyad asked.

"Well," Cyrus said, "in fairness, it was a training exercise, and it was Swift Swords versus Able Axes, and while we were supposed to keep it non-lethal and strictly to more of a 'tag, you're out' system, he didn't play fair. So I killed him."

"Oh," Nyad said with a distant sort of nod, "so it was an accident."

"No," Cyrus said, and took another sip of his stew, "I knew full well what I was doing. I bludgeoned him with a tree branch until his head split open."

"But ..." Nyad's voice came again into the quiet. No one else was eating now. "... You did it for your team, then? To win the game? For the ... Swift Swords?"

"I wasn't on the Swift Swords team," Cyrus said, and this time he did feel a pinch of emotion, but he took another sip of the stew anyway.

"So you killed your own teammate?" J'anda asked, watching him carefully.

"No," Cyrus said and finally felt the burn of it. He looked to his left to see Aisling watching him, curiosity in her eyes. *So she doesn't know, either.* He looked to Martaina. *But she does.* He slowly looked around the circle and saw only Scuddar In'shara nodding in agreement. "I was on my own, you see."

There was a steely quiet that was finally broken by J'anda. "I admit my understanding of the Society of Arms is somewhat ... flawed. But I was given to understand that every single child brought in was given a Blood Family—for kinship, for a familial structure and familiarity." The enchanter spread his arms wide. "For support. So that even while learning the hardness of battle, you are not ever fully alone."

"True," Cyrus said, and put his patera aside, the stew now gone. "But occasionally an inductee is deemed unworthy of having a Blood Family and is separated out to survive on their own." He felt a tightness in his jaw. "I was one of those."

There was a silence. "But ..." J'anda said, "they would have all been arrayed against you, yes?" He stared at Cyrus, and there was a horror behind the enchanter's eyes. "They base everything in their training off of Blood Families?" Cyrus nodded. "Every exercise pits the Blood Families against each other?" J'anda kept on, and Cyrus nodded every time. "So if you are without a Blood Family, then you huddle with the others who are without one? Make your own sort of small circle?"

Cyrus smiled, but there was no warmth to it. "It's a rare thing, being without a Blood Family. I was the first in five years. The one before me died two months into the training. Typically 'outcasts,' as they're called, don't survive six months." He gave a slight nod. "And I do mean survive. They're usually found dead in the morning hours, well past the time when a resurrection spell would be able to bring them back."

"Murder," Nyad said with a quiet whisper. "Nothing more than child murder."

"Aye," Longwell said, arms folded where he sat on a log. "That's pretty savage, even for a guild that trains warriors."

Cyrus shrugged. "If you know that's how outcasts die going in—

and they do tell you, by the way, probably as a suggestion to the Able Axes and Swift Swords, but I took it as a warning to me to be scarce during the nighttime hours—it makes it that much easier to avoid that sort of death."

"Barbaric," Nyad said, shuddering. "Absolutely barbaric."

"I'm certain that back when Pharesia had a Society of Arms, they did it the same way," Cyrus said lacksadaisically. "But it's all rather irrelevant now."

"How is this irrelevant?" J'anda said. "How did you survive? Most don't make it six months? You were there for ... twelve years?"

Cyrus shrugged. "I fended them off. I did what I did on that training exercise after the first year and gave the Able Axes a string of injuries that made them afraid of me. And I held the Swift Swords at bay until Cass Ward came of an age to keep them off me."

"He was your friend, then?" Aisling spoke up at last. "Cass? He's an officer of The Daring, right? But he was your friend?"

"No," Cyrus said with a slight smile. "An outcast lives and dies alone in the Society of Arms. They're not considered *of* the Society, you see, not part of the family. So you're not allowed to talk to them. But he respected me because we fought together. We didn't speak until after we graduated; but I did know him. Friends? Hardly. I didn't have friend until ..." Cyrus swallowed heavily. "Until Narstron. Or at least Imina, if you want to count her as that."

There was a deadened silence after that, a quiet that settled on their party that no one seemed to want to break, so Cyrus did it himself. "Come on. This was all years ago. I don't feel sorry for myself about it, so none of you should, either."

"Sorry," J'anda said, with a weak smile, "it's just ... uh ... that is truly appalling. It might take a bit of adjustment to get over that. I'm no stranger to the cruelties that others may deal out, but that ... is a special sort of disturbing, if I may say so."

Cyrus felt a cool settle over him, like the waters deep in his soul became placid. "It was life. It made me who I am today."

"The only one without a Blood Family to ever graduate the Society of Arms," Martaina said from behind the stew pot; her gaze was not accusatory, but something else, her words tinged with slightest awe. "To survive being an outcast."

Cyrus shrugged. "You do what you have to. It was just a day-to-day struggle, like everyone else experiences in life—" He held up a hand to stop Nyad's protest, "a different level of struggle, perhaps, but a struggle. Everyone has adversities. I made it through, and we don't really need to go sift it. I wouldn't be who I am now if I hadn't faced what I faced then."

"And they do teach you how to be fearless?" Longwell asked, perked up with interest. Cyrus saw the others, as well, easing up, paying attention, waiting for his answer.

"As close as they can get," Cyrus said. "They expose you to it, over and over, things that scare you, and it just gradually fades away, like night turning to day. Snakes, bugs, battle, blood, everything, all the major things. They talk about fear all the time, how it can hurt you, how it can make you flinch. Fear is death on the battlefield, the surety of injury and failure because you'll hesitate at the wrong moment and it'll cost you."

"Interesting," J'anda said, as though he wanted to say more, but didn't. "I believe ... I have reached my end for the evening. With a nod to each of them, he spoke once more. "Good night, all."

"I should probably turn in as well," Cyrus said, and stood, grasping his patera.

"I'll wash that for you if you want," Martaina said from behind the cauldron. "I have to stay awake a little longer anyway, and I'm going to take care of the cauldron before I go to bed."

"Sure," Cyrus said and set it next to her. Aisling did the same a moment after him, and he walked behind a tree, about twenty feet from the campfire, where he had set his bedroll alongside Aisling's.

"You never had a friend until after you left the Society?" She watched him closely as he took to a knee, preparing to brush himself off and remove his armor. Her hand rested on his shoulder, and he could only just feel her touch through the metal.

He pulled the snaps and freed his neck from the gorget, then slid his pauldrons off before unfastening his breastplate. "It's true."

Her hand was on his chainmail now, and he could feel the lightness of her touch as her slightly elongated fingernails rose to his neck and applied the gentlest of pressure. "No lovers either, then?"

He shook his head. "Not until Imina." He unsnapped his greaves, then slid off the chainmail pants and shirt while she watched. He looked at her, gauged her expression. "You're feeling sorry for me, aren't you?"

"Not too bad," she said with a whisper. "More sorry that you didn't have much of a life for all those years. That you didn't get to feel so many things ..." Her fingernails danced down the cloth that still covered his chest, and she tugged it up over his head, then ran her fingers down his chest hair, gently pulling the strands. "Like making love in the autumn woods as the leaves fell down around you."

"Oh?" He took a look around, and a breeze came rustling through, shaking a few leaves loose and causing one of them to land in her hair. "It would appear to be autumn now, and leaves are falling around us."

"You caught that too, huh?" She didn't bother to pull the leaf out of her hair, just left it there as she kissed him. Even through the activity that followed, it stayed there as though some sort of badge until the breeze kicked up the following morning and it was carried it off on the winds in a way that Cyrus's past never could be.

Chapter 72

The towers of Vernadam were higher than Cyrus remembered, as the castle appeared on the horizon the day after they passed over the bridge at Harrow's Crossing. The former battlefield had been quiet, the dead all cleared and few reminders to show that there had even been a clash there some eight months earlier. It was a clear day, with little of the chill that had been so prevalent farther north.

They rode through the town at the base of the hill that Vernadam was built upon, and it was quiet as well, as though everything had died down after the harvest. There were no soldiers, no women plying their wares outside the inn. The market was much less active than when last they had been through, and by the time they were climbing the switchback road that led up to the castle, Cyrus wondered if Galbadien's army was even still stationed in the area.

At the castle gates they met no resistance. Guards saluted Longwell, who led the procession. "It would appear we are expected," J'anda said.

"They watch the roads," Longwell said. "No one gets this far unless they're wanted. Apparently, my father is amenable to my visit."

There was a stir at the far side of the courtyard as they rode in, and Cyrus saw Odau Genner's bulk coming down the long stairs that led up to the keep. He was flanked on either side by guards with polearms.

"Hail, Odau Genner," Longwell said as he handed the reins of his horse to a stableboy. "How fare thee?"

"I fare well enough, Lord Longwell," Odau Genner said, "though I admit my surprise to see you."

Longwell frowned at him. "Surely you were apprised of my journey here by your spies."

"Oh, certainly," Genner said, making a sweeping bow as he reached the bottom steps. "We knew of your crossing all the way up at Gundrun. That you came at the head of such a small force while your army remains engaged north of Enrant Monge was of some interest, however."

"You know that they are engaged in battle, then?" Longwell asked. "Do you know what they battle?"

"Some form of creatures," Genner said slowly, "or so the rumor goes."

"The reports your spies give you about my passage through our land are treated as certainty," Longwell said, his fingers hanging upon his prominent chin, still smooth from the shave he had given it that very morning, as Cyrus watched with some amusement. "Yet the words of your spies about a threat that will swallow our entire Kingdom whole are said to be rumors. Very interesting, your somewhat schismatic approach to gathering intelligence."

"Well," Odau Genner said, nervously, "we have had several descriptions, but of course His Majesty says—"

"You need not acquaint me with what 'His Majesty' has said about the whole endeavor," Longwell said dryly, "for I suspect that it will be almost as nonsensical as an army of the living dead sweeping south out of the mountains, killing every living thing in sight. Of course," he went on, "at least the latter has the actuality of truth on its side; whatever my father has said has only the grounding of a throne and crown that count for less and less as the days go by."

"That ... is a very ... unkind thing to say about your father," Odau Genner said.

"It's also fairly accurate," Longwell said. "I have need to speak with the King. Is he about?"

"He remains in his throne room," Odau Genner said. "I am told that there are quarters prepared for you, that you may wash the dust of your journey off, and that you may then be seen for dinner. If you would care to follow me," Genner said with a sweep of his hand.

Cyrus gestured for Longwell to lead the way then followed up the long, wide stairs that took them into the foyer, the massive tile and marble entry to the castle. Stewards waited, taking each of them in turn. Cyrus followed his and felt Aisling shadowing just behind him. He turned and saw Martaina beyond, her sharp eyes looking in all directions at once, head swiveling around to keep watch on everything. He started to ask her if she expected an ambush but dismissed the idea; *only a fool would not be paranoid here, especially given how we parted last from the King.*

They wandered through the corridors, following the stewards. No guards were in sight, something Cyrus thought slightly odd, and it increased to his worry. They were led along the back side of the castle, to the hallway where Cyrus had stayed during his previous visit. He felt the bite of tension as the steward led him straight to the door of the suite where he had stayed when last he had been at Vernadam, and he turned to give Aisling a hopeful smile. She seemed unaffected, cool, still there at his left elbow, just behind him.

"Your room, sir," the steward said. He was a teenager, but his voice was high like a eunuch's, and Cyrus didn't pause to ponder that possibility too deeply.

"Thank you," Cyrus said, and gestured for Aisling to enter first. "I don't need a tour."

"Very well, sir," came the high-pitched response. "I'll be back for you in two hours, when dinner is about to be served."

"Thank you," Cyrus said, and shut the door.

Aisling was already slinking around, her shoes padding on the marble floors as she examined the tapestries near the window. "Very impressive," she said. "Much better than my accomodations last time I was here."

"Oh?" Cyrus's eyes caught on the rug before the hearth, where a flame was already lit and the logs were piled high inside. The rug was just as he recalled it, a fluffy mass of fur. He recalled the softness of it to the touch, the feeling of what he had been experiencing when last he had been here.

"Yes," she said, jarring his gaze up to her. "You got one of the most impressive suites, according to one of the stewards I spoke with last time."

"Is that so?" Cyrus muttered. "Apparently I'm still just as honored a guest as I was last time. I assumed this time it'd be the stables for certain."

"For the hero of Harrow's Crossing?" Aisling said demurely, sliding behind a curtain in front of the window, then stepping out of the other side, smiling. "Surely a welcome of the sort you deserve is in order."

"Surely," Cyrus said weakly. "I suppose we'll have to dress more formally for the dinner."

"That does seem to be the norm," she said. "Though your armor wouldn't be out of the norm at all for you ..."

"I suppose not," he said, and his feet carried him to the bedroom door, where he nudged it open to reveal the familiar space; lush carpets, fine furniture. It was still shadowed in darkness, and he was reminded of the first night he had spent here, with Cattrine—*before I knew who she was. Back when I thought I knew who she was.*

"Fond memories?" Aisling's voice came from behind his shoulder this time, and he started when he realized she was close behind him.

He began to answer but faltered. "Some, I suppose. Some not." He looked around the room. "Do you find it ... uncomfortable ... knowing that when last I was here I—"

"No," she said, and pushed past him gently to enter the bedroom. Her belt came off, daggers and all, and she left it on the vanity on the other side of the bed, the clink of metal scabbards on the wood as loud in this room as any shout he might have been able to recall from when last he was here. She grabbed a brush off the smooth wooden surface and ran it through her tangles of white, putting it all into lines, easy curves coming off her forehead. She put down the brush after a minute and then unstrapped her leather armor and undressed before a full-length mirror. "You may have been here with her last time, but you're not here with her now, and I trust you're grounded enough in reality to tell the difference." She delicately made her way across the floor. "I care less about the fact that she once held you; I care more about the fact that I hold you now." She kissed him, long and deep, luxuriant, smooth, and he was reminded for a flash of the soft fur of the rug against his naked skin, of the caress of his fingers against scarred flesh in the bed.

She took him by the hand, and led him there to lie down. "Besides, whatever memories you have of what happened before are a welcome challenge." She swayed over, pushed him onto his back and then climbed astride him. "I have no doubt of which you'll remember more strongly when you leave this time, after all."

Chapter 73

When the steward arrived to collect them only an hour or so later, it was after Cyrus had had a bath drawn and luxuriated in it for a while. He wore his armor—*as though I could have escaped it,* he thought, as they marched along the corridor. The others were with him, all dressed in their battle garb, though with slight adjustments.

"I don't suppose any of you could find it in yourselves to wear the more elaborate dress clothing they left for us?" Cyrus asked, sotto voce, as they came around a corner and two servants jumped back against the wall, flattening themselves against it so the Sanctuary procession could pass.

"I wore the scarf they left with my ensemble," J'anda said, his fingers tracing down a purple silk piece of finery that Cyrus had to concede went well with his robes. "Is this not dressy enough for you?"

"The hospitality of my father's dining room called for a certain sort of fashion," Longwell said in a muted tone, his armor clinking. "I dressed appropriately."

"Perhaps you should have worn a scarf as well," J'anda said.

They were led into the room off the foyer, the long space looking the same as last time, with its plaster walls hiding the stone that Cyrus knew was back there. The fires were burning and there were fewer chairs around the table this time; there were however, Cyrus noted, just as many servants hovering around the table.

After being seated, Cyrus waited, his nose already flooded with the smells of the kitchen, a symphony of delights to the olfactory sense. The King's seat to his right remained empty when the servants came through with the first course, a soup that was thinner yet more satisfactory than the last he had been served in this very room. It was heavy on the broth, and when he sniffed it, the spices reminded him of Arkaria.

Odau Genner made his way into the room with another man, taking their seats without fanfare or announcement. Count Ewen Ranson made his way across from Cyrus and seated himself without any assistance from the servants, who fawned and fussed over him. He spread his own napkin in his lap as Cyrus watched the older warrior brush them off.

"It is of course a pleasure to see you again, Count Ranson," Cyrus said, halting his spoon halfway to his mouth.

Ranson looked up at him, hesitant at first, looking to the empty chair to Cyrus's right as if for approval. "And you as well, Lord Davidon of Perdamun, Warden of the Southern Plains." He gave Cyrus a half-hearted smile as he said the full title. "I trust all goes in the north as we have heard?"

Cyrus looked back down to the soup. "I suspect so. Have you heard that these enemies will be the end of your entire land?"

Ranson's face shifted not at all, but his eyes fell to his own bowl. "That would be the gist of what I have heard, yes."

"Yet your army remains idle here," Cyrus said then took a sip from his spoon. It was hot but not too hot, and the scent of the tomato that flavored it was perfect, no hint of acidity to be found.

"My army remains as my King commands," Ranson said stiffly, and then lapsed into a silence with the rest of the table.

It was not until the main course of duck was brought out that the King finally made his appearance, looking even more drawn than when Cyrus had last seen him. Cyrus noted for the first time that Samwen Longwell was seated considerably down the table from him, where before he had been seated at the right hand of his father. Cyrus wondered at his place directly left of the King, and Ranson across from him. Aisling was to his left, but she seemed to be keeping quiet, and he could not hear even the faintest slurp as she daintily attacked her soup. He began to make comment to her about this then decided the better of it, finding no tactful way to tell her that she could suck more quietly than any woman he'd ever known.

The duck was soft, slightly greasy but succulent, as Cyrus chewed the meat. The King had entered to little enough fanfare, but he had said nothing since seating himself. He was far from jovial normally, and now he seemed even more downtrodden and quieter than ever he had been before. His paunch was still obvious, but the rest of his body was skeletal, shriveled, as though all the life had gone out all of him but his belly. His skin was badly settled on his bones and he carried an ill humor about him.

"King Longwell," Cyrus said, halfway through his duck breast, "might I speak with you about the situation in the north, sir?"

"Speak all you would care to," the King said, "and I can even guarantee that I will listen—until such time as I want to hear no more."

Cyrus chose his words carefully. "Surely you know, as wise and informed as you are, that we have come from the battlefield up north where Syloreas and Actaluere have faced this new threat to Luukessia. You have heard that our armies were beaten back by this enemy, nearly broken, and survive only through sheer force of will." Cyrus leaned heavily on the table with his elbow, trying to get the King to give him his attention. The King was plucking at the duck breast with his fingers, tearing strips of meat from it. "These beasts are coming south, even now, and will surely reach the gates of Vernadamn by this time next year, at the latest."

"What of it?" King Longwell said, looking up as he took a bite of duck. Flecks of half-chewed food fell upon the table, landing just short of where Cyrus's gauntlet rested. "Let them come, I say. Let them chew up the Tiernans, those whores, and the Ungers, those brutish fools. Let them eat Syloreas and Actaluere whole." Utter distaste dripped from his words. "I welcome them. Let them come, this … scourge. Let it scour the land, cleanse it, and when it is done, we will march forth from Vernadam and destroy them, unifying all of Luukkesia under the banners of Galbadien. He cracked an odd, loathing smile. "Don't you see? These things, they are the vessel of our ancestors, a sacred cleansing for a land torn asunder. This is our destiny. This is that which will deliver us from the fools that have run us aground with their dishonor and lies. Let them come. Galbadien has stood for ten thousand years. We shall rule the land of Luukessia for the next ten thousand."

There was a quiet that settled over the dining room, one that lasted for almost a minute unbroken, until J'anda spoke. "Oh."

"Oh?" King Longwell said, looking up from his duck breast, another strip of meat clutched in his greasy fingers. "That is what you bring me? 'Oh?' Such a measured reaction, such a clever deduction, really."

"I think it was probably just shock," Cyrus said, "considering I just heard the most wholly unbelievable idiocy I have ever heard breathed, and it came out of the mouth of a King."

There was quiet again, and J'anda's voice was heard once more.

"Oh. My."

King Longwell's putrid loathing turned toward Cyrus. "You come into my hall and insult me. You have done nothing but insult me since the day you arrived—"

"And save your Kingdom from your own incompetence," Cyrus said, interrupting the King, who did not stop speaking. "Don't forget that."

"—the day you arrived with your arrogance," King Longwell said, his speech now heated, "and bringing with you these westerners, these— these— magicians," he imparted a sort of vitriol to the word that made it sound like the lowest form of insult, "and in the company of the great whore of Actaluere—"

Cyrus stood at that, his chair falling over behind him, the sound of wood cracking and splintering upon landing on the marble floor. He kept his hand well clear of his sword but glared down at the King. "Just because you're a King, it doesn't give you license to speak that way of her."

Aron Longwell looked up at Cyrus with a malignant glee buried under sheerest loathing. "Doesn't it? Didn't you as much as say so yourself to her? Did you not cast her back to her husband's loving embrace? Did she not fill your ears with lies and poisons even as she lured you to her bed and kept you entranced with her feminine wiles? Is she not the whollest example of a harlot run amok, doing the bidding of her husband and brother, stirring chaos, whoring herself to a man with power, drawing him in while she worked her way into your confidence—"

"I consider myself a patient man—" Cyrus said.

"Though none of the rest of us would," J'anda breathed quietly— but not so quietly that most of the table didn't hear him, even over the crosstalk.

"Amen," Aisling said.

"—but you are rapidly straining any patience I might have," Cyrus said.

"As though I give any sort of a damn," King Longwell said, and slid his seat back with great effort. He stood to look Cyrus in the eye. "You were a man ensnared not months ago, and now you come to my court, to my house, and think to speak to me of all you know? You are a fool and you think to tell me how to run a Kingdom. You think to tell me what threatens me, when you could not see a threat with your own eyes as it dangled tantalizingly in front of you. You know nothing, Cyrus Davidon. Nothing," the King repeated. "Nothing of our land, nothing of our ways, nothing of us. You think we are easily defeated by some creatures that come from the north." He waved a hand at Cyrus. "Go back to your land, fool. Take the Tiernan harlot with you, if you wish to be further deceived. This is Luukessia, where reign the men supreme, the architects of our own fate, keepers of our own lands and counsel. I'll be damned if some western fool that falls for the first thing dangled in front of his crotch will tell me there's a threat to my Kingdom when nothing is of worry to me—"

"You are the fool, Father," Samwen Longwell said, standing abruptly. His chair did not fall, Cyrus noted, though the dragoon stood with force of his own. "You spend all your time crafting insults and none of your time trying to use your wits. Your Kingdom—our Kingdom," he said, and drew a vengeful glare from his father, "was mere days from falling when the army of Sanctuary came to our aid. You could not even save your own land without help, but now you insult the man who led his army here to save us."

"I am the King!" Aron Longwell's shout echoed over the dining hall, quelling all other noise save for a servant dropping a ladle. "I am made to rule this land, guide our people, to restore us to the rightful stewardship of Luukessia. You are nothing but an ungrateful whelp who should count himself fortunate to have been begat from his lowborn mother!" With the last of his shout carrying through the room, Aron Longwell's face deteriorated, his mask of rage boiling off into one of uncertainty, his gaze falling, his eyes looking away. "She never should have left. Never. Ungrateful ..."

"She didn't leave, Father," Samwen Longwell said from his place down the quiet table. "She died." Aron Longwell recoiled slightly at his son's words. "She died, Father. She didn't leave, she was taken by death. Do you recall? Do you remember her wasting away?" He slid free of his place at the table, started a slow advance on his father. "Do you remember her bony, frail hands, at the end? How light she became as she turned to skin and bone?" Longwell's face was flushed, and he took each step slowly, each one driving metal against marble, and they echoed as if to underscore the cadence of his words. "Do you recall? She didn't leave us, Father, not willingly. She was taken. Taken by death, ripped away, torn from our caring hands by the beast."

"I ..." Aron Longwell looked down at his plate, his fingers shining in the light of the reflected chandelier's candles. "I ... cannot ... I ... no ..."

"Do you remember, Father?" Samwen cocked his head as he looked at the King. "Do you remember death? Do you remember watching it, the predator, as it stalked her down? I remember sitting in that room, the still air, with the windows shut. I remember it, remember thinking as a boy that it was coming for her, that it would devour her whole and that I would have to watch it." He was close to his father now, and stopped at arm's length. "Do you recall? Did you see it, too?"

"No," the elder Longwell shook his head, lips shut tight, eyes closed, shaking his head. "No, no, she left, she left us—"

"She was taken by death month by month, day by day," Samwen said, and his hand went to his father's shoulder. Cyrus saw the gauntlet land gently on the King's green finery, and watched the son stroke the father's arm in reassurance. "We watched it happen. And now, we will watch again." The King's head came up, and Cyrus saw the tears in his eyes, welling there unfallen. "Death comes for Luukessia, Father," Samwen said, and Cyrus watched the gauntlet tighten on his father's arm. "It creeps up, and it will eat this whole land bite by bite. You will watch as your northern reaches are taken first. Then," he waved a gauntlet slowly in front of his father's face as though trying to hypnotize him, "when you see them at your throat, that is when they will tear the heart from your Kingdom and destroy Vernadam." He let his hand fall as Aron Longwell watched, spellbound, "and the rest of this land will fall behind it all the way to the shores of the sea."

A deep quiet that settled, a dread silence that no one wanted to break, waiting as they were for the King to speak. His face wavered and moved, the wrinkles crinkling at the corners of his eyes, the breaths coming short and shallow from him. A tear dripped down his face first, then another on the other cheek. "My son," he croaked at last, and his weathered hand came up to Samwen's face, ran over it, a finger tracing a line like he was connecting the dots between the younger Longwell's freckles. "Your face ... reminds me of her," he said, voice cracking.

"You ... you ... remind me of her." The King's face hardened, grew spiteful once more, the lines solidifying into loathing. "And you left ... just ... like ... her." He left a fiery residue with each syllable, hate flowing out of them.

"I'm sorry, Father," Samwen Longwell said, and Cyrus saw the emotion in his eyes. He laid a hand on his father's face, and the old man's eyes fluttered at his touch, at the metal soft against his skin. "Truly sorry. Sorry I disappointed you. Sorry I left." Longwell's eyes crinkled at the edges. "And sorrier still for what you have become." He glanced away for just a beat, and Cyrus caught a flash of something. "But I will remain the sorriest for what I do now."

There was no warning, just a shift in the atmosphere of the hall, as though the candles were all blown by the wind at once. Samwen Longwell, the dragoon of Galbadien, leaned forward and kissed his father on the cheek. The older man flinched as though he'd been struck, though Cyrus saw he plainly hadn't. There was no movement at all, save for a very subtle one of Samwen's hand, reaching under the plate of his armor. In a movement quicker than an eyeblink, a dagger emerged and was plunged into the King's chest. The strength of the dragoon held it true and straight, and there was only a gasp from the King as the blade entered his heart.

"I'm sorry, Father," Samwen Longwell said as the King sagged on his feet, and his son held him up, keeping him close, not letting any see what he'd done. "I am so sorry." The King moaned, but Samwen held him tighter, no one else moving, perhaps some suspecting but not a word of protest voiced. They stood like that for some minutes, the father being held by the son, until the King of Galbadien finally laid the body of Aron Longwell back in his seat.

Chapter 74

Vara

Day 102 of the Siege of Sanctuary

The plains were windblown, a hard, driving rain coming down around them. It was cold, rattling off her armor as the fury of the land itself descended upon Vara. She could hear the steady clatter of it against her helm, the mad tapping as it went along, watched forked lightning cut across the sky in an arc, followed by a crash as loud as if someone had hit a warhammer against armor.

"If I get hit by lightning," Erith yelled into the maelstrom of the storm, "someone please cast a resurrection spell on me!"

"I just assumed you'd rather remain dead for a time," Vaste yelled back. "It is rather reminiscent of your 'lie there and take it' approach to the bedroom, after all."

The rain rattled Vara's helm, followed by a burst of wind. "I do wish you both would keep your damnable thoughts to yourselves," Vara shouted to be heard, "as there are some things that I would truly prefer to remain ignorant about."

"Yes, well, you've had enough of those moments in the last couple months, I suppose," Erith called back. Vara turned to look at her as the rain patted upon her face, running down her cheeks. It was not a new sensation of late, the feel of water making its way down her face. It was not normally so cold, though.

"Will we even be able to see the enemy convoys in this mess?" Ryin spoke now, his horse just down the line from Vara's. "Visibility is a hundred feet at best."

Vara had to concede the druid's point; the rain fell in sheets, lines of water visible when it was heavier. A gust picked up and suddenly the wind blew sideways for a moment, and she turned her head as though she could shield her face from the drenching.

"Perhaps if there was some master of the magics of nature who could command the elements, and suspend this thunderstorm," Vaste said with no small amount of irony, "then we could go about our business only as wet as we presently are, and not completely drenched with all the waters of the entire land."

"I think the land has given us all it has and then added the entirety of the Torrid Sea for good effect," Erith said. No one found cause to disagree with her.

"I can only control so much," Ryin spoke louder, his voice cut off in the middle by another crack of booming thunder; Vara's sensitive ears echoed yet still she heard every bit of it. "To try and stop a light summer shower is very doable for a druid of my power. To stop a normal thunderstorm is straining it a bit. To try and put the cease to this tempest?" The druid shrugged, and the water ran off the shoulders of his overcoat in drenching sluices.

"I would not allow you to do so in any case," Vara shouted to make herself heard, and she drew confused looks. "This weather is murder on convoys, and the roads are nothing but long stretches of mud that will bog them down. For the next day we'll be able to ambush a number of them simply by riding up on them in the night where they remain stuck."

"Yes," Vaste agreed, "but we have to be able to see them, else it becomes a fine opportunity for us to stumble into a fight that we're not prepared for."

A shadow appeared in front of them, lit by a flash of lightning; Vara saw it for only a second as the sky illuminated the ground, but it was a wagon, and other shapes were around it, and suddenly an arrow flew past her ear.

"See?" Vaste called. "Like that."

Vara urged her horse forward, sword in hand, and when the next flash lit the world around, she brought her blade down upon the dark elf she saw before her. By the time of the thunderclap he was already falling, bleeding on his way to the ground. The next flash of lightning followed shortly thereafter, and before her was a field in motion, more soldiers than she'd seen before around a convoy; *there have to be near five hundred, she* thought as she rode on toward a thick cluster of them, and let out her hand, following it with a spell that shot forth into the dark night.

It made a light of its own as it left her palm, and she watched it make contact with three dark elven soldiers, flinging them into the air. A bolt of lightning came from behind her, not above, and she felt the air blister with electricity as it passed. It hit five of the enemy and she could see their shadows jerk with the surge of power, dancing in the oddest fashion before they fell still in the mud.

She rode forward and felt something solid hit her horse, a jarring feel that caused the animal to jerk then start to fall. *Oh, dear,* was all that had a chance to make it through her mind before she was thrown. Her shoulder hit the mud and all her weight came down on it and then her head, driving her helm and her armor into her soft skin. She heard a crunch upon the impact, and for just a second it felt as though her legs were dangling in the air above her before momentum carried them forward and she felt her back and lower body hit the ground with unmerciful hardness. There was a splash that barely registered, and then shooting pains started from her hips and buttocks, but none worse than the one that raged along her shoulder and neck.

Sweet Goddess of Life. Her lips anchored closed against the cry she felt rising from within. *They stabbed my horse with a spear or lance, surely. Damn them. Bloody damn them all to the hells of legend.* She tried to move but the pain was suffocating. There was movement all around her, too much to track, and her anguish necessitated she squeeze her eyes closed even as she raised a hand, chanting words under her breath that were as familiar to her as her own name, that had been drilled into her so often that they were rote memory by now, called upon in time of trouble.

The healing spell was minor, at best, compared to the power of the one a healer could call upon. Still, she felt some of the pain subside, the fire in her shoulder was reduced, and she moved it without a scream of agony. She stirred, bringing her sword across the nearest shape to her, a leg in the darkness. She heard a howl of pain when it struck true, and a dark figure began to fall toward her. She rolled left, knocking the legs from underneath the dark elves around her, causing them to teeter. She brought her sword around and made them fall, limbs gushing blood that was not visible in the dark. She pushed them off and got to her feet, looking about as the lightning flashed and the thunder drowned out all the sound of battle that was raging around her.

She stabbed into another dark elf, whose surprise was obvious as his mouth dropped open and exposed the blackness in the gaping back of his mouth. She drew her sword out of him and hit the next, then sensed, rather than saw, someone coming at her from behind. She twirled her open hand and fired the spell that was closer to memory than the healing incantation. It flashed, separate from the lightning, and she watched a surprised face carried through the air where it became pained after the body it was attached to broke upon contact with a wagon.

Vara crouched down then leapt straight up as four enemies came at her all at once. She watched them crash into each other, swords gone awry and striking their own fellows. She landed with both boots hard on the back of two of the survivors' necks then used her sword to make certain none of them lived. The dark elven escort was visible in flashes, as though someone were taking a candle and holding thick parchment over it, pulling it back and forth rapidly, lighting and unlighting the world.

There was not much to be heard other than the screams, the wet sopping smell of the mud on her armor, the blood already washed away. She leaned into the fight, throwing all her power into each thrust of the sword. She could feel her allies at work somewhere behind her, but for now, she knew, she was on her own and surrounded by enemies. She smiled as she let an attack carry her through. *What a marvelous way to spend such an evening. I suppose the God of War would be pleased.*

That thought did not chill her near as much as the rain, and with every flash of lightning she took another dark elf's life, or two or more, and though the tempest raged until long after the last of her enemies was dead, in truth it never stopped, not within her, and she wondered if it ever would.

Chapter 75

Cyrus

The dining hall was cleared out, the servants all urged out the door by Odau Genner, who finally lost his temper at the last of them as they stood staring at the body of Aron Longwell, slumped in his seat. "OUT!" Genner shouted, and threw his napkin at the man for good measure. The swinging door closed behind him.

"This is quite a mess you've thrust us into," Ewen Ranson said from his place at the table, still sitting at the right hand of the corpse, his head bowed and his hands resting atop his head, fingers pinching tufts of greying hair between them as though the Count were preparing to yank them out. He looked down and to his left, to where Samwen Longwell knelt in front of his father's seat, his gauntlets gone and his hands on his father's legs, looking up at the slack face with no expression on his own.

"He's thrust us into?" Genner said from the kitchen door. "He bloody well killed the King!" Genner's voice was a furious whisper, muted enough to not be heard, but near apoplectic with the red blood filling his face, giving him the look of a tomato with a mustache. "And there's not one of THEM—" he waved a hand at the door of the kitchen, "that doesn't know it, even if they didn't see the dagger and the blood!"

"He killed the King?" Nyad stood up from her place near the end of the table, a look of flush horror upon her cheeks. "Oh, Samwen ... what did you do?"

"Killed his father," Aisling said without any sort of concern, daintily cutting away at the duck breast she had purloined from Genner's plate next to her. "What did you think we were here to do?"

"Speaking for myself," J'anda said, wide-eyed, "I thought we were here to persuade them to enter the war—you know, to save their homeland. Call it enlightened self-interest, that idea that they may want to get involved."

"You heard him," Martaina said from her place across the table from Genner's empty seat. "He wanted no part of it. The old King was mad. He'd watch his Kingdom eaten alive by the scourge sooner than he'd order his troops to ally with his enemies. There was no other road but this one."

"But you don't know where this road leads yet," Count Ranson said, raising his head, hands now clenching the side of his face. "What do you expect will happen now?" He threw an accusing hand toward Samwen. "The boy—excuse me, I still think of him as such—he killed the rightful King of Galbadien." Ranson's eyes darted from the Longwells to Cyrus. "I don't know how you conduct things in Arkaria, but here, that sort of action is treason, murder, and all who would be party to it are conspirators worthy of being hanged." He closed his eyes and slumped in his seat again. "To kill one's own kin is the worst sort of murder." His hands proceeded to his eyes, and covered them, muffling his next words. "The most horrid part is, I'm not even certain he was wrong to do what he did."

There hung a stark silence. "Do you know what is coming?" Cyrus asked, but Ranson did not stir. He looked then to Genner, who seemed deflated. "Do you know what is happening in the north right now?" He waited a pause. "What do you believe—"

"I believe we are about to face the single greatest threat to the land of Luukessia that has ever been seen," Ranson's head came up and there was a light in his eyes, a fire, "that what comes down those northern plains is the worst doom to ever visit itself upon this land, worse than the breaking of the Kingdoms. I believe that it slides upon us like the death he described," a finger pointed to Samwen again, "and that if we do nothing, we are not only damned in the eyes of our ancestors for doing nothing, but twice damned because we will see our people blotted out by it and thrice damned as our own eyes are eaten out of our very heads by those things."

"Then would you have stood by and let your liege drop your Kingdom right into the waiting mouths of the scourge?" Cyrus looked at Ranson. Ranson looked back at him accusingly. A sidelong glance at Genner revealed only nervousness, nerves and sadness, expressed on his rounded face through a slightly open mouth as he licked his lips. "Would you?"

"We had not ... decided the course to take, yet," Ranson answered for both of them. Genner was in the background now, Cyrus realized, almost useless, for his part in things.

"Yet you know—you saw!—that these things are a blight across the very surface of the land," Cyrus said. "They will come whether you act or not, and every day you hesitated in making your decision was another day in which they had free reign to whittle down the numbers of men left to fight them. The time is now, gentlemen." He looked from Ranson to Genner. "Acknowledge Samwen as the new King, and let us be on about the business of saving your Kingdom from utter ruination."

"I'm not certain I want the crown," Samwen said at last, still huddled by the body of his father.

"Then this was perhaps a poor course of action to pick," J'anda said.

"No," Longwell said, rising, his cheeks streaked with tears. "My duty was to save Galbadien. If I had to die to do so, then so be it, I would pay that price and more, willingly. I know full well," he gestured at Ranson, "that my father's successors, regardless of whether it was me or not, would do what is necessary and rally us for war. I could not sit by and allow my realm to fall to the scourge, and yet my father would do exactly that. My course, then, became obvious, when I realized he would die before acting—"

"I can get well past the decision," Ranson said in a whisper. "Aron Longwell is hardly the first King of Galbadien to be displaced by their own blood in such a way—though we do not condone it! But we must not speak of this any longer, we must keep it confined to this room, let it die here with Aron Longwell."

"You think you could hide the truth of this?" Cyrus exchanged a look with Aisling, whose eyes flickered amusement. "Good luck. Word is likely already spreading."

"To seat a King who slew the last, and openly no less," Genner croaked. "These are dark days indeed."

"I care not how dark the days grow," Samwen Longwell said turning to look at Odau Genner, "so long as Galbadien survives to see the dawn."

"We'll arrange it," Ranson said quickly and tossed a look at Genner. "A quick coronation before we ride north." Ranson seemed to be thinking it all through quickly, as though it was a plan he had been holding in, waiting to execute. "Where do we go?"

"Enrant Monge," Cyrus said. "We rally there; Actaluere is sending for the rest of their armies, and Syloreas is evacuating everything they have south. Enrant Monge will be the site of the battle, and we'll have to break them there."

"How do you know these creatures will come there?" Genner said, softly, almost like a child asking a plaintive question of a parent.

"They seem to follow life as a moth follows the fire," Longwell said. "The Syloreans are running their entire population there, as many of them as can move from the east, from the north. Some of them in the west are moving south, but other than that, they're rallying there, every able-bodied man."

"That's a poor place to keep their civilians," Ranson said, thinking it over. "What if you should fail—if *we* should fail? They'll need to be moved, south, ahead of the horde."

"These people are refugees," J'anda said, "they'll be hungry, starving. They aren't an army, yet they march on their stomachs. We have spellcasters that can conjure food and drink for them, at least enough to be getting on with. But any evacuation will be slow, and will need to be covered by the army we have."

"I don't mean to suggest we'll fail," Ranson said, "as I'm confident we'll succeed, but—"

"Only a fool doesn't have a fallback plan," Cyrus said. "Agreed. We'll need to work on it. But we'll have a month's ride to get to Enrant Monge. Hopefully the armies can hold back the tide of the enemy for that long." He stared at Ranson. "When can you send for your armies, start assembling them?"

Ranson looked up at him, and a slight smile creased his face. "I sent the orders almost two weeks ago, when it was clear you were coming here. The barons have already begun to assemble west of here at a crossroads town called Callis. We'll be ready to march for Enrant Monge in three days."

Cyrus regarded Ranson carefully. "So you were going to take action."

"Soon enough," Ranson agreed. "And now, as the King has said," he nodded to Samwen Longwell, "our course is set."

Chapter 76

The coronation was a short-lived and short-noticed affair, attended by few enough of the nobility and fewer still of the castle staff. Ranson did the honors, administering an oath in the long, hollow-spaced throne room as the first light of the next morning streamed down through the high windows.

"Do you swear to give all your life, all your judgment, all your honor, and all your strength to the prosperity of this Kingdom?" Ranson asked, finishing the last in a long series of questions.

"I do," Samwen Longwell said, and an attendant placed the simple crown of golden leaves strung together by a circlet upon his head.

"Ladies and Gentlemen, I give you the King of Galbadien, the Garden Kingdom—Samwen Longwell the Eighth." Ranson stepped back, letting the King stand upon the platform by himself. It would have been better in effect, Cyrus supposed, if there had been anyone there besides Ranson, Genner, two attendants, and the Sanctuary party to see it happen.

"Not much pomp for such auspicious circumstances," J'anda said once the ceremony was concluded—which was announced by Odau Genner muttering to himself as he left the throne room, still red-faced and looking to be much out of sorts. "I would have expected more."

"He killed the last King," Cyrus said, looking at Longwell, who sat upon the throne with his fingers templed in front of him in a way that evoked a memory of Alaric at the table in the Council Chambers, "and they're about to send every man they have into a war that's likely to claim a high number, if not all of them. If they fail, their homeland will fall." Cyrus cast J'anda a glance. "I'm surprised he got as much pomp as he did; I would have thought it would have been dispensed with in favor of riding out as quickly as possible."

They rode out two days later, down the great man-made hill that Vernadam rested on. It was pleasant enough, Cyrus thought, a fall day back home by the weather, and yet near winter for the calendar. *Reikonos must have had their first snow by now. The autumn will have brought storms along the plains near Sanctuary. Yet here I am, in this cool place.* He rode quietly down the first switchback, relaxed upon the back of Windrider.

Part of the way down the next curve, Samwen Longwell came alongside him, his crown shining. "Here we go," he said, no mirth in him, and nearly enough to no life as to be indistinguishable.

"Here we go," Cyrus agreed. "You're about to look on your lands as a King for the first time; I would try to put some sort of happy face on for your subjects, considering that with what we are up against, yours will likely be the one that they look to. Whether they take hope or sorrow from your countenance is entirely up to you, my friend, but a King seems more ... disposed ... to one rather than the other."

Longwell did not answer him for a moment, as if pondering. "You are right, of course. But how do I ... how do I shed this misery that falls on me?" His face contorted as Cyrus watched. "I think of what I did, and I weep for my soul; I am unworthy to stand before my ancestors after death, now. What I have done is the horror of all horrors."

"Listen to me," Cyrus said, and pulled Windrider's reins so he stopped. "What you did is save your Kingdom. What you did was make the hardest choice of anyone I've ever met. He wouldn't step aside, and you knew it. You made a sacrifice that few would have made—"

"You would have made it," Longwell said, turning to look straight ahead. "In my place, I believe you would have done the same." He flicked his gaze back to Cyrus, as though he were looking for approval. "You have had the courage to do things I would not have thought possible before."

"There's a far distance," Cyrus said, "between standing on a bridge and knowing you'll die and having to sacrifice the person you care for most in the world." A flash ran through Cyrus's mind—of the Fields of Paxis in the Realm of Death, of the rotting grass, and steps in the distance, of a god as tall as a building, of his threat and the movement of his hand, stirring toward Vara, her head bowed. "I couldn't do what you did. I didn't ... do what you did. Thank the gods that you were the man in the place now, Samwen, because you made the choice I couldn't, and hopefully your choice will redeem mine."

They were quiet, then, on the way down the rest of the hill, Longwell seeming to try and reconcile the thoughts he'd been given.

When they reached the bottom, the townsfolk were already turned out, and they saw a monarch who waved at them with pride, with confidence, and not a single hint—to Cyrus's practiced eye, anyhow—of any threads of doubt.

Chapter 77

Vara

Day 141 of the Siege of Sanctuary

"The good news is that our plan is working," Ryin said, his hushed voice still seeming to echo in the quiet Council Chambers. "The bad news is that our plan is working but not as well as we might have hoped."

Alaric was a still statue—*it might as well have been one in his chair for as little as he moved,* Vara thought. His expression was dark, as though carved from stone, and he appeared not only weary but less expressive than usual. "Explain it to us."

Ryin sighed. "I've run sorties from the nearby portals to scout convoys passing through the Plains of Perdamun. Their sentries have finally reached the point in the last week where it is no longer safe to hit them with a raiding party. I'm observing escorts of five hundred to a thousand soldiers marching along with each convoy, larger convoys now than there used to be, and spellcasters intermixed with them. I suspect they're also using wizards and druids to teleport some of the richer convoys directly, even though that's likely to tie up considerable amounts of their resources. Our raiding days have come to an end is what I'm telling you." He looked around the table. "In addition, there appears to be no appreciable change in the numbers of the horde that surrounds us. All we've managed to do is pull more dark elves into the Plains of Perdamun."

Alaric's eyes flashed back and forth, assimilating this. "Vara?" he asked. "Have you heard anything from your sister?"

"Only to echo that the battle lines around Reikonos remain quiet," Vara said, finding the words most disagreeable. "The only good news is that the humans are preparing for a major offensive in the coming weeks, after the New Year passes and the Winter Solstice has gone by. Perhaps that will relieve some of the pressure around us?"

"I have doubts about that," Alaric breathed, as though he meant for them not to hear it. "The line remains unchanged for the elves as well, bottled up behind the River Perda, staring at their foes across the water. The bridges between Termina and Santir remain a 'No Man's Land,' and I have my suspicions that King Danay will not find the courage to change that anytime soon, given his ..." Alaric sighed, "... personnel challenges."

"You mean the fact that any elven soldier killed can't possibly be replaced?" Vaste asked—*with his usual flair for the annoying,* Vara thought.

"Yes," Alaric said without a trace of amusement, "that was what I was referring to. Unless Danay finds himself in possession of a rather extreme amount of pluck, I wonder that they will prosecute this war further, putting themselves on the line to dubious purpose for the humans. Vengeance for Termina would seem to be his only motivation for going forward."

"But if the Confederation and the Kingdom don't work together," Erith said, shaking her head, "it seems that the Sovereignty will eventually break them both."

"Probably not the elves," Vara said quietly. "Oh, they'll glare at the dark elves across the river, certainly, but now that their army is massed, the Sovereign will have a devil of a time putting his troops across the Perda, and Danay knows that. The rest of Arkaria could well burn, and the Elven Kingdom would be able to sit apart from them, quite safe, all things considered, and simply wait out the war."

"Until they all grew old and infirm and the Sovereign could simply march over the bridge and take the entire Kingdom without any sort of fight that didn't involve a cane being smacked over someone's head," Vaste said.

"Yes," Vara replied acidly. "Until then. But as that is several thousand years off, I very much doubt that is something we shall have to ponder too deeply in the immediate future."

Alaric was unmoved, again, quiet for a piece. "The humans wait too long, then. By the time the Sovereign strengthens his grip here, in the Plains of Perdamun, he'll have all the supplies he needs to deal a final, crushing blow to Reikonos. Without Reikonos, it seems likely that the Riverlands and Northlands will fragment and argue amongst themselves. At best, they could rally, but they would have a hard time defending against the dark elven onslaught. There are simply too few good spots to mount a defense of the Northlands or Riverlands. If Reikonos falls, so too does the best chance to face the dark elves in a decisive battle that could turn them back."

"Except here," Vara said, turning their heads. She shrugged when they looked at her. "A hundred thousand at least surrounding us, another fifty thousand or more spread out around the plains; that is no small host, and its loss or breaking would likely hamper the Sovereign's war efforts."

"Oh yes," Vaste said, "his mysterious and seemingly unlimited army. How many soldiers does he have, anyway? Anyone?"

"At least one more," Erith said with a smile. "He has more than anyone has been able to predict thus far. Who knows how many he has in reserve? One thing I can tell you ..." She hesitated. "I probably shouldn't, but since we're all dead anyway if the dark elven army breaks down the gates—Saekaj Sovar was an overcrowded mess when I left twenty years ago."

"I'm sorry, what?" Ryin blinked at her. "You're talking about the diaspora? When dark elves began to migrate out of the homeland again, twenty years ago?"

"Yes," Erith said. "It was at capacity, the streets were choked with waste, and the tribunal that ruled in the Sovereign's absence finally approved the opening of the city. People weren't exactly starving, but there was heavy rationing. That's why you saw so many dark elves start cropping up at once—those of us who were more opportunity-minded wanted to get the hell out, take a chance elsewhere, somewhere that you weren't living twelve people in a room a quarter this size." She shook her head. "The average citizens were stacked on top of each other, four and five to a straw bed half the size of this table. Ticks were rampant, fleas. The meat we ate was that of the vek'tag and their milk was the drink of choice, and it was old mushrooms baked into bread three times a day most of the time. The noble houses lived fat and had more space, the lower classes scrapped for every damned thing we could lay our hands on." She shrugged. "It was nice to get out of there, even nicer when I finally got my own room in the Daring's guildhall. Living here was like a dream."

"And the point of that wildly veering narrative?" Vaste asked, feigning a yawn.

Erith favored the troll with a sour look. "That Saekaj Sovar is huge. Massive. When I left, the population was easily over two million." She looked around the table in patient expectation.

Ryin was the first to show his reaction. "Well, then that means ... oh. Oh, damn." His head pivoted to Vaste. "It means—"

"Yes," Vaste said, "I got it right off. Millions of people means hundreds of thousands of soldiers if need be."

"Yes," Erith said, "and keeping in mind that the Sovereignty is a society where you can live a thousand years and not really feel the strain of age until you are over eight hundred—"

"They have a larger population of war-ready men to draw from than any other nation." Ryin looked at Vaste again.

"I said I understood the first time," Vaste looked back at the druid intently. "Why do you keep staring at me? I know how dark elves age, probably better than you do."

"I'm sorry, I didn't mean to look *at* you!" Ryin said. "I'm just ..." his gaze swept the table and found Vara. "Did you know about this?"

"No," she said, finding herself somewhat hoarse. "No, but it is hardly a great surprise now, is it? The dark elves have a big army. The sky is blue, water is wet. They've paraded countless number of soldiers through the world, are fighting a war on three fronts and they don't seem to be suffering greatly for it." She tried to shrug from indifference, and found that it wasn't hard to find. "They have us outmatched. Their enemies are not fighting them at present, largely out of fear. They have us surrounded, and they have thrown a hundred and fifty thousand troops at the bothersome fly we have become to keep us from continuing to bind them down here in the plains." There was a certain hopelessness that came with her pronouncement, but she wasn't sure she could entirely feel it.

"None of it is good news," Alaric said finally. "But neither is it the worst. We may be outmatched, but they have yet to find a way to reasonably break through our fortifications." He smiled. "Take heart, friends. We will protect our foyer as we have, we will keep them held off at the wall, keep them at a distance, and we will remain here until the situation changes." There was only a hint of hope in Alaric's tone, but it was there, Vara could hear it. "In a battle against the entire world,

I still believe that the Sovereign has bitten off more than he can possibly hope to digest." Alaric steepled his fingers in front of him. Now, let us hope that the rest of the world discovers that exact same truth ... before it becomes too late to take advantage of his misstep."

Chapter 78

Cyrus

The road to Enrant Monge was longer than he remembered, though they traveled at a brisker pace. They went to the west first, crossing under the leaves of trees that still showed their green, meeting up with the armies of Galbadien's barons in the town called Callis, which Cyrus could not remember at all from when last he had been there, and they rode on.

"There are not so many of them as I hoped for," Cyrus said, riding next to Count Ranson under a blue, clear sky, on their way out of Callis.

"We just came out of a war," Ranson said, "one that was particularly costly to us in terms of lives." He gestured his head back behind them, where followed some twenty thousand men, half on horseback. "We have a great many dragoons, though, and we lost few enough in the last battle. Some of the men are long-time veterans—"

"Meaning they've seen too much combat," Cyrus added.

"—and some new blood," Ranson finished with a raised eyebrow.

"Meaning they've seen too little."

Ranson sighed. "Aye. It would have been more convenient if this scourge had come before we had our little war with Syloreas. Instead, they picked the first time in a decade when both of us were well and truly ground down. Our eastern armies will meet us a bit farther on, the ones we moved to the Actaluere border. That will swell our numbers somewhat."

They rode on. The sun rose and set what felt like a hundred times, but was more probably only thirty. The air turned colder as they hooked north on the road that led past the shores of an enormous lake. Cyrus went to his bedroll with Aisling every night and awoke with her next to him in the morning, putting out of his head all the troubles and worries of the battle ahead. The numbness inside was still there, but he managed it, thinking about it sometimes late at night when she lay against his side, and he listened to her slow, soft breathing.

As the mornings became bitterly cold, the scenery began to change;

there came a morning where there was frost on the ground, glittering in the early morning sunrise like diamonds sprinkled in the grasses, and Cyrus could have sworn that he had been there recently. He had, he realized, been this way only months before, with a smaller army at his back.

After so many days of numbing, wearying travel, one arrived where he found himself staring into the distance and staring back at him at the top of a crest was the familiar shape of Enrant Monge. He heard a few whoops from behind him as the men of the Galbadien army let out their pent-up emotion at seeing their destination after a long journey.

"I will not be sorry to be done riding," J'anda said, his hand rubbing the outside of his robes just below his back. "This is quite enough for a while."

"I never get tired of riding," Aisling said with a lascivious smile toward Cyrus.

He glanced back at her. "You haven't done that in a long time."

She shrugged, and he thought he caught a hint of disappointment. "Before I was trying to work to entice you. Now, I scarcely have to entice you at all."

They left the army behind on the flat grounds before the woods, left them to set camp in an open space as Cyrus rode with Longwell and the others into the big, wide gate on the western facing of Enrant Monge. There were Sylorean refugees along every bit of the ride, as there had been for the last few hundred miles of the journey, sunken-eyed beggar folk with weary looks.

"Do you suppose we'll finally ride through the Unity gate now?" Longwell asked, and Cyrus watched the new King, who maintained an air of guarded skepticism.

"This would be the closest we've ever gotten, my King," Count Ranson answered after a second's reflection. "Perhaps not as anticipated, in a new Kingdom of Union for all Luukessia, but united in common purpose."

"Seems more genuine than with a monarch at your head," Cyrus said, "ruling through fear."

"The last Kings of all Luukessia were hardly tyrants," Ranson said, as though delivering a history lesson to an interested student. "The Kings of Old Enrant Monge were good men, fair men, who ruled with strength and honor, and who delegated most of their power to the three Grand Dukes. When the last King died and his only son, Lord Garrick, went missing after an expedition, the three Grand Dukes broke with formality, argued among themselves, and each declared himself the new King in turn. They made their protestations, but none would see the other for the true ruler of Luukessia, and so each left Enrant Monge in turn, so furious with the others that they went out through their own gate, to consolidate and hold their own seats of power, and then each raged at the others in turn, in wars, for the next ten thousand years, returning to Enrant Monge and the old guardians of the King of Luukessia—the Brothers of the Broken Blade, who remained there to mediate disputes, and to hold the castle against the predations of the the three Kingdoms."

"So it was your forerunners who were the tyrants," Cyrus said with a half-smile.

Ranson seemed to take the jest in the spirit it was intended. "Not my forerunners, no."

They galloped through the inner gate. The refugees watched the column and the King of Galbadien with awe as he passed into the courtyard, which had masses of the careworn gathered around its walls, their hungry eyes quieted by the food that members of the Brotherhood of the Broken Blade were dispensing to them from a station in the corner. There were dark clouds overhead, putting the whole of the world in a dim glow. The stones of the castle that had been a shining orange when Cyrus saw them in sunlight were greyed now, the overcast light tingeing them. The smell of sodden hay was even sharper in the crisp air, the smell of the horses potent as they approached the small stables. There were a few boys milling about, caring for the animals, and Cyrus could hear one of the horses whicker as they approached. He gave a reassuring pat as he dismounted, to which Windrider responded with a whinny.

"It's you, m'lord," said the boy who rushed out to take the reins of the horse from Cyrus. He was familiar, and it took only a second for Cyrus to realize that it was the same lad who had spoken to him when last he'd left Enrant Monge. "You've come back to us again."

"I have," Cyrus said, feeling the stress in him as he recalled the lad's words when last they'd spoke.

"You're going to save us," the boy said, in awe. "You're going to save Luukessia from them ... from those things."

Cyrus didn't answer at first, looking back to see if anyone had heard. The others of his party were met by additional lads from the stable, boys collecting the reins to more than one horse, leading the animals away. Ranson and Longwell stood apart, off to the side, as though trying to make a decision. J'anda was the only one watching him, listening; J'anda and perhaps Aisling, though her back was turned and he knew not what she was doing.

"I'm going to try," Cyrus said at last, handing the reins to the boy.

"You'll do it," the boy said with utmost faith, surprisingly cheerful to Cyrus's ears. The boy favored him with a smile. "You're him. You'll do it."

Cyrus tried to smile back but failed; a little bitter grimace of half-effort was all he managed. He followed the others as they went, the chill seeping into him. There was a trace of snow here and there as they walked, gathered into near-insubstantial piles on the ground; Cyrus wondered how deep the snow would get here, if it would turn bad at all. He looked north\ toward the wall of the courtyard, where he knew a gate led to Syloreas's courtyard. *How far away are they now?*

There was a quiet in the castle as they entered the tower; none of the Brothers were in sight, and Cyrus wondered where the keepers of the castle were. They made their way forward toward the center of the structure, toward the Garden of Serenity. Still, there were no Brethren so they entered the long tunnel to the garden. There were voices within, echoing from the hallway, distorted. Cyrus recalled the listing of names, of accolades shouted by heralds in this very place. Now there was only talk on the other end, low, discontented, and just as bitter to his ears as the wind when it picked up and raced through.

When Cyrus emerged behind Ranson and Longwell, the voices died down, and he could see men huddled around the amphitheater at the center of the Garden of Serenity. He recognized Milos Tiernan immediately then saw Briyce Unger standing in his usual place, his face puckered with a new scar. Brother Grenwald Ivess stood at the west facing of seats, where he had been when last they had met. Eyes swiveled toward the entourage from Galbadien, and Cyrus saw the frown from Unger and the soft dissolve to impartiality on Tiernan's face as they came down.

There were other figures, too, Cyrus realized as they descended into the amphitheater; Curatio and Terian waited in the place where the Galbadien delegation was usually seated. Curatio gave him a half-hearted smile when they began to descend the steps. Cyrus kept his gaze on Terian, though, and the dark knight kept his on Cyrus, their eyes locked as the meeting came to a halt while the new arrivals took their seats.

"We are well pleased to see you," Grenwald Ivess said as Cyrus shuffled past Terian. Ranson and Longwell remained standing at the front row, and Curatio stayed forward with them, though he gave a short bow and stepped aside so they could take the center of the bench. Longwell stood there, still in his blued armor, his helm being carried by Odau Genner, who hovered in the second row, his red face glowing in the grey day.

"May I present the King of Galbadien," Count Ranson said, drawing a look of surprise from Briyce Unger and Grenwald Ivess. Tiernan, for his part, remained nearly inscrutable, only a small smile making its way from behind his facade.

"Your Majesty," Grenwald Ivess said with a nod and the slightest bow. "You have, I fear, run into the middle of our discussion at an inopportune moment, but your arrival will perhaps make it more opportune than it was. You have brought some forces, I take it?"

"I have brought everything that Galbadien holds," Longwell said. "Every man who can ride with a spear or lance, every man who can stand and fight with sword or shield, and every boy and grey-haired fellow to boot. Whatever Galbadien holds, I have committed to this defense—to Luukessia."

Briyce Unger straightened, nodding at Longwell. "Every man I could summon to escape, save for those escorting our women and children south, I have brought here or to the to fight to our north. Syloreas has fallen, but our men fight on—for Luukessia."

Milos Tiernan gave a sigh. "Every man I command, from here to the southern seas, I have summoned to me. Every one who has responded is here and is willing to fight to defend this place in the hopes that this scourge will never touch their homes or their families." He hesitated. "For Luukessia—and for us all."

"We commit to this fight everything that we have brought with us," Curatio said, speaking in Cyrus's place. The warrior considered standing and dismissed the thought; *to move to the front would expose my back to Terian. Best to let Curatio do the speaking for us, since he is the Elder—and a better spokesman than I, in any case.* "We have asked for additional aid and should it come, it will be pledged to your cause, to defend your land." The elf gave a slight nod. "For Luukessia."

Grenwald Ivess took it all in, and Cyrus had a feeling that the Brother was almost letting it steep like tea leaves in water, allowing the words to run into the ears of all present, to let them take it all in. "The Brotherhood of the Broken Blade has maintained Enrant Monge as the last vestige of the old world of Luukessia; the days when our Kingdoms were one. We have also kept our presence here to defend this remnant against those who would attack it. We have on the grounds over one thousand knights in our sworn service, volunteers all and well-trained. We commit them to this effort to save our homeland.

"I appreciate the sacrifices that all of you have made to come here," Ivess said, "and to bring with you all you have. The people of Luukessia are losing their homes, their lands, and their lives at so startling a speed that it is barely fathomable. The men who stand before me are the last hope of this land. You men, who once upon a time vied for yourselves and your Kingdoms, I see now before me united against this common foe. It is well that you think of Luukessia at a time like this, even those of you who have been scarcely touched by this menace as yet.

"Let this be the place where the unity of Luukessia was made final," Grenwald Ivess said, hitting his stride, his rich baritone echoing in the garden, "let this be the place where ten thousand years of bitterness and enmity were put aside for the good of our people. Let us unite once more in hopes that our combined efforts may stave off this disaster that brews, that sits outside our door even now. Let us gather together, stand together—that we may not be divided. That we may not fall."

Chapter 79

The day was filled with planning; when night fell, it was almost sweet relief of its own kind. Cyrus woke in the middle of the small hours, Aisling settled in next to him in the quiet, nothing audible in the tower room but her breathing. The smell of the air was stale, and the last taste of the night's stew was still with him. There was a chill in the room, as it had only a small hearth of its own and the fire had died down. He tossed a log upon it and stirred, feeling the slight weight of the poker in his hand as the ashes came back to life slowly over the next minutes and were roaring again soon enough.

Aisling did not move, and he watched her for a few minutes in the quiet, her white hair catching the orange glow of the fire. *She looks so ... small,* he thought, and wondered about it only until he remembered that she was short, shorter than—

Cyrus's fingers came to his face, rubbed his eyes, as though he could strike the vision out of them, rub the image of the blond-haired elf from them. *It has been near a year since last I saw her. One would think I would be well and truly done with her by now.* He looked back to Aisling, who lay under the blankets, her blue skin dull against the grey cloth. *I am different. Things are different, now. She told me flatly that it would never work, could never work.* He squeezed his bare hand against the cold stone floor, pressed it, felt the smoothness of it. *Why is it so hard to be rid of her?*

He stewed for only another minute before he stood, quietly dressed and went out the door. He gave a last look at his lover before he left; if she was awake, she had the good grace to say nothing. *Another reason she's vastly superior to ... her. Sometimes I just need to be alone with my thoughts.*

His steps carried him along the spiral staircase to a lower landing. The lamps were low, dim, and Cyrus saw a glow of color outside a translucent window, something faintly orange and red. He stopped at the landing and stepped toward the door, which he knew led outside, onto the castle's interconnected ramparts.

With a squeak the door opened, and he grimaced at the sound. He shut it back carefully then looked around. The ramparts led in either direction; to his right he knew he could find himself overlooking the Garden of Serenity with only a few twists and turns. To his left, however, was the outer wall, and all that lay beyond. He went left, felt the chill of the night air. He drew his heavy cloak around him, trying to hold in the warmth escaping through the cracks in his armor.

His feet carried him along and he looked up into the sky, where an aurora lit the blackness like a fire of its own. It was a magnificent red and orange glow, shimmering faintly, stronger, like a snake of fire sliding its way across the night. He took a breath and exhaled, watching the air steam in front of him. The sky was clear above, but the wisps of clouds were visible in the distance, lit by the aurora. The smell of the night air drew into his nose, freezing it, giving it the smell of cold, all in itself. *How is it that cold has a smell?*

His walk took him around the perimeter; there were guards, here and there, and they nodded to him as he passed. He found himself at the east wall and looked out, across the small valley beyond. Lit campfires waited below, the entirety of Galbadien's army laid out before him. *Tomorrow they will move north, a half-day's ride ... and a day from now, perhaps two ... it will begin.*

He let his gauntlet slide along the uneven ramparts, clanking as he dropped it off a crenellation. He followed the curtain wall, though in truth it was all one massive structure. *How has this stood for ten thousand years? It is the most magnificent and detailed castle I can recall ever seeing—other than perhaps Vernadam.* He thought, too, of Scylax, high upon a mountain. *I wonder what Caenalys must be like? Where she was raised—*

He let out a small, angry hiss at himself. *Can I not be rid of the thoughts of these women? It has been nearly five months since I have seen her, yet she does not leave me be, either ...*

He walked on toward the north, toward tomorrow. *We set out tomorrow. We face them on the day after.* He felt a chill, more than the cold. *Can we best them?* He did not press the answer to that question, almost afraid to know it.

Another guard passed with a nod. Their helms were a simpler things that partially covered their faces. *Like the Termina Guard,* Cyrus thought, and wondered if he should banish that thought as well, for all its unpleasant associations.

There was a figure on the northern rampart, on the wall segment that jutted out allowing archers to cover the north gate in a siege; the armor was familiar even at this distance, though Cyrus had been so wrapped up in his own thoughts that he had come to within twenty feet and not even realized it. The outline was visible against the aurora above, spikes shadowed behind hues of fiery orange and flaming red. His helm was off, lying on the nearest crenellation, a spiked crown of its own sort, as pointed as the personality of its wearer.

"I'm not going to kill you now," Terian said, turning to Cyrus, his black hair flowing in the wind. The dark elf had an accumulation of stubble that might have been more easily visible on a human. As it was, it gave the dark knight a shadowed look about his jaw and lips. "I gave my word to Curatio that I would not settle my personal grudge with you until this was all over."

"I'm trying to decide if I should take comfort in the word of a dark knight," Cyrus said, his hand already on Praelior's hilt, "especially one who has already attempted to murder me without warning."

"There was plenty of warning," Terian said, turning back to look over the edge of the wall, toward the north, "you were just so wrapped up in your own petty concerns that you didn't notice it."

"Petty concerns?" Cyrus asked. "Like coming here, winning the Sylorean war, assaulting Green Hill?"

Terian chuckled lightly. "As though you devoted more than a few hours of thought over the course of our months-long journey to any of those things. No, Cyrus, you know very well of what I speak—Vara, Cattrine, and Aisling. These women that you stumble to, one after the other, hoping they'll pick you up and fill that shallow, empty place in your chest where you used to keep your conviction." He cast a sidelong glance at Cyrus, who took tentative steps to stand down the wall from him. "They won't, you know."

"I hardly think that I'm looking for them to fill some gap in my belief," Cyrus said, staring at the northern reaches; there were no fires here, just vast, empty woods. There was light in the distance, though, something like a fire, but it was far off.

"Truly?" Terian asked. "Is it possible that the great Cyrus Davidon, that shining light of all virtue, has finally come to the point where all he looks to a woman for is the physical? Because I believe we had a conversation about this some time ago, my friend—"

"I think we stopped being friends when you cursed me and left me to die," Cyrus said quietly.

There was a pause. "True enough," Terian said, and Cyrus watched him clutch the edge of the wall, and the image of a man clinging to something for life sprang to mind.

"Shouldn't you be happy about that, if it's true?" Cyrus asked, flicking his gaze back to the empty lands in front of him. "You were the one who chided me to ignore the idea of deep feelings or of any kind of resistance to baser appetites. You were the one who wanted me to come to whorehouses with you, to 'scratch the itch,' as it were, with any woman freely available. Now that I've done it, you say I've lost something—what? You were the one urging me down that path all along; I think it a bit late now to fret about some irrelevant consequence of me doing what you suggested, however unwittingly I might have come to it."

"I never thought you would," Terian said quietly. "Not in a hundred years, not in a thousand. Cyrus the Unbroken, wallowing about in the filth, fallen from his iconic high?" He turned to gaze directly at Cyrus. "I think I erred in trying to kill you."

Cyrus snorted. "You erred? You slit the throat of my horse after casting a spell on me that caused immense pain and left me surrounded by enemies. You betrayed a guildmate and a friend who had no idea he had wronged you; yes, Terian, I would say you erred. Badly."

"That's not quite what I meant," the dark knight said, a quiet sadness held firm on his face, his pointed nose angling just away from Cyrus. "What I meant was ... revenge on you might have been a foolish notion, seeing how much you've suffered this last year. Perhaps a more fitting punishment was to let you live in this strange, fallen state of anguish you seem to have gathered to yourself."

"'Fallen state of anguish'?" Cyrus repeated. "That's poetic."

"No," the dark knight said, "I mean it. Truly. As a friend, killing you might have been more merciful—"

"You have a strange notion of mercy, 'friend.'"

"Think about it," Terian said, and Cyrus watched him anchor his hands on the wall, holding them there as though he might fall if he didn't. "Everything horrible that could have happened to you this year has just about happened. The woman you loved rejected you in spectacularly brutal fashion. Your mentor and father figure berated you for the first time in your history, you came thousands of miles from home, trying to find some soothing balm for your tortured soul, and instead the woman you started to fall in love with lies to you about who she is and you cast her away over it." He laughed, but it was a sad, pitying sound. "I could not have orchestrated a worse punishment for you than all that."

"This is pathetic, even for you," Cyrus said. "Merely reminding me of the less pleasant turns of events that have occurred this last year is hardly the stuff required to break my spirit, though it brings me no joy. But you might consider adding to your list the moment when one of my sworn and chosen brothers tried to kill me himself."

"There was that, true," Terian said. "I could also make mention of your decapitation, or the fact that Alaric has yet to send even an acknowledgment of your pleas for aid, but why? The worst of it," and Terian's voice dripped with a sort of sad sincerity, "the real torturous prize is not the pain they caused, but the scars they left." Terian shrugged, as though trying to shake off some unpleasantness or warm up from the chill wind that blew by. "You don't see it, but you've changed, Cyrus. And not for the better. You've become a harder, colder sort of person."

"I'm becoming you, in other words."

"Yes!" Terian said and clinked his gauntlet while snapping his finger and pointing it as Cyrus. "Your soul is calloused, my friend, and all those things that you carried with you into the Realm of Death—the illusion of what you were fighting for, the idea of a future with Vara—you walked out of the gates of Sanctuary on the journey here without any of them. Whoever you were last year—when I *was* your friend—that man is gone. I don't even recognize the one in front of me anymore."

"Yet still you'll kill me when this is done?" Cyrus asked.

There was a twist in Terian's face, the hint of something unpleasant as his face stretched, lips pursed, in a sort of pained grimace. "Perhaps. Not until this is over, but ... perhaps."

"Then it really doesn't matter how I've changed, does it?" Cyrus asked, and let his hand drift over the crenellation, let it settle as the first snowflake drifted down by the aurora's light; clouds were moving over now, the red and orange had begun to be covered by tge dark, grey shapes drifting across the sky, threatening to overcome the entirety of it. "I'm still the man you want to kill."

"Maybe," Terian said, and the first flakes came down to rest upon his armor, soft symbols next to the spikes and edges of that which protected him from harm. "But the other Cyrus—the one who killed my father—I wanted to hurt him. I wanted to see him bleed his righteous life out in front of me, suffer for what he'd done."

"And now?" Cyrus looked at him expectantly. "You think I've suffered enough?"

"I don't think you have any idea how much you've suffered," Terian said, turning away from him as the snowfall intensified. "I don't think you have any idea how much you will continue to, as the man you are now. The changes you've made, that have happened to you, this jading, this winnowing of decency—I don't know how to explain it other than that—you're an empty man, walking forward with each step following a path laid out long ago." The dark knight smiled, but there was no mirth in it. "What do you even believe in anymore?" He gave Cyrus a ghostly grin across the rampart.

"Duty," Cyrus said. "Loyalty. To my brethren in Sanctuary. I believe I unleashed this scourge that is costing a great many people their lives, and I aim to correct it."

"And what after that?" Terian asked, but his head was bowed and he no longer looked at the warrior. The snow had begun to accumulate now, just a little bit, a faint white dusting, but it came down heavily enough that all the land was cut before him, and Cyrus could see only a hundred feet off the wall at best. "What will you do if you fail?" He blinked and turned his head to Cyrus. "What will you do if you succeed? Where will you go? What will you fight for?"

"I'll go home," Cyrus said, but he didn't feel it, not really, not in the emptiness within. "I'll fight whoever next crosses the path of Sanctuary—just like I always have." He turned away, brushing the wet snow from his shoulders as he began to make his way back to the tower. "What about you, Terian?" he asked as he walked away. "You're no longer welcome in Sanctuary, unless Alaric finds some measure of deep pity for you. What will you do? Where will you go?" He turned and looked back, but the dark knight was all shadow now, just an outline, a silhouette in the rising frenzy of the snowstorm as it blew around him. "What will you fight for?"

"The same thing I have been since the days when I lost all my belief and care, like you have," Terian answered, the wind muffling him as he spoke. "Myself. And I'll go wherever the road takes me." He turned away, and the next words were nearly lost to the wind. "If I'm not much mistaken, it won't be that long before you do exactly the same."

Chapter 80

The snow had come heavily, all through the night. Cyrus did not sleep, but he lay down next to Aisling in the tower room, the fire crackling and shedding warmth now. The sweet smell of wood smoke harkened him back to thoughts of Sanctuary, but he found less comfort in them than he would have imagined. A dull, gnawing feeling ate at him from the thought of it, of going home, he realized. The smell of meat pies came back to him, whether from thoughts of Sanctuary or memories of the days before, when he was a child in a home of his own, with a mother and father, he knew not which. *Alone. It's how I lived, from the day Belkan dropped me at the Society to the day I ... what? Made my first prayer to Bellarum? Met Narstron? Perhaps. Married Imina?* He grimaced. *Doubtful. She knew I felt the call to war more than to stay with her. From the day I ...*

There was the flash again, in his mind, of blond hair, of a sword in motion, laying open foes on a battlefied. Of a sharp voice and sharper wit, of her fluid motion in a fight, and of her face ... *oh gods, her face ...*

From the day I joined Sanctuary. Even the echo of the words only in his mind was as loud as any battle; it resonated in the quiet night of his chamber, and even the presence of Aisling against his side, almost purring, was no consolation.

Dawn found him unrested, and he wondered if he had shut his eyes at all after returning to bed. Terian's words rattled in his head, thoughts of the man he was plagued him, of who he had been.

He rose, ate breakfast with the others in a somber feast in a room at the bottom of the stairs, the brothers quietly bringing them porridge. No one spoke, not even Martaina, though she looked to be of a mind to say something at one point. When finished, they filed outside. The courtyard had filled with snow during the early morning hours, and still it came down heavily, lying already in drifts up to mid-calf on the women, Cyrus noted upon seeing Aisling slip into it. She cringed and he knew that wet slush had fallen into her leather shoes, low as they ran to the ground.

The horses were saddled and waiting, and the same stable boy brought Cyrus his reins. He took them wordlessly, the lad's shining face not adding any brightness to an already dim mood. The snowfall was lighter now than it had been last night, but the crunch of it underfoot, the way it drowned out all the distant noises and made the land still and quiet was deeply unnerving, especially before battle. The remnants of his cinnamon porridge, sweetened with cream, still hung on his moustache and beard, and he could taste the sugar still lingering on his tongue. He pulled tight his cloak again once he was on Windrider's back, and the horse started off right away, without even a prompting from him, heading toward the north courtyard, following Longwell's lead in this case.

Briyce Unger and Milos Tiernan were already waiting, having a quiet conversation with aides behind them, ahorse. As Longwell approached they each gave a nod of courtesy and were off, toward the gate north, out through it and then the second gate beyond, where the world opened up before them. The snowflakes forced Cyrus's eyes to squint every few minutes. He blinked them away when needed, but a few minutes later they would return, and he would brush them off his face. It was a steady path to madness, he was certain, but his coat began to become wet, and his armor chill, the inside padding saving him from the worst of the cold.

They rode out, and the army of Galbadien joined them past the forest road, falling into line behind them. Others rode out from the east as well, the other armies of Actaluere that had filtered up. Cyrus rode at the front—*the tip of the spear,* he liked to think of it—with the Kings and his own command. He looked back and wondered, trying to see through the snow, stealing a look at the army of Actaluere.

Tiernan caught his eye when he looked back around, and there was a slight smile on the King of Actaluere's face. "He's not here, of course."

Cyrus blinked at Milos Tiernan. "Who?"

"Hoygraf," Tiernan said with a smug look. "Can't be of much good since you gutted him; he remains in his lands, along with a considerable contingent of Actaluere's troops." The smile was gone now, and it became somewhat shrewd as a look, giving Cyrus the slightest hint that the King was holding something back.

"Wouldn't we be better off with his men coming along with us?" Cyrus asked, keeping his eye on Tiernan.

"We have about a third of them with us," Tiernan replied, now turned to look in the direction he was riding, giving Cyrus a sideways profile. He had not noticed before, but the King's chin was weak, withdrawn. "The rest remain as a sort of reserve—insurance, if you will, against any sort of strike by Galbadien or Syloreas against our holdings."

"Speaking for Galbadien," Longwell said from his place not far away, on the other side of Cyrus, "we have no intention to strike at you, nor do we have any forces left in our country with which to do so if we wanted." He shrugged, his pointed helm with a hawklike visor giving him a predatory edge. "Though I suppose if you wanted to, Baron—I'm sorry, Grand Duke Hoygraf—could just about march to Vernadam without any sort of serious opposition."

"Good to know," Tiernan said without any sort of pleasure. "But my greater concern is the refugees of Syloreas that pour through my borders unfettered even now. We give them all the charity we can, but it is a risk, however slight, that they may decide to turn on my people. The troops who remain are there to keep the peace. Refugees are hungry, after all, and sometimes desperate, and I don't wish to see my people bear the brunt of an angry, starving mass cutting a rugged path across our landscape."

"What exactly do you think they'll be doing," Briyce Unger asked, "this hungry, starving mass of desperation?" The umbrage was obvious from the way he said it. "Capturing Caenalys? Sacking your treasure room?"

"I worry more about the farmers in the northern reaches," Tiernan said bluntly. "Starving people do desperate things—like, say, murder a man for food. Form a mob and destroy a town while trying to get fed. I am doing what I can for charity, but I must also preserve my people's safety. I would hope, were our roles reversed, you would understand that."

Cyrus could see that Unger did not, but the King of Syloreas did not voice whatever irritation he held. He guided his horse away from the discussion, though, away from Tiernan and back to a thick knot of his aides who rode at the front of the formation. Cyrus could see them casting glances every now and again, though, and he did not like the look of them at all.

With the snow slowing their pace, and even more the walking speed of the men on foot, the great army of Luukessia took the better part of the day to get to the flat lands that had been marked for the site of their battle. There were no tents set up when they arrived, but fires were set. The whole camp was a buzz of subdued activity; quiet in the gloom, the snow still coming down. There were whispers, rumors, flat-out lies, and all of them reached Cyrus's ears as he walked through the encampment, alone, his feet crunching through the snow. Men were huddled near fires for warmth; and every once in a good while he saw a woman in armor or with a sword. There was thin stew cooking and not much else. A skin of ice was broken off a nearby creek for drinking water and for boiling, and latrines were set up over a hill to the rear. Coming back from them, Terian said, "I suggest we try and lead the scourge in that direction when they come; it'll be certain to send them running back to the north."

"Even on such a cold day as this?" Martaina had her bow out and was fletching, working on arrows, putting tips upon shafts she had carved while gathering wood earlier. The shafts had a wet look to them, and when she caught Cyrus looking she shrugged. "I work with what I have."

The night came upon them early, and no sign of the aurora was to be had under the cloudy, still-snowing skies. It was quiet in the camp, though Cyrus wondered how many men were actually sleeping. The snows came down on them, and still no tents had been set up; the need for mobility and a quick retreat trumped comfort, and so tens of thousands of men and a few hundred women lay beneath a sky that wafted snow down upon them. Aisling lay next to him, of course, and as much as she had tried to take his mind off of all matters, it had not worked as it did before, and he lay awake again, unease hanging over him as he hoped sleep would claim him, yet knowing that it would not.

Dawn was a grim affair, and the snow went ever on, unhalting, now almost a foot deep. It flurried hard in spurts then reduced to a manageable few flakes before picking up again. The wind howled, sending icy slaps hard against the men who were standing around fires that were whipped with every gust. They kept their heads low, their cowls and collars up to get warmth by any means they could find.

The first messenger for the army came an hour after daybreak, when pickled eggs, hard cheese and bread were being eaten by the armies of Actaluere and Galbadien. The Sanctuary members ate conjured bread and water with their supplies. An uneasy quiet hung in the air until the messenger appeared, a half-elf, half-human warrior whom Cyrus knew only in passing. The man was exhausted, it was obvious, his eyes red with fatigue. He whispered a few words to Curatio and then stumbled into the nearest bedroll, not even bothering to care that it wasn't his own.

"They'll be here within hours," Curatio said. "Perhaps two, perhaps a little more, depending on how well our efforts to hold them back go. The whole line is exhausted; which should not be surprising, as they've been performing a strategy of engaging and falling back for months now. When we left them a week ago," he gave a quick nod to Terian, "I wondered if they'd be able to hold for as long as it would take. I suppose they have."

"How is our force doing?" Cyrus asked.

"Faring well," Curatio said, snow turning his hair white. "They've never once been the cause of a retreat. It's become obvious, though, that these things are drawn to life, absolutely drawn to it. They doggedly come at us, ignore the possibility of pulling a wide flanking maneuver; we've seen them break off in numbers when we pass a village that still has occupants. They go, they slaughter, they return with bloodied faces. I honestly thought they'd take longer to get here, but it would appear the army is wearier than even I thought."

Cyrus looked at the messenger, already well asleep. "We'll give them as much rest as we can afford. Hopefully this fresh army pouring into the fight will allow us to push forward."

Curatio smiled and nodded. "Let us hope."

"They've changed," came the muffled words of the man laying on the bedroll, the half-elf. "They're more dogged now, trying to flank more." He didn't roll over, but turned his head slightly. "They come at our weaknesses, too; not that they didn't before, but Odellan says it's worse now, as though they can exploit them, sense their flaws and approaches. More strategy, less brutal anger. There's something else, too." The half elf rolled over and looked at Cyrus through half-lidded eyes. "There's a master, we think. One that stays in the distance, but we see him. Tall as two men, a four-legged creature, and it bears a mark of sorts. It stands off, growls at the others, and they move almost like it tells them to. We've had archers try and kill it, but it stays out of range of spells and arrows." He looked directly at Cyrus. "We think it's their General, the thing that leads them."

Cyrus felt the cold wind pick up in a gust just then, carrying the sounds around his ears like a howling of the wind. The snow fell on, down around them, and the quiet descended again, except for the wind, as he sat there near the fire—and derived no warmth from it at all.

Chapter 81

The snowfall was at a blessed slowdown as they stood all in a line, a quarter mile from the campsite. Cyrus's nose hairs felt well frozen, and every breath just added to the searing pain behind his cheeks and eyes, as though someone had taken a frozen hammer and tapped behind them gently for quite some time. His sweat had frozen to his skin, and whatever breakfast he'd eaten—he could little recall now what it had been—was sitting poorly, and threatening to come back up. The cold had seeped to the bone and all was quiet save for the roar of the wind when it picked up. It ran with near continuousness now, driving the snow sideways at its worst and at a forty-five degree angle at best.

It was the sound that reached them first, the yells and battle cries of men weary and desperate. They saw them shortly thereafter, in the distance, through the haze made by the snow.

"This is an ill time and place for a fight," Terian said, and Cyrus glanced over to realize that the dark knight was next to him.

"Because we can see little, our cavalry is unable to operate in the heavy snow and our infantry is slowed to being unable to advance?" Cyrus let the irony seep in as he said it.

"Also, it's colder than your elven girlfriend's touch and we're relieving an army that's likely to break from fatigue as soon as they realize we're here to take up for them." His eyes glittered in the bare light of a sun that none of them could see. "If they manage to let us take over as the front line without breaking, it will be a miracle of military discipline of the highest order."

Cyrus looked forward to the line stretched in front of him, and saw others closer, the walking wounded, and a few carrying men on makeshift stretchers made of bedrolls and all manner of other things. "Would I be wrong in assuming there won't be many wounded?"

"Most have been left behind," Terian answered. "It became obvious after you left that our healers were not nearly enough to handle the entire army under sustained assault; they lacked the magical energy to come close to saving everyone. The Luukessians played it carefully after that; if a man fell and ended up behind the enemy's line, he was given up lost so as not to cost five more trying to recover him." The dark knight set his jaw. "It's an ugly thing, what they do to those who fall. I wouldn't wish it on anybody. Our rangers nearly ran out of arrows putting the poor bastards out of their misery."

"We lose any of ours that way?" Cyrus asked, not really wanting to know the answer.

"Couple of disappearances," Curatio said from behind Cyrus. The army of Galbadien and Actaluere sandwiched the small group of them on either side. "Likely fell in the night and we didn't see or hear them, you know ... in the heat of the battle."

You mean in the midst of all the men screaming, Cyrus thought, but did not say. *Hard to tell if the scream comes from a man of Sanctuary or one of the Luukessians when you're bunched tight together along a front line.*

The army before them was still falling back in tatters, only a few scant rows deep. Cyrus could see the Sanctuary numbers, the largest part of the force. The army of Actaluere was much reduced over when last he saw it, easily a quarter the size. There were almost none of the Sylorean civilians remaining, the farmers and villagers that had been on his right when they'd fought at Filsharron. The Sylorean army looked smaller, too, and ragged, though it was hard to tell since they had been the most ragged at the outset of the fight.

"It's the New Year today, did you know that?" Terian looked over at Cyrus. "The Solstice will be here in only a week or so." He flashed his gaze to the fight, now only a few hundred feet away. "Do you suppose this will be over by then?"

Cyrus felt his jaw tighten; talking to Terian was the most natural thing in the world when he didn't think about it. When he did ... "I doubt it. Depends on how many there are, I suppose."

Terian gave him a pinched smile. "Do you suppose we'll ever get to that cave with the portal?"

"That's the goal," Cyrus said, irritated.

"Do *you* believe we'll get there?" Terian turned to him as Cyrus tensed; the battle was close now, only a minute or two away.

"Yes," Cyrus lied, "now make ready."

"Hm," Terian said, watching him for just a second longer before turning back to the madness unfolding in front of them. It was clearer now, the snow disappating the closer they got, painting a fuller picture in broad strokes, the clarity increasing. "I almost believe you. You truly have changed; used to be you couldn't lie worth a damn."

The ranks of battle closed, and Cyrus saw the backs of those in front of him, the line retreating. Furtive looks came his way now, men and women with bone-weariness settled in their eyes, their sunken eye sockets peering at him. Their shoulders hung low, but still they fought, those up front, those behind. It was the army of Actaluere that broke first, their back line disintegrating, and only the four or five disorganized rows in front of them to hold up. The press of the scourge forward meant that the front rows fell back even harder, and Cyrus saw a body tossed into the air, saw the motion of grey flesh ahead of all the humans and dark elves and all else that blocked the smaller creatures from his sight.

The smell of death was pungent now in the cold, and the shiver up his spine was at least as much from the knowledge that the unceasing beasts were trying to clamp down on him even now, that they were coming. *They don't stop, they don't quit when you hurt them, they only give up when you kill them.* He clenched a hand, trying to remember the training of years gone by, the words he learned in the Society when he banished fear from his life. *Throw yourself into what you fear, and the death of fear is a certainty. Fear is a ghost, a shadow for lesser beings who worry of death. It is not your enemy but your tool, your business, that which you deal with sword and axe and spear and knife. Death is yours to wield, and it should be your enemy who fears death, not you. Embrace death.* The notion of holding onto the corpse of Mortus flashed before his eyes, that strange, shrunken figure that the God of Death turned into at the end, as he faded from life. *Death is your talent, your profession, and the end result of your call to war. Death is your blessing, your gift, and your strength in time of trial. All men die, and women too, but few live without fear.*

He said the last of the Warrior's Creed in his head. He had not had need to repeat it to himself in years. Unease settled within him, the acidic taste in his mouth was still there and he spat, trying to rid himself of it. The last rank of the Sanctuary army, unbroken in spite of the sudden fleeing of the Syloreans on one side and the Actaluereans on the other, was only feet away now. He took his first step toward them, watched them watch him. *They will not yield an inch,* he willed them, *not even when all else falls apart around them. I should be proud of them,* he thought, dimly aware that that particular emotion was strangely lacking, buried perhaps somewhere beneath his creed.

Praelior came up as the back line folded; the Actaluereans and Galbadiens on either side of him were already moving hard now, trying to stream through the press of their own retreating brethren to form a new front line; it was ugly, a dance of chaos and madness, with men who had been fighting for weeks and months, desperate to escape it. Their tiredness was obvious, their steps in the deepening snow were slow, they dragged, they looked skinny and worn, had been fighting on and off and sleeping in spurts and retreating in others.

Cyrus came up to the second line of the Sanctuary army, perfectly organized, the model of discipline in the heart of the storm. He saw in the motion ahead of him the helm of Odellan, the points of it extending like wings on either side of his head, and his hair moving in the wind. He spun, attacked, parried, and thrust, killing two of the scourge in his next move. Cyrus's small band came up, Terian next to him, Scuddar just down the row, easing through the tight Sanctuary formation. Longwell was there, too, at the head of his army, his lance in hand, strange-looking without his horse. For a flash Cyrus remembered fighting with Longwell at his side, in the dark, on a bridge, with ash streaming down around them like the snow did now, and it heartened him.

With a last deep breath, Cyrus took the step free of the second line and became one with the front rank. The scourge was here, was upon him now, too numerous to count, filling his sight line all the way to where the haze became too great to see any more of them. He let the breath all out in one great battlecry, and swung Praelior into action, to war, to battle—to life and death—once more.

Chapter 82

Vara

Day 150 of the Siege of Sanctuary

"It's not the idea of being cooped up here that I object to," Partus said, in the closest imitation to whining that Vara could imagine without actually being a whine, "it's the fact of it. I know you've sent expeditions to other places to gather food, to get relief and supplies, and yet I wasn't offered a chance to go along with them."

Vara listened, waiting for the dwarf to say more. When he didn't, she let herself take a breath and count to five before answering. "As we have discussed, I would be more than happy to send you along to Fertiss with not only the utmost haste but also with a bounty of gold simply to be rid of you." She caught the cockeyed gaze of the dwarf, and wondered if he was as insulted by that as she had intended him to be. "Unfortunately, Alaric seems to be of a different opinion—and, in a stunning reversal of his previous nature to this point, he is keeping that decision secret for reasons that I cannot possibly fathom." She shrugged broadly, trying—*Oh, how I try*—to keep it amusing. "I wish he would send you away. Were it in my power, I would send you away. I would walk you to the gate right now, open it up, roll you under it, and be done with it. Unfortunately, it is not in my power, nor the other officers of Sanctuary either, because—"

"Alaric has some ill intention toward me that he has no desire to disclose to the rest of you," Partus said, still squinting at her with one eye half-closed. "I see how it is. He knows strength when he sees it, and he knows you're in a dire situation. He thinks by backing me into this corner with you, I'll have no choice but to fight for Sanctuary when the time comes. You know what? The sneaky bastard is probably right. I've got no love for the dark elves, not after Aurastra, and they don't take prisoners, as well you know. Well, they take the women ones, but not like—"

"Thank you, for that," Vara said, wondering if her fake smile was holding. *Alaric compelled me to be nice to this one. I cannot imagine what reason he might have for that, nor why he would ask it of me, OF ALL PEOPLE.* She felt the strain inside, the desire to scream, to raise a booted foot and punt the little blighter—but she resisted. *He's a strong paladin,* she grudgingly admitted, *stronger than me.* Two days earlier, the dark elves had begun constructing siege towers from logs hauled to within sight of the Sanctuary walls; Partus, in an annoyingly boastful show of force had bragged that he could destroy every single one of them before they had started moving. No one had believed it. There had been bets placed, gold wagered. Partus had taken all of it and left fifteen siege towers in wreckage, showering splinters into the army of dark elves huddled around them. There were bodies lying there, too numerous to count, from the explosive force with which the wood had splintered into both the engineers and laborers that had built the things, and also warriors and fighters that had been standing nearby. *He's a wealthy little git now, eager to spend his newfound winnings and make his escape while the getting is good; he's unlikely to manage another gambling win such as that.*

"You know that no other paladin could match my power—other than Alaric, of course." Partus gave her a wink, causing Vara to restrain an explosive fury of her own. *I could surely blast him at least a quarter of the distance he managed to send his spell; far enough to kill him, perhaps.* Instead, she rolled her eyes and realized that the smile had long since vanished, and that now all she wore was a look of undisguised loathing.

"I recognize that you are quite strong in the powers of the white knight," she answered, "though it mystifies me that you can even call yourself one given that you seem to believe in nothing, and certainly have no sort of crusade, if you ever did—"

Partus let out a soft laugh. "You're a young one, aren't you? Being a paladin has little enough to do with having a crusade or a cause." Vara bristled at this, and Partus laughed further. "It doesn't matter what you believe in, some god or cause or nothing at all. All that matters is that you know how to use the spells to their maximum effect. That you put in the practice to push them to the limits of what they can do."

Vara listened to him, taking care not to grind her teeth. "Is that so? Believe in nothing—"

"But yourself," Partus said, correcting her not at all gently, "if you're into saying it that way, I suppose."

Vara let her eyes slip sideways, darting around the foyer. "And how would you say it?" She watched him shift on his short legs; he only came up to her chest in height, a fact that was not lost on her. Or him. "If you were forced to describe it."

"If I were forced to describe it," Partus said slowly, "I would say it's believing in power. Not in yourself, exactly," he cringed, his face turned mocking, "because that's a little elven and weak for my tastes, frankly—no offense. Your people make good mystics and warriors, but they talk such a pitiful line of effeteness when it comes to yourselves. You have to see your ability to cast a spell that mighty—" He held his hand out in front of him, aimed it just past her. She kept her cool, and realized he was watching for her reaction, his palm pointed into the lounge. "It's all to do with seeing it, saying it, bringing it to form. It's not just the words." He ran the back of his hand over his brow. "Then, after you've done it once, you know you can, so then it's about stretching your magical energy to accomodate, exercising your abilities to adapt to casting it more often." He used his tongue to suck at something stuck in his teeth. "Then, it's about practice. Constant, diligent practice."

She eyed his short frame, at the slight paunch that hung over his belt. "And you did this? Practiced diligently?"

"Aye," Partus said, "I may not look it now, but I put in thousands of hours of effort when I was at the Holy Brethren. More than anyone else, that's certain."

"Yes," Vara said with a trace of irony, "I'm certain you practiced by yourself constantly, until you became a tremendous master."

Partus caught the hint of insincerity and squinted at it, then shrugged it off. "It doesn't matter that you believe I did it, you can see the results for yourself. Care, don't, pay attention, heed me not, it's all the same to me until those dark elves come crashing in; then you might wish you'd done things a bit differently."

With that, the dwarf wandered off, toward the lounge and the casks of ale that remained there, even in this time of crisis. Vara wanted to sigh but she didn't, instead letting the smell of the hearth burning give her a moment's peace, that slight homey feeling to calm her nerves, then she turned to see Vaste watching her by the stairwell. She hesitated, unsure of what to do. *He's standing right in my path. Should I avoid him entirely?* The troll watched, giving her a slight smile, then continued to speak with the human he had been talking to. *It would appear he's focused upon his own matters; just as well, I do not know that I could handle much more in the way of sympathy from him at this point.*

She headed for the stairs, her head involuntarily moving to look in the open doors of the Great Hall. Larana waited within, seated at a table inside. The druid looked more ragged than usual, her face smudged with a little dirt or grease, and her hair in a muss—that part was usual. Vara pondered speaking to the chief cook, but she sat alone, by herself, and seemed to be working on nothing at all. *I haven't said more than a dozen words to her since I came here. This seems an ill time to start, simply because I know she may be the only other one in Sanctuary who misses ...* she cringed ... *who wishes Cyrus were here.* She felt the physical reaction in her face as she thought it; a tightening of the muscles into a scowl, the lowering of an eyelid, the muscles straining and causing it to twitch.

She made for the stairs instead, keeping her pace slow, neutral, until she had passed Vaste. Then she sped up, taking the steps two and three at a time, letting her frustration come out in a near-aggression. She reached the Council Chambers and paused; the door was parted slightly, as though someone had left it open for some purpose. She stopped, pondering, then opened the door and stepped inside.

It was quiet, of course; no motion within. The hearths were dead, only the faint glow of fading embers showing any sign of life. The shadows were long inside, the sun was behind the clouds outside. There was little light, only what came in through the windows. *Strange, the torches typically light themselves—*

"Shut the door," came a voice in the darkness, originating from Alaric's chair at the head of the table. It was quiet but full of command, and she heeded it immediately, drawing the door closed behind her. There was less light now, and Vara stared into the shadow of the massive seat at the head of the table, peering into it with her superior vision. *If he is there, I should see him, even in this, unless—*

There was a faint hint of haziness in the room, she realized, a lack of clarity as though a mist had seeped in around her. It hung low, around her feet. "It is easier this way, sometimes," came the voice of Alaric from his chair, "to keep one foot in the world of men and the other in the world of the ethereal, existing fully in neither." There was a slight sound, barely audible to her ears, a rushing of air, and then he was visible, his outline, the helm and armor. There was a clink of metal on the wood of the table and his chair. "Do you think it would be easier to live in this world if you could leave it at any time you wanted?" There was no mirth in Alaric's statement. "It isn't, actually. It might be harder, if such a thing were possible."

"Alaric?" she asked, still uncertain—uncertain what to say, what to do, why he was here—*I cannot recall having heard him like this before. He almost sounds ... like ...* "Have you been drinking?"

When the reply came, it was filled with amusement. "On this occasion, no. I think there is quite enough going on around us at this point to fill one's mind with a certain heady sensation, something to make one feel lighter than air. Of course, when one can already become lighter than air with only a thought, it becomes redundant, but ... perhaps you get the point."

"Perhaps not," Vara said, easing closer to the table from where she stood by the door. "What has happened to you, Alaric? You have never been so ... bizarre."

There was a pause. "I am merely musing. Contemplating what has happened, what has gone before. On who I am, on what I have done— the triumphs and the failures. The failures, I think, are the things upon which I most often dwell, but occasionally I think of the triumphs as well." He paused. "Time is running out, you know."

Vara blinked. "For Sanctuary?"

"For all of us." There was clarity in Alaric's voice now, a disturbing note that was foreign to his usual tone.

"What do you see?" She took another step in, resting her hand on the back of the nearest chair. Cyrus's chair, she realized.

"I see much," Alaric replied, and now the fatigue had bled into his voice. "More than most, less than the gods. Enough to disquiet me. I see that which I want to see, and that which I don't care to see, and that which no one thinks I can see. All of these things."

"Is that how you know so much?" Vara asked. "Is that how you're always so vague and mysterious and all-seeing?"

"I am hardly all-seeing," Alaric replied. "There are many, many things beyond my sight. For example, I can no longer see ... him. He passed beyond my vision when he went across the bridge. Beyond the boundaries." The Ghost's hand gestured vaguely in Vara's direction, and it took a moment for her to realize that he indicated Cyrus's chair and not her.

"Cyrus?" She stared at him, then the seat. "You could see him? Before he left the shores of Arkaria?"

"I could watch him," Alaric said, "just as I can watch a great many things whileethereal. But no more, now."

"How do you do it?" She slid the chair quietly, and it made a screech that to her ears sounded as loud as if someone had scraped wood across stone harshly next to her head.

There was a moment of quiet as the sound of the chair sliding died away. "I suppose it would be asking too much for me to say it is merely magic and have you believe it?"

She thought about it for a moment. "There are things beyond magic in this world, Alaric."

"There is nothing beyond magic in this world. Only things that you do not understand that you wrongly attribute to being beyond magic." The shadows seemed to deepen in the room with his answer, as though he had summoned them to wrap him up in a cloak.

"What strains you so?" Vara asked, leaning forward in her seat, trying to see him. "What has you on edge for the first time since I've known you?"

There was a pause and a quiet settling over the room like the shadows, draping themselves over everything. Alaric's answer was calm, measured, and covered over with the same quiet, but layered with deceit, she thought. "Nothing, child."

"I am hardly a child," she bristled. "Never before have you condescended to call me 'child' even though you knew I was the youngest of my race. You know I don't care for that appellation and never have, and to apply it now, of all times, you had to know would raise my umbrage and suspicions in equal measure. So what is it, Alaric? Why do you sit here in the darkness, alone, meditating on the idea of leaving this world behind?"

She could almost hear the raising of his eyebrow. "I leave this world frequently; you have seen it many times. The meditation, perhaps, is new to you but not to me, I assure you. As for being alone ... are there any of us here that are not so?" She waited as he finished, and could almost hear him add, "my child," to the end of the question, though it remained unspoken.

"We are not all alone," Vara said, "there are many among our number who have found companionship with each other, as friends, comrades ..." the next words stuck, but finally came loose, "lovers, spouses. So, no, we are not all alone. And most of us do not spend our time considering abilities that we do not have—for example, the power to become insubstantial and watch others as they go about their business."

There was a shrug from the figure in the shadows. "I assure you it is not as ominous as you make it sound; it actually is quite banal. But to the earlier point, about being alone ... well, you are correct, after a fashion. There are friends here, companions, those who guard our gates against the outside world, who watch each others' backs, find friendly company herein, and more perhaps—love, laughter, all these things. Yet when we leave this world, we do so alone. When we wander through it, much as we might make of having companions there, many of us do not share the load, shoulder the burdens of others. Then again, this should be no great mystery to you ... since you have chosen to do so all the days I have known you."

"I was betrayed," she said quietly. "It takes a bit of time after that to—"

"I realize." He was unflinching, she heard it in his tone. "But once you did move past it, you let your fear take hold of you, you acted on it without consideration—"

She laughed, a high, empty sound that was no more real than Alaric when he was transformed into mist. "It feels peculiar that you should lecture me about this."

There was a quiet in the darkness. "I don't mean to lecture." Alaric leaned forward, suddenly, his chin visible through the gap at the jaw of his helm, and he was urgent now. "I only mean to tell you that however long you think your life is, if you go through it alone, it will drag. It will crush you, the weight of it, like a wagon filled to the top with no wheels to carry it on, pulled by a team of old horses. Those things you attribute to others—love, friendship, companionship—these are the wheels that make your passage go easy. True, there are ruts in the road that you would not experience had your wagon no wheels, but that is only because the day-to-day passage of the hours is all rut, all scrape, no smoothness." The light in the room shifted and illuminated the holes where his eyes were, and she saw they were wild. "You made choices in fear because of what you lost. You threw away everything you had left, and like a fool I said nothing, too wrapped up in my own problems to acknowledge or intervene. But the day has come where you regret what you have done, where you know it was foolish, and yet I know you— and I know pride—and you are the second most prideful and stubborn invidual I have ever met in my long life. I warn you now—cast it aside. Be done with it. Your pride, your fear, is keeping you from the life you might have, is dividing you from all you could want." He seemed to recede then, pull back in his chair, leaving only his hand stretched out across the table, as though he were reaching out to her.

She sat stiffly upright in the chair, his chair, her head pressed against the wood behind her. Her eyes burned from holding them open, so she let them close, and the darkness was little more than what she had already been looking at. The weight of her armor was more pronounced now that she was settled in the chair, and there was a gaping sound in her ears, a silence; even her breathing was not audible. "I hear your words," she said. "But it occurs to me, Alaric, in all the years I have been here, that I have never seen you try to do what you encourage me to do now, that you have never moved beyond Raifa—"

"And I tell you this," Alaric said in a hiss, "so as to steer you around my mistakes. Just as I always have in other areas, now I want to—need to—attend to this last concern." He waved a hand and the torches flared to life, the hearth came roaring back to fire, and Vara's eyes snapped open at the glow of orange. "Life does not last forever, unimpeded," he said, and she saw the blaze in his eyes through the holes of his helm, as though the torches were reflected in them. "Not yours, not mine, not his. You have talked to others of regrets, of the ones you feared should he die first, and I tell you now, as someone who has felt it—I would not have given her up, not cast out her memory or done away with it had I a chance. I embrace the pain for the rest of my days in spite of it and would not wish to be rid of it if the alternative was to have never had it happen at all." He flinched at his own words. "She was everything to me, Vara, and her loss has haunted me all these years. You say it seems strange to come from me because I live now as though I were dead inside, never moved beyond her. This is true; when she died, a part of me died with her, a part that will never come back to life. But if I had it to do all over, I would do it exactly the same, even if it meant experiencing the pain once more, because the alternative ..." he swallowed heavily, "... would be to never have lived at all, truly." He looked back up at her. "Consider what I have said." She started to speak, and he waved her off. "Consider it." With that, his eyes closed, and he began to fade, becoming smoke and mist, which drifted, slowly, out the crack under the door behind her.

The hearth flickered, and so did the torches at the last great rush of air as he left her behind, his presence departing and changing the currents in the room as he did so. She sat there for quite some time, wondering at his words, wondering at his change, and for some time after that ... wondering what had prompted such musings on the finite lives of mortals.

Chapter 83

Cyrus

The battles were long, the snow was deep and the cold was bitter. Cyrus had come off the front line after just under twenty-four hours; he had fought through the night, slaughtering more of the scourge than he could count. It was midday now, the snows had stopped but the wind blew, causing it to drift, blowing sideways over the flat lands upon which they battled. His nose was cold, frigid enough to feel like it was frozen stiff, but he sat in front of a warm fire now, a mile behind the battle, and heard the sound of the war in the distance.

"This is a peculiar way to fight," J'anda said in the midday gloom. The clouds hanging over them were meager cover, casting a shroud of grey over everything. The enchanter had bread in his hand, nibbling at it. "I have never been part of a battle so large that it rages while you can leave it behind, take a break, use the latrines, then come back to find it still going."

"It's not exactly like anything I've ever done before, either," Cyrus said, Aisling next to him, chewing on the nub of bread she held in her hands. "Can you imagine taking a breather like this in the midst of fighting the Dragonlord? Or the goblins in the depths of Enterra? Or on the bridge in Termina?" He shook his head and sipped from a skin of water that had been filled by Nyad with a touch and a word as he passed, dragging himself off the front line of battle.

"These things are utter madness," J'anda said, looking to Curatio, who sat next to him, unspeaking, and Terian, who sat idly, not saying anything but staring at his gauntlets. "They throw countless numbers at us, watch them get ground up and die, but throw more yet. I was not exaggerating when I said that I could not determine how they think. There is no guessing, not from what I saw inside the mind of the one I tried to commune with. If our soldier was right, that there is a General of some sort out there, that may be the key." He looked to Cyrus. "My view was somewhat obstructed, sitting in the back of the lines and of very little use for the first time in my life. Did you see it while you were up there?"

Cyrus thought about it for a minute then shook his head. "I saw something out there, big, but far in the distance. It never got close enough for me to catch much more than a shadow, even in the best light today."

"I saw it," Aisling said.

"Me too." Terian did not look up from his gauntlets.

"Must be nice to have such fine eyesight," Cyrus said. "What did it look like?"

"Like one of them," Terian said, waving his hand in the direction of the battle, "but writ large; four legs, walking around like a dragon without wings. It kept low, though, lower than I think it normally would have, like it knew we had archers and it wanted to be low profile. It was out on the edge of sight, and it stayed there during most of the fight."

"Most?" Cyrus asked.

"It came closer once," Aisling took over for Terian. "Not much, but a little. At the beginning of the fight, when we got to the front of the line. That's when I noticed it, when I felt its presence. After that it receded, like it didn't want to be seen."

Cyrus chewed that one over for a minute. "You think this thing is the mastermind? The brain of the operation?"

Terian chuckled. "If this operation has any brains other than the ones it eats on the field of battle, yes."

"What if we made a direct assault at it?" Cyrus asked.

"Sounds like a fine way to lose your body," Curatio murmured. "Have you seen what happens when these things start to lose any ground? They throw more at you, more of their numbers. Failing that, they hit you on either side, drive back the lines around you so you end up bulged, in a little pocket, sticking out like an arm, Then they winnow it, chopping into the sides at your weakest point until they can surround you; then it is over." He slapped his hands together and the echoing noise was loud enough to startle Martaina, who had been sleeping nearby, into jumping to her feet, bow drawn and arrow already nocked. "Sorry," Curatio breathed, and the ranger nodded, replaced the arrow and bow across her chest, and lay back down.

"You don't think it's possible to stage an assault on that thing without getting swallowed by the scourge army and destroyed?" Cyrus asked, chewing on a stubbornly hard piece of bread. The grains cracked in his teeth and the yeasty flavor lingered on his tongue. He stook a swig out of the water skin to wash it out.

"I think that you're talking about trying to storm something alive as though it's a fortification," Curatio said carefully. "It moves, Cyrus. Let us assume you managed to cut your way across the field of battle towards it: what's to stop it from retreating once it realizes what you're up to? Soon enough you're on a chase to wherever it leads, which, by the way, is halfway to perdition and with the whole of its army surrounding you." He angled his head. "Unless you have some idea of how to escape that, which I am unaware of."

Cyrus ran a hand over his chin, brushing the crumbs out of his beard. He let the faintest hint of a smile tug at the corner of his mouth, and stared straight ahead as the others gradually stopped what they were doing and looked at him, at the curious hint of something long gone, now appearing upon his face. *A smile? How long has it been ...*

"Well, you know ... I actually do have an idea ..."

Chapter 84

The battle raged on; it came evenfall and darkness, and they returned to the front as the line worked its way back to them. The smell of the latrines had grown strong in the hours Cyrus waited with the others—resting, most of them did, lying in their bedrolls. He and Aisling had burned off nervous energy, as always, but he had not joined her in sleep. Also as always, of late. He lay awake in the clouded afternoon light and felt the snowy ground beneath him. The cold seeped, but not too badly; it seemed warmer today than it had the day before for whatever reason, even in spite of the lack of sun. The lingering taste of the water and bread was little enough for sustenance, but he had eaten plenty. Sleep would not come, however, not with the calls of battle growing ever nearer, and the snoring of Terian just across the fire. The thought of his plan rustled around in his mind like a cat trapped in a sack, twisting every way possible to get loose of what held it.

Soon enough it was time to go again, and someone shook his shoulder, waking him out of a sleep he didn't even realize he had fallen into. It was Aisling, already dressed. She leaned down and kissed him, and for a moment the smell of her sweat from battle and their lovemaking overpowered everything else in the camp. When she broke free of him he sat up and began to put on his armor. She did not help, having already moved on, heading over the hill in the direction of the latrines.

The lines were almost upon them now, Cyrus realized, the sound of fighting coming from only a few hundred feet away. *This will be a long and yet short few days, and then we shall be backed against Enrant Monge, forced into the walls of the keep for safety if we cannot turn them back. Then what? They can breach the walls, surely, as they did at Scylax, and then we will find ourselves surrounded.* He thought of the stableboy, of what he had said, and of the refugees that filled the keep, of their slow, dragging procession out of the gates and toward the south. *This will go ill for them if we cannot hold back the tide of these things; they will run out of places to go.*

He waited once his armor was on; the others lingered as well, as though afraid somehow to be on about the day. The line of battle came ever closer, and when they could ignore it no more, Cyrus pulled to his feet, drew his blade and stepped toward the fight. He heard the others with him, and cast a look back to see some stewards and young boys gathering up the things they had left behind, throwing them in the backs of wagons that waited across the camp, horses snorting into the cold air. The wagons began to move as Cyrus reached the back line of the fight, and he wondered how far away they would retreat, and how long it would be before he went back to rest again—or at least try.

He took long, crunching steps through the lines until he reached the front. He began to use his blade to fend off the scourge as they made their way forward, inexorably, open mouths ravenous to take life, to bleed it out on the snow in great red stains. He hacked the head from one, tore limbs from another, then made a move at yet another still that charged him before a perfectly aimed arrow took its eye and caused it to fall still as it slid across the snow to his feet.

The battle turns to a slog, he thought, *nothing more than a steady expectation that we will retreat, that there is no momentum to be had. What madness is this that we fight a battle with no expectation to win?* Praelior gleamed with its soft glow, and the blood he spilled did not remain on it.

"So are we going forward with this blatant ploy to have ourselves all declared mad?" Terian was close beside him. "Because otherwise I'm quite content to remain here, gradually retreating."

"The problem with gradually giving ground," Cyrus said as he slammed his blade home in one of the creature's ribs, "is that sooner or later, no matter how gradually you're doing it, you run out of ground to give." Three sprang at him like dogs and he sliced them out of the air with little thought and only instinct to guide him. "We move now."

"Oh, good," Terian said lightly, "I didn't really want to go on living anyway. Dull existence, you know, drinking, whoring, eating nice foods in pleasant places ..."

"You've been locked in chains for months when you haven't been eating conjured bread and water and fighting these things," Aisling said from Cyrus's left as her daggers danced while she spun aside to let a charging scourge brush past her. Her daggers hit it four times as it went by and it collapsed, knocking down a warrior behind her as it slid to a stop. "And if you've had any woman in that time, I'd be shocked—"

"Fine," Terian said, and Cyrus could hear the scowl in the way he said it. "I really don't care if I go on living since I've been deprived of all those things anyway, but it would have been nice to have a last meal—not insubstantial bread—before we went forward with this idiocy."

"Now, Terian," Cyrus said, "if we'd had a so-called last meal for that purpose, where would your motivation be to fight your way back after what we're about to do? Nowhere, that's where; you'd have peaked in your life, and with nothing before you but the dim, boringness of being a soulless mercenary, you'd probably just lie down and let them eat you right there."

"Wow." Terian's answer sounded slightly shocked and partially amused. "I think I miss the dour and sour Cyrus Davidon, the one who didn't know what to do with a woman in his bedroll. I thought you were truly heading toward the path to desperation and I was eager to see what you did when you got there." He waved a hand vaguely at Aisling as he brought his sword down in the middle of a scourge's head. "Other than her, I mean."

"I think I'm just coming back to myself now," Cyrus said with a slash that sent a scourge screeching away from him missing a limb. "I want to live. At least long enough to get some hard drink, like Reikonosian whiskey, and throw down a toast to the ones we lost without even knowing it."

There was a pause then Terian spoke again. "You're beginning to sound more and more like a mercenary every day, Davidon; loose women, hard drink, strong battle, reckless chances—why soon enough, you'll ask for money in exchange for fighting something." Terian paused and let that hang in the air. "Not that I'm knocking it, because as you can tell, the mercenary's life seems to have pretty much everything I want."

"Then why didn't you go do that after you left Sanctuary?" Cyrus asked, turning his hips to level a scourge with a sideways slash. Cyrus got busy afterwards as three more of the grey-pallored scourge jumped at him, one going low at his legs, one coming at him from the side and another head-on in a jump. He swiped the two in front of him and turned to deal with the other when Terian's sword sliced it in two in midair, sending the pieces tumbling past Cyrus, who stepped adroitly out of the way to avoid them.

"Because ..." Terian said, and Cyrus saw a hollowness in his eyes that matched what he saw in the pits of eyes that the scourge possessed, "... Alaric asked me to return."

"What about before that?" Cyrus didn't let up, cutting apart a scourge then turning back to Terian. "You were gone six months. Six months you walked the face of Arkaria, could have done anything you wanted. Been anything you wanted. So what was it, Terian? You walked the path of your father in those days, didn't you? Found out how it was, truly was, to stand in his shadow for a good long while, to see all it entailed?"

The dark elf flinched at Cyrus's words. "Who told you?"

"No one 'told' me, at least not in as many words," Cyrus said, and with a shake of his head was back at the battle, sword in motion. "The Gatekeeper told me, when he stunned you to silence with a subtle accusation. Partus told me, when he said the word Aurastra and you reacted—as though rumors of that one hadn't percolated around. That was enough, really, to put it together. You said you were in the Sovereignty before you came back to Sanctuary, that you knew the Sovereign had returned because of it. You were working with your father then. You were doing his bidding."

"Aye," Terian said, after a long, strained pause of minutes. "I was."

"But you came back to us," Cyrus said, and turned his attention forward again.

"I did."

"Why?" Cyrus asked, looking out over the field of the enemy, coming at them like onrushing death, their limitless numbers only broken by the countless corpses left on the ground as the front line retreated.

There was another long pause, and Cyrus prepared to issue the advancing order when the answer came, quiet, subtle. "I told you. Because Alaric asked me to."

Cyrus shook his head. "All right—let's go!" He leaned into the next one of the beasts that came at him, moving forward instead of back, taking an offensive posture instead of staying with the line. This time, however, the line moved around him. The second rank stepped up, and others came with him—Curatio, mace in hand, smashing the skull of one of the foes that crossed him. Nyad was in the center of the formation, her staff at the ready, two druids alongside her, ready to blaze fire and create a gap if needed. Aisling was at his side, as was Terian at the other. Martaina and Scuddar had blades in hand and were fighting their way through as well. A few others were along, but it was a tight-knit formation, a seed pod in the midst of roiling winds of chaos, and as Scuddar and Martaina pulled away from the front line it became a contained little bubble only so wide, a circular line of their own, now separated from the ranks of their fellows.

Cyrus saw Longwell down the line of defense that they had just left, his lance skewering two of the scourge while his men covered him. The dragoon looked up and saw Cyrus, and hesitated for only a moment before pulling his lance free and attacking the next enemy that came against the Galbadien army that backed him. *He does well at the head of an army of his own; he would make a fine General for Sanctuary.* Cyrus looked back and saw Odellan leading a force of men and women to cover Cyrus's advance, keeping the increasing numbers of scourge from pushing them back, fighting desperately to keep forward, to not surrender an inch of ground. *He'll hold til we get back—another fine General.*

They were away from the front rank now by fifty feet, surrounded by the enemy, who came at them two and three deep, crawling over each other trying to attack them. Cyrus's sword remained in motion, constant, flowing, cutting their foes to ribbons of blood in the snow, blooming black flowers of death on the trampled ground of the battlefield.

"It's moving," Martaina said cautiously, her short swords a flurry of motion. "Looks like it's heading away."

"How far are we gonna pursue this thing?" Terian asked. "And please don't say all the way to the depths of the Realm of Death, because we've been there, and it's no party."

"I don't know," Cyrus said, his weapon moving in front of him, where he stood at the head of the attack party. "If it's going to constantly circle away from us, I don't see much need to keep going because there's no way we can chop through these things fast enough to catch it." He brought his sword aloft for a long, swinging chop across an enemy leaping at him, and he watched Praelior glimmer faintly in the close of day.

"Whoa," Terian said, "it stopped."

"Sudden, too," Aisling added. "It was looking at us and just froze." She let her hands work in a blur, cutting at the scourge that was coming for her; she caught it across the face with a quick thrust, then spun low and opened its neck.

There was a quiet that fell over them, then Cyrus saw the shadow in the distance that jutted over the heads of the creatures, and it rose higher, at least four times the height of the beasts around it. "Not small," he breathed.

"It's looking ... right ... at us," Terian said quietly. "I find that very, very unnerving."

"I don't blame you," Aisling said.

Cyrus brought his sword up again and drove Praelior into the skull of a running scourge that came at him. He brought the blade up in the air again and let it descend in a hacking motion, the faint blue glow along the length of the blade gleaming in the early, cloudy twilight.

"Whatever you're doing," Aisling said tightly, "is pissing him off. That thing is looking right at us."

"I'm killing its fellows," Cyrus said, keeping his weapon light and attacking the beasts that continued to come at him. "This is hardly new."

"His eyes are right on you," Terian agreed. "I mean, anchored. It's watching you, not us."

"Do you think it senses he's the General?" Nyad asked.

"Could be," Aisling answered.

"Fine," Cyrus said, raising his sword again into a high guard and slashing a leaping scourge into halves in front of him. "Whatever the reason, let him come—"

"It's your sword," Aisling said as the ground rumbled beneath them, "that's what's catching his attention; and it looks like you get your wish because here he—"

The rumble grew loud now, the shadow in the distance that was as large as a small house was crossing the snowy ground, chewing it up with surprising speed. Where Cyrus would have imagined the creature be ponderously slowly, it was anything but, rumpled skin becoming plain as it closed on them, the same grey of dead flesh covering its massive bones. *It really is the size of a dragon with no wings.* "Are you sure it's my sword that's catching it?"

"Pretty sure," Aisling said, steadying herself as she parried the attack of another one of the creatures. "Every time you raised it where he could see the flash, he watched closer. Now that he's gotten a look at it three times, he's charging us."

"I can't argue with her logic," Terian said, "her judgment in men, but not her logic. It happened exactly as she describes."

"If that thing hits our line he's going to trample his way through," Curatio said as they held there, the beast traveling toward them. "You might want to—"

"Martaina," Cyrus said warningly, "Nyad—"

Arrows were already in flight before he could finish his thoughts; the spells followed, a flame spell that shot in a small burst. It was hardly enough to compare to the long, flaming lines that had blocked scourge advances, but it was enough to light up the sky, to slow the massive creature as it barreled toward them, legs like tree trunks pounding feet the size of stumps against the ground, leaving tracks as big in diameter as Cyrus's shoulders. He clutched Praelior close but kept it moving; *even with this thing charging them down, the smaller ones keep coming, their onslaught always threatening to overpower our defense.*

It grew closer now, a hundred feet away, thundering across the snowy plain like a dead rhino, its eyes different than the others. There was red in them, reminding him of the eye of a white rat he had once looked into when just a boy. There was intelligence burning in there, too, something far beyond the simple ravening hunger of the others, the mass. This one came for him, watched him, not the others. He could see the exhalations of steaming breath as it came forward, jagged teeth as long as his forearm.

"Nyad!" Cyrus called. "Stop him!" *Too fast, he's not slowing enough from the fire and arrows, and if he splits us, we're dead, damned sure guaranteed to be overrun in seconds—*

There was a flash of light, blinding, from behind Cyrus, white in its intensity, and hands yanked him to the side as the thing burst through the center of them, a grey, blurred leg missing him by inches. Cyrus staggered into Aisling, who had pulled him along, and the thing thundered past, stopping just beyond them, snorting into the air as it shook its head. The others, Cyrus realized, had dodged as well, breaking their small formation down the center. They surged back together now, quickly, and a wall of flame burst forth in front of them, in the open, crushed-down snow where the largest of the scourge had charged through, and it half-circled them in a hundred and eighty degrees of protection.

"A little wall," Nyad said, her voice strained, "to minimize the vectors of attack. I won't be able to hold it long."

"He's pinned between us and our army," Cyrus said. "CHARGE!" he called out over the lines. "CHARGE!" There was movement on the line, and Cyrus could see them begin to fight forward, on the Galbadien side and in the middle of the Sanctuary forces. With Nyad's flames stymieing the advance of the scourge behind them, Cyrus moved back toward the army, slicing his way toward the creature—the General, he thought of it—as it stood, shaking its head as though it were trying to get its senses back. It took faltering steps, crushing some of its own kind underfoot.

"Be wary," Curatio said, grasping Cyrus's arm. "That is no ordinary creature. No ordinary soul."

"What is it?" Cyrus asked, pausing for just a second, unable to take his eyes off the beast, standing as it was almost three times his height, with such a massive torso as he had not seen on a creature since Mortus himself or Purgatory before it.

"I have only suspicions," Curatio said icily. "Be careful. There is more to this thing than is readily apparent."

As though it heard them, it turned, red eyes almost aglow. There was another flash of light, and Cyrus realized it was Curatio blinding the creature, which screeched at them in a high bellowing noise of pain and anger, then came at them in a head-down charge that Cyrus only missed by throwing himself aside at the last second. He skidded in the snow and returned to his feet, clearing the ground around him with a sweep of his sword and ending three more of the scourge in the process.

The General of the scourge was now before him again, halted before the wall of fire. The line was close by, now, and Cyrus watched them advance, thinning steadily decreasing numbers in the middle of the battlefield that were pincered between the front rank and Cyrus's separated group. *Less to worry about here, and maybe I can kill this thing before it gets its bearings again.* He took off at a slow run, approaching quietly, sword in hand as the beast tried to blink its eyes back to normal once more, heavy, grey lids shuttering over the red pupils, irises and everything else.

As Cyrus reached it, he jumped—a hop to take him to the lower hindquarters of the thing, where he plunged his blade into the muscle of the left rear thigh. He drew a shriek of rage more than pain, and the leg moved abruptly where he had planted his feet upon landing, jarring him and his sword loose. He fell the five feet or so to the ground, hit the snow and rolled backward and to his feet again. He spun the sword in his grasp, back to facing upright, and brought it forward into a slicing attack as the creature turned into him. He narrowly dodged a butt of its head as it lashed back at him in a sideways motion.

Cyrus brought a sword slash across the side of its wrinkled, rotted face and it let out a roar that flooded his senses with the smell of dead things; a rot of bodies that made him gag and taste the return of his bread and water with stomach bile mixed in for good measure. His ears rang with the sound of it.

A leaping attack onto the giant scourge's back caused it to arch its spine and howl. Aisling landed with her blades buried into the flesh and for a moment it bucked onto its back legs. Cyrus watched the sultry grin of the dark elf vanish as she was flung away. She landed on her feet and slithered quickly back while killing two scourge that blocked her retreat.

There were arrows sticking out of the General's back and head. Cyrus could not see Martaina on the other side of the thing, but her handiwork was obvious when it exposed its other side to him. It came at him, ignoring all else, mouth open and teeth exposed. Cyrus met it head on, driving the sword into its face as it snapped at him. He missed the eyes but caught the snouted nose, leaving a great gash between the nostrils.

"Thick-skinned!" Terian shouted from somewhere to his right. Cyrus saw Scuddar In'shara attack with his curved blade on the end of the tail. Cyrus started to tell the desert man not to bother but was forced to dodge another snap of the jaws.

"Reminds me of a dragon," Cyrus shouted back to Terian. "Any chance this is Ashan'agar? He's dead and was none too happy with me when last we parted."

"Or Kalam," Terian replied, now visible in Cyrus's peripheral vision, fending off the smaller scourge while Cyrus focused on the General. "You did kill him twice, and you sleep on a bed made of his bones."

"It's not what you think," Curatio said, appearing between the two of them. His hand came out, glowed briefly, and Cyrus felt the banal wounds of the fight thus far disappear, minor scrapes knitting themselves shut. He clutched his mace in both hands, holding it ready, and swung it around to crush the skull of one of the scourge, causing it to go dead and fall, twitching, into a pile.

"I think I've killed a couple dragons," Cyrus said, waiting for the beast in front of him to make its next move. It seemed almost overwhelmed, looking at the assault coming at it from all directions— Scuddar had cut off its tail six feet from the tip, Nyad was bombarding it with spells, Martaina had expended a dozen or more arrows around its face. Cyrus watched Terian and Aisling keeping the remaining scourge back while the two druids maintained the wall of flames routing the other scourge away from them and toward the rest of the battle line, which was holding. "This thing looks big enough to be one of them— and it also seems to be carrying one hell of a grudge against me." Cyrus met the gaze of the thing and it honed in on him again, the red eyes flicked downward, off his, away from all the other distractions and locked on to his hands.

"Don't you see?" Curatio said, to his right. "It doesn't care about you at all! It's your sword—that's what it cares about—and not that it's your sword, but that it's Praelior."

There was a bellow from the creature at that moment, deafening, at the sound of Curatio's words. Cyrus blinked and stared at it, holding his blade forward as it stared back at him, ignoring the attacks of all the others that surrounded the dead creature. "Praelior," Cyrus said, and another bellow was loosed, this one louder, more violent, and the beast turned its head down, ready to charge. "It's the sword," Cyrus whispered. "But why?"

"Because," Curatio said, as the General of the scourge began its charge toward them, "it was HIS once upon a time."

Cyrus dodged out of the way as though the creature were a bull, but only just. It was fast, fast enough that the grey head skipped off his elbow, causing it to go numb even as he rolled out of the way of the charge. "No ..." Cyrus muttered, looking at the creature as it turned around, its red eyes finding him again, finding the blade in his hands, his lifeline. "It can't be ..."

"It is," Curatio said simply. "You face all that remains of Drettanden—the God of Courage."

Chapter 85

"Mortus, you bastard," Cyrus said as the Drettanden-scourge turned to come at him again. "What the hell were you doing with these things?"

"Feeding off of them," Curatio answered, and Cyrus heard the tension in his voice. "Ten thousand years in the Realm of Death being used like that and I expect you'd be a bit put out as well."

"God of Courage," Cyrus said, whipping Praelior in front of him. "Well. I believe I've killed gods before."

"Don't—"

Curatio's words were lost as the Drettanden beast charged at him again and Cyrus answered with a bellowing warcry of his own and charged, feeling the strength of Praelior. *Fear is weakness, fear is undue caution, fear of pain is deadly ...*

He vaulted, leaping as the enormous scourge put its head down to ram him, dragging his sword beneath him. *This is how I used to fight, when I was fearless. No timidity, no concern, no worries to bog me down. No ...* He blinked, and thought of Vara. *No worries for the future.* He whipped the blade around as he landed on the other side of Drettanden, and dragged a cut through the beast's hindquarters. "Of all the gods I've met," Cyrus said as he came back to his feet and the creature came around with a roar, "you're actually only the second-most dead." Cyrus frowned. "Does that mean we're going to see Mortus dolled up like this?"

"I rather doubt it," Curatio called from across the field, "since it would appear he was the one trapping the souls that have been loosed here. It would have been difficult for him to trap himself, what with being preoccupied with dying and all, especially since these lot were breaking free roundabout that very time."

"Are there more like you?" Cyrus asked, waving the blade in front of him. "Alaric said that other gods died." There was a bellow from the Drettanden creature at that, and he came at Cyrus again, faster this time, if it was possible. Cyrus started to throw himself to the side and run his blade out but the head came to meet him, the snout landing hard on the inside of his ribcage. Cyrus felt it hit, sending pain shooting through his side and a sudden numbness in his arm. His blade was at full extension; he had been aiming Praelior for the creature's eye as he dodged.

The stinging agony of the blow sent a numbness up his arm, and when he felt the beast's snout come up it jarred his already loosened grip. Praelior went spinning into the air and so did Cyrus, but in the opposite direction. He hit the ground hard, at a bad angle, and heard his shoulder break as he did so, rolling poorly out of it in a way that snapped his neck to the side and left him with a tingling numbness below his waist. *That ... was not good ...*

He rolled as best he could; his eyes alighted on Praelior on the other side of Drettanden. It was aglow, shining against the white snow. Cyrus breathed heavily into the mush pressed into his beard and tried to lift himself up, but failed. A healing spell landed upon him and he felt his strength return, the feeling in his legs come back and he was already in motion, clawing back to his feet, making his own charge at the beast, which was distracted, torn between him and the sword. A flare of flame caught it in the face and turned it away from him, toward the blade, as Cyrus slipped between its legs and leapt for it, landing in a desperate roll as his fingers clinched around the hilt.

He came up with the blade pointed back just in time to see the creature charging again. His sword caught it full in the face as it hit him, and he felt the full fury of its effects this time. There was no abatement of the blow, the full force of the multi-ton creature hit him with solid bone against his armor. His armor held, but pushed the impact into his chest where he felt his ribs shatter against the padding.

Cyrus maintained his grip on Praelior but little else; he was flung through the air in much the same way a doll tossed by a child in rage might. He watched himself arc over the line of his forces, saw them stare at him as he flew overhead like he was on a Griffon or some other such beast. The ground came at him, suddenly, and he was reminded of riding the back of Ashan'agar when he hurtled toward the earth—

Chapter 86

Vara

Day 162 of the Siege of Sanctuary

They're at the walls, she thought as she ran out of her chambers, vaulting down the stairs. The alarm was blaring, of course, had been for a few minutes, but she'd been asleep, deeply, and for some reason the horn hadn't sounded real. The stairs were not terribly crowded, but there was fighting below. *Perhaps not the walls but the foyer. Again.*

She burst out of the last steps to find the full melee in action. Her eyes widened as she did so, because there was something she did not anticipate waiting for her.

Trolls. Full-blooded trolls, taller than Vaste and armored to the maximum. They swung maces and sent men flying; spells hit them and did little enough damage without hitting collaterally and hurting Sanctuary members. A fire was going in the middle of the floor and Vara was amazed, blinking the shock out of her eyes as she stared, stunned—the Sanctuary force was losing.

She pulled her sword and rushed into the fight. *There have to be close to a hundred of them. A hundred trolls. Is the Sovereign mad? He's been keeping his own troll strike force?* The smell was overwhelming, a kind of musty mildew and body odor more rancid than anything she'd ever scented. She made a move to strike the nearest enemy but her sword glanced off his armor. *And mystical armor? What madness is this ...?*

The troll she struck dealt a murderous blow to a warrior with his mace, and Vara watched the man's head sag on a broken neck, limp and loose in a way she'd never seen save for when a paladin she'd trained with broke a shin so badly that the heel of his foot was pointed upward and the bone jutted out of the skin. She swallowed her nausea and looked for the weak point; the trolls were in a formation, though they had appeared to have made a jolly game of the first attacks. There were dead everywhere, more than she could safely count. *More than we could stand to lose and still defend this place.*

A burst of flame came from behind her, carefully targeted at the troll's face. It hit him dead on and he screamed, dropping his weapons and clawing at his helm. It was a full helm, one that completely covered his eyes and his face, and the flame had heated the helm or slipped through the eyeholes. He screamed and threw it off, bending low while holding himself.

Vara took the opening and leapt; the troll was tall, taller than Vaste even by at least a head, but her leap was long. She brought her sword down and struck true. The hearty blow did not remove the head, but made it through enough to get the job done. The troll hit the ground as Vara landed, and she felt the impact through the padding in her boots, as well as the aftershock of the troll slumping over.

She glanced back to see Larana at the entrance to the Great Hall, another spell already in motion. *Goddess help us should they send another round, we'll be bloody dead.*

The trolls were aligned, formed into a rank, with the forward line carrying shields and the back containing at least one dark elven healer, she realized, seeing movement of white robes through the tall, green armored beasts that were backing toward the doors under a timid onslaught from Sanctuary's defenders. *A healer. Bloody hell. We're f—*

There was a glow from Vara's left and she looked to Larana again; there was a blazing ball of fire forming in front of the cook, bigger than a person, and it launched like a catapulted stone right over the top of the formation and into the middle of the trolls. It burst like a blast of water but flooded outward as though it were splashed, a rain of lava coming down on everything inside the troll formation then moving outward to the armored periphery. There were screams louder than any she'd heard and the line broke, trolls running left and right to escape the fires that had shot out from Larana's spell.

"What ... the hells ... was that?" Ryin Ayend said, turning to look at the timid druid. Larana flushed under her frizzed hair and turned away from him, running to the side of the foyer near the stairs.

"I give less than a damn," Vara said, advancing on the trolls, whose formation was broken, as they tried to reform. There were bodies amongst them where the flaming blast from Larana had hit; the healers, dark elves, scorched away to near-nothingness, only bones and ash remained. A few of the trolls had similarly been afflicted, and there was a molten slag of steel wrapped around the remains of charred green flesh where their armor had melted around them.

Her next thought was interrupted by a howl of outrage. A body flew through the massive entrance doors over the heads of the trolls that were blocking it. The body was overlarge, green, and came to rest in the middle of the floor after hitting and rolling. There was a shout from outside, one near-deafening that stopped the action in place. "STAY AWAY FROM LORD VASTE'S FLOWERS!"

Vara shot forward at the nearest troll and aimed for the joint of his armor at the knee, plunging her sword into the open crack while he was still turned toward the commotion outside. She buried the blade up to the hilt and he shrieked, turned and hit her with a short backhand that sent her to the floor. She hit the ground and slid, the feeling of blood rushing warm down her nose. She wiped her face with the back of her gauntlet, and it came back red. The flavor of it was on her lips, tangy with iron, and she spat. *My nose is broken.* She knew it from the pain, from the crack that had accompanied the hit. Her nostrils gushed with it, a warm stream flowed down her front as she rose to a squat and looked at the troll who glared back at her.

With a shout, she launched herself at him, darting under his reach as he swiped for her and tried to catch her with his gauntleted paws. She grabbed her sword from where it remained lodged in his knee and yanked down. She twisted it and prompted another howl from him and then jerked the sword free as she slid around behind him. The troll staggered forward and she saw the gap at the back of his armor and lunged up, sticking it in. She felt it resist and hammered it as hard as she could. He dropped with a squeal and she pulled the weapon out and down, feeling the torsion on it as though it were a pry bar with too much weight against it. She knew it was cutting him terribly inside and she did not care; she listened to his scream as she finished withdrawing it, remembering how it had felt when Archenous Derregnault did it to her. *Curious. I don't remember screaming that much.* With a kick, she pulled it free and sent him forward onto his face, unprotesting. She brought her sword over her head and rammed the blade into the back of his neck.

There were other fights still going on around the foyer, she saw.

Larana had three of the enemy boxed into the corner. Lighting forked out from her hands, causing her foes to jerk and twitch on the ground. The druid's green eyes were cold, colder than Vara could ever recall seeing on the woman before. She let the lightning flow out of her and smoke had begun to pour off the trolls. Vara started to say something but shrugged; there were a dozen more still on their feet around the room in various states of attack. Most were contained; a few were not. She watched as one seized an elven ranger by the neck and shook him then threw him bodily into the hearth, which exploded and knocked the ranger free with a minimum of fire.

"This is not going our way," Vara said quietly and launched herself at one of the trolls who was half bent, slumped over. She brought her sword down into the side of his neck perfectly. The combination of her weight and swing did the trick, and she dragged him down to death. She looked left and saw Mendicant, quietly lurking next to the stonework around the hearth. His hands were extended and Vara could see a group of trolls being frozen solid by his ice spell. Belkan attacked them one by one, shattering their hands, their bodies, and then their heads last of all.

There was a misting just then that swept through as though carried on a strong breeze. Buffeted by a crack of thunder from Larana's lightning spell, Alaric Garaunt appeared, his blade flashing motion, impaling a troll through the back, causing a grunting scream from the creature. Guts spilled upon the floor. The Ghost's eyes were afire, and he moved with his customary speed between battles, mist and then not, solid form striking, attacking, killing all that opposed. When the fight was finished, he stood in the midst of the carnage, his sword dripping blood.

Erith Frostmoor was there, Vara realized, quietly making her way among the bodies, bringing them back to life where needed, casting healing in other places. The carnage was great, the smell of blood and gore filled the room, along with other smells—emptied bowels and bladders and troll stink, the like of which she had not experienced.

"Larana," Alaric said quietly, and Vara's head snapped around to see the druid, lightning still flaring from her fingertips at the bodies of three dead trolls that were near fried, blackened from her magic. "Enough." The mousy druid looked up, and Vara saw the blaze in her eyes, the light coupled with horror of a depth she had not remembered seeing ever before.

"Alaric," Erith said, rising to her feet from healing a ranger who had been gushing blood, "We must close the portal."

Alaric stood stock still in the middle of the room, waiting, his shoulders slumped, his weapon still dripping blood on the floor, drop by drop, onto the great seal in the middle of the room. "To do so would leave our guildmates in Luukessia with no way to return to us."

"If we leave it open," Erith said, "the Sovereign will continue to send wave after wave of enemies upon us. These are mere forays, designed to push us, to test us. His forces are assaulting the wall even now because he's trying things out. If we leave the portal open for when his final assault comes, we're simply making it all the easier for him to crush us."

Alaric's head came up and found Vara, looking her in the eyes. There was not a word exchanged between the two of them, but even behind Alaric's helm Vara could see the eyes, the grey eyes, and saw the flicker that revealed the thoughts. *No. Please, no.*

"Aye," Alaric said, and slowly slid Aterum back into the scabbard at his side. "We cannot continue to fight the enemy at our gates as it grows in strength, and the enemies that would come at our bellies with a dagger in the night."

"Alaric," Vara said, alarmed, "please consider—"

"All I have done is consider," Alaric said, his hand sweeping to encompass the foyer, the carnage around them. "Hundreds dead, and the Sovereign has yet to visit a true horror upon us, one of the choicer delights he has at his command. They come at us from outside the wall right now as well." He shook his head. "I do not wish to abandon our guildmates, but if we do not close the portal ..."

He stopped speaking, and the world around seemed to become louder for Vara, as though a great sweltering hum filled the air. *Chanting. From the army outside. They are making another assault on the gates. Right now. They keep coming ... and coming ...* She bowed her head.

"If we do not close the portal," Alaric said, shaking his head sadly, "they may not have a guild to return to."

Chapter 87

Cyrus

The darkness was total, complete, save for the flashes of spells around him. The battle had gone on for days. They had not seen the Drettanden beast, not since the first time, but that had been plenty enough. Cyrus had died, killed upon impact with the ground, and when he woke up later, behind the lines, he'd found only Calene Raverle at his bedside.

"What happened?" he'd asked in a grog.

"You died," she said simply and handed him a skin of water, which he drank from. The sounds of battle had carried from beyond. He had not asked her anything else, the strike of swords and cries of wounded answering all his further questions and filling in any gaps.

It was days later now. Cyrus had lost count of how many times he'd stood on the front lines since, sword in hand. Drettanden was out there, he could feel the creature instinctively, but it kept well back from the fighting. *And a good thing, too. I need another clash with that beast like I need to be splattered all over the snow.*

"Second rank, coming up!" came a call from behind him. Odellan, he thought, as he swung his sword through the face of a scourge. *Time for relief.* Cyrus eased back into a defensive posture, hacking apart the next scourge to jump at him. It was all he did, anymore, hit these creatures with his sword, stare into their black and soulless eyes and hit another one. *Kill it, kill the next, kill another.* Day after day until this moment had come. He found a dry sort of relief sprinkle over him at the thought of going back behind the lines, of eating something, even bread, possibly some hard cheese. There had been nothing but cheese, all the meat having been consumed by the refugees, but that was to be expected. Bread was enough to go with, bread and water and perhaps some jerky or salted pork every now and again.

Cyrus let himself fade between the next rank of combatants as the second rank took up the battle, and he let his shoulders slump as he placed Praelior back into his scabbard. *How long has it been? Did I ask that this morning? Or was it last night? Two days ago?*

It was dark enough that he could not see the horizon; a few torches lit the way for him, the people behind him carrying them to brighten the battlefield, to cast a little illumination on the moonless night. Heavy clouds hung overhead, and the smell of unwashed armies was heavy. Infection, pain and death were faint, but stronger the farther one got behind the lines.

"How long have we been doing this?" Terian asked, rattling into place beside Cyrus.

"Three weeks," Curatio said, "this time." The elder elf walked slower than usual, his seemingly inexhaustible nature oddly subdued; Cyrus suspected he had been burning life energy again. *That'll cost him over time. Even he can't do that forever without repercussions. Can he?* "Three weeks since we started the defense of Enrant Monge."

There was movement all around them, the armies holding the fight to the field. "I could use a break," Cyrus admitted, and he saw a flash of green ahead in the darkness as a shadow broke toward him, female. "Nyad," he said, acknowledging the wizard with a nod. She hobbled toward him with her staff, coming from behind the lines with a few others, looking only slightly less haggard than he himself—*though she probably just finished a rest. Bad sign for all of us, I think.*

"I have a message for you," she said, brushing blond hair back behind her pointed ears. He watched the motion she made, and it stirred Vara to his tired mind, if only for a second. "The Kings of Luukessia request your presence for a moot."

"A moot, eh?" Cyrus asked. "I suppose it's about time we discussed strategy, seeing as how we've been going about this for a few weeks without much success." She shrugged, and started to brush past him. "Is that it?" he asked, watching her go.

"That's all I've got," the Princess of the Elven Kingdom said, favoring him with a weary smile, "but then I'm rather tired."

"Aren't we all," Cyrus said as he started his path back to the rear of the lines, a few others in tow, "aren't we all."

He found J'anda waiting beside a fire with a few loaves of bread that he wordlessly handed to the new arrivals as they strew themselves around the campsite. The dark elf's face flickered in the light, and he wore no illusion of late. *I wonder why not? He doesn't go to the front because there's no use for him there, you'd think all he'd have to do is sit around and play with illusions.* Cyrus took the bread offered to him wordlessly. "I have a meeting to attend—I'm sorry, a moot." His fingers came up to his eyes and tried to brush away the sleep, but found only dried blood encrusted on his forehead. *I don't even know if that's mine or not.* "I'll return when I'm done."

"I was figuring you'd just collapse wherever you were standing when it was over," Terian said, staring down at the bread clasped between his gauntlets. He stared at it as though it were an adversary; Cyrus knew well what he was feeling, as the taste of it had grown quite old for him as well. "You know, from exhaustion."

"I'll be waiting for you to get back," Aisling said, her eyes glistening in the firelight.

"Or possibly something venereal," Terian muttered. "I don't know where you find the energy," he said, a little louder.

Cyrus didn't answer, instead turning his face toward the largest fire behind the lines, a roaring blaze off in the distance. It was a bonfire, almost, and he could see a few figures gathered around it. *That'll be where they are,* he thought, taking the first trudging steps toward it. *I hope they speak quickly, though I have my doubts that they'll do any such thing.*

The snows had grown deep around his feet but were packed down from having an army treading constantly over them. He heard the crunch with each step and huddled tighter against his cloak, trying to find shelter within it from the wind. He tried to keep his head down, eyes directly off the fires that punctuated the dark around him. The moonless night gave him little enough to see by, and every time he gazed directly into a flame he was forced to blink the afterimage of it out of his sight for a few seconds in order to see the path he was walking. *The only good news is that every bit of foliage that can be burned has already been cleared to do so. I expect they've taken to chopping down the woods around Enrant Monge itself by now, sending it north to us by wagon along with whatever meager supplies they have remaining.*

His nose adjusted to the cold air, to the smell of wood fires burning and nothing cooking. The army was subdued. All joking and laughter seemed to have fled long ago, blanketed over and suppressed like the night sky that wrapped the world above them. *They are weary. These men have fought for weeks, some of them for months. If I'm this tired, I cannot imagine how someone like Odellan feels, having done this now for so long.*

He reached the fire at last, the largest one, and there was a small circle of men in armor standing guard around it. They didn't stop him, stepping aside when his face became visible. He entered the circle and found Longwell sitting on the ground next to Tiernan, both facing the roaring flames. Briyce Unger was there as well, though he was standing. Cyrus did not bother greeting them with anything more than a nod before dropping onto the melting snow next to Longwell. He heard the light squish of the muddied ground, and realized that he truly did not care.

"I see you're in as fine a state as the rest of us, Lord Davidon," Milos Tiernan said.

"Indeed," Longwell said, scarcely turning his head, "we are truly a kingly lot, we masters of Luukessia. Sitting here, far from our halls—" He looked at Unger, a look laced with profound apology, "we who still have halls, that is—sorry—and watch our lands swallowed up a day at a time."

Cyrus felt a stir of pity. *I've felt the same, remembering the dark elves coming to Reikonos. Home.* He felt a slight pang, deep within, buried under layers of weariness. *It's been so long.* "How many more days until we reach Enrant Monge?"

"One," Unger answered, waving behind them. "You can't see it now, because of the darkness, but we're in sight of it."

"In sight of it?" Cyrus sat up, a cold clutch of surprise pushing back the weariness. "The refugees—"

"Evacuated," Tiernan said, staring into the fire. "They've been moved south, toward Actaluere." The King of Actaluere looked up from the flames. "Does anyone want to say it yet?"

There was a pause and a silence, then Briyce Unger spoke. "You speak of the fact that nearly half of Luukessia has been devoured by these things."

"Aye," Tiernan replied. "I received a messenger from Grenwald Ivess today with missives from border towns to the west; the scourge advances along a line, taking the towns south of Actaluere's border with

Syloreas. They are eating my realm now, and my citizenry are moving south as quickly as possible." He looked expectantly at Longwell.

Longwell was glum, but did not look up from the fire. "Much the same to the east. They will be at Harrow's Crossing in another few weeks. Their advance is slower there, in fewer numbers, but enough to consume what remains. The villages and towns have emptied, and the people are in full flight before them. They seem to be following the lead of the battle here, letting their fellows who hammer us on this front be the guiding force for their advance. It gives us time to evacuate the cities and towns, but ... to what purpose?" Longwell gave a weary shrug. "We are soon to run out of land to give them in exchange for the time we buy."

Briyce Unger waved into the darkness. "It seems likely that they'll take Enrant Monge within a day or two of enveloping it—which I suspect will be tomorrow evening, the following morn at the latest. We'll be forced to divide, or perhaps retreat and reform beyond it, adapting to the woodlands to the south as we make our moves." He shook his head. "This is a slow-burning nightmare, like watching Syloreas swept away all over again. I see these things when I sleep, like the avalanches in the passes near Scylax, and everything they touch as they rumble down is dragged with them, to the underworld. Ancestors," he cursed. "We shan't be making so much as a stop to them. We've fought them from Filsharron and have yet to stymie them to delay for so much as a night. They come on, more and more. How many have we killed now?"

"Hundreds of thousands," came Tiernan's hollow reply. "A million or more, perhaps. How many can there be?"

"Of the dead?" Cyrus asked. "Because that's what these things are, the dead, unleashed, furious, ready to consume the still-living. Countless dead. The spirits of all your ancestors and mine, for all we know, unremembering—" He thought of the Drettanden beast, of the attacks it mounted on him, holding the sword that had once been wielded by the God of Courage himself. "Or perhaps not unremembering but beyond reason. Mad with desire and craving life, that elusive thing they've lost."

"We cannot reach the portal," Unger said quietly. "All hope of that is lost. So what now?"

"Keep running," Tiernan said. "Go south. Buy time until we can find some new stratagem."

"There is no new stratagem," Longwell said, his voice edged with sorrow. "This land will be destroyed, filled with the bodies of the dead, with the wreckage of those creatures as they continue to eat us piecemeal."

"Do not lose hope," Cyrus said, but weakly, as though he did not feel it in himself.

Longwell let out a short, sharp bark of a laugh. "Why should I not? Tell me, Cyrus, what is there left to hope for? What is there to believe in besides a long, slow death? Every inch of Luukessia will be covered in these things, and where have we to go? What have we left?"

"Your people," Cyrus answered. "They live yet. They look to each of you for guidance. Show them the way to safety."

"There is no way to safety," Unger said quietly.

"Arkaria," Cyrus said, and the three Kings looked to him. "You are correct, they will continue to come. But perhaps, if we can keep going south, leave the lane of retreat open to the Endless Bridge, we can allow your people to escape. Perhaps if—"

"Perhaps, perhaps, perhaps," Longwell said, and Cyrus could hear the light desperation in his voice as well. "Perhaps we can get to the bridge, perhaps we can herd our entire surviving people over it—those who haven't dropped dead from exposure, from lack of food, from the journey of miles to get there from all over the land—and then we give them ... what? A fool's hope that we can defend the bridge against the onslaught of these things that cannot be stopped? A frantic hope that perhaps they won't follow?"

"What else would you have them do?" Cyrus asked. "Lay down in the snow and wait for death?"

"I could at least believe in the truth of that," Longwell said, folding his hands before him, rubbing his fingers together before the fire, as though he could feel no warmness within them. "I do not believe we will survive these things. I do not believe we were ever meant to."

"A strange thought from a man who only a year ago told me that he didn't believe in gods that controlled our actions."

"It's been a long year," Longwell said and didn't look up.

"Even if we could get ... a portion of our people to the bridge,"

Tiernan spoke up, "and that's a very large 'if,' considering that those traveling from the north have been walking for months already, we could still march them into Arkaria and have these things follow and be no better off than we were before. We would only be prolonging the inevitable."

"What is the alternative?" Unger said, and Cyrus was surprised at the strength of the Sylorean King's conviction. "To yield all hope up as lost?" Unger reached back for his maul and slapped the handle against his hand, a whomping noise that did little more than cause Tiernan and Longwell to look at him. "If we are to lose Luukessia—and I agree, it seems likely—I mean to make these beasts choke on that loss. I won't simply bow down and be chewed up by the unrelenting mouth of this thing. I will take as many of them with me as I can, and I'll fall to my death proud that I went to my last breath fighting for something greater than those things will ever conceive of—my people. My land. My Kingdom. My brethren. Come to it, these things die like beasts, all trying to chew up their next meal. I'll take my death and go willingly, as a man, and for a reason. For Luukkessia." Unger set his jaw and slapped the handle of the maul against his palm again.

There was a silence until Tiernan spoke. "I've never much seen the margin in war. Nor in these endless battles we fight; oh, certainly I'll take what I can get, expand my territory and my tax revenue, but I never understood the call to war. But this ... this slaughter they intend for us, this is truly the most grotesque thing I can remember." He ran a hand through his hair, smoothing it back over his shoulder. "I swore when I took the throne to do my best by my people. I never thought it would require much more than fighting you lot," he waved a hand from Unger to Longwell. "Now we find ourselves staunchest allies, with an enemy that the three of us combined may not be able to defeat. I will fight these things to the death. I gave a sacred oath to protect my Kingdom, and I took it meaning every word I said. I will not go back on it now simply because all that I anticipated has faded away and drawn me into something unimaginable." He pointed toward the southwest, toward his Kingdom. "They are good people, my citizens. Hard workers, not all virtuous but on the whole good people, unworthy of the fate this scourge would visit upon them. I would be a willing sacrifice to stop these things, to stem their advance. I would die in the fight with these monsters, but not til I've given every last drop of my blood for these people." He stood. "I never thought I would say that. Never thought I'd ever see an enemy so horrid that I would stand with the two of you and be willing to die to stop it, but … here we are."

Cyrus waited to see if Longwell would speak. He did not, and after a moment Unger spoke again. "Should we even try to defend Enrant Monge when the moment comes?"

"If the pattern holds," Cyrus said, "they'll envelop it, and perhaps crawl over the top, I don't know. If we defend it, expect to die doing so. Enrant Monge is nothing compared to Scylax."

"You need not worry about Enrant Monge." The voice came from behind them, and Cyrus turned, blinded by the light of the fire still flashing in his eyes. When it faded, a grey cloak was obvious, and a bearded man emerged from the darkness.

"Grenwald Ivess," Briyce Unger said, stepping forward to offer his hand. "What brings you out of the castle?"

"It has hardly escaped our attention that you are nearly upon us," Brother Ivess said, keeping his hands joined together within his sleeves. "I came to speak with you, to discuss our next moves."

"We have decided to retreat toward the Endless Bridge," Tiernan said, still standing, his back now to the fire, shadowing the man. "We will reform south of Enrant Monge and continue the defense, fighting for every inch of ground to give the people time to make their escape."

Grenwald Ivess gave a short nod. "You are brave, I will give you that. The Brotherhood will remain at Enrant Monge as you withdraw, and we will buy you the time to remake your formations."

"That is unnecessary," Unger spoke, his beard shifting as he ran a hand through it. "With the Arkarian magics to cover our retreats and hold lines, you should leave the castle. It is vulnerable and will cause you naught but death when they come. Get your men out, head them toward the southwest, and have your soldiers help the civilians make their way."

Ivess stood still, but Cyrus noted the subtle vibration of his body under the robe. "I'm afraid I cannot do that. The Brotherhood has kept Enrant Monge against all challenges for ten thousand years. We will not abandon it now."

There was a moment of silence before Longwell spoke. "Brother

Ivess, the purpose of Enrant Monge was unity of Luukessia, is it not?"

"It is," Ivess replied.

"We have achieved unity," Longwell said, gesturing to Unger and Tiernan. "We stand united against the darkness before us. There is no need for your Brotherhood to die now for a place, even Enrant Monge. The people of Luukessia are the true beating heart of our land, not some castle, no matter how old it is. We could make much use of your soldiers in our retreat."

"And you shall," Ivess said. "I will send seven hundred and fifty of my thousand with you. The others have all refused to leave. We will remain to defend Enrant Monge against this enemy." He held up a hand as the three Kings began to speak as one. "You must remember, our order is old and set in its ways. To die in defense of Enrant Monge is no great burden for us. It is what we have been living for all our lives. And it is a small thing, really, having seen this day come. You are quite right," he said, looking to Longwell. "We have sought the unification of Luukessia for ten thousand years. Though this is not how we would have hoped it would play out, it is what has happened. Those of us who remain will do so gladly, having known our purpose was fulfilled and that we stood against the single greatest threat our land has ever known."

"I feel as though I should clap," Longwell said, finally standing for himself, "but I suppose instead I will have to content myself with bidding you farewell, Brother Ivess."

"I am not leaving quite yet," Ivess said, and then looked to Tiernan. "I have some unfortunate tidings to deliver as well." His hands emerged from his sleeves, breaking them apart, and he handed a small envelope to Milos Tiernan, who took it and walked back to the fire with it in his hands, ripping it open to pull free a letter, which he proceeded to read.

"What is it?" Unger asked under his breath.

"I am not free to speak for the King of Actaluere," Grenwald Ivess said. "If he means to have you know, he will—"

"DAMN THE MAN!" Milos Tiernan's voice echoed across the camp. He took the note, crumpled it and tossed it into the fire.

"Luukessia is already beset upon by the most fearsome beasts we have ever known," Unger said, "and we've just decided to tell every man, woman and child of our Kingdoms to flee to the edge of the sea and cross it on a bridge that will take us to a foreign land that likely has no place for us. Something tells me that whatever the contents of that letter, they would have to be powerfully bad tidings to agitate King Tiernan after all that's already transpired here tonight."

Tiernan paced, staring for a moment at the flames, regretfully, as though he could snatch back the letter he had cast into it. Grenwald Ivess stared at him quietly, as did Longwell, while Unger stood with his arms folded. "Well?" the King of Syloreas asked. "Out with it."

"Hoygraf," Tiernan said, and it came as more of a curse than any word Cyrus had ever heard spoken. A flash of irritation passed through him, and he thought of the dark haired Baron—*Grand Duke,* he corrected himself—and thought of the faded memory of the last time he'd seen the man, knife in hand.

"Oh, yes, that pestilence," Unger spoke again. "What is your dear brother-in-law up to now? It must be a powerful irritant if it can inspire such rage in you after we've already had such a down evening—"

"Oh, it is," Tiernan said, now pacing before the fire. His head snapped up and he looked to Cyrus. "You."

Cyrus blinked at him. "Me, what?"

"You must come with me," Tiernan said, and took two steps forward to grasp Cyrus by the forearm. Cyrus did not stop him, but stared in mild curiosity at the King's grip on him.

"Come with you where?" Cyrus asked. "We have a battle ahead of us, in case you forgot? So unless it's to the front—"

"To Caenalys," Tiernan said, and Cyrus could feel the slight squeeze of the King's hand even through his armor.

"Your capital?" Cyrus asked. "Any particular reason why?"

"The weather there is bound to be better than it is here," Unger said under his breath.

"Because that's where Hoygraf is," Tiernan said. "He's taken my sister and captured my city with his forces," Cyrus felt a cold sensation plunge through him in spite of the warm fire nearby. "He holds her hostage, claiming to be the new King of Actaluere." Tiernan's cold eyes burned into Cyrus. "He says that if I attempt to reclaim Caenalys, he will kill her."

Chapter 88

Cyrus's walk back to the fire that he shared with the others was long and stumbling. The cold bit at him in a way that felt foreign, as though he hadn't been exposed to it for weeks now. His eyes even felt cold, the air freezing the moisture within them. He cracked his knuckles and moved his tongue around in his dry mouth, as though the bread he'd eaten had formed a coating of yeast around it. The smell of the cold air and the dead around him was overwhelming, and he felt himself stagger from the weariness.

She's his problem now. She's the one who went willingly back to him—for whatever reason. He mentally kicked himself for even thinking it. *She went back for Luukessia. To save her land, to turn her brother loose for war. She went back for—*

"Are you lost?" An arm snugged into the crook of his elbow, giving him strength. He smelled the surprising scent of sweat and—faintly—greenery.

"Martaina," Cyrus said, recovering from a near-stumble. "Watching out for me again?"

"Someone has to."

He took a few steps with her. "You heard?"

She had her cowl up, but he could see her lips present themselves in a pursing motion. "I did."

"You have an opinion."

She smiled, and at this she was almost impish. "Have you ever met a woman who didn't?"

He chuckled in spite of the fatigue. "You think I should go to Caenalys."

She waited before answering and came to a halt, their boots crunching against the packed snow, which still gave a little at every step as Cyrus put his weight onto it. "I think that if Milos Tiernan goes to retake his capital in order to save the hundred thousand people that live within the walls, if he doesn't have some form of magical assistance, then Cattrine Hoygraf will be quite dead by the end of the endeavor."

"I see," Cyrus said, and nodded. "And that raises the likelihood that Hoygraf's army will cause even more damage in Caenalys before he is defeated."

"Tiernan will have to pull more away from this battle in order to break open the city walls and save those people from Hoygraf's delusions," Martaina said. "The man will make Caenalys a mass grave site, bottling himself up with the scourge coming."

"So I would go for the people of the city?" Cyrus asked, watching her without emotion.

"No," Martaina said, "you should go because if you don't, you'll regret it to the day you die." Cyrus opened his mouth to speak and her gloved hand came up and a single finger lay across his lips. "You need not posture before me—the others, perhaps, but there is no fooling someone who has watched you so close as I have. You would have an easier time fooling yourself than me—and you have. You feel for her, even now." She did not break away from staring him down. "In spite of all, just like Vara, it is there. You will regret it to your grave if you don't save her."

With that, Martaina turned loose his arm, and he felt as though a weight had been attached to it instead of lifted, as though she had given him strength and taken it all away at once. "Why?" he asked, in the hush of the night, with the battle still raging somewhere in front of them, and the campfires burning all around him. "I wanted so hard to be rid of her, to be rid of both of them—her and Vara, and yet they still torment me so. Why can't it be ..." he let his voice crack slightly, "simple."

"I believe you have confused matters of the heart with something much different, like fletching, perhaps," she said, drawing an arrow from her quiver. "Make an arrow, put a head on it, make them of uniform length and material for the same purpose, and be done with it. This is not an occupation. It is not a job, or something that you would do in your spare time. This is love, whether you admit it or not. She was there for you in a time of great sorrow, and allowed you to feel something that you had thought lost. Imagined slights and betrayals aside, you gave her your word."

"She went back to him," Cyrus said. "To save her homeland—"

"To save you," Martaina said sharply. "It was for you that she gave herself back. It was for her home that she remained there under the most odious tortures I have ever seen." Martaina took a step closer to him and seized his arm again, and he felt for a moment as though a parent were lecturing him. "Do you know the last time I saw her? We came upon her being whipped while tied to a pillar that your head was stuck upon. She was given your head and told to walk it back to Sanctuary. Aisling managed to rush it back in time, but J'anda and I carried her, bleeding, broken, back to our camp so she could be healed. And she went back to him willingly. Yes, she stayed with him for her homeland, but the bargain was struck to save you." Her hand came loose of him again. "Don't be a fool. However much you may be doubting everything else right now, believe this—she loved you."

Martaina turned and began to walk away, back toward a fire that was not so far off, her feet making no sound on the snow as she went. "You were the first for her, I think." The wind whistled through, but he heard her nonetheless, and shivered as she spoke. "And while you do not owe her your love, you do—in spite of all else—owe her your life."

Chapter 89

The night was terribly cold, and when he lay down next to Aisling, he did what she wanted, perfunctorily, tired, with aching bones and pain in his heart, and he kept himself together through it only by focusing on the smells, the sweat, closing his eyes and remembering the bed in Vernadam. He ran his fingers over her skin, and imagined a back filled with the ripple of scars. Her hands came up to his face, and it was as though he were there again, and the window shone in over him, and a light flashed as he caught his breath, the cold air hitting his lungs, his skin almost as though it were going to burst into flames from overheating. He rolled to his back, off her, and lay there under the bedroll, breathing deep breaths into the air, watching as they fogged in front of him in the firelight.

"That was ... more than I expected from a weary man," Aisling said, pressing the bedroll over her chest but leaving her arms exposed to the night air.

"Yes," Terian said from a few feet away, "it was very impressive. The rest of us are trying to sleep, though, so maybe save the pillow talk for another time?"

"Most of us are polite enough not to comment," J'anda said, "recognizing that in a space like this, where there is no actual privacy, the least we can do is respect each other enough to pretend."

"Gods, man, how much pretending can you do when she's caterwauling like that?" Terian asked. "Ever since they got back from Galbadien, I've been afraid that someone set loose a ghoul from the Waking Woods in our camp. I wake up ready to draw my sword."

"I thought it sounded lovely," Martaina mumbled. "I'm left to be a bit envious over here—"

"Come on," Cyrus said. "I like J'anda's philosophy. We ignore it from the rank and file, you people can't ignore it from me?"

"Usually, yes," Terian said. "Tonight's round of ... I don't even know how to describe that. I'm fair certain you tried to stuff an angry raccoon into your bedroll, not a full-blooded dark elven woman."

Aisling froze next to Cyrus. "I doubt you'd know the difference at this point, as cavalier as you are."

"Oh, I'd know the difference." Cyrus could hear the grin in Terian's voice. "More bite and scratch marks from the dark elf."

There was a pause, and Cyrus looked at Aisling. "Thank you for not biting and scratching," he said. "Much."

She shrugged. "I try to be considerate."

"But not of your neighbors in camp," Terian mumbled.

"Would all of you shut up?" Curatio said. "Please. As mentioned, this is hardly the first time any of us have heard a couple being intimate in our midst. This isn't anything new, I assure you—"

"I'm pretty sure I just heard something done that was new to me," Martaina mumbled.

Curatio glared at her. "And we all have a long day ahead of us. Go to sleep."

There was a murmured assent to the healer's words, and Cyrus felt Aisling next to him but not leaning into him tonight. She was like that sometimes, preferring her space. He lay there, eyes open, staring up at the sky as the first flake of snow made its way down onto his forehead. He felt the next on his cheek, and the one that followed landed on his nose. The fire caught them as they descended, more and more of them now, and Cyrus shook out of the bedroll and quickly dressed, strapping his armor on. That done, he sat by the fire and stared into the flames as they licked at the logs in their midst. He paused and found the nearby pile, brushed the newly fallen snow off of it and threw one on the fire.

"I'm surprised you can't sleep after all that." Cyrus's eyes jumped to the voice, sitting opposite him. It was Curatio, his fair hair highlighted by the dancing flames, watching the fire.

"Things on my mind," Cyrus replied. "You?"

Curatio had his mace lying across his lap and flicked the button to cause the spikes to roll out. "A thing or two I'm thinking about, yes."

"You could have saved the elves," Cyrus said, a thought hitting him out of nowhere. "You and your fellow Old Ones. You could have had a mountain of kids with elven women, and the curse would be beaten out by your own efforts."

Curatio looked at him and raised an eyebrow. "In spite of your obvious efforts at practice, I'm going to hazard a guess you've never had children of your own." He waited for Cyrus's shake of the head. "I couldn't do that, just have a hundred or two hundred children and leave them to be raised by someone else. I had two, only seventy years ago. Two very fine daughters, and it was a chore for me to leave them when they had reached the age of human maturity." He shook his head. "Besides, that wouldn't have saved the elven people. Not really. Our Kingdom has slouched toward death, become stagnant. The people grow old in spirit but only slowly in body. They live long enough to become fearful for their mortality but not immortal enough to take some reckless chances. Their craving for security over all else makes them weak."

"Weak?" Cyrus chuckled. "They aren't that weak."

"They are," Curatio said. "The whole Kingdom totters from it. It'll fall in another thousand years or less, even absent the curse. They need new blood. Having to have their women breed with humans will be good for them. It'll water down that long life, perhaps force them to innovate and grow again instead of always moving too damned slowly to do anything differently. The world is changing around them and if they don't change with it, they'll be irrelevant anyway."

"Pretty cavalier attitude for someone whose race is dying."

Curatio snorted. "My race is already dead. We Old Ones were elves, true elves, if you want to get into an argument of blood purity. The elves that live now are almost as much human as they are elf, when you compare them to me. I am the last of the purebloods, remember? I don't consider this change a bad thing, and it's certainly not as dire of a watering-down as those in Pharesia make it out to be." He shrugged his shoulders. "I don't see it as a problem."

"But you wanted to cure the curse," Cyrus said. "You—"

"I did," Curatio said. "But I've had a year to think about it. Now I wish we'd never gone to the Realm of Death. It was a foolish, fruitless endeavor, and greater than the curse visited upon the elven race is the ill luck that Mortus returned to his realm when he did."

Cyrus let that rest for a moment as he smelled the smoke, felt the curious sensation of the heat on his front from the fire and the cold at his back from the lack. "Curatio ..." The healer's eyes found him in the dark. "I think about that day all the time. If I had ..." Cyrus heard his voice crack. "If I had let her die ... none of this would have happened.

These people wouldn't be losing their country. These people wouldn't have died." The smoke was heavy now, for some reason, and Cyrus felt his words choke off in the back of his throat.

"I was rather hoping you wouldn't see it that way," Curatio said quietly, and the healer looked up. Cyrus saw sparkles on Curatio's cheeks in the light of the campfire, twin streams down toward his chin. "Because all I've been able to think about since we found out what they are is that if Vara had simply let me die ... if I'd been more fearless, stepped up to Mortus and shoved her aside ... none of this would have happened." He stared into the fire. "I would not wish that guilt on anyone. Certainly not you."

"We're going to lose, aren't we?" There was no doubt in Cyrus's voice, but he kept it low, as though he could prevent the very thought from reaching any ears but his and the ones they were intended for.

"You were at the moot," Curatio said, moving his face behind the fire. "I presume you all came to that conclusion."

"Aye," Cyrus said and felt a stir within. "We'll fight to the end, but the aura of defeat is ... it's upon us. We cannot push this foe back, can't seem to stagger them at all. All we do is lose ground, and so the Kings are resolved to give every man, woman and child as much time as possible by fighting a slow retreat to the Endless Bridge." Cyrus swallowed heavily. "We'll bottleneck them there, or try to outrun them, hope they won't cross the water. But Curatio, if they do—"

"You think of Arkaria," Curatio said. "Of them scourging across it as they have this land."

"How can I not?" Cyrus asked, his voice hushed. "How can I not look at what I have wrought—or you, if you prefer to argue it that way, but regardless, the culpability is here at this fire—and not think about how this falls upon us? We may very well have caused the destruction of not only this land but also our own if these things follow across the Sea of Carmas."

Curatio was quiet, the air of a lecturer upon him. "You asked if we are going lose ... I have been in many battles, some more hopeless than this, if you can believe it. I was there at the end of the War of the Gods, when the city of the ancients was destroyed, everything but the Citadel. It was held by the Guildmaster of Requiem, a most stubborn fellow, as a place where the humans of the city—slaves at the time, most of them, stayed to avoid the devastation." Curatio's head came up, and he looked out into the darkness. "That was an impossible fight, if ever there was one. In no way should we have won that. Yet we did; the long night passed and the Citadel still stood where little else remained." He looked back at Cyrus. "You ask me if we're going to lose? I don't think so. The odds are steep, but sometimes all it takes to win is to continue fighting until the odds change for some reason. There is temptation to call it a miracle when that happens. It is not, not always. Something changes, something little, something unexpected in many cases. But when it does change, victory goes to those who endure. We have not lost this fight yet, and we might not. I would tell you the same thing that I told the Guildmaster of Requiem that night in the Citadel when he wavered— 'Do not be afraid.'"

Cyrus blinked and stared at the fire for a spell. "I didn't feel fear for the longest time, you know? They carved it out of me at the Society of Arms, made it so that I didn't feel it anymore. They taught me how to vanquish it, to make myself the master of it and turn it against others."

"No, they didn't," Curatio said quietly. "They taught you how to not care about anything, how to cut yourself off from thoughts of a future, of the idea of people you loved, of having things to believe in beyond the God of War and the path of chaos."

Cyrus stiffened and gave it a moment's thought. "So what if they did? Fearlessness is the most prized attribute of a warrior; it allows you to throw yourself into battles you know you can't win, to give a full commitment to the fight of a sort that an undecided, fearful person won't."

Curatio cleared his throat. "Forgive me for contradicting your years of training, but you're quite wrong. I've seen your Society of Arms at work, and they certainly produce some impressive warriors. But I haven't seen any of them fight half as hard as I saw that Guildmaster fight for his people. No one has the indomitable spirit of a man with a cause in his heart. I've watched Society-trained mercenaries go up against half their number of men defending their homeland and seen the lesser win. You think fearlessness is some strength? It is a lie; it is deception at its most base. A man who has nothing to live for can be fearless because he has nothing to lose. But a man who fears and throws himself into the battle regardless ..." He shrugged lightly. "That is a man I wouldn't care to face in a fight. And I've faced more than my share."

Cyrus ran a hand along his beard. *How can that be right?* "That doesn't make any sense, Curatio. A man filled with fear would be paralyzed, halted in his tracks, hesitant—"

"No," Curatio said. "A man filled with fear who surrenders to it would be all that you describe. But that is the great lie—you see a man charge into battle without hesitation, with great strength, against impossible odds, and you label him fearless. But if you talk to him afterwards, many a man of those would tell you he felt fear the entire time—but greater than his fear of what would happen to him was another—that he would not be there for his brethren in a battle, that he would let them down, that his homeland would be destroyed if he failed to act." He waved his hand around. "These men of Luukessia? Most of them have no hope of one of our healers bringing them back from death, yet they fight to the death and most of them in a manner you might call fearless, yes?"

Cyrus nodded. "Close enough. Some hesitation, not much. But a few, yes."

"You think them fearless?" Curatio smiled grimly. "They are driven by the greatest fear of all—the loss of their homes, their families. They fight hard, harder than our own in many cases. A man fights harder for what he believes in, that's a simple fact. It drives him to overcome that fear, to not let it paralyze him. No, Cyrus, I tell you right now that being fearless is never what would make you a great warrior. Being fearless could make you a great mercenary, perhaps. Believing in something so deeply that you'd not only fight and die for it but that you'd see yourself thrown down for it a hundred times, and get back up a hundred and one—that's what would make you a great warrior." He blinked. "That's what made *him* great."

Cyrus let the quiet wash over him. The smell of the fire and its crackle was all that consumed him; he felt as though his bones were roasting over it. *Cattrine.* He imagined her in Caenalys, tied to a stake. *I've been a fool.* He rose unexpectedly.

"Going somewhere?" Curatio asked, watching him shrewdly.

"Can our army continue to hold the center without me?" Cyrus asked.

"It could." Curatio looked around the flames.

"I have to go to Caenalys," Cyrus said. "I have to …" He felt his cheeks flush. "I have stop Hoygraf from killing Cattrine."

"Hmmm," Curatio said, nodding slowly. "Caenalys is a long ride from here. A far distance."

"It doesn't matter," Cyrus said. He hesitated. "How far would you go to fix a mistake, Curatio?"

The elf raised an eyebrow, but his seriousness never wavered. "All the way to the end, of course."

Cyrus frowned. "The end of what?"

"The end of the world," Curatio said, "or the end of me, whichever came first. When the cost is high enough, could you pledge any less?"

"No," Cyrus said, shaking his head. "Take over command for me, will you? I have to leave."

"Right now?" Curatio asked. "Tonight?"

"Yes," Cyrus said. "Tiernan rode hours ago, with a good portion of his army. I'll need to catch him."

Curatio frowned. "With much of Actaluere's army gone, we will give ground faster. But you already know that, don't you?"

"I do." Cyrus said, feeling for Praelior's hilt. "I'll rejoin you as quickly as I can, and perhaps I'll be able to send back the rest of Actaluere's army when I do."

"That would be good," Curatio said. "As I suspect we'll need them before the end."

"The end of what?" Cyrus said with dry amusement. "The end of you or the end of the world?"

Curatio's smile was there but it was thin. "I'm beginning to think that they may just be one and the same."

Chapter 90

Vara

Day 198 of the Siege of Sanctuary

The Council Chambers were quiet, again, the hearth crackling through the silence. Vara sat at her seat at the table, along with Vaste, who wore a black robe this day, Ryin, Erith, Thad—who was present in his capacity as castellan—and Alaric at the head of the table. Grimness was all that was present; even Vaste seemed to be starved of his usual aura of mischief. He leaned back in his chair, staring out the window behind Alaric. There was a smell of defeat in the air, bitter, and it choked Vara, filled her throat with bile and anger.

"Shall we go through it again?" Ryin asked.

"Has something dramatically changed?" Vaste replied, still staring out the window, emotionless.

"We've been besieged at our very walls eight times in the last thirty days," Ryin said.

"Being neither deaf nor stupid, I not only counted when each of those attempts were made," Vaste said, "but I also heard it moments ago when Thad mentioned that number." The troll's arms were folded across his chest. "I remain unimpressed as they have yet to breach the gates and we have four weeks worth of rotting dark elven carcasses piling up outside our walls. The smell of those is the most fearsome of our worries thus far."

"When will it end?" Ryin asked, and this time no one answered. After he waited a spell, the druid turned around the table. "Can we finally discuss it?"

"If by 'it,' you mean the delightful fashions that will be on display in Reikonos when spring rolls around, then yes, and the sooner we start discussing those lovely and cheery frocks, the better," Vaste answered. "If you mean what I suspect you mean, then no."

"I have no appetite for discussion of frocks—" Vara began.

"Big surprise, there," Vaste said.

She looked daggers at him. "But perhaps there is some merit to considering what the druid is suggesting."

Ryin gave her a wary eye. "I love that you call me 'the druid' instead of using my actual name. I do have one, by the way."

Vara let out a small exhalation. "Very well. Perhaps we should consider what the odious pile of troll dung is suggesting."

"My defecation is not so preposterous as he," Vaste said, "and it smells sweeter, too, like freshly baked cinnamon bread."

"Is it really that difficult," Ryin said, with barely constrained desperation, "to consider evacuating Sanctuary for neutral territory—"

Alaric's hand slammed into the table and the whole thing jumped slightly, causing everyone sitting at it to jump in fright—all save for Thad, who merely continued to watch the whole proceeding without blanching. "We will not abandon Sanctuary."

Vaste looked at the Ghost, his eyebrows raised. "And I thought I was reacting poorly to this entire line of discussion."

"You are," Ryin said, wide-eyed, his entire focus on Alaric, "but I believe our esteemed Guildmaster just aced you quite easily."

"Our walls have held against everything that the dark elves have thrown at us," Alaric said, his face dark, "and we have yet to lose more than a few unfortunate souls in these assaults. I see no reason to consider discussing alarmist measures."

"Alarmist?" Ryin asked. "We're surrounded by the foremost army in the world. They're battering on our door with increasing frequency, aiming to take our keep and burn it to the ground. I'm not ready to retreat either, but it might be useful to have a contingency plan in place should we need to evacuate—"

"There will be no evacuation," Alaric said menacingly, and Vara heard a darker edge to his voice than she had ever known before. "We remain secure with our portal closed, and we will continue to turn back any advances. Let them stay out there, rallied around us. That will keep them from mustering any sort of a counterstroke against Reikonos or the elves, and give the others time to perhaps find their courage and begin to take the war to the Sovereign."

Vara heard him and felt a tingle of despair. She looked to Erith and saw the healer match her own expression. *No one is going to rise against the Sovereign; they've felt the taste of defeat against him, and it is a heavy sauce to flavor the stew. The dwarves and the gnomes will not intervene, and we will sit here as the years tick by, waiting for the Sovereign to lose interest—which he won't.*

"And when the century rolls past," Ryin said calmly, "and some of us are dead of old age or from battle—"

"Or from eating conjured bread and water every day for our entire lives," Vaste interrupted. "And never meeting that special woman who appreciates you for the brilliant, witty, especially handsome green man that you are?" He flicked a look around the table. "That last one is probably just for me."

"How long, Alaric?" Ryin asked. "Sooner or later, the members will grow sick of being trapped here, without true food to eat, or a life to live. Will we ever discuss it? I would even settle for being promised a discussion 'in the fullness of time' at this point. It would be better than thinking we will never—"

"We will not," Alaric said, "yield. Not Sanctuary." There was an unmistakable hardness to the Guildmaster's voice.

"We are all officers here, Alaric," Ryin said quietly. "It should be put to a vote."

"Vote, if you must," Alaric replied, "but I am the Master of Sanctuary. If you wish to flee, you may. Take any who want to go with you. But we will not evacuate entirely; I will not halt our defense. I will not surrender to the dark elves. Not when this place is all that stands ... it is the last bastion that holds against them marshaling their forces and striking the head from the Human Confederation from Reikonos. I will remain here, manning the wall, destroying the Sovereign's every soldier until I can do so no longer." The Ghost's eyes blazed with fire, and Vara could hear the forged steel in his tone. "We will not discuss evacuation because it is not a guild matter, it is a matter of individual choice. If someone chooses to leave, that is their business and they may conduct it. But until such time as the wall breaks and the dark elven hordes pour in upon us, there will be no discussion of abandoning our home—my home—to these chaos-bringers so that they may have their way with it and be on about destroying the next unfortunate target on their army's list."

There was a long and ringing silence, into which no one spoke before Alaric did again. "You are all you dismissed." Without another word, he puffed into a light cloud of smoke and dissolved, more abruptly than Vara had seen him do so before.

There was a slow movement toward the door; Vara stood, not wanting to be the first nor the last. She found herself next to Thad—*that cursed idiot*—and wandered down the stairs awkwardly next to him, trying to speed up just as he did, resulting in an uncomfortable silence between the two of them as they settled into walking down the stairs roughly next to each other. *I should make a conversation attempt, I suppose.* "You, uh—"

His head snapped up at the sound of her voice, and he looked at her in near-shock. "Yes?"

"Sorry," she said. "You had mentioned before that you were of the … Swift Swords when you were in the Society of Arms."

"Indeed I was," he said with a nod.

"I see," Vara said. "And was Cyrus … uhm … a Swift Sword with you as well?"

Thad frowned; she cursed herself for asking as his earnest face crumpled, forehead lined and eyes slightly squinted. "No, ma'am."

"Ah," she said with a nod to the younger man. "He was an Able Axe, then. I'm certain you faced him in those fabled child slaughter games that they presented you lot with under the guise of practices."

"No, ma'am, he wasn't an Able Axe, either," Thad said, shaking his head. "I didn't typically face him in the exercises because they always had the older kids band together to fight him when it was called for."

Vara ran his response through her mind, trying to make sense of it. "I'm sorry. You said he wasn't a Swift Sword and then you said he wasn't an Able Axe. But I remember distinctly being told that every single member of the Society is assigned a Blood Family, for training purposes, for espirit de corps. So if he wasn't either of those, then … was there a perhaps a third Blood Family I am unaware of?"

"Ah, no," Thad said with an almost embarrassed shake of the head.

I am dealing with a moron of some sort, as I have always suspected. Perhaps I should speak slowly in order for him to understand me. "Then he was … not a member of the Society of Arms in Reikonos?"

"No, he was," Thad said. The warrior cocked his head at her. "You don't know, do you?"

Vara felt the slow, hammering burn of annoyance in her cheeks, the sound of blood rushing into her ears flared and she restrained her hand from doing that familiar thing again, seeking the hilt of her sword. *Why must I continue to be like him in this damnable habit? I'm not actually going to strike this fool down, after all, much as it might entice me ...* "No, I suppose I don't know what you're hinting at. Perhaps you'd be so kind as to enlighten me rather than standing there and making me feel like a complete fool."

Thad's mouth opened wide and then shut abruptly. "I'm sorry," he stammered. "I thought everyone knew by now, with the rumors that went around awhile back."

Vara felt a surge of impatience. "I seem like the sort who trades in rumors, do I? Do you see me with an abundance of people to keep me informed of the latest tidbits of gossip?"

"No!" A slight look of shock ran over his face. "I don't mean suggest you're the disagreeable sort or anything of that nature—"

Vara leaned in closer to the warrior in red, causing him to shut up immediately. "I am ... very disagreeable. And I am about to become much more so if the next words out of your mouth aren't a succinct explanation of that which you clearly realize I do not know regarding Cyrus and the Society of Arms."

"He was never in a Blood Family," Thad said. "It happens, rarely, that a recruit for whatever reason isn't given one, because the instructors want him to be killed off in the training process."

Vara frowned at him; no difficult feat since her natural state was to be somewhat displeased. "Yet he clearly has survived to this point, so it cannot have been all that bad—"

"He was the first," Thad said with a gulp. "The first to make it past a year without a Blood Family, the first to *graduate* without one. The strongest warrior they ever graduated, I think, because he did it all on his own."

She stared at him through half-lidded eyes. "No family? None?"

He shook his head. "He slept on his own, hid in a different place every night. Took all his meals by himself." Thad's jaw moved, but no words came out for a moment. "I don't ... I mean, the instructors would talk to him when they gave him orders, but uh ... no one else was allowed to say anything to him. No fraternizing with the enemy, you know, it's Blood Family law ..."

Vara felt a sudden dryness in her mouth, the taste of bitter acrimony faded away. "And he was there from the time he was ..."

"Six," Thad said helpfully. "One of the youngest. He's legend there, I mean ... *legend*."

"Yet unable to find a guild when he left," she said quietly, pondering.

"Oh, that was because of the Guildmaster of the Society," Thad said. "I mean, League recommendation counts for a lot in most guilds. I doubt he even knew it, but I heard a couple warriors in my last guild talk about it. Cyrus got struck down every guild he applied to—they'd use him for a while, an application period, and then cast him off, him and the other two with him. That's why they ended up starting their own guild." Thad blanched. "Don't tell him I told you that; like I said, I don't think he knows he was blacklisted by the Society. I'm actually a little surprised that Alaric wouldn't have checked with the Society Guildmaster before—"

All Thad's words fell upon a great deafness in Vara's ears; they came, she heard them vaguely, but they faded in the background, as though he were speaking to her at a distance of miles instead of a foot away. *No father. No mother since he was six. Not a friend nor a confidant until age eighteen? A wife who left him, a best friend who died. Goddess, I hate pity. Truly, I hate it. Yet there it is, all the same. Pity and a great swell of ... sympathy.* She did not acknowledge Thad again, merely started her way back up the stairs. He mouthed some words behind her but she waved him off with one hand and climbed, passing the others who were finally descending, went all the way up to her quarters and lay down on the bed.

And for some reason she could not explain, even when she thought about it at great length, she cried over the thought of Cyrus Davidon's upbringing for the next several hours, and when she stopped, it was only because she had no tears left to shed.

Chapter 91

Cyrus

The sun rose on trees glazed with ice on the branches. It caught Cyrus riding south, fatigue catching him ahorse, bumping along to the briskness of early morning. The snowstorm he had ridden through in the night had settled into a winter's mix, and his beard was as frosted as the tree branches, though he had used his fingers to attempt to brush it loose every now and again. *At least the rest of me is warm.* He tugged on Windrider's reins; the horse was at no more than a canter now. Looking back, he saw Enrant Monge just barely on the horizon, a boxy shape behind him on a hill.

Enrant Monge is a majestic castle, no doubt. A tremendous place, and one so wrapped up in the glories of Luukessia that I can see why the Brothers are willing to die for it. He felt a tug of regret. *And die they shall, if Scylax is any sort of indication. All it would take is for Drettanden—if that's what that thing truly is—to come charging at the gates and I suspect they would buckle after only a few good hits. Still,* he looked back, *the majesty of that place is not to be underestimated.* Even as a shape on the horizon, the squarish nature of the outside walls, the soaring towers and the meaning behind it all gave him a feeling of sadness. *They're going to lose ... everything.*

He started to turn again to the road ahead but blinked and looked back, down the barely noticeable track that he knew to be the road. Wagon ruts were the only sign that this was a path, and they were partially covered over from the snowstorms. There were figures coming up behind him, on horses, their hooves struggling through the snow. They were moving faster than he was, and he pondered, just for a moment, pulling Praelior out and readying for them. Then he caught the first sight of deep blue skin under robes, and waited instead, keeping Windrider in place.

"You left without saying goodbye," J'anda said as his horse trotted along, each step a slight struggle with the snowy road. "If there is one thing I simply cannot abide, it is the thought of a trusted comrade and friend throwing himself into oblivion without so much as a 'fare thee well' before doing so."

Cyrus watched the others who were with him; Aisling was easy enough to pick out, with her sullen eyes, her easy smile long gone, no trace of it left on her face. Martaina, too, though her eyes were hidden by her cowl. "So you came to say goodbye?" Cyrus asked.

"No, fool, we came to go with you." J'anda waved a hand at him dismissively. "My talents are wasted here, conjuring bread all the day long. But sieging the city by the sea? You may have use for an enchanter's skill yet." He said it with a twinkle in his eye.

"And you?" Cyrus asked Martaina.

"I'm here to keep an eye on you," she said grudgingly, "as I said I would. I expect you'll be easier to keep an eye on if you remain alive and in close range."

Cyrus looked to Aisling but didn't say anything. She smoldered, looking back at him. "I told you," she said finally, "I'm here to give you what you need, no questions."

Cyrus looked back at her. "Aisling ... I'm s—"

"Don't." It was only a little pointed, the way she said it. She didn't flinch, didn't react, just took the reins of her horse and urged it forward to lead the way along the snowy road.

"How far is it to Caenalys?" J'anda asked, starting his horse forward, the smooth landscape a long, rolling plain of white broken only by the snow-wrapped trees, jutting out of it like an ocean of bones.

"A moon's change, at least," Martaina replied, coming alongside him. Aisling was ahead of them both now, and Cyrus was only just turning Windrider around to follow.

"A month?" J'anda asked. "With those two in a snit? Hm." The enchanter shook his head. "Well, that won't be dreadfully uncomfortable."

Chapter 92

They caught up with the Army of Actaluere on the following day, and outrode them three days later, packs on their backs and laden with provisions. The sky remained a dreary color for the most part; only the occasional daybreak found beauteous pink in the sky with the dawn. Most mornings it was grey all the way through, and the snowy ground persisted for the first week, the brisk air chilling Cyrus's nose until they could set the fire every evening.

The flavor of hard cheese was long familiar to them by the second week, coupled with the conjured bread that J'anda could provide, and the smaller servings of salted pork and pickled eggs that helped break the monotony. The snow began to disappear in the second week, becoming patchier and more occasional until one day it yielded to brown earth and bare trees, with leaves still on the ground, uncovered. They rode through deep brown woods that smelled of fresh air, found empty houses and inns along the way that had been stripped of everything edible by the masses of refugees passing down the highway. They began to run across stragglers and slow-moving bands a day later. By the end of the week they traveled on full roads, and every soul they encountered was a beggar, starving for the most part.

The smell was overwhelming, a stink of a people who had not bathed in a month, coupled with horses, manure, and all manner of other things—poor food, muddy roads. The sound of them was incredible, babies and children crying from hunger. J'anda conjured bread from morning until long after the sun had gone down and yet still had not enough to provision the people they encountered. Cyrus watched the faces that came to them, tired, beleaguered, desperate in some cases.

Martaina killed a cutthroat who crept into their camp in the dead of night with a sword. A few nights later a haggard man had tried to corner Aisling when she had gone off into the woods on her own, and when she returned she casually mentioned that someone had tried to "force his way with her." After an alarmed query from Cyrus, she led them to the place where the body lay, already stripped of its belongings. Though he cast a sidelong glance at her, Cyrus did not bother to ask her whether the man had any possessions of note before he had died.

Aisling had not forgiven Cyrus in the truest sense of the word, he could tell. She had not, however, withheld her favors from him, not even for a night after rejoining him. She did, however, become less charitable and—he noted one morning while feeling the shape of a bruise on his neck—more vengeful. He did not complain, continuing to lie with her at night.

By the third week of their journey, the ground had returned to a somewhat green state, albeit a darkened one. Some of the trees retained their leaves, and the roads became choked with refugees. Cyrus watched one day as J'anda's spells to conjure bread turned from their usual white aura to a reddish one and he shook the enchanter by the shoulder. "Stop," Cyrus said.

"I can't," the dark elf said, his lower lip quivering, "these people are starving."

"You won't do them any good if you kill yourself trying to feed them." Cyrus watched the enchanter carefully for the rest of the trip and warned Martaina to do the same. He rode in silence, for the most part, the perpetual glimmer gone from his eyes, staring ahead in silence. He conjured bread at every occasion, and water too when necessary, for anyone he could as they passed.

On the fourth week, the sun came out and the land turned flatter, the road less winding. "We'll have entered the lands around Caenalys by now," Martaina said, studying a hand-drawn map that had guided them thus far. "There is a signpost ahead just a bit farther, and it will put us upon the last leg of the way." She let her jaw tighten. "After that, we'll be at the gates soon enough."

"Are you certain about this?" Aisling asked, flicking her eyes to him in the barest hint of impatience.

Cyrus paused. "Certain as I can be. The people of this city deserve a chance to flee, to survive, and the Baroness ..." he felt his throat constrict. "I owe her a debt."

"Is that all?" Aisling asked.

Cyrus looked down. "It's all I've got for now. If that army has to besiege the city, she dies. She suffered a lot to make sure I lived. I owe her."

"She wasn't the only one who helped bring you back to life," Aisling said quietly. "Don't forget that."

He looked at her evenly. "I haven't."

That night she was particularly vicious, more frenzied than before, and he felt the pain of it in the following morning's ride, with scabbed-over nail marks along his back. He felt them pulse and sear with each step of the horse, each bump in the road.

The land was green now, green with spring, grasses gone dormant for the winter returning to life. "This is canal country," Martaina said to him as they rode along, "we are likely no more than two days' ride from the city."

"And an army," Cyrus said.

"I haven't forgotten them, I assure you," Martaina said with a roll of the eyes.

The flat lands and coastal swamps gave them a day of blessed warmth at the next dawn. The sun shone down and Cyrus felt the heat upon his armor at midday, and realized that he felt warm for the first time outside the presence of a fire in months.

"I could become used to this," J'anda said, turning his face to the sun, closing his eyes and letting his horse meander down the path."

"What can we expect when we get there?" Aisling asked.

"We should be outside the city gates in a few hours," Cyrus said, though he saw no sign of any city on the flat horizon. There were few enough travelers and refugees here, most having turned southeast at the previous crossroads. There were scarcely any travelers at all, and their number grew sparser as the day went on.

"It's a fishing town, a seaport," Martaina said, repeating the same information that Milos Tiernan had given them before they departed the army. "But the port is closed, I suppose, and the gates under watch."

"If King Hoygraf can't hold the city voluntarily," Cyrus said, "he'll squeeze it to death by force."

J'anda looked at Cyrus accusingly. "When you pick an enemy, you don't do it in half measures, do you?"

"My only regret is only half-killing him," Cyrus said.

Martaina cast him a cocked eyebrow. "That's your only regret? Not—" She stopped and looked to Aisling, who glanced at her sideways without turning her head. "Never mind."

Night fell, the skies darkened, and soon enough the swaying of the trees was only visible by moonlight. They rode on, quietly. The gates of the city grew larger in the distance, braziers lit all around the perimeter of the wall to give the city an imposing feel. It was wide, huge.

"Any bets on them seeing this coming?" J'anda said.

"I'm not much of a gambler these days," Martaina replied, tense.

The walls were wide and flat, and reached a hundred feet up. There was nothing visible behind them save for a few lanterns hung in high towers. *We should have come in the daylight. It would have been more glorious to see this city the way Cattrine described it to me.*

The thundering hooves of the horses around Cyrus lulled him into the quiet as they went. "Are you sure you've got this, J'anda?"

"Fear not," the enchanter said. "You have never looked more unthreatening than you do right now."

"Glorious," Cyrus said, "my life's ambition, fulfilled."

"Look at me," Martaina said, "I'm no different than I was."

"I am," Aisling said, holding out a tanned, browned hand. "Human is not a good look for me." She swiveled to look at Cyrus. "Is it?"

He favored her with a once-over. "I don't mind it. You look good."

She gave him a slow nod. "Maybe I'll keep it on. For later. Variety, you know."

There was a silence around them, broken only by the sound of the horses' hooves hitting the road. "What a fabulously misplaced use for my beautiful magics," J'anda said mournfully.

"Try and pretend you haven't used them for the same purposes or worse," Aisling snapped at him. The enchanter shrugged with a slight smile of mystery.

The flat, dark colors of the stone wall were rising at them. The gates were open—*thank the gods*—as they came along the last few hundred feet. Guards were in the shadows, Cyrus could sense them, and they stepped out upon the approach of the party on horseback. Cyrus stared at them.

"What have we got here?" the head guard asked, utterly disinterested.

"I'm escorting a party of holy women into the Temple of Our Forebearers," J'anda said. "You know, helpers to prepare the dead for their departure."

One of the guards shot his partner a look. "You know the city is closed to exit? Once you go in, you don't come out until it reopens."

"I'm quite fine with that," J'anda's human face smiled. "Once I've dropped the ladies off, there are a few locations I'm keen to visit. Traveling with holy women ... you understand. It provides little enough comfort."

The guard guffawed. "All right, then. In you go. It's after dark, and martial law is in force, so be quick to your destination. No loitering about in the streets, or you'll be arrested." He lowered his voice and leaned toward J'anda. "If it's female companionship you're looking for, try the Scalded Dog out near the seaport. Very fine wenches there and reasonable as well."

"Oh, I've heard good things," J'anda said. "But as I believe your sailors say, 'any old port in a storm,' yes?"

The guards shared a laugh at that one. "Too right. Be on your way, then. Don't dawdle."

"Oh, I shan't," J'anda said, spurring his horse forward to lead the way. "I'm in too much of a hurry to get where I'm going to linger for long."

Another laugh filled the night as they went on, crossing through the torchlit dark under the portcullis. There were murder holes above, Cyrus saw, archers with arrows pointed down at them as they passed. Cyrus kept his mouth shut, waiting for the tension to subside.

There was a definite quiet as they went, and when the tunnel underpass for the wall opened up, they found themselves on a wide avenue. Small buildings lined either side of it, most of them three stories, set back off a dirt path in the center that was deeply rutted with wagon tracks. It had turned to mud, Cyrus realized, from spring rains.

Ahead was clearly the palace, and palatial it was, with columns and a dome that reached into the sky. There was a bridge ahead, one that dipped over a canal running through the city. *There are dozens of them, allowing the citizens to navigate on water as easily as they do on the streets.*

There was a commotion behind them, something atop the wall, and Cyrus turned to listen. He saw Martaina freeze, her face hidden behind a conjured mask that covered her features save for her eyes. That was plenty enough to give Cyrus the impression that something was desperately wrong. Just behind them, the clanking of the portcullis as it began to descend and the shouts of "ALARUM!" rang over the wall.

"What is it?" Cyrus asked, grasping at Martaina's shoulder. "What's wrong? Is the Army of Actaluere here already?"

"No," she said with a shake of the head. "Worse."

There was scurrying atop the walls, and screams, shouts that were undistinguishable to Cyrus's ears. Bells began to ring in the streets, and suddenly an aroma hit him, overpowering, with the wind that rushed through the rapidly closing portcullis—death, rot ... fear. In the blackness beyond the lowering gate he could see nothing but the tingle ran over his flesh nonetheless and his mouth filled with a bitter, acrid flavor as the blood pumped through his veins. He watched as the gates began to close behind that latticed portcullis, as it clanged to the ground and reverberated through the tunnel. A single word bubbled to his lips, and he knew by all that happened around him that he was right, even before Martaina confirmed it.

"Scourge."

Chapter 93

Vara

Day 209 of the Siege of Sanctuary

The rattle of the remaining siege engines rolling away from the wall was loud, but not overpowering. Vara stood on the heights, smelling the fetid waste in the no man's land below her, watched the last few surviving siege towers limping away across the muddied plain and breathed a sigh that came out of her slowly, as though she could scarcely believe it was through. *Another done. Another repelled.*

"That's right!" A voice cried to her left. She turned to see Thad, standing there in his red armor, waving his sword over the wall at the backs of the retreating dark elven army. "Remember this! This is what happens when you mess with the best!"

"Or in your case," Vara said acidly, "the barely competent." She tasted the burning on her lips of the words, as though they were real, as though they were vile in truth as well as content, and she shrugged involuntarily. She leaned heavily against the tooth of the battlement before her and felt her whole weight lean with her, armor and all. It felt heavy, in spite of the enchantments. *It's not the weight of the armor, it's the weight of the burden. The defense of this place is dragging me down, it becomes all I've ever lived and all I'm living for.* She ran a hand across her face and flipped up the nose guard on her helm, removing the little line from her vision where it sat to protect her face from harm. *It is almost as though I can remember nothing before this.*

"Nasty bit of business, isn't it?" She turned her gaze to the side, where she caught Partus looking at her with a gap-toothed grin. "They keep coming, we keep slaying them. The Sovereign has to have thrown away fifteen, twenty thousand lives here thus far, and all on these half-arsed attacks we keep turning back. You'd think he'd make a concerted push sooner or later."

"I don't think I wish to see your definition of a concerted push."

"It'd involve throwing more and more men at the gate," Partus said, "taking up where their brethren fell, grabbing the battering ram when the men who hold it drop it—"

"Would you want to grab that?" she pointed to the gate where the last battering ram the dark elves had used was lying. It was long, about thirty feet, a felled tree with the ends sawed off, a massive log. The men who carried it lay dead around it, all of them in flames, as was the ram.

"Not as it is, no," the dwarf said with a shrug. "But you put a wizard and a druid close up by it, they use a water spell to extinguish it, you throw another forty men under it and keep hammering until the gates give."

"Our gates do not give," she said simply, but her eyes remained on the flaming ram, where it burned on the once clearly defined dirt road that led to the Sanctuary gates. It had become indistinguishable from the fields around it, however, because of attacks during rainy times, and the entire verdant plain for several hundred feet around the Sanctuary walls had become nothing but a slick mudscape, a messy pit of dead bodies, discarded armor and weapons, and only a few stubborn patches of grass that had not yet been wiped out.

"Every gate gives if you hammer it hard enough and long enough," Partus said, still looking at her and not the battlefield. "Take you, for instance—" She gave him a disgusted, scathing look and he held up his hands before him in surrender, with amusement. "Now, now. We've known each other a good long time, Vara, since the days of Alliance yore. I've always respected you—"

"You've rarely seen me, since I attended few enough Alliance functions and never went to the meetings."

"Not after a time," Partus said with a grin, "but at first you did, when you were new and sweetly innocent to the way things ran." He ignored her searing look at the remark. "Anyhow, you've always had such a charming personality, I just can't tell you how amazed I was when I heard that the one who finally broke down your gates was that blockhead Davidon—"

"Stop talking," she said. This time there was no menace to her voice, only a whisper that sounded like thunder to her ears.

"Ooooh," Partus said, hands still up in front of him. He wiggled his fingers and made an amused sound. "So it's true, is it? I had always wondered if you'd ever melt for a man, but Davidon? Really? What is it about him that has women throwing themselves at his feet? The Princess of Actaluere, that smutty little rogue dark elf, and you—"

"Stop what you're saying right now," Vara raised her hand at him, "or I'll—"

"Now, now," Partus replied, waving his own hand, which was still pointed at her, "let's not be hostile about things. Assuming you *could* fire off a blast before I did, which is a bit iffy because I've seen you work your magic and you're just not that fast—but assuming you did, I don't think it would end out well for you, my dear, because you know I wouldn't go far, and I'd be back in mere moments to slaughter you—"

There was the sound of an explosive blast, and Partus was launched to the side, smashing into the battlement wall. Vara heard the crack of his bones as his leg and hip hit the stone and broke. His upper body was carried by the force of the spell into a flip, his hip the center of gravity. He tipped upside down and was flung, end over end, off the wall. Vara leaned over to look and saw the dwarf fall in a spiral from his momentum, and when he landed with a crack, he did not stir, eyes wide, staring up at the battlements, dead.

"You wished to leave Sanctuary, Partus," came Alaric's voice, to Vara's right. She turned and saw him there, his hand still extended, even as he spoke to the empty space where the dwarf had stood only a moment before. "Now I have granted your wish." Without bothering to look over the battlement at the fallen dwarf, the Ghost turned, walking back to the tower nearest them, and disappeared into the darkness without another word.

Chapter 94

Cyrus

The sound of troops filled the street, guards shouting, men marching in armor. The clatter of the gates shutting was complete, and the smells of death were cut off abruptly, replaced with the city scents—old baked bread from communal ovens, torch oil, and latrines. Cyrus whipped his head around, and saw more soldiers running toward them, toward the walls, the gates, and felt the padding of his armor brush against him as he tried to decide what to do next. "The palace," Cyrus said. "If the scourge is coming now, they'll be pulling defenses. We need to go."

"No time like the present," J'anda said as the first wave of guards began to pass them. He waved his hand, and Cyrus saw the enchanter's appearance change from a human man in robes to an armored guard wearing the livery of Grand Duke Hoygraf's Green Hill guard. Cyrus looked down and saw his armor masked in the same way. Martaina and Aisling were now absent, but beside him on horseback were two others, similarly clad.

"Let's go," Cyrus said, and urged Windrider forward, holding as close to the side of the street as possible. The soldiers made way for them as they passed, the hooves of their horses splattering in the muddy street. The steady clang of armored men on the march echoed off the houses to either side, and Cyrus watched as the lines of infantry maintained their formations, holding to their discipline as they headed for the gates. "That'll be important for them," he said out loud, "especially as those things come over the walls."

"This is not going to end pretty," Martaina said, glancing back nervously, her Actaluerean helm sitting atop a blond man's head. That her soft voice came through in a husky whisper was even stranger to Cyrus, who had to think about it for a moment to remember it was, in fact, her.

They rode on, down an alley onto a side street and on toward the palace, with its columns and massive steps. Guards were peeling off from the gates as they got close, the dirt streets an unpleasantly muddy place to be. They rode through without being questioned or inspected, the chaos wild around them. There was a harbor visible to their left, dark waters lapping at the piers; the palace was built on the water but rose stories above it, high enough that the entire side was protected by the sheer face of the palace's eastern walls. The back of it was against the ocean too, Cyrus realized as they entered the courtyard; he wondered if there was an easy way out. The shouts of the palace guard filled the air, crackling as the portcullis to the palace's smaller curtain wall began to crank slowly shut. A few more guards rushed to beat the closing.

"Let us hope there is another way out," J'anda said, eyeing the gate closing behind them. "If it truly is the scourge, then I don't expect we'll be going out the front."

"Aye," Martaina said. "We're bottled up now."

"Well, let's be quick about this, then," Cyrus said, eyeing the palace steps. "Aw, hells, why be polite and shy?" He urged Windrider forward and the horse began to climb the front steps, a few at a time with a neigh. Cyrus heard the clopping of hooves on the stone and knew the others were following behind. The palace steps narrowed toward the top, running into a column-lined portico and within moments Cyrus was under it, a few guards staring at him in shock. "Urgent message for the King," he called as he passed. "Urgent!" At a checkpoint ahead he saw two guards stare at him, crossed poleaxes ineffectually blocking his path. At the sound of his cry, they uncrossed them, then stepped aside as he thundered into the palace on Windrider's back.

"What are you going to do when they find out you don't have a message?" he heard Martaina say behind him.

"I actually do have a message for King Hoygraf," Cyrus said tersely.

"I don't think he's going to want to hear that one," Martaina replied.

"No one ever wants to hear bad news," Cyrus said. "It still shows up anyway. Urgent message for the King!" he called, and a bevy of guards ahead of him parted in a slow sea, the two closest to the bronze doors behind them opening them for Cyrus to pass. As the doors opened, he could see a throne room ahead, a high seat in a wider room than Vernadam's. Columns lined either side of the room and to his left there was an open balcony that overlooked the sea running the length of the room. There were a few guards scattered about that came to attention as he entered, and Cyrus dismounted swiftly, saluting Hoygraf as he did so.

Hoygraf rose from his seat on the great throne as Cyrus dismounted. The man still carried his obsidian cane, leaning heavily upon it as he pulled up. Cyrus froze for only a beat as he looked to the seat next to Hoygraf; Cattrine sat there, upon a grand throne with a teal backing. Hoygraf's seat was teal as well, and the ocean's salt air seemed to fill the room around them as Cyrus stared at Cattrine. Her hair was only neck-length, now. She watched him without interest, slumped slightly to the side in her chair, her neck limp and angled, as though even sitting were some great effort for her. Her left eye was blacked, and there was a crust of blood at her lip. Her hand came up self-consciously to daub at her face as Cyrus began to stride across the wide, blue carpet toward the throne, his head bowed.

"Your majesty," Cyrus said, traversing the carpet in quick steps, struggling to remain nonchalant and keep his hands free from his sword belt. *One chance at this. The minute I draw on him I'm going to have a fight on my hands. Ballsy effort has taken us this far, I just need a minute to make this happen.*

"That's close enough," Hoygraf said, stopping at the edge of the rise of steps. He leaned heavily on his cane for support, stooping over like an old man.

"As you wish, m'lord," Cyrus said, and knelt to one knee roughly ten feet away from the man, bowing his head.

"You ride horses into my throne room," Hoygraf said, straining at each word. "If you have an urgent message, deliver it."

"Yes, m'lord," Cyrus said, adding a tone of contrition. "M'lord, the scourge appears on the horizon."

Hoygraf let out a small hiss of disbelief. "Yes, I know that, you idiot. We have lookouts posted that rode back here with that message long before you." Hoygraf frowned at him. "Is that your only message? Why didn't you report that to a guard captain?"

"Because, m'lord," Cyrus said, and bowed lower, obscuring his upper body as he reached for his sword, "I have a further message to deliver, one meant for you and you alone."

Hoygraf's voice bled caution, and Cyrus could hear the man standing up straighter. "Oh? And what might that be?"

"That the westerner, Cyrus Davidon, even now rides for Caenalys and means to strike you down in your own throne room," Cyrus said, his hand finding Praelior's hilt even under the illusion."

"Well," Hoygraf said with dark amusement, "I doubt he'll be getting through the hundreds of thousands of those beasts filling every square inch of ground outside our city gates, but I do welcome him to try. I don't fear that petty coward, who hides his vileness and impotence behind western magics and wickedness."

"I believe if you were to consult with your Lady, you'd find he's anything but impotent," Cyrus said, raising his head with a smile, "but you are quite right that he hides behind western magics. But only because sometimes ... it's the fastest way into your enemy's throne room." Cyrus stood, letting his blade hang by his side. "Oh, and not to correct the faux-King in his own chambers, but ... you do fear me. You always have, since the day I put a sword in your belly and left you to die."

Hoygraf reached for the tip of his cane and ripped it aside, revealing a narrow blade. "Perhaps you mistake hate for fear; I fear no man, especially not a man I have personally removed the head from in the past and shall again. Guards!" He called out, his voice reverberating through the chamber.

Cyrus looked left and right, and in the eye of every guard he saw the same dead expression, their faces blank, drool dripping down a few of their chins. "I don't think you'll be finding much help within their ranks at the moment." He smiled, and with a nod at J'anda, said, "Western magic. You know how it goes."

"So it's to be the two of us, then?" Hoygraf said, wavering on his legs, from one side to the other, balancing tentatively as he held the narrow blade of his cane aloft. "I welcome the opportunity to have a chance to gut you as you've gutted me."

"You cannot be serious," Cyrus said, staring at him. "You can barely stand."

"I will surprise you with my strength," Hoygraf said. "My resolve is not to be questioned, nor is my prowess—"

"Much like the idea of you living to rule this puppet kingdom you've set up," Cyrus said, "the idea of you lasting more than a second in a sword fight with me is simply delusion."

"Puppet kingdom?" Hoygraf spat. "I will have you know that this moment is the culmination of a lifetime of planning, of waiting for so rich an opportunity. This land is mine, now, and no Arkarian filth is going to ruin my moment. I will finish you, and then my men and I will end this scourge that you and yours couldn't find the balls to deal with. This is the beginning of a thousand year reign for my house!"

Cyrus looked at him blankly then blinked his eyes, twice. "When you called me impotent, earlier, you were really talking about yourself, weren't you?"

Hoygraf's hand made a swift gesture, waving at him. "Come at me, fool. Let us see what sort of power you have against a God-King. This is my destiny. This is the moment I was born for—" With a sudden choking noise, he looked down, then sideways.

"I agree," Cattrine said, her hand on his shoulder, the other behind his back. "You were born for this very moment. You've lived your whole life leading up to it, and now you're here. It is a culmination, husband of mine, a reaping of all the seeds of discord you've sown throughout the great and small moments along the way." Her other hand came from behind his back, now, and a long, bloodstained dagger was clenched in it, and she rested it on his throat. "Enjoy the reaping, dear." She ran it across his neck, opening his throat to a gasping noise as he collapsed. "Enjoy your moment." He fell to the ground and blood washed out onto the blue carpet, his mouth still open in shock as his eyes went from her to Cyrus, then his face grew still.

"You all right?" Cyrus asked, staring at Cattrine. Her blue gown was stained with crimson she stared at the knife in her hands with empty, hollow eyes. "Cattrine?"

She looked up and found him again. "I didn't dare to hope you'd come. I dreamed it, at night, when I hoped he wouldn't hear me thinking it. I thought of you in the worst of moments, the darkest of them. I thought of you."

"Are you all right?" he asked again, and closed the distance between them with two long steps. He took hold of her arms, gently, and watched the shock on her face dissolve as she leaned into him, kissed him, on the lips, and he could taste the spattered blood on her as she did it, smelled the court perfumes. His free hand ran across her back, gently, his gauntlet feeling the soft flesh beneath, and he wondered how many new scars she had now, how many he had let her acquire by abandoning her ...

Cyrus broke away from her as Aisling cleared her throat. He turned and looked at the dark elf, who was back to her normal appearance, white hair and all. Her face was only slightly less inscrutable than of old, but he knew betrayal when he saw it. "We have to get out of here," he said, and heard Windrider whinny in agreement.

"The city is surrounded?" Cattrine asked. Cyrus nodded. "There is a small dock in the bottom of the castle, there is a spiral ramp just outside the throne room—"

"The city is going to be destroyed unless we do something," Cyrus said. "The scourge will consume it whole. We need to save these people."

"Whatever we do," J'anda said, his hands still waving vaguely in the motions of a seamstress spinning a tapestry, "may I suggest we do quickly? I grow weary of this, and I suspect these soldiers will not be happy that we are standing here in the midst of a floor covered in their anointed King's blood."

"Easily fixed," Aisling said, and turned to the nearest guard, running a dagger across his throat. A spray of blood caused Cyrus to blanch, and by then she had killed three more the same way. "What?" she gave a caustic look over her shoulder at the silence as she killed another. "They would have happily done the same to us and still will when they awaken if we're here and unwilling to fight them."

Cyrus exchanged a look with Cattrine, who gave him the faintest nod of approval. He started toward the line of soldiers that was in front of the balcony, but Martaina ran swiftly and cut all their throats in seconds. Cyrus blinked at her. "I guess Terian was right about that one thing ..." She gave him a frown, and he shrugged.

"In terms of a plan?" J'anda asked, grabbing the reins of his horse and turning it around toward the large bronze doors they had entered through. They were open, and braziers lit the antechamber outside, though the door beyond had been shut, the one that led to the main hall's chamber.

"We rally the people of Caenalys," Cyrus said, taking Windrider's reins purposefully and striding forward. He looked back and took Cattrine's hand with his other after sheathing Praelior. "With luck, the scourge will still be outside the city walls—"

There came the loudest of noises, a shattering that nearly defied explanation, as the doors to the main hall broke open off their hinges and skittered across the floor of the antechamber to the throne room. The floor shook as they landed, twelve-foot tall pieces of lumber that had been carved with intricate patterns that reminded Cyrus of fish and seas.

Replacing them was Drettanden, a beast that took up the entirety of the doorframe, from marbled floor to crown-moulded ceiling, breathing at them, flooding the antechamber with the smell of rotting flesh so rancid it made Cyrus nearly gag, infesting his very sense of taste and hanging on his tongue as though he had kissed a rotted corpse. A steady breathing filled the air like a starving dog panting for food, and there came a drop of sweat that rolled down his back, so acute he felt it, like the gentle kiss of a lover.

"Or," J'anda said, breaking the quiet shock that permeated the antechamber, "we could just run for our lives."

Chapter 95

Vara

Day 209 of the Siege of Sanctuary

She stalked across the lawns, green now at least, though footpaths had been worn between the front steps of Sanctuary and the guard towers on the wall, brown strips of ground where the green had simply been lost from overtravel. A rain had started, one that made everything smell more pungent somehow, fresh earth on the path as though it had been tilled. She watched him disappear inside and she followed at a jog, trying to catch him. "Alaric!" she called. She quickened her pace, breaking into a run, feeling the first droplets splash her cheeks as she did so. There was a peal of thunder in the far distance, and she ignored it as she climbed the steps and entered the foyer.

The doors were open, shedding the grey light of day into the room. It was quiet now, of course, with nearly everyone out on the wall from repelling the latest attack. Larana was visible in the opening to the Great Hall, along with—*Aha!* He was speaking to her in a hushed whisper even Vara couldn't hear. The druid nodded once then locked eyes with Vara for a split second before bowing her head in shyness and mousing away toward the kitchens. "Alaric," Vara called again, more quietly this time and more accusing.

"Yes?" The Ghost did not turn to face her, leaving his armored back in her full view, his bucket-shaped helm only slightly twisted as if to acknowledge her. "What can I do for you, Vara?" It was slow death, his every word, a sort of weariness she recognized in her own soul.

"You killed him." She heard the bluntness and was surprised at the lack of accusation. "For nearly nothing—"

"He raised his hand to you," Alaric said, and his helm slid so that he was facing once more toward the officer's table at the far end of the Great Hall. "I found that unacceptable."

"A great many men and beasts have raised a hand at me," Vara said. "I should think you would find it to be a full-time occupation to kill them all."

"But a worthy one, I believe," the Ghost said, quietly.

Vara let her boots clink step by step toward him. "This is unlike you, Alaric. Snapping in Council. Killing an annoying dwarf who but raised a hand to me. Slaughtering prisoners as they surrender. What has happened to you? Where is this burgeoning darkness coming from?"

The helm came around again, and she saw his chin in profile, his mouth a thin line. "Perhaps it has always been here."

"No." She took a last quiet step and laid a hand upon his shoulder. "I have known you for years. Seen you in one of the darkest periods of your life, in fact, which was upon the day we met. This? I have never seen this from you. Not you."

His helm slid away, hiding his face wholly from her. "You know nothing of my darkness."

She blanched at his response. "Were you not the man who counseled me away from deadly action? Were you not the one who guided me back to the path of the light after my fall? Did you not say that vengeance leads to dark roads, roads that are not worth walking?"

There was a quiet for a moment before he responded. "Sometimes," he said, "you look down upon a road that you've chosen in earnest, with best intent, and it leads to a far different place than you thought it might when you chose it. Dark roads, yes, they are not worth walking. But sometimes the path turns dark of its own accord, long after you've begun your walk down it."

"This is not the path," she said and tried to step around him to look him in the face, but he turned so abruptly it threw her off balance. "Why will you not look me in the eyes when I talk to you?"

He took a step away from her, still giving her nothing but his back. "I hear you just fine. Finish speaking your mind."

She let her mouth drop slightly open. "But do you listen?"

He swung around on her then, and she saw the fury burning within him. "I listen. All I do is listen. To you. To your guildmates. Your fears, your worries. Will the dark elves break down the gates? Will I die here, in Sanctuary, still but a bloom not yet come to flower?" His face went from frightful to neutral, which made her stomach lurch alarmingly, giving her more than a pinch of fear. "How many crises must I lead you through? How much counsel must I give that is ignored? How many times must I watch others die undeserving—" His voice broke, and she flinched at it. "How many sacrifices must I make before the end? How many times must I give all to you and to your brethren here?"

He brought his hand up and slammed his gauntlet into his chest in a fist, and it made a dreadful clank that echoed through the Great Hall. "I have fought for this guild. Believed in this guild, in our purpose, believed in it when no one else did. I have bled for it, and I would die for it." He waved a hand around him, as though to encompass the entirety of Sanctuary, and all the people standing out on the walls. "Yet I have an army who worries for their lives. Not for the world that will burn if we fail but for themselves." He sagged, and she saw the fight go out of his eyes. "And I fear for them as well. For them, and for all Arkaria."

His hand came up, and she saw his long fingers clutch at his chin. "I cannot keep carrying the purpose of this guild all on my back; I cannot keep believing when no one else does." He raised a hand out, as though he were going to point, and then let it fall to his side. "I cannot do it all on my own." He seemed to recede then, as if he was stepping away from her, but she realized that he was not; he began to dim, to turn translucent in the lighting. "I will carry it as long as I can, as far as I can, until I reach my limits, and then, I think you will find ... I will merely fade away."

The mist rose up around her, encircling her for a moment, and then disappeared, just as he said, into nothingness.

Chapter 96

Cyrus

"Drettanden," Cyrus whispered, and his fingers wrapped around the hilt of Praelior, the sword in his hand before he finished speaking.

The enormous scourge-beast stood before him. He handed Windrider's reins to Cattrine as Drettanden snorted, filling the air with the reek of death again, bad enough that Cattrine gagged as it hit them. "Take this," he said, pressing the leather into her fingers. "Be ready to lead them down to this dock."

"And the people of Caenalys?" Cattrine muttered, coughing from the stench.

"If this thing is here," Cyrus said darkly, watching as Drettanden stared at him, unmoving, "the streets are already flooded with his brethren. This battle is over."

"Cyrus," Martaina said quietly, still watching Drettanden as it stared at them.

"Go with her," Cyrus said to Martaina then let his gaze flick to Aisling. "You too. We have no healer and the two of you carry short blades that won't even make a dent in this thing's hide. Get out of here. I'll cover your retreat."

"And an escape plan for yourself?" J'anda said, sotto voce.

"I expect I'll be diving off the balcony in the throne room in five minutes or less," Cyrus said. "It would be lovely if someone were there to fish me out of the water."

"Five minutes?" Martaina let out a low whistle, and Drettanden growled menacingly to match it. "You're feeling optimistic about your chances against that thing?"

"I like my odds," Cyrus said, never breaking eye contact with the thing that stared at him. "Go. Now." He clutched Praelior as Cattrine brushed a hand against his shoulder, so softly he couldn't feel it. With a subtle look she went to his right, and he saw Martaina cast a regretful look as well, then slip away quietly along with her, horse in tow. Aisling went next, then J'anda. Cyrus listened for their quiet footsteps as they angled through a small, open door to where he could see a flat ramp spiral downward, and watched as the last of them faded into the darkness of it.

"So ..." Cyrus said, looking at the scourge creature which stared back at him. It took a step forward, taking a deep breath, then exhaling so strongly Cyrus found himself wanting to retch. "Please stop that, will you?" The red eyes widened at him. "Do you have any idea what your breath smells like? Corpses. Yeesh. Do you eat everything you come across? Because you could stand to digest a field of mint, my friend—"

The grey lips came apart and Drettanden filled the air with a screeching roar, leering at Cyrus with a hard-edged gaze, mouth hanging open and enormous teeth exposed.

"Yeah, I know," Cyrus said, overcoming the desire to gag, and waved Praelior in front of him. "It's this, isn't it?" He watched red eyes follow it. "This was yours when you were alive? Well, I didn't take it from you, and I didn't kill you. I put this together myself, after following a quest given to me by Bellarum—"

The beast roared and sprung at Cyrus at the last, jaws snapping as Cyrus dodged out of the way. Drettanden took two steps and sprung, crashing through the pillar and supporting wall as Cy fell back, rolling into the throne room. Dust and plaster came down, rock and stone as well, and Cyrus felt a rough shift in the palace above as he came back to his feet, sword in hand. "Hey, if you're gonna charge at everything like a bull, could you at least look out for the load-bearing walls? Or do you want to kill me so bad you're willing to risk killing yourself in the process?" Cyrus circled, putting his back to the balcony. "Because, if so, we could just keep going in this direction. It'd be great. Soft landing too, in the water."

There was a flick of the red eyes, and Cyrus caught it. "Water. You don't like the water, do you?" He waved Praelior and watched the eyes follow it. "But you want your sword back, don't you? It's a little small for you now, don't you think?" There came another snap of the jaws at him. "That, surprisingly, was not a taunt or a goad, but just a simple statement of fact." With dizzying speed, Drettanden came at him in a quick motion, leaping off its back feet and Cyrus dodged aside again, this time leaving his arm extended with the blade. It caught the scourge across the side of the neck and raked the grey flesh. Black blood oozed out, peppering the white marble floor as Cyrus put a foot on the first step below the throne.

"Welcome to the throne room of Actaluere," Cyrus said, keeping the sword pointed at Drettanden. He stepped over the unmoving corpse of Hoygraf, which lay with its eyes wide, a small pool of blood gathered around it. "This was the self-proclaimed king, if you by chance wanted to have a bite of royalty while you're here—" Cyrus dodged as it came for him again, this time leaping back onto the throne, then jumping high over the back of the creature, where he ran with his sword down along the spine, ripping open flesh until he jumped off at the end.

Cyrus landed with a flourish, spinning perfectly, ready to defend himself against another attack. There was none, however, and Drettanden had yet to turn back to him; the creature's head was down, on the steps, and there was a sickening sound of bones crunching as blood dribbled down the stairs. "Really?" Cyrus asked, looking at the spectacle, dumbstruck. "The saddest part of this is that it's not even the most unbelievable thing I've seen in this room in the last half hour."

Drettanden spun, mouth still full of Hoygraf's corpse, an arm and a leg hanging out of the grey lips and red staining the teeth. "You really do eat the dead," Cyrus said, shaking his head. "You feed on life. You've come a long way from being the God of Courage," Cyrus watched a slight reaction at the edges of the red eyes, "to being the exterminator of as much of it as you can. Quite the fall, I suppose."

There was motion to Cyrus's left and he turned; five more of the smaller scourge were there at the smashed entry door, easing into the room. "Right," Cyrus said. "Not as bad as the one I'm about to take, though ..."

They all snapped into motion at roughly the same time; the five creatures at the door jumped for him like a pack of wild dogs, and Drettanden, at his right, came at him at full tilt. The scourges' claws gave them poor traction, and Cyrus watched as they tried to spring and failed. He ran, every step of his boots pounding as he made for the edge of the balcony. Teeth were snapping behind him as he reached the open doors to the outside, and the smell of death was overwhelming as he thrust his foot upon the railing and vaulted.

The wind caught his hair, even through his helm, and tugged the strap against his chin. It ran all across his body as he felt the fall take over. With a look back he saw the scourge, looking over the railing and down at him as he fell, the smell receding as the air rushed past his ears, deafening him. *Please don't let there be rocks down there.* His eyes forced themselves shut as he hit the water with painful force, pushing the air out of his lungs and shoving him into the depths.

There was only a faint flicker of orange light above him as he swam, Praelior in hand to give him strength, until he broke the surface, taking a breath of air, tinged with smoke and wetness. He turned his head to see a boat cutting through the water toward him, and looking far up above, he saw the balcony, and the scourge looking down at him. One of them fell and splashed; he waited, clutching the hilt of Praelior to see if it surfaced again. Tension. Anticipation. It never came up.

"Ahoy!" Cyrus watched the boat as the oars stroked out the sides toward him. It was long, at least fifty feet in length, with a mast and sail and a few crew members. He swam up to it at the approach, seized the side and hauled himself out of the water with a hand from Martaina. He fell upon the deck and looked up to the pillared balcony far above. Drettanden remained, standing, head draped over the railing, eyes following Cyrus on the boat.

"That thing ..." Cattrine said from beside him, "it seems quite fixated on you."

"Yeah," Cyrus said. "This is what happens when you insult a guy's mother when you're three. Old grudges die hard."

She frowned. "You're joking. This hardly seems the time."

Cyrus shook his head, wiping water from his beard. "I don't know what else to say."

Cattrine stood as they came further out into the sea from the palace. There was light to their left, and Cyrus turned from looking at the crew of a half dozen rowers on the small lower deck to the city, where lights blazed, and his mouth fell open.

It burned. Half the city was on fire, blazing strips of light where smoke drifted in the corners against the walls. Against the fiery backdrop, figures were visible, running around on four legs, striking people down. The docks were a frenzy of activity, ships casting off, battles being fought. The fires cast light on the walls of the city, and Cyrus realized to some surprise that they crawled, covered over with scourge scaling them as easily as he might climb a ladder.

"Look at them go," Martaina whispered, and the crew stopped rowing. Other boats were launching out of the docks as quickly as they could steer out of the harbor with crews rowing madly. Cyrus watched as a scourge ran to the end of the docks and leapt into a boat. The screams carried over the water.

"They came because of him," Cyrus said, looking up into the air, to the outline of Drettanden, still watching him from the balcony. "He came because of me. We brought death to Caenalys." He bowed his head and felt Cattrine's hand on his wet hair, stroking it gently off his brow where it crept out from beneath his helm.

"It was coming anyway," Cattrine whispered, and he felt her kneel next to him. "My brother would have laid siege to the city trying to get the walls open, and it would have taken months. The scourge would have come around behind him and taken his army then the city, anyway." She looked in concern. "Where is my brother?"

Cyrus felt a surge of guilt. "We rode ahead of his army three weeks ago. They would have arrived here in another week." He swallowed heavily. "I don't ... I have no idea whether they met the scourge or not. We had thought these creatures bottled up, fighting our armies at Enrant Monge while we planned to evacuate the rest of Luukessia." Blackness climbed into his mind. *They followed me. I changed the rules and ruined all our battle plans, all our assumptions. I've failed again, and hundreds of thousands have died for that failure.*

"Where do we go now?" Aisling asked quietly as they sat there, drenched in the glow and the noise.

"West," Cyrus answered, and he saw the men at the oars put them back in the water after a nod from Cattrine. "If the armies of Luukessia are still out there, they'll have to flee toward the bridge. Hopefully we'll meet up with them there."

J'anda let the quiet remain in place for an additional moment before he spoke. "While I love the conditional 'hopefully,' what's your plan if they're not?"

Cyrus felt his jaw clench. "Then I guess we'll have to cover the retreat of the last civilians ourselves ... and hope the scourge don't follow us over the bridge."

He cast his eyes back toward Caenalys, even as they rowed away, past the palace and toward the west. The city burned, a little at a time. The air was cold, not like winter but the distant fires gave no warmth at all. The smell of death was heavy in the air, along with the smoke that came in drifts off the city. Cyrus sat there, dripping, breathing it all in, and watched as the Kingdom of Actaluere reached its end.

Chapter 97

They rowed on through the night, through a swell and a rain that chilled Cyrus through, spattering on his armor. They went west, and when he took his turn at the oars, Cyrus felt the pull of them over and over on his hands, the knotty pine of the wood smoothed and making callouses in places he hadn't had them before. The rain washed away the smell of death, sapped the salt from the air and went slightly chill but nothing in comparison to what they had braved in the winter up north. There was still the taste of salt permeating in Cyrus's mouth from the air before the rain, and he rowed on, with the others, until he tired, then he clutched Praelior in his hand and pinned it against the oar, using the strength to keep going long past when he might otherwise have quit.

The slow tapping of the rain on his helm died in the wee small hours of the next day. They had a lamp at the fore, and stars came out to guide them. Cyrus felt the press of the bench he was seated upon, and he kept an even stroke, matching his motions to the other men rowing with him, all swarthy men of the sea, with olive skin and dark hair.

There came a sound next to him as someone sat, someone covered in a heavy boat cloak, and when Cattrine's delicate features peeked out from beneath the cowl he was unsurprised. "Hello," she said just loud enough to be heard over the rain.

"Hello," he repeated back to her. He let a healthy silence fall between them then thought to speak. "I'm sorry about—"

"I'm so glad you came," she said, halting as they spoke over one another. "No, I'm sorry, I didn't mean to interrupt you. You were saying?"

"I'm sorry about Caenalys," Cyrus said. "It feels as though everywhere we go, destruction follows—"

"The city was doomed," Cattrine said. "If they hadn't come with you, they would have been along within weeks anyhow, and it would have been just as bad." Her eyes found his. "You saved my life, at least. I thank you for that."

"It was the least I could do," Cyrus said quietly, trying to focus on the steady rhythm of rowing. "I heard that you made a bargain for my life, to return my head to my guild for resurrection." He lowered his voice. "A terrible bargain, with a terrible price."

"It was not all for you," she said, "though I confess your life was the thing that tipped the scales." She stared straight ahead, toward the bow, and he saw her delicate features in profile. Her lip was still swollen, scabbed, and he could see by the lantern light hanging on the ship that her eye had a trace of black under it.

But she was still pretty. Still Cattrine. He resisted the urge to kiss her again and again. "I wish you hadn't. Not for me." He bowed his head, even as he kept the steady stroke of the oar going. "Why did you do it?" he asked, shaking his head, feeling the mournful sadness in his soul as he considered what she had likely been through. "For me—"

"Because I loved you, idiot." She spoke in an outburst of relief, as though it were all she could do to get it out, and a sob followed it. "I did all I did because I felt it, as I thought you did, but did not wish to say it because of your beloved Vara." Her hand came up to his face, stroked his bearded cheek. "I saw the struggle in your eyes the whole time we were at Vernadam, and I wanted to let you heal and become whole again before throwing another burden upon you." She blinked and turned her head away. "It was the same reason I did not tell you who I was. I only wanted you to be able to feel ... normal again. To begin to believe you could feel for another again."

"I did," he said quietly. "I did because of you. As hard as I tried to forget you, to stay away, I still found myself like a boomerang in flight, curving right back to where I had come from. He shook his head and felt the droplets of rain that had collected in his beard fall. "I ... missed you." He tugged in the oar, and laid it across his lap. He reached over and kissed her, fully, totally, and felt her return the same to him.

She broke from him quickly but with hesitation, her hand still held to his face. "Are you not with Aisling now?"

Cyrus paused, and felt his head bow unexpectedly. "I ... I don't know where I stand with Aisling."

"Do you love her?" There was quiet expectation and disappointment in the way she said it.

Cyrus looked back to the rear of the boat, and Aisling was there, eyes closed, asleep. "I don't know. I've come to a place where things have become beyond complicated. I don't know how I feel about her. She's been such balm to me over these last months, but it's almost as though I've become so empty inside that it did me little good."

"I wouldn't tell her that if I were you," Catrrine said.

"Not high on my list of things to do," Cyrus said with a grunt. The ship bobbed in the water, and she leaned toward him. "I don't entirely know where I stand with you, either. This land is about to fall." He looked back. "I think there are other boats following us as well, which is probably wise on their part. There is little I recognize as safe, stable or normal right now. It feels as though everything is danger and trouble."

"I don't expect you to untangle all these emotions now," she said, not meeting his eyes. "It's quite enough that you came for me. To hear you say that you felt the same ... it gives me the possibility of hope."

Cyrus gave her a slow nod. "I'm sorry I can't give you any more than that. I'm still ... sifting through the wreckage inside."

"And when you finish," she asked, "what do you think you'll find?"

"I don't know," he said with a shake of the head, slipping the oar back into the water and matching the rowing of the other men. "I'd like to believe in something again, something more than just fighting my way through life. I'd like a certainty to cling to, something that will always be around, no matter how bad things get. It used to be me; when things would get bad, I could look inside, and I knew which direction to go. When you worship the God of War, it's a simple matter to just turn yourself toward battle. But it's not that simple anymore. Now battle is a given, especially after these things," he waved toward the dark shore, to their right, "came unto the land."

"I'm not certain I understand," Cattrine replied. "You believe in war, in conflict, in battle, yet ... you look for what? Something else?"

"Something else, yes," Cyrus said. "I let myself hope for a future with a woman I didn't really have a true hope with. It shook my world. I believed in a greater purpose for myself through my guild, in the idea that I would fight to protect those who couldn't protect themselves, but everything I have done in this last year has caused the opposite of that. It's put more people in danger and makes me question everything about this purpose I embraced." He shook his head. "Is there really any good I can do when everything I do seems to come out wrong?" He turned his head away from her. "That seems especially true when I consider the women in my life."

"For my part," she said quietly after a moment's pause, "although I wished things had gone differently between us, I have never seen you do anything less than your best with what you had available at the time."

"Isn't that what all of us do, though?" Cyrus asked. "Our best? Most people's best doesn't involve releasing a plague of death upon an entire land, though."

She didn't say anything for a long space after that. "You couldn't have predicted it. No one could."

"You're right," he said. "But I'm still responsible. That means it's up to me to salvage all I can from my failure."

"How do you think ... you'll go about that?" Her eyes cast ahead, in the direction of an unseen shore.

"I don't know," Cyrus said. "I really ... just don't know."

She laid a hand upon his shoulder. "I am grateful to you for coming, regardless of all else that has happened. These things you have become embroiled in, these matters of gods and the dead, are beyond my understanding and almost my belief. I only know that absent your arrival, these things would have swept us away completely. Had you not come to Caenalys, I would surely have died there."

"You don't know that," Cyrus said, looking down, putting his shoulders into the work. "Your dear husband seems like the sort of crazed rat who might have abandoned the city given a chance. He might have dragged you into a boat and taken you off to the west."

"Where we would still eventually be killed by those things, I'd wager." She didn't sound sad when she said it, though it was hard to be sure in the wind. "And if not, I'd still have been with him. I might have preferred to stay in Caenalys."

Cyrus bowed his head. "I don't know that I've done you any favors. What's coming ... if they manage to cross the bridge, I don't think there is any safe ground after that. Arkaria will fight them, eventually, if they have enough will left to do so after the war. It may be that I've spared you death in your homeland so that you can come and die in mine."

She pursed her lips, thinking about it. "I don't think so. Since the day I have met you, you have consistently defied all expectations, including mine. Even when I was certain I would never see you again, you came for me. Even when I thought all faith between us had been broken." She smiled, just a little one. "I suppose what I'm trying to say, Cyrus Davidon, is that thus far, you've come through on every occasion for me." Her eyes were deep, lost in his. "I believe in you. Perhaps more than you believe in yourself just now, but I do. And I believe that if there is any man, in any land, that can find a way to save us from this menace—it is you." With that, she kissed him again passionately, with a hand on his cheek to hold his face. Then she broke from him with a lingering touch, a long one, and went back to the rear of the boat where the others waited for her.

For a long time after that, Cyrus continued to row his oar in time with the others—and let his mind try desperately to find a way to correct his gravest of errors.

Chapter 98

They made landfall a few days later. Because the peninsula that Caenalys was built on and the one that connected the Endless Bridge to Arkaria were close together, they made an easy transit of the shortest distance between the two, and came ashore on a beach that was overgrown with long, green swamp grass. Cyrus waded in and helped Cattrine onto the sulphur-smelling shore, where rotting seaweed lay upon the beach. It festooned the sands, a curious red and green tinge to it. The wind whipped along, carrying only the faintest bite of the winter that had picked at him for months; it was clearly spring, and in a southern locale. *Now at least we don't have to fight in the snow.*

The boat crew launched off a few minutes later, leaving Cyrus, Aisling, Cattrine, J'anda and Martaina along with their horses on the shore. The sand was packed tightly beneath Cyrus's boots, and every step yielded a little, reminding him of walking on shallow snow.

"We have four horses and five people," J'anda said, turning his blue face into the wind and to Cattrine. "Why don't you ride with Aisling, since she's the smallest of us?" The enchanter turned to give the ranger a wicked smile and found her expressionless, though her eyes did tack toward Cyrus, hard and pointed. "I kid. I'm not that heavy, you can ride with me unless you'd prefer to strain his horse," he chucked a thumb at Cyrus.

"That's a very kind invitation," Cattrine said with a bow of her head. "I accept, though perhaps after a while I will switch, just to spare your horses from such a heavy burden all day long."

Cyrus left Aisling's sidewards glare behind and climbed the berm at the edge of the beach, where a field of heavy, tall grass blocked the sight of the other side. Below was an easy spread, flatlands with sparse short grass interspersed with fields of longer grass and hummocks of trees. There appeared to be a coastal swamp in the distance to the left and almost out of sight, Cyrus could see a road ahead, at the edge of his vision. There was movement on it, a steady line of refugees trudging, their darker clothes and human shapes separating them from the horizon line. They stretched from one side of his vision to the other, trailing off, a sad line with only the occasional horse to differentiate from the stooped-back figures.

"It would appear that the evacuation of Luukessia is well underway," J'anda said from next to him.

They climbed onto their horses, Cyrus leading the way as they galloped toward the road. Cyrus could smell the people as they got close; some of them looked to have been walking for a considerable distance. Cyrus passed a child who looked no older than eight, a ragged waif whose shoes were worn to holes. The animal skins he wore were from a mountain goat, as was the horn strapped to his back. *Sylorean. Gods, how far has he walked?*

There was a stir in the line as they approached, and fingers pointed toward J'anda as a whisper went through the crowd. Smiles appeared, and gasps of relief were heard. "Never seen a group of humans so glad to see a dark elf," J'anda said as his hands began to glow, spells already being cast.

"I have," Aisling said sardonically, "but it was at a brothel." She kept a straight face. "It was pretty much exactly like this."

"I'll try not to be too insulted by that since these people are starving," J'anda said, handing off a loaf of conjured bread to a family who held it up, crying with happiness. Cyrus saw the woman he handed it to immediately break it to pieces and begin to pass it around to a large group of children. He saw one of the boys in a ragged old surcoat with the livery of Galbadien upon it. *This whole land, emptying.*

There was a rising cry, and J'anda waved to Cyrus. "I think I'm going to be here for a while."

"You," Cyrus said to a man nearby, a swarthy fellow with dark hair and skin. "Have you seen any armies about?"

"Yes, m'lord," he said with a bow to Cyrus as J'anda gave the man a loaf of bread. "The dragoons of Galbadien are just up the road a piece, perhaps a day's ride. They were waiting on a flat stretch of land to hit those monsters that are destroying everything."

"Who was leading them?" Cyrus asked, focusing in on the man.

"The King of Galbadien," the man said with a bow of his head. "Saw him with my own eyes, the new one, the young one. They say the western army is farther out with the Syloreans and the rest of our

Actaluerean army, fighting to hold the things back while we escape. The man shook his head. "I heard tell from a Sylorean that the monsters are all the way up to the neck of the peninsula and still coming."

Cyrus felt a chill. "How far to the bridge?"

"Straight ahead, another day, sir," the man said. "I've been there before, a couple times."

Cyrus shot a look at his party. "We need to go."

"I'm going to stay with these people," J'anda said. "I'm of no use to you with those things anyway. I will walk to the bridge with these folk, keep them fed and try to do some good along the way."

Cyrus looked at him evenly. "Are you sure?"

"I'll go with him," Cattrine said, and Cyrus heard the man he had been talking to whisper, "Lady Hoygraf," to the crowd. "I can be of little aid to you," she said, "but of much trouble were I to get in the way."

"Get to the bridge," Cyrus said. "If the dragoons are only a day away and the rest of the army only a bit past that, it's not going to be more than a week before we've fallen back all the way." He felt his jaw tighten. "If that."

"Aye," J'anda said. "Here." He tossed them each a loaf of bread and looked at Cyrus seriously, the wind stirring his hair. "Take care up there. We'll be waiting for you at the bridge."

"Understood," Cyrus said and urged Windrider forward, riding along the side of the road and listening to the crowds shout their joy at the sight of J'anda on his horse.

"I'm going to stay with them," Aisling said, halting her horse just a few paces along. Cyrus pulled Windrider to a stop and came around to face her. "I'm not much use on the battlefield, not against those things. It's a fight for proper swords and I'm really more of a daggers and sneaking kind of girl."

"You've been doing pretty well so far," Cyrus said, watching the dark elf's eyes. She was cagey, avoiding his gaze.

"I've been lucky and good in equal measure," she said. "But these things notice me more than most people, and I'm tired of pressing my luck. I'm sure you'll do just fine."

"All right," Cyrus said with a slow nod. "We'll see you at the bridge, then."

"Yeah," she said, and her horse moved forward alongside him. "We will."

He stared at her for a moment, at her hard, flinty gaze, inscrutable as she was. "I'm sorry," he said.

She didn't seem to react, just kept watching him. "I know."

He started to look away but didn't, keeping his eye on the purple irises that reminded him so much of a storm. "I don't know ... what I would have done without you on this expedition."

"Died," she said quickly. "That's the short answer." She let the slyest hint of a smile show through her grim facade.

"True enough. But I meant besides that." He held out a hand to her, but she made no move to take it. "I meant ... in all the other ways you've carried me through this time of trial. All the things you've—"

She leaned over and kissed him, maintaining her perfect grip on the horse. It was rough and heavy, a press with enough weight and feral savagery behind it that he wondered if she were about to bite him too. She broke from him and balanced back on her horse. "Don't ever forget what I can be to you, then. Remember it while you're mulling through ... whatever you're mulling."

He gave her a slow nod of acknowledgment. "I will. Be safe." He flicked a look toward J'anda and Cattrine, mobbed by the crowd, whose upthrust hands were gently clawing at them, waiting for bread. "Take care of them, will you?"

"J'anda I can promise I'll take care of." A dark look flickered over her. "The other ... I'll try." She said it so grudgingly, it sounded as though she'd been turned upside down and had it shaken out.

"Yes," Cyrus said. "Try. For me."

There was a sigh of near-disgust and Aisling turned her horse around. "The things I do for you ..."

Windrider began to move again without any action from Cyrus, and the warrior looked down in surprise. "Well, all right then."

"You think they'll be okay?" Martaina asked, coming alongside him as they rode, the wind coming from the north now, and carrying that faintest hint of the breath of Drettanden, that smell of death.

"We're the ones who are riding toward the scourge, not away from it," Cyrus said. "I'd be more worried about us, frankly."

"I'm always worried about us," Martaina said as the horses broke into a gallop, the line of refugees in front of them a thick column of filthy clothes and dirty faces. "I just figured I'd add a little variety."

"You're always worried about us?" Cyrus asked, cocking an eyebrow and looking over at her. "That feels like a commentary on my leadership in some way."

"Your leadership is just fine, sir," Martaina said. "But it does seem to point us in the direction of trouble more often than not. You're like a bloodhound for trouble; you can't stay away from it. I believe you might even thrive on it in some small way."

He looked back to the horizon, at the downtrodden, the people without a home or hearth to call their own, fleeing their land and trying to escape death itself. "I think I've had quite enough of trouble for the sake of trouble after this excursion," Cyrus said. "But I can't deny that it seems to follow me about." He looked back and could just barely see the shapes of Aisling in the distance, along with Cattrine and J'anda, still in the midst of the crowd. "In every possible way."

Chapter 99

It was less than a day later when they reached the dragoons. Flat plains of sparse grass broken by lowlands and patches of swamp grass with hummocks of trees gave way to a large stretch of open ground. It was there that they found the horses and men, tens of thousands of them, enough that the camp was a sight in and of itself. The smell of food was in the air, real food, bread, even some meat. The wagons were just being reloaded when they arrived, tents being broken down. Refugees were being turned away, but there was only a trickle of them now, and Cyrus felt a grim discomfort at the thought of what that meant. *That is the last of them, then. The rest have been taken by these things, by the last gasp of the God of Death.* He watched the stragglers go, lingering as though they hoped to draw protection from the army of horsemen that remained in the fields and saw the supplymen shoo them away after tossing them odds and ends to eat, directing them toward the bridge. *The last of the Luukessians.*

When he asked a soldier, he was directed toward a cluster of men in the distance. The surcoats were familiar, of course, the majority of them being Galbadien soldiers. A few were men of Actaluere and Syloreas but very few. *Galbadien was the Kingdom of the horsed cavalry. Now it's an empty land, I suppose, desolate and filled with those ... things, grazing on the remains of the dead, like crows.* Cyrus pictured the scene of the loping fields of Galbadien in his head, tilled ground, green grass, the smell of death in the air, bodies choking the rivers and streams, and the scourge feeding on all of it. The sound of their screeches filled his ears as he imagined it, and he nearly choked at the thought.

They rode up to a small circle, and Longwell was there with Ranson, and both rose to meet them. "General," Samwen Longwell said as Cyrus dismounted and took the proffered hand of the King of Galbadien—*the Garden of Death, now.* "We'd heard Caenalys was cut off," Longwell said, "Actaluere's army barely met up with our main force in time to save them from being shredded. We thought you dead," he said with barely disguised relief.

"You know it takes more than a few of these scourge to kill me," Cyrus said. "They came wide around Enrant Monge, didn't they? Ended up flanking our holding action?"

Longwell nodded. "Two days after you left. They sent another army even wider around, through Galbadien, and it tore through the Kingdom. We had no warning to speak of." Longwell shook his head, disgust etched on his face. "We saw the fall of Enrant Monge as we rode out of the unity gate. Those things ... they climb walls as though they were—"

"I know," Cyrus said. "We saw it at Caenalys. We had just gotten into the city when they hit, barely made it out via boat."

There was a flicker of concern from Longwell. "The Baroness?"

"She's safe. She, J'anda and Aisling stayed along the route to give bread to the refugees." Cyrus let his hand fall on Praelior's hilt. "We, on the other hand, figured we'd give whatever aid we could here. How far away are they?"

"Hours," Ranson said, speaking up now. "We're looking to use our horsed cavalry for the first time against them. With the snows around Enrant Monge and the rapid fallback over mostly wooded land, the flanking actions—we haven't really had a chance to have a go at them. It's our hope that the increased mobility of our horsemen will start to turn the tide of this war." He caught the skepticism from Cyrus. "All right, well, we don't think the tide will turn, but we're hoping to do as much damage as possible before we reach the bridge." His expression hardened. "I'd certainly like to pay these things back for the loss of my homeland."

"You and countless others, I'm sure," Cyrus said. "We'll wait here with you, then, try and relieve the foot army when they arrive. I expect the melee will turn interesting fast, depending on how these things react to horsemen. The best we can hope for is to give the last of the refugees time to start across the bridge. If the scourge don't decide to turn back, at least we've got an easily defended corridor."

Longwell looked at him carefully. "You mean to orchestrate another bridge defense. Like Termina."

"I mean to," Cyrus said. "I mean to make it the last stand. I want to take so many of those things with us, cause so much havoc and destruction that by the time we reach the other side they've got a wall of their own corpses so high to crawl over that they'll never make it without sliding into the sea."

There was a pause and silence for a moment. "Lofty goal," Ranson said.

"The alternative," Cyrus said, "is letting them start to visit the same destruction on Arkaria as they've wrought here in Luukessia." He felt a tired weight land upon him. "I cannot let that happen. There is nothing but broken ground between the Endless Bridge and the settlements of southeastern Arkaria. They can surely cross the Inculta Desert without great difficulty, and we'd be at a disadvantage fighting on the beaches, the forests, the sands and the mountains. Everything but flat plains, the scourge has mobility to beat anything we have for them." He waved a hand at a densely clustered group of horsemen nearby. "Our only hope right now is that your dragoons can run over them like cavalry over infantry. Otherwise, we're going to get driven back to a bridge that's likely crammed so full of people it'll be a slaughter, a shoving match where people get tossed over the edge without regard as panic sets in and they begin to stampede to get away."

Quiet greeted this statement. Martaina spoke a moment later. "How many people would you estimate have gotten to the bridge?"

Ranson and Longwell exchanged a brief and telling glance. "Few enough," Ranson said. "We have no real idea how many people lived in Luukessia before all this, of course, but the guesses were in the millions. I would estimate that only a hundred thousand, perhaps many less, as few as fifty, have made it out of the area that the scourge now dominate."

Cyrus swallowed heavily and tasted the bile in the back of his throat threatening to come back up. *Fifty thousand? Even a hundred thousand is a pitiful amount—one in ten or twenty or thirty survivors of this land? Imagine if only one in ten members of Sanctuary survived some attack upon them.* "That ... is a pittance."

Longwell nodded grimly. "I would estimate more started and were trapped along the roads or caught behind the lines as the scourge moved to sweep down along the eastern road through Galbadien. Those people are trapped behind the scourge now, and nothing can save them. They're exposed, and the scourge will have at them at will. There is no effective fighting force outside of this peninsula left on Luukessia. We can only hope that perhaps a few of them made it to boats and can make the slow way around the land unfettered by those things."

"They can't swim," Cyrus said. "We found that out in Caenalys. Unless they can walk along the bottom of the sea, I think we're safe from them across bodies of water."

"They breathe," Longwell said. "I've found that out from the stink of their breath and the realization that they cease breathing when they die. I doubt they'll be able to do much on the bottom of the sea save for drown, like the rest of us."

"Quite an assumption," Cyrus said, "but I'm hoping you're right." He looked east, to the horizon, where the midday sun was just starting to come down from its apogee. "Only hours til they get here? I suppose we should rest for a piece, and make ready." He felt the set of his jaw as it got heavy, and the slightest bit of determination from somewhere inside crept up, like a friend he hadn't seen in a long time. "Because it's going to be a long fight after this."

Chapter 100

Vara

Day 214 of the Siege of Sanctuary

She sat in the lounge, staring at the front window as the spring rain drizzled down outside, little speckling turning the glass into refractions, tilting the little bit of light that came down in different directions. The smell of home cooking was in the air, Larana's finest efforts at turning pickled eggs, conjured bread and old mead into something palatable seemed to be working; in fact, Vara could not much tell the difference between the smell of what the druid was creating now from what she created with the freshest meats and vegetables. *In the case of most, that would be a damning criticism indeed. In her case, it's praise.* Her mouth watered as she took a deep sniff of the air around.

The sound of a dozen practice swordfights being conducted in the foyer were like a steady clank of metal in her ears, deafening in their way, causing her to clutch the stuffed arms of the chair with all their padding. It was a soft touch against her hands; her gauntlets lay at the table to her side, along with her book, *The Crusader and the Champion. Can't seem to get into it at all. I haven't been able to since ... since he left.*

There was a shout of triumph, and she turned her head to see Belkan with his blade at Thad's neck. "You may be one of our best," the old armorer said to the red-clad warrior, whose face was as scarlet as his armor, "but age and experience still beats youth and speed from time to time."

She let her mind drift back. Her eyes drifted to the window, still spotted with the rain. *Will he ever come back? It's been a year and more, now.* She chided herself for a fool. *Even if he wanted to return, the portal is closed. He would have to go to Reikonos and wait there until the embargo was lifted.* A glumness lay upon her, deep sadness draped over her shoulders like a shawl on a chill day. *We are truly cut off from the outside world. That is the lasting legacy of what the*

Sovereign has wrought here, to place us under his thumb once and for all, without any way to come back and forth, to get supplies—she thought of Isabelle, and the briefest hint of sadness grew—*to see family, friends. He means to drive us out, to kill us, or worse. How Alaric sees all this and still manages to believe so strongly in the mission, in the ideal of disrupting and holding against the Sovereign ...*

Then again, should we fall, we lose our home.

There was a stir behind her, a quiet that settled over the foyer, and she turned her head to see Alaric come out of the Great Hall, walking. *He rarely walks these days, flitting from place to place in his ethereal mists—or whatever they are.* She stood, grabbing her gauntlets and book, and marched toward the entry doors as Alaric headed toward them, nodding at those he passed and speaking to a few.

"Well done, Belkan," Alaric said as he passed the space where the armorer was sparring with Thad. "You continue to prove that skill and ability are ageless things and that a heart and willingness are enough for a fight."

"Let us hope we don't have to prove your theory correct in an all-out battle," Belkan said to Alaric. "I'd just as soon stay in the armory with a dead quiet than continue to have to sharpen these young ones for a battle I'd rather not fight."

"Agreed," Alaric said, passing between the two of them smoothly, clapping each on the shoulder with great assurance and with none of the darkness of the soul he'd exhibited when last he'd spoken with Vara privately. She had not seen much of the Ghost since then. There had been no Council meetings and no change, the wall continuing to be assailed in earnest every few days. "The purpose of this guild was never to sit here and defend our own keep, and that it has come to this is a measure of the depths that Arkaria finds itself in rather than a commentary on us, I think." He gave a slight nod. "I think."

He graced Thad and Belkan with a smile and then kept on, giving a ranger he passed a slap on the shoulder for good measure, causing the man, a dwarf, to smile and blush at the acknowledgment of his guild leader. *He's so good at this when he wants to be. They respect him, they love him, even though he maintains his air of mysteriousness and aloofness. They would follow him into the Realm of Death on a whim, just like—*

She felt the stab of pain inside and ignored it, placing herself before the door and directly in Alaric's path. He noted her but did not adjust his course and did not look up until he was nearly upon her. "Lass," he said as he came to the doors.

"Alaric," she said.

"I'm going to inspect the inner walls," he said, gesturing toward the door she was blocking. "If there's something on your mind, perhaps you'd care to accompany me as I go."

She gave a very subtle half turn to look at the door before realizing how pointless it was to look at a closed door in indecision. "It's raining."

"A true deluge," Alaric admitted. "And exactly why I am going now. The run of the water will apprise us of any breaches, any places where the drainage is poor, any areas of concern. The water shows us the truth of the wall, I think, and the strength of our barrier."

"Yes, very well," she said, and looked back to the table just inside the foyer. Laying her book upon it, she pulled her gauntlets on, one by one, and grasped the door handle, opening it for her Guildmaster. "Shall we?"

He eyed her curiously, dismissed the fact that she was holding the door open for him and walked through. She followed and the patter of the rain upon her helm began a moment later. Alaric paused outside the door on the first step as the rain fell upon him. He raised his face skyward, as though he were trying to expose himself to the drowning sky, and Vara watched, huddling closer to the door, trying to shelter herself using the slight indent of the main doors to protect her from the downpour. It was only minimally effective.

"Do you feel the liberation that the rains grant?" He turned to look at her, a solemnity and peace visible on the part of his face she could see. "It is spring, and the rains mean growth and the coming green of summer. All the vestiges of the hard winter will be washed away as though they were our past sins, and we will be left left with nothing but a new field, freshly tilled, ready to be planted with whatever we will."

"My field appears ill-tilled and filled to the brimming with dark elves," she said sourly. "But perhaps I'm seeing it wrong. Though I would consider myself very fortunate if the spring rains would wash them all away and leave me with an empty field once more."

Alaric gave the slightest chuckle. "So would we all, but that is not always the point of the storm. When the real downpours begin, you cannot always control what is washed away. Sometimes you lose a part of your field, of your crop. It would certainly be easier if such things did not happen, but since we see it always in nature, I find it hard to believe it would not carry over into every other facet of life."

She watched the steady stream of water come down, smelled the freshness of the rain, dissipating the last aromas of the dinner being prepared inside, as though she had taken a drink of water to cleanse her palate between courses of a sumptuous meal. "Yes, I have heard you talk of these philosophies before, of how we grow in storms, in times of trouble. I daresay we will be doing some considerable growing here." He looked over his shoulder at her briefly, then settled back into his position, arms up, palms tilted skyward as though he could capture the rains for himself. "Alaric, I must tell you something."

He did not move, still drawing strength from the waters coming down around him. "All right," he said. "Go on."

"What you talked about before," she said. "About taking our purpose to its natural conclusion—to defending this place to the last. I wanted to tell you ... I have believed in you as a leader and a friend since the days when I was so ground up inside that it felt as though there was nothing left within me but shattered glass. My sword has served you in noble cause all the days since the first, when I swore my allegiance to Sanctuary—and it shall not falter now."

"I never doubted you for a moment," he said, still not turning. "But I admit I am curious; why this profession to me now?"

"Because," she said at a whisper, "I saw you. You doubted yourself, and that is not something I am accustomed to from you, Alaric. You have been ever the constant to me, since the day you carried me back here from the Realm of Purgatory. I am used to seeing all manner of breakage around here—from the days of Orion and ... what the hells was that gnome's name, the troublesome one? I have seen everyone go to pieces at one time or another, myself included. But not you, Alaric. Your title is Guildmaster, and you are affectionately known as the Master of Sanctuary, but it is better said that you are the Master of yourself. You do not fall apart, not ever. Not when the Dragonlord threatens to consume the entire north, not when every power in Arkaria rallies to destroy us, not when we stood before the God of Death himself and you bartered for our very lives. Yet now, in this time, you begin to show the signs of strain." She watched him, saw the rain cascading off his pauldrons of battered steel in sheets as the tempo of the rains began to increase. "You … falter. You crack. I wanted you to realize that you have my support—and my affection—for all that you have done and do. That I have ever considered you a friend and a mentor, and that I will follow you in this crusade of being the stopgap against the fall of Arkaria until its conclusion, whatever that may be."

There was no response at first, and then Alaric brought a hand to gesture her forward. "Come out to me." He began to walk forward, down the steps, toward the lawn.

She let out an impatient hiss. "Alaric, it is a deluge out there."

He turned back and stared at her with wry amusement. "You say you will follow me into death yet fear to tread in the rain. What am I to think of your level of conviction?" The corner of his mouth contained the barest hint of an upward creep, as though he were holding in a smile, rueful or otherwise.

She sighed and stepped out of the slight cover she was under. The rain began to patter upon her helm, and she took another step forward, reminded all at once of the sound of rain tapping on windows when she was a child in Termina. *I do not see what sort of commitment can be tested by a mere walk in the rain. There's not even any lightning to be wary of.*

"Very good," Alaric said as she reached the bottom of the steps where he waited. "There is a lesson in all this, you realize." He looked to a tree to their right, a good ways off, a tall one, one that Vara had sat under more than once on summer days while reading. "In the winds of the storm, the boughs of a tree spring back and forth, they bend in the gale. Sometimes, when the wind is strong, they crack. If you are close, you might perceive the sound. If it were a good break, it may be obvious to the sight. If a small one, it could go unnoticed." He raised an eyebrow. "If you are not particularly close to the source, then you may not see the strain, hear the crack, until the branch falls." She saw the pulse of a spell leave his hand, a weak burst, and it jarred a branch near the top of the tree, which was considerably high. A small bough broke loose and tumbled, catching in the upper branches until it fell, finally, to the earth. "Yet it cracks nonetheless. You simply do not see it until it is too late."

She tore her eyes from the branch on the ground to Alaric, straining to hear him over the disconcerting sound of the rain hammering at her head and body. "You keep everyone at a distance. You maintain the vague and mysterious allure of a man whom no one knows. I suppose no one would be close enough to hear you strain and crack, would they?"

He smiled slightly. "Perhaps."

"What would you have me learn from this, teacher?" She tried to keep the sarcasm out of her reply but somewhat failed, she knew. "A gardening lesson, perhaps? Tend to every branch of the tree, keep watch on them lest they fall at an inopportune time?"

He glanced upward and nodded his head, a flat expression of surprise on his lower face. "That is ... not bad, actually. I was aiming more for a visual representation of the idea that you never know what lies beneath the surface of a body of water until you've been in it, but I did not wish to walk all the way around to the pond."

She let a small laugh escape. "So it was merely a lesson in being vague and mysterious and keeping people at a distance in order to keep them from seeing you bend and break."

He nodded with a slight smile of his own. "Close enough. I have endeavored in the last years to get you to soften that edge you keep about you, the one that holds others at a distance. I told you before in your dealings with Cyrus that your protective instincts would drive him away. I have no desire to keep harping on what I perceive as your attempts to sabotage your own happiness, especially as you are aware of them. The lesson closest to what I want to tell you is this—" He stepped closer to her and placed both hands on her shoulders, looked her in the eyes with the cool grey of his, and took a deep breath. "If you allow no one to stand close to you, no one will know when you are straining, when you are close to breaking, or the reason why. While I thought once, perhaps, this was a fine posture for a leader to maintain, I now doubt its efficacy, both as a leadership method and as a fulfilling way to live one's life." He glanced past her to the tree. "Also, it seems somewhat dangerous in its illustrative purposes. That branch could have hit someone, after all."

She chuckled again. "You jest. You couch your lessons in jests. Truly, this is rare indeed. You stumble between morbidity and a clarity of thought that I can scarcely fathom and then go right back to humor, all in the space of seconds."

He smiled. "I only wish to convey to you the mistakes I have made."

"You've been a very good Guildmaster," she said.

"I have made errors," he said gravely, and she felt the squeeze of his hands as they clinked on her pauldrons. "Grave ones. Foolish ones. Almost all preventable, almost all brought about by my failure to trust my guildmates with things I should have told them. I have believed in you as well, all of you, that you were better than me. I felt my role here was to be secret-keeper, to mete and dole the things I had learned and acquired in their own time, fearing these secrets might be too much for anyone else to bear, that they might break you all or cause you to be under the same duress as myself. All it has done is isolate me, to put me off to the side, and make me shoulder every ounce of the burden. Indeed, now I am left to wonder if any of the things I held back ever had any real purpose at all, if it would not have been better for me to say plainly everything I knew and let the officers at least react with their own best judgment." He sagged. "But that is a discussion that is entirely esoteric at this point; we are too far down the road now for anything less."

"If you have no one to speak to about these things," she said, "I would listen, as you have for me all these years."

"I have rarely done that for you, my friend," Alaric said with a smile. "And I am not totally bereft of those with which to speak some of my mind." The smile disappeared. "Though I do miss Curatio at moments such as this. His wisdom was as great as his discretion, and there were things I could talk about with him that I dare not with anyone else." There was a slight twinkle in his eye at her. "Well, almost."

They lapsed into quiet, and Alaric withdrew his hands from her shoulders. She thought on what he had said as the rain continued to fall around them. *Isolated. Alone. Filled with regret. Yet still there is something he won't say, things he won't talk about.* She cast a sidelong glance at him, wondering. "Alaric?" she asked. "For all these you have said, the things you have told us will come to us 'in the fullness of time'? Will we ever actually hear the answers?"

His face darkened, and he stared at the tree as the rains washed over it. The air was clear now and fresh, the smell of all else washed away and replaced with the scent of good mud and earth. There was a flash of lightning on the horizon, and then a solid crack of thunder followed a few seconds later. She did not have to strain to hear him but only just. "Perhaps," he said, his voice fading as he spoke. "Perhaps you will indeed. But the day may come when you do ... that you wish you had not." He was stoic, still, and looking at the wall before them and all that it held back, the army on the other side. "For not all secrets are prizes to be revealed, celebrated and reveled in. Some are dark, and dangerous, and when the door is open to them," he pointed to the gate in the wall, sealed against the predations of the dark elves, "they wreak nothing but destruction on everyone—everyone—that they touch."

Chapter 101

Cyrus

It was a slaughter, Cyrus knew, as night fell. The dragoons had filled the air with the smell of horses, of manure, so thick that he could scarcely breathe it without thinking of stables and wet hay. The sky had been clear, and when the sun set, the first fires to the east had been easy to see, the sight of spellcasters burning ground to slow the scourge's advance and cover a rally. They had come an hour or so after that, the army on a march. He had seen them from a distance, faint heads and bodies blending into the outlines that were illuminated by the fires behind them, but the number was few enough. *It was an army of thousands, and now it is half or less what it was when last I saw it. Actaluere, Galbadien, Syloreas and Sanctuary combined.* It was hard to see detail, silhouettes against the only light source; when the moon came up the picture became clearer—but no less disheartening.

The sound of the horses was heavy too, hoofbeats, rallying, the soldiers burning off nervous energy as they waited. The trouble was coming, it was close at hand. The dragoons formed up, and the horses snorted in the still, warm night, the first Cyrus could recall in what seemed like years. *How many have we lost of Sanctuary? How many have we left?* He felt the pull of worry at his innards. *How many have I lost? They are mine to command, after all, even if I have abdicated that responsibility a great deal of late.* The touch of the warm night air on his skin was palpable, a reminder that winter had subsided and spring was roaring through with intent to carry summer with it.

When the armies drew closer, it was near to midnight, and the full moon gave them a clearer idea still. "Were there so many missing when last you saw them?" Cyrus asked Longwell, who was alongside him on his horse.

"Aye," Longwell said. "The flanking action was terrible, and the Actaluereans were caught on the march by the scourge when they swept through from the west. They were separated from us and the Sanctuary army by too wide a distance; they had to flee without fire spells to cover them and lost three-quarters of their men before they met up with us." He shook his head. "Your Baron Hoygraf's ambitions cost a great many lives, it seems."

My failure to kill him, you mean. But Cyrus did not voice the thought, true as it was. *What good can I do here when all I seem to be able to achieve are failures that embolden the enemy and turn every silly mistake of mine into another thousand or hundred thousand dead? How many must die before I stop giving these things more room to kill us?*

There was movement at the back line of the retreating army, the leading edge of a few wagons and men carrying the supplies. They came out of the darkness, speaking little to the dragoons as they passed, trying to edge around the army on horseback. He saw tired faces, downturned, going about their labor. Some seemed more familiar than others, and he knew they had been part of the wagon train at Enrant Monge and perhaps earlier, at Filsharron. One of them came out of the dark on a pony and approached him, face cracking into a smile. It was a young man who looked vaguely familiar. "It's you," the lad said. "I knew you'd be back."

"Oh?" Cyrus looked at him until something clicked in his mind. "You tended the horses at Enrant Monge."

"Aye, I did," the young man said. "Been doing it for the army since, taking care of the ones that haul the wagons. The Brothers had me leave before the castle fell." He shook his head. "Never thought it would happen. They've taken it all, haven't they? The whole land?"

"Aye," Cyrus said with greatest reluctance, "they have."

The boy seemed to absorb that. "It's all right. You'll save us."

There was such a moment of absurd intensity that Cyrus felt almost compelled to laugh. "I haven't exactly done a bang-up job of that so far, kid."

The boy shrugged as if to say *no matter.* "I believe in you. You're him, after all. You're him, returned, like me mum used to talk about."

Cyrus quelled a deep sigh. "Kid, I'm not your 'Baron Darrick,' or whatever his name is."

"Lord Garrick?" Longwell said from next to Cyrus, raising an eyebrow at the warrior. "You speak of the legend of Garrick's return?"

"Aye," the boy said with a hint of pride. "It's him, I tell you. He's the one. He'll save us."

Longwell gave Cyrus a pitying look of understanding then a nod of surrender. "If ever there was a man who could find a way where there was no way, this would be the man."

Cyrus frowned. "You cannot be serious."

Longwell shrugged. "No, I believe it. You've done impossible things in the past. You're a human man who brought down the Dragonlord—"

"Through luck," Cyrus said.

"—you led a nearly untested army into the Trials of Purgatory and came out a victor—"

"Through some good fortune and the skill of my comrades."

"—you broke the Goblin Imperium and threw one of the most prestigious guilds in Arkaria into shame—"

"Thanks to a sword forged by a god."

Longwell shrugged. "Held a bridge against an army of a hundred thousand."

"With your help. And ... Vara's."

"Killed a god," Longwell said. "Something that hasn't been done in living memory." He paused. "Except Curatio's."

"Because of Alaric," Cyrus said, annoyed. "And also the cause of all our current problems."

Longwell locked eyes with the stableboy, ignoring Cyrus. "You've got a good eye, lad. If ever there was a man born today who embodied Garrick's dauntlessness, his fighting ability, his indomitable spirit, this is the one."

"Aye, Your Majesty," the stableboy said, and bowed so low he nearly fell off his horse.

"Run along now," Longwell said. "Take care of yourself, and stay clear of the fighting. You get to that bridge and stay well out in front of everyone else, do you hear?"

"Yes, Your Majesty," the boy said again, and started his horse forward, looking back with awstruck eyes at Cyrus and Longwell.

Cyrus waited until he was out of earshot before turning on the King of Galbadien. "You didn't have to feed his delusion."

Longwell let out a mirthless guffaw. "Delusion, nothing. All I did was recount a piece of your legend." He waved in the direction of the stableboy's retreating back. "Tell me what harm it does to give that lad a hope in a land that has nearly had it struck out of it. We're about to surrender our last foothold here. I would have him believe as we do so that we're not retreating just so we can die on the other side of the sea. I would have him believe he can have a future free of these things. I would rather surrender our last square of land here a thousand times over, to feel the pain of that loss, than surrender our hope. Hope is a powerful thing. Belief is a powerful thing, too. It hurts him little to believe that you are the legend of Lord Garrick returned to us." Longwell's face darkened. "And it certainly is our darkest hour, when it was said he would return. We all could use a little hope right now."

Cyrus took a long glance at Longwell, the King. "As you wish," he said simply. The last of the suppliers had passed now, and it was down to the army, clumped ahead of them, lines of fire on either side."

"Would you like to argue it further?" Longwell said with an impish smile as he started his horse forward.

Cyrus drew Praelior as he watched Longwell heft his lance. "Not at present," Cyrus said. "But I expect you'll be whistling quite a different tune when we're on the other side of the sea."

"I dearly hope not," Longwell said as the army before them opened ranks to channel the horses through as they fell back. Cyrus rode past the Actaluerean army, through its midst, three short rows before he hit the scourge, coming forward in the darkness, advancing into the last hundred miles of Luukessia that was left.

Chapter 102

"Well, that was effective," Terian said beside the fire as the sun was rising nearby. Martaina was there, as well as Curatio and Nyad, who was sacked out already. Calene Raverle and Scuddar In'shara shared the fire with them, the desert man strangely quiet—*though not strangely for him,* Cyrus reflected. The battle had lasted most of the night. "I've never seen that many scourge die so quickly."

"Yet, we still find ourselves a mile back from where we started the night," Curatio said, studying a book draped across his lap. "Tens of thousands of the enemy dead but ultimately irrelevant. Even with the effectiveness of the dragoons, we'll be seeing the Endless Bridge inside of a week."

Cyrus sat staring at the fire in front of them. "That means we'll see the end of the bridge in a week or so after that. And after that …" He let his words trail off. "There's no holding them back at that point. They can flank us in the jungle and we'll have a hell of a time doing much other than forming a line on the beach and fighting with our backs to the waves." A thought occurred to him. "Actually … we might try that here, on the shores of Luukessia."

"Not a bad idea," came a voice from behind him, and Longwell trudged up, lance in hand, his helm under the other arm. He threw down his weapon, careful not to hit anyone. The smell of activity came with him, the strong scent of sweat. Cyrus knew it well, having smelled it on himself earlier, but it had faded away now, blended into the background behind the smell of the logs burning. The crack and pop of them owned the air while they waited for Longwell to speak again. "A last stand against the shores of the sea might just produce some killing results."

"For the day or so you lasted," Curatio agreed, "yes. Then, when you became too tired to fight any longer, you'd likely be up to your chest in water already, and left with no options save one: drown."

"Perhaps," Longwell said. "But to take as many of those things down with you as possible before the end, to have them keep coming and to refuse to yield, to not leave Luukessia's shores and lay down your life for the country?" He gave a subtle nod as he fixed on the fire. "I could think of worse ways to go. Besides, if those things do make the choice to crawl over the bridge," he waved a hand behind them in the direction of the Endless Bridge, "our days are over soon enough anyhow. I don't expect drowning would be much worse than being devoured by one of them."

Curatio looked up from his book with a raised eyebrow. "Drowning is agony."

"And being ripped apart and crushed in the jaws of one of those creatures is a fun and easy way to leave this life?" Calene Raverle asked, looking at the healer.

"Point," Curatio said. "The only thing I was suggesting was that of all the ways I could pick to go out, drowning is not a good one. You struggle for breath for agonizing minutes, fighting to get air, and it lasts what seems like forever."

"Drowned to death once or twice in your life, have you Curatio?" Terian asked.

"Just the once," Curatio said. "I wouldn't do it again."

"I'm now taking recommendations for ways to die," Calene said. "I will say that hanging wasn't terrible," she shuddered, "though what came before it was a bit … much."

"Do you remember it?" Martaina asked. The ranger's eyes were on her counterpart, and Calene Raverle seemed to focus on a distant point behind them.

"Sort of," Raverle said. "I mean, yes. But it's almost as though it happened to someone else. It feels … very long ago, very far away."

Cyrus did not say anything; he just kept his head down and watched the fire.

"I believe it's time for me to sleep," Terian said as he stood, and his spiked profile receded into the darkness.

"Not staying by the fire?" Martaina teased as she stood, disappearing into the black as well.

"Gods, no," Terian replied. "Too hot."

"I kind of figured that out for myself," Martaina said with a roll of her eyes.

"I mean I'm too hot," Terian said with a wicked grin. "Wouldn't want any of the rest of you to get—"

"All right, that's enough for me," Curatio said as he stood, and then walked off in the other direction.

"It seems likely we'll be awakened in the middle of the night," Longwell said, and grabbed his lance, using it to push himself to his feet. "To move back or come to the front. The advance is harsh, and the dragoons are doing great damage, but not nearly enough, I think."

"How much more flat ground do they have to fight on?" Cyrus asked.

"A day's worth, perhaps," Longwell said with a shrug. "After that, the land becomes swampy, the grasses hide water and soft ground, and we'll need to withdraw. "We'll do as much damage as we can for as long as we can, but in another day, we might as well be infantry for all the good we'll do."

"Your day will come again," Cyrus said. "On the other side of the bridge, I think. We'll need to move you out to flat ground if we're to carry on. Perhaps use a wizard to teleport your men to Taymor or one of the portals northwest of there. You can assemble on the flatlands north of the Inculta desert and make another defense there as these things come north."

"I don't love the turn of inevitability this conversation has taken," Calene said from across the fire.

"Nor do I," Scuddar said quietly from behind his cowl.

Cyrus stared at the two of them; though he had shared a fire with both of them on numerous occasions, he could hardly say he knew them well. "I'm sorry. But this is not going well, and I think we have to conclude that we need a plan to deal with what's about to happen."

"And what's that?" Calene asked. Scuddar's eyes watched as well, silently accusing.

"We're going to get pushed back to the bridge," Cyrus said. "And once we're on the bridge, we'll be pushed back all the way to Arkaria."

"Why?" Scuddar was the one who asked this time.

"Because," Cyrus said, feeling as though he were explaining the concept to children, "there are more of them than there are of us. Because the viciousness of their attack inevitably requires us to give ground."

"Why?" Scuddar asked.

Now I really am explaining to a child. "You've fought them,"

Cyrus said. "They come at you, they lunge, you kill one, you parry another, the next comes, you have to take a step back to avoid getting hit. There's push. It's a natural part of the battle."

"It's a natural part of losing a battle, seems to me," Calene said quietly, avoiding Cyrus's eyes.

"Which makes sense," Cyrus said with as much patience as he could find, "since we are losing this battle. This war, really. As much as I'd like to rail against the inevitability of loss, I can't find an example to point to of when we've ever pushed them back. We've only seen the opposite happen."

"It would seem we lack only belief and hope," Scuddar said quietly.

Cyrus tried to avoid rolling his eyes but only succeeded in looking to Longwell, who shrugged in some agreement. "Really?" he asked the King.

"He makes a point," Longwell said. "We retreat because we accept the inevitability of their advance. We don't fight to push them back because we believe they're going to keep coming long past the point when we're willing to stand and die to push them back. Because that's what it would take—a full-blooded, mystic-bladed warrior with the conviction that they could singlehandedly cut the enemy down if they advance one step further." He shrugged. "You put someone like that in front of the scourge—on a bridge, no less, where all their myriad numbers count for less—I believe they'll buckle before the warrior."

Cyrus hid a foolish grin, a patronizing one, behind his hand. *You cannot be serious.* "I don't know where you'd find this warrior—"

"It's you," Calene said without hesitation, causing Cyrus to freeze in place. "It's always been you."

He pursed his lips and felt the guilt well up. "I appreciate that, really I do, more than you know. But that's a vote of confidence I don't think I deserve. If anyone on this expedition should be skeptical of me and my ability to command effectively it should be you, after what you went through—"

"After what I went through?" She bristled. "I got captured by the enemy, a cruel, vicious and subhuman one. He did some nasty things, things that made me feel like less than a person." She leaned forward. "But you weren't him. And you didn't let him get away with it, either.

You came for me, and you didn't have to. Anyone else would have left us behind, or struggled to get us back. You saved me. You saved the others—"

"But not until after—"

"After what happened had already happened," she said, and Cyrus heard the razored steel in her voice. "You saved us. Led us out and made him suffer." She sat back and looked at him coolly. "I believe in you."

Cyrus put a hand against his face. "Everyone keeps saying that. I'm not even sure I know what it means anymore."

She stared back at him, quiet, then looked at Scuddar, then Longwell. "Haven't you ever had someone you knew you could count on before? That no matter how bad it got, you knew they'd be there with you, no matter what?"

Cyrus felt an icy chill run through his gut and a memory flitter. *They all left, one by one. Left me alone. Father. Mother. Imina. Narstron. Orion. Niamh.* He looked around the fire. *And this lot ... they're the ones counting on me. Who am I supposed to count on?*

Vara. He blinked away the thought. "I don't know," he said at last, almost mumbling.

"Belief in others is a powerful thing," Scuddar said, his quiet, deep timbre. "Hope is sometimes all we have. There's an old legend among my people, the story of the Ark. Have you heard it?"

"No," Cyrus said with a shake of his head.

"When the world was first new," Scuddar began, "there were only two gods who ruled over it—the God of Good, and the God of Evil. They divided among themselves all the attributes and aspects that each prized. Courage, Light, Knowledge, Life—these were but a few of the virtues held by the followers of good." His countenance darkened in the firelight. "Darkness, Despair, Death and War—those and others were held high in esteem by the God of Evil. It was a mighty struggle, waged day and night over the surface of the bare land. But the forces were too evenly matched, as evil had captured the hearts and souls of mortal beings to even the score. Mortals began to despair, so wracked were they with the darkness sent from evil. And so the God of Good sent forth his last gift to mortals—the Ark. It was to be what they looked to in times of trouble, as within they could find that most ephemeral of all the virtues."

Cyrus stared across the fire at the desert man, heard the pop of the logs, felt the smoke fill the air around him as though the words were taking on a mystical quality of their own. He took a deep inhalation through his nose and the smell of the wood fire took him back, as though he were around a campfire in the days when the story was happening. He listened on as his skin prickled from the back of his neck and up his scalp, and he watched through the flames as the man of the desert moved his hands in time with the story, as though he had told it numerous times before. "What was it?" Cyrus asked, and realized that if Scuddar had, in fact, told this story numerous times before, he had paused and was waiting for someone to answer.

"Hope." Scuddar's hands came down. "It is in our darkest hours that we let despair creep in, let it drain us of any faith in ourselves. Hope is our respite, the answer to our cries. The belief that darkness can be destroyed by the light, that despair can be turned back if we believe—if we have hope for a brighter day ahead."

Cyrus ran his hand up to his long hair, tangled and matted. *How many days has it been since I bathed? Since I breathed? Since I slept in my own bed, lived in my own walls, breathed air that didn't have even the slightest tinge of decay and wondered if these things would be coming? How long since I first started to lose ... hope?* The thought came easy: *It was the day I carried her to her room and listened to her say that we would never be together—could never be together. Everything since has made me question every action taken, every consequence I've set loose.* "How can you dare to hope ..." Cyrus began, "... when you know that all you have wrought is ... darkness ... and despair ... and death?"

Scuddar leaned forward over the fire, and his eyes caught the light; they were yellow, and Cyrus had never noticed that before, but they glowed. "Because darkness ... and despair and death ... these are things all rooted in your past. Hope ... is about a future. You need not live your whole life governed by them. That road is despair. Futility. Hope is the idea that no matter what evil you might have done, willing or unwilling—it can redeemed."

Cyrus felt the gut clench of emotion. "I fear that there are some things so wrong, so dark, that there is no redemption for them."

Scuddar's yellow eyes narrowed. "Well, that is not really up to you now, is it?"

"Didn't you believe in the God of War, once upon a time?" Longwell asked, breaking Cyrus out of his trance and turning his head away from Scuddar. "In battle and chaos, destruction and death?"

"For combatants, yes," Cyrus said. "Not for the innocent. For those who wanted it, for those who thrived on battle, the clash of blade, the evangelism of the trial by fire."

"Those things are combatants," Longwell said, pointing him toward the field of battle, somewhere ahead in the darkness, barely visible beyond the fire-lit camp. "You don't believe they deserve to die?"

"They're already dead," Cyrus said, "but yes, they deserve to die. And I'll kill as many as I can."

"Ah," Scuddar said. "So you believe in something, at least. Even something so minor as that. It's a start."

"And what do you believe?" Cyrus asked, watching the smoke waft between him and Scuddar, between the night and those yellow eyes.

"I believe that when you come to the moment when you believe all hope is gone," Scuddar said, "you will be forced to reach down inside yourself, to touch whatever remains within you. I believe in that moment, General … you'll find the embers of whatever is left. You'll find what you truly believe in. And I think …" the desert man smiled, "… that whatever it is, our enemy will have cause to fear. Because a man can only live with despair for so long before hope resurges."

Chapter 103

The next day was a long battle, one that grated and dragged along him, like a whip taken to flesh. He could feel the pain in his muscles at the close of the day, the smell of death fixed in his nose as though he had swallowed it, the stench hanging in the back of his throat and threatening to gag him with every breath. The sound of swords tearing flesh was in his ears as was the guttural screaming of the scourge, their cries echoing in the night even now, far behind the lines. Cyrus was arrayed in a council, Curatio and Martaina with him along with Terian. Opposite him were Longwell and Ranson, directly across, Briyce Unger to his left and Milos Tiernan to his right, a fearsome scarring present on Tiernan's face.

"Before we begin," Tiernan said, nodding in acknowledgment to Cyrus, "I owe you my thanks for saving my sister."

"I only wish it hadn't cost you Caenalys in the process," Cyrus said. Tiernan's jaw clamped shut; he said nothing.

Silence reigned for almost a full minute. "Well, we've come to it at last," Unger said. The mountain King's shoulders were slumped, as though one of the fabled avalanches had finally come down on him.

"Aye," Longwell said. "Our flat ground is done; from here to the bridge it's a swampy corridor of peninsula. Our last advantage is gone." He made as if to turn and look to the fields of recent battle. "It was a good fight while it lasted, though." He turned serious, sober. "We could have the dragoons dismount and fight as foot infantry—"

"Foolish," Unger said, shaking his enormous head.

"A waste," Tiernan agreed. There was a somber spirit of dejection upon them, but Tiernan seemed to brush it aside. "The time has come to plan the next phase. To see our people safely across to the west. We have the foot troops to hold the last of the peninsula for a time." The King of Actaluere set his jaw. "I've discussed it with my men, and many of them have no desire to leave these shores. I mean to stay, to water these last miles with my blood and tears, and to give our people as great a head start as we can."

The silence filled the air. "I never thought an Actaluerean would leave aside merchant sensibility for something so ..." Unger smiled, "... deeply felt. I've lost my homeland. Few enough of my people have made it over that bridge." He shook his head. "I have no desire to keep fighting this battle into a new land when I've already lost my own." His eyes flicked toward Longwell.

"Aye," Samwen Longwell said, and Cyrus saw the full weight of a crown that wasn't there, weighing down his head. "I have seen things ... *done* things ... to try and save this land ... things I don't wish to carry with me to the west. I was born in Luukessia, and I wish to die here." He looked up at Cyrus. "Will you lead my men—my dragoons—into the west and help them to protect our people as best you can? We will buy you as much time as our bodies allow," he said with a grim smile.

Cyrus looked from Tiernan to Unger then to Longwell. "I obviously can't stay with you gentlemen, much as I might like. My land has yet to be hit by these things, but we all know it's coming. Yes, I will protect your citizenry in their retreat with everything I have left," he said, without much feeling. "I'll take whatever men you have who don't wish to die in the last defense of Luukessia and into battle in Arkaria." He settled in, a glum feeling hanging over him. "And perhaps we'll ... find a way, over there, to stem the tide of these things. If they follow."

"There's no guarantee they will, after all," Longwell said, but with enough of a kernel of disbelief that Cyrus knew that the dragoon didn't believe it either. "If we give you enough time, perhaps the smell of life will be lost among their fear of the waters."

"A faint hope," Cyrus said with a slight smile, "but one I'm clinging to right now."

There hung a moment of silence as the four of them all looked to one another. Tiernan broke it when he stood first, and gestured toward Cyrus, who stood and stepped closer to take the King of Actaluere's outstretched hand.

"I trust you'll continue to see to my sister," Tiernan said, "and make certain she's kept well out of the danger that comes?"

"I will," Cyrus said.

"Your word," Tiernan said firmly. "I'd like it, please."

Cyrus felt a pinch inside. "I give you my word I'll protect her for as long as I'm able."

He smiled tightly. "Thank you." He shook Cyrus's hand hard and stepped aside.

Unger stood and stepped over to Cyrus. "Thank you for believing me when no one else would. Without your help, we'd not have gotten much of anyone out of Syloreas before the fall."

Cyrus felt a clutch of pain inside. *If not for me, you'd still have a Kingdom.* "I'm sorry we couldn't do more."

Unger gave a slow shake of his head. "You've done quite enough. More than I likely would have done were our situations reversed. I'd have fled and not looked back."

Longwell stood last and his crossing was slow, the King of Galbadien looking down at his feet, his helm clutched under his arm. When his head came up, Cyrus saw him biting his lower lip. "I owe you great thanks for all you've done. You've shown me a world I never would have believed. That you came here in the name of our friendship, out of loyalty to me, when you didn't need to—it means everything."

"I wish I'd had purer motives in doing so," Cyrus said.

"Whatever your motives when you started," Longwell said, "you stayed when you didn't have to. You went north to Syloreas when you had no reason to think you were responsible in any way. And you've fought—ancestors! How you've fought." He seized Cyrus's hand, hard. "I believe in you—that if anyone will find a way to stop them, it's you. If anyone could hold that bridge ..." Longwell's face tightened. "Well. I'm sorry I won't be there to help you this time—"

There came a crack from behind Samwen, and the dragoon slumped, falling abruptly to Cyrus's feet. Ranson stood behind him and unclenched his gauntlet. "Enough of that," the Count said. "Take him with you, would you please? This is not a place for a young man to die, especially one whom you know could help you hold that bridge."

Cyrus looked at the fallen figure of Longwell, out cold on the ground. "You could have ... made your case to him about that."

Ranson scoffed. "I've served his family for all my life. Served Galbadien for my entire life. I'll die here, willingly, but I'll not have the last vestige of our old ways destroyed because he's got a foolish desire to spend himself before his time. If he truly wants to die, he can do it across the sea—after he's ensured the safety of our people. It's his last duty as King of Galbadien." Ranson cocked an eyebrow. "You tell him I said that, when he wakes up."

Cyrus looked between the Kings of Luukessia. "All right. We'll pull back to the bridge with the dragoons and any men you want to send our way, and we'll hold there until the last are on it. After that, we'll go and cover the retreat—and hope that we make it far enough, fast enough to leave those bastards behind."

"We'll give you all the time we can spare," Milos Tiernan said. "We're placing the last of our Kingdoms in your hands—the last of the Luukessians. I dearly hope you'll save them." He looked from Ranson to Unger, then back to Cyrus. "After all," the King of Actaluere said with a smile, "you are our last hope."

Chapter 104

With the dawn they were headed west, Cyrus and the Sanctuary army, on a slow march along the road. The sound of combat faded behind them as the morning wore on, and they set out pickets that night after sunset. The territory was familiar in appearance, the coastal ground they'd trod in their first days in Luukessia. The crickets sang in the grasses, the winds blew sea air fresh across them from the south, a salt breeze that reminded Cyrus of the boat, or of a day on the beach long ago—the first day he had been in Luukessia. The swaying grass and short sight lines reminded him of plains, just briefly. *Of home. Or whatever Sanctuary is to me now.*

There was a sound, a low moan. Cyrus turned to look and saw Longwell clutching his head nearby, stirring from the place where he was bound with rope. He had been thrown unceremoniously on the back of a horse and left there for a good portion of the day after a healing spell from Curatio. Cyrus had looked at the damage done by Ranson before the healing spell had been cast; privately he did not envy the dragoon.

"What happened?" Longwell said, trying to sit up and struggling against the rope.

Cyrus looked him over. "Ranson knocked you out and asked me to take you with us."

Longwell blinked and looked at the ropes that bound him. "You must surely be joking."

Cyrus shrugged. "I think you'll agree I haven't been in much of a joking mood of late. More brooding, I think."

"Are you going to let me loose?" Longwell said, struggling against the bonds that bound him under his armor.

"In another day or so," Cyrus said, taking a drink from a skin of water and then holding it up to Longwell to let him sip from it. "Wouldn't want you trying to escape and go back to throw yourself into a massacre, after all."

Longwell finished his drink, giving Cyrus a measured glare. "So this is how you would treat me, after all this time? Bind me like a criminal?" He eyed Terian, who sat nearby and cocked his head at the comment. "Sorry." He switched his gaze back to Cyrus. "You would strike my ability to choose for myself?"

"Yep," Cyrus said. "I hope you understand. I'm going to need your help on that bridge." He favored Longwell with a look, a cool, understated one.

"I ... what?"

"The bridge," Cyrus said. "I need someone at my side who can handle this situation. Someone who's been in a fight like this before because if these things end up crossing, we're the last line of defense. Your horsemen are going to be useless in a fight of this sort. The Sanctuary army can do some good if we fail, but we need to be the stone wall upon which the scourge breaks—for as long as it takes to get your people off that bridge and headed north to the portal, where we can evacuate them quickly." He took another sip. "Hopefully some of them have already reached the other side and started to head that way."

"You want me by your side for this again," Longwell said, letting his bound hands hang in front of him.

"I need your help," Cyrus said. "You, Scuddar, Odellan," he darted a look backwards, "Terian, probably. This could be days of fighting. I have a lot of veterans thanks to our army being in a near-constant battle these last few months, but I need an elite, a front rank that won't buckle, no matter what."

Longwell settled, his struggle with the bonds done. "It almost sounds as though you mean to try and drive them back; to stand and fight and make them feel the pain and blink."

Cyrus looked at Longwell out of the corner of his eye, just for a moment, then back to the dark, swampy night. "Maybe I do. Maybe I do."

Longwell gave a short nod after a moment of thought. "Very well, then. I cede the wisdom of your proposal. I will fight alongside you on the bridge." He held out his hand. "You may release me now; I won't go anywhere."

Cyrus pulled the water skin from between his lips. "I know you won't. Because you're going to stay roped until we get to the bridge."

Even in the dark, Cyrus could see the disbelief as Longwell's face fell. "What? But I gave you my word."

"Yeah," Cyrus agreed. "But a man desperate to die in the defense of his homeland might be possessed to say some untruths. After all, who's gonna care if he lied after he's dead?"

"But," Longwell said, sputtering, looking around for some sort of support. "I'm the King of Galbadien!"

"Right you are, Your Majesty," Cyrus said, and bowed his head. "Would you like some more water?"

Longwell's expression turned from disbelief to fury, then slowed to irritation, then finally to a long, sustained eyeroll. "Very well."

Chapter 105

Two days later, they crossed the berm to see the bridge spanning the sea before them. The last of the straggling refugees were already upon it, barely visible on the horizon. At the base of the span, though, waited a familiar party—two blue-skinned figures at the side of the bridge along with another, her brown hair above her shoulders. Cyrus rode up to them, felt the salt spray of the tide hitting his face, and gazed upon J'anda's face in shock. His own gasp filled his ears, and a feeling like someone had jammed a rod into his spine set him upright in the saddle. After a moment it subsided, as he got closer, and looked at the lined, worn skin on the enchanter's face. "You burned through your magical energy," Cyrus said, "and started trading your life for bread."

There was a nod from the enchanter, whose hair was now streaked with a faded grey. "Worth it, I think," he said, voice raspy. "A few hundred years of my life to spare thousands of lives." He shrugged. "In mere days, it may not matter anyway."

"Very laudable," Curatio pronounced as he arrived.

Cyrus shook his head at J'anda. "It's your life, I suppose."

"I did what I thought was right," J'anda said with another shrug. "I regret nothing."

Cyrus waved toward Longwell, who sat at the front of a line of horsemen. "Start them across. They'll be able to catch the back line of those refugees fairly easily. Tell them not to hurry, not to push. We don't want to start a stampede, and we've got some time." He paused. "I think."

Longwell tossed him a mock salute with only a little acrimony and motioned for the horsemen to start across.

"How many horsemen do you have?" Cattrine asked, with a look of slightly shocked awe as she looked at the perfectly formed lines, moving up the bridge at faster than a walk.

Cyrus dismounted and landed his hand on her shoulder, giving it a squeeze. "More than ten thousand. Enough to give the scourge a fight if we can get to open ground on the other side of the sea. Transport will be a problem because you can't teleport nearly that many in one bunch with one wizard, but if we can get to the portal two days north of the other side of the bridge, we can transport everyone fast—in half an hour or so—back to Sanctuary."

"Your magic still amazes me," Cattrine said with a shake of the head.

"I don't have any magic," Cyrus said. He gave Aisling a nod of greeting, which was returned with some reserve. He looked Cattrine in the eyes. "I'm sending you with the second regiment of dragoons."

She looked to him, and her head went from leaning forward, eager to see him, to relaxed and falling back as her face did the same; it fell. "I wouldn't want to be a bother, I suppose."

"Not a bother," Cyrus said. "But I promised your brother I would see to your safety, and I need to keep my word."

"Very well," she said. "Did he send any other message?"

He let his jaw relax. "Just to see you to safety. His last worries, aside from wanting to die fighting the good fight for Luukessia, were about you."

She gave a slow nod and started to turn away toward the horsemen marching up the bridge. "I don't suppose he gave a thought to what would happen to our people in this new land? Of how he should have stayed to lead them?"

"I don't think he much wanted to contemplate a new land," Cyrus said. "I believe the pain of the loss of the old was the sort of wound he would not ever have been able to put aside." There was a sting in his words, as though he were rubbing salt on a wound of his own. "That's my suspicion, at least."

"I'm certain you have no idea what that feels like," Cattrine said, her eyes warm, but her tone slightly sardonic. *She knows.* "I'll take my leave of you now, Lord Davidon, so you might fight whatever battle comes without concern for my safety." She stepped to him, gave him a peck on the cheek, then a longer, fuller kiss on the lips. "I do hope to see you on the other side." She lifted her skirts and trod across the beach, her feet leaving impressions in the sand.

The horsemen went on for the rest of the day. As the night began to fall, the Sanctuary army moved onto the bridge at last, the back ranks going first—the most wearied, in Cyrus's eyes, along with Windrider and the other horses. Curatio and a few of the others came toward the end, with their spellcasters, and finally Cyrus himself, along with Odellan, Longwell, Martaina, Scuddar, and Terian.

After the first hour, Terian eased over to Cyrus. "You haven't asked me to fight alongside you."

"You've been fighting alongside me on and off since Enrant Monge," Cyrus said, unimpressed. "What's different now? You finally going to try and kill me again?"

"Not today," Terian replied. The clank of his boots and Cyrus's, and countless others, was soft in the night, and somewhere far below the splash of water against the pilings of the bridge could be heard. "Maybe tomorrow, though," the dark knight said with a wicked grin.

"You don't even really believe it anymore," Cyrus said.

"Hm," Terian said with only a trace of amusement. "I think it's more accurate to say I don't know what I believe anymore."

"Lot of that going around."

"Indeed there is," Terian said. "We're still not done yet though, you and I."

"No," Cyrus said, "I suppose we're not. I'm fine with that, so long as it doesn't bleed into this."

"No," Terian said somberly, "I won't let my personal vendetta against you stop us from saving these people as best we can."

"'As best we can?'" Cyrus mused. "I don't know, Lepos, maybe there's some hope for you yet."

Terian shot him a scathing glance. "Why? Do you think there's some chance for redemption for me, even after I tried to kill you? Because if you say 'yes,' I may have to kill you now, outside of my promise, just on the principle of it."

"I don't know about that," Cyrus said. "Redemption's a funny thing."

"Oh?" Terian said with a scowl. "What's so funny about it?"

"I don't know." Cyrus looked back over his shoulder, into the darkness, to the long, empty stretch of stone behind him. "The Kings— Unger, Tiernan, Longwell," he looked to the side and gestured to Samwen, who trudged alone quietly to their left, "and Ranson, I suppose. They thought they'd failed to protect their Kingdoms, the places they were sworn to serve. They failed their lands, their people.

They were Kings, supposed to be the most exalted, but they understood that basic truth that they were supposed to serve their people. Their redemption for that was to stand at the last edge of their land and die trying to stop these things from coming any farther." Cyrus shrugged. "I don't know. Maybe the willingness to fight that hard, to die for what you believe in … maybe that brings its own sort of redemption. And peace, I would hope."

Terian looked back now, as though he could see the scourge behind them. "I don't know what peace death brings, not after all we've seen this year. Those things. I don't know what sort of redemption there is out there for those of us who have …" He bowed his head. "Erred, let's call it."

"I don't suppose you'd consider your attempt to kill me in that category, would you?"

"Don't push it, Davidon," Terian said irritably. "I'm already having the sort of conversation with you that I don't comfortably have with anyone else."

"But because you're going to kill me, it's almost like you're not talking to anyone at all, huh?"

"No one keeps secrets like the dead," Terian quipped.

They walked on in peace for two more days after that, a solemn, quiet, cool breeze coming off the sea of Carmas in gusts that ran through the cracks in Cyrus's mail. The salt air was good, a pleasant smell, but it left a film on his armor. The nights were long and he spent them alone. Aisling looked at him from across the army a few times, as though she were waiting for him to beckon her forward. He did not, though, and instead lay awake staring at the stars until his eyes finally drooped into sleep.

It was at the close of the third day that the wind shifted directions, from out of the south. Cyrus could feel it, tangible, a change in current. The stone bridge went on into infinity before him, packed tightly with men and horses as far as he could see. When he turned back, as he had every few minutes for the entire journey, afraid that his next moment would be the one when a scourge jumped onto his back and dragged him down, he still saw nothing but the faint distortion of a mirage in the distance. The sun was falling in the sky but it was surprisingly hot, the southern breeze doing little to shift the air. *Early summer weather? It's not even finished being spring yet.*

There was movement to his left and he turned to see Martaina, her cowl falling behind her head and exposing her hair to flutter in the breeze. She stared into the distance behind them, peering carefully, then dropped to the ground and put her ear against the surface of the bridge.

"Interesting place to sleep," Terian said with a grin.

She waved at him for silence, and they waited. A moment later she sprang up and looked at Cyrus, deadly serious. "They're coming."

He tensed. "Are you sure?"

She nodded. "I can hear their claws. Much different sound than horses clip-clopping along ahead of us. It's faint, but there. A whole bunch of them, too, coming on fast. They'll catch up to us in a few hours, maybe a half-day at most."

"We're only two days from the shores of Arkaria. We need to buy time," Cyrus said, thinking. "Nyad!"

"Buy time for what?" Terian asked. "Once those things hit the shore, we're done. Good luck bottling them up again, or beating them in the jungle as they sweep north. Once the cork comes out of the bottle, the wine is going to escape all over your new dress."

"I don't wear a dress," Cyrus said as Nyad appeared at his side. "Go back to Sanctuary and warn Alaric that these things are coming and we need help, now, at the bridge. No time to waste. Don't take any excuses; these things aren't on Luukessia anymore, they're coming, and they will destroy our land if we don't stop them. You need to make him understand. Got it?"

She nodded, and closed her eyes, lips moving in subtle ways as she repeated the incantation. Her hands glowed slightly, and there was a burst of green energy that exploded over them, causing Cyrus to turn his head and avert his eyes. When he opened them again and looked back, Nyad remained standing in the same place, a look of puzzlement upon her face. She closed her eyes again and began to cast the spell, the glow came forth once more, the light burst with sparkles, and when the spots cleared from Cyrus's vision she still stood in the middle of the Endless Bridge.

"Maybe I should send someone else?" Cyrus asked.

"No," Nyad said with a shake of her head. "It's not that. It's not me. It's the spell—the portal! It's not working."

"What do you mean it's not working?" Terian asked, his eyebrows knitted together in a deep furrow. "How does a spell not work?"

Nyad seemed to consider this for a moment, staring off at the horizon. "There are only two reasons why the spell wouldn't work. Either the portal has been shut down, or—" She stopped speaking and paled, her complexion looking a flushed orange in the light of the late afternoon, as her voice dropped to a hushed whisper. "Or it's been destroyed."

Chapter 106

Vara

Day 221 of the Siege of Sanctuary

The battlements were in motion, a steady flow of people. The smell of them was strong, unwashed after a few days of long watches; Vara could even smell herself from under the armor. There had been only time for a few hours of sleep per night as the dark elves had begun a near-constant assault on the front gates. She looked down on the battering ram they were currently employing, hundreds of arrows sticking out of it in all directions, as the twenty or so dark elves carrying it were surrounded by an additional phalanx with shields to protect them. *This situation needs Alaric's touch. I dearly hope he's on his way.*

The sound was riotous, a hundred thousand enemies surrounding them, ladders flung upward to the top of the wall every few minutes with a clack of wood against stone and thrown back down only moments later with screams. Of course, some of the screams came from atop the wall as well, Vara knew, as there were volleys of arrows coming at them thickly, like a diagonal rainstorm of shafts, fletchings, and arrowheads. She kept her head down and heard them whistling all around her, the occasional scream close by attesting to another poor soul who'd caught one. One came from beside her, presently, and she heard a scuffle. A ranger had an arrow sticking out of his eye and was shouting, his bow cast aside from where he had been using it to aim at the shielded enemy.

"Healer!" Vara called without looking back. She plucked the bow and arrow off the ground and fired blindly over the ramparts.

"You called, Shelas'akur?" Vaste's droll voice came up behind her. "Ow, this one looks like it hurts. Eyeball, eh? Wouldn't want him to end up as Alaric the Second." A scream came from behind her but she didn't bother to look, just plucked another arrow and fired. "Well, hold still, damn you," Vaste said. "This arrow isn't going to pull itself out, and I can't exactly heal you with it still in your eye, can I? Oh, dammit!"

There was a sound of a hard hit behind her and she jumped, looking back, forcing her back against the crenellation of stone. Vaste smiled weakly over the fallen ranger, who was unconscious with a blatantly broken jaw. "Sorry. I had to knock him out. I'll fix it now."

"Try not to enjoy yourself too much harming our allies," Vara said, snagging the ranger's quiver from his back and pulling it free, then blind-firing another arrow over the battlements.

"I can't imagine you're doing much good shooting like that," Vaste said, his hands beginning to glow.

"I can't imagine I'm not hitting something," she replied, releasing another arrow, "seeing as the dark elves are filling the ground before us all the way to the horizon."

"More of a random act of hoping to hit something?" Vaste asked, his healing spell complete, the ranger's eye now open, unfocused, and returned to normal. "Sounds like a metaphor for my love life."

"I would have to miss considerably more to make that an accurate metaphor."

"So cruel," Vaste said. He glanced to the left and right. "Need any more healing done here? Other than your bitterness-encrusted heart?"

"I would laugh," Vara said tightly, firing again, "but I seem to be in the midst of a crisis that has my attention. Be assured, though, I am remembering this moment for later, and I will certainly give it due amusement at that time. By which I mean I'll be sitting around later whilst reading and will perhaps spare a moment to frown at your ridiculousness."

"So long as we all live to see that moment, I'm fine with that," Vaste said, still on his knees. "If you'll excuse me, I have to crawl down the ramparts a ways," he pointed toward the gates to the left, "and assist that poor bastard who has an arrow sticking out of his buttock." The troll sighed. "One would think that armor would protect against that sort of thing. And who do you think will have to pull it out? Why couldn't it have happened to a short, swarthy human woman? I like those."

Vara rolled her eyes. "I have things to be getting on with, troll. Be about your business."

"Oh, I'm sorry," Vaste said, beginning to crawl left, "I didn't realize it was my presence keeping you from looking at where you were firing, I thought it was the ten thousand arrows that were filling the air like the worst cloud of mosquitos ever visited upon a swamp."

She shook her head as he left. *This is ridiculous, this press of the attack.* She stuck her head out of the rampart for one second only, and saw that the battering ram was down again, wreathed in flames, and she spared only a little smile. *Not today, Sovereign. Not today.*

"They come again," the voice was shot through with fatigue, but the figure appeared in a cloud of smoke, wafting off him in waves. "I see they've already fallen," Alaric said, peering over the rampart as arrows flew through his exposed face and upper body. "Let us make this moderately more difficult on them." Vara leaned her eyes over and felt an arrow *clink!* off her helm, causing her to blanch. She looked down upon the battering ram as Alaric's force blast hit it and sent it rolling as though it had been kicked by a titan; it hit the ground and bounced five feet into the air and off the trodden road, bowling over a knot of dark elven soldiers, landing on them while still on fire. Their agonized screams blended into the chorus already filling the air. He fired another burst and the ram bounced again into the air from the force of his spell, this time even higher, almost ten feet, before it came down into another thicket of men.

Vara eyed the chaos that the paladin's spell had caused; *that injured over a hundred men and killed quite a few of them.* "Satisfied yet?" she asked.

"No," Alaric's voice was gruff, uncaring. "Wizards! Druids!" he called, as though his words were amplified beyond a shout. "SEND THEM RUNNING!"

She watched as the flames rose around the walls, a burning, roiling firestorm ten feet high of interconnected fire spells that ate into the dark elven army surrounding them like little she had seen. It was not terribly thick—*not like Mother's*—but it burned with a fury, lancing into the thickest concentrations of soldiers and raising the volume of screaming that filled the air by a considerable amount. Some began to flee, throwing the knot of soldiers around them into disarray and chaos, and Vara watched as a soldier fell and was trampled while attempting to escape. She ducked back behind the teeth of the wall and put her back against it. "Not bad, Alaric."

"I told you," the Ghost said, "they will not breach our walls."

"Thanks to you," she said.

"Courtesy of our wizards and druids," he replied. "I have little to do with it save for sending their battering ram off course in a fit of pique. It will take them a few attempts to get it back to the road and in position again. That will cost them a few men."

Vara gave him a nod. "A few men indee—" she tore her eyes from him at a blur of motion that came out of the tower to her right, a leather-clad figure who ran surefootedly, bent double, keeping her white hair low as she crossed the top of the rampart to reach them. Vara blinked in surprise as she registered recognition. "YOU!"

"Me," the woman said, coming to a rest and kneeling next to where Alaric stood. "And you wouldn't believe what I had to do to get here." Her white hair was caked with dirt as was the rest of her outfit, leather armor and all.

"Aisling," Alaric said mildly, peering down at the ranger. "You have returned to us. I would ask how, but I suspect 'Why?' is the more important question."

"There's a waste tunnel that leads to the river over there," she waved in the distance toward the river Perda's split, which rolled by outside the walls almost a mile away. "It's a tight squeeze over a long distance, but I managed. Nyad, too—she teleported us in behind the army through the portal over there —" she waved out the direction of the gate, "but she's a little slower than I am after that trek." She looked up at Alaric in seriousness. "Cyrus sent me to plead for your help. They've evacuated the whole of Luukessia."

Alaric blinked at her, but said nothing. "Excuse me," Vara said. "Did you say—"

"The whole land of Luukessia has fallen, yes," Aisling said. "They've taken it, from one side to the other, killing ..." There was a moment's pause as the dark elf seemed to waver then compose herself. "We've managed to get the last of the survivors onto the bridge, and Cyrus and the others are staging a slow withdrawal and bridge defense, but ..." she shook her head, "they need help. They need an army before the scourge breaks loose of the Endless Bridge ... or we'll be facing the same fight here that cost us Luukessia."

Alaric stood silent, and Vara looked to him for guidance. He did not react openly, but she could see even in the slight twitch of his mouth that something roiled beneath the surface. "Alaric?" she asked. "The dark elves—"

"The lesser threat, now, I think," Alaric said quietly. "How long until this scourge make landfall?"

"A day," Aisling said. "Perhaps two. They're strong, Alaric, too strong for us to hold back the tide of them forever."

Alaric nodded. "Very well." He looked out across the panorama of the army surrounding the curtain wall. The volume of arrows still flying through the air was considerably decreased. "I need you to find Ryin Ayend and bring him to me. He will be just down the wall in that direction, I think," and the Ghost pointed to his right. "Tell him to hurry."

Aisling nodded and was off at a run, bent over and moving at incredible speed and with enough grace that Vara felt a surge of jealousy as she had a flash where she saw Cyrus pressed against the dark elf in her mind, naked— "Alaric," she said, throwing cold water upon that thought, "what do you intend?"

"It would appear Cyrus Davidon requires assistance," Alaric said calmly, and he crouched down next to her. "I will go to him myself to render it."

She frowned at him as though he were insane. "Alaric, one man will not be able to turn back the tide of these things that are coming, not if Cyrus's reports or that diseased harpy," she waved at Aisling's retreating—*and firm,* she noted irritably—backside, "are to be believed. These things swept our army and the armies of three nations before them. What makes you think that they'll do any different to you?"

Alaric stared at her through his helm, calmly impassive, but only for a moment before he smiled. "Have faith, Vara. I will take care of this. It is upon you to hold our home safe until my return." His smile flickered. "Take care of yourself—and the others."

She lay her head back against the wall behind her and caught a sudden waft of death far below. "How long will you be gone?"

He hesitated, an unusual thing for him to do. "As long as need be and not a moment more," he answered finally. She saw movement out of the corner of her eye and Ryin appeared, led by Aisling. She gave the dark elven woman a sneer, but it was halfhearted and she received only a coldly satisfied gaze in return. Alaric gave Ryin a nod. "Ladies," Alaric said, "take care while I am away." With that, the winds carried up around them, sweeping like a tornado around the ramparts, stirring Vara's hair and rushing through the cracks in her armor to touch her skin while roaring in her ears. There was the taste of bitterness in her mouth as the wind settled, and Alaric was gone.

Chapter 107

Cyrus

The slog was hard, the salt air on his tongue along with the sweat that fell in drops with his exertion. The breeze kept him cool under the sun, but with every swing of Praelior he let another exhalation out, another muted curse at the things that came at him, black eyes, foul breath, no souls, and he took his fury out upon them. *I've faced them for months, relentlessly, with all I had. This is the first time I can recall feeling so angry at them.* He chanced a look back behind him; there was the faintest outline of land, far, far in the distance, barely visible even in the morning light. *Hard to believe, that.*

"You know," Terian said conversationally, to his right, "I honestly thought that at some point, after as many of these things as we've killed, that they would eventually run out of them. But no, I guess thousands of years of dead kind of pile up, huh?"

"Less talking," Longwell said, swinging his spear wide and sweeping five of the scourge over the edge of the bridge; he was to Cyrus's far right, past Terian. Odellan and Scuddar were to his immediate left. *I anchor the line in the middle.* Another three came at him, all teeth. *Where they aim their onslaught hardest.* "More killing."

There were black stains running along the stone they stood upon, the fresh evidence of the chaos they'd unleashed. It ran along the slight grade toward Arkaria, filling the carved lines in the bridge, the infinitesimally small gaps that didn't seem like gaps at all to Cyrus, more like lines in the stone. *Perfectly joined. No sign of mortar. The ancients must have been impressive indeed to have built this.*

"Augh!" There was a cry to Cyrus's left, and he saw Odellan fall, his arm in the mouth of one of the creatures. Cyrus slashed forward, tightening his distance to the elf. He felt Terian move a little closer to the center of the bridge to compensate.

"It's all right," Curatio called from behind them. "I've got him." There was a moment that passed, as Cyrus cut the head from the scourge that had Odellan's wrist, and he watched it fall away. "As much as they keep pushing you back," the healer called, "be thankful that they don't do much damage."

"At this point I'm just thankful that we have ground left to give," Odellan said, looking back behind them before unleashing a savage flurry on the next scourge to come forward at him in a lunge. "Thank you," he said to Cyrus.

"Not a problem," Cyrus replied, moving back to the center. He could sense Terian ease back to his lane of the bridge, as though they were moving in perfect synch. "Just like old times, huh?"

"I'm afraid that this is playing out much more like my defense of the Northbridge than your defense of the Grand Span," Odellan said tensely as he brought his sword around and parried one of the scourge, letting it carry past him and into the waiting blades of the second line. Martaina and two warriors killed it quickly, before it had a chance to halt its forward momentum from the jump or turn on any of them.

"Aye," Cyrus said. "And that's not the best of signs for any of us, considering how it all turned out on the balance."

"At least they can't flank us," Terian said. "Unless somehow they can crawl under the surface of the bridge." His voice turned pensive. "Please tell me they can't do that."

"Let's hope not," Cyrus said, running Praelior across the face of a scourge and then taking the left shoulder off another before stomping it in the face, caving in its skull and killing it. He shot a look at the dark knight. "I know you're not doing this for me, but I appreciate you being here nonetheless."

"You're welcome," Terian said simply. "And you're right." He brought the red sword down in a long arc that caught a leaping scourge across the nose as it jumped, its momentum arrested and thrown off to the side with the power of Terian's stroke. "I'm not doing this for you."

"Then what are you doing it for?" Cyrus asked as he was forced to take another step back to parry a particularly aggressive and coordinated swiping attack from three scourge.

"I have my reasons," Terian muttered, almost too low to be heard.

The sun rose higher in the sky as the day wore on. They gave ground steadily, and with every step and every furtive look back, Cyrus's unease grew. The tension in his belly became intense, roiling, meshing with the acid in his stomach that allowed him to ignore the fact that he hadn't eaten since the battle had begun earlier in the day. The horsemen were well out of sight now, the only remaining forces were the Sanctuary army—*the last line of defense before these things hit Arkaria. And we're failing. Slowly, but just as sure as if it were quick.*

The sun began to set as Cyrus's muscles grew weary. He watched as his comrades grew slower, their arms wearying, but carrying on. Others came up, here and there, to spell them for a bit. Cyrus waved them off each time, the relief strong but not strong enough. *Not as strong as me. Not as determined. They lose ground quicker.* He tried to push forward and a scourge leapt forward and smashed into him. He held, swinging his blade at the beast, putting it through its heart, and he took another step forward but was driven back by a scampering rush of two of them, coming at him like dogs, their claws clicking on the stone as they tried to bowl him over. He ended them both with quick sword thrusts, dodging the teeth as they came at him but losing two feet in the process.

Two feet might as well be a mile, because it adds up to one when you lose it enough times. The sun had set, and he could no longer see the outline of Arkaria's shore, but he saw lights upon it in the distance, campfires from the Luukessian refugees. *Driven from their homes into ours, and they may still die here.* "Flame!" Cyrus called, and spells swept forward across the bridge, creating a scouring line as he took a deep breath, in and out. He watched Odellan slump, taking the moment's respite. Scuddar seemed to stand stiffly straight, while Longwell leaned on his lance. Terian stood next to Cyrus, though, hands on his sword, blade planted down, as though he were drawing strength directly from the stone of the bridge.

Night came, swirling with a thousand stars in the sky. Cyrus called for flame as often as he could, sucking down a skin full of water each time, making water when needed, taking a loaf of bread and eating as much as he could during the small breaks they were afforded, never more than five minutes or so at a time so as to give the small number of druids and wizards that remained a chance to refresh themselves.

It went on, the smell of death and fire, of roasted, rotted flesh all combined into one. The screams of the scourge dying rolled on, too, along with the lapping of the water against the pillars of the bridge in quieter moments and the crackle when the flame spells came down, roaring and raging against the enemy that came, unstoppably, before them.

"This may be the longest night of my life," Cyrus muttered to himself as the fire roared to life again. He saw black eyes watching him through the inferno, waiting, pacing on the other side.

"Worse than Termina?" Terian asked, winded, to his right. "You know, I wasn't there for that, and I have to say ... I am not sorry I missed it."

"You didn't miss much," Cyrus said. "The worst parts were when an Unter'adon nearly ripped my head off with a ball and chain—"

"He brought his wife to the fight?" Odellan asked quietly. Heads swiveled, and the elf shrugged. "I can joke, too. It just happens infrequently."

"Let me guess," Terian said. "The other bad part was when a dark knight nearly ripped you in half with a sword."

"Aye," Cyrus said as the wall of flame began to fade. "I had leapt into the midst of the army of dark elves because they had healers. They kept saving our enemies—I'd chop one down and he'd spring back up behind me a moment later. I took one out, but there was another. I ripped into the middle of their line, threw myself forward, killed him, but I got stabbed a few times in the process." He raised Praelior and took the blade to the first scourge to charge off the line, severing the head and ripping the jaw off the next, causing it to make a guttural scream. "It was then that I was attacked by the dark knight."

"Bad timing," Terian muttered. "If he'd caught you fresh it would have been a hell of a fight. Maybe even one for the ages."

"Maybe not," Cyrus said. "His spells were doubtless strong; he might have just been the end of me with that one that rips the breath of life out of you."

"Oh, yes," Terian said and extended his hand to a scourge, let it glow slightly purple and a scream tore out of the scourge's lips as it fell to the ground, dead. "That's a good one. But you had a healer, didn't you?"

"I was out of their range when the fight started," Cyrus said. "Being behind the enemy lines and all."

"Still," Terian said, "as a dark knight, I expect to beat a warrior with a healer, not independently." He stiffened as he cut another scourge to pieces mid-leap with his blade, which he brandished in front of him. It glowed in the dark, reflecting against him, revealing a solemnity Cyrus had rarely seen on the dark elf's face. "It's how I was trained." He swung the blade back into motion.

"Did he teach you everything?" Cyrus asked, forced to parry an incoming scourge that went too low for him to effectively hit. "About how to fight?"

Terian did not respond for a long moment, and the sounds of his heavy exertions hung in the air between them instead. "No. Not nearly everything."

The night dragged on as did the war for ground. When the first rays of the sun crept over the horizon, there was a gasp when Cyrus looked back; the green and verdant shores of Arkaria were well in sight, the jungle past the beach was visible, the trees swaying in the wind.

"Hours," Odellan said next to him. "Few enough of them, too."

Cyrus felt his teeth grit unintentionally. *Damn it.* He felt the strength in his arms return, the weariness fade, replaced by an anger that brewed deep inside. He looked back to the enemy. Breathing deep, furious breaths, he clutched Praelior tighter and ripped into the flesh of the first of them that came at him, shredding it and sending it mewling to the side of the bridge and over the edge with the fury of his attack; it took two others with it from sheer force. Cyrus let out a warcry, a soul-deep shout of rage that did not even slow the scourge as it advanced at him. There was a rumble after that, and he both heard and felt it, a shake in his legs from the motion, and it gave him pause.

The breeze cut over from the sea, just for a moment, shifting off the scourge's stink of death. It felt warm, as though the chill of the night had dissipated. Cyrus's eyes sharpened, his ears listened closer for the sound of thunder in the distance. *No. Not thunder.* He looked, and beyond the farthest reach of the enemy he could see it, a massive head and body, lengths above the height of a normal scourge. A cold chill came over him, the clutch of something unpredictable—unfelt—unexpected.

Fear.

Chapter 108

Vara

Day 223 of the Siege of Sanctuary

"Is this all you have?" she shouted over the crenellation of the wall, through the gap between it and the next, the teeth of the rampart. She threw an arm out and sent a blast of force at the nearest tower to her and watched it hit, blasting the supports out of the second level of it. She cast again, a quick incantation, and scored another hit as the siege machine crashed down upon the dark elves below it. Bodies fell in a wave all around it, like a stone dropping into the water sends out ripples.

She took a breath; the smell had worsened atop the wall, both from the unwashed bodies above and the dead in rot below. *They keep pressing toward the mark, though, don't they?* And they surely did; the advance had not relented since Alaric had left two days earlier.

The sound was still an uproar, a hundred thousand enemies surrounding them yet, minus however many were dead around the walls. She let her hand clink against her armor, bracing herself against the battlements. "Come on, then," she whispered, more to herself than them. "Is this all you have?"

"You just have to go and tempt the gods with that, don't you?" She turned to see Andren slumped, much as she had seen him before, his flask in hand, taking a swig while shaking his head at her. "They're vengeful, you know. Lightning and fire and all that. They'll get you back for that."

"I welcome them to try," she said, looking back over the rampart. "Hmm. They've brought more of their armored trolls, it would appear." Lightning streaked past her head from a spell. "And wizards, too."

She chanced a look at Andren, who shook his head. "Lightning. I warned you."

She breathed again deeply, twice, and dipped her head and hand over the wall. Another siege tower rolled forward and she aimed for it but pulled back as it burst into flame. Down the wall she saw Larana throw fire at another one then dodge behind a crenellation as a volley of arrows targeted her segment for bombardment.

"Don't they know by now we can kill their siege towers?" Andren asked, looking slightly sideways, just for a second, around the battlement, before dodging back as an arrow shot past his head. For that, he took another drink.

"Certainly," she replied and dodged out to fire twice at ladder-bearing enemies. The two in front were blasted clear and the ladder dipped, hitting the ground and causing the dark elves at the back to stumble. "But every one they push forward is another distraction for us." She turned her head to look at the gates. "Soon enough they'll have their battering ram back in service ..." She let her voice trail off as she stared at the battering ram. It was unmoving, with only a few dark elves hiding behind it for cover. "That's odd."

"We're being bombarded by enemy arrows numbering in the millions," Andren said, "siege towers are rolling across our fields as fast as the dark elves can push them. Tell me, in the midst of all that, what is odd? Flying mounts? Because I've seen those before." He looked skyward for just a moment. "Actually, I'm surprised I don't see them right now."

"They're rare and valuable enough that surely the Sovereign wants to keep them for an assault on the Elven Kingdom if he needs to," she answered almost by rote instinct. "No, they're not making any efforts with the battering ram." She turned to look at the siege towers. "But neither are their siege towers making the sort of progress which would inspire one to halt their efforts there." She frowned. "Which begs the question of why—"

It was not even before she got the words out that the explosion rocked the battlements and the stone arch above the gate disintegrated in a cloud of flame and debris. Her head ached and she realized she was lying flat, her cheek pressed against the stone of the curtain wall. She lifted herself up, tasted blood in her mouth and felt the sting on her lip where she must surely have bit it. There was a ringing in her ears, as though someone was calling her to worship with a bell just outside her helm, and she had to blink to see clearly. Somewhere, faintly, in the distance, there was a roar, and as she pushed herself to her feet she felt a deep disquiet, a certainty—*fear,* she realized, as she whipped around to look at the gate, where the dust and cloud of smoke had already begun to clear, leaving a twenty-foot-wide gap in the wall where the gate had fallen, and already there rushed an onslaught of dark elves—banding up, filling in, like water rushing forward into a crack.

The dark elves had entered the grounds of Sanctuary.

Chapter 109

Cyrus

The fear did not pass, not as Cyrus expected it to. *Imagine the arena, imagine the sand beneath my feet, the smell of—* All that came to his mind was left behind as Drettanden, the God of Courage—*or what remains of him*—came forth, knocking aside his own allies, clearing the bridge as he went.

"Not good," Odellan said. "Any plan to stop this thing?"

"Flame!" Cyrus called out, and a moment later the wall of fire dropped down in front of them, ten feet high. Cyrus could see through the jumping inferno as the smaller scourge stopped. He blinked; *He's not stopping!*

Drettanden kept on, charging along the bridge, and sped up as he came to the flames. With only a second's warning, he jumped, half clearing the massive wall of fire that crossed the stone bridge, dividing it off.

"DIVE!" Cyrus called and jumped sideways, slamming into Terian, who reacted just a second more slowly than he had. Cyrus's head hit the inside of his armor, hard, and jarred him as it did so. The two of them spun off, just out of the way of the beast's massive paw as it came down where Cyrus had been only a moment before. He watched the one on the other side catch Odellan in the chest, and the elf had only the briefest chance to scream before he was caught underfoot in a sickening crunch of bone and blood, as red liquid squirted out from the place where Drettanden had landed.

"You SON OF A BITCH!" Cyrus forced himself upright, sword in hand. He waved Praelior in the sunlight at the creature, "you see this?" Drettanden's head snapped into line with him. "Was this yours? Well, it's mine now!" He brought it back, ready to swing. "If you want it, come and take it."

"Bad idea," Terian said from behind him. "That thing's pretty big, it might just do it—"

Without warning, Drettanden swiped out with a paw the size of a dwarf, and Cyrus used all the speed that Praelior gave him to surge forward and attack it. He met the blow head-on, sword extended—*Just like with Mortus*—and when it sent him flying he had the momentary satisfaction of knowing that the howl he heard was his foe in pain.

He lay there, staring up at the clouds, the dawn and the horizon. It was bright, the sun, shining down on him, and the sound of sea gulls not far away was almost peaceful somehow. There was pain, but it was distant, already fading. He felt his fingers curled around the weapon in his hand, and the thought came to him. *Praelior, the Champion's Sword. Made by the God of Courage. Did he fight to the death to keep it when they came for him?* He felt a smile crack his face, realized there was a tooth out of place in his mouth and pressed his tongue idly against it. *Did he show courage at the last? Did he fight til the end or cower? Because that would be quite the irony, wouldn't it ...? the God of Courage, filled with fear ...*

"Get up," Curatio said, shaking him.

Cyrus felt the life flood back to his limbs, and the pain went to a dull ache, replaced in his guts with a blinding rage. He vaulted to his feet and came up to the spectacle of a battle on the bridge. Drettanden was covered with arrows all over his grey flesh. A flame spell hit him in the face as he shrugged it off, roaring and snapping into a Sanctuary ranger who Cyrus didn't get a good look at before the man was gone, devoured whole, red staining the teeth and lips of the beast. The wall of flame remained behind Drettanden, cutting off the smaller scourge, keeping the flood of them from coming forward and overwhelming the Sanctuary army, which was already hesitating; he could feel it.

He cried out again, a bellow of fury, and leapt through the air after a few running steps, and buried his sword in an upper leg. *Just like a dragon, only it can't fly. Dangerous mouth.* He could feel his mind breaking it down. *I ran at Kalam, went right at his face. I taunted the Dragonlord into making some stupid mistakes. I came at Mortus head-on, I won—with help. Hacked him to pieces.* "Sanctuary!" Cyrus called out. "To me!" He buried his blade again in the upper thigh and let himself slide down as the leg kicked and kicked again, as though Drettanden were a dog trying to rid himself of a flea.

Cyrus took the chance. He planted both feet then backflipped, withdrawing his sword as he did so. He landed perfectly, the balance granted by Praelior saving him from a catastrophic landing. *Agility. Speed. Hostility. He cannot match me in these ways.* Drettanden let out a roar that flattened the Sanctuary ranger standing in front of him.

Maybe the hostility.

Cyrus brought back the sword and hacked at the tendon at the back of the leg, drawing a sharp cry from Drettanden. Cyrus dodged the back kick that followed and slunk back as the former god swiveled to face him. Cyrus let him come, dodged into the blind spot behind the neck and raked his sword across the fold at the back of the jaw, sending a slick line of black blood whipping across the ground. He struck twice more, pivoting and rolling against the body of Drettanden as the creature turned, bouncing off and using its own momentum against it. *Here's a trick I bet you haven't seen before, outrunning you with your own strength.* At the last move, he spun again out in front and brought his sword across the creature's flat nose, drawing a screech of pain that caused it to buck its head.

The nose hit Cyrus perfectly in the arm, numbing it to the elbow and sending him flying. As he was tossed through the air, he saw the battle unfolding. Odellan, pulled off to the side, alive again but a mess, nowhere near ready for combat. Scuddar, lingering in the shadow of a supporting pillar of the bridge, his scimitar raised and attacking Drettanden's tail. Longwell, backed almost to the firewall, his lance gone—*no, buried in the side of the beast—sticking out like a splinter of wood.* Cyrus felt all the air leave him as he hit the ground, his head slammed against the hard stone, and then felt the ground give way around him.

Edge—

His good hand reached out, scraping against the stone surface, and he caught himself just as he started to fall over. The jarring ran down his whole arm, all the way up to the shoulder where he felt the scream of pain, agonizing, ligaments tearing and protesting as he held his own weight and all that of his armor with one hand. He hung there, fingers tight against the stone, as he fought to get the other up to grip the edge. A blast of foul, rotting breath hit him in the face like a physical blow and he recoiled. His eyes danced toward the shore, miles and miles off. *Not in this armor. Not on a day when I was fully rested, let alone one where I've fought without sleep nor a good meal in over a day ...*

The face of Drettanden appeared over him, at the edge, looking down. The red eyes twitched, and Cyrus could hear pain being inflicted on the creature by the Sanctuary army behind him. *It doesn't care.* It stared at him, two red abysses looking deep into his own eyes, and Cyrus watched the dead god raise his foot, five claws hanging off the grey flesh—raised it and brought it down—

Chapter 110

He remembered the arena in a flash, like the rumored last memory that came before certain death. It was more than a feeling, more than words; it was everything about the experience, all summed up in something that lasted a mere second of time but encompassed so much else beyond that.

Six. I was six.

The man's name was Erkhardt, and Cyrus knew him only in passing. A dwarf he was, the one who had waited outside the Society the night that Cyrus had been brought back as a child. The dwarf smelled of old leather and wafts of something else, a strong, fermented scent. He stood before young Cyrus, in the arena, the quiet all around them. Cyrus shuddered, the chill in the air from winter. His eyes caught the glint of the still-burning candles off the axe slung over the dwarf's shoulder, a battle axe with a blade wider than Cyrus's entire body. He shivered again, rubbing his hands against his bare arms; since being assigned no blood family, the clothing that was fought over once per month when new skins and cloth came in had been too difficult for him to secure. *Blood Families stick together for everything.* Cyrus was small, too small to fight them all. *Put me against the ones my own age and I'd—but I can't, the others are too big, they're just too big, and the Guildmaster will—*

"Listen," the dwarf said.

Cyrus did. He was not allowed to address any of the trainers unless they asked him for a response. None of the others even addressed him individually, let alone found him where he hid in the night and bade him to follow them to the arena.

"Do you hear that?" Erkhardt asked.

"No," Cyrus said, his voice unusually small even to him.

"That's silence, lad," the dwarf said with a slight smile, one finger held in the air. "The silence of rest. You've learned to hide yourself; that's good. It'll be necessary until you get bigger, big enough to fight them. You'll be a big lad too, no doubt. Until then ... you need to learn something."

Cyrus waited, patiently. *I will not speak until spoken to, I will not speak until spoken to,* ran through his head over and over. He felt a weak memory of pain radiating from his lip until that lesson had sunk in. There was a question, though, one that he wanted, needed to ask, couldn't contain anymore. "Can you take my fear away?"

The dwarf blinked at him. "Sorry, what?"

Cyrus swallowed, hard. "What the Guildmaster said on the first day. He said he could teach us to be without fear. I don't … I don't want to be afraid anymore."

Erkhardt surveyed him with a solemn eye. "What are you afraid of?"

Cyrus swallowed, hard. "Everything."

The dwarf gave him a subtle nod. "You need not fear everything. And I don't know that there's any man who is truly fearless."

"But the Guildmaster said—"

"The Guildmaster," Erkhardt says, "fears many things. Bellarum, for one. The Leagues and the Council of Twelve, for others. Listen," he knelt down, just slightly, to put his hand on Cyrus's shoulder. Cyrus stared at the subtle pressure in surprise; no one had touched him since the night he'd returned to the Society for any purpose other than striking him. "The only way a man can be truly fearless is to care for absolutely nothing, including his own life. That's a dark road, and few enough men can become soulless enough to pull it off." He gave Cyrus a reassuring smile. "If you want courage—which is the virtue of being able to look fear in the face in spite of all the daunting it would give you, well, that's something I can tell you about."

Cyrus felt his lips crack open and the words desperately wanted to come out in a plea, begging for the how. Instead he remained silent.

"To put aside fear," Erkhardt said, "you must confront it. Courage is standing up to it, facing it. Pain, suffering," he put a hand on Cyrus's jaw and a slight twinge radiated out from it from where he had been hit a week earlier. "These are normal things to fear. If you want to master fear, stare it in the eyes." Erkhardt stood. "And if you want to be able to face it harder than any other man you know, then find something … something you truly can believe in, put your faith in, your trust in … and you fight for that thing. Or that person." Erkhardt looked out the sidelong path up the arena steps. "They won't tell you that here. They'll tell you about the God of War, they'll tell you to believe in him. I carry my doubts that that's the best way to proceed. But I'll tell you this, a man who's fighting for something he believes in will fight ten times as hard and look worlds more fearless than a man who cares for nothing, believes in nothing. An empty soul means when times become hardest, it doesn't matter that you're fearless, because you're not going to fight for anything but yourself anyway."

Cyrus looked into those dark eyes, saw the warmth in them—*the last warmth I saw for some time after that,* the adult Cyrus remembered—and listened. "Now," Erkhardt says, "there's something you need to learn before I leave this place. Something more important than believing ..."

Cyrus blinked and the memory, the feeling, was no more than that. His fingers strained at the edge of the bridge, the sun beat down overhead on the face of Drettanden, and those red eyes stared back at him. The smell of salt air from the sea wafted under his nose, his knuckles ached and longed to be set loose, and he wondered in that moment if there was, in fact, anything left to believe in.

Chapter 111

Vara

Day 223 of the Siege of Sanctuary

It was broken loose now, all manner of hell, and she knew it from her place on the wall. The smell of something new was in the air, acrid, sharp, oddly chemical, like something from an alchemist's shop but worse. It wafted in the smoke that came from where the wall had exploded, and even now the crater where the gates had stood only moments earlier was filled from the surge of dark elves, clambering across the dead space of the battlefield. The smell of the dead was overwhelming.

She jumped from the top of the wall without thought, hitting at the bottom of the thirty-foot fall and already whispering a healing spell as she heard her leg break. There was a push as the bone realigned itself and thrust her back to her feet, her joint pain subsiding as she ran, charging toward the place where the enemy was coming through into the yard, picking through the debris with shouts and screams of imminent victory. *They smell the blood of their foe. They know it comes soon, the end. But I will show them their end, not ours. Coming through that wall is the worst mistake they have made yet, because now they face the teeth of this tigress.* She didn't smile, but it was close, a white-hot rage at the violation of her home. *And this tigress is bloody hungry.*

Her sword found its first target, a troll warrior who was looking the wrong damned way. Trolls seemed to be the leading edge, ten feet tall, most of them. The smell of swamp wafted off of them in waves, as though they had been freshly plucked out of Gren and its surroundings, fitted with armor, and thrown to the front lines. *A bold move. Savvy, though, O Bastard Sovereign.* She spilled the beast's guts out with a crosswise slash and ran on, clashing next with three dark elven warriors in full armor. She broke the sword of the first with a furious slash, splintering the blade and then the man's helm. She made a stabbing motion toward the next to feint then kicked him with such fury in the chest that his armor dented in and he clutched himself in pain. The third she brought her sword across, aiming for the neck but hitting low and glancing off his armor, leaving a deep crease in the steel. She swung around faster than he could adapt to her angle of attack and came up with a strike that caught him where the legging armor of his greaves met his groin and the armor broke. The man folded, and she finished him with a stroke to the face, plunging her sword into his open-faced helm.

They were coming too fast, though, and she saw others around her; the red armor of Thad, fighting off four of them, Belkan with his sword and shield, battering away at another one. Fortin had waded into the fray and pieces of bodies began to fly through the air with every hit the rock giant levied. Flames shot forth into the new hole in the wall, scorching those that were there, turning back the advance. The dark elven assault had stalled, and the first wave that had besieged the wall was trapped. *Yes. Come forth a few at a time, and we'll destroy you in those small numbers. We'll plunge blades into you, spear you to death, stick your heads upon pikes as warnings to the next to come that this is what happens when you face the might of Sanctuary. You can carry the message back to your Sovereign, with your very deaths, that he ... will ... not ... break ... ME.*

She took a breath as the battle began to subside. There were a few more of them now, and Fortin was wiping the last of them out, holding a dark elf in each hand and listening to them squeal as he crushed the life from their armor, squeezing it in the palm of his hand as she listened to it strain under the screams, heard the cracking of bones and the rending of flesh—and she did not stop him.

"They failed," Thad said, a rough smile on his face. "They made their bid, some new magic and horror, that—but they failed. We held them back." He nodded to the hole in the wall, blocked by fire, then looked to Mendicant. "Can you maintain that?"

"For a time," the goblin agreed.

"Then drop it," Vara said, "and let them come forth for a while before you raise it again. "We'll disassemble them piecemeal, a hundred at a time, and in a thousand cycles of this we'll have them killed." She wore a grim smile. "We can hold them back like this, we can defeat them. The Sovereign will come to rue the day he ever set upon us here—"

The explosion whistled first then loudly blew down the section of wall a few hundred feet to the left of the gate. Vara covered her head instinctively but looked back quickly and saw that another fifty-foot gap of wall had been removed, smoke in its place, and the first surge of dark elves came through, wildly, screaming their victory. And they came even as another explosion rocked the ground from the wall far down to the other side and then another and another.

Chapter 112

Cyrus

There was nothing but the soulless eyes of death, staring at him, waiting, looking him down. The teeth were exposed, and something dripped onto his face—blood, he realized as it speckled him, spattered on his black armor, the strong smell of it came to his nose along with the wet, disgusting feeling of the sticky saliva mixed with it. It was enough to make him want to let go, to let his fingers, screaming with pain, release, but he held on. He stared back into the red eyes, heard the low growl that Drettanden made, and wondered where his army was, what they were doing. There were screams in the distance, of pain or surprise, he couldn't tell, but they were there.

The pain in his knuckles was near unbearable. Even the cushioning in the gauntlets did not assuage it, the searing ache that radiated out from having the entirety of his weight relying on the one hand. He tried to readjust, staring back at Drettanden, lifting his other arm, still numb from the scourge-god's blow, and trying to reach up to the bridge. He failed and nearly lost his grip. *I can't do this. I can't hold on. Why am I bothering? It's over. He's broken through our line. The minute that fire drops, his friends will join him and that'll be it. They'll be on Arkaria, and there will be no stopping them, even if we could get everyone allied and cooperating. This is the end. I've failed.* He looked from the red eyes, the hopeless feeling they conveyed, to the sea below, blue-green waves lapping against the support. *I could drop, fall in, all the way down to the bottom ... and it'd all be over ...*

And why not? He looked up at the face of the former god, at the paw poised to destroy strike him down, hovering, and wondered. *Why should I not go? What is there to stay for? What is there to live for? To see my people destroyed one slow step at a time? To watch as this thing overcomes us and kills everything in its path? What is there to fight for, to believe in ...?* The scourge-god looked at him and seemed to smile, the jagged teeth dripping with malice as his clawed foot began to descend on Cyrus ...

There was a blast of force and Drettanden blew sideways, a sudden shock in its eyes as it was flung, slipping, into the nearby pillar atop the bridge. Cyrus heard the stone break along with bone, and the mewling scream from the scourge creature was louder than any he had heard since a dragon had shouted at him.

It's not over.

He swung his other arm around again, clamped the other hand onto the side of the bridge. *No leverage. I'll have to pull myself all the way up if I'm to do this.* He blinked and looked down at the water again, and it looked so appealing, the dark and mysterious depths.

"That is not the way," a voice said from above him, and he felt a hand upon his—strong, clenching at his gauntlet. He looked up and felt a wash of relief at the sight, the half of a face that showed from beneath the old helm; the battered armor was recognizable in an instant.

"Alaric," Cyrus said and pulled as the Guildmaster stood, dragging him up. For the knight it appeared no struggle at all, and he lifted Cyrus back upon the bridge and nearly to his feet without effort. He stared at the old knight's chin, at his grey eye sparkling beneath the slit in the helm. "Alaric ... you came."

"I could not leave you to face these foes alone," the Ghost said, turning back to Drettanden. "I see you have run into ... difficulties." There was a roar from Drettanden as it staggered off the broken pillar and turned toward Cyrus and Alaric, snorting and spitting blood, both red and black, upon the stone bridge.

"That's Drettanden," Cyrus said, looking at the creature. "Or what's left of him."

"Indeed," Alaric said coolly, and Cyrus felt pressure in his palm as Alaric pressed Praelior into his hand. "You'll be needing this, then."

"Aye," Cyrus said and took a fighting stance, sword in hand. "You could just hit him again, you know?" He looked to Alaric. "Sweep him off the bridge and into the water, end this?"

The eyes behind the helm did not blink. "I think he would always hold some mastery over you if I were to do that. Do not fear to face that which confounds you. Look it in the eyes and strike it down."

Cyrus took a ragged breath and looked back at the God of Courage, fallen as he was, a distorted and pathetic creature, snarling at Alaric.

"All right." He took a step forward, then another, breaking into an attacking run. He let the air fill his lungs again, the anger course through his veins. *They'll destroy my land. They'll crush everything that matters to me. They'll break my home, and the entirety of my world will be consumed by death ...*

He brought the blade around as Drettanden snapped at him. He sunk it into the nose and across the lips, snagging it on a tooth, which broke free when he ripped hard at the hilt. A paw came up at him to strike but he dodged and blocked with his blade, letting the glow of it guide him to the grey and pallid skin. He heard the screech of a good block, listened to the pain, and roared himself as he struck again at the face, that soulless face with empty eyes. He saw the flash of his blade in them, the glow reflected as he ripped into the creature's cheek, gouging the mouth wider with his strike.

The head came around again but Cyrus was ready. Instead of dodging, he threw himself at it, blade first. He buried the sword in the side of the head, and Drettanden halted his forward momentum quickly, screeching, jerking away rather than following through with a headbutt that would have sent Cyrus flying. *Strike at your fear, and it will recoil.* He worked the sword free, prompting Drettanden to retreat three steps to swing about to face him. *Grasp at it and it will dissolve in the sunlight. Confront it, make it your own ... and make it fear you.*

He let out a cry of rage and emotion, jumping into the air and striking down with the blade again. A streak of black blood welled up on the face of the dead god, and he backed up again toward the still-standing wall of fire, toward the foes that waited beyond, a chorus of wailing voices and gnashing teeth. Cyrus pressed the attack and Drettanden moved into the fire and recoiled, screaming in a voice that was almost human but very definitely not. With three quick strikes, Cyrus carved into the face of the beast, and when it tried to bat at him, he slipped low and waited for the paw to land. *You are faster than your fears. You need not outrun them when you can outfight them, conquer them, make them yours ...* He threw everything into the thrust, all his strength, the full twist of his hips and back, and he landed the blow at the ankle joint of Drettanden's front leg. Praelior buried itself into the grey flesh all the way to the bone. Cyrus forced it in, harder now, gritting his teeth and pushing with all his strength as the creature lifted its foot.

With a surge forward, Cyrus felt the flesh and bone give first, and the foot came free, as did his sword. He stumbled forward then dodged to his left as Drettanden fell, squealing all the way down. The scourge-god landed heavily on his face, now missing a foot to stand on. Cyrus whirled about, saw the creature lying splayed out, and he spun his sword around. "You wanted to make me fear you. You thought you could drive me before you, keep running me." Cyrus clenched his hand over the grip of the sword as he reversed it. "You think this is your sword, but it's not. I won it through a price paid you can't imagine, through sacrifice you probably can't even conceive of anymore. This is Praelior, the Champion's Sword. And I'm going to give it back to you—right now."

Cyrus leapt, his arc taking him high above the creature. He landed heavily on the back of its neck as it struggled to stand. Without warning he plunged the blade down into the top of Drettanden's skull, and he couldn't even feel the resistance as he shoved it into the head of what once had been the God of Courage. There was a sound almost like a sizzle as the blade cut through the flesh, broke through bone, and then a sickening lurch as the creature's balance shifted. As its legs collapsed, Cyrus withdrew the sword and vaulted off, coming to a landing and hitting with his shoulder, sliding into a forward roll that carried him back to his feet, armor clinking against the stone surface of the bridge.

He came up and Alaric was waiting, standing there peacefully calm, watching. Odellan was there, ghastly pale but alive, Longwell next to him, holding his side and using his lance to keep him upright. Scuddar watched as well, and Terian; the others stood back a ways, and Cyrus could see a druid straining, red glow around his hands.

"You may cease the fire now," Alaric said to the druid, who dropped mercifully to the ground at that. Martaina caught the man in her arms and began to drag him backward. "You seem to have come up against your fears and won."

"Aye," Cyrus said. "I suppose I did, at that."

"You couldn't have done that at Enrant Monge?" Terian asked, shaking his head and rolling his eyes. "Might have made it easier on the rest of us."

"Sorry," Cyrus said, spinning about as the line of fire began to disappear from the bridge. "I don't think it quite works that way."

"Figures," the dark knight said. "You're so screwed up it took you a year to get the idea ironed out in your head that you're the greatest warrior walking the land of Arkaria." Cyrus looked at him in surprise, and the dark knight shook his head. "Or so I've heard others say."

"They come," Longwell said. "That big one might be dead, but there's a whole host behind him that isn't letting up."

Cyrus looked back at them, and the smell of death washed over him. It was familiar and horrible—but no longer fearsome. He saw the black eyes and the emptiness within them, but instead of fear, he felt a curiosity, a pity—*They didn't ask to become this. To end them is a mercy.* A cool reserve found him, a confidence, a glacial sense of inevitability. *We will strike down many today. Kill many.* They were loosed now, the fire no longer holding them back. They rushed forward in a mad dash, coming at Cyrus, at the others. He hefted Praelior in his hand, felt the weight of the blade, heard the scamper of the claws on the stone, and could taste the desire to break them as fast as they could come at him. *Come on, then. Send all that you have, and I'll fight them. To the death—mine or theirs. And I'd wager theirs comes long before mine.*

I'm not afraid of you.

Chapter 113

Vara

Day 223 of the Siege of Sanctuary

They came in a flood now, from all directions, from holes in the wall that were beyond number. The Sanctuary defenders were forced up against the front steps in retreat, and there was fighting everywhere within the walls. *There is only room in this space for a few thousand, but a few thousand we have and more. A few thousand of ours trying to beat them back, a few thousand of theirs trying to come forward, and we'll be left with a few thousand dead on each side by the time this is through—a better bargain for them with their more than a hundred thousand in number than us with our less than four.*

The striking of swords, the guttural cries of men and women at war: these were the things that dominated the space around her. Clash of weapon against weapon, of blade on blade and against armor, shield and gauntlet. It was frenzied chaos, wall to wall, a shoving match and a swordfight all in one, and the smell of the dead filled her nose until she could taste it, death and despair in equal measure, and no matter how many times she plunged her sword into a dark elf, it did not cease.

Fortin was at the gap, the closest one, where the gate had once stood, and he was holding out, armored bodies flung through the air every few seconds. She saw spells arcing toward him but the rock giant appeared unmoved by them, and another armored dark elf hit the wrecked wall, cracking and screaming as he fell back to the earth.

A fire burst held the next gap, surging, almost a living flame, reminding her of the bit of magic she'd seen used against the trolls at the last assault on the foyer. *We're losing. Too many of them, too few of us, and all the time in the world helps us little.* She felt a nick against her arm as a dagger bit into it and she gasped but did not halt her swing. She killed the wielder of the blade and was prepared to deal death to the next dark elf in line when a face popped into her view.

"This is not going well," Aisling said to her, wrenching a dagger across the throat of an unsuspecting dark elf who stood between her and Vara.

"Ah, so your talent for understatement is what Cyrus finds attractive about you," Vara muttered, striking down another dark elf with even more fury than she thought she had in her.

"Actually, it's my talent for—" The dark elf was forced to parry a strike by a troll, rolling between his legs and coming up behind him to strike him in the kidneys with two blades. "Well," she called back to Vara as the troll toppled over, clutching his back. "You know."

Vara did not answer, but a bout of fury overcame her and the next enemy who crossed her sight line ended up bisected at the waist from an unrelenting strike. As the upper body fell, she parlayed it into a diagonal cross strike of her next foe, and she saw the blood shining from his exposed ribs as he fell. *Go on, bitch. Say it again. Tell me all about it, I could use some rage to fuel my fire.* She raised a hand at the gap in the wall to their left and mentally repeated the incantation she knew by heart; at the last moment a bit of excess anger bled into her thoughts and something hiccupped from her hand, a blast of pure, furious force that ballooned wider than she'd ever made it go before. It surged forward, knocking flat half a hundred dark elves flooding through the gap, flinging countless numbers of them into the air and into their fellows to sounds of bones breaking, men screaming in pain, and bodies falling from their apogee, some launched as far as twenty feet into the air. She blinked and looked back to Aisling in surprise.

The dark elf stared back at her, openmouthed. "Would it help if I taunted you again?"

"It wouldn't help you," Vara growled, and turned back to the enemies that came at her in two prongs. Her sword was a blaze of motion, and the frenzy was more than she could stand. *He held her, touched her, was—WITH her—smelling her white hair, pressing his skin against hers.* She fought off the urge to feel anything but the rage and turned it loose, sword a blur of fury, blood scything through the air around her.

"We can't hold them back!" The voice broke into her consciousness after several minutes and she seemed to come back to herself. It was darkening, the skies above them, and not with rain. The sun was nearly below the wall and the sky was dimming. *How long have we been fighting?* The lawn was strewn with bodies, countless dark elves and more than a few of her own. *Healers are mitigating that. If they weren't, we'd be matching them corpse for corpse.* "We need to retreat!" She looked to the source of the voice and realized it was Vaste, his staff in hand, at the top of the Sanctuary steps only feet away. The troll whipped his staff across the face of a dark elf that charged up at him then grabbed the man and flung him off the top of the stairs. "Vara, do you hear me?"

"Just ... keep healing us!" she called back, at the base of the stairs herself. She blinked in surprise. *Wasn't I at the left break in the wall just a moment ago?*

"We've been doing so for hours," Vaste called back. "We're nearly dry of magical energy. Call the retreat and barricade the doors while we recover, or every soldier you lose will be lost for good."

The world spun about her, filling her vision with cracks and a whirl, as though the sky had taken up its own rotation. *We can't lose. We can't fall, not now.* She looked to the front gate, where it had stood; even Fortin had moved back now, only thirty feet in front of her, and a solid wall of dark elves was pushing forward. The rock giant wobbled, and black liquid ran down the surface of his body as he battled with three trolls simultaneously. They were all of a height and looked like titans fighting in the middle of the battlefield.

"Retreat," she whispered, so low only she could hear it at first, or so she thought. Aisling's head snapped around to gape at her in shock. "RETREAT!" she called again, louder this time, and heard other Sanctuary voices take up the call, weary ones, almost drowned out by the screams of victory by the dark elves around them, screams that echoed off the remains of the walls of Sanctuary and up and up, until she was certain that they could be heard the whole world over.

Chapter 114

Cyrus

It was nearing night now, and the end of the bridge was close, perhaps a quarter of a mile away. The sweat poured off him in gallons, he was certain, as though his whole skin were drenched with it and the blood of the scourge, that foul-black stuff that had smelled of death only this morning. The gasping of those fighting on the line beside him was strong but not overwhelming, and Cyrus could scarcely feel his arms but to know that they were there, and that Praelior was in a death-grip in his right hand, ready to deal out whatever destruction he saw fit to mete.

"Running out of time," Terian's call was calm, calmer than Cyrus thought it should be given the circumstances.

"And to think," Longwell said, driving a lance through three of the scourge to the far right of Cyrus, "I could have been mouldering and dead on the shores of my homeland right now. Instead I get to watch us fail here and see these things delivered upon the shores of Arkaria." He almost sounded mocking, but there was no joy in it. "I can't thank you enough for saving me so I could witness this day. Truly, it will haunt me for all the rest of my life, all six months of it, should the pattern of Luukessia hold."

"I don't wish to see these days, either," Odellan said darkly. "To think of what we've wrought on the people already dead is almost too much to bear. To add Arkaria to it is a frightful thing, not worthy of contemplation. I would rather die here than watch my land go slowly into the devouring mouths of these things the way we watched Luukessia go. Better to finish out swiftly than the slow slide, like ailing to death."

There was silence for only a moment before Alaric spoke from Cyrus's left, his blade always in motion and faster than even Cyrus's had been. "I find it dispiriting, your lack of faith that we can stop these beasts before they reach the shore."

Terian answered. "No offense, Alaric, but they've been pushing us back just as hard since you got here as they were before. Cyrus killed the King Daddy and they're still coming like they didn't feel it. Their numbers make me think the bridge is filled clear back to Luukessia and likely beyond that." The dark knight parried an attack and cast a spell that left a scourge choking on bile, green sludge pouring out of its mouth. "If you have a solution to stop them, I think we'd all be keen to hear it. If it's to continue what we're doing ..." Terian looked around at the others on the line with him and met Cyrus's eyes; the warrior saw defeat in the dark knight's look, an utterly dispirited expression that he'd never seen from Terian before. "I believe we're about to be done. We failed."

Alaric's next blow sent a corpse ten feet into the air, and the paladin gritted his teeth as he leveled a swipe that killed four scourge and sent their bodies falling back into the charging ranks of the next run of them. "Do you truly believe that? All of you?"

"I'm afraid so," Longwell answered.

"I don't see a victory here." Odellan dodged a scourge coming at him and buried his sword up to the hilt in the beast then kicked another one free long enough to bring around his sword and stop it.

"And Scuddar In'shara?" Alaric asked the desert man, whose scimitar was still a blur of motion, hacking the enemy to pieces.

"I believe," Scuddar said in his deep intonation, "that we are not on the shore yet, and there is still fight left within us."

"Spoken like a man whose village is first in the path of destruction for these things," Terian said, driving his sword into one of them. "It ain't gonna happen, Alaric. They're going to eat Arkaria whole. There's no stopping them now."

"Do you truly believe that?" Alaric said, not looking up from dispatching two more of the scourge in a row.

"Yes," Terian said quietly, casting a spell on the next beast to attack him. "There's no path to victory from here."

Alaric was strangely quiet then, but his sword never stopped moving. "Back up, all of you." He moved forward, his weapon dancing so fast he carved his way through the scourge that came forward in waves to attack him, making a pocket of death as he took another step forward, pushing into the enemy ranks, the bodies piling up around him.

Cyrus felt the weariness in his arms and pushed it aside, trying to command Praelior the way he saw Alaric wield Aterum; it almost worked, he was nearly as fast, fast enough to keep the enemy at bay, but barely. He looked back, just a glance, and saw the others behind him, the scourge surging between them all, creating a solid packed line between Cyrus and the others, and Alaric still ten feet in front of him.

"What are you doing, brother?" Alaric said, looking back at Cyrus as a thick burst of black blood spattered across his helm.

"I'm coming with you," Cyrus said. "I believe in you; we can do this."

There was silence between the screams, just for a beat. "Thank you," Alaric said. "But you need not believe in me for my sake; it was I who believed in you when no one else did. I and others, some of whom you do not even know, who saw the seeds of that greatness in you. Your faith returned means more to me than you know, and I ... apologize for speaking to you so brusquely when last we talked at Sanctuary." The paladin's face fell, and he held out a hand. The concussive force blast jumped forward from his palm, scattering the scourge for twenty feet in front of him, sending countless number of them flying off the bridge, clawing as they went, others struggling to stay on. "One tends to become attached to life the longer one lives it, you understand."

"Sure," Cyrus said, batting away the scourge that lingered behind them, pinned between them and the others. "No one wants to die."

"True enough," Alaric said, now still, the scourge before him regarding him carefully. "But most fear to tread on its ground, fear to go into it." He swept a hand to the horde of scourge around them. "And why should they not, when this appears to be their future? The worst of it, the worst fear, to become something you don't wish to be, to live in torment and agony for the rest of your days, to be reduced to less than yourself, a mindless thing with no purpose, no desire but to destroy." He took a step toward Cyrus. "Thank you for your faith in me, my friend, my brother. I have something for you."

Cyrus blinked. "I'm sorry ... what?"

Alaric reached up. With his hand, he unfastened his gorget and removed it from his neck and grasped at a chain that lay across the back of it. He pulled it up, still keeping a wary eye on the scourge, cowed for the first time and staying at a distance, growling, waiting as their numbers reformed, their line gaining strength. Cyrus could see them preparing to charge, but he could not tear his eyes off Alaric, even as the Guildmaster removed the chain from his neck and brought with it a pendant, a small, circular object that was shadowed in the dark. He held it out to Cyrus, who looked at it for only a moment before glancing back to Alaric's eyes under the helm.

"Take it," the Ghost said and used the hilt of his sword to push his helm up, then off the back of his head. It fell to the ground with a thunk and his face was exposed, long hair flapping behind him in the salt breeze. "Please." Cyrus reached out and grasped the pendant by the chain, holding it up to look at it in the light. "Now hold tight to it," Alaric said.

Cyrus squinted past it, at Alaric. "What are you doing?"

The Ghost looked at the enemy arrayed before them then back to the army of Sanctuary, which had moved back even a bit more, braced for the next attack of the scourge—relentless, unceasing. "My duty. You will see them to safety and protect Sanctuary."

Cyrus blinked. "What? Alaric—"

The Ghost's hand closed across Cyrus's gauntleted arm. "Do as I ask. And one other thing." Cyrus saw the warmth in Alaric's eyes now, the regard, and it stirred something within him, goosepimples across his flesh, across his scalp. "Don't be afraid."

With that, he pushed Cyrus back, causing the warrior to stumble and fall onto the hard stone of the bridge. Without looking back, Alaric took a step toward the scourge, letting his sword rest at his side behind him. The wind picked up, blowing across now from the west, from land, a hot breeze that whipped Alaric's long hair all around him. He held up his hand at the scourge, and now they were charging again, twenty across, four-legged beasts galloping across the bridge toward Alaric, their tongues out and hanging low, salivating at the unguarded man there for the taking.

The Ghost's hand dipped, and Cyrus tensed; it would not hit the scourge, would not throw them back, and Alaric was undefended. He pushed hard against the ground, started to get up, but before he could, Alaric's hand pulsed with a glow and the spell broke forth from it, slamming into the stone bridge.

The effect was immediate; Alaric disappeared as the bridge broke and crumbled all around. Cyrus felt the ground shift underneath him and he was falling, falling down. He felt the cold splash of the water only a moment later, heard chunks of rock and stone from the bridge falling around him and swam madly to the side, as fast as he could, the waters roiling around him. He felt something threaten to suck him down as it passed to his right, and then he swam toward the light above, the brightness of the sun.

His head broke the water and he gasped for breath, looking back to where he had come from. It was a spectacle of horror and amazement; the bridge had broken, and he could see the Sanctuary army still standing on the last segment of it remaining; the rest, stretching east toward Luukessia was gone, fallen into the sea, a white, churning foam and a few supports sticking out of the water the only sign that it had been there.

"You all right down there?" Longwell's voice reached him, and he looked up at the dragoon standing a hundred feet above him. "Can you swim?"

"I'm fine," Cyrus said and slid Praelior into its scabbard to use both hands to tread water. He felt oddly weightless, as though his head were swimming as well, floating in the water all on its own. "Do you see Alaric?" he called back to Longwell.

The dragoon hesitated, and Terian's head came over the side to look at him as well, followed by Odellan. "No," Longwell said. "He's ..." The dragoon didn't finish his thought, and he didn't need to. "You need to start swimming, Cyrus. It'll be a miracle if you make it to shore already without drowning ..."

But Cyrus couldn't, wouldn't. He swam toward the bridge, toward the nearest support pillar, and when he reached it he threw his hand up to grasp hold, and something clinked in his palm. He held up his hand, and something dangled from it, on a length of chain that was twisted around his wrist. It was a round medallion, no bigger than a large coin, with a pattern carved into it that he could not see in the shaded light under the bridge. He hesitated for only a moment before placing it over his head and around his neck, then grabbed hold of the support pillar and waited. *I could swim down, perhaps.* He cursed. *In full armor? Foolish.*

The weight of the chain around his neck was almost insignificant, and yet it felt heavier than anything he had ever carried. Cyrus waited, watching the water where the bridge had stood, for minutes that turned into hours. He waited until past sundown for the Master of Sanctuary to rise from the depths, waited until his arms had begun to tire and his legs screamed they could hold him against the pillar no more. When there was no light to see by but the fires on the shore in the distance, he finally kicked loose of where he waited for the man they called the Ghost and began the long, slow swim toward home.

Chapter 115

Vara

Day 223 of the Siege of Sanctuary

She could hear the dark elves as they battered away at the doors outside. It was nearly a miracle that the defenders of Sanctuary had managed to do what they had, fought back to within the halls of Sanctuary and barred them shut. Their enemies clattered at the big, heavy, wooden doors, but she knew when they retreated that it would take time to move the battering ram inside the walls, time to take it forward, to carry it up the stairs and position it to break them down. *And it would appear that the time has come—and ours has run out.*

She closed her eyes and could feel the fear around her in the huddled masses. "Nyad," she said, and the elven princess came forth, startling her with her appearance. "Can you teleport us out of here—all of us? Somewhere safe, like Fertiss."

Nyad was always pale; she was paler than usual, now. "No," she said simply. "The dark elves have positioned wizards outside; this entire area is under the effect of cessation spells.

Vara looked at her in alarm, and held up her hand, casting the most elementary healing spell. There was no tingle, no power, nothing. "So this is it," she whispered.

"Nowhere to run," came the rumble of Fortin, standing just behind the door, arms folded, his chest a scarring of dark, oozing substance that was thick as magma. "I like it better that way."

"I always prefer to have somewhere to run," Vaste said, clutching his staff. "Of course, I'm not quite the fighter that you are, and perhaps a bit squishier, so that might have something to do with it."

There was a scream as the battering ram hit the doors again and a crack appeared in the wood. Vara composed herself, closing her eyes for a moment, taking a breath. When she opened them again, she spoke. "There is no escape," she said, loudly, to all of them. "They mean to have us dead, or worse, as prisoners."

"Prisoners is worse?" Vaste asked, sotto voce. She shot him a blazing look. "Right," he said. "Worse."

"I mean to leave them with nothing," she said. "I will fight for every inch of this place, and they will kill me before taking me prisoner. If you wish to surrender, go to the basement, lock yourself inside and await your fate there. If you truly believe that letting them score a painless victory here will do the world we leave behind one bit of good, then flee. I, for one, find the thought of letting them leave here without a gaping, bloody scar to be so unpalatable I'm willing to throw myself in the path of this meatgrinder, to put a stick in the eye of the Sovereign's war machine." She bit down on her spite, choked on it. "I will make this bastard pay for every life he takes with ten of his own, and I will not yield until the last breath has fled my body. When they have hurt me so badly I can no longer walk, I will crawl, dagger in hand, in the direction of their boots and bury my blade in their ankles, pull them to my level and murder them unexpectedly."

There was a shocked silence before the battering ram hit the door again, and the door cracked slightly wider. "That's the spirit," Vaste said with false upbeatness. "Go for the ankles. They'll need those for marching and stomping on our corpses. That'll put a kink in the Sovereign's efforts."

"If you want to leave," Vara said, "now's your chance. None of us will look down on you because you don't want to die here, like this."

"Some of us actually will," Vaste said, "but you should do it anyway, because embracing your inner coward in these last few moments will probably give you something to regret for the span of time it takes the dark elves to rape you to death. You know, like they do with all their prisoners."

There was a shocked silence as the battering ram hit home. "Stop helping me!" Vara hissed at him.

The crowd grew quiet, no one daring to speak. Swords were drawn and clattered about against armor as people clutched them tight. Vara saw wizards pull daggers, druids grab logs from beside the fire to use as clubs, as her eyes slid over the crowd. Mendicant was nearby, clicking his claws together noiselessly as he shed his robes, joining a few of his fellow goblins nearby. They crouched low to the ground, skittering toward the doors, prepared to ambush the first enemies through. She felt a surge of pride in them. Andren was nearby, too, just behind them, a tankard in one hand and a knife in the other. Belkan and Thad, both bleeding profusely, stood just behind Fortin. There was a growling noise, a subtle one, and Vara noticed the wolves of Menlos Irontooth in the middle of the foyer, ready to spring. *Alaric would be proud. We'll not go down without a fight.* Larana stood next to Erith and Nyad; the wizard and the healer held weapons of their own, a small blade in both cases, but the druid's eyes were closed, a tear dripping down her cheek as she stood in utter silence, the very picture of despair.

Aisling slipped between them all, sliding into the shadows near the door, and all Vara could see of the dark elf was the glistening of her blades, ready to strike at an exposed back. *Let her have at it. I need all the help I can get at this point.*

She felt someone at her side and looked up to see Vaste, staring down at her, his staff in hand. "If it had to end this way," Vaste said, "I'm glad it was you here to lead us. I can't imagine a better voice of inspiration and fortitude than yours, here at the end of all our days."

She stared at him briefly then blinked as her face dissolved into disbelief. "You utter arse," she said. "Can you not be serious for even one moment now, at the end?"

His face stiffened in shock. "I know it's hard to believe, but I actually was being serious. Just this once. Don't tell anyone."

The battering ram hit home once more and the brace that held shut the great doors of Sanctuary broke loose along with the doors themselves. There was a cacophony from outside as the dark elves started in, around the fringes of the battering ram, streaming in at the sides, and were attacked by Fortin on one side and low-to-the-ground goblins on the other side. The first wave of the enemy fell quickly as the crew of the battering ram tried to remove the giant obstruction from the battle.

"Why, Vaste," she said, holding her sword high above her head, "whoever would I tell?" She let out a cry that was matched by a thousand more around her, and let her feet carry her forward, into what she knew beyond reason would be the last fight of her life.

Chapter 116

Cyrus

He pulled himself ashore, barely there, crawling on all fours onto the sand. He spat the salt water out. It had begun to fill his nose, his mouth, and all else. He coughed, bringing it up. The bridge was to his right, but there were fires in front of him, spread out all along the shore, but more to the north than south of the bridge, where he had come ashore. He looked toward the camp in front of him, but lay down on his back, studying the dancing flame from the top of his field of vision. He heard voices in that direction, but he cared little for who they might be or that they called out in alarm, met with voices from the bridge.

Alaric ...

"Cyrus!" The sharp, clear voice was feminine and all too familiar. He looked up and saw figures running toward him across the sand, and he felt the tide come in again and wash over him. There was a strong whinny of a horse above him, and he dimly realized it was Windrider, standing above him with others. He blinked, and recognized Cattrine, who was now by his side, her face close to his. "Are you all right?"

"I'm still alive," Cyrus managed to get out. "Which is more than I can say for ..." he almost choked on his words, "... some."

"What happened?" Cattrine asked. There were others, he could hear them, talking. "We saw the bridge come down, and then Windrider went mad, stamping and snorting. He didn't stop until just a moment ago, when he went charging off down the shore and led us to you."

"Alaric came," Cyrus said. "My Guildmaster. He ..." Cyrus felt a lump in his throat and swallowed. "He destroyed the bridge, drowned the scourge. And he ..." Cyrus let his voice trail off.

Cattrine's eyes flickered in the light of a torch someone was carrying nearby. "Oh, Cyrus ... I'm so sorry."

"He saved us," Cyrus said numbly, pushing himself to sit upright. "He saved us all."

There was noise at the base of the bridge, commotion and shouting, and Cyrus grasped Windrider's reins, which dangled before him, and without warning the horse pulled him to standing then snorted at him. "Okay, then," Cyrus said.

"Where is he?" came the voice from the bridge. "Has anyone seen Cyrus?"

"I'm over here!" Cyrus called and felt his feet sink into the sand with every step forward. He kept his hand on Windrider's reins. "I'm here."

There were torches atop the bridge, lighting the edges of it as it sloped toward the sands at the end where it met the ground. They followed off in a procession. The twilight turned dark now, night having fallen. He felt Cattrine next to him rather than saw her, sensed her presence as he moved through the night, and the water that drenched his underclothes sloshed in his boots and on his person as he walked. The water was beginning to cool on him, to chill him, like the winter at Enrant Monge.

The torches grew closer, and Cyrus could see the faces lit by them now—Terian, Longwell, Odellan. Martaina was there as well, and he saw the relief pass over her face as he appeared to them. Curatio broke into a smile at Cyrus's appearance. Cyrus blinked in surprise at the sight of Ryin Ayend, who stood next to J'anda. "Ryin," he said in acknowledgment.

"Cyrus," Terian said, standing apart from the others. He had broken off from them and stood at an angle to the side. Cyrus stared closer at him, saw the faint red glow in the torchlight and felt a whisper of menace through him as he drew Praelior, causing the others to halt their advance toward him.

Cyrus walked slowly toward Terian, angling himself away from the others. "Now, Terian?"

"No," Terian said, choked, as he raised his blade and pointed it at Cyrus. "Not now. I did what you asked. I fought to the end. Now ... I'm not going back with you. Not to Sanctuary. Not so you can put me on trial like some kind of circus or example. I'm leaving."

"Terian," Curatio said menacingly, "you tried to murder a fellow officer. If you think you can simply walk away from that—"

"No," Cyrus said and pointed Praelior at the dark knight's shade, his blue face almost fading into the background of the jungle behind him. "He can go."

"I wasn't asking your permission," Terian snapped.

"I wasn't giving permission," Cyrus said slowly. "I was releasing you from the charge of attempting to murder me. Go on. Be about your business, then; we have no more between us now to deal with, it's all settled on my end."

Terian gave him a slow, hard nod. "Not on mine. This isn't over between us. Not yet."

Cyrus gave a long sigh. "Fine. But at least do me the courtesy of not coming at me like a sidewinder next time. Try it head-on, like a man. I'll give you the fight you're looking for."

Terian said nothing but started to back away, up the slope of the beach, until he finally turned, sheathed his sword and entered the jungle. Cyrus watched him go until he disappeared and felt a familiar chill he could not define as he watched the darkness of the space between the trees. He wondered if Terian had turned around, was watching him, was giving him that eerie feeling.

"Cyrus," Ryin said, jarring the warrior out of his reflection.

"Ryin," Cyrus said. "You brought Alaric here?"

"Aye," the druid said. "When we left, the dark elves were hitting Sanctuary's walls with a strong attack, trying desperately to break through."

"Gods," Curatio said, sagging. "First Alaric, now this. How many of the enemy?"

"At least a hundred thousand," Ryin said. "And no way for us to get back behind the walls. And no way to dislodge an army of that size, with only your thousand or so remaining."

Cyrus's head spun at the thought. *A hundred thousand encamped around Sanctuary, hell-bent on breaking down that wall.* "What kind of soldiers?"

"Infantry, mostly," Ryin said. "Some trolls, for variety. They've been launching staggered attacks at us, but they were warming up for the finale when we left two days ago. They kept coming, aiming for the gate, trying to break it down." He ran a hand through his hair. "I don't know what we'll do."

"A hundred thousand," J'anda said in quiet awe. "We would need an army of our own of at least similar size in order to break them loose from around the wall ... at least as many ..."

Cyrus felt his jaw set in determination, felt the fury flood his veins. *Attack Sanctuary, will you?* The words came back to him now, the ones Alaric had said—

Protect Sanctuary.

There were hushed voices, raising discussion around him, unsure, starting to argue.

"Enough," he said, and they ceased, every head turning toward him. "We have no time for argument."

"Cyrus," Odellan said, "I appreciate your desire for harmony at this moment of all moments, but this is in serious need of discussion. Sanctuary under siege from such a superior army is cause for great concern. With the portal closed, it seems unlikely we'll be able to relieve our beleaguered comrades; to get back inside—"

"Sure we will," Cyrus said, and began to walk past them all, his hands still on Windrider's reins, toward the bridge.

"Uh, Cyrus?" Longwell said, speaking up. "Maybe you didn't hear Ryin. There are a hundred thousand foot infantry surrounding them, and we can't get back inside by teleportation."

"I heard," Cyrus said. "I don't want to get back inside by teleportation. I want to ride through the front gate."

Curatio coughed, but still they all followed him, even as he picked up speed and curved around the bottom of the bridge, beginning to run. He stepped up onto the arc of it, the bottom, and ran up the slope of it ten feet, using the height to give him a higher perspective. *Please let them have remained. Let them have stayed in the order we sent them in.* He crested, reached a high enough height to see, under the moonlight a thousand fires scattered along the beach, saw what he needed to, heard the noise of them—and he smiled.

"Cyrus," Curatio said, coughing politely. "A hundred thousand dark elven warriors stand between us and the front gate of Sanctuary, and with the portal shut down, about six months' ride for us, assuming we wanted to walk right up to their army of a hundred thousand and try to kill them with our thousand."

Cyrus's eyes surveyed the scene before him. "We don't have an army of a thousand, Curatio. And it doesn't matter how many *infantry* they have." He flicked a gaze back at them, then let their eyes wander where his had been only a moment earlier. Longwell and Odellan got it first, the elf letting an "Ahhh ..." in recognition. "They have a hundred thousand men on foot, pinned against the walls of Sanctuary. And I mean to *ride* through the front gate." He smiled and saw the slow dawning of understanding catch on Curatio's face as well. Martaina wore a subtle smile, and Ryin still looked around in confusion.

"I don't understand," Cattrine said, from just behind him. "You're outmatched, yes? A hundred thousand soldiers would seem to be a tremendous disadvantage to run up against."

"If I were going to stand and fight them by myself, you are correct," Cyrus said. "But I don't mean to stand toe to toe with them; and I don't mean to give them an even chance." He looked at the officers before him, surveying them quietly. "Longwell ... you know what to do—rally. Odellan, get our army together. They'll be marching in behind. Ready the wizards; this will be a hell of a feat for them." He looked back out over the edge of the bridge, to the sand and fires below, through the moonlit night, and the last hope of Sanctuary, and he knew deep within him what he was fighting for now, knew to the core. *I believe.*

"Let's go home."

Chapter 117

Vara

Day 223 of the Siege of Sanctuary

She wanted to weep but she killed another dark elf instead, striking his head from his body with enough force that it flew through the air and hit one of his fellows. The door had been open for less than thirty seconds, but already the dead were beginning to pile up, slippery on the floor where the blood was spilled. There was sound in the distance, too, trumpets heralding some sort of advance. She could barely hear it, but it both infuriated her and demoralized her, and not in equal measure. The fury won out, and another dark elf failed to survive his day of victory.

Aisling slipped out from behind one of her enemies and punched twin holes through a dark elf's back, then thrust one knife in the back of another's neck. The goblins were spitting and screeching in the corner in some sort of frenzy, joined by Irontooth's wolves, and blood was flying thick through the air and streaking the walls. Vara watched a gnome no more than three feet tall, charge forward, a cane in his knubby fists, slamming it down on a troll's foot, dashing between its legs and away as Belkan drove a sword through its belly while it was distracted.

She saw red armor fly through the air and Thad hit the wall near the hearth. He fell to the ground and did not move, and she knew he was dead. A troll bellowed, then slung a sword again and sent Menlos Irontooth smashing to the ground, guts opened to the air and grunting in agony.

We'll lose, she thought. *This is it. Only a minute of battle in here, and we're already decided.* The horn sounded in the distance again, and she bowed her head slightly. It was faint, but something about it prickled at her mind. *Why would it be far off? Their army is here now.* She felt a tingle and raised her sword again, cutting through the dark elf who appeared in front of her. She listened harder over the sounds of the battle, and faintly, near the edge of the walls, she could hear the worried cries of the enemy, looking out over the battlements. The horn sounded again as a ripple of uncertainty ran through the army that was outside but within the walls; she could barely hear it over the chaos in the foyer, but it was there—a rumor of something approaching.

The horn sounded again, louder this time, loud enough for others to hear it faintly. The battle did not pause, but it slowed for a moment, even in the foyer, as everyone assessed. She looked out the door, straight down the path toward the open crater where the front gate used to be, and in the darkness she saw movement over the heads of the dark elves. Torches burned in procession, cutting a wide V through the middle of the dark elf army at the gate. The torches seemed to split, surging out into three prongs, riding through the heart of the dark elves, with the largest prong still coming forth.

It was just inside the walls now, and Vara slashed aside a dark elf who came at her, shoving his corpse out of the way to keep her eyes upon the disturbance. The horn blew again, louder this time, at the fore of the movement, somewhere at the front of the torches that were coming toward them now, coming for them …

All motion seemed to come to a halt outside. She saw the armored dark elves who had queued up toward the steps to Sanctuary, waiting their turn to plunge inside and attack, begin to shuffle back and turn toward the approaching disturbance. The torches kept coming, moving erratically up and down but inexorably forward. Her eyes strained to make out what was behind them, what could be moving so fast to carry them forth. They were just inside the curtain wall now and had only slowed slightly; screams and cries from their wake were just now audible to her ears, along with the sound of battle, the clash of steel on steel.

There was a faint blue glow at the front, in the shape of a blade. She pushed a dark elf out of the way, shoved him roughly down, stabbed him in the back of the neck and then placed a boot atop him as she levered herself up to look over the crowd. The blue glow moved up and down with alarming speed, and it grew closer, more distinct. She watched as dark elves lined up on the lawn fell before it in waves, the momentum of the thing bringing it forward with the others, with the torches, as though it were being carried—

On horseback. By cavalry. She blinked at the sight of the

destruction outside, stretching back past the walls, at the cries of anguish and agony and the swath of destruction cut whole through the dark elven army. *It would take ... thousands of cavalry to do that ... who could manage such a thing ...?* Her eyes alighted on the blue glow, the sword, and she felt a rush as she killed another dark elf, shoving her way forward through the knot of them, recognition flooding her heart with relief.

The sword shape came at the head of the cavalry, riding down the dark elves on the lawn even as his army fanned out behind him. When he reached the broken doors she saw him in profile, rugged as always, Praelior at his side, and watched as he dismounted, killing three enemies on his drop to the ground. Her gasp of recognition was drowned out by the calls of others shouting his name, screaming it as he cut down a troll from behind, then another, blocking the door to the outside all by himself as those in the foyer turned on the limited number of enemies within their midst and began to slaughter them.

There was other noise, too, the sounds of "RETREAT! RETREAT!" being shouted from outside, but in the dark elven tongue, not human standard. The fighting in the foyer had begun to die down already, and the dark elves who tried to retreat were cut down in the doorway while attempting to flee by the same blue blade that he had carried for years as he took up the defense himself. The courtyard behind him was already emptying, she could see, corpses strewn across it all the way to the broken wall. There were still torches moving outside it, visible, fast horsemen riding down footmen without any challenge at all. Now the momentum had shifted, the dark elves were afraid and broken, running out the holes in the wall and pouring out onto the plains in all different directions.

He stood in silhouette, the moonlight glaring down from behind him, putting his face in shadow as he watched out the front doors at the last vestiges of the fight concluding outside. There was little enough battle on the lawn now, and the cavalry, which had struck through and driven the dark elves out, was streaming back through the wall now as well, following the retreating army of the Sovereign. Cyrus Davidon watched them—and she watched him.

She started toward him but something stopped her, a notion that something was about to go wrong. His head was bowed as he looked out over the remains of the fight, and someone came up to him in that moment, before Vara could overcome her fear and move forward again; a dark elf, small, catlike—Aisling with her white hair and leather armor slunk up to him and curled herself around him in a tight embrace. Vara recoiled at the sight as though something had burned her, and it only worsened when the dark elven ranger leaned up and kissed him, full and with feeling, deeply, and he returned her kiss, his hand upon her back.

Vara turned away, her legs carrying her unintended up the steps of the staircase, toward the Council Chambers—and away, away from him.

Chapter 118

Cyrus

There were slaps on the back enough to satisfy the largest ego, but Cyrus felt them hardly at all and not because of his armor. He watched as the dark elves were broken in their advance, driven out of the wall, leaving their dead behind them. Aisling had kissed him, he dimly remembered, but his thoughts were not of her, not at that moment—they were on the dead.

And Alaric.

"I need healers," he said, taking the first strides down onto the lawn, caked so thickly with bodies it could scarcely be believed. "We need to work starting at the gates and move inward, I need resurrection spells—" He paused, and noticed Andren at his side. "Hey."

"Oh, and a fine hello to you as well," the healer said, glaring at him. "Remember when you said you would be back in a few months? You know, something on the order of a year ago?"

"I got a bit sidetracked," Cyrus said. "You know, there are a lot of people here who could use your talents—"

"Fine," the healer huffed. "But don't be thinking that our conversation is done. We need to have a discussion, you and I."

"I look forward to it," Cyrus said, exhausted, as the healer moved away, upturning bodies as the members of Sanctuary began to look among the dead for their own. Calls of finds filled his ears, but he filed them all away, not really taking anything in.

A horseman appeared in the dimness, under the light of the moon, dismounting as he reached Cyrus. Cyrus blinked then recognized was Odellan by the winged helm. He greeted the elf with a nod. "Report."

"They're broken and fleeing," Odellan said. "You were right; they were utterly unprepared to be flanked while they were trying to lay siege to the keep. We rode them down, took minimal losses, and our men are running them through the plains even now, making merry slaughter of them." He sighed and looked at the gap in the wall where the gate had once stood. "They won't get away, you know. Our Luukessian cavalry friends seem to be relishing the opportunity to pay us back for their perceived debt. They're pursuing with an aggressiveness I'd find disquieting if not for the fact that the dark elves are completely in disarray. One of our thrusts hit their command tent and cut it to pieces. There are the bodies of at least four generals on the pile, along with more adjutants and colonels than I'd care to count. High-ups in their army, too, ones I read reports on when I was an Endrenshan." He looked out over the chaos. "They must have placed most of their force here in the Plains of Perdamun. We've dealt the Sovereign a hell of a blow tonight, and it'll be all the worse when we've finished. He'll be lucky to get a thousand of them back at the rate we're riding them down."

"Good," Cyrus said numbly. "I need a Council meeting of ... whoever's left."

Odellan nodded at him. "I'll see who I can rally together for you. A time?"

Cyrus looked at the destruction around him. "Give it an hour. That'll be enough time to bring back all the dead that'll be coming back." He saw Erith Frostmoor casting a spell in the distance as members of Sanctuary dragged the bodies of their comrades over to her. "Odellan—make sure any of our Luukessian friends who might have died in the charge get brought back, will you?"

"I already have soldiers bringing their bodies together," the elf said and saluted with a tight smile. "It was a great victory, you know. The scourge and the dark elves vanquished in a single day."

Cyrus nodded as the elf walked off into the Sanctuary foyer. *Then why does it feel like a defeat?* He recalled the bridge, Alaric disappearing as the stone broke apart around him and he fell ... *Right. That's why.*

He looked up at the moon, staring at the pale disk hanging in the sky above. It almost seemed as though it were slightly red, tinged with blood. He stared at it for only a moment more before he began to pick his way through the bodies, moving aside the countless corpses of dead dark elves in hopes of finding a few familiar faces before it was too late.

Chapter 119

The Council Chamber was quiet when he arrived. There was a stir as he entered, motion around the table as they stood to greet him. It was a somber silence, though, with a kiss on the cheek from Erith, her eyes filled with regret. Nyad gave him the same, and Cyrus saw the tears from her. Vaste stood before him, an imposing figure, and he stared up at the troll's impassive face for a moment, started to say something but was swept from his feet in a bear hug that pressed him against the healer's tattered and stained robe.

"I missed you, too, Vaste," Cyrus said as the troll pulled him tight. "But perhaps not that much."

Vaste turned him loose. "Oh, sorry," he said with aplomb. "I was just trying to burp you. You look like you could use a good burping."

"Thanks," Cyrus said with a nod as he took his seat. It squeaked when he eased himself into it. The smell of wood burning in the hearth was especially strong, and familiar, but still, something was off, something that kept it from feeling like …

Home.

There was a quiet, and the darkness outside the windows was impenetrable, though Cyrus knew that out there the Luukessians were still running down the enemy and that druids and wizards were bringing more and more of the refugees into the Plains via the portal in Sanctuary's foyer, newly reactivated, as well as the one a few minutes north of the gates. Sanctuary troops and scouts were spread out in a pattern around it, and the foyer was packed with guardians, all facing the seal in the center. *The Sovereign won't soon try that again, not without an army at the gates. It would be pointless now.*

Curatio sat at his usual place next to Alaric's empty seat, which was a gaping thing, a missing piece that made the whole place seem strangely empty. Cyrus's eyes darted to Terian's seat as well, also empty. *Terian. Niamh. Alaric.* He bowed his head.

"I call this Council to order," Curatio said quietly, somberly, "in my capacity as the Sanctuary Elder and acting Guildmaster." The elf's mouth became a thin line. "And it grieves me so to do it, let it be known."

"So noted," Nyad said, with her parchment in front of her and an inkwell at her side.

"We find ourselves in an unusual situation," Curatio began. "How goes the pursuit of the enemy?"

"A hundred thousand or more killed," Longwell said with a shrug. "Very few still alive. Hard to outrun men on horseback when you don't have any for yourself. We managed to hit their cavalry at the outset of the battle and caught them unhorsed, so they had no horses with which to flee or fight back. A few wizards took some of ours out but only in small groups. There are likely a few hiding here and there, but sunrise will essentially see the end of that campaign." His eyes were half-lidded, as though he had lost any interest in it, though there was a little fire remaining. "What does that mean for the war?"

Vara cleared her throat, and Cyrus's eyes were drawn to her for the first time since he had returned. She looked worn, scuffed, a healed gash left dried blood under her eye. Her ponytail was back as always, but a few strands were out of place—*well, more than a few*. She leaned against the back of her chair, looking down her face at all of them as though she would fall asleep at any moment. She did not look at Cyrus. "The Sovereign threw the bulk of his forces at us here, hoping to capture the plains to feed his armies as he marched them in conquest. To have lost ... even ninety percent of them will cost him dearly and stall their progress on the other fronts." She shrugged, lightly, as though it were a matter of no consequence. "I should find it hard to imagine he will be able to continue the war in its present form, not without some other source of troops. There are simply not enough remaining for him to be anything but defensive."

"You don't know that for certain," Erith said. "This was a massive upset, true, but we don't know the disposition of the dark elven forces. And it would certainly be in our best interest to get the wall repaired as soon as possible."

"Because it held so marvelously against whatever devilry he employed on it this time," Vara muttered.

"We captured some prisoners," Longwell said, "his intellectuals, if you will. They spoke of a kind of powder, black as the night itself, that when lit afire, explodes. It was no magic, according to them, but some form of alchemy."

"Whatever it was," Vaste said, "it was a fearsome power to unleash. It blasted those holes in the wall; took some of our people with it, I suspect." He glanced toward Erith, who nodded.

"At least a couple hundred unaccounted for," Erith said. "Some of their bodies might still be out there, but if any of them got caught in that—alchemy—then there's probably not enough left of them to resurrect."

"I hate to even speak of it at a time such as this," Nyad said from her place at the table, holding the quill, "but it seems unlikely that even with the siege broken, we'll be seeing much in the way of applicants at the moment. Who wants to be part of a guild that's likely to be blockaded by dark elves at some point in the future?"

There was a stark silence. "I hate that you spoke of it, too," Vaste said. "Because now I'm thinking about it, and I wish I weren't." The troll leaned his face into his hands, elbows on the table. "Can we not have ... can we not mourn for just a small amount of time? Think of how many we've lost, how much battle we've seen ..." He scanned the table, eyes coming to a rest on Cyrus. "I mean ... some of you just watched an entire land—three whole Kingdoms—go down in flames."

"Aye," Longwell said, "and some of us will never forget it, not for the rest of our lives."

No one spoke for a long time after that. When the silence was finally broken, it was Cyrus who did it. "We have a lot of survivors of Luukessia who have no homes and no place to go. We can feed them here for a time, but—" He shrugged. "I doubt they'd want to settle close by here. We seem to be a magnet for trouble of late. Especially of late."

"I had an idea about that," Longwell said, looking up. "As you may recall, in addition to being the King of a land now lost," he said with a sharp taste of bitterness, "I am also a Lord of the Elven Kingdom with a very nice holding not far from a portal in a green, verdant, and unfarmed land." He looked around the table. "I have spoken with some of the dragoon captains, and with a few leaders among the survivors. If I can secure King Danay's permission, I will settle the survivors there on my land." He looked to Nyad.

"He'll likely consent, especially if you get them to pay taxes of some form," Nyad said. "He'll agree to just about anything if it increases his coffers right now. The destruction of Termina and the war have left them quite dry, I suspect."

"I doubt your people have much in the way of money," Cyrus said quietly.

"They do not," Longwell said, "but I think I know of a way they might earn their keep, might add some value in a place that could grant them incomes."

Cyrus watched the dragoon cannily. "Go on."

"If you would care to have tens of thousands of new applicants to Sanctuary," Longwell said, drawing the silence around him as surely as if he had slammed a sword into the table, "I believe we would be quite content to put our weapons to your service."

Vaste rubbed the bridge of his nose. "I can see we're going to move right past that mourning and on to the next conquest."

"Aye," Cyrus said. "We'll mourn. But we need to focus on something other than grief before it chokes us to death." He scanned the table. "Alaric believed that we of Sanctuary had a greater purpose than merely acquiring wealth and fighting enemies to take from them. He believed we were supposed to protect the helpless and give aid to those who need it." He looked each of them in the eye in turn. "How might we give aid if we have no money to give it with?" He waited for an answer but found none. "We'll go to Purgatory again with the new applicants from Luukessia. We'll get them equipped, build our guild bank, get some coin dispersed among our people again to make up for this catastrophic year." He held his head high when he spoke, though he didn't feel it. *I'll protect Sanctuary, Alaric. I'll do it however I have to.* "We'll rebuild, become what we were before but stronger. We just won an epic battle against the dark elves. That has to be worth something in the eyes of the people of Arkaria. That has to enhance our reputation at least some. We need to keep growing." He felt his voice crack as he said the last. "It's what Alaric would have wanted."

Chapter 120

The Council broke in silence, some to their duties, some to their beds. Cyrus waited, though, head down at the table, hearing them file out one by one. There was a taste of bitterness in his mouth, an acid in the back of his throat that caused him to realize he had not eaten a substantive meal in a day or perhaps two. *Yet I do not hunger.* His mouth was parched, he realized, but he didn't care.

"Cyrus," Longwell said, and he blinked at the dragoon. "The first groups of survivors have begun to come through the portal. I wanted you to know." He hesitated then looked across the table as though guilty of some crime, and Cyrus's gaze followed his to where Vara sat, in her seat, still reclined, watching them both.

"Out with it," Cyrus said, but Longwell hesitated, casting a look at Vara, uncertain. "Go on."

"Cattrine is with them," Longwell said. "I have ... allocated her quarters here in Sanctuary for the night. I did not wish to overstep my bounds, but as she was of the royal family of Actaluere, it seemed ... appropriate, somehow—"

"That's fine," Cyrus said, with a dismissive hand.

Longwell nodded slowly then stepped aside, walking out the door. Behind him, J'anda remained, as did Curatio. Vara was still in her seat, Cyrus noted, still looking quite weathered—and beautiful. *Always beautiful, even when she's been through hell.* Her cheeks looked thinner, but when she looked at him in response to his stare, he did not look away afterward.

J'anda coughed. "I don't mean to interrupt your long, meaningful look at each other, but I did want to ..." he paused. "Well, I had to show someone."

"Show someone what?" Vara said slowly, as though she were so tired that she were pushing the words out one syllable at a time.

"I stayed behind with the Luukessians on the beach when the cavalry teleported back here," J'anda said. "Myself and one of the druids went back with a couple rangers, back to the site of the bridge destruction, to go underwater, to see if we could find anything." He looked down, chagrined. "We used Nessalima's light, as brightly as we could, and spells that allowed us to breathe underwater. We searched for two hours, shifted some of the rubble—"

"Did you find anything?" Cyrus cut him off, leaning forward. "Did you see—" He stopped, and felt the pressure build in the back of his throat.

"We found the bodies of more scourge than you would care to count," J'anda said quietly. "And this." He reached into his robes and pulled something out, something rounded, and set it upon the table with a thunk, right where it usually sat on the table next to its owner—

Alaric's helm.

Cyrus sagged back into his seat, felt the weight of the thing, the true loss it represented. He stared at it, the empty eye slits staring back at him, accusing him— *If only you had believed sooner. If only you had listened to me in Death's Realm—*

"Thank you," Cyrus said in a choked voice, and J'anda nodded mournfully and shuffled toward the door. It shut quietly behind him, and Cyrus was left staring at the helm with Curatio, whose face was an iron mask of reserve mixed with regret, and Vara, whose lip actually quivered as she stared at it.

"Thus ends an era," Curatio said softly, almost too low to be heard. He placed his hand on the top of the helm and ran his palm across it, closing his eyes and bowing his head for a moment as though he were praying. "So long, old friend," he whispered, and then his long, weighted, shuffling steps were audible as he made his way across the floor of the Council Chambers and out the door. It shut just as quietly behind him.

"He is truly gone, then," Vara said, drawing his eyes toward her. Hers were rooted on the helm, and she stared at it with a little horror before she squinted her eyes shut and lowered her head onto her hand.

"I think so," Cyrus said. "He knew he wasn't going to get away from it. He talked about making sacrifices for what you believe in, and he gave me this," he realized with a start, reaching under his armor and pulling out the pendant. He looked at it in the light. The smooth edges felt strange to his naked palms, and he removed it and set it beside his gauntlet on the table.

"He was a Crusader to the last, then," she said quietly. "Dying for the cause he believed in."

"Yes," Cyrus said. "Yes, he did." But he did not look at her.

"Can we talk?" she asked, almost choking on her words as they came out. He looked at her in surprise. She watched him with greatest hesitation, even fear.

"I think ... we are, right now."

"I meant about us," she said, voice no more than a mere whisper. He strained to hear her, watching her as she spoke.

He blinked twice, stole a sidelong look at the hearth, and then turned his eyes back to the table in front of him, where the medallion rested, perfectly centered in front of him. *No.* "Yes."

She rose, but he tried not to look at her for more than a few seconds at a stretch, always looking back to the medallion in front of him. "It has been over a year since I watched you march out the front gates of Sanctuary ..."

He looked up. "I didn't know you were watching." Calm. Cool. Uncaring.

"I was," she said, placing her hand upon the arm of her chair as she stood, looking for support of some kind. "I watched you go, watched you ride off at the head of the army, and I wished—oh, how I wished— that I had said and done something far, far different when last we spoke. With every report of dismal news from your expedition, my fear worsened. I was certain that I would never see you again, that you would die in some far off place with the memory of our last conversation being what you remembered of me." She took a tentative step toward him, crossing behind the next chair—Nyad's, one of two between them—and putting her hands delicately upon its back. "I did not wish to leave such a dark air between us—"

"I wouldn't worry about it," Cyrus said, clearing his throat abruptly. He shook his head but still kept his eyes upon the surface of the table. "You said what you needed to say. I can hardly fault you for feeling as you did, especially in the wake of ... all that happened in Termina—"

"I was afraid," she said, and eased another step closer, behind Vaste's chair, using her hands to almost pull herself nearer to him. "I let fear guide my actions toward you, let my mother's fears—my fears—

carry me along a path I don't wish to go down—"

"It's only natural," Cyrus said, shaking his head, keeping his eyes away from hers, looking at the lines of the medallion, "only natural to listen to reasonable instincts warning you away. I won't live as long as you, after all—"

"You very nearly outlived me today," she said, interrupting him. "If it hadn't been for you, for this army you brought with you, these eastern cavalrymen, I would have been dead. We live in dangerous times, and a dangerous sort of life—"

"Right," he said, "all the more reason to be cautious in our personal lives—"

"Listen to me," she snapped at him then eased closer behind Longwell's seat, the last between them. "I'm sorry, I didn't mean to ... I just ... please, let me say this." Cyrus nodded, but did not interrupt her. "I let fear rule me. The fear of losing something very precious to me, more precious than ... anything else. Anyone else." She took a breath, composed herself. "I lost my parents within days of each other. Lost my home. You already know my past, the things that happened to make me untrusting. None of these are excuses, but ... after all that ... I couldn't bear the thought of losing someone else, someone who has perhaps grown more important to me than any of the others—"

"We all feel the loss of Alaric," Cyrus said, templing his fingers in front of him and bowing his head. "And it is particularly acute now—"

"I'm not talking about Alaric—" She ground the words out, practically in his ear, and he was forced to look up at her at last. She stared down at him, disbelieving. "I am talking about you." Her face changed, softening. "You have come to mean more to me than anyone else in my life." Her hand came down upon his shoulder awkwardly and eased up to his cheek. He looked at her in surprise, not quite openmouthed but wide-eyed. "I pushed you away once before because I was afraid. Afraid after so many losses that I would lose ... a good man. That I would lose you, perhaps not now but in the future, and feel that pain for the rest of my days, so sharply." Her hand shook as it came to rest on his cheek, brushing against the stubble there. "I could not bear the thought of that loss. So I pushed you away. And I am ..." her face crumpled, "so ... sorry. So sorry I drove you away."

"It's all right," Cyrus said and rose slowly. She eased toward him, wrapping her arms around him as he stood, pressing her face against his shoulder, against the blackened armor there. He felt the weight and press of her, smelled the aroma of battle that clung to her after days of fighting. It was a soothing feeling, having her close, and only a year earlier he would have welcomed it happily, exclaimed it inside with such fervent joy—

But now he felt only emptiness as he held her, the fire crackling in the hearth behind her. "It's okay," he said. "I would have gone anyway, out of a sense of loyalty to Longwell, to help him. And I still would have stayed, because everything that happened afterward was my fault. I had to be there. It was my duty."

She looked up at him, lifting her head off his shoulder. "But I could have—should have—been at your side. Been with you."

He shook his head slowly. "No. You did well, you held Sanctuary together while I was gone. That was the task appointed you, and you did it marvelously, better than anyone else could have in your stead."

"But ..." she whispered, "... after all that's happened ... after all we've been through ... do you think that there's a chance ... that you still feel for me the way you did on that bridge in Termina?"

He took a deep breath, pondering his answer. "I don't know. There was a time when I believed in the idea of us—you and me—with everything in me. I believed that you and I could be together, could be something more, something greater than anything else I'd ever experienced in my life. I went to war for you, I killed for you, and I even tried to die in your stead, because I ... loved you." He said it slowly, and bits of it came out as though he were awakening to them. "I felt it so deeply in my bones, in my heart, that I would have done anything for you." He lowered his head. "I don't believe that anymore."

She nodded sharply, almost in denial. "And ... do you believe ... you could ever feel that way about me ... again?"

He breathed out, slowly, felt the emptiness and the fatigue deep inside. "I don't know. I don't know anything right now, really ... except my duty. Except the promises I made." He blinked, as though he were coming out of a trance. "I haven't slept in days, or eaten. I'm so tired ... I just don't know. I'm sorry."

"Yes, well," she started to withdraw from him, from his arms. Her hand remained rested on his breastplate, just above his heart, as though she could somehow touch it through the layers of armor and clothing. "I understand," she said, her face firming up, settling into a mask of sorts into straight lines, the emotion sapping out of it, replaced with the face of the Vara he had come to know—*back when I knew her. I haven't seen her in over a year.* "I understand completely. It has been ... some time, after all. And there have been ... others ... in the interim." She said "others" with a pang of regret so loud to his ears that it cried out to him.

"Yes," he admitted. "But I don't know where I stand with them, either." He placed his fingers over his face, massaging his temples. "I'm sorry I have no answer for you."

"It's quite all right," she said, and the regret now belonged to him as she slipped back to her old self. "I shouldn't have expected any less from our conquering General, weary from the battles he's fought to preserve us all from harm." She gave him a quick nod. "Perhaps we'll speak again later—once you're ... recovered." She snapped to a more precise stance and walked toward the door, her back ramrod straight.

As he watched her go, it was her walk that gave her away. She had always been precise in her stride, evenly measured, crisp, almost marching. As she made her way to the door she kept the same stride but he could see the struggle in each step, as though she were having to drag her feet along away from him. It was a difference measured in time that would have been unnoticeable by most ... and meant more to him than anything else she had said.

Chapter 121

The knock at the door had stirred him out of sleep, a long, wearying sleep filled with old dreams, red eyes, and worse. The smell of his room was there when he snapped out of the deep weariness, opening his eyes and finding the stone ceilings above him, surrounding him. It took a moment to reacclimate, to adjust to his surroundings, to the fire in the hearth in front of him, filling the room with its smoky smell of home, to lick his lips and realize that the taste of the meat pie Larana had brought up to him was still on them, still hearty and good, better than anything he'd had while he had been away. The sheets were cool against his bare, clean skin, the shower in his own bathroom having done its job, the running water a beautiful luxury after his time away.

The knock jarred him again, reminded him why he'd awakened, and he forced his legs out from beneath the sheets. He wore fresh underclothes, for the first time in—*too long*. He blinked the sleep away, then rubbed his eyes, and wondered who might be at the door. *Longwell or Odellan with a report on the pursuit.* He took a sharp intake of breath. *Or someone else—perhaps with news of Alaric.* His feet carried him to the door, bare feet padding across the cool stone, his step a little quicker with anticipation, and he threw open the door—

"You," he said dully, the fatigue biting back down on him, hard.

"You sound disappointed," she said haltingly, staring at him over the threshold.

"No," he said. "Just surprised."

She stared at him coolly, hesitant. "May I come in?"

There was only a moment's thought on his part. "Yes." He stepped aside to let her in, but as she passed, something clicked in him and he leaned forward, his hand landing on her cheek and pulling her face to his. He kissed her, long, passionately, and she returned the kiss with all enthusiasm, one hand on his chest and the other tugging at his shirt, lifting it up as she broke from him for a moment. He lifted hers as well, kicking the door shut with his foot while he undressed her, leading her to the bed as he felt her slip his cloth pants off. His naked back hit the bed when she pushed him. The last of her clothing came off a moment later and she was upon him, kissing him deeply, the flavor of her in his mouth, then he pushed his lips against her neck. She rolled over and he was leaning atop her now. Their passions took over, and it was as though everything he had ever wanted were here, in this room, in this moment.

She kissed him, brought him close, and they made love, loudly and long into the night. When they were done, he fell asleep contented, his rest now dreamless and all his worries relieved, her head lying on his shoulder.

NOW

Epilogue

The noise was subtle but there. Cyrus heard it, out of the archives, on the staircase, the scrape of a shoe against stone. He put the journals aside and pulled a blade. Letting it point in front of him, he felt the strength surge through him from it. There was an odor blowing through now from the darkened plains outside. It smelled of decay, of rot—*out of the east, no doubt.*

He took a step forward, letting his armored boot land on the floor as quietly as he could make it. There was no fear in him, now, only caution. He could feel the weight of the sword in his grasp, the strength it gave him—and the slightest twinge of hunger from his stomach, protesting loudly at having not eaten for hours. It sent a swell of dryness to his mouth, and reminded him to take a drink of water at his next convenience—*a strange thought for a man who has just heard an intruder in a dead place.* He stepped out of the archive into the Council Chambers, letting his eyes ease around the room. The fire was going in the hearth, the torches were all lit, and he waited, trying not to even breathe, listening for the sound outside the half-opened door, which was hanging partially off its hinges. He was at an angle where it was not possible to see the stairs, though he knew that whoever was climbing them—or had already done so—would have to enter his field of vision in moments.

Cyrus tensed, bringing his sword back for a swing. The weight of it was solid in his hand, and he held it straight back, ready. He let his breath out slowly then took another as quietly as he could.

"You know," came the voice through the open door, "if you're going to invite someone to a place, it's not really very sporting to sit just inside the door, waiting to ambush them."

Cyrus felt his breath all come out in a rush. "You."

"Me," the voice came again from the room outside. "Would you mind lowering your sword so I can come in without fear of being filleted?"

Cyrus chuckled darkly and lowered the blade, putting it back into the scabbard that waited for it on the right side of his belt. "Come in."

"About time," came the voice again, and the man who said it was only a moment behind it, stepping in past the broken doors, avoiding hitting his head on the low-hanging arch of the trim. "Place looks like hell," the man said—*though I wouldn't always have called him a man,* Cyrus thought. *Troll, in fact, would have been the preferred insult for quite some time.*

"Vaste," Cyrus said with a nod. "It's good to see you."

"Thanks," Vaste replied. "I get the feeling you don't say that much anymore."

Cyrus shrugged, turning his back to the troll and walking toward the window. "Perhaps I might out of politeness. But meaning it? No. Not since ..." he cast a hesitant, regretful look back. "Well. You know."

"I know." There was a pause. "You left poor Windrider meandering about outside. I felt bad for him. He looked lonely."

"He knows the way to the stables," Cyrus said idly, staring out into the dark.

"Because there's so much for a living horse to do in there," Vaste quipped. He eyed his old chair at the table and bent over, picking it up and setting it upright again. "What are the odds that this old thing will still hold my—" He pulled his hand away from it and it promptly broke in half along a split at the back, then the bottom collapsed under its own weight. "Well, damn."

"There's a chair in the other room if you're of a mind to sit," Cyrus said, waving at the archive.

"I don't really *want* to sit, but my body would appreciate it after a few days of unpleasant travel. Hard to find a ride down here nowadays."

"Do you blame 'em?" Cyrus asked, looking over his shoulder dully at the troll.

Vaste pursed his lips. "No. Not particularly. Not after what happened. Still, made it damned inconvenient to get here." He stood in the middle of the room and looked around. "So ... before I go get that chair ... you *were* serious, weren't you?"

"About what?"

"In your letter."

Cyrus waved vaguely at the walls around them. "Clearly."

"But, I mean ... the other—"

"Yes," Cyrus said quietly. "Yes, I meant it." He waited for Vaste to say something, something light and funny, something to redeem the darkness of the moment that felt as though it had seeped in from outside unchecked by the candles. "It really is good to see you, by the way." He looked and caught the troll staring back at him. "I meant it when I said it to you. I wasn't just being polite this time. It's ... good to see another one of us around."

"One of us?" Vaste said mockingly. "You mean ... one of the handsome? The debonair?"

There was that lightness I was looking for. Cyrus looked around the wrecked Council Chambers, felt the pervading sense of grief and loss that came with the memories of this place. *It didn't have quite the effect I was looking for,* he decided, looking back out the window. *It never does anymore.* "No," he said, and his eyes took in the world outside— darker than it had been a few years ago—*and with ... so much less to believe in.* "That's not what I meant. I meant—"

"I know what you meant," Vaste said. Cyrus felt the troll's tall presence next to him, and they looked out into the darkness together. *Just like we always have.* "I know what you meant. You meant ..." The troll's scarred face grimaced, and his onyx eyes flicked toward Cyrus, the light dancing off them.

"Survivors."

Author's Note

Well, that took about forever to get out. Sorry. I hope you think it was worth the wait. It ended up a heck of a lot longer than I thought it was gonna be, and of course my other series took off like gangbusters, and since I do actually have to pay the bills, the adventures of Cyrus and Vara took a back seat for a bit. Sorry again. These books take a good long while to write, which is why it will be until 2014 before I can get volume five out. BUT! Don't despair too much, because I have a few Sanctuary offerings to hopefully whet your appetite between now and then. I've added a novel starring everyone's favorite (or least favorite) dark knight to my schedule (check out the teaser on the next page - it started as a novel but is pretty much a trilogy now) as well as a novel starring Aisling (that one's just a standalone novel - for now). They won't be as long as Crusader, obviously, or book five (teaser is on the same page as the one for the Terian novel) so I can write them more quickly and get them out to you without having to dedicate *months* to working on nothing but them (as I did with Crusader).

Anyway, again, I'm sorry for those of you who are waiting. I'd love to finish these main books (Volumes 5-8) sooner, but it's just not possible right now, not with the numbers it's selling. I will finish this series (and even add additional side books/trilogies and short stories) because I love the world of Arkaria and all its occupants, but it's going to be slower because of how big these books are. Thanks for your patience (if you have patience - I *really* appreciate it if you do) and if for some reason this series were to explode the way the other has (The Girl in the Box), selling tons and tons of books, I can pretty well promise I will be back to finish it sooner. I'm nothing if not a ruthless mercenary. Meat pies don't pay for themselves, after all...

If you want to know as soon as the next volumes are released, sign up for my mailing list. I promise I won't spam you (I only send an email when I have a new book released) and I'll never sell your info. You can also unsubscribe at any time.

Thanks for your support and thanks for reading!

Robert J. Crane

About the Author

Robert J. Crane was born and raised on Florida's Space Coast before moving to the upper midwest in search of cooler climates and more palatable beer. He graduated from the University of Central Florida with a degree in English Creative Writing. He worked for a year as a substitute teacher and worked in the financial services field for seven years while writing in his spare time. He makes his home in the Twin Cities area of Minnesota.

He can be **contacted** in several ways:
Via email at cyrusdavidon@gmail.com
Follow him on Twitter – @robertJcrane
Connect on Facebook – robertJcrane (Author)
Website – http://www.robertJcrane.com
Blog – http://robertJcrane.blogspot.com
Become a fan on Goodreads – http://www.goodreads.com/RobertJCrane

Cyrus Davidon will return in

MASTER

THE SANCTUARY SERIES, VOLUME FIVE

The disappearance and presumed death of Alaric Garaunt has thrown the guild of Sanctuary into chaos. Added to the upheaval are the sudden disappearance of Sanctuary's old allies, The Daring, the resurgence of the Dark Elves in the war, and a mystery brought to Cyrus Davidon by an old friend. As the darkness rises in the land of Arkaria, Sanctuary must find a way through their struggles to unify, even as a battle between two pillars of the guild threatens to tear them asunder once and for all.

Coming in 2014

But first...

THY FATHER'S SHADOW

A SANCTUARY NOVEL
BOOK ONE OF THE KNIGHT OF SHADOWS TRILOGY

Terian Lepos is a man without a home. Cast out of Sanctuary, he wanders the land of Arkaria until a messenger arrives with a curious offer, one that will take Terian into the darkness of Saekaj Sovar, a place he thought he had long ago left behind, and into the service of the Dark Elven Sovereignty, where he will face his worst fear - his father, and the secret that drove him from his homeland once before.

Coming Autumn 2013!

Other Works by Robert J. Crane

The Sanctuary Series
Epic Fantasy
Defender: The Sanctuary Series, Volume One
Avenger: The Sanctuary Series, Volume Two
Champion: The Sanctuary Series, Volume Three
Crusader: The Sanctuary Series, Volume Four
Master: The Sanctuary Series, Volume Five*
Thy Father's Shadow: A Sanctuary Novel*
Savages: A Sanctuary Short Story
A Familiar Face: A Sanctuary Short Story

The Girl in the Box
Contemporary Urban Fantasy
Alone: The Girl in the Box, Book 1
Untouched: The Girl in the Box, Book 2
Soulless: The Girl in the Box, Book 3
Family: The Girl in the Box, Book 4
Omega: The Girl in the Box, Book 5
Broken: The Girl in the Box, Book 6
Enemies: The Girl in the Box, Book 7*
Legacy: The Girl in the Box, Book 8*

Southern Watch
Contemporary Urban Fantasy
Called: Southern Watch, Book 1*

*Forthcoming

9 780615 858692